O F
LOVE
AND
LIFE

OF
LOVE
AND
LIFE

Three novels selected and condensed
by Reader's Digest

CONDENSED BOOKS DIVISION

The Reader's Digest Association Limited, London

The Reader's Digest Association Limited
11 Westferry Circus, Canary Wharf, London E14 4HE

www.readersdigest.co.uk

ISBN 0-276-42530-8

CONTENTS

MAEVE BINCHY

Scarlet Feather

It is New Year's Eve and for Cathy Scarlet there is only one blot on the horizon—she has agreed to do the catering for her highly critical mother-in-law's party. Cathy and her business partner, Tom Feather, need to make contacts for their newly launched catering company, Scarlet Feather, but for Cathy there is a more personal reason—she wants to impress her mother-in-law, who has always disapproved of her son's choice of wife . . .

New Year's Eve

ON THE RADIO SHOW they were asking people what kind of a New Year's Eve did they *really* want. It was very predictable. Those who were staying at home doing nothing wanted to be out partying, those who were too busy and rushed wanted to go to bed with a cup of tea and be asleep before the festivities began.

Cathy Scarlet smiled grimly as she packed more trays of food into the white van. There could be hardly anyone in Ireland who would answer the question by saying that they really and truly wanted to spend the night catering a supper party for a mother-in-law. Now that was the punishment posting tonight, feeding Jock and Hannah Mitchell's guests at Oaklands. Why was she doing it then? Partly for practice, *and* of course it would be a good way to meet potential customers. But mainly she was doing it because she wanted to prove to Hannah Mitchell that she could. That Cathy, daughter of poor Lizzie Scarlet, the maid who cleaned Oaklands, who had married their only son, Neil, was well able to run her own business and hold her head as high as any of them.

Neil Mitchell was in his car when he heard the radio programme. It annoyed him greatly. Anyone looking at him from another car would have seen his sharp, handsome face frown. People often thought they recognised him; his face was familiar from television, pushing the hair out of his eyes, passionate, concerned and caring, always the spokesperson for the underdog. He had the bright burning eyes of a crusader. This kind of whining really drove him mad. People who had everything, a home, a job, a family, all telephoning a radio station to complain about the pressures of life. They were all so lucky and just too selfish to realise it. Unlike the man that Neil was going to see now. A Nigerian whose papers were not in order and there was grave danger he would have to leave Ireland. Neil, who was a member of a barristers' group set up to protect refugees, had been asked to come to a strategy meeting. It could go on for several hours. His mother had warned him not to be late at Oaklands.

'I do hope that poor Cathy will be able to manage it,' she had said to Neil.

'Don't let her hear you calling her "poor Cathy", if you want your guests to get any food,' he had laughed.

It was idiotic, this nonsense between his mother and his wife.

Tom Feather was going through the property section of the newspaper yet again. He lay across the small sofa—there was never room for his long limbs and big frame unless he draped himself somehow over the whole thing. He shook out the newspaper. There had to be some kind of premises with a room that could be made into a catering kitchen. He and Cathy Scarlet had worked so hard to make this happen. Since their first year at catering college they were going to set up Dublin's best home catering company. The whole idea of serving people great food in their own homes at reasonable prices was something that fired them both. They had worked so hard, and now they had got the funding, all they needed was somewhere to operate from. Cathy and Neil's little town house in Waterview, though very elegant, was far too small, and the flat in Stoneyfield, where he lived with Marcella, was even tinier. They had to find somewhere soon. He was half listening to the radio programme. What would he really like to do on this New Year's Eve? Find the perfect place for their company to set itself up. But that wasn't going to happen.

Marcella Malone worked in the beauty salon of Hayward's Store. She was possibly the most beautiful manicurist that any of the clients had ever seen. Tall and willowy, with a cloud of dark hair, she had that kind of oval face and olive skin that schoolgirls dreamed of having. At the same time, she had a quiet, unthreatening way about her that made uglier, fatter people take to her despite her beauty.

They had the radio on in the salon, and people there were talking about New Year's Eve. Marcella bent her beautiful face over the nails that she was doing and thought how lucky she was. She had Tom Feather, the most handsome and loving man that any girl could want. And she had been photographed recently in a knitwear promotion and at a charity fashion show. This looked like the year it could all happen for her. She had a very good portfolio of pictures now, and Ricky, the photographer who had taken them, was giving a very glitzy party. A lot of media people would be there and she and Tom had been invited. If things worked well she would have a proper agent and a proper modelling contract, and she would not be working as a manicurist in Hayward's by this time next year.

It would have been lovely for Cathy if Tom could have come with her to Oaklands. It would have halved the work, but Tom had to go to some do with Marcella. Neil had said he would help her and they had hired Walter, Neil's cousin, to be barman. She had kept it fairly simple, she and Tom had slaved on it all morning.

'There's *nothing* in this lot that could make anyone sick, is there?' Cathy had a vision of all Hannah Mitchell's guests groaning with some terrible food poisoning. Tom had said she was getting sillier by the hour, and he must be mad himself to have such an unhinged business partner.

'Give yourself plenty of time, fill the van with swirling music to calm yourself down and ring me tomorrow,' he soothed her. 'This time next year—imagine . . .' he said.

'I know, a great success story,' Cathy said looking much brighter than she actually felt.

It had been the way they got by. One being over-cheery and optimistic when the other was down. And now the van was packed. Neil wasn't home, he had to go to a consultation. He wasn't like an ordinary barrister, she thought proudly; he didn't have office hours or large consultancy fees. If someone was in trouble, he was there. It was as simple as that. It was why she loved him.

They had known each other since they were children but had hardly ever met. During all the years that Cathy's mother had worked at Oaklands, Neil had been away at boarding school and then college. It was such a chance that she should have met him again in Greece. If she had been cooking at one of the other villas, they would never have got to know each other and never have fallen in love. And wouldn't Hannah Mitchell have been a happier woman tonight? Cathy told herself to put it out of her mind. She was still much too early to go to Oaklands. She would call and see her own parents. That would calm her down.

Maurice and Elizabeth Scarlet, known to all as Muttie and Lizzie, lived in the inner city of Dublin in a semicircle of old, stone, two-storey houses. It was called St Jarlath's Crescent, and once the dwellings had all been occupied by factory workers who were woken by a siren each morning. Although it was only twenty minutes from Cathy and Neil's town house, it could have been a thousand miles, and a million miles from the rarefied world of Oaklands, where she was going tonight.

They were delighted to see Cathy. What were they doing to see the New Year in, she wondered? They were going out to a pub nearby where a lot of Muttie's associates would gather. The associates were actually the men he met up with in Sandy Keane's betting shop, but they all took their day's business very seriously and Cathy knew better than to joke about them.

'Will there be food?' she asked.

'At midnight they're going to give us chicken in a basket.' Muttie Scarlet was pleased at the generosity of the pub.

Cathy's father was small and round, his hair stood in wisps and his face was set in a permanent smile. He was fifty years of age and she had never known him work. His back had been too bad, but never quite too bad for him to get up to Sandy Keane's to put something on a cert in the three fifteen.

Lizzie Scarlet looked as she had always looked, small and strong and wiry. Her hair was set in a tight perm, which she had done four times a year in her cousin's hair salon.

'There's going to be a pub quiz with prizes, too,' Lizzie said. Cathy felt her heart go out to her undemanding parents who were so easily pleased.

'And have they all rung in from Chicago?' she asked. Cathy's two brothers and two sisters had all emigrated.

'Every one of them,' Lizzie said proudly.

'Well, I'd like to be with you tonight,' Cathy said truthfully. 'But instead I'll be disappointing Hannah with whatever food I produce.'

'Please be polite to her, Cathy, I've found over all the years it's better to humour her.'

'Relax, Mam. I agreed to do it, and if it kills me I will do it well and with a smile on my face.' Cathy kissed them goodbye and practised her smile as she drove to Oaklands.

Hannah Mitchell's husband Jock stopped on the way home from his office to have a drink. He felt he needed one before facing Hannah. She was always tense before a party but this time it would be magnified many times—she so hated having Cathy doing the catering.

He drank his single malt Scotch and wished that he didn't have to worry about this as well as everything else. Today his nephew Walter, an idle layabout, the eldest son of Jock's brother Kenneth, had revealed that all was not well at The Beeches, his family home. His father had gone to

England just before Christmas and had left no indication of his where-abouts. Walter's mother, Kay, not known to be a strong character, was reacting to this by a heavy reliance on vodka. What was happening to the nine-year-old twins, Simon and Maud? Walter shrugged; they were managing, he implied. Jock Mitchell sighed again.

As she arrived at Oaklands, Cathy's mobile phone rang.

'Hon, I'm not going to be there to help you unload.'

'Neil, it doesn't matter, I knew it would go on a bit.'

'It's more complicated than we thought. Listen, ask my dad to help you in with all those crates. Walter should be there . . .'

'If I were to wait for Walter to help me unload and set up, the party would be halfway through . . . Stop fussing and go back to what you have to do.'

Cathy told herself that there were only six hours or so of this year left, only six hours or so of being nice to Hannah. She looked down the tree-lined drive to the house. A gentleman's residence, 150 years old, with its four bedroom windows above the large front door and the bay windows on either side of it. Ivy and Virginia creeper covered the walls. It was a house as different from St Jarlath's Crescent as you could imagine.

Shona Burke often stayed late in her office up on the management floors of Hayward's. She had listened to the radio programme and was wondering if she had a choice about how she would spend New Year's Eve. Long ago in a happier life there would have been a celebration, but not in the last few years. She would make the hospital visit out of duty, of course, but it was pointless, she wouldn't be recognised or acknowledged.

Then she would go to Ricky's party in his studio. A pleasant, easy-going photographer, Ricky would gather a lot of people and make a buzz for them all. She was unlikely to meet the love of her life, but still Shona would dress up and go simply because she did not see herself as the kind of person who would sit alone in her apartment in Glenstar.

The question nagged her, what would she *really* like to be doing tonight? It was so hard to answer because everything had changed so much. The good days were over, and it was impossible to imagine doing something that would make her really happy. So in the absence of that, Ricky's would do fine.

Marcella was painting her toenails. She had new evening sandals which she'd bought at a thrift shop. She showed them proudly to Tom.

'They must have cost a fortune new,' she said, examining them carefully.

'Are you happy?' Tom asked.

'Very,' she said. 'And you?'

'Oh, very, very,' he laughed. Just looking at her made him happy. He couldn't really believe that such a beautiful girl, who could have had anyone she wanted, really found him enough for her.

Marcella picked up a tiny red garment from the back of a chair and put it on. It was actually a dress, short and tight, clinging to her and leaving nothing to the imagination.

'Marcella, are you really wearing that to the party?'

'Don't you like it?' her face clouded over immediately.

'Well, of course I like it. You look beautiful. It's just that maybe I'd like you to wear it here, for us, not for everyone else as well to see you.'

'But, Tom, it's a party dress,' she cried, stricken.

He pulled himself together at once.

'Of course it is, and you'll be the success of the night.'

'I thought you'd be proud of me,' she said.

'I am so proud you'll never know,' he reassured her.

Hannah Mitchell stood in her navy wool dress, her hair hard and lacquered from her New Year's Eve visit to Hayward's.

She watched Cathy carry in all the boxes and crates to the kitchen, standing in her way and fussing, hoping the crates wouldn't mark the wallpaper, and wondering where would Cathy put the van so that it would be out of the way when people came. Grimly, Cathy turned on the ovens, placed her bag of ice in the freezer and began to sort out the food. It would be useless asking Hannah Mitchell to leave her alone. She would stay put, fuss and irritate until the guests arrived.

'Will Mr Mitchell be home shortly?'

'I don't know, Cathy; really, it's not up to me to police Mr Mitchell about what time he comes home.' Cathy felt her neck redden in rage. How dare this woman be so offensive and patronising? But she knew her mother would beg her not to annoy Mrs Mitchell. Even her aunt Geraldine, who could normally be relied on for encouragement and support, would say Hannah Mitchell was an insecure nobody, not anyone to waste time worrying over. Cathy began to peel the foil from the dishes she had prepared.

'Is that fish? Not everyone eats it, you know.'

'I know, Mrs Mitchell, which is why there's a choice, you see. I'll be serving, so I'll tell them.'

'Tell them?' Hannah Mitchell was bewildered.

Cathy wondered was her mother-in-law a half-wit.

'Like asking them would they like fish in a seafood sauce, or herbed chicken, or the vegetarian goulash,' she said.

Mrs Mitchell tried but found it hard to find fault with this.

'Yes, well,' she said eventually.

Neil looked at his watch. Every single person in this room had some kind of New Year's function to go to except the student that they had all gathered to protect. Neil was trying to reassure this young Nigerian that there would be justice and a welcome for him in Ireland.

'When we're through here, you can come back to my parents' house,' Neil said. 'A barrel of laughs it won't be, but the food will be good.'

'I'm OK, Neil, truly, you're doing so much for me . . .'

'We'll go through it once more,' Neil said to the meeting, 'then Jonathan and I will go and party.' He saw them look at him in admiration. Neil Mitchell really went the distance. He felt a bit guilty at not being there to help Cathy as he had promised, but this was much more important—she'd understand.

Hannah still hovered, which meant that Cathy had to talk, answer inane questions and pat down unnecessary worries. She could have got things done faster had she not been under the scrutiny of the most critical eyes in the Western Hemisphere.

'It's seven thirty. Walter will be here any minute,' Cathy said desperately.

'Oh, Walter! Like all young people, I'm sure he'll be late.'

'I don't think so, Mrs Mitchell, not tonight. It's a professional engagement. I'm certain he won't let us down.' Cathy wasn't at all sure of this; she had no evidence that Walter Mitchell was reliable.

At that moment Jock Mitchell came into the kitchen rubbing his hands.

'I say, Hannah, isn't this an amazing spread?'

'Welcome home, Mr Mitchell.' Cathy said. 'Did Walter leave the office at the same time as you, by any chance?'

'Ages earlier,' her father-in-law said. 'Boy keeps his own time. I'm getting a bit of stick from the partners over him, as it happens.'

Hannah Mitchell hated family business being discussed in front of Cathy.

'Why don't you come upstairs and have a shower, dear? The guests will be here in half an hour,' she said crisply.

'Fine, fine. Don't you want any help, Cathy?'

'No, not at all. Neil will be along when he can.'

She was alone in the kitchen. Cathy unpacked the glasses, filled thirty of them with a sugar lump and a teaspoon of brandy and laid them on a tray. Later, once the guests arrived, she would top the glasses up with champagne. Walter was meant to be doing this while she got her canapés ready. Cathy caught a sight of herself in the hall mirror—she looked flushed and uneasy. Wisps of hair were escaping from the ribbon that tied it back. This would not do.

She went into the downstairs cloakroom and dampened her hair and tied it back more expertly. She put on her clean white shirt and her scarlet skirt. It looked a *bit* better, she thought. How wonderful if she got a lot of business out of this party! Please may it be a success.

Ricky's studio was in a basement, three rooms opening into each other, drink in one, food in another, dancing in a third. You didn't so much come in, you made an entrance down a big, brightly lit staircase.

Tom felt every eye in the room was on Marcella in her little red dress as she walked gracefully ahead of him down the stairs, with her beautiful long legs and the gold evening sandals. Every other woman seemed suddenly drab by comparison.

Marcella never ate or drank at these functions. She might have a glass of fizzy water. But she genuinely wasn't hungry, she said, with such sincerity that people believed her. Tom, however, was dying to see the food, to compare it to what he and Cathy would have done. Ricky's caterers seemed to have endless plates of insubstantial and tired-looking finger food. Smoked salmon already drying and hardening on bread, some kind of paté spread sparsely on unappetising-looking biscuits. But bit by bit he tasted and examined.

'Tom, stop tearing those unfortunate things to bits,' Marcella giggled at him. 'Come and dance with me.'

'In a moment,' he said, poking around the plates.

'Would you like to dance with me?' A boy of nineteen was staring at Marcella in disbelief.

'Tom?'

'Go ahead. I'll drag you away in a minute,' Tom grinned.

It was considerably later, and after three glasses of inferior wine, that he found his way to the little dance floor. Marcella was dancing with a man with a big red face and big hands, spread over Marcella's bottom. Tom moved up to them.

'I've come to drag you away,' he said.

'Hey,' the man said, 'fair's fair, find your own girl.'

'Oh, this is my girl,' Tom said firmly. 'If you don't mind . . .'

'Let's just finish this dance,' Marcella said.

He moved away, annoyed. He saw Shona Burke, a nice girl from Hayward's and one of the many people in Dublin who had been asked to look out for premises for the new catering company.

'Would you like me to get you a glass of red ink and a piece of cardboard with a scrape of meat paste on it?' he offered.

Shona laughed. 'Now, you're not going to get anywhere by badmouthing the opposition,' she said.

Tom's glance went back to Marcella, who was still dancing.

'It's all right, Tom, she has eyes for no one except you.'

Tom was embarrassed to have been so obvious. 'Would you like to dance?'

'No, Tom, I'm not going to be any part of this. Go and get Marcella.'

But by the time he came over, another man had asked her to dance. Tom went off to have another glass of the unspeakable wine.

Walter arrived at eight thirty, when there were ten guests already installed in the sitting room of Oaklands. He came in cheerfully kissing his aunt on both cheeks.

'Now let me give you a hand, Aunt Hannah,' he said with a smile.

'Such a nice boy, isn't he?' said Mrs Ryan to Cathy.

'Indeed,' Cathy managed to say.

Mrs Ryan and her husband had been the first guests to arrive. She was full of admiration for the canapés and had plenty of small talk.

Cathy was looking at Walter, small and handsome like all the Mitchells, and trying hard to keep her temper under control. He was being praised by people like her mother-in-law for having turned up one whole hour late. She was barely listening to Mrs Ryan.

'One thing they always wanted was apple strudels, and I just wouldn't know where to begin.'

Cathy brought her mind back. The woman was having some business friends of her husband's to coffee and cake next week. Was it possible for Cathy to deliver something?

It was their first booking. Nine o'clock and she had got a job already.

'Do you intend to stop dancing with strangers at all tonight?'

'Tom. At last,' Marcella said, excusing herself with a smile from a man.

'But maybe I'm not good enough to dance with,' he said.

'Don't be such a fool, put your arms around me,' she said.

'Is that what you say to all the lads?' he asked.

'Why are you being like this?' she was hurt and upset.

'You've lurched around half naked with half of Dublin,' he said.

'That's not fair.' Marcella was stung. 'It's a party, people ask other people to dance, that's what it's about. What's wrong, Tom?'

'I don't know, Marcella. I realise that I'm a spoilsport, but would you come home.'

'Come *home*?' she was astounded. 'We've only just got here. And we want to meet people, be seen a bit.'

'Yes, I know,' he said glumly.

'Do you not feel well?' she asked.

'No. I drank too much very cheap wine too quickly and ate five strange things that tasted like cement.'

'Well, will you sit down until it passes over.' Marcella had no intention of leaving. She had dressed up for this, looked forward to it.

'I might go home a bit before you,' he said.

'Don't do that; see the New Year in here, with all our friends,' she begged. 'Have another cement sandwich and cheer up.'

Cathy tried to show Walter how to make the champagne cocktails.

'Sure, sure, I know,' he said.

'And once they have started to drink the red and white with the supper, can you collect all the champagne flutes and get them into the kitchen. They need to be washed because champagne will be served again at midnight.'

'I'm paid to help pass things around, not be a washer-up.'

'You're being paid to help me for four hours to do whatever I ask you to do.' Cathy heard the tremble in her voice.

'Five hours,' he said.

'Four,' she said, looking him in the eye. 'You got here an hour late. When Neil comes, we'll discuss it with him. Meanwhile, please take this tray out to your uncle's guests.'

Cathy lifted trays of food from the oven. This night would end, some time.

Eventually Neil got away from his meeting. He drove Jonathan through the streets of Dublin and out to where Oaklands stood. He parked the Volvo and ran in the back door. Cathy was surrounded by plates and glasses. How could anyone do this for a living and stay sane . . .?

'Cathy, I'm sorry things took longer, this is Jonathan. Jonathan, this is Cathy.'

She shook hands with the tall Nigerian.

'I hope I'm not causing you additional problems by coming here,' he said.

'No, heavens no, Jonathan,' Cathy protested, wondering what her mother-in-law's reaction would be. 'You're most welcome.'

'Happy New Year, hon.' Neil put his arms around her. 'Is it going all right in there?' Neil nodded towards the front rooms.

'OK, I think. Go on in. Take Jonathan to meet people and distract your mother.'

She could hear cries of excitement as people welcomed the son and heir of Oaklands.

'I think I'll go home,' Tom Feather said aloud to himself. 'Will you tell Marcella that I've gone home,' he said to Ricky.

'Not a lovers' quarrel on New Year's Eve, please.' Ricky always put on a slightly camp accent. It was part of the way he went on. 'Come on. It's under an hour to midnight.'

'I'm in no form for it, I'm only bringing other people down.'

'I'll see Marcella gets back safely,' Ricky said.

'Thanks, mate.' And he was gone, out into the streets of Dublin. Everything about the party annoyed him; all this insecurity that he wasn't good enough for Marcella would keep bubbling back to the surface.

He didn't go straight home. He walked instead up and down little streets that he had never walked before, the lanes, mews and even back-yards. Somewhere in this city of a million people there was a place which he and Cathy could find to start their catering company.

The phone rang in the hall of Oaklands.

Hannah Mitchell hastened out to answer it. She was confused: Neil had brought this African man to the party. People kept asking who he was, and she didn't really know. One of Neil's clients, she said over and over. It was a relief to escape.

'I'm sure that's Amanda phoning from Canada,' she trilled. It was not her daughter.

'Jock, it's Kenneth's children, apparently they're in the house on their own tonight. You talk to them. I told them Walter was here but they didn't think he'd be any help.'

'Well, well, tell me the problem,' Jock said wearily down the phone.

Cathy moved among the guests, passing little plates of a rich choco-late cake and a spoonful of fruit pavlova on the side. She saw Jonathan standing alone and awkward at the window, while Neil went round the room greeting his parents' friends. She spoke to him as often as she could without making it look as if she was trying to mind him. Cathy moved on and found herself within earshot of Jock on the phone.

'That's fine then, children, I'll put Walter on to you and I'll come round tomorrow. Good children, now.'

Cathy listened as the boy talked to his brother and sister, who were over ten years younger than he was.

'Now *listen* to me. I will be home. I'm not sure what time, because I have to go somewhere when I leave here, but I *will* be there some time. So just go to bed, for heaven's sake.'

He turned round and saw Cathy watching him.

'There's a crisis at home, so I'm afraid I'm off duty. Suppose I just take what's owing to me . . . Four hours will do,' he said grudgingly.

'You haven't even been here for three hours,' she said. 'You're not going straight home, you're going to a party somewhere.'

'Three hours then, cheapskate.'

'No, that's what I am most certainly not. Come into the kitchen.'

Her heart sank when she saw the washing-up, including the champagne glasses that would be needed at midnight.

'Good night, Walter.'

'Good night, Scrooge,' he said, and ran out of the house.

Tom stood by the canal and watched two swans gliding by.

'They mate for life, swans, did you know that?' he said to a passing girl.

'Do they now? Lucky old them,' she said. She was small and thin, he noticed; a druggy prostitute with an anxious face.

'Don't suppose you'd like any casual mating yourself,' she said hopefully.

'No, no, sorry,' Tom said.

'Happy New Year anyway,' she said.

'And to you,' he said, feeling hopeless.

The doorbell rang in Oaklands.

Hannah teetered out on her high heels, wondering who else it could be, arriving so late. Cathy leaned against a table at the back of the hall to support her tired legs and to see if it was a late guest wanting food.

It appeared to be two children in a taxi which they didn't have the money to pay for. Cathy almost felt sorry for Hannah. A Nigerian student, and now two waifs. What else would the night throw at her?

'Please get Mr Mitchell immediately, Cathy,' Hannah ordered.

'Is that the maid?' the little boy asked. He was pale and aged about eight or nine. Like his sister, he had dead straight fair hair and everything looked the same colour—his sweater, his hair, his face and the small canvas bag he carried.

Cathy had never seen them before. Jock Mitchell and his brother Kenneth were not close; the nearest they had ever come to solidarity was in the apprenticeship of Walter in his uncle's office.

Jock was not enthusiastic at the sight of them.

'Well?' he began. 'What have we here?'

'We had nowhere to go,' the boy explained.

Jock looked bewildered. 'Cathy,' he said eventually, 'these are Walter's brother and sister, can you give them something to eat in the kitchen?'

'Certainly, Mr Mitchell, I'll look after them.'

'*Are* you the maid?' the boy asked again.

'No. I'm Cathy, married to Neil, your cousin. How do you do?' They looked at her solemnly. 'And perhaps you might give me your names?' Maud and Simon, it turned out. 'Come into the kitchen,' she said wearily. 'Do you like herbed chicken?'

'No', said Maud.

Cathy noticed them putting some chocolate biscuits in their pockets.

'Put those back,' she said sharply. 'There'll be no stealing,' she said.

'It's not stealing, you were told to give us something to eat,' Maud countered with spirit.

'And I will—so just put them back this minute.'

Grudgingly, they put the already crushed and crumbly biscuits back on the silver tray. Swiftly Cathy made them sandwiches and poured them a glass of milk each. They ate hungrily.

'In your lives so far did anyone mention the words "thank you" at all?' she asked.

'Thank you,' they said ungraciously.

'You're most welcome,' she said with exaggerated politeness.

'What will we do now?' Simon asked.

'Well, I think you might sit here—unless you wanted to help me wash up?'

'Not really, to be honest,' Maud said.

Hannah came into the kitchen, with her tottering, tiny steps which always set Cathy's teeth on edge.

'Oh, you're sitting here, Cathy, I think people's glasses need . . .'

'Of course, Mrs Mitchell, I'll go and see to it . . .'

Cathy paused just long enough to hear Maud asking, 'What rooms will we have, Aunt Hannah, we've brought our pyjamas and everything . . .'

Cathy worked and worked. She removed plates, picked up scrunched-up napkins, emptied ashtrays, kept things moving. Soon it would be midnight and things might begin to wind down. She looked towards the window where she had left Jonathan to fend for himself. He was talking animatedly to someone. Cathy looked again. The twins were in deep conversation with him.

'Jock, *what* are we going to do with them? They can't stay here.'

'Well, not for ever, Hannah, no. But until we get them settled.'

'And how long will that be?'

'Soon, soon. Put them in Neil's and Mandy's rooms, or wherever. Haven't we a house full of bedrooms, for heaven's sake.'

Hannah went over to the ill-assorted group at the window. 'Now children, don't annoy Neil's client, Mr . . . um . . .' she began.

'Oh, but they're not annoying me at all—delightful company,' Jonathan begged.

'Time for bed, anyway,' Hannah said.

Hannah ushered the children up the broad, sweeping staircase of Oaklands. She showed them their bedroom and said they were to remain there quietly in the morning.

'Are your nerves bad? Like our mother's?' Maud asked.

'Of course they're not,' Hannah snapped. Then she recovered herself. 'Now it's all been very upsetting for you but it will get sorted out.'

'Which is my room?'

'Whichever one you like.' Hannah pointed to Amanda's and Neil's old bedrooms.

'Good night, now. We'll talk about everything in the morning.'

'Which room will you have?' Simon asked. They had done a complete tour.

'I'd like the one with all the coats in it,' Maud said.

'But . . . It could be their own bedroom. Look, it opens into a bathroom.'

'She said wherever we liked. We could put the coats on chairs.' Maud was determined. They stood in Jock and Hannah Mitchell's large bedroom.

'Look, she has all this make-up that mother used to have on her dressing table before her nerves got bad.' Maud picked up some lipsticks.

'What are the black things?'

'They're for eyebrows.'

Simon drew heavy dark eyebrows and then a moustache. Maud put on a dark red lipstick and then used a pinker shade to make little spots on her cheeks. She picked up a cut-glass atomiser and began to spray.

'Hey, that got in my eye,' Simon said, picking up what looked like a large can of hair lacquer in retaliation. It turned out to be some kind of mousse. It went all over the dressing table.

There were long earrings which Maud tried on. Simon found a short fur jacket and put it on with a man's hat. They were bouncing happily on the two large beds with white counterpanes when two women came into the bedroom.

They gasped and one of them screamed when she saw Simon wearing her jacket. Her screams frightened Maud and Simon, who screamed back, and Hannah and Jock came running up the stairs to find out what had happened.

Tom walked on up from the canal and down a lane he had never been down before. And that's where he saw it. A wrought-iron gate leading into a cobbled courtyard, and what looked like an old coach house that had been converted for some business. He pushed open the iron gate and went up to the door where there was a piece of cardboard on which someone had written 'FOR SALE' and a phone number. Bells were ringing all over Dublin, it was midnight, a new year had arrived. Tom peered through the windows. He had found their premises.

Cathy filled the champagne glasses for midnight, and as the bells rang over the city they all toasted each other and sang 'Auld Lang Syne'. Hannah Mitchell looked almost pleased with it all.

Cathy cleared and washed and dried in the kitchen, she packed crates and took them to the van and neatly arranged several little dishes of goodies for Hannah to discover the next day, in the refrigerator. The bulk of the work was done. Now all she had to worry about was serving more coffee. She felt tired in every one of her bones. She heard the telephone ring, thank God. Neil's sister had finally called them. Then she heard Hannah say in tones of disbelief, '*Cathy*. You want to talk to Cathy?' She moved to the hall.

'It's for you,' her mother-in-law said, astounded.

'Cathy,' said Tom, 'I've found it.'

'Found what?' she asked.

'The premises,' he said. 'I've found the place where Scarlet Feather is going to live.'

TOM FEATHER GOT some cold orange juice from the fridge, and fixed a flower to the glass with some sticky tape. He marched straight into the bedroom.

'Happy New Year to the most beautiful, saintly and forgiving woman in the world,' he said.

Marcella woke and rubbed her eyes. 'I'm not saintly and forgiving. I'm furious with you,' she began.

'But you haven't denied that you are beautiful, and I have totally forgiven *you,*' he said happily.

'What do you mean? There was nothing to forgive *me* for.' She was very indignant indeed.

'Quite right, I should thank you instead, because last night I found the premises. If you hadn't forced me to leave that party, I'd never have found the place. I'll take you to see it as soon as you're dressed—'

'If you think I'm going to leap out of bed and—'

'You're so right. I do not think that for one moment. Instead I think *I'm* going to leap *into* bed.' And he had his crumpled clothes off as he spoke.

In Neil and Cathy's house at Waterview the phone rang. 'It's your mother, saying all the guests are dead from salmonella,' Cathy said.

'More likely to be some shrink saying that you've been committed to a mental home for advanced paranoia,' Neil said.

It wasn't, it was about Jonathan.

'Tell them I'm on my way,' Neil was saying.

Cathy put coffee in a flask as he dressed.

'Take it with you, you can drink it in the car,' she said.

He took the flask and kissed her. 'I'm very sorry, hon. I *did* want to go and see this place with you this morning, you know I did.'

'I know, this is more important. Go.'

'Don't sign anything or accept anything until we've had someone take a look at it.'

'No, Mr Barrister, you know I won't! Now go and save Jonathan before it's too late.'

Cathy watched him from the window. He must have known she would be watching. He waved up at her. Jonathan was lucky: Neil would worry at the case like a dog with a bone.

'God that was a good party.' Jock groaned. 'I feel it not exactly in my bones, more in the front left-side of my head.'

'I'm not surprised,' Hannah was terse. 'But, Jock, those children are not staying another night in this house.'

'Don't be hasty,' he pleaded.

'I'm not being hasty. I was a saint out of heaven, not breaking every bone in their body when I saw the wreckage in here last night.'

'Where else can they go? They're my brother's children. He seems to have abandoned them.'

'It's too much,' Hannah protested. 'And they were very rude, both of them, no apology, saying I'd said they could have any room and they had chosen this one. Enough to crucify anyone at what was meant to be a party, a celebration.'

'Well, didn't Cathy do that very well. I heard a lot of praise for—'

'What do men know of what needs to be done?'

'She left the place like a new pin.' He tried to defend his daughter-in-law.

'Well, at least some of the training I gave her poor mother must have paid off eventually.'

'True,' Jock said, getting up to get a painkiller.

Geraldine O'Connor had been up since seven o'clock. She had been alone in the Glenstar swimming pool: usually she would have had the company of half a dozen other Glenstar residents, but New Year's Eve had taken its toll. Geraldine did her twelve lengths, washed her hair and went through the arrangements again for today's big charity lunch. She had been wise to leave the photographer's party early last night. There had been nobody that interested her to talk to, a lot of them much younger than she was. Cathy and Neil would have been there, but of course Cathy had been catering that Mitchells' party last night. Geraldine hoped that it had gone well and that there had been a chance to make some useful contacts. Geraldine wished they could find premises soon. She had agreed to back them, as had Joe Feather, Tom's rather shady elder brother. All they had to do was find the place. And then brave, gutsy Cathy wouldn't have to nail a smile on her face and work in the kitchen of her mother-in-law's house. One of the advantages of being single was that there were no mothers-in-law to cope with, Geraldine thought as she poured more coffee.

In a different part of the Glenstar apartments, Shona Burke woke up and thought about the year ahead. Many other women of twenty-six would wake today with a comforting body on the other side of the bed. In fact, she was sick of people asking her when she was going to settle down. It was so intrusive.

As it happened, at last night's party at Ricky's she had had one very definite offer and two suggestions. But these would not have been people she could trust or rely on. And Shona Burke was not one to trust easily. She would get up soon and go out to Dun Laoghaire for a brisk walk.

In the garden flat of a big Victorian house in Rathgar, James Byrne was up and at his desk. Ever since he had retired he had continued the routine of working life. Breakfast of a boiled egg, tea and toast, ten minutes, minimal tidying his three-room apartment. It had been useful when he worked in the big accountancy firm. Cleared his head, sorted his priorities before he got into the office. Now of course there was less to do, but he could always find something. To his surprise the telephone rang. Very few people telephoned James Byrne at any time, and he certainly hadn't expected a call at ten o'clock on New Year's Day. It was a girl.

'Mr Byrne? Is it too early to talk?'

'No, no. How can I help you?'

The voice was very excited. 'It's about the premises, Mr Byrne, we're so interested. Is there any chance we could see them today?'

'Premises?' James Byrne was confused. 'What premises?'

He listened as she explained. It was the Maguires' old place, the printing works they hadn't even entered since the accident. Now, apparently, they had disappeared, leaving a 'FOR SALE' sign on their gate and James Byrne's phone number.

'Let me see if I can find the keys, Miss Scarlet,' James said. 'I'll call you back within the hour.'

Cathy put the phone down carefully and looked around her in Tom's apartment, where the little group had been following every word of the conversation. Tom, leaning forward, like their father always did to a radio when he wanted to hear who was winning a race. Marcella in an old shirt of Tom's and black jeans, her dark eyes and clouds of black hair making her look more and more like the top model she yearned to be. Geraldine, crisp and elegant, dressed for her smart lunch but still giving time to be present for the great phone call and what it might deliver.

'He's not an estate agent, he's an accountant, he knows the people who own it and he'll ring us back in an hour,' she said, eyes shining.

It felt like three hours, but Geraldine told them it was only thirty-six minutes. Then the call came. This time Tom took it. James Byrne had been in touch with his friends in England. They reported they really did intend to sell. James Byrne had been asked to set it all in train. And as quickly as possible. Cathy looked at Tom in disbelief. They were the first potential buyers in there with a chance.

'Of course you will understand that my first loyalty lies with the Maguires who own the premises. I will have to try to get them the best price possible.'

'Yes, of course,' Tom sounded deflated.

Geraldine was scribbling something on the back of an envelope and showing it to him.

'Is there any chance you could show us inside the place, do you think?' Tom asked.

There was a pause. 'Certainly,' the man said. 'That would be no problem. Suppose we meet there in an hour?'

Small and rather precise-looking, wearing a navy overcoat and gloves, James Byrne was a man in his sixties who might have been cast in a film as a worried bank manager. He introduced himself formally and shook hands with everyone.

They walked through in wonder. The place that could be Scarlet Feather's new home. First home.

All this middle section could be the main kitchen; this would be the freezer section, and they would have storage here. And a small room where they could greet clients. Everything was what they had hoped. And it was so run-down; perhaps others might not realise the potential. Cathy was aware that she had clasped her hands and closed her eyes only when she heard James Byrne clear his throat. She knew she must reassure him.

'It's all right, Mr Byrne, I do know it's not ours. This is only the first step of a very long journey,' she smiled at him warmly.

James Byrne smiled back at her. 'It might not be too long a journey, Ms Scarlet. The Maguires want a quick sale. It might move much more quickly than you all think.'

Their house at number seven Waterview was described as a town house. A stupid word that just added several thousands pounds to the small two-bedroom house and tiny garden, built for people like Neil and Cathy, young couples with two jobs and no children as yet.

Hannah Mitchell had particularly disapproved of their having no dining room, Cathy had immediately decided that the room should be a study, since they would eat in the kitchen. The study had three walls lined with bookshelves and two tables where they worked late hours together. It was one of the great strengths they had, the ability to work side by side companionably. They had friends who often complained that one or the other was working to the exclusion of their having a good time. But Cathy and Neil had never felt like that. From the very first time they had got to know each other out in Greece, they had had very few misunderstandings. Neil had understood that Cathy wanted to run her own business. Cathy had known that he wanted a certain kind of law practice. There would be no short cuts for Neil Mitchell, no pretending that he was somehow doing business by being out on a golf course. They would talk late into the night about the dyslexic defendant who had never had a chance because he had never understood the forms that were sent to him. Or they would go through the budgets yet again for Scarlet Feather, and Neil would get out his calculator.

Cathy let herself into number 7 Waterview, sat quietly in the kitchen and looked up at their art collection. Everything there had been painted by someone they knew. The Greek sunrise by the old man in the taverna where they had stayed. The prison cell by the woman on a murder charge that Neil had got acquitted.

A telephone in a quiet house can sound like an alarm bell.

'Is Neil there?' her mother-in-law snapped.

'I'm afraid he's out with Jonathan.'

'Cathy, he has to come here at once . . . I need Neil to get those children out of here. They left bath taps running and most of the kitchen ceiling has come down. We haven't had a moment's peace—and as for you, Cathy, those children have eaten entirely unsuitable rich desserts and have been sick. I need to talk to Neil. Now.'

'I can't contact him for you, I really can't. But I know he'd say we'll take them here. So that's what we'll do.' Cathy sighed.

'Can you, Cathy?' The relief in Hannah's voice was clear. 'I don't want Neil to say I put them on to you . . .'

'It won't be like that.'

'No. But get him to ring me the moment you can.'

Cathy dialled Neil's mobile phone and left a message. 'Sorry to disturb you with trivia, but the twins have apparently brought down the ceiling in Oaklands. Ring your mother soonest.'

Tom rang to say he wanted to borrow the van.

'I want to go up into the mountains. It's just I can't think or talk about anything but the premises and I'm afraid I'll drive Marcella demented. Do you want to come? Is Neil bearing up?'

'He's still out fighting the good fight. I'd better not come with you, though. The twins from hell who turned up at Oaklands last night are probably getting ready to come to Waterview as we speak.'

'Cathy, they can't!' Tom was aghast. 'You don't have room, apart from anything else.'

'Don't I know it, but as my father would say, even money we see them here tonight.'

'I'll just sneak in and take the van away,' Tom said.

'Don't look up at a window, they could fire something at you,' she said with a laugh.

28

'Just one word of warning, Cathy, and then I'll shut up about it all. Don't let Neil take them on and then go off saving the world and leaving them to you.'

She sighed. 'And will you take one word of warning from me. Drive carefully, we haven't finished paying for that van yet.'

Cathy made a cup of tea and thought about Tom. They had met on her first day at catering college and his enthusiasm and the light in his eyes had been the keynote of their years on the course.

There had been the picnics and barbecues where Tom insisted they must be true to their calling and insisted on marinating kebabs when others would have been content with burnt sausages. Cathy could almost smell those nights full of food and herbs and wine on the beaches around Dublin.

He had never been short of girlfriends but took none of them seriously. He had a way of looking at people that seemed to suggest no one else in the world existed. He was interested in the most trivial things people told him and he was afraid of no one.

They had been talking about Scarlet Feather from the earliest days. While their friends wanted to do hotel work, be celebrity restaurant chefs, Tom and Cathy had this dream of serving top-grade food in people's homes.

They worked together in restaurants to get the feel for the kind of food people liked. Cathy was amused at how casually Tom took the compliments and the come-on glances directed his way. Even the stern Brenda Brennan in Quentin's was sometimes heard to say she wished she were twenty years younger.

Had Cathy fancied him herself in those days? Well, yes, in a way. And it might well have come to something. She smiled at the recollection.

They had planned to go to Paris on a very cheap flight. They had listed the restaurants they would visit: some to admire from the window, one to tour the kitchens because a fellow student had got a job there and two where they might actually eat dinner. They hadn't exactly said that this was the trip when they might become lovers. But it was in the air. Cathy had her legs waxed and bought a very expensive lacy slip. They had been all set to leave on a Friday afternoon and then that morning Lizzie Scarlet fell off a ladder in Oaklands and was taken to hospital by ambulance, Tom was offered a weekend's work at Quentin's and Cathy was called to interview for a job cooking in a Greek villa for the summer.

They told themselves that Paris would always be there.

Cathy went to the Greek island and met Neil Mitchell, a guest in the villa. And Tom met Marcella Malone.

Cathy heard a key turn in the door.

'Where are the twins?' she called.

'They're in the car,' Neil answered sheepishly. 'You knew they were coming? Mother said you did, but I didn't really believe her.' His face was alight now, as if he had expected a protest. 'And you don't mind?'

'I didn't say that. But you had to bring them. How was Jonathan?'

'It looks as though it's going to be OK.'

'Well done.'

'It was a group effort, teamwork,' he said as always. 'I'll get the twins.'

She watched them coming up the steps, muttering to each other that it was a much smaller house, wondering was there a television in the bedroom. Cathy forced herself to remember that they were nine, frightened, and had been abandoned by their father, mother and brother.

'This is the Last Chance Saloon,' she said pleasantly as they came in. 'You have one small bedroom between you with no television. We have a very stern policy on bathrooms here, leaving them clean but not overflowing for the next person, and there's an endless amount of please and thank you going on but apart from that you'll have a great time.'

They looked at her doubtfully.

'The food is terrific, for one thing.'

'That's for sure,' said Neil.

'Did you marry her because she was a good cook?' Simon asked.

'Or did it just turn out that she was a good cook?' wondered Maud.

'And my name is Cathy Scarlet. I am married to your cousin Neil so from now on I won't be referred to as "she" or "her".'

'Why don't you have Neil's name if you're married to him?' Maud wanted everything cleared up.

'Because I am a woman of fiercely independent nature and I need my own name for my work,' Cathy explained. This seemed to satisfy them.

'Right, could we see the room?' Simon said.

'I beg your pardon?' Cathy was icy.

He got it. 'I mean, please can we see the room. Thank you.' He looked pale and tired; they both did.

'Come on, then, I'll show you,' she said.

'How did you get on today?' Neil asked eventually when the children were asleep.'

'It was exactly what we want . . . But we have to be patient.'

The days crawled by after that. They waited and waited. And then finally, 'James Byrne here, Miss Scarlet.'

'Mr Byrne?'

'You did say that it was fine to call either of you.'

'Please, is there any news?' Cathy wanted to scream at him.

'Now, the Maguire family are going to accept your offer, subject to—'

'Mr Byrne, what do we do now?'

'You'll tell Mr Feather, I imagine, Ms Scarlet, and then you both get your lawyer and your bank, and then we go to contract.'

And everything began to move very quickly after that. Too quickly. There were not enough minutes in any hour to cope with all that had to be done. When Cathy was sitting with Geraldine and the bank manager, she should have been meeting Tom and his father at JT Feather's builder's yard. When she should have been at the solicitor's, she was making spaghetti bolognese for Maud and Simon Mitchell.

Why had she agreed to take those monstrous children into Waterview at this of all times because of some vague marital disharmony in their home? There was marital disharmony in every home in the Western world at the beginning of January. Why couldn't their big brother Walter look after them? Why bother asking that question? Walter wouldn't have known where to find their cornflakes in the morning, that was supposing he was ever home by breakfast.

They asked disconcerting questions . . .

'Do you have a drinking problem, Cathy?' Simon asked.

'Only problem is getting enough time to drink these days,' Cathy said cheerfully. Then she remembered the danger of being ironic with children. 'Why exactly did you wonder that?'

'You seem kind of anxious,' Simon explained.

'And there's a big bottle of brandy on the kitchen table,' Maud added.

'Oh! I see . . . no, that's for putting in Mrs Ryan's apple strudels not for drinking. And I'm anxious because I'm buying a business.'

'Why are you buying a business? Why don't you stay at home and have children instead?' Maud wondered.

Cathy looked at them. With their pale, straight hair and pasty little faces, they lacked their elder brother's charm, but they also lacked his selfishness. They did genuinely seem interested in her predicament, and she must answer them truthfully. 'I'd like to have something of my own. So that's why I want a business. And Neil and I may well have children some time, maybe in a few years . . .'

'Wouldn't you be too old to have children then?'

'I don't think so, Maud,' Cathy said. 'I did check.'

'Suppose they came earlier, by accident?' Simon frowned.

'We arranged that they won't arrive until we're ready for them.'

Tom was sympathetic about the twins, but the day they were going to see the lawyers he became suddenly anxious.

'I wonder can we leave them anywhere else today, Cathy . . .'

'Jesus, Tom, I can't leave two children in a house on their own all day.'

'Are you suggesting that they come and negotiate some of the finer points of the contract with the solicitor?'

'Tom, stop picking on me. You're nervous, I'm nervous. Where else can I take them?'

'Take them to your mother and father's.'

'And have my dad take their pocket money to put on something with three legs?'

'Warn them about your dad. Cathy, we *can't* take them to the lawyer.'

'How are you, Simon?' Muttie gave a manly handshake.

'What's your name?' Simon was suspicious.

'Muttie.'

'Right. How are you, Muttie?' Simon asked.

'Or even Mr Scarlet, possibly,' Tom suggested.

'Muttie's fine,' said Cathy's father. 'And this is Maud. You're very welcome, child.'

'What are we going to do today?' Maud asked ungraciously.

'I thought we'd take a little walk,' Muttie began. 'You see, I have one or two things to do, and maybe I could persuade you . . .'

'No, Da,' Cathy cried. 'And kids, remember what I told you?'

'I know he's an addict,' Simon said.

Cathy closed her eyes.

'A what?' Muttie asked.

Simon was clear on his instructions. 'You can't help it, it's like being a drug addict. You think if someone has a pound you need it to put on a horse, and Cathy says we have to buy magazines or sweets as quick as we can if you suggest it.'

'You know I didn't put it quite like that, Da.'

As they left for the lawyer's office Cathy heard Simon asking her father casually. 'Do you have an addiction to drink too, Muttie? My mother has, she can't help it, you see.'

Cathy leaped into the white van. 'I want to be out of here before we hear him inviting the twins down to a good pub on the docks.'

It went so smoothly at the lawyer's that Tom and Cathy were worried. There should have been some hold-up.

There was one message each on their mobile phones when they got back to the van. Cathy was to ring her aunt Geraldine. Urgently. Tom was to ring his father. They stood at either end of the van, talking. They finished and came back to sit down, both in good humour.

'Well, you first, *was* it a crisis?' he asked.

'Absolutely not. It was great news, she knows a restaurant selling up a load of kitchen equipment, cookers as good as new, an enormous chest freezer. We can go over and look at them today.'

Tom said his father had agreed to do the building job. 'He's around at the premises already. The Maguires want their equipment moved out and sold, so Da and the others are clearing the place.'

There were very few people looking at the kitchen equipment. It was almost exactly what they wanted.

'Isn't it kind of sad?' Cathy said in a whisper.

'I know,' Tom agreed. 'I was just thinking that. Someone else's dreams gone up in smoke.'

'It won't happen to us.' She sounded braver than she felt.

And all day their mobile phones kept ringing. Something else the lawyers needed, some problem JT Feather had unearthed, James Byrne looking for another detail. At none of the places they visited was there ever any proper parking. Nobody they called was ever at a desk. At four o'clock they were very hungry but there was no time to stop, so Tom got them two bars of chocolate and a banana each. Somehow they got through the day, and Cathy realised guiltily as she drove to St Jarlath's Crescent that she had left those children there for far too long.

The twins were alone in the kitchen, staring at the oven and covered with flour. They had made pastry, they said, and Muttie's wife had helped them make a steak and kidney pie which they were going to take home with them because the shoemaker's children were never shod.

'Did you enjoy it?' Cathy asked. She had loved helping her mother to cook.

'Not much,' Simon said arrogantly.

'He thinks it's not men's work,' Maud explained.

'It's just I didn't expect to be doing this. We don't do this at home,' Simon complained.

'It's always good to learn things,' Cathy said, wanting to slap him. All he could do was complain. 'What did you learn today?'

'I learned you need sharp knives to cut up the meat. Have you got any sharp knives for your waitressing business?'

'Catering business, actually. Yes, I do, thank you, Simon.'

'Muttie's wife has a great way to put salt and pepper in the flour,' Maud began. 'You shake it all up in a paper bag together.'

'Oh, for Christ's sake call her Lizzie,' cried Cathy.

'We didn't know her name, you see,' Maud explained, startled. 'Anyway,' Maud added, 'we told them that this is better than Oaklands and we could keep coming here until things got back to normal at The Beeches.'

Cathy looked at them in disbelief. What amazingly self-possessed, confident children. They were sure of their welcome anywhere, free to criticise and comment. That's what being a Mitchell did for you.

'And what did they say?'

'Muttie said that he didn't have any problem with it, and his wife Lizzie said that it would all depend on Aunt Hannah.'

'Where are they now?' Cathy asked.

'Muttie said he was slipping out to the shoemaker . . .'

'Bookmaker,' Simon corrected Maud.

'And his wife Lizzie is upstairs on the phone because her daughter telephoned from Chicago.'

Cathy sat down. It could be a lot worse, she supposed.

'We have to watch as it goes golden brown,' Simon said.

'Who is the bookmaker, and why was he never shod?' Maud wanted to know.

'It's a sort of saying, really. A shoemaker makes so many pairs of shoes for other people that he never has time to make any for his own children.'

'Why don't they get shoes in the shops?' Maud asked.

'Is he coming to dinner with us? Is that why we made the pie?' Simon wondered.

'Not tonight,' Cathy said wearily.

Neil's court case was all over the papers. Prominent civil rights leaders had come to court, there was talk of a big protest march, a stay had been given for three months. Cathy had time only for a quick glance at the evening paper as she settled the children in the kitchen with instructions on how to set the table, and grabbed a shower. She was just pulling on a clean T-shirt and jeans when Neil came into the bedroom.

'Well done, I saw in the paper you're a hero. Was he delighted?'

'He was more stunned than anything else I think, but the great thing is we've mobilised a lot of support. It won't be so easy for them the next time.' Neil's face was animated and excited. Cathy hung her head slightly. Her own day seemed suddenly trivial.

Neil stroked her cheek. 'You look lovely, you know. What a pity we don't have time to . . .'

'I don't think we'll have time for that sort of thing in the foreseeable future. Let's go and eat dinner and celebrate.'

Simon had the table set. 'Are we sure the shoemaker isn't coming?' he asked, slightly worried.

'The shoemaker?' Neil paused in drawing the cork from a bottle of wine.

'Don't ask, please don't ask,' said Cathy.

'Were the cookers suitable?' Geraldine wanted to know next morning.

'Perfect, we're going to take two plus a fridge, a freezer, a deep-fat fryer and a lot of saucepans.'

'Great stuff. Have you time for lunch?'

'I'd love it, Geraldine, but I haven't a minute, we have to meet the insurance broker again, and there's a good January sale on. I thought I might have a quick hunt for curtain material before we meet James Byrne again up at the premises.'

'You're killing yourself.'

'Early days, busy days.' Cathy sounded cheerful.

'And why are these awful children not going back to their own people?' Geraldine was disapproving.

'There *are* no own people, Geraldine, so what can we do?' Cathy wailed. 'We can't let them go into a home.'

'So they're in your home instead. I bet that's a barrel of laughs.'

'Don't worry, Geraldine, it's not going to last for ever.'

'Mam, I really owe you for this,' Cathy said, falling into a chair.

'Not at all, they kept your father out of the betting shop.' Lizzie poured them mugs of tea. 'He took them to the zoo, no less.'

'Where are they?'

'Drawing away, there's not a word out of them.'

Muttie had given them paper to draw their favourite animal at the zoo. Simon had done ten drawings of snakes. Maud had done six owls.

'Muttie says he sees no reason why we couldn't have an owl at home,' Maud greeted Cathy.

'He doesn't? Maybe he could explain it to your mother and father when they get back to The Beeches.'

'They might never be back,' Simon said cheerfully. 'There's no word of our father, and our mother's nerves are pretty bad this time, I think.'

Cathy went back to her mother. 'What am I going to do, Mam?'

'I'll tell you one thing, a couple of days here and that is fine, but long-term you're not doing yourself any favours taking those children in. Can't you see it's showing her up as well . . . as well as everything else?'

'What do you mean, Mam? "As well as everything else?"'

'Well, you know, all this setting up a business. People like that expect you to be staying at home and making Neil a good wife.'

'Oh, Mam, for God's sake. Tell me what's so good about Hannah Mitchell, a woman who won't even take two unfortunate brats who are part of her husband's family. I hate that woman for the way she turned her back on them. I know they're monsters and they're both as daft as brushes but they're not the worst, and it's not *their* fault that nobody wants them.' She broke off because of the frozen look on her mother's face. Simon and Maud stood behind her open-mouthed in the doorway, having heard every single word.

The white van stopped for an ice cream. Cathy bought three cones and they settled down companionably to eat them in the van.

'Why do you hate Aunt Hannah?' Simon asked.

'She doesn't like my being married to Neil, she thinks that my family and I have no class. That annoys me.'

'Do you want to have class?' Maud wanted to know.

'No, no way. I don't give three blind damns what she thinks about *me*. But she looked down on my mother, and I can't forgive her for that. Now let's go and buy some supper, since you didn't make us a pie today.'

In the Chinese restaurant the children studied the menu carefully.

'Are you and Neil rich or poor?' Simon asked.

'If you don't mind my saying so, it's not a question you ask people—'

'But I need to know in order to know how many dishes we can order,' Simon said.

'Oh, I see. Well, we could have Imperial Menu A.'

'You must be very rich indeed, richer than your father.'

'What?' She was exhausted.

'Do you hear things in your head, like he does?' asked Maud.

'I didn't know he heard things in his head.'

'Yes, all the time. The sound of hooves, thundering hooves. He says they go at the same rhythm as your heart. Did you know that, Cathy?'

'I'm not sure I did, Maud.'

'*And* Muttie says that the sound makes your blood run faster in your veins and gives you a better life,' said Simon.

'Oh, it does? We must try that then,' she said as she grabbed the price list and ordered Imperial Menu A.

'I don't think it's something you try. You have it or you don't. We both have it, as it turns out,' Simon smirked.

'Well, I'm very sorry if you do,' Cathy said grimly. 'Because you'll spend the rest of your lives deafened by the hooves, and have no time or money for anything else.'

'Tell me something, Neil,' she said that night in bed.

He put down the copy of the law reports he was reading and turned to face her. 'I know the question you are going to ask.'

'What am I going to ask?' Cathy laughed.

'What plans did I make for the twins today?' he smiled ruefully. 'Honey, it was a desperate day.'

'I know; mine was fairly filled, too,' she said.

'I know, I know, and then I was late home, but, Cathy, I can't work while they're here, I just sat in a café. They keep asking question after question. I'm going to get them made wards of court,' he said simply.

She looked at him, shocked. 'But they'd have to go into care, a home, a foster family, total strangers. They're family.'

'Not yours and mine.' Neil was trying to sound firm and in control. 'I can't *have* this,' he said. 'It's not just my work alone, it's your work too. We've put too much in to let it be wrecked by children.'

'I suppose that's happening all over the world.'

'People's own children *might* be different, though I must say this has proved to me very clearly that we are totally right not to want them. But truly, Cathy, I'll get them out of your hair. There has to be *some* money there, we'll mortgage The Beeches, something to borrow against. We could still keep an eye on them.'

'You know we'll have no say in where they're sent. Leave it for a few days until we know more.'

He reached out for her. And she lay awake with her eyes open for a long time afterwards.

By the end of the week, the electrical appliances had all been installed, and Tom and Cathy were waiting for the rest of the equipment. The window frames and door had been painted a vivid red. James Byrne had told them that the Maguires had professed themselves satisfied with everything. Tom and Cathy's solicitor said that nothing untoward was showing up in the search on the company title. Geraldine, who had her own PR agency, was already coming up with names of contacts. Cathy and Neil had decided that there was now no way they could immediately abandon Simon and Maud, but that living permanently in Waterview was proving too much of a strain. Lizzie and Muttie, on the other hand, seemed perfectly content with them and found them jobs to do around the house. Next week they would be going back to school. It was a compromise. Neil had told them that an unofficial carer's allowance had been arranged. In fact, it was guilt money put up by Jock and Hannah until the situation sorted itself out. The arrangement was that Muttie and Lizzie would mind Simon and Maud after school, and they would sleep alternately in Waterview and St Jarlath's.

'I'll never be able to thank you, Mam,' Cathy said to her mother.

'Don't go on like that, Cathy, doesn't it give Muttie some shape to his days. He's very fond of them.'

'Let's go out tonight and have a coffee and make a list for the reception.'

Tom and Cathy had taken to doing their Scarlet Feather work away from home. It wasn't fair on Neil to have his whole study commandeered, nor on Marcella to keep her out of her own sitting room.

'I think we should include friends and family, don't you?' Tom began.

'Of course I do, though it has to be said hardly any of *my* family and friends will put any business our way, not much demand for caterers down on the morning shift in my dad's bookies.'

'Nor mine,' Tom said. 'But that's not the point.'

'Can we do a quick deal, the pair of us? If you don't ask your in-laws, I won't ask mine,' Cathy pleaded.

'I don't *have* any in-laws, as you very well know, and you *have* to ask your in-laws.'

Cathy sighed. 'My mother-in-law will make it a misery for everyone there if she does come, and she'll sulk for six months if she's not asked. But we will have Geraldine working the room for us, and talking us up to everyone.'

'How *did* she earn enough to be able to give us a whack like that?' Tom wondered.

'No idea. Just invested well, I think. And you've got that sexy brother of yours to keep all the women happy. Let's hope he goes into one of his charm routines.'

'I was always afraid that Marcella would fall for him when she met him, but mercifully she didn't,' Tom said.

'Marcella? Fall for Joe when she could have you?' Cathy laughed. 'Marcella's too bright for that.' Marcella had been extremely helpful, coming on from her work at Hayward's, changing into jeans and taking out her rubber gloves: she did all the menial jobs anyone could give her. But she utterly refused to serve and help at the party.

'Listen, Cathy, you should understand about having a dream. I want to be a model. I know I can do it, I believe I'm as good as anyone else. I

just *can't* be seen in public as a waitress or that's all I'll ever be, a manicurist and a waitress.'

'You could be worse things.' Cathy had been curt.

'And you could have been a typist or a shop girl, but you wanted
more,' Marcella had answered with spirit. There was no moving her so
Cathy didn't try.

'What will we do at the party?' Maud asked.

'I don't think you'll be there,' Cathy said. 'It's really for older people.'

'But where would we go? You're going, Neil's going, Muttie and Lizzie
are going, Aunt Hannah and Uncle Jock. There won't be anyone left to
look after us.'

'We could take the coats. Muttie thought that might be a good job for
us,' Simon said.

James Byrne said yes, he would come to the party.

'And of course if there's anyone else that you'd . . . um, like to . . .um,
bring with you,' Cathy said hesitantly.

'Thank you, but I'll come on my own.'

They were finally on first-name terms with each other, not that it
seemed to sit easily with the older man. He was so courteous and old-
fashioned. And so extremely reticent. They did, however, know a little
more about him.

He had been an accountant in a large provincial town for most of his
life, and had only come to Dublin in the last five years. He was now
retired and lived in a flat in Rathgar. They didn't dare ask him had he
any family. Their conversations, though relaxed, were always professional. One day Tom had asked whether he might know someone who
would act as a bookkeeper for them.

'I'd be very happy to do it,' he said. 'If that would suit you. Two hours
a week should be adequate at the start.'

Cathy sensed he was lonely and had nothing else to do. 'But of course,
if you would take us on a trial period we would be delighted,' she had
said. And an unaccustomed smile came across James Byrne's face.

'Oh, Geraldine, *what* am I going to do with those children?'

'There must be some neighbour in St Jarlath's Crescent.'

'Of course, there are a dozen people, but Mam has reservations about
all of them, and I don't want her like a hen on a hot griddle all night
wondering are they all right.'

'All right, I'll get them into the child-sitting service at Peter Murphy's

39

hotel. Chicken nuggets and chips, suitable video and a swim in a heated pool if they want one.'

'Would you really?'

'Of course. I have to protect my investment tomorrow night, don't I?'

Neil was up and dressed when Cathy woke with a start. 'God almighty, it's not even seven yet. Why are you up?'

'This is the big day,' he said.

The launch party, Scarlet Feather up and ready for business.

'I know, I can hardly believe it.' Cathy rubbed her eyes.

'I know he's only a junior minister, but it's very big for him to come to the breakfast, and it'll give the whole thing some attention.'

She realised that it was a big day for Neil because a group of them had managed to get a government minister to meet them about prisoners of conscience.

'I hope it's a great success, anyway,' she said in a flat voice.

He looked at her, startled at the tone, but she said nothing by way of explanation. 'So I must run,' he said eventually.

'See you tonight,' she said.

'Oh yes, of course, the do. It will be great, honey, don't have a worry in the world about it.' He gave her a quick hug. 'I'm very proud of you, you know.'

'I know, Neil,' she said. But she wished that it were more important to him than a quick hug and a pat on the back.

Ricky sent one of his photographers down to the premises to do a few food shots an hour before people were expected. One of Cathy's friends from schooldays, June, was kitted out in a white shirt with the Scarlet Feather logo. They all posed beside the plates of dressed salmon, colourful salads and baskets of bread.

The front room looked terrific tonight. How right they had been to have old-fashioned sofas and chairs. It was a peaceful place where they hoped that customers would sit and discuss menus. Nothing of the shining white and steel of the kitchens here: that was all beyond the door, and they had cleared spaces for people to stand and later to dance. Tonight the front room was acting as a cloakroom and a ravishing-looking redhead who worked in Geraldine's office was hanging coats neatly on two great rails and giving people tickets for them.

June stood with trays of welcoming drinks leaving Tom and Cathy free to greet and welcome.

One moment there seemed to be nobody except the staff and the next the place was teeming with people. Cathy's parents were there, awkward and out of place. Her father twisting his cap and roaming the room with his eyes looking for someone he might talk to. Her mother in a soft, flattering green wool dress had no idea how attractive she looked. Instead, her eyes scanned the room for somewhere to hide. Tom's parents, JT and Maura Feather, didn't look as if they were having fun either. Now there was an idea. Cathy made the introductions.

The mood was getting more relaxed by the moment. Geraldine was in there talking and enthusing and broadening the circle. The noise level was much higher now. Cathy looked around her at the guests. One was missing: James Byrne had phoned at the last moment to say he couldn't come. Marcella looked just exquisite in a beautifully cut silk jacket and long black skirt. She was the centre of admiring glances, and Tom looked on proudly.

Then she saw Neil's parents arrive. Hannah wore a harsh, dark purple dress that somehow drained the colour from her face. She looked affronted before she even came in the door. There was nothing here that she could fault, Cathy thought triumphantly. Nothing at all. She had, however, known Mrs Mitchell for too long not to be able to read her face. The woman was spoiling for a fight.

Cathy noticed her father deep in conversation with a sports journalist, and her mother sitting happily with Mrs Keane, a neighbour from Waterview, on two chairs a little away from the general throng. To Cathy's amazement, Hannah Mitchell approached them.

'Ah, good to see you, Lizzie, give me that chair, will you, like a dear, and get me a plate of mixed nibbles.' Poor Lizzie Scarlet stumbled to her feet and apologised. She was still Mrs Mitchell's cleaner, and she had been caught sitting down. 'Yes, Mrs Mitchell, sorry, Mrs Mitchell.' Cathy had never been so angry. In an icy voice, she ordered her mother to sit down. Out of sheer shock Lizzie did just that, and Cathy manipulated Hannah Mitchell to the other side of the room. Then she seated her mother-in-law in an area where she could see everyone.

'There was no need to push me across the room, Cathy, really.'

'I know, isn't it just terrible when places become so crowded? But you wanted a chair.' She smiled until the sides of her face hurt.

'I had a perfectly good chair where I was.'

'Sadly no, that was my mother's chair, but can I leave you for a moment? I do hope you like the premises.' And she was gone.

Neil, who had noticed nothing amiss, was talking to his cousin Walter, jumpy and restless as ever. Cathy saw Tom's brother Joe come in.

'What a great job—you've done it, I smell success everywhere.' Tom and

Cathy beamed at him, he had such a knack for saying the right thing.

They turned the background music level up slightly. They all seemed to love the food: it had been worthwhile showing off their wares. Tom and Cathy were congratulated on all sides, and could hardly take it in. Some early leavers were beginning to get their coats, but the hard core would be there for much, much longer.

Geraldine had arranged a taxi, which would collect Muttie and Lizzie and take them to the hotel to pick up Simon and Maud. But just as the Scarlets had got to the front room, Hannah moved in on them again.

'There you are, Lizzie, get my coat for me, will you, dear?'

'Certainly Mrs Mitchell, is it your fur?'

Cathy moved in quickly. 'Mam, your taxi is getting restless. I'll get Hannah's coat for her.' Together with Geraldine she got her parents into the taxi.

Cathy walked over to the cloakroom girl and pointed out her mother-in-law's coat. 'May I have that black one, please?' She held it open, but Hannah made no attempt to put it on. So Cathy laid it on a chair. They were alone in the foyer at this stage.

'You've gone too far, Cathy Scarlet. You'll regret your behaviour tonight, mark my words.'

'And I very much hope that you will regret yours, Mrs Mitchell, trying to humiliate my mother as a way to annoy me. Yes, it *did* annoy me, but you couldn't humiliate her. She has a decent, generous soul, and because she took your money for years for hard, menial work she thinks she still owes you.' Hannah gasped and Cathy went on. 'I want you to know that my days of being polite to you are over.'

'You were *never* polite to me, you common little . . . little . . .' Words failed Hannah at this point.

'When I married Neil I tried very hard. I didn't want to make things difficult for him and actually I was sorry for you, because you were so very disappointed in the wife he brought home. But I was never in my whole life afraid of you. You just don't have any power over me. It's a new Ireland, a country where maids' children marry who they bloody well like—'

Hannah interrupted her. 'When you apologise, Cathy, as you will, I am not going to forgive you . . .'

'Oh, no, I will never apologise, believe me, I meant everything I said.' Cathy spoke icily. 'If you, on the other hand, apologise about the way you insulted my mother twice tonight, I will consider it. Otherwise we will behave courteously to each other in public and communicate not at all in private. Now, you can either come in and join your husband or leave. Suit yourself.' And Cathy turned and went, head high, back to the party. Inside, she saw Geraldine looking at her anxiously.

'She still has a pulse, Geraldine, don't worry.' Cathy Scarlet had her first drink of the night. A very large glass of red wine. Her instinct was that Hannah would say nothing. Reporting the insolence of her daughter-in-law would mean putting the spotlight on her own behaviour. Hannah wouldn't risk it.

The music was louder. Tom moved to hold the beautiful face of Marcella in his two hands and began to dance with her. Dreamily, Cathy put out her hand towards Neil and they held each other tight. And then she closed her eyes and danced with the man she loved.

'TELL ME THAT WE CLEARED the place up,' Tom asked Marcella sleepily next morning. 'Tell me we didn't just walk out and leave everything as it was.'

Marcella laughed. 'Surely you remember. You had us all running in and out like a fast-forward film, and by the time the taxis came everything was put into the right places and the dishwasher was turned on.'

'I'm a genius,' Tom said happily. 'However, I really laid into the wine, I'm afraid.'

'You and Cathy deserved it.' She stroked his forehead and began to get out of bed.

'You're never leaving me alone in the morning of my triumph?'

'Tom, it's my dance class,' she said.

'Of course.' He had forgotten. Marcella didn't need this two hour-class in movement every Saturday. She was a lithe, gorgeous girl who turned heads. But she was convinced that these were all part of her apprenticeship.

Tom knew he should go into the premises, but it was still early and he deserved another cup of coffee.

Cathy was there when Tom arrived. She was with those terrible children.

'You're late,' said Simon.

'Where's your girlfriend?' asked Maud.

Cathy came out and gave him a hug. 'Wasn't that a night to remember,' she said. Then, looking at the children, she said in an entirely different voice, 'Tom is not late, his girlfriend Marcella is at her dance class, and what did I say about greeting people in a civilised society? Tell me this minute.'

'We say hello and pretend to be glad to see them,' said Simon.

'We use their name if we know it,' added Maud.

'OK. Sorry Tom, could you go out and come in again.'

Tom went back outside.

'Good morning,' he said as he re-entered.

Simon, with a nightmare rictus grin on his face came out to shake hands. 'Good morning, Tom,' he said.

'You are most welcome, Tom,' Maud said.

'Thank you . . . um . . . Maud and Simon,' said Tom. 'And to what exactly do we owe the pleasure of your company?' They looked at him without an idea of what he was talking about.

Cathy explained. 'My mother isn't all that well this morning.'

'Too much wine here last night,' Simon explained.

Cathy interrupted, 'And so I thought it would all be for the best if they came to help me here . . . And if you have no objections, they are about to unload the dishwashers. *Now*,' she barked suddenly at the children, who scuttled away to get on with it.

'Sorry,' she whispered to Tom. 'I really had to. I've never seen my poor mother so shook. My fault, I kept tanking her up so that she wouldn't hear that old bitch Hannah Mitchell patronising her.'

'Cathy, whatever you want, believe me, it *was* a great night last night,' he said. 'I really do think we're going to be all right, don't you?'

'I think we'll be millionaires,' said Cathy, just as Joe Feather came in through the open door.

'That's what I like to hear,' said Joe. He took Cathy up in his arms and swung her round in a circle. 'Well done, Cathy Scarlet, you and my brother here have really got the right touch. You've a great set-up there, it's very professional, really it is. Geraldine and I think our investment is one of the best we've ever made.'

Maud and Simon peered out of the kitchen. 'Good morning, I'm Maud Mitchell and this is my brother Simon. You're very welcome.'

'I'm Joe Feather. Delighted to make your acquaintance,' Joe said.

'Are you Tom's father?' Simon asked interested.

'Not quite, more his brother,' Joe said agreeably.

'And do you have children and grandchildren of your own?' Maud wanted to be clear on everything too.

'No, I'm a bachelor, that's a man never lucky enough to marry,' said Joe. 'And I live by myself in London in an apartment in Ealing. I go to work by the Central Line every day to Oxford Circus, where I sell clothes.'

'Do you sell them in a shop or in a street?'

'It's more an office really. You see, they come in to me and then I send them out again,' Joe explained. 'It's how I earn my money.'

There was silence. 'Are we talking too much?' Simon asked Cathy.

'No, truly, but why don't you go into the kitchen again and sort the cutlery? Like now.' Maud and Simon went out immediately.

'They're extraordinary,' Joe said. 'Who are they?' he asked.

'You don't have time. Why don't you two go have a coffee somewhere sane, and we'll do this place.'

'Come on, Joe, we'll go to Bewley's,' Tom said.

Tom and Cathy sat for hours dreaming up menus for a christening, a first night party and a business lunch. The christening would have a very flash, moneyed crowd at it, people who could spend. They would have to lay out a bit more on the actual presentation. The theatre party was on a very low budget; what they wanted was something much nicer than sausages and crisps but at the price that sausages and crisps would cost. It needed a lot of thought. There would be no profit in it but it was very dear to Tom's heart. He also wanted to help Cathy with the business lunch.

Cathy had asked if Marcella would consider serving at this first one, just to start them off. Nobody would be likely to forget Marcella pouring their mineral water and smiling her dazzling smile. But Tom knew that Marcella just would not do it.

'She must have a stab at this modelling, you know, no matter how hard she pushes herself. I hardly ever see her.'

'I know what you mean.' Cathy shrugged. 'But you're going to have to get used to it when she does become a model, because she'll be off at different shows all the time.'

Tom realised with a shock that he had probably thought Marcella would never make it. He had somehow seen a future where he and Marcella would marry and have two children. But perhaps he was just fooling himself.

'Where will we be in ten years' time, do you think, Cathy?' he asked her suddenly.

'I'd say we'll still be here working out this bloody menu, and the child will be nearly grown up and walking round a pagan because he never got christened at all,' she said. 'Come on, Tom, let's cost it out . . .'

45

Cathy and Tom had been trained to do their accounting very carefully, pricing their ingredients, labour and staff precisely. On the theatre job they lost a total of seventy-six pounds. Tom was shaken.

'It's a one-off, it will lead to other things,' Cathy soothed.

'No, Cathy, it won't, it was to please my theatre friends, that's all. *And* we had to pay June two extra hours because she worked them. I had no idea it was going on so late.' Tom was contrite.

'OK, three jobs this month and we lost seventy-six pounds on the first. How *not* to go into business.'

'It all looked so simple in theory, didn't it?' Tom sounded less cheerful.

'What we need just now is one of those strokes of luck we kept saying that we were having,' Cathy said.

The phone rang. Cathy was nearer.

'Oh, yes, James, how are you?' Tom watched as Cathy frowned.

'Yes, of course, James, it would be a pleasure.' She put the receiver down. 'You'll never guess what James wants.'

'It's not one of those strokes of luck is it?'

'I don't think so,' Cathy said slowly. 'He wants us to teach him to make a supper for two people, three courses at his place. He's costing our time at fifteen pounds an hour. Minimum four hours, including the shopping.'

'When does he want it?' Tom asked. 'We're very busy this week . . .'

'It's ages away, but he's going to pay us a hundred and twenty pounds to make a dinner,' Cathy said, knowing James was only trying to put some money into their bank account.

'He's off his skull.'

'I suppose it's for some woman; he did say that discretion was to be a part of it,' Cathy said.

'Good. Then let's not let Simon and Maud know; they'd have it on the six o'clock news,' said Tom happily.

They had no idea how hard it was to make contacts. People either didn't consider themselves in the league that hired a caterer, or if they did then they already knew someone who was doing just fine. They drew blank after blank.

Sometimes, after a fruitless day of searching for work, Cathy would say that it was only Tom's enthusiasm that kept her going. And it was sincere: he really believed they were so good, it was only a matter of time until everyone recognised them for what they were. Tom never sat back; he was always looking, asking and hunting.

'Geraldine, could I come and spend just thirty minutes going through your client list again?'

'It does my street cred good to have a handsome young man come to the apartments,' Geraldine said. 'Come round on Sunday morning.'

The Glenstar apartment block was immaculately kept. There was regular landscape gardening and a smart commissionaire stood in the hall. Tom wondered how much the residents paid a year in services charges. Then he reminded himself not always to think in terms of how much things cost and how much they might bring in.

Geraldine looked magnificent: she wore a dark green velvet track suit, her hair was still slightly damp from swimming. The smell of coffee filled her big sitting room.

Geraldine got down to business at once, and they spent an hour at her dining table seeing where any opportunity might lie. 'Peter Murphy's hotel is useless, or course, since all their functions are catered by themselves. The garden centre never wants to spend any money, they serve thimbles of warm white wine and that's that. But these now are a bit more lively . . .' She gave Tom the address of an import agency. 'They take a lot of clothes, even some from your brother, he was telling me the other night. They need an upmarket party.'

'And Hayward's?' Tom said hopefully.

'No, not a chance. Shona Burke and I have talked about it over and over. She's done her very best but they have a café, you see, so it doesn't make any sense for them to bring in an outsider.'

They went through the list of names. Tom admired the matter-of-fact way Geraldine went about her business. She spoke affectionately, even discreetly, about her clients. She emphasised to Tom that this was all in confidence, but she was in no way impressed by any of them. She was afraid of nobody. He remembered asking Cathy how Geraldine had got the money together to buy this PR agency, but it wasn't a question he would ever put to her. He frowned to himself.

'What on earth are you making faces about, Tom?'

'I was thinking about money, actually, and why it mustn't be a god in itself, but if you don't keep an eye on it you go down the tube.'

'I know what you mean. Money itself is not important at all, but in order to make it and get the life you want you have to pretend that it is for a while, just to keep it rolling on in.' Her face looked hard for a moment.

Tom said no more on the subject. When he took his coffee cup into the kitchen he saw ingredients for a lunch set out there. 'Have you a busy day?' he asked.

'A friend to lunch,' she said briskly. 'Which reminds me, find a few canapés that freeze well and give them to me, then I can talk you up all round the place.'

'Of course, but why don't you let us *do* a lunch for you, any time, it's the very least we can do.'

'You're sweet, Tom, but the kind of guys I entertain like to think that I cooked everything with my own fair hands.'

Shona Burke was getting out of her little car, and she called out to him as he left Glenstar. 'Do you have your brother's phone number?'

'No, not you too. What do you all see in him?' he groaned.

'Purely business,' she said. 'They're doing a young people's promotion in Hayward's in late spring, and he told me that he might just have a line of what he called fun clothes. Swimwear, lingerie, you know.'

He looked up Joe's London phone number for her in his diary.

'You don't know it?'

'No, I don't call him that much. Have you got sisters and brothers?'

Shona hesitated. 'Well, yes, in a way I do.'

It was an odd response but Tom let it go. Some people hated to be interrogated about their families; Marcella did. Her mother was dead and her father, who had married again, just wasn't interested, she said. Cathy, on the other hand, had something to say every day about her parents: she loved Muttie and Lizzie, n spite of her mother's humble, grateful attitude to life. Cathy would also go on about her sisters and brothers in Chicago, particularly Marian, the eldest, who had done well in banking but poorly in her love life until recently, and was now going to marry a man called Harry who looked like a film star. Tom got into his van and waved Shona goodbye. She stood there taking no notice of the light rain that had begun to fall, not covering up her hair as most women would, looking oddly lonely and vulnerable.

Marcella came home from Hayward's beauty salon the following evening and told Tom amazing news. This woman had come in and said she was going to a drop-dead-cert smart christening party on Saturday, and there were going to be fancy caterers at it. Tom could hardly believe it. People were talking about them. He couldn't wait to ring Cathy. But tonight she and Neil were taking those children to see their mother in some drying-out place.

'Will we celebrate?' he asked Marcella.

'Ah, love, I'm just off to the gym,' she said.

'Couldn't you . . . Just for one night . . .?'

'Tom, we *agreed.* The only way to get any value is for me to go every day.'

'Sure,' he said, then knew he must sound a little warmer. 'You're absolutely right,' he said. 'And as soon as we really are a fancy caterers, then you'll come to every classy, fancy thing we do and get yourself photographed all over the place.'

'You'll be a great big success . . . you do know that, don't you?' she said, and he thought he saw tears in her eyes.

'Of course I know,' he said, and he held her close to him.

Ricky rang. He had the pictures: six black and white arty studies of food which they were going to put up in the premises. He could bring them round tomorrow if the picture rail was up, and did Tom want the measurements? Tom did and got his paper and pencil.

'I was going to give them to you tonight at the do, but I figure it makes us look idiotic talking work at a party,' Ricky explained.

'Party?'

'Yeah, you know, the new club?'

'No, I never heard about it.'

'Well, Marcella said you'd both be there.' Ricky was puzzled. Tom could feel his heart beating faster.

'Misunderstanding,' he mumbled.

'Sure. Now I'll give you the top-to-bottom measurements first. Your father's getting a rail made, isn't he?'

Tom wrote down numbers on his pad, but his mind was on autopilot. He could not believe that she had just left pretending to go to the gym, and was in fact heading off to something without him. He felt such a shock at the betrayal that he could hardly hear Ricky's words.

'Right, see you tomorrow, OK?'

'OK, Ricky, thank you a million times,' Tom Feather said to the cheerful photographer who had just broken his heart.

He needed to give his father the measurements for the picture rail. He dialled his parents' number.

'Yes?' It was a woman with a bark that nearly lifted him off the phone.

'Sorry,' Tom began, 'I've got the wrong number. I was dialling the Feathers.'

'This is the Feathers. Who's that?'

'Tom, their son. What's happened . . .?' Tom could hear voices in the background. Something must have happened. Eventually, he learned that his father had chest pains and his mother had run out into the street to get help. Almost all the neighbours in the small street had come into his mother and father's house, and someone had gone to the hospital when the ambulance came, and others had stayed making tea with poor Maura.

Tom grabbed up his car keys and coat. He paused for a moment to write a note. He couldn't forgive Marcella for lying to him. *My father's not well. Gone to see him, hope you enjoyed the party*, he wrote. That would show her. He drove to the hospital.

Unless his father had another heart attack tonight the prognosis was fairly good, they told him in Intensive Care. A nurse asked him gently if he would perhaps like to take a seat outside.

'He's resting now. He's fine.'

Tom went out into the cold night to get some fresh air and telephoned his mother on his mobile.

'He looks fine, Mam.'

'What do you mean, he looks fine? Didn't I see him with my own two eyes clutching his chest, fighting for his breath? He's finished, Tom, you know he is. He shouldn't be up ladders at his age, he was just desperate to get that place right for you.'

'Mam, I'll ring you back when I know more.'

It was freezing out here, but it was better than the heat and noise and medical smells of the hospital. He went to a bicycle shed and sheltered there against the wind, huddled in the corner, and willed his father to get well. He saw someone very like Shona Burke locking a car and then walking purposefully towards Reception. It was Shona. He moved back. He didn't want to tell her about his father before he knew what there was to tell. But Shona had seen him and called out.

'You look shivery, Tom.'

'I know, but still it's too hot inside there.'

'Oh, don't I know all about it, I come here quite a lot . . .'

'I'm sorry, is it . . .?'

'It's all right, Tom.' She spoke gently, letting him know that there would be no discussion on who she was visiting. 'But you look terrible. Is it something bad?'

'My father, chest pains, angina. It all depends on tonight—if he makes it through till tomorrow he'll have a great chance.'

'Poor Tom, when did it happen?'

'I just heard about it over an hour ago.'

'That means Marcella doesn't know yet, does she?'

'No,' his voice was flat.

'Oh, poor Marcella. I offered to drive her home from the gym but she said no, she was getting a bus, buying you a potted plant as a surprise.'

In front of everyone in the Reception area, Tom gave a whoop of delight. 'She was at the gym?' he cried. 'Tonight?'

He drove home so fast he was amazed that there wasn't a police siren following him the whole way. He let himself in the door and she was sitting there at the table.

'Marcella!' he said.

'How is your father?' her voice was icy.

'He'll be fine, it's all under control . . . You were at the gym?'

'As I told you I was going to be.' Her face was like a mask.

'Marcella, if you knew . . . you see, I thought . . . you'd gone to a party, to a club . . . Ricky said . . .'

'But I didn't want to go, because you're too busy and I knew you'd hate it, so I went to the gym as I told you.'

'I'm so sorry. You see, I didn't think . . . I didn't think you could love me enough to give up something like that for me.'

'I did, yes, of course I did.' Her voice was very level.

'You do love me, I know it now.'

'No, Tom, I said I did, not I do.' She picked up the note. 'You are the most bitter, mistrustful man I ever met. How could anyone love you?' She stood up and went to the bedroom.

'Marcella, you're not leaving?' He stood at the bedroom door, looking at her.

'If you imagine that I could stay a night here with you when you think I'm a liar.'

She moved towards the bathroom, then stopped to pick up the phone.

'Where will you stay?'

'I have friends. I'll find somewhere to stay.'

'Please, Marcella.'

She phoned for a taxi then walked into the bathroom and closed the door. Later, when she heard the doorbell ring, she came out.

'I am so sorry,' he said.

'So you should be, Tom, seriously sorry, because I have *always* told you the truth.'

And she was gone. Eventually the phone rang. It was his mother.

'You said you'd ring in an hour, I had to ring the hospital myself.'

'Is he all right, Mam?'

'He is for the moment. Tom, what will we do if he dies?'

'I'm coming round, Mam,' he said.

Before he left he rang Joe and left a message on his answering machine. Then he sat down to write a note to leave on their table: *I hope and pray you come back, and if you do, darling, darling Marcella, just know that I didn't know the meaning of love before I met you, and that I can't see much point in life without your love.*

Tom kept his mobile phone on all night, and not long after dawn he stopped at another builder's yard to make the pole to hang the pictures on, and drove to the premises. Cathy was there already.

'What does the other fellow look like?' she asked.

'What?' He looked at her blankly.

'God, Tom, it was a joke. It's what you say to somebody who's been in a fight. You're worse than Simon and Maud. Were you on the whiskey or something?'

'No, I've been up all night with my father. He had a coronary and Marcella has left me.'

'What happened?' Cathy was both kind and unbelieving. Tom was about to lose it and to break down when Ricky arrived with the pictures.

'Jesus, did you miss a wild night,' Ricky said, holding his head. 'You were wise not to come to that particular party, my friend.'

'That's me, Mr Wise Guy,' said Tom Feather sadly.

The christening was what Cathy said should be called The Function from Hell. They had been asked to cater for fifty, but there were at least seventy people there. The kitchen hadn't been cleaned properly, so Cathy, June and Tom had to spend the first twenty minutes wiping surfaces and putting down a disinfectant. When they tried to set up the buffet, the two small dogs of the house began a game of pulling the tablecloths.

'People who don't like animals are really not my kind of people,' said the baby's mother, who was three gins in before they had left for the church.

The ceremony had been forty minutes shorter than Cathy and Tom were told, so their bar wasn't ready.

'I was told you were top-drawer,' said the baby's father. 'We're in business just as you are, and we don't pay for what we don't get.'

They had ordered kedgeree as a starter, but before it got under way, the baby's mother began telling everyone, 'Don't bother eating all this rice and fish stuff, they have a proper roast coming later.' So a lot of people obediently put down their half-finished starters. Tom and Cathy looked at each other. Their only hope had been that people would stock up on the kedgeree. Now they were waiting for the miracle of the loaves and the fishes.

'What in the name of God will we do?' Cathy asked him.

'Get them drunk,' Tom suggested.

And they did. Spectacularly.

Cathy Scarlet approached the baby's father firmly.

'May I suggest something? You guests seem to be enjoying themselves enormously, and you have chosen some particularly good wine.'

'Yes, yes, what?'

'It's all going so well here, may I ask you to sign permission to bring out more wine?'

'Do what you want.' Larry Riordan was a small, fat man with small, piggy eyes. 'Just keep getting the drink round.'

'Thank you. You are a wonderful host,' Cathy said through tightly clenched teeth.

Tom eased his way through the guests, smiling and telling them that the kedgeree was delicious.

'You're pretty delicious yourself,' said a woman with chocolate smeared over her face. Tom thanked her for the compliment.

'You've got such a lovely dress,' he said. 'Is it from Hayward's designer room?'

'Yes, it is.' She was stupidly flattered.

'Come here to the mirror, you've got some kind of mark on your face.' He offered her a tissue, and she wiped the smears away hastily.

'That was nice of you to do that,' Cathy said. 'Listen, give June a hand over there. I'll ring my father and get him to provide taxis.'

'Muttie? Taxis?'

'Have we time to start looking up taxis at this stage? Half the people my father bets with drive taxis.'

'You're brilliant, Cathy!'

'Excuse me?'

'Yes, Mr Riordan?'

'Don't we know each other?'

'Well, Mr Riordan, I'm the caterer . . .'

'We met at a party a couple of months ago, New Year's Eve . . . I just wanted to say that that sort of thing rarely happens. It was the drink, I felt very odd after it. I think they deliberately mixed the drinks there.'

Then Tom remembered him. He was the man who had been pawing Marcella at Ricky's party.

'Oh, yes, yes indeed, Mr Riordan, of course I remember you.'

'You did from the beginning,' Larry Riordan said. 'Come on, you've had a load of attitude since you came in the door, you knew you had one over me.'

'No, I knew you had made a mistake about the number of guests you had invited. I didn't realise until now you were the happily married man I met on New Year's Eve,' Tom said. Larry Riordan shrank in front of him.

'The whole thing was a total misunderstanding, of course . . . due entirely . . . What I wanted to say was that if there was any offence—'

'Oh, there was great offence at the time.'

'But not now, I hope.'

'Now I shall continue to do this job professionally for you and your wife. In fact I *was* going to ask your wife—'

'No need to ask her anything. Just ask me.'

'Relax, Mr Riordan, I was only going to ask her did she think we should arrange some taxis for later? Many of your guests will have to leave their cars behind.'

'Do whatever you like,' said the host, loosening his collar.

'Thank you, now if you'll excuse me . . .'

They gave everyone in sight their business card, and tidied the house to within an inch of its life. They lined the bottles up in the back garden in ranks like soldiers, so that there would be no dispute about the number ordered and drunk. Muttie had sent five taxi-driver friends to the scene and they did a shuttle service all evening.

'Is there anything wrong, Neil?' Cathy said. 'Your mind was a million miles away when I was telling you about the party.'

'Sorry,' he said. 'It's not definite yet, but I hear that I *could* be offered this amazing position . . .'

She looked at him open-mouthed as he told her about a committee that worked with the UN High Commission for Refugees.

'Are you trying to tell me that you would consider taking a job abroad now?'

'Not immediately. In about five or six months, I imagine. That's if it comes to anything, but it's only fair to tell you about it now.'

'But this was never on the cards, Neil, never part of any plan.'

'You don't know anything about it yet. And you'd love it, you've never had a chance to travel.'

'Oh, but I have travelled. To Greece, didn't I, where I met you.'

'But, honey, that was only a Mickey Mouse summer job.'

Her face hardened. 'But I don't have a Mickey Mouse job now, I have a company,' she said.

'Yes, but you can't expect to think—'

'Think what?' she asked.

'It's not the right time to talk now, it's too late.' He stood up.

'One sentence isn't finished. You said I can't expect to think . . .' She looked up at him.

'I didn't know how it was going to end,' he said, anxious to be out of it all.

'Will I finish it for you?' She sounded calm, too calm. 'We can't expect to think that you'd ask me to give up my whole life's work and dream any more than I would ever expect you to. Was it something like that?'

'It needs a lot more thought and discussion,' he said.

'You're right,' she said, and they went to bed, where they slept so far from each other that not even a toe touched.

Back at Stoneyfield, Tom was in better humour—his father was definitely on the mend. The Riordans sent a message that the account was all in order and the bill for the christening would be paid in full that afternoon. There had been a note from Marcella saying that Shona had told her of Mr Feather's heart attack, and she sent her sympathy and hoped that he was getting on well. The bad news was that there had been no word of response from Joe Feather, whose father could well have died and been buried.

Tom put on the Lou Reed record he loved because it showed other people had lives as confused as his own. There was a ring at the door. He answered it, and it was Marcella.

'You have a key,' he said quietly through the intercom.

'I wouldn't use it, unless . . .' Her voice faltered.

'Unless what, Marcella?'

'Unless you wanted me to come in.'

'Well, I've been just waiting for you all those days, hours, minutes, seconds, however long it's been,' he said.

'Tom, I wanted to tell you that I do know you love me, and that we both made silly mistakes along the way. Would that let me come home, do you think?' He knew she was crying, and he didn't care if she knew that he was crying too as he ran down the stairs to bring her back home.

Next morning there was a call from the woman at the party whose face Tom had rescued. She said that she wanted to book them for a silver wedding party weeks ahead. Geraldine booked them for a lunch for a group of estate agents who wanted to get into the villa market and would like a buffet with a Spanish theme. The hospital called to say that Mr JT Feather would be going home today. Cathy got an email from her sister Marian in Chicago, asking Scarlet Feather to cater for a lavish Dublin wedding in August. Cathy had also received a letter from Hannah Mitchell in which her mother-in-law had suggested a little lunch in Quentin's to clear up any outstanding difficulties. And when Cathy rang Tom to tell him this last and most amazing piece of information, the phone was answered by Marcella.

'Oh, Tom,' Cathy said with a lump in her throat when Marcella passed the phone to him. 'I'm so happy for you.'

March

'MRS MITCHELL, MISS SCARLET,' Brenda Brennan greeted them in her calm, measured way.

'You *know* my daughter-in-law?' Hannah was annoyed as always that she had not been able to make the introduction.

'It's always a pleasure to see both of you,' Brenda murmured as she left them the menus. She had not mentioned that Cathy had washed plates in the kitchen, served tables and was far better known here, at Quentin's, often described as Dublin's best restaurant, than the elegant Hannah would ever be. Mrs Mitchell was special only for habitually changing her table, sending food back or querying the bill.

'It is nice to have time to have a little chat like this,' Hannah began.

'It's very kind of you, and a lovely break for me, certainly,' said Cathy, who had told herself twenty-five times already that there was no point going to this lunch at all unless she remained calm and courteous.

'Possibly you work too hard. You should have a few more breaks,' Hannah said.

'Possibly indeed.'

'So you agree you might be overworked, a little tense, ready to fly off the handle, then?'

Cathy saw now where her mother-in-law was coming from.

'Funnily, Neil and I were saying this the other day. At our time of life we all have to work so hard running just to keep up, that by the time we get to your age and Mr Mitchell's, our life will be so much calmer.'

'You were saying that?'

'Yes. We were noting the way Mr Mitchell can spend so much time on the golf course, and you have all these hours to give to charity lunches. Our day, for all that, will come too.' Cathy smiled broadly.

Mrs Mitchell was put out. This was not the way she had intended the conversation to go. 'Yes, dear, but don't you think you might be . . . how shall I put this . . . directing too much energy into this?'

'You're probably right. I am devoting a lot of energy to the new company, but that's natural. Once we get it off the ground we hope to relax a little more.'

'But, my dear, what about your life with Neil?'

'Neil's working almost every night too, either at home or at some consultation. It's just the way things are.'

'I think it's just the way you've let things become, dear.'

Cathy remembered that tone. It was the way Mrs Mitchell had spoken to her mother. 'Sorry, Lizzie dear, I don't think we were terribly thorough cleaning the bath, were we?' Cathy had wanted to kill the woman then. The feeling was hardly less strong now.

'Do explain what you mean, Mrs Mitchell.'

'It's just that I'm asking myself, *why* does Neil go out so much for work, why do you not have a social life, give dinner parties, go to clubs? I wondered, perhaps, if you were to . . .' She seemed to lose the words.

'If I were to what, Mrs Mitchell?' Cathy was genuinely interested now. What on earth was the woman going to suggest?

'Well, that you should smarten yourself up a little. It's just that possibly you've been so busy with work and everything . . . that you haven't had time to stop and take a good long look at yourself.'

Cathy did not know whether to feel humiliated or amused. 'And where do you think I should start?' she asked in a level voice.

'Well, your hair, of course, and to show how much I really mean it I've got a token for Hayward's.' Mrs Mitchell pulled out an envelope.

'I can't possibly accept this,' Cathy began.

'But you *must*. I don't think I gave you a proper Christmas present, and let this be it. You did such a delightful job catering for our New Year's Eve party. The very least I can do is start you off on some kind of make-over.'

Cathy stared glumly at the envelope. 'Truly I am grateful for your kindness, Mrs Mitchell. And for this lunch. I'll certainly think about the hairdo.'

As Cathy listened to the wisdom of having a regular facial and not let the muscles get saggy, she wondered to herself, as she had so often before, how this empty, sad, envious woman had given birth to Neil. Cathy almost wished they could have gone back to the days of straightforward hostility. It was far easier to cope with.

'What did you eat at Quentin's?' Tom asked.

'I can't remember. I was with Hannah.'

'Is there blood all over the place?'

'No, she just wanted to cut my hair,' said Cathy.

Tom found this puzzling. 'But she didn't?' he said eventually.

'She did.' Cathy tapped her handbag. 'She gave me a voucher for it. Tom, do I need my hair cut?'

'I don't know. Do *you* want to?'

'No, not particularly.'

'Then don't.' It was simple for men. Simple for anyone who hadn't taken Hannah Mitchell's money.

'I'm going to give this hairdressing voucher to June.'

'How much is it for?' asked Tom, and when she showed him he pretended to reel around the premises. 'Do people really spend that much money on hair?' he asked.

'Apparently.' Cathy laughed.

'Marian was on again about the wedding entertainment,' Cathy said to her mother. 'They want a pageboy and a flower girl, Mam, and they want them to do some Irish dancing.'

'Well, they can't have them,' Cathy's mother said. 'We don't have anyone that age in the family.'

'We have Maud and Simon,' Cathy said. 'Marian would love them.'

'Cathy, that wouldn't do at all, you know *she* wouldn't stand for it, not for a moment.'

'Well *she* has nothing to do with it, Mam. Let's discuss it with Maud and Simon. They loved *Riverdance*.'

'Everyone loved *Riverdance* but I told you Hannah Mitchell wouldn't hear of it.'

'Mam, *she* is not important. Let's ask the kids.'

'They're not here,' Lizzie said.

'Of course they're here, Mam, they're always here, listening, spying, stealing food. That's what they do all day, isn't it?'

'That's not fair, Cathy, you sound as if you hate them. They're only children who didn't have a proper home.'

'No, I don't hate them. I've got to like them a bit more recently. But they still steal food. *And* they listen at doors. Don't you, Maud?'

'I was just passing by,' said poor Maud.

'Please, it was only four sausages and a couple of packets of cornflakes just in case,' Simon said.

'In case what?'

'In case there would be no more,' said Simon, ashen-faced.

'I had lunch with your mother today,' Cathy said that evening.

'Oh, good.' Neil didn't look up from his papers.

'It's not a usual occurrence. I thought you'd wonder why.'

'Well, why then?'

'Don't know.' Cathy shrugged.

'Listen, Cathy, you told me you had to work out a silver wedding menu and a Spanish buffet tonight, so I took all this stuff home . . .'

'Sorry.'

'Don't be like that.'

'No, you're quite right, I did say that . . .'

She meant it, she wasn't even sulking. They did tell each other in advance what their plans for the evening were. He was justified in being put out. Yet this was so huge a fact she had just told him, and he wasn't mildly interested. His own mother, who had waged war on her for years, had invited her to Quentin's for God's sake. Neil had not even registered it.

'No, I'm sorry I was a bit short with you . . . It's another bloody complicated thing, and we'll be in court over it tomorrow. I'm for the tenant who broke his back on a faulty stairway . . .'

Cathy held up her hands. She really was contrite. 'I'm sorry. I'm going out anyway. I just came in to leave the shopping. I'll be back in a couple of hours and we'll have supper.'

Cathy hadn't intended to go out, but now she drove to Glenstar apartments and dialled Geraldine on the mobile phone. The answering machine was on. Stupid to have come without ringing first, Cathy thought, looking up at her aunt's flat. There were two figures in the room. Geraldine was entertaining someone. A man. She was about to pull out of the parking bay when she saw someone waving. It was Shona Burke.

'I saw your van. Well, who could miss it, with its distinctive scarlet feather on the side?' Shona laughed. 'Do you want to come in for some coffee?'

Cathy looked around as Shona got the coffee. Similar to her aunt's flat, but totally different furnishings. A lot of brightly coloured rugs and embroidered cushions. There were no family pictures on the wall and Cathy wondered how Shona could afford the mortgage. Perhaps she came from rich people. Shona Burke would never tell.

'You're very far away,' Shona said, coming back to join her.

'I was thinking about Simon and Maud,' Cathy lied. 'Neil's nephew and niece. We appear to have adopted them, my mother and I.' She laughed a little grimly and explained. To her surprise Shona didn't find any of it funny or praise them like other people did. She just listened.

'So that's it,' Cathy finished. 'Neil and his father got some kind of order which releases money from the estate to my mam and dad, and I suppose some even comes to us if we need it.'

'And what about their social worker?'

'She's happy enough with the set-up, she knows they're well looked after.'

'It's terribly unfair on the children,' Shona said.

'Life's unfair, Shona. Of course I'd prefer them to have a nice mummy and daddy who cared for them, but they don't, so we have to pick up the pieces.'

'And then will they go back to hopeless Mummy and Daddy, and what then?' Shona asked.

'I wish I knew.'

Tom said that the whole trick for the estate agents' reception was setting up the Spanish atmosphere. He was busy chasing up Spanish hats, castanets, a guitarist and a flamenco dancer. All they wanted was the feel that they were actually in Spain already. Cathy said that was all very well certainly, but they must have a whole range of tapas to start. Followed by a knockout paella. She worked out that they should have two paellas, one with shellfish and one less authentic one without. Cathy wanted little labels on the individual plates of tapas showing how typically Spanish they were. They were showing off to potential clients and the press.

'Would it be educational for us to go to it, do you think?' Simon wondered the night before.

'No,' said Cathy briefly, and saw their two disappointed faces. 'Actually it would be boring for you. Have I ever told you a lie?'

They paused to consider this question. 'No,' they said at exactly the same time. 'Will there be leftovers, do you think?'

'Not at St Jarlath's tomorrow, Maud. Your aunt Hannah is coming to Waterview tomorrow, to supper with Neil and myself. I'm going to serve some delicious Spanish food and try to make my hair look good.'

'Why would she want to see your hair?' Maud asked.

'I'm not sure, Maud, but she does, and often when people want things that are quite easy it's probably best to do them, it saves trouble in the long run.'

The estate agents loved the lunch. None of them mentioned the food; they all talked about the atmosphere.

'Right again, Tom,' Cathy said, admiringly. He got things so right.

The Mitchells were in good time, and of course Neil wasn't home. Cathy had laid out little dishes of black olives.

'Thought we'd be getting these,' Jock Mitchell laughed his bluff, loud laugh. 'Had a drink with a couple of lads from the golf club and they said you had done this slap-up Spanish meal, and I said to Hannah what's the betting we get the taste of España tonight.'

Cathy's face took on a set look. 'Ah, but I hope you didn't have *real* money on it because you'd have been wrong, Mr Mitchell,' she said triumphantly. 'Just these lovely fat olives. I thought I'd save a few for you.'

Hannah was busy hanging up her coat and hadn't seen Cathy properly since she came in.

'Oh dear, Cathy, no time to get the little job done on the hair yet?' she said, more in sorrow than in anger.

'Alas no, but I have given it a lot of thought,' she said.

Neil came in at that moment. Cathy spoke in an unnatural voice. 'Neil, *great* you're back. I have to do just five minutes' work and send something by taxi somewhere. Can you entertain your parents for a minute?'

'Sure,' he said agreeably.

She called her local taxi firm and wrote a note to Brenda Brennan at Quentin's: *Can you send me with this taxi driver four portions of anything at all I can give my bloody mother-in-law? Love from a distraught Cathy.*

'This is lovely,' Hannah said, and Cathy smiled serenely. 'I knew it wouldn't be reheated Spanish food,' Hannah continued. 'Jock can be way off-beam sometimes.'

'Sorry,' said Jock.

Tom was a great audience next morning when Cathy told the tale. They sat companionably drinking mugs of coffee and trying out his new date and walnut bread.

'Quentin's sent proper dishes. All I had to do was put them straight on the table.' She was gleeful about it all.

'And what did you do with the Spanish food?'

'I asked the same taxi driver to take it straight round to St Jarlath's. I don't care *what* it all cost, it was worth it, Tom,' Cathy said, delighted with the little victory.

A pinger sounded, so Cathy reached into the oven to take out more bread and screamed with pain. Tom leaped up to take the tray from her.

'I've told you a hundred times to put on those long gloves,' he fussed.

'I know, it's just that I was trying to be quick.'

'That's what you always say, and is it? Here, let me see.'

He held her two arms under the cold-water tap and let the water flow over the red patches.

'It's nothing, Tom, stop clucking like a hen.'

'Someone has to cluck or you'll be as much use as the Venus de Milo.'

'What?'

'The one with no arms. It was a joke.'

'I know, you eejit, it's just that Hannah and Jock were only talking about it last night. It was an argument between Neil and his father.'

Tom laughed, 'And what did you and Hannah talk about?'

'My hair,' Cathy said simply. To her rage, she felt tears in her eyes.

'Oh, Cathy,' he said.

'Tell me, Tom, is it stupid or something? I don't know.'

'No, it's gorgeous.'

'What's it like? Go on, close your eyes, tell me.'

Tom closed his eyes. 'Let me see, it's fair, sort of honey fair, very thick and it's tied behind your back, and little bits curl over your ears and it smells of shampoo and it's just fine.'

Peter Murphy called Geraldine in the office.

'Awkward thing to ask you,' he began.

'My speciality, awkward things,' she said.

Peter Murphy's estranged wife had died that morning. Geraldine had already been told this. It would be either asking her to attend the funeral or not to. It was a matter of indifference to her, they were old history as a couple; there had been many ladies in his life since she had been there. They were truly just good friends now. She listened and made what she hoped were the appropriate sounds of regret, coming as they did from a former mistress. It turned out that Quentin's wouldn't do the catering for the funeral, they were passing such work over to Scarlet Feather. Would this be embarrassing for Geraldine?

'Absolutely not, and I'm sure they'll do it very well,' she said.

'It will be on Saturday morning . . . um . . . at what is . . . was . . . well, her house . . . Her friends would expect . . .'

'Yes, Peter, and what would be best . . .?' Geraldine waited. He was unwilling to decide. 'Perhaps I shouldn't come to the house. I didn't really know her personally, after all.' She could hear his sigh of relief, echoed by her own. Yet she *would* like to know who turned up.

'I've got a question for you Simon,' Lizzie said. 'You and Maud have to say yes or no to Marian's wedding today. If you say yes, then you get dancing lessons and outfits. If you say no then that's fine. It's got to be your decision, the pair of you.'

'Then I say no,' Simon said.

'Right. Maud will be disappointed. She said yes, she wanted to dress up.'

'Well, I don't,' he said.

'Fine. Cathy will be relieved.' This was part of a plan.

'Why?' He didn't like playing into Cathy's hands.

'She says you'd have been no good. Muttie and I didn't agree and it would have been a great day out, but there, it's your choice.'

'I suppose I *could* do it, I mean, if Maud wants it so much.'

'And you do have to learn the dances and wear a kilt?' Lizzie was making sure there were no grey areas.

'Well, I suppose. There's not going to be anyone from school there, after all.' He was talking himself into it. 'Do you know when the wedding is, Lizzie?'

'Yes, it's in the summer,' she said.

'Can I help you out on Saturday at the Murphy funeral? I want to be in the kitchen out of sight, buttering bread and washing dishes.'

'Why?' Cathy was surprised by Geraldine's strange request.

'Because you're a businesswoman. Where will you get a better offer, a pair of hands free for four hours?'

'No, you're doing this for some horrible reason.'

'Only pure curiosity. I used to have a fling with the grieving widower. I'd like to see at first hand how many people turn up and who they are.'

This was their first funeral, and they must do it right. Brenda Brennan at Quentin's said there was a lot of work in that area. You just had to be terribly nice and considerate to the family concerned, and keep everyone else fed and supplied with drink. The problem, of course, was that nobody could tell them how many people to expect.

They would cook two hams, Tom decided, just produce one and carve it in the dining room, keeping the other in reserve. They would have salads ready to make on the premises, a selection of Tom's breads ready to warm up in the oven. There would be big plates of Irish cheese served with apples and grapes. Desserts might make it somehow too festive. *Inappropriate* was the word they kept using to each other.

The family of the late Mrs Murphy were back at the house first. Cathy took their coats and hung them on her mobile coat rack in the hall. Then Walter, who was being the barman once again, offered them a drink, and they moved into the drawing room.

They looked around amazed. In all the years that she had lived here their mother would never have entertained like this. And the big rooms looked so well today; these caterers had added small touches, and certainly managed to show the place at its best.

'It must be very poignant for all,' Cathy said. 'So many memories all coming together.' They looked at each other, surprised. 'I'm sure she would have been very pleased that you opened up her lovely house to everyone . . .' Cathy went on. She saw them relaxing.

Tom kept looking out of the window, giving a running commentary.

'They're coming very slowly, but I think there's just enough to take the bare look off the place. No, wait, there's three more cars pulling up outside, we might have a decent house after all.'

'Geraldine, do we sympathise with Mr Murphy or not?' Cathy said.

Geraldine paused in her work, spreading pâté on small round biscuits. 'I think the words "Upsetting day for you" should cover it perfectly,' she said briskly, and peered again through the little service hatch. 'Hardly anyone here from Peter's hotel. I don't suppose they know what the protocol is.'

The lunch party didn't last long, and soon people were saying goodbye to the daughters. Peter Murphy had left; he never knew that Geraldine was there. The invoice would be presented to his hotel. Cathy wondered whether Geraldine was pleased or disappointed by the small turnout at the funeral of the woman whom she must have hated at one time. But it was impossible to know: Geraldine gave little away.

'Will we freeze the ham, or wheel it out again out for Mrs Hayes, do you think?'

Tom and Cathy had dropped Walter off at the top of Grafton Street, where he was going to spend his pittance, as he called his three hours' wages. They were driving June back with them to the premises, since she was to stack the dishwashers.

'Mrs Who?'

'The lady that had chocolate all over her face and who has booked us for her silver wedding.'

'Oh, yes, of course. No, let's freeze this fellow, I say. They want gooey, creamy things. A nice lean ham would be much too healthy for them.'

Cathy looked at him questioningly and he nodded. They were, as so often, in agreement.

Back at the premises, they turned on the answering machine: three requests for brochures. Then a booking: a ladies' lunch for eight, just to deliver and leave for the Riordans.

'No address, no phone number. Great,' Tom fumed.

'Come on, Tom, we *know* them. *You* know, we did the christening there, you kept referring to him afterwards as Mr Bloody Family Man.'

'Oh, *him*, yes indeed.'

'What will we give them?' Cathy asked.

'A lecture on the subject that there ain't no good in men,' Tom offered.

'No, silly. To eat. And anyway, that's not true. There's plenty of good in men. My father's buying a puppy for the twins to keep in St Jarlath's

Crescent, though he'll have to do all the work training it and cleaning up after it. My husband has got us two great tickets for the opera tonight, even though he doesn't really like it. James Byrne's going to give up his Sunday morning to do the books for us just because we couldn't meet him today. So I haven't one thing against men at the moment,' she laughed at him.

There was a note on the table: *Now I know you'll think I'm trying to wriggle out of culture, but when you hear what's happened you'll agree . . .* He was sorry . . . very sorry. He would make it up to her. The tickets were on the table. Could she find someone else?' Cathy was furious. Could she find someone else to go to the opera with her at five o' clock in the evening? She could feel the start of tears of annoyance and disappointment, but she fought them back. It was only about a night out.

'Geraldine? Would you like to stand in for Neil at the opera tonight?'

'I'd love it. Is it sad?'

'Pretty hopeless set-up, yes. Heroine marries a guy she doesn't love, she kills him. The guy she *does* loves kills himself. That sort of thing, low in communication skills, fairly typical of opera.'

'Fairly typical of life, I'd say,' Geraldine said crisply.

'I'll take you to Quentin's for supper afterwards.'

You did a fantastic job, today. I was very proud of you,' Geraldine said.

'Were you pleased not to see a big crowd there?'

'No, I was indifferent really, just objectively interested, that's all.'

'But if you loved him once, you must have felt something.'

'I never loved Peter Murphy,' Geraldine said simply.

'But weren't you . . .' Cathy's voice trailed away.

'Certainly I was. For over five years. But that doesn't mean I loved him.'

'Then what? Why?' Cathy stopped again. 'I'm sorry, Geraldine, it's none of my business.'

'No, I don't mind . . . I was having a nice time with a pleasant companion who also introduced me to a lot of people and helped me build my business up. Why not? *And* he got me the apartment in Glenstar.'

Cathy looked at her. 'He *got* it for you?'

'You're a big girl now, Cathy, stop being the round-eyed innocent. If people want to give me presents, should I throw them back?'

'Of course not, but a *flat*, Geraldine?'

'It was the same builder who was doing his hotel extension, and it didn't cost him as much as it would have cost other people. It was very generous, though, and as you know, we have remained good friends.'

'But he doesn't think he can come round and . . .'

'No, of course he doesn't, Cathy. Please.'

'But most men don't do things like that, do they?'

'I find that most men do,' Geraldine said. 'I got the car as a present, and that CD player you admire so much.'

'You got all those things from different men at different times?'

'Do you think less of me?' Geraldine asked.

'No, *no*, of course not,' Cathy said emphatically. But she did. Greatly less. The aunt that she had so much admired, who had made it all on her own from a working-class background to a position of power and elegance, turned out to be no more than a courtesan. She was getting presents for sex. It was one small step away from being paid for it.

'Good, I'd hate you to get all pious on me.'

'Me? Pious? Never,' said Cathy with a weak grin. Cathy sought to change the subject. 'Hey, is that a new watch? It's gorgeous.'

'It *is* nice, isn't it.' Geraldine twisted it to make it catch the light. 'That nice estate agent, Freddie Flynn, gave it to me last week.'

They had all the food they could freeze for the silver wedding ready.

'I might even buy you a beer just to get us out of here . . .' Tom began, as someone knocked on the door. It was Neil.

'I was in the area, so I thought if I offered my wife lunch she might forgive me for standing her up at the opera,' he called out.

Cathy came out to the front room.

'There was nothing to forgive, Neil. None of this is necessary.'

'It *is* necessary. I promised something I didn't deliver. Can I deliver a lunch instead?'

'Go, Cathy. Go to one of the posher places and steal ideas,' Tom urged.

They sat opposite each other in a very trendy place and gradually she got over her annoyance. He really *did* feel badly about letting her down.

'They've heard from Uncle Kenneth. He's coming home, apparently.'

'I don't believe it, and what about Aunt Kay in the clinic?'

'Getting stronger by the minute, I hear.'

There was a lump of lead in Cathy's chest. 'It doesn't mean they'll be in any shape to take Maud and Simon back?' she asked fearfully.

'Well, not this very moment I'd say, but of course they will have to go back some time, Cathy.'

Cathy was aware of her very mixed feelings.

These people were not going to look after their children properly. She had taught them some manners, her mam and dad had taught them love and friendship. The return of the prodigal parents had always been something for which she had devoutly hoped. Now that it was beginning to be a reality, Cathy was not so sure.

'Anyway.' Neil was changing the subject. 'None of that is really important. You and I have to talk about the job.'

'Tom, it's Walter. Can I come in and have a word?'

Tom swallowed the sandwich he was eating and pressed the buzzer to let him in. The boy was basically harmless, Tom thought. No hard worker, a little overswift to find his jacket at the end of a job rather than help to carry the plates and glasses out to the van. Still, they had decided not to ask him to do the Hayes silver wedding. Instead they were going to try out a barman they had met, a red-headed boy called Con with a friendly smile.

'Can I do anything for you?'

'This gig, this do . . . whatever . . . on Wednesday. I want to know, is it dinner jacket for me to wear, and what time should I turn up?'

'I don't think we made any arrangement—' Tom began.

'It's just that I was hoping you could give me something in advance now. Towards getting geared up and all.'

Cathy would *not* have booked her husband's cousin without telling him.

'We didn't book you for Wednesday,' he said, 'so there's no question of any advance, I'm afraid. I'm sorry if you got the wrong end of the stick.'

'What? You told me all about it, you spoke about it in front of me— what was I meant to think?'

'What are *we* meant to think, Walter? You describe the wages we give you as a pittance, you don't enjoy the work. How were we meant to be inspired with the idea that you want to work at the Hayes silver wedding?'

'Oh, this is what it's all about. It was a joke, it's what people do, they don't expect people to take a light-hearted remark seriously. But now I see it's a matter of bowing down to the ground and thanking you for the privilege of being allowed to work with you.'

How long could Cathy's lunch take? Tom wondered. Was she ever coming back?

'The job abroad?' Cathy looked at Neil across the table.

'Yes. You and I sort of got started on it the wrong way. I wanted to tell you what it's all about.'

'Do,' she said.

'No, not if you're going to put on that clipped tone with me.'

'Neil, I said tell me about it.'

Just then, the waitress asked if they would like a cocktail.

'I'd love one of those silvery things over there with the frosting on the glass,' Cathy said.

'Why do you want that?' Neil was amazed.

'We're doing this silver wedding. This drink might be just the thing,' she said.

And she waited while he told her about the chance to change the whole thrust of immigration law. It was new and exciting, and it mattered so much. There was only so much individuals could do in their own countries. Too often countries looked the other way when there was oil involved, or if they were selling arms to the area. This international agency would be above all that.

'Where from?' Cathy asked.

'Initially The Hague,' he said.

'You want us to live in Holland?'

'There will be travel, of course, and you can come with me. You'll see places, Cathy, places that you never dreamed of.'

'What will you do every day, Neil?' Her voice felt disembodied; she needed to buy time to think about this. He really expected that she would drop everything and go with him. As he struggled to paint a picture on how he saw their days shaping out, she wondered if anyone truly knew anyone else. She heard words somewhere around her in the air as she tasted the silvery cocktail, which turned out to be a disaster.

'You're very quiet,' Neil said eventually.

'I'm thinking about it, letting it all sink in.'

'I knew you would, if we had time. Back in Waterview you had boxing gloves up in the air in confrontation, your-job-my-job sort of thing. It's not about that, it's about our life. Believe me, I know you'll love it. They want you to come out with me for a week, to see first hand where we'd be living. Cathy, you *love* a challenge.'

'We need a lot more discussion about this. A lot more,' she said.

'Of course we do.' He patted her hand.

Neil seemed to think the conversation had gone well.

To their surprise, Walter was installed at the premises and Cathy noticed that Tom was looking hassled.

'Hey, are you better?' Neil asked Walter.

'Yeah, I'm OK.' Walter said, shrugging.

'He had a fall and hurt his back,' Neil explained. 'Dad was telling me. He's been out of the office a week.'

Tom and Cathy knew there had been no fall, but they said nothing. At that moment the phone rang. It was Mrs Hayes. They had decided they wanted two waiters for Wednesday. Would that be any problem?

'No problem at all, Mrs Hayes.' Tom hung up and turned to look at Walter. 'Usual pittance, Wednesday, Walter, turn up here at six thirty to help stack the van, no money up front, no need to hire a dinner jacket, you already have one. OK?'

'OK,' Walter said, smiling. 'I knew you really meant me to work.'

Muttie had planned the surprise for weeks. And he wanted as many people to witness it as possible. So he asked Cathy and Neil if they could drop in about six o' clock on Tuesday, and Geraldine. The little black Labrador puppy was going to be already hidden up in the bedroom. The conversation would be brought around gradually to dogs. Maud and Simon would say yet again how much they'd love a puppy, and then Muttie would produce the little fellow . . .

It didn't suit Cathy because she and Tom had to collect their dishes from the Riordan ladies' lunch. It didn't suit Geraldine because Freddie Flynn said he might be able to call round to the Glenstar apartment after work. But they all tried to fit it in. Geraldine told Freddie that she'd be a little delayed. Neil said that he'd try to be there, but he'd have to be out of St Jarlath's Crescent by six thirty. Cathy said that she and Tom could call before they went to pick up the dishes.

'Is something happening?' Simon asked when they all sat down at the kitchen table. 'Everyone here's sort of waiting.'

'No, Simon, we're sitting round a table having tea.' Cathy continued her attempt to improve the twins' manners. 'And making general conversation rather than centring everything on ourselves.'

'Is everybody all right for sugar and milk?' Maud said obediently.

Muttie cleared his throat. 'There's nothing better than a family sitting down round a table,' he began as if reading lines from a play. 'All over Dublin there's people sitting down to their tea now, watched by their cats and dogs.' He waited, but the children said nothing.

Tom felt he had to fill in the gap. 'You've got a point there, Muttie, a family could be watched by all kinds of things, a hamster, a rabbit, and a dog, of course.'

Still not a word from Maud and Simon.

Muttie was desperate now. 'But there was never a dog in this house, of course, not having been in the past a family of dog lovers.'

Then the twins leaped up.

'It *is*,' cried Simon.

'I *knew* it,' shouted Maud, and in a flash they were up the stairs. There were sounds of barks and screams, and then they arrived carrying the puppy, all black fur and wagging tail.

'It's beautiful,' said Maud.

'It's a he, I looked.' Simon was looking again in case there should be any misunderstanding. 'Is it for us?' he asked, hardly daring to hope.

'It's for the pair of you,' Muttie said, beaming all over his face.

'To keep for ever?' Maud said, unbelieving.

'Sure, of course.'

'You know we were hoping you might get a dog,' Maud said. 'And—'

'We heard it whimpering inside the door.' Simon took up the story.

'And I said maybe it was a puppy.'

'And I said yes, Muttie *could* have got himself a puppy, but also it could be just some old person grunting on the floor of Muttie's bedroom and we'd better not go in.'

'But we never knew it was for us,' Maud said.

Cathy realised that this was the moment when the twins actually changed their personality. The way they stroked the puppy and laughed aloud at its antics would have melted the hardest heart. They had the little animal on the table now, flopping about on its fat little paws. Tom put a newspaper under him, just in time.

'We'll show you how to train him,' said Lizzie.

'And what are you going to call him?' Tom wanted to know.

'Hooves,' said Simon, and Maud nodded eagerly. There was a silence. 'Hooves Mitchell,' Maud elaborated.

'And . . . um . . . why exactly did you think of this . . . um . . . interesting name?' Tom voiced everyone's thoughts.

'It's what Muttie always says is the best thing in the world . . . the thundering hooves that match your heartbeat,' said Simon.

Muttie blew his nose very loudly.

Neil called Cathy on the mobile just as they were leaving.

'I'm so sorry.'

'It doesn't matter, Neil. They just love the puppy . . .'

'That's what I was calling about, Cathy. Uncle Kenneth is back cleaning up The Beeches, Kay is getting out of hospital at the weekend . . . This can't last here, all this make-believe.'

'It's not make-believe, it's a home. What kind of a home is that uncle of yours making for children?'

'According to Dad and Walter, not too bad a fist of it. Walter even suggested that they get some food from you for the freezer.'

'I'll tell them what to do with food for the freezer,' Cathy said.

'Cathy, please, we'll talk later.'

'It's just not fair,' Tom said. They were driving into the Riordans' house. There were definite sounds of a party.

'They swore they'd be finished by five o' clock. What will we do?'

'Leave it to me,' Tom said. 'Stay in the van. It might take half an hour.'

She heard Tom rummaging in the back of the van for something and then saw him running up the steps with a package.

Mrs Riordan came to the door. 'Oh God, is that the time?'

'Must have been a wonderful party.' Tom nailed his happiest, most enthusiastic smile to his face. 'Can I go in and say hello to the ladies? I brought them a gift.'

'What? Yes, of course, come in.'

'Good evening, ladies,' he said pleasantly to a group of eleven women who had drunk too much wine. 'I thought you'd like . . .'

'A stripper!' screamed one of the women happily.

'Sadly no,' he said hastily. 'I've hurt my back. I wouldn't be able to give you a proper performance at all, but I *did* come with a gift of petits fours.'

They thought this was wonderful, even though they contained four hundred calories a bite.

'And why don't I give you more room to enjoy things?' Adroitly he started to clear the table. The women rushed to help him. In the kitchen, they saw him begin to stack the plates in the crate.

'We must wash them first,' Mrs Riordan said.

'No, no, we do that back at base, all part of the service,' he said.

But they insisted. A sinkful of hot, soapy water, another for rinsing, two ladies drying. The party was in the kitchen now.

'Your back doesn't look all that bad to me,' said the woman who had hoped Tom was a stripper.

'Wait till I'm on real form,' he said to her roguishly, and she blushed with excitement.

They helped him carry the crates down to the van.

'You're a pair of angels,' said Mrs Riordan, pushing two twenty-pound notes at them. 'Go on, go out and have a drink on me.'

They spent the forty pounds in a Chinese restaurant. Cathy noticed that Marcella had three prawns, no rice, no stir fry, no sweet and sour pork. Tom noticed that Neil was concerned because the Chinese waiters were probably not in trade unions. They told the story of Hooves.

'Isn't The Beeches a big house with a garden?' Marcella asked. 'They might be able to have it with them there.'

'No—those two would freak if they had to cope with a dog as well as children,' Cathy said.

'But maybe they won't be going back there for ages.'

Neil said that it would be much sooner than anyone thought; the law actually did move quickly in restoring children to their homes.

'It seems a pity if they're happy where they are,' said Tom.

'That's not the point.' Neil was very strong on that. 'At least nowadays the importance of the birth parents is actually recognised.'

Cathy thought that this was being overrecognised in this particular case. But she did nothing. There were so many other things to be discussed with Neil.

The Hayes household was up to high doh when they arrived at six thirty. Two discontented sons were hanging around, unsure of what to do. An equally discontented daughter was saying that there was no way she could use the ironing board in the kitchen. Mrs Hayes said they were to call her Molly, and her husband was Shay. He was a plump, somewhat anxious man, who obviously felt the need to bark out orders.

Cathy had switched on the kettle, asked June to take the ironing board and iron up to the spare room, and got the boys to put the two Persian cats into a place from which they could not emerge and eat the salmon. By the time the kettle had boiled, Cathy had persuaded Molly to go upstairs and rest with her feet slightly raised.

'But setting everything up . . . ?' Molly begged.

'Is exactly what you are paying us well to do,' Cathy said firmly.

She heard Tom telling Shay that they had a chain of command, a checklist, a routine to follow, and it was wise if they were left to themselves to do it. He had always thought it good for the family to come down at seven thirty, half an hour before the first guests arrived, so they could check everything was all in order. Shay nodded, it made sense. And soon the Hayes family had all gone to their rooms. Tom and Cathy got into action. At exactly seven o' clock the two barmen arrived. Con, the cheerful redhead, and Walter, sulkier and moodier than ever.

'They'll be having champagne cocktails to start,' Cathy explained.

'How naff,' Walter said.

Cathy's face was hard. 'You know how to do them, and fill them up very shortly before the guests arrive with champagne.'

'Or what passes for champagne,' said Walter, lifting up a bottle.

Cathy now addressed herself entirely to Con. 'I'd like you to get forty glasses ready and can you see that Walter opens twelve bottles of white and twelve bottles of red.'

'Excuse me, Cathy, do you have a problem talking to me? Should I leave?' He looked so supercilious she wanted to hit him. He knew that she couldn't let him go now. Not just before the guests arrived. Or could she?

'Either change your attitude or get your coat,' she said crisply.

'And where will you get a replacement at this hour?'

'Your cousin,' she said simply, and took out her mobile phone.

'Neil? You wouldn't.'

She began dialling.

'OK, sorry I was out of order.'

'No, I'm sorry, Walter, I can't rely on you. This is a big job for us.'

Suddenly he realised that she meant it.

'Walter's actually doing some work for once,' Tom said admiringly, watching the wine bottles moving swiftly as requested.

'I put the frighteners on him,' Cathy said, with some satisfaction.

Just then the Hayes family all appeared downstairs.

'We have a little tradition, which is to take a family photograph before everyone comes,' said Tom, and he posed them next to the cake by the buffet table, accepting their first champagne cocktail of the night.

Only an hour in they knew it was going to be a roaring success. 'Fantastic, these things,' said Shay to everyone about the little choux pastries each filled with horseradish sauce and cream, and cold rare beef.

'Did you invent these, Cathy?' a man asked her.

It was Freddie Flynn, her aunt's friend. Mrs Flynn was there, small and jewelled. She smiled at them both.

'No, alas, I didn't. But I did see them somewhere and remembered them! Is that as good?'

'Certainly,' he said. He had a nice smile. 'Darling, this is Cathy Feather, she's a sort of cousin of Geraldine, you know, who does our PR. Cathy, this is my wife, Pauline.'

'You might do *our* silver wedding,' the woman said.

'Oh indeed, we'd be honoured. Now excuse me, I must . . .'

She moved away, seething. They were going to have a silver wedding party. And according to Geraldine, this was meant to be a dead marriage. God, it would make you sick.

Molly had said wistfully that she thought they would all feel too old to dance, but Tom had brought the *Best of Abba* just in case. First he put on Leo Sayer 'When I Need You' and then 'Don't Cry For Me, Argentina'.

When he heard people joining in and when the desserts had been cleared away he let rip with 'Mamma Mia' and they were all on their feet.

Tom and Cathy paused to have a coffee in the kitchen. Around them the dishes had been collected and stacked. Soon it would be midnight, time to pay the two barmen their five hours.

The van had been filled, the kitchen was immaculate and only a hard core of ten people remained. Con asked if he could speak to Tom for a moment.

'Very awkward, this,' he began.

'What?' Tom hoped Con wasn't going to ask for more money.

'It's just that . . . I think you should have a look at that sports bag over there. God, I hate saying this . . .' the boy looked really distressed. Tom unzipped the bag. There, on top of Walter's sweater, were four silver ladles and two silver cruets.

'Thanks,' he said. 'You go off now, quick as you can. I found this bag myself, do you understand, and thank you again.'

Cathy came into the kitchen and took off her Scarlet Feather apron.

'Cathy, Walter stole the silver. His sports bag there, filled with their stuff, look for yourself.'

The colour left her face. 'Where is he?'

'Still in the dining room, chatting up Molly and Shay's daughter.'

'We sort this out here and now, Tom, get the guards if necessary, if he denies it.'

'You're not going the distance on this?' Tom was amazed at her courage.

'If I have to I will.' Cathy went into the dining room.

'Walter, I need you in the kitchen, straight away,' she said.

When he saw the open bag, Walter began to bluster. 'How *dare* you root in my private things . . .' he began.

'An explanation, Walter.'

'I didn't put them there, *you* did. You both hate me.'

'We haven't touched them. The guards will be here shortly and will tell us whose fingerprints are on them.'

'You're never going to call the guards?' His face was white.

Cathy lifted her phone. 'I'm going to wait for you to call your cousin first because you're going to need someone to speak for you, Walter.'

He looked at her, unbelieving.

'Go on, make the call. It's preset. You just dial one.'

They watched him as Neil answered. The kitchen door was closed; they could hear both ends of the conversation.

'Neil, sorry . . . sorry for ringing you, it's Walter.'

'What is it? Is Cathy all right?'

'Actually, I'm in a bit of trouble. There was a bit of a misunderstand-ing . . . We're still at this house, you see, and Tom went rummaging in my private bag and he says he found some silver there . . . belonging to the house, as it were . . .' Walter paused but there was no response. 'And now, Neil, they're talking about calling the guards, Tom and Cathy are. Uncle Jock will kill me, you have to help me . . .'

'Take off your jacket and hand it to Tom.'

'What?'

'Do it, Walter.'

He did it. There was a rattle as he struggled out of his dinner jacket. Tom shook it again. There were silver teaspoons in the pocket, a watch and a paper knife.

'Is it done?' Neil asked.

'Yes, there seem to be . . .'

'I was sure there might have been,' Neil said.

'What happens now?'

'Not up to me, I'm afraid. It is up to you. Cathy and Tom and the people whose silver you stole. Good luck, then.'

'What do you mean, "Good luck"? Aren't you going to help me?'

'No, I most certainly am not.'

'Cathy's here, Neil; let me pass you over to her . . . Please, Neil.'

'Cathy and Tom run their business, Walter. They had the bad luck to employ a thief. Anything they do is fine with me.' And he hung up.

There was a silence. 'I want him done for this, every bit of me wants that,' Cathy said. 'There are just two things against it. I don't want to spoil Molly and Shay's evening, and I don't want to tell those children I was the one who put their brother in jail and added to all the problems the unfortunates already have.'

'So you'll not call the guards?' Walter grabbed at the lifeline he saw.

'Tom?'

'I'm with you,' Tom said.

'I'm sorry, Cathy.'

'You're just sorry you were caught, Walter. Why did you do it? Jock pays you plenty.'

'I'm in debt,' he said.

'Well, at least you're not in the Garda station,' she said.

'I'll never forget this, Cathy.'

'Go now,' said Tom.

He left. Cathy sat there, very still.

'You were great,' Tom said. 'And Neil was great too.'

'I knew he wouldn't defend Walter,' Cathy said.

'I didn't. I thought he'd see him as the underdog.'

'No, *we* were the underdogs, Neil could see that straight away. Our entire business could have gone under.'

'He has an extraordinary sense of justice,' Tom said admiringly.

'Do you get the feeling this night went on for days and days?' Cathy asked wearily.

'I do. Weeks and weeks actually. Come on, let's go home,' he said.

April

THEY HAD WORKED HARD this morning, the preparations were all done for the two delivery jobs: a fancy bridge tea for twelve people—tiny sandwiches and little cakes to go to a private house—and a supper for a woman who was pretending to her in-laws she had cooked the meal herself. Now, as they sat down to have a coffee after a buying spree in the mid-season sale at Hayward's, Cathy saw Shona Burke, sitting alone and reading a book. She was eating a small salad and drinking something from the health juice bar. She looked lonely and rather prim. She finished her lunch, closed the book, looked at her watch and was about to go back to her work when she spotted them.

'Aha, Scarlet Feather undercover in our café,' Shona said.

'Your breads are rubbish compared to mine,' Tom teased her.

To his surprise she nodded. 'You're absolutely right, that's what I was saying last Friday at a meeting. Lovely soups and salads here, but just the plainest and dullest of bread. You know *that's* how I'm going to get you in here. They can put up a notice saying that the breadbasket is by Scarlet Feather. Listen, there's a meeting tomorrow at ten thirty. Let me have a selection of your best, and I'll suggest it.'

They talked about prices and presentation and quantities and delivery. The enthusiasm was enormous. Shona became anxious.

'Don't be too disappointed if it doesn't work, but I'll give it my very best shot for you both, and I think it would be really good for the restaurant too.'

'You're a star, Shona,' Tom said, gathering up his bags.

'Are you back to the kitchens to start baking now?' she laughed.

'No, now I'm going to see my father. I'll go into the premises tomorrow, early . . .'

'How *is* your father?' Shona asked.

'Oh, he's fine thanks, Shona. He's taking it a little easier, which is no harm. Listen, I'm going to run up to the salon and see Marcella for a quick word before we go. I'll see you in the van in ten minutes, Cathy.' He was gone. The two women watched him, and saw the admiring glances as he moved like an athlete through the tables.

'He has absolutely no idea the effect he creates,' Cathy said.

'When he and Marcella go anywhere together they're just like film stars, the pair of them,' Shona said, getting up to leave.

Cathy picked up her parcels and said, 'Tom said you had family in the hospital when he went to see his father?'

'Yes, that's right.'

'And is it all right . . . for them, too?'

Shona looked at her. 'No, no, she died.'

'Oh, I'm very sorry to hear that.'

'Thank you, Cathy.'

Marcella was sitting doing nail extensions for a very elegant woman who was busy holding out her hands and admiring them. She was delighted to see Tom. She looked so gorgeous in her short white uniform, her long slim legs in dark navy tights and her cloud of dark hair like a halo round her face.

'Will I get a video, or would you like to go out?' he whispered.

'There's a book launch,' she said.

'Let's hit that, then,' he said with a good-natured shrug. He knew not to ask Marcella what book. A book launch was a photo opportunity. Someone might take a very glamorous picture of Marcella, which could appear in the Among Those Attending column.

The twins were doing their homework in the kitchen when Cathy arrived at St Jarlath's. Her mother had begun making their wedding outfits, and had the sewing machine whirring away. Her father was out in the back painting the kennel that one of his pals had made for Hooves.

'You're welcome, Cathy, but this is a house of hard industry at the moment until after six thirty, if you know what I mean.'

'I'm just going to do my accounts at the table,' Cathy said quickly, and sat down opposite Maud and Simon. 'Hello,' she whispered, and they all went back to work. She didn't even see the figures, they were just a blur. She had phoned Neil just before coming here. Simon and Maud's mother and father were looking forward to seeing their children again, and were expecting them to come home at the weekend.

At half past six they all went on a tour of inspection of the snow-white kennel.

'A palace for Hooves,' Simon said with awe.

'But of course he can't get into it until the paint is dried,' Muttie explained.

'Or he'll look like a Dalmatian, all white spots,' said Cathy.

'Dalmatians are actually white with black spots,' Simon corrected her. Then he remembered that you didn't correct people. 'At least, I meant to say . . . that some of them are white with black spots.'

'Good boy, Simon,' Cathy said with sudden tears in her eyes. They had taught these children so much, and for what? So that they could be sent back to their dysfunctional parents?

'Are you crying?' Maud asked with interest.

'Sort of. People of my age do cry sometimes, quite unexpectedly. It's a nuisance,' she said matter-of-factly and blew her nose.

'Our mother used to cry like that in the hospital, and she didn't know why either,' Maud said kindly, as a sort of reassurance.

She hadn't realised just how very much she was going to miss them.

'Come on, kids, let's take Hooves for a walk.'

Up and down St Jarlath's Crescent they went, telling the people that they met about the puppy.

'I never thought we'd have a real puppy of our own, living in the house,' said Simon, when it was Maud's turn to hold the lead.

'Sure, and he'll always be yours. The actual *house* where Hooves sleeps isn't as important as the fact that he belongs to you.'

Simon looked up at her, troubled. 'Why do you say that?'

'Well, you know,' she shrugged vaguely.

'I know now,' he said. The old solemn look was back.

'What do you know?' she asked fearfully.

Simon spoke very slowly and deliberately. 'Father has come back from his travels, Mother is coming out of the nervous hospital and we'll be going back to live with them and leave Hooves behind us.'

There was a silence. 'It's your turn with Hooves,' Maud said.

'I don't want him Maud, thank you,' Simon said, and walked ahead. His shoulders were hunched and his head was down. Cathy knew that he was trying very hard not to show how upset he was.

'Are we really going to be leaving St Jarlath's Crescent and you and Neil, Cathy?' Maud's face was paler than ever.

'It's not really *leaving*, you know. Friends don't leave each other. You'll be coming back to us and, who knows, maybe you can take Hooves with you.'

'You didn't know Mother, did you? Her nerves would never let her make a home for Hooves,' Maud said sadly.

Marcella was talking earnestly to Ricky, but her face lit up when Tom came into the bookshop.

'You'll never guess what Ricky's going to try and get,' she said.

'No, tell me.' Tom was tired. His mother had worn him out, the passivity of his father had depressed him, he feared they hadn't costed the breads right for tomorrow's demonstration. Cathy had rung him on the mobile to say that St Jarlath's Crescent was plunged into gloom and did he fancy a cheering drink.

'I'm on my way to have one, come and join us. We might make a pitch for the bookshop trade as well,' he'd offered, and she'd agreed.

'Tom, don't look now,' Marcella warned, 'but that woman over there in the hat. She's the editor of the new magazine I was telling you about. Well, Ricky thinks he could sell her a picture story. Big, hunky photos of you. Huge publicity for Scarlet Feather, too . . . at home, at work or wherever.'

'Yeah, I mentioned it to her, she seems to be interested. I'll think she'll bite.'

'You do, Ricky?' Tom's eyes lit up. This would be truly wonderful. Everyone who was ever going to hire a caterer read this publication. They would never in a million years be able to get this kind of coverage.

'He's going to ask her to come over and meet you in a minute—give her your biggest smile,' Marcella begged. She looked so beautiful, but extra lively and happy tonight in a very smart short, dark grey and white dress he had never seen before.

She was like a toddler at a birthday party she was so thrilled with it all. Just then he saw Cathy. She looked bedraggled in her raincoat, and she had an elastic band holding her hair back. She wore no make-up and she had lines under her eyes.

Cathy smiled. 'Lead me to the red wine and let me loose on it.'

The woman in the silly hat approached and was introduced by Ricky. 'This is the celebrated Tom Feather I told you about.'

'Mmm,' she said, looking Tom up and down.

'I hear the magazine's doing really well,' he said.

'And your business too.' Again she seemed to let her eyes run all over Tom's body slowly and appreciatively.

'Yes, well, let me introduce you to the other half of the business, half of Scarlet Feather, Cathy Scarlet.'

'Great to meet you,' Cathy said pleasantly.

The woman looked somewhat puzzled. 'How nice,' she said.

'We'd be very happy to cooperate in anything . . . everything,' Tom said with his huge smile.

'Well, *that* sounds like the best offer I've had all night,' she said, moving on. She had a strange manner, this woman. Full of innuendo. Cathy thought she was grotesque. But she had gone now, so it was immaterial.

'Wait till you know what's going to happen, thanks to Ricky.' Tom couldn't wait a moment longer.

'What?' Cathy had rarely seen him so excited.

'That woman's the head of the new magazine we couldn't afford to advertise in, and, wait for it, there's going to be a photo feature about Scarlet Feather in it.'

'Well, Tom . . .' Ricky began.

'*No!* You're not serious.' She was going to have to do so much, borrow some clothes, get a professional make-up . . . But it would all be worth it. 'When do they want to do it?' she asked, as excited as Tom was.

'Well, you see, actually . . .' Ricky began looking ill at ease.

Marcella explained. 'Ricky was telling me she's a very difficult woman, she blows hot and cold, we won't really know when or what form it will take for quite some time.'

'Sure,' Ricky said. 'Marcella tells it as it is. Stay in this part of the room, honey. I'll get one of the guys from the Sundays to come over to snap you.'

'Why did Ricky change his tack so suddenly? A few minutes ago he was saying it was in the bag.' Tom was puzzled and annoyed.

'There's been a misunderstanding,' Marcella looked awkward.

'Go on Marcella.' Cathy was gentle.

'Ricky was selling her a feature for a kind of Glamorous Couples thing. You know, you the big, gorgeous gourmet cook, me the model, our home, pics of you serving a meal to me, me at the gym, you piping cream on a dessert . . . So you see . . .'

'It's not about Scarlet Feather at all.' He was bitterly disappointed.

'Well, of course it is in part . . . people will get to know your name.'

'But it's all a fake. I don't cook you meals, Marcella . . . you don't *eat* any meals.' Tom's face was red with indignation.

'Oh, come on, Tom. This is the chance I need. They can't *have* a feature on the business alone, that would be just advertising.'

Cathy turned to go away, and saw herself reflected in a glass door. Of course it had been ridiculous to think that a glossy magazine would have wanted her in it.

'Don't go, Cathy, you wanted a drink and to be cheered up.'

'Well I *am* cheered up, very.' Her eyes were very bright, overbright. 'We've got a load of great publicity ahead of us.'

'I'm sorry. I thought it was the two of us.'

'I'm not . . . I'm totally relieved.' And she was out of the bookshop.

Cathy was around at the premises at dawn the next day.

'I'm not here to interfere, just to make coffee and tidy up after you. This is your show,' she explained.

Tom was overjoyed to see her. 'I'm having awful second thoughts about the fruit and nutty bread.'

'But everyone loves that,' Cathy protested.

'They love it when they've paid for it in advance and they can't give it back,' Tom wailed, 'but will they love it if they have to pay so much a slice?'

'I think it's a great idea . . . Come on, strong, strong coffee and lots of backbone . . . How's Marcella?'

'I proposed again last night. I said if we have to do this idiotic photo shoot let's make it an engagement celebration, but she says she won't marry me until she's successful, until she believes that I'm getting as good a bargain as she is.'

There was a ping on the oven timer and the bread came out. It all looked perfect as it went onto the wire trays. 'It's bloody great, Tom, I *know* we're into Hayward's today.'

They delivered the baskets to Shona just before the big meeting. Shona looked very much in control. You didn't stay in a senior job at Hayward's just by looking pretty.

'It smells utterly magical, but you know it's not down to me. I can only hope for you,' she said, and she was gone.

They would meet in the café at noon to hear the result. They would go to the market to buy the ingredients for James Byrne's cookery lesson that evening. They would price little breadbaskets in the market too, just in case they got the Hayward's job. That would fill their time until Shona was able to tell them the news.

Shona came running into the café. Not only had they bought it as an idea, they had eaten it all at their coffee break. They could start next week on a six-week trial period.

'Can we use our name?' Tom asked.

'Yes, but a bit smaller than you wanted. They'd like "Baked fresh every day especially for Hayward's", and then your name. And they accept the price.'

Tom and Cathy looked at each other in disbelief.

'Back to the market,' she said.

'To buy the breadbaskets,' Tom said with a great whoop of joy.

James Byrne had explained to them that he wanted three cookery lessons. And that he would need to master a starter, a main course and a dessert at each lesson. Then he could mix and match, and when the time came he could serve whatever he liked best.

It was a big house, back from the road, with a well-kept gravelled space for cars. James Byrne had said to ring the Garden Flat bell. It was a basement with iron bars on the window. Fairly typical of his cautious behaviour. Be prepared for burglars, clients with laundered money, random tax inspections.

He opened the door to them and smiled his usual grave smile. Dressed formally—no sweater and sloppy corduroy for James Byrne at home. They carried in their bags of ingredients through a dark narrow hall. On the right was a sitting room, and on the left a kitchen. It was mainly a dark muddy-brown colour, and even with the April sunset peeping through the dark curtains there was nowhere that the light seemed to land on a cheerful corner. The kitchen had an awkward table, an old-fashioned oven, and a fridge that took up a great amount of room. Cathy ached to get it all torn out. But this man would live with these hopeless, outdated appliances for ever. He had never said if he was single, married, divorced or widowed. His flat gave absolutely no sign of any lifestyle. You would not know what chair he sat in in the evening. A low table had a pile of neatly stacked newspapers and magazines on it. Dull pictures on the walls of mountains and lakes. Just two shelves of old books, a desk with some papers on it and an old-fashioned blotter. Cathy shook herself.

'Right. The lesson starts here, James: put on your pinny.'

Triumphantly she produced a Scarlet Feather apron. He seemed bashful as he tied its strings round his waist.

'That was very nice of her, wasn't it, Tom?' he said. 'Trust a woman to have a nice little touch.'

'Don't ever let the females think they have a monopoly on little touches, James. I brought you a great big oven glove so that you won't burn your arm like some people I know.'

He was very pleased with this. 'Looks as if it's all going to be much more intensive than I thought,' he said.

They did a smoked mackerel starter in little ramekins. Cathy flaked the fish expertly and added the cream.

'It seems a very easy thing to make.' James Byrne was suspicious.

'It tastes as if it were very difficult to make, I assure you.' Cathy patted him down.

'I've had it in restaurants, and you know I thought there was an awful lot of cooking in it.' He shook his head in wonder.

'Wait till we deconstruct chicken tarragon for you, James,' Tom laughed. 'You'll never trust a cook again.'

They sat and ate together, the three of them. Cathy had written out everything step by step. James said it was all quite delicious, and what's more, he thought he could do it on his own. They talked easily, touching on a lot of subjects: politics, prisons, drugs and eventually opera. James said he used to go a lot to the opera when he was a student, but somehow since then . . . His voice trailed away. Neither of them asked why he couldn't go now. Or indeed, in the years in between.

The photo shoot was endless. Tom just could not believe that grown-up people spent such huge amounts of time doing something so trivial that would result in five or six photographs in a magazine. He felt sure there had been some mistake, and that a multimillion-dollar movie was being made in the small apartment. Marcella arrived home with a selection of Hayward's garments for both of them.

'It's all with Shona's blessing . . . It's an advertisement for them. And you are so gorgeous I'm going to have trouble beating them all off you, the make-up artists, the hairstylists, the lighting people.' She laughed excitedly.

Marcella sat motionless as they applied yet more make-up. When asked to smile, she did so with a radiance he could hardly believe. It didn't matter how many times she had to do it, the same smile was delivered as fresh as if it had come from the heart. Tom, on the other hand, felt awkward.

It was beginning to happen for her, the work dream coming true. Tom would do his utmost to smile and look rugged, or whatever they wanted if it would help Marcella's career.

That night, Neil told Cathy that Kenneth and Kay Mitchell were now installed, and everything was in place; they were ready and waiting.

'I told the social worker, Sara, that it would be a bit hard on the kids to go straight back in, and she agrees entirely. She says that we should bring them to visit their parents once or twice before leaving them there. She'll come with us.'

'OK, I'll fix a time to take them to the House of Horrors,' Cathy said.

They told Hooves that they were only going out for a visit, and that they would be back later on.

'I know it sounds silly, but I think he does understand,' Maud said.

Nothing would make Cathy believe that this was the just or fair thing to do. But she had to go along with it.

'Come on, kids, into the van, and take me to see your house.'

'Could Muttie and his wife come too?' Simon hung back.

'One day they'll come to see it, but today it's just us,' said Cathy, refusing to look at her parents watching the children leave.

The Beeches was a large, shabby, ill-kept house 150 years old, a gentleman's residence which had seen better days. Not as imposing as Oaklands, but attractive, with good proportions. A disused tennis court and a broken garden shed showed how grand it must have been at some stage.

Kenneth Mitchell welcomed them in as if they were the most honoured guests, rather than the two children he had abandoned.

'How perfectly splendid,' he said.

'Hello, Father,' Simon said.

'Simon, good chap. Good boy,' his father said, 'and Maud too, excellent.' He looked at Cathy vaguely as if trying to place her. He was quite like his brother Jock in appearance, but he had not run to fat. There was no sign of his wife.

'Well, Kenneth, shall we wait for Kay and Sara before we do the tour?'

'Tour? Sara . . . um, Kay?' He was bewildered. 'Oh, yes, she'll be here in a moment, she's getting ready.'

Maud seemed to feel uneasy as well.

'What time is Sara coming?' she asked.

Kenneth Mitchell looked confused. 'Sara?'

'The social worker,' Cathy said in a level voice.

'But I thought *you* were the social worker,' he said.

'No, Kenneth, I am Cathy Scarlet, I am married to Neil, who is your brother Jock's son.'

His embarrassment, if he had any, was spared by the sound of the bell ringing. They heard Kenneth out in the hall welcoming the social worker with great charm and even greater confusion. A very tall, handsome girl with flaming hair and big laced boots, she seemed altogether confident.

'Hi, Maud, Simon, everything OK?' she asked. 'I mean, have you been to the bedrooms to check all your things are there?'

'Well, Sara, we haven't been here very long, you see,' Simon said.

'We haven't even seen Mother yet,' Maud added.

'OK, go and check the rooms and then come back to me.'

They scampered up the stairs obediently.

'How're you, Cathy? I believe you hate my guts,' Sara said companionably. 'Your husband seemed to think you had problems with their returning home.'

'No, Sara, I don't think I have any problems with it at all. I brought them along here for a visit, their father thought that I was the social worker and their mother wasn't here to greet them, which I found odd. Listen, I'm doing everything by the book. Why don't you inspect the visit and leave me out of it? I'm going to be out of it anyway when they come back here.'

'And where is Walter?' Sara asked, looking at her notes. 'The whole family was meant to be here,' Sara said.

'Walter?' asked Kenneth vaguely. 'I expect he's at work.' Kenneth looked anxious to be helping in an ever more confusing world. The children came in at that moment, holding their mother by the hand. Kay Mitchell looked frail and as if a wind would blow her away. She had a nice smile.

'Hello, how nice to see you,' she said to Cathy.

'You look much stronger now,' Cathy said.

'Do I? That's good. Did you come to see me in hospital?'

'Yes, from time to time. Any sign of your brother Walter?' Cathy asked the children.

'He sort of made the beds for us,' Simon said.

'It was just the sheets and pillowcases left at the end of the beds actually. They were very damp, so Mother has been helping us put them into the hot press,' Maud explained.

'So now it's only Walter we're waiting for, is that right? This is his home?'

'Well, he's an adult man of course, he doesn't have to check in every night. But his room is here . . .'

'Locked,' said Simon.

'How do you know?' Sara was interested.

'We had a rocking horse and an old black and white telly. I thought maybe Walter had borrowed them . . . which would have been fine with

85

us.' Simon didn't want to get anyone into any trouble.

'When will we be coming back here for good?' Maud asked.

'Whenever you like.' Her father beamed.

'The sooner the better.' Her mother's smile was wide.

'When all the paperwork is complete,' Sara said.

'And Cathy, were you able to explain properly to Sara all about Hooves visiting, and the wedding of Lizzie's daughter,' asked Simon.

'I say—' Kenneth began.

He was saved from having to say anything by the arrival of Walter.

'Hi, kids, Mother, Father, Cathy.' He nodded to them all, then he put on the Mitchell smile. 'And you must be Sara? Aren't you terribly young and, um, gorgeous to be doing this job?'

Cathy looked at him in despair. *Please* may Sara not fall for it.

'You were meant to be here forty-five minutes ago.' Sara was stern. She called the meeting to order with a cough. 'Can we run through the arrangements, please? Can we start with school. Last September there was a problem. The twins missed a lot of days. But since they went to stay in St Jarlath's Crescent they have been doing well. You are content that they continue where they are and there is a bus journey if nobody can collect them.'

'Good to become familiar with buses,' said Kenneth.

'Quite. And meals. Will you do the cooking, Mrs Mitchell?'

'Well, of course I will, and there's a Mrs . . . Mrs . . . Somebody who is coming to help, isn't she?'

'Mrs Barry,' Sara said. 'Now you say there are damp sheets on the beds.'

'Which will be aired, of course, by the time they come home,' Kay said.

'Yes, indeed. And there's a matter of a missing rocking horse and a black and white television set.'

'I didn't say they were missing. They might be in Walter's room. Which is locked.' Simon wanted things to be clear.

'I've every right to lock my room, everyone has.'

'Sure, but can we go and see if the kids' things are in it?' Cathy could sense there was something in that room that Walter didn't want seen.

'Excuse me, Cathy,' he said, 'I thought this was Sara's job.'

'Do you know anything about a rocking horse and a television set?' Sara asked him levelly.

'Oh those. They were very old. I gave them away to friends ages ago. Sorry, you're both much too old for a rocking horse. I didn't know they were still needed.'

Cathy knew he had sold them.

'We're not too old for a television set, though,' Simon said.

'Listen to me, Sara, is this a witch hunt or what?' asked Walter.

He looked so put upon that Cathy could see that Sara was falling for it.

'Of course we don't want to examine your room, but we do want to know what contribution you can make to your brother and sister's return.'

Walter paused to give a slow, triumphant smile in Cathy's direction. There would be no inspection.

There were many more points also answered very vaguely by the children's parents and with enthusiasm by their elder brother. Time now to take Maud and Simon back to St Jarlath's Crescent. There were no hugs; Kay kissed them both on the cheek and looked at them vaguely and proudly. Sara and Walter were outside comparing bicycles.

'Why don't I give you a lift to the office, Sara? I've got the van, and your bike can go in the back,' Cathy said suddenly. 'We can go by St Jarlath's Crescent and see Hooves. Come on, Simon and Maud would love to show you their wedding outfits.'

'That's a great idea, Cathy,' Simon approved as they climbed into the van. 'This way she'll see the really important things.'

James Byrne's second cookery lesson was on Thursday.

'What will we do with James?' Tom asked. 'Parma ham and figs to start, fillet steaks in mushroom and cream sauce?'

'He'll say the starter's too easy, and he'd fuss with the steak.'

'No, he wouldn't, he's much less of a fusser than he used to be.'

'I wonder did he ever have children?' Cathy said. 'It's a funny thing, but I get the impression that he's doing this dinner not for someone he fancies, more for some young person that he wants to prove something to . . .'

'I don't know where you get that notion. Perhaps you should bring a crystal ball to the next party we do.' Tom often thought women were complicated, but this was ridiculous. 'What will we give him as a pudding?'

'Brown-bread ice cream?' she suggested.

'OK, now all we have to do is sell it to him.'

Cathy reached for the telephone.

'But steak? It's too . . . too . . .' James Byrne objected, but Cathy and Tom held fast.

'It's a huge treat, and you can have small steaks. Wait till we show you the sauce.'

'She'll think I bought the ice cream in a delicatessen,' he said.

At least they defined it *was* a she. That was some advance.

'Not when you can tell her how you made it, and honestly, it's great fun,' Cathy begged. She had a lot on her mind; she was sick at heart about

Simon and Maud. She had no idea what they were going to do as a great feast for her sister Marian's wedding in just over two months' time. She was not going to listen to one more word of James Byrne's fears.

'James,' she said in a voice like the crack of a whip. 'Do we question a balance sheet? No. We say James is the particular expert that we are paying for this advice. We are the particular experts that *you* have paid for our advice. See you on Thursday, James.'

She hung up with a loud noise. Tom was looking at her open-mouthed. 'Well?' she asked belligerently.

'Well indeed,' he said.

She laughed. He was such easy company.

'Tom, I need your advice. How am I going to entertain Hannah? I'm trying to build a hedge of olive branches, but I'm no good at it.'

'Do you want her to enjoy it, or do you want to show off?'

'Good question, but actually I'd quite like her to have a good time.'

'OK, why don't you ask her here?'

'Here, to the premises?'

'Sure, ask her for lunch next Monday. I'll serve you, then put the phone on answer and leave. Remember the last time she was here?'

'Oh dear, yes, the opening. I sort of forgot the words we had then.'

'Bet she hasn't, though. Really, Cathy, this would be real olive-branch territory. Go on, ring her now.'

Tom went to pick Marcella up from work.

'Your brother was in today,' she said.

'He's never back twice in a few weeks. What's it all about?'

'He said he's setting up this show . . . Feather Fashions . . . He wants trade to come to it as well as the public. He's full of ideas, he's here to see Shona . . . Tom, you won't believe this, he's putting in a serious word that I should do some modelling during the show.' Her eyes were dancing.

'Just let me tell you that I hope and pray he gets you this job, with all my heart,' Tom said.

'I'm sorry I wasn't able to get up to The Beeches, the case went on for ever,' Neil apologised.

'That's OK, I didn't expect you.' Cathy was preparing supper. 'And anyway, you couldn't have done anything to help, they behaved like the family from hell, but still they're getting the children back.'

'Sara's great, isn't she?' He sounded very enthusiastic.

'Yes, she is actually. I thought she was going to be boot-faced, but she doesn't miss much.'

'I was very impressed with her, and she's going to help on this homeless project. It's good to have a social worker on the team . . .'

Neil was excited about it in a way that slightly turned Cathy's heart. She had been going to tell him all about Walter's locked bedroom, about her plans to entertain his mother at the premises. But they all seemed very trivial compared to the project for the homeless. A long time ago Cathy would have gone to committee meetings, taken notes and typed letters; that was before she had a proper career of her own.

This time the tea tray was on the table when they arrived. Kay poured from the heavy teapot with a frail, shaking hand. Kenneth seemed to be more aware of the fact that his children were not automatically being returned to him. He knew that he had to put on some kind of a show.

'Two charming ladies *and* my beloved twins as well . . . Too much happiness,' he said.

The children looked at him, startled.

Sara spoke first. 'Can we run through a few outstanding matters, Mr Mitchell?' she said briskly.

'I made scones,' Kay cried triumphantly.

Cathy looked at the small shop scones which the woman had heated up in her attempt to make this look like a normal home. She felt a lump in her throat. Kay *had* given birth to Simon and Maud nine years ago. They must mean something to her, even in her confused state of mind.

'Apparently your brother has arranged for this house to be mortgaged and has set up a trust,' Sara said.

'Very good of Jock, sorted it all out,' Kenneth nodded. 'He gave me these figures, and it's agreed that this proportion goes towards their clothes, school needs, books, bus fares, and so on.'

'By the way, Walter left you a note about his room . . .' Kenneth offered her a letter without an envelope, 'one that all were meant to see.'

Sara read it out. '"Dear Sara, I have tidied up my bedroom, ready for inspection. Please feel free to go in as you please." No need, of course, but very courteous of him,' Sara murmured.

'No need now,' said Cathy, half under her breath. Whatever Walter had been fearful that they should see had been moved. They did a tour of the house, checked the bedrooms, saw that the linen had been aired, the bathroom properly cared for. Sara was very thorough; she checked that the washing machine worked, examined the dates on items in the freezer and even checked the garden shed.

'Nothing to cut the grass with,' she observed.

'We used to have a big motor mower.' Kenneth was startled. 'It was quite new, actually. Children, do you remember a motor mower?'

'Walter took it to be mended,' Simon said. 'Ages ago, when we were living here.' he said. 'I think it was a secret.'

'Why did you think that?' Cathy was gentle.

'I don't know. I thought he had broken it himself, you see, and he wanted to get it mended before Mother and Father found out,'

'Walter sold the grass-cutting machine. And the kids' things,' Cathy said as she and Sara walked through the garden.

'We've no proof whatsoever of that, Cathy.'

'Let's ask Neil, Sara, when he gets here,' Cathy said.

In her heart she thought, If he gets here. But she was wrong: when they got back to the house he was there.

'Uncle Kenneth, have you been through the house to make sure that nothing went missing while you were away?' he asked crisply.

'But how could it have? I mean, Walter was here.'

'You know how hopeless young people are.'

'I did wonder had we put away the little carriage clock so carefully that we couldn't find it,' poor Kay trilled.

'And I can't seem to see those silver brushes I had.' Kenneth seemed puzzled.

'Maybe we should make a list.' Neil was very firm. 'You see, when we were assessing the value of your estate, we took all the possessions into account. We'll have to assess downwards if some things turn out to be missing. We'll go round the house and see what's not where it should be. Can you help, Maud and Simon? Your sharp young eyes will be terrific.'

'Please can I have a board like Sara's to write on?' Maud asked.

Sara immediately ripped some pages off and handed the clipboard and pad to the child. Neil smiled at her in gratitude, and Cathy then saw the look that Sara gave him in return. It was naked admiration.

'Cathy, it's Geraldine.'

'I was just thinking about phoning you five minutes ago.'

'You weren't thinking about Sunday lunch tomorrow, by any chance?' Geraldine asked.

'No, but you're very welcome. We'd love to see you.'

'I meant here, it's a working lunch . . . I really think it's time someone did something about Marian's August wedding. We should have a council of war. Shona's coming, she's a great help at things like this, and Joe Feather will be here about a fashion show he's setting up, but he might have a few ideas about the party as well.'

'That would be great, Geraldine. See you tomorrow.'

'No, love, I can't go,' Neil said.

'OK.'

'No, Cathy, don't be like that . . .'

'Neil . . . I said OK. I thought we might go to the pictures afterwards. But if you have too much to do then I understand.'

She called Geraldine to tell her there would be one less, but the number was engaged. She'd tell her when she got there.

But when she got to the Glenstar apartment the table was only set for four. Cathy was puzzled.

'Did Neil ring you then. To say he couldn't come?'

'Neil? No, I didn't expect him to come . . .' Geraldine said. 'Of course he was invited, but he never turns up at things, does he?' Geraldine said, going back to the kitchen.

'Ah, he does, Geraldine, he was marvellous out with the twins yesterday. He was just like a dog with a bone, nothing would deter him.'

'And if I wanted a barrister for any cause whatsoever, he'd be first on my list, that's without a doubt.'

'But this wasn't a case, it was family.'

'*His* family, Cathy. He's too busy for other things.'

The buzzer went and Shona had arrived, followed, minutes later, by Joe. Cathy had to drag her mind back to the conversation. Why hadn't she forced Neil to come today? He would have if she had told him that she needed him. Cathy wondered was she getting flu; she had been feeling tired and slightly weepy for a few days now. Suddenly a terrifying thought came to her. There was no wild possibility that she could be pregnant? She grabbed her diary. Her period was three days late. But it often was, Cathy told herself firmly, and forced herself to listen.

Joe Feather was very focused at the lunch. He wanted to be sure why Hayward's thought it a good idea to go downmarket when they had designer rooms and a very wealthy clientele. He listened intelligently while Shona explained that Hayward's was busy encouraging the younger shopper, women in their twenties who would buy three or four outfits for summer or a whole holiday wardrobe rather than those who paid a fortune for two items. Geraldine reeled through plans for a press party before the fashion show, advance photographs taken by Ricky and sent to papers and magazines, models, make-up, hairdressing.

'Let me work out a proposal and email it first so that we all know what it is we *are* talking about,' Geraldine said, 'by eleven tomorrow. Is that all right, Joe?'

'Super-efficient.' He raised his glass to her.

They were unexpectedly helpful, it turned out, on the subject of the Dublin wedding. Cathy's hand raced across her notebook writing things down. The church hall they had hired could be used as two areas, one for the reception and drinks and the other for the food, then the first one would be cleared for dancing. It would hold a hundred people comfortably. They could decorate it as they liked—Marian had suggested she would like an Irish-American theme, and maybe flags. Joe said that he thought it was over the top to drape the hall with US and Irish flags. Shona said it wasn't over the top at all, it was exactly what they would like. The Americans were travelling many thousands of miles for a ceremony; it must be marked. Cathy thought that Marian would prefer it to be as traditionally Irish as possible; people often thought like that when they had left home.

'But does she *know* what she wants? She thinks Ireland is coming down with Irish dancers leaping up into the air and she's probably told all the Americans that the place is like Maureen O'Hara's in *The Quiet Man*.'

'Well, give it to her,' Joe said, as if it were obvious.

'The customer's always right,' said Shona.

'The atmosphere is more important than the food,' Geraldine said.

Geraldine was brisk. She summed up all the arguments for and against every suggestion they made. No wonder she had got on so well in business, she had a very clear mind. Cathy finally had a proper plan in front of her.

Shortly afterwards, Shona and Joe left to go back to work. Cathy watched them from the window. Geraldine poured two glasses of wine, then sat on the sofa, her legs tucked underneath her.

'Sit down, please, Cathy.' The voice was firm.

'Sure.'

'What is it, Cathy? Tell me, please.'

'What do you mean?' she blustered.

'I've known you since the day you were born, so you won't go on pretending that's everything's all right. Either I have offended you by something I did, or else you're in some bad trouble.'

'All right,' Cathy said eventually. 'It's neither and both in a way. I was upset when you told me you took presents from men.'

Geraldine looked at her. 'You think less of me? Me, your friend, because I accepted gifts?'

'Yes, I do, it's so tacky. You haven't loved any of these men, they're just . . . a meal ticket, but you don't need a meal ticket, you have your own business.'

'I loved Teddy,' Geraldine said.

'Teddy?'

'It was twenty-two years ago. Teddy said he would leave his wife for me, and I believed he would, particularly when I was pregnant.' Cathy stared at her. 'But it turned out not to be the case.' The voice was very flat. 'And we agreed that the timing was all spectacularly bad, I can't remember what, one of his children going to school or leaving school or hating school or loving school. Some bloody thing.' Cathy took a sharp breath. 'But it meant that there could be no baby.' A long pause. 'I *could* have kept the baby. But then I knew I'd lose Teddy. A friend of his was a doctor, not a great doctor, as it happened, and I had left it too late so that complicated it. So after that, no more babies, ever.'

'Geraldine.' Cathy was stricken. This was horrifying.

'So after that, as you can understand, I was a bit low, but I thought I'd have Teddy to comfort me, but as it happened I didn't. He took his family and went abroad. So, Cathy, I didn't allow myself to wallow too much in the luxury of love after that. The men I've known since like my company and conversation just as much as my bed. I have not been dependent on *any* of them for *any* thing. They can't offer me commitment or a home, so they give me presents. I'm sorry if it *upsets* you and you think *less* of me, but it doesn't offend me, and it's my life.'

'I'm so ashamed I could die,' Cathy said.

Geraldine sighed. 'Leave it, Cathy. You had guts to say it, I give you that much. What was the other thing that was upsetting you?'

Cathy spoke slowly. 'I don't suppose there could be any more inappropriate thing to tell you, but I think I might be pregnant, and it's the last thing on earth I want now.'

June

'WHAT TIME is she coming?' Tom asked.

'Who?'

'Well, excuse *me*, but I thought all this shining and polishing was to impress your mother-in-law,' Tom said.

'Oh, sorry, Tom, I was miles away. About half past twelve.'

'Let's get the skates on then, and go and make some soup.'

Cathy leaped up guiltily. Tom had been here since five o'clock in the morning, having the bread delivered to Hayward's, stopped at the fish shop on the way back, got all the vegetables and a huge lamb bone for a big soup order, and she had done nothing. After the hours of crying in Geraldine's flat she had felt drained. Of course she hadn't told Neil, he had been distracted. She must get a Predictor first, from the chemist, it might be a false alarm.

'Tom, I'm so sorry. I'll start chopping the basil and tomatoes.'

'I don't think you should have a knife in your hand this morning,' Tom said. 'You'll be in ribbons by the time she comes. Leave the dangerous stuff to me.'

'Great. So what do I do?'

'Set the table, get some flowers. And start practising your smile.'

'You're a very sweet girl, you know, Geraldine,' Freddie said as they had coffee together in her office. They were talking about his party, for which Geraldine's niece and her partner were going to do the catering. 'You're as anxious as I am that the party Pauline and I are having will be a success.'

'But why ever not, Freddie? I don't want anything from you except what I have; your company, your interest. You know what the French say about a mistress: she must be discreet, and never, ever do anything that would upset the man's family, his children and his property . . .' She laughed engagingly at him.

'You ask so little, Geraldine.' Freddie Flynn had not come across such women before.

'But that's not true, and truly I have so much.' She waved her hand around the office, the business that was hers alone.

James Byrne had decided to cook a dinner that night. Not the real one, but just to see whether he could or not. And as it happened, Martin Maguire was going to be in Dublin. Martin Maguire would be very surprised indeed to be presented with such a gourmet meal. And it would be great practice for James. He had enjoyed his two evenings with Tom and Cathy enormously, and wished he could think of an excuse for more. But he must remember that this had been his undoing before. Becoming too fond of people, too dependent.

'Come in, Mrs Mitchell.' Tom's smile rarely failed to hit its target. 'How well you're looking, if I may say so.'

She patted her hair. It was so wise to go to a good salon regularly. Cathy was so foolish in this regard, as in so many things.

'You're are a kind boy,' she said.

Cathy stood waiting, her face as white as a sheet, her hair tied back with an elastic band.

'You're welcome, Hannah,' she said in a flat voice.

'My goodness, doesn't the place look nice!'

Tom hoped that Cathy would respond warmly to her, otherwise all this would be in vain. To his relief, Cathy was smiling.

'This is our front room, where we sit clients down and persuade them to have much bigger parties than they intended,' she said.

'Very nicely done,' Hannah looked around her with grudging admiration. 'Nice colours, too.'

'My mother made the curtains and covers,' Cathy said proudly.

Hannah looked at them in disbelief. 'Oh, Lizzie was always . . . marvellous with her hands,' she said eventually.

Tom sighed with relief, poured them a sherry and went to the kitchen.

'Tom, will you stop analysing that sandwich,' Joe said.

'Look at what they charge for that, Joe. A tired tomato, a piece of plastic cheese.'

'Oh, shut up and eat something else,' Joe said good-naturedly. 'What am I going to do about Mam? She wants to come to the fashion show.'

'Well, let her, can't you?'

'Of course I can't.'

'I'll keep an eye on her.'

'No, not that, the clothes. Ma can't see them.'

'But why not?'

'It's swimwear, lingerie, half-naked girls all over the place . . . Mam would only drop stone dead.'

'It's not *all* that, is it?' Tom asked with a hollow feeling in his stomach.

'Most of it.' Joe looked at his brother's face. 'Marcella told you, didn't she?' he said.

'That was delicious, that tomato soup, and my heavens, that's good, that bread . . . you hardly ate any,' Hannah said.

'Hannah, I'm eating it all day, and all night . . .'

'And what do we have now?'

Was there a time when she had dreaded this woman? How long ago it all seemed. 'It's monkfish, I think you'll like it.'

'I brought you this.' Hannah spoke gruffly, and thrust across the table a gift-wrapped Hayward's parcel.

Cathy knew she must open it, however ill-timed; the monkfish with its saffron sauce, the green beans with tiny lardons of bacon and toasted almonds, the potatoes and ginger were all wafting up their vapours at them. It was time to savour the food. But she unpicked the elegant wrapping. From the paper came a pungent smell of incense.

'It's wonderful, Hannah, what exactly . . . ?'

'It's one of those aromatic oils for the shower . . .' Hannah began.

It was too much, the heady smell of that and the food. Cathy ran from the table, and knelt vomiting into the lavatory pan. She heard her mother-in-law calling outside the door.

'Cathy, let me in, are you all right?'

Marcella looked up from arranging bottles of nail colour and saw Joe Feather in the salon.

'I sort of let slip to Tom that the lines you'll be modelling are fairly sexy . . . And to be honest, I don't think he knew that.'

She looked at him, surprised.

'Now I'm getting out of it and letting you take it from here, Marcella.'

'Sure.' She was very calm.

'It's just that he adores you . . . you see.'

'Thank you, Joe,' she said in a voice that made him feel small.

'I'm so sorry, Hannah, I've had an upset tummy.'

'But you should have said, you should have cancelled the lunch . . .'

'No, please, Hannah, look, I'm fine now.' Cathy forked herself a help-ing of the monkfish, which tasted like soap in her mouth, and forced herself to swallow it. Eventually she felt her stomach return to normal. They talked about how the twins were adapting to their return to The Beeches and how genuinely good Lizzie had been. Good and generous, all the right words. Hannah remarked that Cathy hadn't found time yet to go to the Hayward's salon, and Cathy looked her in the eye, promis-ing that she would go soon. They talked about Neil and how hard he worked. Soon Hannah made a move to leave.

'Won't you have more coffee?'

'No, indeed, it was all quite perfect. I really enjoyed this lunch, and you look much better now, dear.'

Cathy watched as Hannah left. In all those years of fighting this woman, she never could have envisaged a day like today.

'Please come in, Muttie,' Maud begged.

'No, child, honestly. I thought you'd need to be settled onto that bus, for the first day anyway, Hooves and I will get another bus back.'

'But we want to show you our house. *Please*, Muttie.'

'Another time, son, not the first day.'

He was firm. It wasn't sensible. He didn't want it to look as if he and Lizzie were trying to muscle in.

'But you will come in *sometime*, will you, Muttie?' Simon begged.

'Of course I will, son, when you're more settled.'

'And we're definitely coming to St Jarlath's Crescent at the weekend, that's agreed with Sara,' Maud said anxiously.

'Of course you are, child, and Lizzie and I are looking forward to it greatly, so we are. So in you go now, like a good girl.'

'I had lunch with Hannah,' Cathy said to Neil that evening.

'Well done.' He poured two glasses of chardonnay.

'She was fine. Listen, are you going to sit down with that wine, or are you going to take it to work with you?'

'I'm taking it to work with me, by which I mean next door. I have a hell of a lot to finish on this homeless thing . . . I met Sara today with the twins, by the way, and she's a lot of help . . .'

'Oh, how did it all go? Sit down for a minute and tell me.'

Neil sat down. 'She explained that there *is* funding, but that no one can really get at it.'

'Funding?' Cathy was bewildered.

He explained at length about a European Union grant that might be available for the homeless. Eventually, after a lot of details of strategy, there was a moment when she could get in a word about Maud and Simon.

'Oh, they were fine,' he said, getting up to leave the table.

'No, sit down and tell me, did they have a meal for them?'

'Yes, they had sandwiches.'

'Is that all?'

'The twins were so funny, they kept asking about their real tea. Sara took over, it's under control.'

And that was all she was going to hear. And it seemed it was not the night to tell him about anything else.

Tom was looking for the right way to mention the fashion show to Marcella. A way that would not reveal the sick feeling at the base of his stomach that she was going to be walking around half naked in front of strangers. He knew that this kind of suspicion and possessiveness was what had made her walk out before; he *must* keep it under control. To his surprise, she brought the subject up herself.

'You won't believe the colours for the show, lime greens and fuchsias—

nobody could want to wear that kind of underwear.'

Tom let his breath out slowly. At least she was telling him that it was lingerie. 'No, give me basic black lacy stuff any day,' he smiled.

'Just so that you realise it's all a bit of fun,' she.said.

'Of course.' His heart was heavy. She was preparing him. 'And the swimwear, what colour is that?'

'The same, mad, wild colours, almost luminous. Joe either hasn't a clue what he's doing, or else he's got it just right. There's a very fine line between the two.'

He stared at her. She really was obsessed by the whole fashion business. It didn't have anything at all to do with stripping off in public.

'**D**arling, you'll never believe who was just on the phone!' Kenneth Mitchell said to his wife. 'Old Barty ringing up out of the blue.'

'Barty? Our best man?' she cried, pleased.

'Yes, I told him he could stay. He says he'll take us all for a spin in the car on Saturday. You kids too.' He looked at them, proud of the treat.

'But on Saturday we go to St Jarlath's Crescent,' Maud said.

'No, darling, you can go another day. Those people won't mind,' their mother said.

'We can't go another day, they're making a proper tea and everything, we asked for sausages.'

Maud was almost tearful.

'Well telephone them and say it's off, that's a good girl.' Her father was brisk.

Simon and Maud looked at each other. 'Let's ring Cathy,' they both said at the same time.

'**N**eil, this is *not* going to happen,' Cathy fumed at him after Simon and Maud's phone call.

'Hey, I'm on *your* side, of course it's not going to happen. I'll ring Sara,' he said.

'But she's not at work now, surely?'

'I have her mobile number,' Neil said.

'**T**he dancing teacher's coming round tonight,' Lizzie told the twins.

'Oh good, will we wear our costumes?' Simon wanted to know.

'No, I don't want them getting all messed up. I've made up cheap kilts and cloaks for you so you can get the swish of it all . . .' Lizzie's face was glowing with pride. 'Suppose you were to take a tape home with you and practise in your kitchen back there?'

'Yes . . . yes, we could.' Simon looked doubtful. 'You see, Father doesn't understand it being a family wedding. I said it was for our cousins coming from Chicago, and he didn't understand that either.'

Muttie hastened to reassure him. 'Oh, isn't Cathy the sister of the bride, and she's married to Neil, your first cousin. What on earth could be closer than that?' Muttie asked. This satisfied the twins totally, and they ran off to teach Hooves a new trick before the dancing teacher came.

Muttie and Lizzie looked at each other.

'We should never have let them leave,' Muttie said.

This time the twins persuaded Muttie to come in and say hello. Walter had come home and old Barty was now in residence. Kay Mitchell was already in bed, and the three men at the table looked up, mildly and politely interested.

'You've had supper at . . . um?' Kenneth said.

And as Maud and Simon began to tell about all the extra things they had with their sausages, Kenneth Mitchell's interest flagged.

'You're so kind to look after them so well,' he said to Muttie, and shook his hand firmly. Muttie opened his hand. A pound coin was there. Muttie's face flushed a dark red.

'Thank you very much indeed, sir,' he said with great difficulty.

Simon and Maud looked on, stricken. 'See you next Saturday, Muttie,' Simon said. 'Thank you for a lovely time.'

Muttie was backing out.

'Do you want to see our rooms, Muttie?' Maud asked.

'Another time, Maud, thanks all the same.' And he was gone.

The twins had thought they might do the reel tonight at home. But they noticed a bottle of whiskey had come onto the table, and their father and brother and old Barty wanted to discuss something other than dancing. Everyone was waiting for the children to go to bed, on a bright summer evening when they had been hoping to be up for ages more. With brief goodnights the twins marched grimly upstairs.

Cathy said they couldn't possibly take on a sales conference lunch for thirty on the very same day as Freddie Flynn's party.

'It will be dead easy,' Tom pleaded. 'They're slave-drivers these people. No lingering and enjoying themselves for the employees. They'll be back working in that hall at two fifteen and we'll be out in half an hour after that. Do we want to get this business up and running?'

'We do, but not by beating ourselves down onto our knees. We're pushing ourselves,' Cathy said.

'Stretching ourselves,' Tom corrected.

'It's easy money, it's a good contact,' said Tom. In his heart he was thinking that if he cleared a few pounds profit on this he'd take Marcella to one of those fancy hotels for a weekend.

'We've always said people go under if they take on too much. Their standards fall,' Cathy said. She was thinking that truthfully she could barely manage as things were, the nausea was still there, and she still hadn't found or made the time to tell Neil. The Predictor from the chemist had said yes, but people knew it was often wrong. She had an appointment with the doctor next week. Supposing it were true.

'Let's go to arbitration,' Tom said.

They took out a coin. Solemnly they watched as the coin spun round and waited until it fell. Tom picked it up.

'So I won, but I promise you'll be glad.'

'Can we come to England with you?' Simon stood at Walter's door, as Walter packed for a few days at the races.

'Of course you can't,' Walter said impatiently. 'Kids, I'm sorry, I have to get on.'

'Are you going today?' Maud asked, disappointed. It was marginally more lively here when Walter was around.

'Tonight or tomorrow. I have some work to do with Father.'

'So if Father's out and Mother's going to stay in bed . . . what will *we* do?' Simon and Maud looked at each other blankly. There had been so many things to do in St Jarlath's Crescent.

'You could get a job,' Walter suggested.

'I don't think we're old enough,' Maud said.

'No, doing kids' jobs: stacking shelves, collecting trolleys in a super-market . . . those kind of things . . .' said Walter vaguely, having never attempted them.

'We might be able to wash up for Cathy and Tom,' Simon said.

'It's worth a try,' said Maud.

When Cathy saw the two faces arrive at the premises, she racked her brains to think of something that the twins could do to help, where they couldn't do too much harm.

'Chopping anything . . . ?' Con suggested.

'They're worse than I am, the place would be running with blood. I know, they can shine up the silver and count the forks.'

Maud and Simon were installed in the storeroom. They chattered on happily; sometimes Cathy leaned against the door and listened. There were bits about Father's business with Barty, and whether Muttie would ever come to visit them at their home again after what Father had done. Cathy sighed. She had resented them so much a few short months ago. But now everything had changed. Again and again she went over when exactly it must have happened. Neil would be furious. Once it would have been unthinkable to keep something this important from him. It was still unthinkable. She would tell him tonight.

Tom and June came back from the sales luncheon in high spirits. Fifty people, all of them as obedient as mice, start eating, continue eating, finish eating. If only the whole world was run like this.

'Ah, but it was so easy, Cathy, you've no idea. They'd have eaten a paper plate smeared with jam, believe me.'

'They must have been *very* hungry,' Maud said, shocked.

'Well, *hello*, we have help.' Tom was surprised and pleased.

'We've been polishing your good silver,' Simon said proudly.

'Well, that's great, because everything we own, all our treasures, are tied up in these four walls.'

'Is it all very valuable?' Maud asked.

'Some of it is irreplaceable, like that punchbowl,' Cathy said. 'I won that at a competition at college, we use it everywhere now.'

'And what's the next most valuable thing?' Simon wondered.

Tom, Cathy and June joked about whether it was the book of contacts, the double oven, or the chest freezer . . .

'We never thought we'd own such a huge amount,' Cathy said.

'Like Muttie thinks he'll never win an accumulator,' Simon said, eager to show he was on her wavelength.

'But he never will, Simon,' Cathy implored. 'We worked for it, night after long night . . .'

'Muttie works at the bookmaker's, he learns about form and he lets the sound of hooves get in on his brain.'

'Of course he does,' Tom said gently.

'Are you insured, in case anyone came in and took all your treasures?' Maud worried.

'Very well insured. James Byrne made us take out a very big insurance policy,' Cathy reassured her.

But Simon had one more worry. 'Do you lock up properly when you leave?' he wanted to know.

'Yes, Simon, two locks, an alarm with a code and all.'

'And do you remember the code? Do you have your birthday?' Simon asked. 'Or your lucky number?'

'No, they told us not to,' Tom said. 'We have the two initials of Scarlet

Feather. S is nineteen and F is six. If we forget, all we have to do is go through the alphabet.'

They agreed to drive the children back to The Beeches, since it was on the way to Freddie Flynn's house. Solemnly Simon and Maud watched as the alarm code was set and Tom completed a checklist.

'OK, ceremony of the keys.'

Simon and Maud watched fascinated as they hung the keys to the premises carefully on a hidden hook at the back of the van.

'Whichever of us takes the van back needs to be able to open the place up, so we always have the ceremony of the keys . . .' Cathy explained.

They watched as the two children ran into the big house.

'They have to be with their own parents, don't they?' Tom asked.

'To be honest, I've never exactly seen why,' Cathy said.

Freddie Flynn was most welcoming when they got there. 'Now I know you hate people saying to you this is the hot tap, this is the cold tap . . .'

'You wouldn't ever do that, Mr Flynn,' Cathy smiled up at him from under her eyelashes.

Tom let out a low whistle when he'd gone. 'And you say that I put on the charm for the ladies . . . I never saw anything like that performance,' he teased her.

'I promised Auntie Geraldine he'd get the full treatment.'

At that moment Freddie's small, plump wife Pauline came in. 'Freddie says I'm not to fuss, and I promise I won't, but somehow it seems like cheating to let you do it all,' she said.

Cathy felt a lump in her throat. This woman was being deceived by Frederick Flynn, important Dublin businessman, purchaser of a diamond watch for Cathy's aunt. 'Not a bit of it, Mrs Flynn. Now, your husband tells me you don't want anyone to take the coats?'

'Yes, you see, we got the upstairs all decorated, and I sort of hoped they might go up and see it so that I could show it off.'

'Let me see where I'm to direct them.' Cathy ran lightly up the stairs and saw the magnificent bedroom. It was in beautiful shades of pale green and blue, and there was an elegant white dressing table. It wasn't exactly a four-poster bed, but there was a ring with cascading curtains over the top; lace-trimmed pillowcases. This place had all the appearance of an altar built to the god of pleasure.

'Lovely room,' Cathy said in a slightly strangled voice.

'I'm glad you like it. I'm old and silly, I know, but it's what I always wanted and Freddie seems to think it's nice too, and that's what pleases me most of all.'

'Hello, Walter.'

'Hello,' Walter grunted.

There was a silence. 'We got a job like you said,' Simon said eventually.

'Good for you. Where?'

'With Cathy and Tom . . . They have a fortune in their premises, it's full of their treasures.' Simon wanted to impress his older brother. 'They have two keys and a code lock in case anyone gets in.'

'Oh yeah, I bet the whole world is trying to get in there and steal catering plates and paper napkins.' Walter laughed.

'They have a solid-silver punchbowl, it's beyond price. They have loads of things,' Maud said.

'I'm sure it's very impressive, but do you mind moving off for a bit, I've a lot to think about now.'

'OK.' Simon and Maud were good-tempered.

'Cathy gave us something for the microwave,' said Maud. 'Do you want some? There's plenty for the three of us.'

'Thanks.' Walter was gruff.

They sat at the table. The twins talked happily on.

'Do you think we should get a burglar alarm here, Walter?'

'Nothing for a burglar to break in here for,' he said glumly.

'We could set it before we went out and disarm it when we got back.' Maud didn't want to let the notion go entirely.

'Yeah, can you see Mother and Father doing that?'

'But it's so simple,' Simon said. 'We know how to get into Cathy and Tom's premises just after seeing it once.'

'Sure, but do you have the keys?' Walter took his plate across the kitchen to the sink.

'No, but we know where they are,' Maud said.

Walter came back and sat down with them again.

Walter had looked up the Flynns' address in the phone book. It wasn't far away. He parked his borrowed car beside the van and found the keys exactly where the twins had said.

Wearing black cotton gloves, he let himself in and used the code to disarm the alarm. Where were all these treasures? He must be quick; he needed to get the stuff hidden in his garden shed and the key back into the van. He pulled out possible items like a toaster and a microwave oven. But these wouldn't bring him a fraction of the money he needed.

On the table in the front room, he saw the punchbowl the children had spoken of; it wasn't solid silver at all. There were boxes of supplies, unopened steamers and saucepans in the storeroom; they might make *something* if he could just unload them on the right person. He began to drag the items towards the front of the premises, and knocked over a tray of glasses as he did so. The splinters of glass were everywhere. They wouldn't like that. Something welled up in him, and he swooped an entire shelf of plates onto the floor. It was somehow satisfying. So, with his elbow, he raised the end of one of the china shelves so that all its contents went in a great crashing slide to the floor. He pulled out the plug of the freezer. He wrenched the answering machine from the wall and stood on it. He packed the car, taking the punchbowl at the last moment. They were so bloody smug, those two. This would show them.

THEY HAD OFTEN HEARD that people who were robbed felt violated. This was what it was like. Cathy saw that her punchbowl was gone from the table. Tom saw all their plates knocked from the shelves. June saw the drawers opened and their contents spilled. They couldn't take it all in. Tom was the first to speak.

'Bastards,' he said. 'Total bastards.'

The guards were mystified. No sign of a break-in, nobody else had access to keys. They had no idea of anyone who harboured malicious feeling towards them. Had they? They couldn't think of anyone at all. One of the young guards who had already asked twice about insurance mentioned it yet once more to Tom.

'Yes, I told you,' Tom said a trifle impatiently. 'But that's not going to sort this out.'

Neil had been asleep when Cathy had called. Now he arrived wearing a sweater and a pair of faded cotton trousers, but as full of authority as if he were wearing his full formal barrister's outfit. The questions were endless and the leads seemed to be non-existent. Back and back the guards went to the keys and the access.

Finally one of them said, 'So all I can say is for you to take things up as best you can with the insurance company.'

'What do you mean, exactly? What has this got to do with finding whoever did all this?' Tom waved his hand around despairingly.

Neil spoke suddenly. 'The Garda is pointing out, Tom, that because there were no signs of a break-in the insurance company is going to have to look into the possibility of it being an inside job.'

There was silence in the room. Nobody thought that things could get any worse than they were, but they had now.

It seemed that all night they were cooking Tom's bread for Hayward's, partly in the small oven in Stoneyfield, while Marcella timed things and lifted out batches, and partly with the better facilities in Waterview, with Neil and June helping.

The night ended, the bread was delivered, and as the rest of Dublin was beginning to wake up and go to work, Neil showered, changed, put on his barrister's gear and went down to the Four Courts, they sent June home in a taxi, and Marcella showered, changed and went to Hayward's.

Tom and Cathy went back the premises. Gradually they picked through the rubble and looked at each other, red-eyed.

'They surely can't think it was an inside job?' she asked.

'Apparently they could think we did it to get the compensation. It's been done before, when companies were going down the tubes.'

'But we're *not* going down the tubes. James could tell them that for one thing,' Cathy said.

James! They had forgotten about him. Was it too early to ring him? They risked that he would be up just before eight o'clock.

'James Byrne.' He was crisp and matter-of-fact when he heard the news. He asked questions, one after the other. Any likely leads? No, no. The plant, cookers and freezers, would Scarlet Feather be able to continue trading? Hard to say. Quite, quite. The insurance. Yes, he assured them, it would cover losses. Then they told him that there had been no break-in, no forced entry.

'I see,' said James.

'You mean they mightn't?' Tom was hardly able to say the words.

'Let's say it may just take longer for them to pay up,' said James.

Shona Burke got them permission to use Hayward's kitchens from now on to do the breads; in fact it worked so well they said it could be permanent. Tom worked there until the store opened. Cathy worked from Waterview.

'I thought a town house was small, but it seems to have become a bedsitter,' grumbled Neil, who had to step over crates and boxes everywhere he moved.

Cathy had forgotten how impossible it was to prepare food in such a small space. There was simply nowhere to leave anything. There wasn't nearly enough room in the freezer or the fridge. Each day was more like a nightmare than the one that went before.

June and Cathy worked as they had never worked before. They did a picnic for Freddie and Pauline Flynn; they did two First Communion buffet-lunch parties on the same day, shuttling from one to the other with Con. They left Tom to deal with putting the pieces back together at the premises. Men from JT Feather's builder's yard came in, but only after James Byrne had insisted on a representative of the insurance company coming to view the destruction. It was going to cost over £2,000 to get the cooking underway again. The frozen food had been given away or destroyed; long weeks of work thrown out at just a stroke.

Among the very first people that they should have told were Geraldine and Joe, their backers. But neither Tom nor Cathy wanted to tell them until it was under control. They had the sickening feeling that they were going to go under. Cathy didn't want Geraldine to hand over more money. Cathy's pride had always meant that it was a debt of honour to repay Geraldine's investment with interest.

Joe was the last person Tom wanted to talk to just now. Joe, who had given Marcella this chance to strut nearly naked in front of half of Dublin. Joe, who had filled Marcella's head up with the chance of meeting some model's agent who would put her on his books and get her jobs 'across the water', as he called it. Joe, who somehow felt guilty about this fashion show, would find funds for Tom as a way of buying himself out of any unpleasantness.

So if they didn't want Geraldine and Joe to know, that meant they couldn't tell a lot of other people either. Shona was sworn to secrecy, and June was asked to keep quiet as well. Neil would fight for them against nameless bureaucrats who always kept the little people waiting for their money. He was being supportive, but Cathy wished that he had been a different kind of help. That he would take her head on his shoulder and stroke her hair. Tell her that he loved her and that they would get through this. And then she could tell him about the baby.

'Cathy, could we come round to the premises to work today, to polish the treasures and things?' Maud asked.

'No, Maud, sorry, today's not a good day.'

'We wouldn't want money or pasta or anything,' Maud begged.

'Sweetheart, we'll do it another time, OK?' She hung up.

'She hung up on me,' Maud said, alarmed. 'What did we do?'

'Maybe we should have written to thank her for the pasta,' Simon said. 'It's very hard to know.'

There was a rehearsal for the Feather Fashion show. Joe made it his business to talk to Marcella.

'Tom OK about everything? All this, you know . . .' He waved his hands at the half-dressed girls around him.

'Fine,' Marcella said.

'It's just that I haven't seen him recently, and I hope he's not pissed off with me for being part of all this.'

'No, no. He's just very busy that's all. I hardly see him myself.'

'Hi Cathy, it's Geraldine.'

'Oh, yes, Geraldine. Oh.' Cathy sounded distracted.

'Sorry, is this a bad time?'

The place was full of people and tension. James Byrne, Neil and the insurance man were all walking around the premises.

'Not great. Why don't I call you?'

'OK. Just tell me, how did it go telling Neil the news?'

'Please, can I ring you back?' Cathy's voice was near breaking.

'Certainly,' Geraldine said, puzzled.

'It will be months before they pay,' Neil said when the insurance man had left.

'How much do we need, James?' Tom's face was hard.

'To get back to where you were when this happened, you need just under twenty thousand,' James said.

'How much is that a week?' Cathy asked.

James told them what the bank repayments would cost.

'We wouldn't make half of that in a week, *and* we have all the other repayments on this place.' Tom's face was hard and sad.

'Before we make or reject any big decisions,' James said, 'will you give me twenty-four hours to prepare some figures? Then you really can see what your options are.' He seemed to know the hurt was too raw and the sense of failure too great for either Tom or Cathy to think rationally.

'I'm sorry, hon,' Neil said in the car as they drove home.

'Neil, are you going to be at home tonight?'

'You know I'm not, hon. You know I have to go to the homeless group. It will be the last before I go to the conference.'

The conference! How *could* she have forgotten that Neil and four

MAEVE BINCHY

lawyers were representing Ireland at an international forum on refugees,
in Africa? He was leaving tomorrow evening.
'I need to talk to you. What time will it be over?'
'How do I know, hon . . . When it's over.'
'Don't go to some awful café talking and yammering all night, *please*.'
He was annoyed now. 'Cathy, I've spent all day down in your office
sorting out the mess there. And don't dismiss my work as going to some
awful café yammering all night. I've never said anything like that about
your work.'
'Neil!' she was aghast.
'I don't want to fight with you, Cathy.'
'I don't want to fight with you either.' She spoke in a small voice.
'I'll try to get away as early as I can. Promise.' He smiled at her. 'And
listen, when I come back from Africa we'll go down to Holly's, that nice
hotel in Wicklow, and we'll have dinner and stay the night.'
'Sure.' She forced a smile back. That's when she would tell him.

The broken glass, china and woodwork had been cleared away. Well,
more or less.
They were always finding some frightening reminder, like the broken
glass at the back of the cutlery drawer. Like realising that the big platter
they had thought was in good shape was cracked all over and disinte-
grated, taking with it an entire dressed salmon. It was all over the floor,
nothing could be rescued. They were left with no main dish for a lunch
party. Wearily, Cathy rang the fishmonger's. Could they do one for her in
two hours?
'It'll cost you, Cathy,' said the man apologetically.
'It would cost us more if we didn't deliver,' she replied. She saw Tom
looking at her. They spent so much time keeping the show on the road,
they had hardly any time to talk to each other honestly.
'Will we survive, Tom? Will we?' she asked sadly.
'I know. There are times I think we won't, too,' he said.

Geraldine let herself into the courtyard of the premises, through the
gate she had oiled herself last January when they were frantically clearing everything up. There was nothing Cathy wouldn't have told her or
discussed with her back then. How had it all changed? She looked
through the window, where normally you saw the little square table
with its silver punchbowl and flowers. There was nothing on the table,
only a lot of broken implements laid out in a line. She could see through
the kitchen door that there seemed to be huge renovations going on

inside. What could have happened to this place since she had been here last? Tentatively she rang the bell.

'Oh, Geraldine,' an exhausted-looking Cathy said without enthusiasm, and with no attempt to invite her in. 'It's not a good time.'

'It never is these days. You always say you'll call me and never do.'

Gently but firmly Geraldine pushed her way in.

'Oh, my God,' Geraldine cried. 'Oh, my God, you poor child, you poor, poor child, who could have done this to you?'

'Come in tomorrow and see a rehearsal, Tom,' Marcella begged.

'No, I don't want to be in the way,' he said.

'You wouldn't, lots of the other girls have their friends in to watch, you'll actually be *in* Hayward's anyway with the bread. All you have to do is come up to the fourth floor. I'd love you to be there.'

She was very anxious that he be a part of it. He was going to have to see it all on Friday next; why not please her? 'You're right, I'd love to get a sneak preview,' he said, and her eyes shone.

A section of the fourth floor had been curtained off for the rehearsal. Tom hung around at the edge. There were a lot of other people milling around equally vaguely. Some of them were involved in setting up lighting. Ricky was there advising photographers. There was no sign as yet of the girls or the garments. He saw Joe in the distance but couldn't catch his eye. They were called to order for a run-through with music.

'We want a lot of hush now,' Joe was saying. 'Right, we're going in ten seconds from now.'

Two men sat down beside Tom. There was a man who owned a model agency who was looking in this week. Marcella had talked of little else. 'Mr Newton himself,' she kept saying. Maybe one of these guys was Mr Newton himself. 'Mr Newton?' he asked.

'Over there, mate,' one of them said, nodding towards a small man. Tom Feather felt pleased to notice that Mr Newton himself looked like a disagreeable little pig. Tom watched as one by one the girls came out in bathing suits. They danced along, hitting a beach ball one to another in time to the music, and there was Marcella bringing up the rear. She wore a white bikini shaped like three shells, one cupping each breast, and one as a tiny G-string. Her flat, tanned stomach and long, tanned legs looked so familiar and yet so alien in this setting. He wanted to do nothing as much as cry. The men beside him seemed to watch her with admiration.

Tom had to say something. 'I know her. She's good, isn't she?'

'Gorgeous,' said one of them.

'Do you think she might make it, big time?' Tom asked, trying to keep his voice neutral.

'No way,' said one. 'She's far too old.'

'She's twenty-five,' Tom said.

'Exactly,' said the man. 'If she were going to make it she should have been out there at sixteen.'

Tom left Marcella a note saying that she was marvellous and he was so proud of her. Then he drove to the canal and sat and watched two swans as they sailed up and down, arching their long, beautiful necks. He didn't realise that he was crying until he went to start the van again, and felt his tears splash on his hand.

Then he drove to the premises. Two envelopes had been delivered by hand. Geraldine had sent a letter to Cathy. She wanted to make another investment in the company, and believed Cathy to be short-sighted by refusing it. However, if that was her intent, she enclosed some details on renting equipment, china and cutlery. Cathy rang her aunt and left a message on the machine. 'Tom and I both think that's a great idea. If we only have to rent it for a few months it will all make sense. Thanks again, Ger. You're great.'

The other was from Joe Feather to Tom. He had heard that they had had a break-in and he wished to offer his condolences and some cash in hand. Tom rang his brother and left a message on the machine. 'Cathy and I thank you from the bottom of our hearts.'

'Did you really think it was good?' Marcella asked when she got home.

'Good, great.'

'It's kind of unbelievable to think that it's all going to happen on this very Friday,' Marcella said.

He looked at her, mute with the fear that those two business associates of Joe might be right, that Marcella was far too old. 'And there's a real possibility that Mr Newton might get you a contract?' he asked her.

'Well, I don't want to be too hopeful, but it looks like it. Apparently it all depends on how you do on the night . . . People can go to pieces in front of an audience.'

'You didn't go to pieces today, and there were lots of people there.' He was begging her to have confidence in herself.

'But there'll be three hundred and more on the night,' Marcella said, hugging herself. 'Still, I think I can do it, all those younger ones there in the group give me great confidence . . .' Marcella hugged herself. 'It's all so wonderful, Tom, really, I can hardly take it all in.'

The letters, faxes and emails were coming in thick and fast from Chicago. Each one was headed simply *Wedding*.

'Nobody ever got married in the world before Marian Scarlet,' Cathy grumbled, looking at the latest message.

'So what are you complaining about? They want fancy, we give them fancy.' Tom was determined to be cheerful.

'No, wait till you hear. They want us to serve corned beef and cabbage. That's what they think is traditional Irish food.'

Tom was aghast. 'We're *not* going to give them corned beef and cabbage.'

'I know.'

'Imagine, we once thought this was going to be an easy number.'

'There's no such thing as an easy number in this game.' Cathy sighed.

'Are you all right?' he asked, concerned at the expression on her face.

'Of course I'm not. We can't go on fooling ourselves. There's no way we can do this wedding.' She was bent double now, her head in her hands, her whole body shaking with tears.

'Cathy, Cathy . . .' He came to kneel down beside her. 'We'll think of something,' he said.

'Why do we have to keep on pretending and saying that everything's all right when it's not.'

'Because that's the only way we stay in business.' He was very gentle and pulled her to him. 'This is not going to go on, it's not, do you hear?'

She cried in his arms as he stroked her hair, and he held her until the sobs died down. She mumbled something he couldn't hear into his sweater.

'What did you say?'

'I said it's over, Tom. We have to face it and tell Marian to get some other leprechaun outfit.'

'There isn't one, we're the only leprechaun outfit in town.' He looked down at her face. There was a half-smile.

'You never thought of quitting?'

'No, not ever.'

'Right then.' She blew her nose loudly. 'Right then, if we're not quitting, then we'll have to redefine Marian's requirements.'

'What, come up with something traditionally Irish that Scarlet Feather can actually live with?' He looked at her. She was better.

Cathy came back from the cash-and-carry and Tom helped her unpack the van.

'Just one message—Simon and Maud want to come and polish your treasures again.'

'They can't come here, they'll tell *everyone*. Everyone would cancel if they knew what we were working out of,' Cathy wailed.

But Tom wouldn't let her get away with it. 'They think you've gone off them, they want to know what they've done.'

'Shit,' said Cathy. 'All right, I'll take them out somewhere.'

'And you're sure we didn't do anything bad?' Maud persisted.

They were having a burger after seeing a movie.

'No, Maud. Remember what I told you about not being the centre of the world.'

'Yes, but we were afraid you thought—'

'I wasn't thinking about you at all; we've been very busy.'

'So how do you know when someone is really cross with you, or if they're just busy and not thinking about you?' Simon wondered.

'It's something that comes with time, Simon.'

The more the children talked about some madman called old Barty and the strange food they ate, and mother being in bed a lot and Father out a lot, she knew it had been a great, great mistake to let those children go. Neil had given the wrong advice there. She knew it. It had nothing to do with flesh and blood. Muttie and Lizzie Scarlet would have made much better parents to these children.

'Marcella, what are you worried about? You look lovely—it's just actor's nerves, I know . . . Mr Newton'll see you perform tomorrow night, he'll *know* you're what he wants.'

'It's a bit different. It's all in their court, they can make or break you. If you play according to their rules, you get to be part of it all. If you don't, you're not allowed to join.' She was twisting her hands uneasily.

'So what's the problem? If you do right tomorrow on that catwalk, as you will, then you *will* be part of it.'

'They say we have to go and party with them tomorrow night back at their hotel,' she said, looking at the floor.'

'But we *can't*. You know I've set up a dinner in the little Italian place, everyone's coming. Geraldine's coming. Ricky and Joe too, I think, Shona and half a dozen more. You'll have to tell them we can't make it.'

'Not you, just me.'

He assumed she was joking and laughed. 'And for an encore?'

'No encore. If I do that, then I'm on his books and that's it.'

He realised it wasn't a joke. She was actually telling him that this guy had made her a gross proposition. *You come round to the hotel and party, or you don't get on my books.*

He looked at her in disbelief. 'You're not remotely serious, are you? You're not some high-class tart he can buy with the thought of a modelling contract,' he said.

'It's not the thought, it's the actual contract,' she said.

'And you'd screw him for that?'

'It won't come to that, you know it won't. Just a party with girls and champagne, that's what they like.'

'He's only calling your bluff, don't fall for it.'

'No, it's one or the other.'

'Well, let it be the other. Tell him to get lost.'

'It's my choice, my future, I'm the one who has to get onto a proper bona fide model agency's books or lose the chance for ever.'

He realised that she meant it. 'So we're not discussing this at all. You're telling me what you're going to do. Is that it?'

'It's not like that. We swore that we would be honest with each other. I never knew that being honest would end up like this. We *have* to be nice to people in business. You do, every single day. Remember that awful woman who ran the magazine that did our photo shoot? She was making great signs of fancying you. I wouldn't have minded if you had had to go to a party with that woman.'

What he said and did now was very important. He must be careful.

'As you said, it's your decision, your choice, your career.' He spoke gently and held her hand. 'But it would break my heart for you to leap to his command as a party girl, and it would lose dignity and respect for both of us, and despite what you say you *don't* need to do this. And under normal circumstances you wouldn't consider it, but these are not normal times, you're so nervous about tomorrow night.'

He looked at her, waiting for her to throw herself into his arms and thank him for his insight and understanding. There was a long, long silence. 'So, then, my love, you'll come to our party?'

'Thank you for everything, for not losing your temper and getting those wild ideas that I'd tell you a lie.'

'I know you wouldn't,' he soothed. But she still hadn't said yes or no.

A lot of the rented equipment had arrived and was being installed at the premises. Men were backing in with freezers while others were taking out the crates that had held cookers and deep-fryers. Tom was supervising it while Cathy and June were getting the finger food ready for the fashion show.

'Most of them won't eat at all: wannabe models like stick insects,' June complained.

'No, you're totally wrong. Apparently people who are far too old and fat for the garments make up the main part of the audience. Right, that's the second last tray. One more and I'll go out and start loading the van.'

'OK,' June said cheerfully. 'You know, I think we should try to get some kind of Christmas menu ready way in advance, a pack of things for eejits to have in the house like canapés and teeny mince pies . . .'

'Like we could deliver them in the van?' Cathy sounded eager.

'But will you still be working at Christmas?' June asked casually.

'What do you mean?' Cathy looked alarmed.

'I mean, when will you be taking leave and everything? We'd need to know, wouldn't we, Tom.'

'Of course we would,' Tom said, understanding nothing.

'And, by the way, were you ever going to tell us about this baby? I mean, were we meant to wait until you asked us to boil some water and time the contractions?'

At Hayward's, things looked very busy. Tom's stomach felt sick about almost everything and it had little to do with the fortunes of Scarlet Feather. He helped Con, June and Cathy set up the press reception and then slipped away and left a small bunch of roses in a vase in the dressing room. He put a card saying, 'Beautiful, lovely Marcella. Good luck on your first night and always.' His hand trembled a little as he left it there.

Cathy had been shocked by this morning's revelation. She had spun them a good story; the whole thing was something she hadn't realised at all herself.

The doctor had only just confirmed it, and she had not been able to tell Neil before he disappeared to Africa. They had backed off admirably.

'Well, we always wanted another pair of hands around the place. As long as the baby starts work at six months, we'll not mention the matter again,' Tom agreed.

'Sure,' June had said. 'Let's keep it really quiet, let's just tell Maud and Simon, is that OK?'

Cathy knew that she could rely on them.

Tom could hardly remember the show. He remembered a few gasps here and there and a lot of applause. He saw Joe look across at him and put his thumb up in the air a couple of times when Marcella was on stage. He forced a smile onto his face. Please may Marcella stumble, he thought, or do it all wrong. Then immediately he felt guilty: what a terrible thing to call down bad spirits on someone's first night. And then there was the applause, and the buyers from different parts of the country lining up for more details and information about stock, and a watchful eye on it all being kept by Mr Newton himself. Tom worked like an automaton, passing filo-wrapped prawns here and Thai fish cakes there.

Gradually the crowd thinned.

'Don't fill their glasses any more, Con, they'll never go home,' he pleaded.

'Suits me, Mr F,' Con said, and began clearing up the empties.

After ages they were ready, the restaurant was only minutes away. Tom begged Cathy to take the others with her, to order the house Frascati and get it all started. Security men and caretakers were going around checking Hayward's. Tom knew a lot of them from his early-morning bread-making visits.

'I'm just running up to the dressing rooms, Sean,' he said to one of them. 'Got to pick up Marcella.'

'Nobody there, Tom, they're all gone,' said the man.

Tom went downstairs, mystified. She must be going straight to the restaurant, but why hadn't she said? And here was Shona.

'I was just looking for Marcella,' he said.

'Oh, she left half an hour ago. She left with Joe and his pals and that Mr Newton. They all have to go to some do back in the hotel. She said that you *knew* she had to go. Didn't you?'

'Yes, deep down I did,' said Tom.

TOM LET HIMSELF into the flat with a heavy heart. How had he managed to keep cheerful all night, talking about everything under the sun except the fact that Marcella hadn't come to her own party? The others had taken in the situation immediately. The beautiful model had gone with the important people. They had all tried to behave as if it was an acceptable thing to do. Of course she had to, part of the job, they all went on, fussing about which pasta to choose. And he urged them to stay longer for more wine. He didn't want to go back to that empty flat and wonder when she would be home.

Cathy said as they were leaving, 'She's probably at home already, furious that she couldn't be with us.'

'I'd say that's where she is all right,' he said.

Of course she wasn't at home. It was one o'clock, and Mr Newton's party would only be getting going. He sat down and nodded off at the kitchen table. And woke suddenly to hear the phone ringing.

'Tom?'

'Yes, Marcella?'

'Tom, I'm sorry, but the party is only just getting going here.'

'It's nearly four o'clock in the morning. You're not coming home, is this what you've phoned to tell me?'

'Not immediately, and in fact some of the girls were thinking we should get a room between us and maybe stay . . .'

'Good night,' he said.

'Are you cross?'

'No, that's not the word,' he said.

It was an extraordinary Saturday morning. Tom was busy, saying nothing whatsoever about Marcella not having come home last night, or Cathy's pregnancy and all it would involve for the company. He couldn't believe that Neil still didn't know about this news and he didn't like the lines of anxiety in Cathy's face. Cathy was busy saying nothing whatsoever about not having spoken to Neil, or Marcella's non-appearance at the supper last night and all it might involve in Tom's life. So they talked instead about the Dublin wedding, now under three weeks away.

'The message from Chicago sounded a bit pissed off about the typically Irish fare,' Tom said.

'Yes, a huff has been taken, not to me personally mind, but behind my back to Mam. The "Wouldn't you think Cathy would know what's expected" sort of thing.'

'We'd better send another email,' he said. 'Should we try pushing a choice of glorious Irish lamb and Irish salmon? We could even send them pictures of that dressed salmon we did a few weeks back, it was gorgeous.'

He was standing beside her, cutting vegetables. They had exactly the same stroke, the same rhythm. It was as if they were rowing a boat together. There was something companionable and calming about it all. They couldn't brood if there was the wedding of the century to organise.

James Byrne came in to go over the accounts.

'How did the fashion show go last night?' he asked politely.

'Fine,' Tom said.

'When will Neil be back?' he asked innocently.

'Tomorrow,' said Cathy.

James Byrne looked from one to the other, surprised at the curt response. These two used to be the happiest of youngsters to work with.

He turned to a different and hopefully less tense subject. 'I want to check that you have work upcoming that will be paid at the time; we can't afford to give anyone ninety days' credit at the moment.'

'Yes, my brother paid half in advance, and when he gets the final wine list on Monday he'll pay at once,' Tom said.

'And then there's my sister's wedding, they'll pay on the dot too,' Cathy added.

'Hayward's pays for the bread by the month,' Tom said.

'Good, good.' James nodded gravely at their list.

'Is it serious, the cash flow, the situation?' Cathy asked.

'Very serious,' said James. 'Very serious indeed.'

When Cathy got home at lunchtime there was a message on the answering machine saying that Neil's plane would be delayed on Sunday, but that he'd still love to go to the hotel in Wicklow, and he loved her.

When Tom got home at lunchtime there was a message from Marcella saying she'd be back soon, and maybe they might go out somewhere and have a nice cheerful lunch, and that she loved him.

'Hello, is that Mr . . . er . . . Maurice Scarlet?'

'Muttie here. Who's that?'

'It's Mr Mitchell. Simon and Maud's father.'

'Oh, good, Mr Mitchell. We're here waiting for the twins to arrive any minute, but they're not here yet.'

'No, and they won't be there, I mean, they weren't able to go.'

'They're not coming? And are they sick or something?'

'Yes and no to that. Let's say that their mother is not at all well, due to them, so they have to stay here to look after her.'

Shona sat in her flat and read the letter for the thirtieth time. She was being invited to a dinner party on August 19 by someone she had never thought she would see again.

Lizzie said to Muttie that he must not disturb Cathy: the girl was the colour of a sheet these days. Muttie said you had to fight now or give up for ever. That man who had pressed a pound coin into his hand would walk over them unless they made a stand. And the dancing teacher was waiting for the twins in the kitchen. He was going to ring Cathy this moment. He tried the premises.

Tom Feather had left Stoneyfield. He couldn't bear to be there when Marcella came back. He answered the phone. 'You missed Cathy, Muttie. She's taken herself off for the afternoon.'

'It's just that I've a bit of a problem here.'

'Tell me the story,' Tom pleaded. Anything was better than being left with his thoughts. He listened to the tale.

'I'll go and get them for you,' he said. 'Just give me the address.'

'Good day, Mr Mitchell. I'm Tom Feather, I work with your nephew's wife Cathy. I'm collecting the children to take them to St Jarlath's Crescent as laid down in the terms of your agreement with the social welfare department.'

'I don't think . . .'

'SIMON! MAUD!' Tom shouted.

The twins had been listening fearfully and came out into the hall.

'We couldn't go, we made Mother ill,' Simon said.

'By practising the dancing, you see,' Maud explained.

'Nonsense, of course you didn't. Right, get your shoes, hop into the van and we'll be off.'

'You have absolutely no right to barge into my house . . .' Kenneth Mitchell began.

'Take it up with the social worker. I'm only the driver,' said Tom, and slammed out of the house and into the Scarlet Feather van.

Cathy thought that when Neil came home she would drive him straight down to Holly's Hotel in Wicklow. She took down all Neil's messages for him on the answering machine, then she packed him an overnight bag. Now he would have no excuse to pause at home and be distracted. She drove the Volvo to the airport and waited as the arriving passengers came through the gate. There he was, slightly tanned. His handsome, animated face full of the conversation he was having.

'Good heavens, you're Scarlet Feather!' one of his colleagues said. 'We were at a dinner you did for Freddie Flynn, simply superb affair. Neil, why didn't you tell us you were married to this genius?'

'Because then you'd have taken your eye off the ball out there and talked about Cathy's food all the time,' he said. But he put his arm around her shoulder. He was proud of her, she could see. It would all be fine, she must not be so nervous about telling him.

Tom came out of the cinema and drove back to the premises and let himself in again. He wondered would he have anything to eat? But food would taste like sawdust in his mouth. He lay down on the sofa in the front office. Tonight was warm, and he needed nothing to cover him. He lay in the dark and looked at the ceiling. Soon he would sleep, and the awful, shocking hurt and jealousy would go away. But all he could see was Marcella. Talk to her, he told himself. She might well be sitting up in Stoneyfield, anguished, waiting for him to come back. But what could he say? With horror Tom realised that there was nothing to talk about any more. They were way beyond that now.

Marcella telephoned four times on Saturday and was amazed to find the answering machine on on each occasion. He had *known* she wasn't coming back on Friday night. She had *told* him, for heaven's sake. Maybe he was sitting sulking, looking like a little boy and needing to be patted down.

'Tom,' she called as she went into the flat, but there was no reply.

The place was quiet, too quiet. Also tidy. She realised that he wasn't at home. There wasn't a note. Marcella sat down and took out a cigarette. For a woman who claimed she didn't smoke, she was getting through rather a lot of cigarettes these days.

It had taken Shona Burke twenty-four hours to know whether she would accept the invitation or not. She didn't want to go, but the wording was very hard to refuse. She wondered how long it had taken to write. Days, possibly. She could not be expected to respond instantly. She would write her letter carefully too.

Holly's Hotel had an old-world charm, a lot of chintz and the same waitresses year after year. Neil and Cathy checked in at the big, old-fashioned desk with all the keys to the rooms hanging there. Behind them were Molly and Shay Hayes.

'Having a little anniversary, are you?' Molly wanted to know.

'No, Neil has just come back from Africa, he was at a forum on refugees,' Cathy explained.

'Hope you sorted them out,' Shay said glumly.

'Well, we did our best. But there was so much red tape.'

'Still, as long as you put the boot in, we've quite enough of our own in need here, without letting a lot of people in . . .'

Neil's mouth was open in astonishment.

'Mr Hayes . . . Molly . . . I haven't seen this man of mine for nine whole days. Do you mind if I drag him upstairs with me?'

'Not at all, I'm all for that sort of thing,' Shay Hayes said approvingly.

They scampered up the stairs and burst into the big sunny room, where they could let themselves laugh properly.

'He's a monster . . . I don't know why we're laughing,' Neil said.

'Listen, forget him. Tell me all about Africa. I want to know what you did there from the moment you arrived.'

He sat down to tell her, the words tumbling out. Cathy ordered a bottle of wine and a plate of sandwiches to be sent up to the bedroom as he told of what was being done and what an amazing amount there still was to do. Then he said he'd have a shower.

He called out from the bathroom, 'Hardly any point my getting clean gear on, is there? You'll only be tearing it off me, won't you?'

'Do put something on just for the moment,' she called back. 'And come and sit here, it's so gorgeous.'

He came out, clean, glowing in the dark blue shirt she had packed for him. He was so attractive. She poured a glass of wine for them both. This was the time to tell him.

'There's something I've been wanting so much to tell you.'

He came and sat opposite her and held her hand. He smiled at her.

'Neil, I'm pregnant,' she said.

Neil looked at her, stunned. 'You're not,' he said.

'Oh, I am.' She was smiling broadly but searching his face, wanting to see the answering smile and not finding it.

'How did this happen?' Neil asked.

'Like the way it always happens. One night when we thought it was a safe time of the month. We *did* discuss it.'

'Oh yes, I'm sure we did. I'm afraid that I just can't take it in.'

A lump of fear began to grow in her heart. 'I thought you'd be pleased.'

'No, you didn't think that, this is not something we agreed.'

He had released her hands and pushed his chair back. He had had a great shock. She knew she must be calm now.

'We did not say we would *never* have children,' she said.

'No, but what we *did* say was that we would discuss it, and we haven't discussed it,' he said. 'How far is . . .'

'About eleven, twelve weeks.'

'Why didn't you tell me sooner? You must have known.'

'I tried several times, but there was never time to talk. You always had to go somewhere, I always had to go somewhere . . .' She wanted to be sure to take equal blame. 'Why do you think I got you down here to tell you? I needed there to be no interruptions.'

'Well, we have to make a decision, don't we?'

'What do you mean?' she asked in a voice that seemed to come from a thousand miles away; but she knew what he meant.

There was a long silence.

'We agreed we wouldn't have children.' He was trying to sound calm. 'But fortunately there's time to reverse this.' He looked at her, his face drawn, his eyes cold.

'You want me to have a termination?' she said.

'I want us to discuss it, yes.'

'I don't believe you.' She was aghast. 'Aren't you at all glad? Aren't you in any way pleased that our . . .' She stroked her stomach.

'It's not fair, Cathy, it's *not* our child yet. Don't talk of it like that. This is only something that could *become* a child.'

She couldn't say anything. She felt almost dizzy at what was unfolding before her. Neil didn't want the baby at all.

'I need some fresh air, I'm going out to the gardens for a while.'

'Don't leave me, not now, not just now,' she cried.

'I'm not leaving you.' He was irritated. 'I need to be on my own and walk a bit, that's all. I'll be back.'

He was gone. She sat in the bedroom, which had seemed so beautiful when they had come into it less than an hour ago, and the tears fell down her face. She knew that no matter how many hours of discussion they might have she would not choose to give up this child.

It seemed a lot darker outside when she heard the door of the room open. But she had no idea how long he had been gone. He seemed different somehow. Not shocked any more. He sat opposite her at the little table, and though he smiled in an attempt at reassurance, she felt a little as if they were barrister and client.

'Cathy, if you have the baby, who will look after it?' he asked.

'Well, I will, of course.'

'But the business?'

'Well, of course I'll make arrangements.' She knew her voice sounded flustered. 'A nanny!'

'And where would she sleep?'

'I don't know, you can get people by the day.'

'But as I see it, most of your functions will be in the evening, so what happens then? I have to work at night, too.'

'We'll work it out when it happens. We'll manage.'

'Like you've managed up to now?'

'I don't know what you mean.' She was alarmed.

121

'Like the business is in great debt and danger, like you are already worked off your feet paddling to keep up. What do we do if there's a child to consider?'

'So you're asking that there should be no child to consider?' She spoke carefully.

He answered just as carefully. 'That is most definitely *not* what I'm asking, Cathy. I have no right, no right whatsoever to deny you a child, and I will not dream of doing so.'

This is what his walk among the roses, hollyhocks and lupins of Holly's Hotel had achieved for him. The kind of honest clarity that always stood him in such good stead.

'But if we are going to have another person in the house we must prepare. We'll have to move. Waterview is so unsuitable for a child,' he said.

'Not yet. It doesn't matter where a baby lives. Later we might think . . . ?'

'But I have committed myself to work in my area, I'm not taking big insurance cases or conveyancing just to make money.'

'We don't need all that much money. We don't need a big house like Oaklands, a big, expensive, fee-paying school. Children don't need luxury, they need to be loved. My mam and dad raised six of us in St Jarlath's Crescent, and did so with no money and no problems.'

'Well, hardly *no* problems. You are always railing that your mother had to go down on her hands and knees to scrub my mother's floors.'

'But I won't have to do that, and neither will you.'

'I suppose I'm just not ready,' he said.

'Neither am I. But loads of people haven't been ready, and look at the great fist they made of it.'

'It's just . . . it's just . . .' He couldn't find the words.

She said nothing.

'Let's be logical, we didn't want children, now you're pregnant.' It was very chilly, very clinical, the way he said it. 'We have been missing each other a lot recently . . .' he went on. 'I misunderstood the depth of your feeling about the company, and I thought that you'd come abroad with me . . . and you thought that I'd automatically come round to being delighted to be a father. We both got it very wrong.'

Suddenly she couldn't help it any more, the remorseless logic, the working out where praise and blame were due. She felt the sobs coming on and couldn't stop them. He watched her aghast as her shoulders heaved with the misery that went right through her.

'Please, Cathy . . .' He reached out to touch her. He hadn't expected this, he had been trying to sum it up as accurately as he could. He had been struggling not to say that he felt a sense of betrayal. He thought it was unjust that he had been somehow bypassed on their bargain, but had tried to concentrate on the practicalities and now, judging by her weeping, that had not been right either. And Cathy wept and wept, saying the same thing over and over. He didn't want the child. There was no instinctive, loving response to the thought of being a father. He had proved not to be a loving, caring, good person after all, only a selfish one, determined to get all that he could achieve in his career. She wept more because she could not and would not believe this of Neil, the man she loved so much. He watched her, his eyes misting with confusion.

'I've never seen you cry like this before. Please, please stop,' he begged.

She made a great effort, and he passed her a box of tissues. She wiped her eyes and blew her nose. He moved her hair out of her eyes and put his arm around her shoulder.

'Cathy, hon?'

'OK. I'm OK now.'

A determination as strong as she had felt all those years ago in Greece came over Cathy. They had been through too much, conquered so many problems, they would not fail now. Not now that the best part, a child, was on the way.

Tom went to Hayward's and made the bread. Was it only two days since he had been in this building? It seemed like for ever, and yet he realised that he was only talking about a mere forty-eight hours.

Back at the premises he was surprised to find Cathy already there.

'Was Neil delighted?' he asked.

'Yes, well, he was startled, that's for sure.' Cathy didn't catch Tom's eye.

It obviously hadn't gone well, this announcement. Tom felt he should say something.

'But he'll be delighted when the shock dies down,' Tom reassured her.

'Of course he will,' Cathy said with a smile.

Tom might be right. Neil had been so kind last night in Holly's after her weeping fit, so gentle, and he had put away the interrogating manner. They had talked long and calmly, and got up very early to drive back. Neil had driven, leaning over to pat her arm occasionally. Yes, when the shock died down it would be fine.

'We decided that we wouldn't tell anyone about it yet,' she explained to Tom. 'So you see . . .'

He understood immediately. 'So the two clairvoyants you work with will keep quiet.' He paused, and she knew he was going to say something important. 'And since you don't ask, which is very good of you, I haven't seen Marcella since Friday and I might sleep here a couple of nights, if that's all right with the company.' He spoke lightly, but she could see his pain. Quietly, she put her arms around him.

Eventually, she said, 'That's fine with the company. Let's open up the emails and see what we've got.'

He moved away as she started up the computer. Then he heard her scream.

'God Almighty, I don't believe this!'

'What is it?'

He came running. Together they read that Marian was throwing the whole wedding party on their mercy for a rehearsal dinner and a recovery lunch. And this had to be booked at the height of the tourist season in just under three weeks.

'It's impossible,' Cathy said.

'We'll have to cater them all ourselves,' said Tom. 'It's as simple as that.'

Walter was furious with Simon and Maud because they had played in the shed.

'That's my shed, stay out of it,' Walter ordered.

'I didn't know it was your shed, Walter, honestly. I thought it belonged to all of us,' Simon said.

'Yes, well, you know now. And give over this dancing business, it's really annoying Dad. He might go away again.'

'Not over our dancing?' Maud was wide-eyed.

'No, but he keeps saying that old Barty's gone to England and he might follow him.'

'And would Mother's nerves get bad and she'd go to hospital again if Father went away?' Maud wondered.

'You can bet on it. Mother's been away with the fairies for days now, you must know that.' Walter said scornfully. 'So cut down on the dancing where anyone can hear you, will you? OK?'

'Sure, Walter.'

'And no whinging to Sara, either. The only hope of keeping this place going at all is not to tell Sara long stories, do you understand?'

'Yes,' the twins said doubtfully.

Cathy went back to Waterview that evening, her head swimming with ideas for the wedding.

'You can't keep working these hours, you're not able to do it,' Neil said. He was very concerned for her. 'Do you have a pain in your back?'

'A bit now and then, not much. I'm fine. Why do you ask?'

'I read a bit about it in a book.'

Her heart soared. The shock bit was wearing off; the father bit must be starting now.

'I went to Oaklands today.'

'You didn't tell them, did you?'

'Of course not, but I was looking at those pictures Mother had on the piano, of when we were children. She had so much help in the house then, and no job, and look at all you have to do. And when my father came home from work he could just close himself away in a study to work.'

'Your father was never home to go to a study. Wasn't he out on the first tee two minutes after he left the office?' Cathy kept it light.

'But it's the principle of it,' Neil insisted.

Neil made some tea, but he was still brooding. He talked on about his mother and father, how Sara had been on to say that some man had left his Georgian house to an organisation for the homeless and all the neighbours were up in arms. The gross selfishness of this city was getting to him. Where he had been in Africa people had different priorities. She looked at him for a long time as he talked.

'Scarlet Feather,' Tom said.

'Tom, don't hang up, please.'

'Marcella.' His voice was flat.

'Can I come round there and talk to you?'

'No, I'm just going out actually.'

'Are you going home?'

'No.'

'But we can't leave it like this . . .' she said in disbelief.

'Why not?' he asked, and hung up. What did she expect him to say?

In Stoneyfield, Marcella sat and looked at the phone. He'd have to talk some time, even to say goodbye. Why couldn't he talk now?

'They are a bit silent about the menus,' Tom said after two days had passed and there was no response from America.

Tom and Cathy had worked very hard on the wedding plans. For the rehearsal dinner they would have the basement in Ricky's studio. For the recovery lunch they would use Geraldine's apartment. The Friday night was going to be a theme party: Ricky's basement would be done up as a speakeasy in Prohibition times; there would be Al Capone pictures on the walls; they would have the Chicago greats in jazz on the music centre.

'Should we ring them?' Cathy wondered. 'We'll have to get going on the props as soon as possible.'

Talking to Marian was like talking to an entirely different person than the one Cathy had spoken to previously. She was alternately tongue-tied, or else speaking in a high-pitched tone about how grateful they all were.

'Here, I can't make head nor tail of this,' Cathy said eventually. 'Tom, will you talk to her, please.'

Tom didn't do much better. *Is she drunk, or high, do you think?* He wrote down on a pad beside the phone. Finally Tom had a brilliant idea. 'Could I talk to Harry about it all, do you think?'

'Harry's here,' said Marian in her normal voice.

'Harry, I'm Tom Feather. I'm no relation of anybody. If you don't like our menus, you tell me now and we'll send you more.'

'Tom, I'm going to say it: everyone here has had to go and lie down even at the thought of a speakeasy party.'

'I see. We thought you'd love it.'

'No, it would be like having the worst theme party you could dream up . . . something about the IRA with bombs and things.'

'Or corned beef and cabbage,' Tom said quickly.

'I hear where you're coming from, Tom.'

'So we trade over this, OK? No speakeasy, no corned beef.'

'It's a done deal,' said Harry.

Sara called quite unexpectedly, and did an inspection of the house. Eyes watched as she opened the refrigerator, looked at the food shelves and checked the laundry.

'Maud and Simon, can I ask you to go and practise your dancing for a little bit,' Sara said, in a falsely cheerful voice. 'When I'm finished here, I'll come and watch you. OK?'

They thought that sounded great, and scurried out.

'Correct me if I'm wrong, but I don't think anyone invited you to order my children about in my house,' Kenneth Mitchell said, deciding to attack first.

'Correct *me* if I'm wrong, but you don't seem to have the remotest idea of how serious your position is, and how you are both on the verge of losing your children. If the fears that I have about their welfare form a substantial part of my report and are accepted, they could be out of your hands by the end of the month.'

'Muttie, do you know why we got to come here to St Jarlath's Crescent as often as we like?' Simon asked.

'I don't, and I tell you that another thing I never do is question anything at all that turns out better than you expect. Remember that day when I lost my concentration down at the "office", and I put an each-way instead of a win? I was so disappointed, and I'd nearly thrown away the ticket, when didn't one of my associates remind me I'd done it for a place as well? I couldn't believe it but I never questioned it; I think that's usually the best way to go.'

Simon thought about it. 'You're probably right, Muttie; it's just that I'd love to know what it was that Sara said to Father which made everything different.'

'We never know half the things that go on in the world.' Muttie shook his head.

Shona came into the Hayward's kitchen long before the store opened officially.

'You're spying on me and trying to steal trade secrets.'

'Lord, no. Little microwave meals for one, that's me.'

They talked companionably about a lot of things, but neither of them asked the question they wanted to ask.

Tom didn't enquire whether Marcella still worked in the nail salon. She had left one more note before moving her things from the flat. *I still love you, and I cannot believe that you will let four years of our life end without a discussion. You owe me that much. Just one conversation.* But it wouldn't be a conversation, it would only be two people sitting there, one saying that something mattered and one saying that something didn't.

Shona for her part wanted to ask Tom to tell her every single thing he could about Mr James Byrne, retired chartered accountant and present-day part-time bookkeeper to Scarlet Feather. But she had kept her own counsel for so long it was hard to ask.

'When are you going to tell your mother that she's going to be a granny again?' asked Geraldine.

'Soon, soon, just let me get the wedding out of her hair first,' Cathy pleaded. 'And we have so much work on. I'm afraid to let Tom out of my sight in case he takes on another booking.'

'He's desperately anxious to make up the money, isn't he?' Geraldine was sympathetic.

'Yes, and to work himself into the ground so that he doesn't have to think about Marcella,' Cathy added. 'He's not sleeping at the premises any more, so I gather she's moved out of the flat.'

'Silly little girl in many ways,' Geraldine said.

'Yes, but he adored her; still does, I think. Who knows anything about men and what they feel?'

'Who does?' Geraldine was slightly clipped.

Cathy opened her mouth and closed it again. They had been in touch with Freddie Flynn about another estate agents' reception. Cathy had asked should they liaise through her aunt as before? There had been a pause, and then he had said it would be simpler to deal with him directly. It looked like Geraldine and Freddie Flynn's affair was over.

Cathy saw James Byrne in Rathgar and tooted the horn of the van.

'Do you want a lift? Are you going home, James?'

'Ah, how nice to see you, Cathy. Yes, I'd love a lift.'

When they got to the elegant house he turned to her. 'Can I ask you something very personal?' he began.

Oh, please God, may it not be that he too had guessed she was pregnant. 'Anything you like,' she said wearily.

'Will you just walk in with me and tell me what you see?'

Cathy's heart sank. All they needed now was for their sane, calm accountant to lose all his marbles and go mad.

'I'll do my very best, James,' said poor Cathy.

Tom was expecting Cathy back at the premises, so he just buzzed the door without looking up.

Someone stood at the door. Marcella. Her face was anxious and upset. She began to speak immediately.

'Do you hate me, Tom?'

'Of course not. Of course I don't hate you.' His voice was gentle. 'But there is nothing more to say.'

'It was just a stupid party.'

'Yes.'

'I told you, Tom, in advance that it was all meaningless. Unimportant.'

'To you, Marcella. And I told you in advance that it was hugely important to me.'

'But you *knew* there was a party, and that I had to go.' She was weeping now. He stood there, his hands by his sides. 'I was so honest, I really was.'

'No, Marcella, you weren't honest. People who are honest wouldn't do that to each other.'

'I told you the truth,' she sobbed.

'That's not the same at all,' said Tom.

'Look everywhere. What do you see?' James asked.

'James, for heaven's sake, what am I meant to be looking for?'

'What does it look like to you? Who would you think lives here?'

'James, you'll have to forgive me but I've had a long day. I *know* who lives here. *You* live here.'

'No, I mean like someone coming to dinner.' He was crestfallen now, and very vulnerable. The cool James Byrne was so ashamed of himself and his raw, nervous state.

'Oh, I see what you mean.' Cathy recovered. 'You're trying to see someone's first impressions, is that it?'

'Exactly.'

'I'm sorry, I didn't quite understand.' She bought time looking around the dark, lifeless apartment with its lack of colour and spirit. 'Listen, I don't want to be too inquisitive, but in order for me to answer this question properly I'd have to know what kind of a guest it is. Like a businessman, or a lady you were inviting on a date.'

He thought about this for a while. 'Long-lost friend is about the nearest,' he said. 'About your age, a woman, as it happens.'

'A few flowers. Some brightly coloured cushions . . . and get your music centre out from under all those magazines.'

'So what it needs is . . .'

'Some sense of colour, of light, a feeling of hope, of somebody actually living here.' She walked round the room as she spoke. Then suddenly realised what she had just said. Tears came to her eyes.

'James, I'm so very sorry,' she said, touching his arm.

'No, please.' He moved away. 'I asked your opinion and I got it; what is there to apologise for?' He spoke stiffly.

'James, I have to apologise. I'm so nervy and anxious that I have upset almost everyone I know these days. Your place is fine. It just needs a little more colour.'

He lost his stiffness and relaxed his shoulders. 'Would you trust me to make us some tea?'

'I'd love that.'

'Is it any one big problem, or a lot of middle-sized ones?'

'It's a lot of very big ones actually, James, but do you know the way that if you don't admit them they sort of go away . . .'

'I know. They don't really go away but they do stay outside the door.'

'You're very kind, James, a restful type of person to be with. I'm sure your dinner will be a big success.'

'I hope so, I really do. So much depends on it, you see.'

Back at the premises she found Tom curiously quiet. 'Anything more I should know about the wedding? Hit me with it if there is.'

'No.' He was far away.

'Right,' she said.

He didn't answer. It was very unlike him to be so taciturn. He had a lot of papers on the worktop. Cathy saw the words 'Dear Marcella' written on one of them. Things were very bad for poor Tom, much worse than they were for her. Without intending to, Cathy gave him a hug. She just came up behind him and threw her arms around his neck.

To her surprise, he grasped her hands and his face moved round a little so that they were cheek to cheek.

'Come in, come in.' James Byrne led Shona into the room where he had carefully placed four brightly coloured cushions and two vases of flowers. She had brought him a bottle of wine.

'My goodness, Australian chardonnay, how wonderful. That looks very good, very interesting indeed.' He studied it as someone might look at a bottle of some vintage wine. It set Shona's teeth on edge. It was a good, supermarket Australian white wine, no more, no less. Why did he have to keep taking off and putting on his glasses? Probably because he was nervous, she realised. As nervous as she was.

'When did you come to live in Dublin?' she asked.

'Five years ago,' he said. 'Just after Una died.'

'She died? I'm sorry.' But the voice was cold.

Shona did not ask what happened, had it been peaceful, had she lingered a long time. None of the questions you ask when someone tells you that a wife has died. The silence hovered between them.

Eventually James spoke. 'Una was never strong, you know, she found ordinary things like going upstairs or making the beds very difficult. Would you have known that now, when you were with us?'

'No, I didn't. I suppose, since it was the only life I knew. I didn't know what other homes were like until I lost the one I had.'

'She was never the same after you left,' he said.

'I didn't leave, I was taken away, sent away.'

'Shona, I didn't ask you here to go over a war of words that did nothing except tear us to pieces half your lifetime ago.'

'Why did you ask me, then?' She had not addressed him by any name. But what name could she call him? Not Daddy, not Mr Byrne.

'I suppose I invited you because I wanted to tell you how great a gap you left in our lives, how nothing was ever, ever the same since the day you were taken away,' he said with tears in his eyes.

'Since the day you handed me over without a struggle, saying it was the law,' Shona said, her face hard.

'But Shona, that's the terrible thing, it *was* the law.'

Harry was a small, round man with a head of dark curly hair and a great warm laugh.

'Muttie, I want you to know that I'm going to look after your little girl,' he said with a strong handshake.

The two men understood each other immediately. It turned out that Harry liked dogs and horses, and Muttie, who read more of the sports pages than people thought, knew all about the Chicago Bears. Marian was so happy and relaxed, saying she had no idea St Jarlath's Crescent was so small, so colourful, so elegant really. Her wedding dress was unpacked and admired, her ring was tried on by all the women, her choice of husband praised to the skies.

'Do you want me to take you on a tour, to show you where all the parties will be?' Cathy offered.

'Not at all, Cathy, I can see you've got it all under control,' Marian said, and Cathy breathed normally for the first time for a few weeks.

'Tom Feather, my old friend, how are you?' Harry clenched Tom's hand at the pre-wedding party with a mighty grip.

'Look, not a sign of a speakeasy,' Tom hissed at him. 'Are there any pitfalls we should know about?'

'My aunt over there, small, hatchet-faced, wearing purple—nothing has ever pleased her . . . Oh, and Cathy's eldest brother Mike's been put off the sauce recently, finds it very hard.'

'Thanks a lot.'

'Tom, do you have a significant other here that I should meet?'

'No, I've just broken up with my significant other,' Tom said.

'I'm sorry. Her doing or your doing?'

'Have you three hours and I'll tell you,' Tom grinned. 'No, seriously, a bit of both, I believe.'

'Right, then you'll survive,' Harry promised.

And for the first time Tom felt that somehow he might.

In the garden flat, they managed a wooden and stilted conversation. He called her to the table and sat her down. They talked of her school life after she had left the convent school. She spoke calmly about the mother she returned to, still lurching between drugs and rehabilitation, the father who had set up with a more stable woman, her older sisters who resented her return. She told of her natural mother's death, how she had dutifully gone to visit her in the hospital but felt nothing. He said that they had always known a foster child was only lent to them, and that if her home circumstances improved she would go back to them. They had unworthily hoped that this would never happen. He said it was impossible to stay in the house after his wife's death, and he had come to Dublin and lost himself in work.

'Well, I did that too,' Shona said as she finished the smoked fish. 'I decided that work was the only answer, that and having something to show as a result. I wanted a place I could be proud of. Glenstar is far too expensive for me, but I like giving that address.'

'And what about love, Shona? Does that play any part in it?'

'The day you stood and let me go without telling me that you loved me and wanted me back, that day killed any thoughts of love that I would ever have.'

The church hall where they had the wedding feast looked magnificent, draped in ribbons and greenery and flowers. There was a glass of champagne offered as soon as the guests came in the door. Tom took charge of Mike, the brother.

'Hi, Mike, I'm Tom Feather, your sister's work partner. Be nice to me, I'm in charge of the food and drink.'

'Drink, huh?' Mike glowered at him.

'I've got something here you'd love. Low-cal cranberry juice with freshly squeezed grapefruit whipped up with a little sugar syrup and white of egg.'

'What's it called?' Mike was still unwilling to thaw.

'It's called, "Let's not show it to the others, let's find something bearable for ourselves".' Tom winked.

Mike was a much-cheered man when Tom left him.

There was a roar of conversation, and as they moved among the guests they realised that it was already a mighty success. They all reported conversations to each other as they flashed by in the kitchen, which was lit up by the late-afternoon sun.

'Simon and Maud have asked us to hold their cake and ice cream, please, until after their dance,' June announced.

'Makes sense,' Con agreed. 'I'd hate to see them bringing up that lot on the floor, wouldn't you?'

'They're devouring the salmon, will there be enough for second helpings?' asked Lucy, the student who was working with them that day.

And eventually there were the speeches, simple and straightforward, thanks being lavished everywhere. And finally, the moment was here for Maud and Simon.

'Now our beautiful flower girl and our elegant pageboy are going to dance for us, and I want you to give them the great big welcome they deserve.'

Maud and Simon strode out confidently in their cloaks, kilts and huge Tara brooches, as if they were totally accustomed to being greeted with such applause.

Simon nodded at the pianist, and they stood, arms high, hands joined and right foot pointed out until the introductory bars were played, and then they were away.

Cathy caught Tom's eye. He raised a glass to her. She smiled.

'You're smiling,' Tom said in mock surprise.

'I know, isn't it amazing? The muscles still work,' Cathy said.

AFTER THE WEDDING, life had to return to normal. And normal wasn't always easy. Tom never finished the letter to Marcella. She didn't say goodbye when she went across the water. He was told that she had left her job in the salon. Two of the kitchen staff at Hayward's had heard she was going to be a model. Geraldine read in the property pages that Freddie Flynn and his wife Pauline had bought a large country house outside Dublin. James Byrne berated himself a dozen times a day for not taking that hurt, withdrawn girl into his arms and crying over the time lost and the pain endured. He had been so afraid that she would push him away. Neil and Cathy put off telling Jock and Hannah about the baby for a few more days. And so they didn't tell Muttie and Lizzie either.

Geraldine asked Scarlet Feather if they could cater for a spur-of-the-moment supper party at Glenstar.

'Any theme?' Tom wondered.

'She's looking for a new sugar daddy; we *could* think up a few sugar-based dishes,' Cathy said.

'You're awful about her,' Tom said.

'No, I'm not. Those are her own words. Freddie Flynn's gone back to his wife full-time, have you noticed? Geraldine was pleased with how well Glenstar looked for the recovery party after the wedding. She's decided to capitalise on it. But, Tom, are we taking on too much, do you think?' she sounded worried.

'No, of course not, we've a load of terrific stuff for a buffet in the freezer already.'

'Yes, but getting it ready, setting it up, serving it.'

'Cathy, June and I will do most of it. Relax, there are bound to be times you're tired. Accept it, will you?'

She smiled wearily. It was great not to have to put on a brave face all the time.

Sara came to The Beeches to ensure that the back-to-school process was going as planned. Kay Mitchell looked at her, bewildered. Sara explained slowly. Textbooks, exercise books, uniform, haircuts.

'There's always so much to do,' Kay sighed. 'It's all quite endless, really, isn't it, Sara?'

'Endless, Mrs Mitchell. Shall we make a list of what has to be done?'

'Why didn't you tell me about the premises getting broken into?' Lizzie demanded. Muttie had met JT Feather by chance.

'Oh, Mam. I didn't want you going on like you're going to go on now.'

'So this isn't the reason why you're killing yourselves and you're looking like a long wet week?'

'Mam.' She felt a surge of gratitude to her mother. She'd tell her about the baby this minute if there was any point, but it would be just one more worry. 'No, Mam, we're absolutely fine,' Cathy lied.

James Byrne had said today that the hopes of getting the insurance company to pay up in the foreseeable future were very slim. They would be renting this expensive stuff for months. They would see no profit, and quite possibly a massive loss at the end of the year.

The room was filling up at Geraldine's apartment.

June went up to Peter Murphy, hotelier and great friend of Geraldine's. 'Lovely party, isn't it, Mr Murphy?' she said to him.

'It is indeed, my dear,' he said distantly, giving the air of never having seen her before in his life.

'I'm no hit with that Peter Murphy,' June complained to Cathy.

'I think he still fancies the hostess,' Cathy said.

'Look who's here now,' June said. Joe Feather had just come in.

'Oh, God Almighty,' said Cathy. This would be the first time the brothers had met since the night of the fashion show.

Shona walked over to the window, to where James Byrne was standing.

'I'm very sorry, I didn't know you'd be here,' she said. 'I'd like to return your hospitality some time soon.'

'Oh, please, don't think you have to do—'

'I don't think I *have* to, I'd like to. Would you like to have lunch with me at Quentin's one day next week?'

'But Shona, that's a very . . .' He spoke softly. But stopped.

She seemed to know what he had been going to say. 'I save my money to pay a posh rent and to have the odd meal in a posh place. I'd love you to be my guest. You pick a day.'

'I'd be proud and delighted to meet you there on Wednesday.'

'All right, Tom?' Joe said in a fake cockney accent.

'All right, mate,' Tom answered in the same cheerful voice.

They looked at each other, not sure what to say next.

'Great place for a party,' Joe said eventually.

'Isn't it just? Have you a drink, or have you gone temperance on us?'

'I'm never going to drink again, Tom. Believe me.'

'Rough night, was it?'

'You bet. Listen, I won't interrupt you here at your work. Maybe we'll have a temperance lunch one day.'

'OK, but I want somewhere with a pint. Right?'

'Con, can you take this tray? I have to sit down,' Cathy said.

'Sure. You're very white, Cathy,' he said. 'Can I do anything?'

'Yes, go and see which of Geraldine's posh bathrooms is free.'

He was back in seconds. 'The near one is free, lean on me, Cathy.'

'Thanks, Con, you're a trooper.' She went in.

'Cathy's in the loo, she doesn't look well,' Con reported in the kitchen.

'Right, you bring in the next lot of dishes, I'll go and check.' June went to the bathroom. 'Cathy, open up the door this minute.'

The bolt was drawn back, and Cathy sat on the side of the bath, her face as white as the white porcelain around her.

'Go back, June,' she said in a weak voice. 'Go back, for Christ's sake, we can't afford to foul up on a good job like this.'

'What's wrong? Just *tell* me,' June said.

'I felt a pain. Look, it's nothing, it's not a haemorrhage or anything.' She grimaced and held her middle.

'Have you passed any blood at all?' June snapped out the words.

'Literally a couple of drops, nothing you would notice.'

'You've got to lie down. In the spare bedroom and now,' June said, scooping up all the towels she could see in the bathroom.

June approached Peter Murphy. 'Mr Murphy, could tell me whether anyone here might be a doctor? I don't want to disturb Geraldine.'

They both looked over to where Geraldine stood talking animatedly to a tall man who seemed very taken with her.

'I don't know half the people here,' Peter Murphy said.

'Why are you looking for a doctor?' Tom had amazing hearing.

'Cathy. She's in the spare bedroom.'

He was in there in a flash. 'Tell me quickly, Cathy, what do we do?'

'There's a bit of blood. I don't know whether it's better to get to a hospital or to stay still.'

'Have you got your mobile?'

'In my bag in the kitchen. But don't go just yet, Tom.'

June was back in the room. 'There *was* a doctor, she's coming in.' She was one of the residents at Glenstar, a small Indian woman with an easy smile. She took in the situation immediately.

'How many weeks?'

'Eleven to twelve, I think.'

'And the pain? The cramps? The blood?' She asked questions without any sense of rush. And nodded, as if pleased with the answers. 'We'll keep you here and make you comfortable for a while, and then we'll think again,' she said.

'Please go back to the party,' Cathy begged. 'I'm all right now.'

'They're coping fine,' Tom soothed her.

'Are you her husband?' the doctor asked.

'No, no. I've rung Neil, but it's the answering machine and I didn't want to leave a message. Can you give me his mobile number, Cathy?'

'Not yet, let's see. Now please go, all of you,' she begged.

They left, and she noticed that the doctor had put still more big bath towels beneath her. The doctor must be expecting to see a lot more blood shortly. Tears rolled down her face.

Geraldine knew that something was wrong but that it was under control. She bade farewell to Nick Ryan, who owned a chain of dry-cleaning outlets around the city. She murmured that she must not monopolise him; he really should circulate. He murmured that he hated to go, but really he had no interest whatsoever in talking to anyone else. She saw Doctor Said moving quietly towards the spare room, and she suddenly realised why she hadn't seen Cathy for the last hour or so.

Only when she got to the hospital did Cathy tell them Neil's mobile number. And by the time he got there it was all over.

Back at the premises Tom, June and Con unpacked the van, washed up, tidied and stored everything. Geraldine said she would call them there when there was any news. They sat and drank coffee in their front room. They were trying to be practical; they would get Lucy in again, and she might even have a couple of friends. Con had a pal who was a good, reliable waiter. Whatever the news, they knew that Cathy would not be able to work for a while and she would need the assurance that Scarlet Feather could survive her absence.

When the phone rang it was two in the morning and Geraldine was ringing to say that Cathy had lost her baby.

Neil came in and sat beside the bed to hold her hand.

'They say you're going to be fine,' he said. 'That's what matters. You're very precious to me.'

'Yes,' she said in a very tired voice.

'And Cathy, I'm very, very sorry. It could sound a little hollow, but I know it's a huge loss, and I *am* sorry that this should happen.'

'Thank you, Neil,' she said.

He stroked her forehead over and over saying, 'Poor Cathy. You'll be fine.' Eventually she closed her eyes. He kissed her and she heard him speaking to the nurse, saying he'd come back next morning.

'Very considerate man, your husband, some fellows who come in are all over the place,' the nurse said.

'That's right,' said Cathy, who realised that some fellows who came in here would be heartbroken if they had lost a stillborn child.

Neil drove her back to Waterview. He suggested that she go to bed; he would work and then bring her supper later. 'It's all right,' he reassured her. 'Tom brought round four little meals for two with instructions on them, so you won't be poisoned!'

The telephone rang. Cathy heard him telling someone that she wasn't there. They must work out a cover story for the next few days. Flu, virus or whatever.

'It was only Simon and Maud, some grouse, some whinge. I headed them off,' he said proudly.

'She *has* gone off us,' Maud said.

'But why? We haven't done anything. Not recently,' Simon said.

They went back over everything. Cathy had been great at the wedding, and had even said she was proud of them. All they wanted to ask her was could they do some more polishing at the premises, because they wanted to earn some money for bus fares. Father had said that old Barty hadn't given him money that was owing, so there could be no pocket money this month.

They chose from the set lunch menu, and ordered a glass of wine each.

'I shouldn't have said that you killed any thoughts of love for me, that was going too far,' Shona began.

'If it was what you felt, and I pray God it will not always be this way, then you were perfectly right to say it,' he replied.

'Did I really have to go back, James?'

'Oh, Shona, you did and they told us that the best thing we could do for you was not to cry and tell you we'd miss you. They told us that it would be hard with your family after ten years without us weeping and wailing and making it worse, so we pretended that this was great news.'

'And I thought, always thought that you were relieved to be rid of me.' Her voice was flat.

'Shona, you were the centre of our lives, and no decision in that house was made without thinking of you. We were left with a great hole in our lives when you had to go.'

'What else could I think? No letters. I looked every day. I couldn't believe you didn't write to me.'

'We were told not to, so as not to unsettle you.' James took out a paper tissue and wiped his eyes.

'You finally realised you don't have to wash hankies. Mum and I used to say that you were the last of the folded-linen variety—'

She stopped abruptly, realising that she had called his dead wife Mum after all these years. She held out her hand at the same time as he did.

'I'm more grateful than I can say that you got in touch,' she said.

'Well, I've learned how to cook three dinners. You've only had one, there are still two to go,' he said, wondering had he gone too far.

'Saturday?' Shona suggested.

'I'm going back to work tomorrow,' Cathy said. She sat in her dressing gown at the kitchen table in Waterview.

'No, it's too soon. You're not fully better.'

'I'm not fully better in my mind because I'm upset, but my body is fine and it needs to get back to working rather than sitting here all day on my own.'

'I'll be home early,' he promised. 'I know it's possibly not the right thing to say but in many ways—'

'Then don't say it.'

'You don't know what I'm going to say.'

'I do, and please don't say it,' she begged.

'Please let me finish. I only wanted to say that in many ways all this sad business has shaken us up, made us take a proper look at ourselves.'

'Yes.'

'And that's all I was going to say. Is it all right?' He looked at her expectantly, waiting for a response.

'It's fine.'

'So after all you *didn't* know what I was going to say.'

'I thought when you began you were going to say it's all for the best, but you didn't, not in so many words. Although that's what you think, Neil,' she said sadly.

'So first I'm on trial for what I'm going to say and then when I don't say it, I'm on trial for what you believe I think.' He looked wounded.

'I'm sorry, Neil, I didn't mean to be harsh.'

'And neither do I mean to be insensitive,' he said from the door.

Cathy wished things could get back to normal, but there seemed to be no way that she and Neil could talk about what had happened without her wanting to scream and rail. She wanted them both to cry over the dead baby; his cool, logical, barrister's way of approaching it was driving her mad. The only place things might be normal was back at work. She'd go today.

They were delighted to see her back, and made a great fuss. They said how much they missed her and how hard they had worked.

'So what's new?'

'A couple aged about a hundred who want to get married next month and can't find a venue to suit them,' June said.

'How old are they, really?'

'Ancient,' June said.

'How about the church hall?' Cathy asked.

'Too big, they don't know how many people they're going to invite. Fifty maybe; but it might only be about twenty-four.'

'They're not very flush with friends, are they?' Cathy asked.

'They're coming in today, you'll love them,' Tom said simply.

Tom was right. Stella O'Brien and Sean Clery were the nicest people you could meet. Aged in their mid-fifties, they had met a year ago at a bridge class. They were devoted to each other. But there was a problem. Stella's son and daughter had assumed their mother would remain a widow, and Sean's three daughters had assumed their father would remain a widower. They might none of them be at the wedding.

Cathy nodded. 'I didn't know on the morning of my wedding day if anyone except five friends and my aunt would turn up. But I look back on it and I think it was a fine day. You will too. Tell me where you would really like to have the reception, and we'll see if we can work out something around that.'

'Do you know Holly's Hotel in Wicklow?' Stella began.

'Yes, indeed,' Cathy said. It was where she had told Neil about the baby.

'Well, they don't do weddings there, sadly. We did ask. But would you know somewhere a bit like that?'

'I'll find you somewhere like that hotel,' Cathy promised.

'Anyone need the van for a couple of hours?' she asked.

Cathy drove south to Wicklow. A beautiful autumn day, it was wonderful to get out of the city. She looked at the tape selection and put on a favourite arias collection. She turned up the volume and sang along to Pavarotti. She thought again of the child who hadn't made it to getting born and the tears poured down her cheeks.

'I can't do it, Ms Scarlet, we don't have the resources,' Miss Holly said. 'I have three waitresses who are as old as I am. We can't take on weddings.'

'Let me do it, Miss Holly. We'll rent the place from you, we'll be in and out, you won't know we were ever here. They're the nicest people.'

'Are they family, or are they blackmailing you?'

'I never met them until this morning, but to tell you the truth I had a miscarriage, and today's my first day back at work and I'm feeling a bit vulnerable. They were so nice, and they said they wanted a place as like this as possible. And I know what they mean.' She was afraid her voice sounded a bit choked.

'You do like it here, you and your husband?'

'It's been our great treat. A place that's worked magic for us.'

'Well, I'll let you have the place, Ms Scarlet.'

'You won't regret it, Miss Holly.'

'Now all we have to do is think of the food for Stella and Sean,' Cathy said when she was back at the premises.

'What do you mean? We have to get a venue first, and it's so hard, given all the limitations.'

'Oh, that's all organised,' Cathy said, her eyes dancing. 'Miss Holly said yes.'

'You drove down there today?'

'Yup,' said Cathy.

'I thought we could manage without her, Tom, but it turns out I was wrong,' said June.

'Not a word from those children,' Muttie said.

'I suppose they have such a great life up at The Beeches.' Lizzie was philosophical.

'They didn't come last Saturday, and never a solitary word out of them,' Muttie said, very upset.

'Well, I rang Cathy and she said they were grown-up enough to make up their own minds,' Lizzie said. 'I think they didn't have their bus fare, that's what I think,' said Muttie, who then sat down and wrote a letter. *Just in case there's a problem about transport between our residences, I enclose £5 (five pounds). We are always here . . . M and L Scarlet.*

Walter picked up the mail. There was an odd-looking letter from someone to the twins. Walter opened it carefully. He found the fiver and pocketed it. He put the letter and envelope into the fire.

Geraldine had dinner at Quentin's with Nick Ryan. He was a very pleasant man. He said it was a treat for him to go out to dinner with a glamorous lady. Normally at this time of the evening he was groaning to his wife about the day at the office and coping with two fairly difficult children. Geraldine nodded her understanding of this. *All* children were difficult. Anyone who said otherwise wasn't a serious parent. This made him feel good, and also the way Geraldine seemed to accept the existence of a wife and family in the life of a man she was having dinner with. She made it clear that she preferred a very independent life, and liked to see a variety of friends.

'And you do have a lot of friends. I was very impressed at your party,' he said. 'Very pleasant gathering indeed.'

'I'm glad you enjoyed it, I hope you met a lot of people,' Geraldine said.

'To be very honest, I wasn't all that interested in meeting other people,' he said.

Mrs Barry wouldn't be at The Beeches for a while, she was going away to her daughter's for three weeks' holiday.

'The press is full of tins of things there for you, and the milkman is paid to the end of the month.'

'Thank you, Mrs Barry.'

'And you know . . . you know your mother's not well. She should have a doctor. I'll give Sara a ring and let her know.'

'No, Mrs Barry, we'll ring Sara,' Maud said.

'Good. That's all right then, she'll be round to see to things.'

Maud and Simon didn't ring Sara. It only upset everyone when Sara came in; it was fine for five minutes, but when she left everyone and everything got worse. And when she called to know was everything all right, they said it was all just fine.

Cathy went to The Beeches.

'You've missed them, I'm afraid,' Kenneth Mitchell barked.

'Oh, really, where are they?'

'I have no idea,' he said.

Cathy's eyes narrowed. 'You're meant to know where they are at all times.'

'All right. They've gone to see their mother in hospital.'

'*What*? She's back in hospital?'

'Only momentarily. She's coming home tomorrow.'

'Where's the hospital?'

'It's none of your business,' Kenneth blustered.

'I wanted to pick up the children, that's all.'

'You needn't do that, I hear them coming in,' he said sulkily.

'I'm sorry your mother isn't well,' Cathy said to the twins.

'We didn't tell her,' Simon said, looking guiltily at his father.

'But you were *meant* to tell Sara or me when things change here.'

They hung their heads.

'I still have to let Sara know. That was the *deal*, Kenneth,' she said.

'Interfering, meddling . . .'

The twins couldn't bear to hear this, so they went out to the garden. Cathy followed them. They sat on a little bench.

'You see, it gets worse if we tell,' Maud said.

'Why haven't you been to see Muttie and Lizzie?' They looked at her guiltily. Eventually she got it out of them; they just didn't have the fare.

'Dad told me that he sent you a fiver. Why didn't you use that?'

'We didn't get it,' Simon said.

Cathy knew without a shadow of a doubt that they spoke the truth. She reached into her handbag. 'It must have got lost in the post.'

'Aren't they such total clowns?' Neil said that night.

She badly wanted to remind him that it was he who had fought for these hopeless people to get their children back. It was Neil Mitchell who had said that they must be restored to their flesh and blood instead of living happily between St Jarlath's Crescent and Waterview. But she left it. However, she did tell him about Muttie's missing fiver.

'I imagine that fool Walter took it,' Neil said casually.

On the Tuesday, Maud telephoned Cathy.

'Excuse me, I don't want to delay you,' she began.

'Good girl, Maud. I am quite busy,' Cathy said.

'It's just that we went up to Muttie and his wife Lizzie, and they told us that some of your treasures were stolen . . .'

'Yes, but don't worry about that.'

'No, it's just I remember how much you liked the silver punchbowl and I saw one in our garden shed. I thought maybe it might be nice for you instead of yours, and I could ask Father—'

'Don't ask anything for the moment, Maud, I beg you. We're up to our tonsils here and we'll get back to you.'

'You said that before, Cathy, and you never came back at all.'

'Jesus, Maud, don't nag, please, please don't nag. If you *knew* the kind of day we're having here. After we've done this wedding tomorrow, I really *will* come and see you. Promise. OK?'

'Who was that?' Tom asked.

'Maud. She was going on and on about some punchbowl hidden in their garden shed.'

Suddenly they looked at each other.

'Oh, my God.' Cathy put her hand over her mouth.

It was a day when they just wouldn't find the five minutes they needed to talk about the possibility of Walter being responsible.

'I can't believe Walter did all that damage,' Cathy said.

'You'd understand him nicking things, it's in his nature. But how did he get *in*?' Tom worried.

And that was it. They had to concentrate on the work ahead.

Tom went ahead to Holly's with the others, and on the way dropped Cathy at the church. It didn't look promising, the gathering. Two very separate groups standing heads close together outside the church, each darting glances over at the other. But Cathy swore to herself that she would do everything in her power to make this day a memorable one for Stella and Sean.

Tom had everything under control when they got to Holly's. Trays of champagne greeted the guests as they came in.

Because of the uncertainty as to who would or would not attend, they had arranged a buffet with open seating. The food went down well and the mazurkas and polkas and whatever else the musicians were playing disguised the fact that this was not the most relaxed and happy of gatherings. Stella and Sean were so happy that they didn't seem to take in the degree of resentment around them. Tom edged them towards the cake and Sean cleared his throat.

'When my wife Helen died, and when Stella's husband Michael died, we both thought our lives were over. And then we got a second chance. Nobody can replace Helen and Michael, and no one is trying to, but we want to thank you for coming out with us this day to celebrate the happiness we had in the past and the happiness we hope is waiting for us in the future. So may I ask you to drink one toast to friendship and the future, and then to join us on the dance floor.'

The musicians struck up with a slow waltz, and Sean led Stella onto the floor. But nobody joined them.

'Take off your pinny,' Tom ordered Cathy.

He dragged her out onto the dance floor. Cathy had never danced with Tom before. She had forgotten how very big he was, her head was way beneath his shoulder. He smelt of soap.

'I'm afraid to look, is anyone dancing?' she muttered.

'Con has Lucy out there, but I think it's time to change partners.' He released her and walked purposefully towards one of Stella's daughters. Cathy pulled a red-faced friend of Sean's from his group, Con and Lucy split up and asked other people. Tom heaved a sigh of relief.

Much later, when the guests began to drift home, Cathy began the usual discreet clearing up. Tom decided to move the van nearer to the kitchen door of the hotel, but it wouldn't start. Not a sound from its engine. They tried jump leads, without success. There wasn't a garage for miles. Miss Holly was hovering in the background, clucking with admiration at the spotless kitchen.

'You two are an example to the whole catering trade,' Miss Holly said approvingly. 'I can't tell you how—'

'Hold the praise, Miss Holly,' Tom said. 'We can't get the van to start. I'm afraid we'll have to stay the night here. I'm terribly sorry.'

'Don't worry, you're in the right place, there are plenty of rooms free. Just take the keys from the rack in the hall.'

Tom and Cathy relaxed in the kitchen at Holly's. They talked and opened a bottle of wine. They would really expand once they had a place like this to do weddings. They talked about giving cookery classes on Wednesday afternoons, about freezer packs for sale at the premises or even through stores. Tom would ring Hayward's early tomorrow morning to get his emergency breads released from the freezer. How wise he had been to set up the system. 'I must ring Neil now.' Cathy took out her mobile. Tom made a move to give her some privacy, but she waved him back to sit down. It was only the answering machine.

'Neil, the van broke down, so I'm going to stay the night here at Holly's. I'll give you a ring in the morning. Hope you're all right. I love you. Bye.'

'You're very independent, both of you.' Tom admired the way they could lead separate lives.

'It usually works, but at the moment it's a bit up and down. He thinks I should go on a holiday with him.'

'Well go,' Tom said.

'I most certainly will not. What have we just been discussing? This is our very busiest time upcoming. We'll have one more glass of wine, Tom.'

'Sure, and a hangover, but why not.' He grinned.

'Let's take it upstairs,' Cathy said.

They took one of the room keys, and, giggling like schoolchildren they went to open a bedroom door. Cathy picked one of the beds, kicked off her shoes and lay down, looking at him.

'We really should have a notebook to write all these things down. We won't remember anything tomorrow.'

'Write what down?' Tom poured the wine. 'Don't spill it, Cathy, you're very drunk.'

She put the glass down beside her and went straight to sleep. Just like a two-year-old would, or a puppy dog. Tom covered her with an eiderdown. He considered going down and getting a second key and finding another room. But they were talking about four hours' sleep, really. He lay down on the other bed.

Walter couldn't believe it. Those *stupid* twins had actually telephoned Cathy Scarlet and told her that some of her stolen stuff was still in his garden shed. Maud had been rooting around when he discovered her. Some story that Cathy was going to call round after a wedding today and see them.

'I told you *never* to go into my shed. You promised me you wouldn't but you are such liars, no wonder no one wants you.'

'People do want us,' Simon said. 'Muttie does and his wife, that's two.'

'They don't want you anywhere near them,' Walter said.

'They do, Cathy said that. And Muttie is taking us to the races for our birthday.' Maud was stung.

'Go to your bedrooms at once,' Walter ordered.

'What are you going to do?' Maud asked.

'I'm leaving this house. I can't bear the sight of you, liars, meddlers.'

They peered out of their bedroom window and saw him filling black sacks full of things from the shed. Then a taxi came and he stacked all the bags in it. He really was going. Father rang and said he had met old Barty, and wouldn't be home until very late tonight so not to send out a full-scale alert for him.

'You will be coming home?' Simon asked.

'You really are the most tiresome child I ever met in my whole life,' Kenneth Mitchell said, and hung up.

'Walter's right,' Simon said. 'Nobody does want us.'

Next morning Kenneth Mitchell came home at dawn from old Barty's club. He found a note on the kitchen table. *We are leaving home. Goodbye, Maud and Simon.*

He called his brother Jock. Jock was not well pleased to be woken at that hour. 'Talk to Neil and Cathy, they'll know,' he said.

Neil listened with no pleasure to the confused story. 'Doesn't Walter know anything?'

'He doesn't appear to be here either,' said Kenneth.

'OK, I'll contact Cathy for you.'

At Holly's Hotel, the receptionist put Neil through to Room Nine.

'Hello?' the voice said. It was Tom Feather.

'Hello?' Neil said again, puzzled. 'Is that Room Nine?'

'Yes, it is. Who's that?' Tom had a headache.

'I was looking for Cathy,' the voice said. It was Neil. Tom was awake immediately. 'Neil, she's down sorting out the van. I just came up here to get her mobile for her.' As he spoke, he began to shake Cathy into wakefulness in the next bed.

'I tried that first. She has it turned off. There's a bit of a crisis here. Can you transfer me back down to the desk?'

'*No!*' Tom shouted. 'No, Neil, hang on, I see her coming up the stairs. Cathy, Cathy,' he shouted loudly. 'Neil is on the phone.'

Cathy had by now sat up, straightened herself and realised where she was. 'Sorry, Neil. Everything OK?' He told her. 'Neil, I'm in the heart of the country with no transport.'

'And of course there's no sign of Walter, the one time you'd need him.'

'*Neil!* I hadn't time to tell you. I think Walter was one of the vandals who broke into the premises. Something Maud saw in the shed, you must check the shed. Listen, I'll ring you later. Why don't you ring Sara?'

Cathy hung up and looked at Tom.

'Quick thinking,' she said. 'But it wasn't really necessary, you know. We could have said what happened. Neil would have understood.'

'I know, but this way was easier,' he said. 'What's happened?'

'The children have run away.'

Simon and Maud got Lizzie on the phone; she was cagey about Muttie's whereabouts, he had gone away for a day or two. This was puzzling. Muttie never went away anywhere. And what about the birthday treat?

'He's not refusing to talk to us or anything?' Maud asked.

'Child, why would he do that?' Lizzie said. It sounded reassuring, but it wasn't a yes or a no.

Muttie Scarlet had spent a night in hospital. He wanted it neither discussed nor known. Lizzie was under strict instructions to say that he was away on business. He came home to find all hell had broken loose. The twins had disappeared. Poor Lizzie was going over every word of the conversation.

'I didn't know they were contemplating anything like this . . . They always said they were fine, I thought they were tired of coming here . . .'

It was an endless morning of negotiating with garages. The fault was identified, the part was found. Cathy phoned Neil.

'Nothing at all, Sara's really worried.'

'Do Mam and Dad know?' Cathy asked.

'They have the whole of St Jarlath's Crescent out with sticks beating bushes by the canal.'

The twins had left a note in the kennel: *We have taken Hooves with us.* It gave no hint of where they were heading. Friends at school could tell them nothing. Kenneth revealed with every sentence he spoke how little he knew of the life that went on at The Beeches. Walter had not shown up at work; Kay, now frightened into sobriety, said he had left earlier, in a taxi with a lot of black bags. But nobody took much notice of what she said. The guards had been called.

Cathy and Tom got back to Dublin in the early afternoon, in no humour to hear of Peter Murphy who wanted to have a cocktail party to annoy Geraldine, nor to discuss a Halloween extravaganza with Shay and Molly Hayes. But they had to do all those things because that was what work was about.

Tom answered a call from Sara, saying it was all in the hands of the guards now. Maud and Simon were assumed to have spent one night sleeping rough and everyone was very worried indeed.

October

'IT'S ALL MY FAULT, I was so short with Maud,' Cathy wept at the kitchen table. 'I kept saying things like "Hurry up", and "If that's all, Maud".' Lizzie, Geraldine, Muttie and Sara all looked at each other helplessly. 'And the awful thing is that she was being so kind, she was trying to get me a punchbowl from the shed and she didn't even realise that it was stolen by Walter.'

Sara looked up sharply. 'You think Walter was your burglar?'

'Yes, he must have been. Maybe this has something to do with the children running away,' she said anxiously.

'His mother thinks he went last night in a taxi . . . carrying a lot of bags,' Sara said.

Then suddenly Sara and Cathy looked at each other as the implication became clear. Sara called the guards again.

The punchbowl was gone when the guards searched the shed, but there were a lot of other things that they asked Cathy to look at. The guards had long decided that there was little future in talking to the children's parents. At first she thought that she could see nothing that belonged to them. Then she saw some salad servers and a linen tablecloth.

'The salad servers were a present from Neil's parents last Christmas, the cloth has our laundry mark on it,' she said in a small, flat voice.

Neil nodded gravely. The guards seemed entirely convinced. The evidence would nail Walter when they found him.

'He never took the children with him,' Cathy said. 'He high-tailed it out of here on his own because he thought we were onto him.'

'They could still get in touch,' said Neil hopefully.

'But who would they ring?' Cathy asked. 'That's the thing that's breaking my heart. They rang everyone and none of us listened.'

'They could be anywhere,' Muttie wailed.

'They're so distinctive, the guards will find them in no time,' Geraldine soothed them as best she could.

'No, the guards haven't a clue where they are, they keep asking us to think of likely places and known companions, and none of us knows anything about their lives, poor little devils.'

'Do you remember them at Marian's wedding? They were so proud of themselves,' Lizzie said, blowing her nose.

'Oh, they're not *dead* for God's sake!' Geraldine said. 'Really and truly, Lizzie, these two are well able to look after themselves.'

'No, they're not, they're real babies,' Lizzie said.

Walter's friend Derek wouldn't let him stay. 'No, you can't leave the stuff. You're too much trouble, Walter, and now you say the law is after you, I can't afford to have any policemen poking round this flat.' There was a fair chance they might find cocaine if they did. 'Take it up to the market,' Derek advised. 'You can unload it there in no time.'

'For peanuts.'

'Well, take the peanuts then and put them on a horse, *then* you're in the clear,' said Derek.

Muttie went in just from sheer habit to the betting shop. 'Don't feel like having a bet today, my mind's distracted,' he said.

'Suit yourself, Muttie, but that was a nice little windfall you got yesterday,' Sandy Keane said dourly.

'I didn't have a bet yesterday, I was preoccupied,' said Muttie.

'Internet Dream,' said Sandy. 'You won seventy pounds on it.'

'Is one of us losing our minds, I wasn't near here yesterday.'

'I know, Muttie, the twins told me.'

'Oh, my God, what time?'

'First race at Wincanton,' Sandy said.

'Can I have the phone? I must ring the guards.'

'You're going to bring the guards in here and tell them that I took a bet from minors? You're off your head, Muttie.'

'No, Sandy.' Muttie had begun to dial. 'You don't understand. These children have been missing for two days.'

It didn't in fact bring them very much further down the line. So the children had hung around the St Jarlath's Crescent area for the night with the dog, until the betting shop was open for bets.

'I feel a bit better that they had seventy pounds rather than just a fiver,' said Cathy.

'But it does mean they can stay away longer, like now they won't have to come home out of desperation,' Muttie said, biting his lip.

'I mean, nobody would *hurt* children, or anything?' Lizzie asked one of the guards fearfully, as she showed him an endearing picture of Maud and Simon taken outside the church at Marian's wedding.

The guard looked at the two serious little faces and cleared his throat. He hated cases about children. 'We have to hope not, Mrs Scarlet.'

The tears came down her face again. 'You see, you'd really have to know them to realise that they're such an odd little pair. They just get notions and follow them anywhere.'

'And would they trust strangers, do you think?'

'They'd go off with Jack the Ripper if he came to the door with a plan.' She put her head down on the table and wept aloud.

Muttie patted her shoulder awkwardly. 'If we could just think what mad thought was going through their little minds the moment they took off, then we'd find them in no time,' he said.

The twins had no idea of the drama they had created. To them it had been utterly simple. Muttie had promised to take them to the races for their birthday. To hear the real thunder of hooves. *That's* where he had gone, to the races, and his wife Lizzie didn't want to admit it. And so they made their plans. They would go to the races and confront Muttie. Ask him straight out what they had done to annoy him. They packed a plastic carrier bag each to take with them, a big sweater, pyjamas, a pot of jam, a loaf of bread and two slices of ham. Then, shortly after dawn when the first bus passed the end of the road, the twins made their way to St Jarlath's Crescent. They weren't leaving without Hooves. They had five pounds and eighty-three pence, but would it take them all the way to County Kilkenny?

'What do people do when they need money?' Maud wondered.

'There's Muttie's "office", the betting shop,' said Simon.

After that it had all been simple. Mr Keane knew them well.

'How's tricks?' he said, as he always did.

They told him tricks were great and placed the bet. Two pounds to win on Internet Dream.

'I break every rule in the book for the pair of you,' said Mr Keane. 'I let minors into my establishment and a small four-footed beast as well.'

'Muttie has a whole lot of tiring things to do for his wife today, so he asked us to put the bet on for him,' Simon said.

Sandy Keane nodded; this seemed entirely reasonable.

They sat as quiet as mice until the race. Internet Dream won at thirty-five to one and they had their fare to Kilkenny. Hooves loved the train journey, and the other passengers seemed delighted with him.

'What will we do if he wants to pee?' Maud whispered.

'Maybe he'll know you can't go on a train,' Simon said optimistically. Hooves saw a nice leather briefcase and was about to relieve himself against it. Simon and Maud jumped up horrified and alerted the owner of the briefcase, who was reading a newspaper.

'Could you take it away? He thinks it's a lamppost.'

'Easy mistake, often made,' the man said.

'Where should I take him?' Simon asked.

'Just out there where the two carriages sort of join, and look away as if you have nothing to do with it,' the man advised.

They came back and sat down to talk to the man, since he was so pleasant, and told him that they were going to the races.

'We'll be meeting a grown-up there, of course,' Simon said.

'Is that your dad?'

'Sort of stepfather, foster father really.'

'And does he have any tips for today?'

'No, but he'll have been studying form all morning,' Maud explained.

'Great. The important thing is to feel lucky.'

'We've been quite lucky already today, we had Internet Dream, thirty-five to one,' Simon said proudly.

'Well, maybe I should stick with the pair of you,' said the man, who said his name was Jim, known to his friends as Unlucky Jim. Unlucky Jim came on the bus with them to the races. 'You've been very good company. I wonder, would you let me buy you a drink after the third race, the bar beside the tote? Your father, too, if you've made contact.'

'We will, of course,' said Simon.

Simon and Maud searched everywhere for Muttie. They went in and out of bars, they stood near the winning post for one of the races, they went to the parade ring, but with no success. After the third race they went to meet Unlucky Jim.

'Did you have any winners? I'm here depending on you both.'

'We haven't studied form yet,' Maud said.

'And what about your da, did he come up with anything?'

'Not really,' Simon said.

They decided they would pretend they had met Muttie; better let people think they were being looked after.

'What do you fancy in the next one?' Jim asked.

They looked at the race card carefully. 'Lucky Child,' said Maud. 'Look at the weight, and it didn't do badly last time out.' Muttie had taught them to read the vital signs.

'You're right, I'll put fifty each way on it,' said Unlucky Jim.

Maud and Simon went down and willed Lucky Child forward. It was a near thing, but he won. Unlucky Jim searched the place to give the twins a share of the biggest win he'd ever had.

'It's very easy really, isn't it? I wonder why Father and people who have money troubles don't do this all the time,' Simon said.

'Did Muttie *say* which day he had planned to take us?' Maud was tired, and a little worried about the night ahead.

'No, but if he's not here today he'll be here tomorrow.'

So they got a bus back to Kilkenny. They walked and walked to find a suitable place, and then found a big shed with some broken agricultural machinery, tractors and things in it.

It was ideal for them. There was even a car seat ripped from some vehicle that they could sleep on. They gave Hooves one slice of ham, shared the other and had bread and jam. Tomorrow they'd find Muttie.

They slept very well because they were so tired, and woke only at the sound of Hooves barking. They had tied him to the door. They had only stale bread and half a jar of jam.

'Do we have enough money for a breakfast?' Maud asked.

'You mean, go into a place and pay for it?' Simon was horrified.

'We could have bacon and eggs.'

Simon agreed that under the circumstances they should go and look for some breakfast. Somewhere that would let Hooves in. They felt a great deal better after they'd eaten, and having tidied themselves up as best they could they set off for the races again.

Maud sat down. 'I'm tired of looking,' she said. 'Suppose he's not here.'

Now it was out in the open. Now it had been said. Simon got such a shock that he let the lead go, and Hooves took off at a great rate through the crowds. The children were aghast. He would do terrible damage out of sheer fright and a sense of unfamiliar freedom. They pushed their way after him. People had staggered back as Hooves had come at them, barking his head off.

'Please, Hooves, please don't go on the racecourse,' Maud cried.

From every side they were getting shouts of annoyance—no place to bring a dog, the horses might get frightened—Hooves had decided against the actual racetrack and swerved to a reasonably empty area, where there were some cars and horseboxes, and had then run straight under the wheels of a reversing Jeep. The driver couldn't possibly have stopped in time. Hooves was thrown right up in the air and then fell to the ground. He was very still when they got there.

Muttie was having a pint with some of his associates, and opinion was divided about Sandy Keane; should he have taken the children's bet? How could he have refused it? They couldn't live for ever on the winnings, they'd have to come out sooner or later. They could hardly go round all the betting shops in Dublin putting two quid on outsiders, or to a race meeting.

'Oh, my God,' said Muttie. 'I told them I'd take them to Gowran Park for their birthday. They could have gone there.'

The children were taken into the offices. They were told that the dog was being looked after.

Simon was too shocked to talk. Maud had been given hot sweet tea but she wouldn't stop shaking. Eventually they had managed to get the children's first names and an announcement was made.

'Can the adults who are accompanying Maud and Simon please present themselves. They are particularly anxious to meet a Mr Muttie. The Information Office, please, as soon as you can.'

Walter had gone down a line of bookies with the pittance he had got in the marketplace. There were better odds now on Bright Brass Neck than there were at the start. Then he heard the announcement. He couldn't believe it; what *were* those two devil children doing here? There was the usual last-minute crowd around the bookies' stands, and the announcement was made again with a greater sense of urgency. Walter went to the Information Office.

Everything happened then at the same time. The guards in Kilkenny had heard that there was a good chance of the missing children turning up at the race meeting. The race committee and its security staff, who were beginning to despair of discovering who these children were, were relieved at this news, which cast them all in the role of heroes. One of the many vets at the races said that Hooves might be lame but would live. Maud and Simon, already overjoyed with the good news about Hooves, could hardly believe it when Walter came to rescue them. They hugged him tightly, and for the first time in his life he felt cheap and shabby.

'That's Walter, he's our brother,' said Maud proudly.

'He came to find us,' Simon said.

'There is a call for Simon and Maud, Mr Scarlet is on the line.'

'Muttie!' they cried in delight.

And outside, where the races still went on, the Tannoy announced that Bright Brass Neck had won at eleven to one.

Muttie thought of himself as the villain of the hour. Of course he had told those children he'd take them. It was all his fault from start to finish. But he wasn't allowed to take the blame. Cathy insisted it was all *her* fault, she just hadn't realised how dependent they were on people, she should have given them a precise date when she was visiting them after the wedding rather than letting them sit there waiting, disappointed. Neil said a lot of it was down to him, he really *had* thought the principle of blood being best was right. Sara said she had just lost the plot on this one, she had been too involved in the campaign for the homeless to see what was straight in front of her. Kenneth Mitchell said little. Kay had been drinking vodka all day from a bottle which she claimed to be mineral water. Soon somebody would find out. But it didn't really matter because quite obviously Kenneth would be going on his travels again.

Tom Feather had been so pleased to hear the good news that he made a cake and delivered it round to St Jarlath's Crescent. He had attached a card with the words *Happy Birthday and Welcome Home to Maud and Simon and Hooves* on it, and left it with Muttie and Lizzie's neighbours. He was delighted they had been found safe. Such funny little things. He had once said to Marcella that he hoped they'd have children like that one day. He remembered she had smiled indulgently, as if he was saying that one day he'd fly his own spaceship to Mars. Perhaps Marcella had never intended to have children. He had been sorry to hear a cryptic remark from Joe that things were not going well in London for her. It was not what he wanted to hear. The only thing that made sense out of all this hurtful, tragic business was if she got what she wanted, a modelling career.

Shona Burke rang James Byrne. 'Those children have turned up.'

'I *am* pleased to hear that,' he said.

'They're with Muttie and Lizzie Scarlet.'

'Well, please God that's where they'll stay,' James said. 'Let's hope Muttie Scarlet has a lot more courage than I did.'

'Let's hope he has just as much love as you did,' Shona said gently.

James felt better than he had done for a long time. A few minutes later, he got a call from Cathy.

'Good news for once.'

'I've just heard about the twins, isn't it wonderful?' he said.

'No, this good news is actually the guards know now that Walter Mitchell, did the break-in.'

'I don't want to add a sour note . . .'

'But?' Cathy said.

'It wasn't technically a break-in. Your husband's cousin let himself in to your premises with a key. It won't make the insurance company think any less that the whole thing was an inside job.'

Walter called Derek, to say that he was sorry but the heat was on and that the guards would probably land there any day, so to make sure there was no substance in the house that shouldn't be.

'I'm not going to be done for your stolen goods, am I?' Derek said.

'No, it's all out of there.'

'And what are you doing?'

'I'll stay away for a few weeks until it all dies down. See you then, back in Dublin.'

'Take care of yourself, Walter, you're not the worst,' Derek said.

Walter caught the tone and went for a last throw. 'Oh, Derek, in about five hours' time you could report your credit card missing,' he said.

'You never took my credit card?' Derek roared down the phone.

'No, but I know its number and I'm going to book myself a one-way ticket to London.'

Sara seemed very ill at ease when Cathy went to see her.

'What are the chances of Muttie and Lizzie getting the twins? Realistically.'

'You know we're talking about fostering, not adopting, because Maud and Simon's parents are alive and could easily put up a case to have them back, and the law says . . .'

'The law doesn't know its arse from its elbow about things like this,' Cathy said.

'Believe me, I'm with you on this, my work every day is saying what you just said, but not as succinctly.'

'I know. You are tireless about things, just like Neil. Did he tell you, by the way, that he will be free after all to go with you to that conference next February? Remember when I was pregnant, he told you that he couldn't?'

'But won't you be gone by then?' Sara asked.

'Gone where?' Cathy asked. Sara made a big production out of looking for her mobile phone. 'Gone where?' Cathy repeated.

'No, I'm mixing it up with someone else . . . um . . . Take no notice of me, I'm in pieces these days.'

'Was it tiring tonight?' Neil asked after the cocktail reception for Peter Murphy.

'No, I'm fine.'

'What are these?'

'I thought you'd like a few special prawns.'

He seemed pleased with them on their little plate. 'They're great, so light . . .' He didn't ask about the do tonight, he never asked about any do. It was still Cathy's funny job.

'You met Sara today,' he began. He seemed uneasy.

'I wanted to ask about the twins. Like whether there was a real chance of Dad and Mam fostering them full-time.'

'She rang me and said she had let it slip to you that I was still interested in the refugee job.'

'Well of course you are,' she was perplexed. 'I assumed you wouldn't have thought of it so seriously and then suddenly just let it slip out of your mind, I supposed you'd be thinking about it, yes.'

'The thing is, they've put the offer to me again, with different terms. We need to talk about it seriously.'

'Meanwhile you talk to Sara about it seriously.'

'Cathy!'

'I'd love a nice long bath,' she said.

'Please don't be like that.'

'Look, Neil, we'll talk about it seriously, but not at this time of night.'

'COME IN, MARCELLA,' Tom said wearily.

They walked in silence up the stairs to the flat where they had once lived together so happily. Tom sat down at one side of the table, and with his hand, made a gesture for her to sit at the other. There had never been any point in offering Marcella food or drink, so he didn't. He looked at her as he waited for her to speak. She looked very tired.

'Thank you for letting me in,' she said.

'It's late, I'm tired, I have to get up very early to bake bread, you and I don't want to go through it all again, now do we?' He spoke gently, trying to be reasonable.

'I just want to tell you something and then I'll go.' She sounded very beaten and down, as if all the life had gone out of her.

'Then tell me,' he said.

'It's quite hard. Do you think I could have a drink. Anything?' He took a can of lager from the fridge, picked up two tumblers and brought her an ashtray. She seemed to take ages lighting her cigarette. Eventually she began to speak.

'It didn't work at all, not at all, not even from the start.'

She looked so bleak and sad that Tom felt he had to say something. 'Well you *tried* it, that's what you wanted to do.'

'No, I never got a chance to try. Paul Newton didn't want me for that kind of modelling, not for what I thought . . . First he sent me to people who wanted what they called glamour shots, which is topless.' There was such shame and sadness in the story, Tom closed his eyes rather than see her face. 'I said to them there had been a mistake, that I was a real model on Mr Newton's books, and they only laughed, saying I could take it or leave it. I told Paul Newton and he said what else did I expect at my age . . . and I said that he had promised to have me on his books as a model, and he said he *had* done that for God's sake, so what was I complaining about? I must be a big grown-up girl, act my age and get on with it . . . I said, "But you promised", and then he got really annoyed. "I told you the truth", he said, over and over.' And suddenly it was just like my sitting talking to you, where I said I'd been honest with you, that I'd told you the truth, but you said that telling the truth wasn't the same as being honest. I didn't see the difference until then.'

'Oh, Marcella.'

'Yes, so anyway, I had enough money for a month's rent, and then I didn't have any more, so I did the topless pictures, and the money went through Paul Newton's office and I collected it every fortnight. I never saw him, then one day as I was picking up my envelope he asked me into his office. He said he was sorry we had parted bad friends, and that I was very good at what I was doing, and now he had something else to offer me. I thought he had a real job for me at last. I waited and he said that if I wanted to I could earn real money, and he showed me some hard-porn magazines.' She stopped, shaking her head in memory of the shock. 'I said I'd call him the next day and I came home.' A long pause. 'I'm staying at Ricky's for the moment. I've worked in bars, and in a sandwich bar at lunchtime. You know that I'd be a real asset nowadays to Scarlet Feather?' The longing in her voice was almost too much to bear.

But he said what had to be said. 'Please believe me, this is not spite, nor sulking, but it's no.'

'Tom, I want to be back the way we were. Suppose it were *you* that had made the mistake, and had upset me by stretching too far in some direction, and begged me to start again, wouldn't you like me to say something hopeful rather than a cold, blank no?'

'It would all be a pretence, an act, like playing at being in love again. I don't love you any more. I'll never forget all we had together, and if I do ever love someone else, that will always remain special . . .'

'Don't look for someone new. Love *me* all over again.'

He felt no desire for her, nothing but pity.

'Will you come away for a weekend?' Neil had asked.

'Sure, that would be nice,' Cathy had said.

She didn't really like the sound of a weekend away. It sounded dangerously like a honeymoon and she wasn't ready for that yet. The doctor had said that Normal Married Life would of course resume, it took different people different times. Cathy thought that in her case it might take a long time. But it wasn't something she could easily discuss.

They had fallen into a disconcerting habit of one being out when the other was in. Even at weekends they were both out a lot. Cathy often spent time at the premises in the evening, rather than going back home. If Tom noticed, he said nothing. Cathy knew that he occasionally took girls out, but rarely anyone a second time. She knew that Marcella was back in town and staying with Ricky; that's all he had told Cathy. June, however, who heard everything, had it that Marcella was doing all kinds of jobs she would have turned her nose up at.

She had been tempted to tell Tom how much Neil had upset her over the whole pregnancy thing. But she didn't even want to acknowledge it openly. And anyway, a lot of that hurt seemed less sharp now. She and Neil *did* get on very well on many levels. Only this morning he had said how he wished she were free to come to the big demonstration for the homeless, but he knew she had to work.

'Oh, June, how are we going to get through this lunch today? This woman's a monster. We are to use the back entrance to the house, and take the van and park it somewhere so the guests won't see it and we all have to put on house shoes when we come in the back door.'

'Oh, well, if it keeps her happy.'

'Oh, and Mrs Fusspot said that she hoped the staff would be decorous, because some of her guests are embassy wives.'

Tom wasn't coming on this one. There would be Con as barman, June and Cathy to prepare and serve the lunch. He urged them to leave in plenty of time, 'Good luck,' he called after them. 'And, Cathy, stop calling her Mrs Fusspot, will you? You'll say it to her face when you're there!'

'Tom, have you Mrs Frizzell's letter and the map there? I've been to number twenty-seven and they never heard of Mrs Frizzell.'

'You mean you aren't *there* yet? Oh, my God!'

He ran to the desk and took down the file with that week's bookings in it. He came back to the phone and read out the address, with the name of the suburb.

'*What?*' she screamed. There were two streets with the same name. She was on the wrong side of Dublin.

'Tom, what will I do? If I ring her now she'll go to pieces.'

'Just get there, I'm much nearer. I'll go round in a taxi with champagne and smoked salmon and hold them at bay until you get there.'

He had a fairly horrific phone conversation with Mrs Fusspot, where he had to hold the mobile far from his ear. The taxi man looked at him sympathetically.

'You know, your job is nearly as bad as mine,' he commented when Tom had finished his call.

'Give me yours today, I beg you,' Tom replied.

'Not today, you wouldn't want it,' the taxi driver said gloomily. 'There's some kind of protest in the centre of Dublin. People marching from O'Connell Street to St Stephen's Green Park. The one you were talking about with the van of food will be lucky to get there by next weekend.' Tom closed his eyes. He must stay calm.

Mrs Frizzell was around fifty, tiny in an unwise emerald-green wool dress. She had black hair scraped up into an angry-looking chignon and was very bad-tempered when he arrived.

Moving quickly into the kitchen and finding suitable glasses, he said, 'The traffic was terrible, the guests will all be delayed.' Her face was stony. Tom opened one bottle expertly and stood it in ice, then he swiftly arranged the smoked salmon pieces on the buttered brown bread.

'Let me take you back into the very nice sitting room I saw briefly on the way in, and give you a glass of champagne while you wait for your guests,' he said.

The guests were in fact not late at all. He did find a bottle of cheap brandy, and decided to add a few drops to every glass of champagne he served. This was going to be the longest pre-luncheon drink in the history of catering.

'I don't *believe* this,' Cathy cried when the guard on traffic duty told her that the roads were closed. 'Has there been an accident?'

'Oh, no, it's only the homeless and those who care about them to the point of closing the city down,' he said, casting his eyes up to heaven. 'Are you conjurers?' he asked them, interested. They had such a funny van with a red feather on it, they might be children's entertainers.

'No, Guard,' said Cathy before doing a perilous turn. 'But we may have to become conjurers before this day is over.'

'Who could have got them to close the streets?' Con asked.

'My husband,' Cathy said grimly.

Most of the women were very much at ease the moment they came in the door. Tom moved among them, smiling, reassuring that there were *no* calories in smoked salmon. He fought down his own panic. There were twelve women, two of the four bottles of champagne he had brought were empty, the smoked salmon was nearly finished.

Tom ripped open three tins of sardines, and like lightning he spread it over the contents of a packet of biscuits he had also unearthed. He tried to keep a mental note of all he had taken from Mrs Frizzell's stores. He had opened jars of gherkins, chopped a cucumber and made a little bowl of dip out of various yoghurts he found in the fridge. There was no sign whatsoever of the van.

Cathy drove right up to the front door, then remembered and reversed to go to the back door. Tom saw them coming, and thanked God.

'Cold canapés of any kind—no time to heat anything, I have the ovens on, just fling the main course in,' he hissed to Cathy. 'And open more champagne, Con, they've drunk my lot. Quick, June, start the tables.'

Cathy went into the dining room, urged them to have the little asparagus tips with Parma ham. To her amazement, Mrs Frizzell said she was very sorry about those dreadful protesters; Mr Feather had been marvellous. Cathy said she was delighted to hear it, and scooped up some really revolting-looking things on plates.

'God, what on earth are these?' she said scraping them into a bin.

'Those were my best efforts until you arrived with the cavalry,' he said. 'I'll go home now, and leave you to cope.'

'You *can't* go.'

She saw he had only been joking.

'Of course I'll stay, you clown.'

Mrs Frizzell thanked them grudgingly. It had, of course, been very distressing that everyone was so late, and extra precautions really should have been taken on a day when everyone knew that the city traffic would be difficult.

'Ah, but *did* they know?' Tom said. In about eight minutes they would be out of here. Cathy had promised to buy them all a pint to apologise for having got the address wrong.

'Well, apparently they should have; that good-looking barrister son of Jock and Hannah Mitchell you always see spouting on about causes was on breakfast television this morning warning everyone.'

They smiled until their faces hurt, until they got in their van. Then when they had driven out through the gate Cathy asked, 'Anything happen when I was driving the wrong way round Dublin?'

'Yes, Muttie rang and the twins are making an Irish stew as a treat for Lizzie tonight and that handsome barrister rang and said he'd booked you both into Holly's the weekend after next.'

'Well, that's a nonstarter for a variety of reasons,' said Cathy, not catching Tom's eye as he drove to the pub.

Neil came home just in time for the television news.

'It was a huge success, I gather,' Cathy said.

'Yes, people can't pretend any more that they don't know about the problem, and that's good.'

'Let's turn on the television and see what they say.'

She handed him a glass of wine and put a plate of warm Stilton tartlets on the table between them.

'These are nice,' he said. 'Leftovers?'

She was annoyed. She had saved them specially for him in waxed paper. 'Well, I suppose they are in a way.'

'Stop being prickly, hon. How did it go anyway, *your* do?'

'Fine. She knew your parents, as it happens.'

The news came on. 'Shush. Here we go,' he said. The march got very full coverage, and they saw Neil. About twenty seconds' worth of him, young and eager, his hair blowing in the wind.

'Thank you for coming out on the streets today to say that in a country of plenty we are ashamed that people will sleep without a home tonight. Let nobody say that the homeless have sought out their lifestyle. Which one of us here would choose to spend this November night in a doorway or under a bridge?'

As he got down from the platform, supporters grasped him and hugged him. One of the people reaching out to him was Sara.

'You were great,' Cathy said admiringly. And she meant it.

'It just might help to change things. It was great out there, Cathy; I *wish* you had been able to come, to be a part of it.'

And then the phones began to ring. People congratulating him, newspapers and radio programmes wanting him to do more interviews.

When people called him on his mobile, Cathy answered the house phone as the assistant and helpmate he wanted her to be.

'Oh, Sara, good to hear from you. Did it all go well?'

'Well, sure it did, didn't you see, don't you know?'

'I haven't had time to ring my mam yet, but I hear that they're making an Irish stew to mark the day.'

'Who are? I don't understand.' Sara sounded totally confused.

'The twins, you know, my dad told you all about it. The Beeches is being boarded up today.'

'Oh, the *twins*,' Sara said. 'Sorry, Cathy, I meant the march.'

Cathy passed the phone to Neil. She felt very tired, and out of things. In fact, she wanted to go to bed. These calls could go on all night. Yet it looked dismissive and cold to Neil on his big day to show so little interest. So Cathy sat there, listening enthusiastically to Neil's side of phone calls. He waved away any offers of food, the adrenaline was enough. 'It will be real food, not leftovers,' she said. And immediately wished she hadn't.

'Oh, Cathy, you *are* getting very petty about a silly remark. Sorry if it offended you. Anyway, I don't want any more, thanks.'

The phone rang again and he seemed to take the call with some relief. Well, why not? Cathy asked herself. The rest of Ireland thought he was a hero. His wife just made petty remarks.

Next morning Neil was rushing, he had to get into the radio studio to do an interview on *Morning Ireland* before anything else. Cathy didn't tell him then she wouldn't go to Holly's with him. It seemed inappropriate.

'See you at eleven,' she called as he was leaving. 'Remember, the meeting?'

'Meeting?' He looked blank.

'Oh, Neil, at our premises, the bad guys are coming, and James.'

'God yes, of course, I'll be there,' he said.

James Byrne had asked for another meeting with the insurance company. He had been told that the position was still very unsatisfactory; apparently a cousin of one of the partners had let himself into the premises and destroyed everything for no apparent reason. Neil hadn't arrived by eleven. Coffee was served in the front room, and James stepped in to bring them up to date on the way things were progressing. He showed them the meticulous books he kept, the ongoing calendar for work planned and booked. He painted a picture of a decent, hard-working, struggling pair who were anxious only for what was theirs by right and law.

'Law has to be interpreted, defined,' one of the insurance men said.

Cathy wished with a passion that Neil was here to answer him. Then her mobile rang.

'Sorry, hon, you've no idea the impact all this has made. I'm literally besieged . . . I'm really sorry, and please give my sincerest regrets to—'

'*No*, Neil.' Tears had sprung to her eyes. He did this too often. 'We need you . . . They've just said law has to be interpreted, you *should* be here to do that for us.'

Tom and James started to talk loudly, to gloss over what was obviously a husband-and-wife quarrel. But Cathy had turned her phone off.

'Neil wasn't able to make it, so even though I'm furious with him for not being here, I'm passing on his regrets.'

The meeting ended indecisively, the insurance men left saying that they would not come to another meeting or consultation until there was something new to put on the table.

'I could kill him,' Cathy said after they had left.

'Don't,' said James. 'We're in enough trouble already. Unless the insurance pays before Christmas, you won't be able to carry on.'

Cathy was putting off going home. Neil's presence there today would have alerted those people; things might have been moved forward. He must be made to understand that. Without nagging, whinging and being . . . what was that word he used about her recently? Prickly.

She decided to try out one of the new places hidden among the foodie streets in Temple Bar for a snack. To her great surprise she was served by Marcella. She looked very beautiful in a smart black trouser suit and a red necklace around her throat.

'You look lovely, Marcella, but then you always did.'

'For all the good it did me,' Marcella said sadly. There was a sudden awkward silence. 'Are you meeting anyone?' she asked.

'No, I was . . . Well, I just wanted a glass of wine and something small.'

'We have a lovely plate of mixed tapas,' Marcella suggested.

Cathy nodded dumbly. 'That would be fine,' she said.

'And Cathy, I'm just on my break now. Would it annoy you if I sat down with you for ten minutes? I'd love that.'

'So would I,' said Cathy insincerely. Please may Marcella not want to cry and tell the whole story about just wanting to talk to Tom all over again. But in fact it was quite different. Marcella asked about Scarlet Feather and what had happened since she left. There was a lot to tell. Cathy told her about Marian's wedding, and her own pregnancy and miscarriage; she told about the twins' disappearance. .

'I've been rabbiting on about myself. You can tell me or ask anything you like, Marcella. Tom and I never talk about personal things at all, it's just an unwritten rule.'

'Do you think there's a chance he'd have me back?' It was so naked, humble and sad.

'I haven't an idea, Marcella, I really don't.'

'And does he have anyone in particular . . .?'

'No, no one in particular. I know he does take girls out, but I don't hear anything.'

'Thank you.' She got up. 'On me, Cathy.'

Cathy knew that the wages in these places were not good, and there would be no tip. But dignity was also important. 'Thank you.'

They arrived home together, the van pulling in beside the Volvo.

'There's timing,' Neil said, pleased. He walked ahead of her into the house and looked at the number of times the little red light flashed on the answering machine. 'Only three messages. Good,' he said.

'Leave them, Neil.'

He laughed. 'What on earth are you talking about, hon—'

'Please leave them. If you listen to them, you'll have to do something about them,' she said.

'Ah, Cathy, what *is* this?'

'An attempt to talk,' she said simply.

'I *told* you, I booked us into Holly's. We'll talk all weekend there.' He was moving towards the phone.

'I'm not going to Holly's with you,' she said, her voice unexpectedly loud. 'I said I'd like a weekend, I didn't ask you to go ahead and book it without discussion. I don't want to go to Holly's.'

'Why on earth . . .?' he looked at her, bewildered.

'The last time you and I went there I was telling you about how we were going to have a baby. You don't think I want to go back there again, Neil?'

He looked at her, embarrassed. 'I'm afraid I didn't think of that. I'll book us somewhere else tomorrow.'

'Or maybe we could do it after some discussion between us,' she said.

'Is this what this is about? My not running everything past you before we do it? Is that it?'

'No, it's about much, much more. It's about your not turning up today when we really needed you so badly,' she said.

'You knew how much in demand I was today after the march.'

'Then you should have cancelled our meeting.'

'But, Cathy, it wasn't . . .' he began.

She waited. 'It wasn't what, Neil?' she asked, almost defying him.

'It was a matter of priorities,' he said eventually. 'We all have to make decisions every day about what to do and what not to do.'

'And you decided not to come to a very important meeting. Leaving the three of us looking so foolish you wouldn't believe it.'

He stopped being calm now. 'Cathy, please. There were things that had to be done, a joint committee is being set up—'

'*We* needed you at the premises, you had promised to come. They ran rings around us and . . . and you won't believe this, but if they don't pay up in time we could be out of business before the New Year.' She waited for the shock on his face, but it wasn't there.

'Cathy, I know this is a blow for you and Tom, and I'm sorry, of course. But seriously, it's not something I could run away from everything else for. It's only a small business, after all, cooking food for rich people.'

'What?' She looked at him astounded. 'This is my job, Neil. This is what I do.'

'I know, hon, but you can't compare all those discussions about canapés and finger food with what I had to do today. It was not as important as the setting up of a joint committee. Don't get carried away with the importance of a business, Cathy. They come, they go.'

'Even if you've slaved for them and played everything by the book like we've done all the way?'

'Cathy, it seems to me that you are trying for a very high moral ground saying that I should have given up good work in defence of the homeless in order to protect something which in the end is fairly unimportant.'

'You think Scarlet Feather is unimportant. Did you always think this, like, say, a year ago when I was so busy setting it up?' she asked. He sighed heavily. 'I need to know.'

'Well, I thought it pleased you, you know, because of all this nonsense about your mother and mine.'

Cathy was silent. There seemed nothing more to say.

'Cathy, is there anything I could say or do to make things better?' Neil asked.

'No, no, there's not, Neil.'

'I know I'm very insensitive, like that thing about Holly's Hotel.'

'Again, I tell you, it's not important, believe me there, too.'

'I love you,' he said.

'Maybe, Neil.'

'No, really and truly, and I don't want anyone else in the world but you. So yes, I annoyed you today and over the past months. I admit this. But I've come to a decision.'

'Yes?' She looked at him.

'I honestly didn't realise how much that whole baby thing meant to you.' He held both her hands. 'Cathy, if you'd like us to try for another child, then I wouldn't mind, I really wouldn't mind at all.'

'CATHY! YOU'VE PUT SEVENTY into that box, not sixty . . .' June snatched it from her. They were doing their Christmas freezer order, flat boxes of canapés. Sixty per box. 'You're miles away.'

'You're right.' She pulled herself together sharply. 'And we must finish quickly because we're having Power Elevenses, remember?'

'All right. You'll speed up if you put your mind on them.'

And with that they went into fast mode. By eleven o'clock Tom was well back from Hayward's and the cash-and-carry. Con and Lucy had turned up, and they were all sitting in the front room, five Scarlet Feather mugs of coffee on the table.

'Now, Cathy and I thought it only fair that you all realise how near the edge of the precipice we are. Our only hope is to work the arses off ourselves this month. There will be nothing whatsoever to do in January, so our only hope is in the next four weeks. What we have to do is to know how many days and nights we can all work.'

'I can work every night except Christmas Day,' Con said. 'I'm going skiing in January, so I need all the dough I can get.'

'And you, Lucy?'

'Any night except Christmas Day, most lunchtimes too. There's not much on between now and February, when I have to study.'

'June?' Tom said.

'Every night including Christmas night,' she said. 'Jimmy isn't bringing in any money and will be glad of my wages.'

'Cathy?' Tom asked.

'Any night, obviously, and any day. This is our last throw.'

'And I'll be here all the time, so there was hardly any need for a Power Elevenses at all.' They were going to do it, all five of them; they would see that Scarlet Feather didn't go under. All they had to do now was go out and get the bookings.

Cathy went to the market. But most of the stalls and stands didn't look suitable places to advertise their party service. She walked towards a notice board, and on her way she saw a bric-a-brac stall, and noticed a silver punchbowl just like hers. She picked it up and looked at the base.

'Awarded to Catherine Mary Scarlet for Excellence.'

'How much?' she asked the stallholder in a whisper.

'Thirty?' he said doubtfully.

'Twenty?' she suggested, and got it for twenty-five pounds.

'Would you have any idea where you got it?' she asked.

'Not an idea in the world,' he said.

'Do you get enough money to make it all right for us to live here, Muttie?' Simon asked.

'We have plenty, son. We lack for nothing,' Muttie said.

'You lack for a good coat, Muttie, yours is very thin. Father always had a good coat with a velvet collar.'

Simon was distressed at the unequal nature of things.

'Ah, but now, remember, your poor father lost his house and your mother lost her health, so not everyone has everything,' Muttie said.

'There are new people going into The Beeches,' Maud said.

'Will that upset you, child? Will you miss the place?'

'No, Muttie. I mean there's no one there any more. Mother's going to be in a home mainly, Father's travelling with old Barty, and Walter's gone away. There's no one there any more to miss.'

'And this is your home for as long as you like. For ever, really.'

'I wonder where Walter is,' Maud said. 'He was so nice to come and find us, the day you did. I didn't expect him to.'

Muttie decided it was time to change the subject. 'They always say you should never look back. Do I look back to the day I meant to put the tenner on Earl Grey, and I mixed up the names and put it on to King Grey instead? I do not.'

'Tom, don't hang up, it's Marcella. Listen, I can't talk long, there's this television game giving dream prizes, you know, a flight in a helicopter, someone to cook a dinner party for you . . .'

'I know.' Tom sighed. 'Geraldine tried to get us in there, but . . .'

'I'm having dinner with the director. I'm actually at Quentin's with him now. Why don't you and Cathy get down here and I'll introduce you.'

'You're very good to think of it, but—'

'But what, Tom? It's eight o'clock at night. I'll be here with this guy for at least another hour and a bit. Go on, get Cathy.'

They met at Quentin's. Tom was wearing a dark suit and white shirt.

Cathy looked at him with admiration. 'You scrub up very well,' she said. She wore her blue velvet trouser suit, and her hair hung loose on her shoulders.

'And you've put on make-up!' he said.

'Let's only have a starter, we can't afford a whole meal,' she said looking at the menu.

Brenda Brennan came to the table. 'I know what this is about,' she said. 'They're having their coffee now, don't order anything yet and they can sit with you for five minutes on their way out; you don't want the table covered with food.'

'You're a genius,' Cathy whispered.

It worked liked a dream. Marcella showed surprise to see them, Tom begged them to sit down for five minutes. Douglas, the director, who seemed a nice sort of fellow, the only one in the dark about the whole thing, talked easily.

'What are you doing nowadays, Marcella?' Tom asked.

'I hope she'll decorate our television programme as one of the prize-givers,' Douglas said, smiling.

At that point Brenda arrived and congratulated Douglas on having discovered Scarlet Feather, the best-kept catering secret in Ireland. 'Patrick and I always quiver when they come in here. They have such high standards.'

'Tell me, what kind of a dinner party would you cook for eight people?' Douglas began. And they knew it was theirs.

'It's just that we're so busy now, you wouldn't believe it.'

There wasn't a free moment for anyone. The television dinner party was on . . . Tom and Cathy would be in the studio . . . The leaflets were beginning to yield some results.

'I would believe it. I heard Muttie telling Lizzie that, with the amount of hours you're working, the two of you will be in your coffins before St Patrick's Day . . .' Maud said on the telephone.

'He said that?' Tom reached over and grabbed a saucepan just before it began to burn. 'Maud, it is nice to have a chat from time to time, but—'

'We have a day off school on Friday and we wondered could we come and polish your treasures. We want to earn money to buy Muttie a coat.'

'I don't think you'd earn enough in an afternoon, to be honest.' Poor Tom was desperate.

'There's a coat in the thrift shop for three pounds,' said Maud.

'Oh, well then, we'll see you Friday,' Tom said, and hung up.

'Well, come on, take off your hat. Let's see the new you.' Cathy had decided on a new image for the television show tomorrow.

'I look like a ploughboy with a straw in his mouth,' Cathy said.

'I know, you've always looked like that, but let's see your hair.' June was giving no quarter.

Cathy took off her hat.

Tom, June, Lucy and Con looked at her in silence.

'Oh, Jesus, is it as bad as that?'

'You look beautiful,' June said simply.

'Beautiful,' Tom agreed.

Con and Lucy clapped and beat saucepan lids.

'That's enough, I will not be mocked,' she threatened them. But they could see she was pleased, and when she got a chance she went into the cloakroom and looked at it herself. It wasn't at all bad. It was shiny and sort of glamorous. She must send a postcard to Gerard to thank him. Now all she had to do was cook a dinner in front of half a million people.

The day in the studio passed in a horrible blur. Hot lights melted things, the food had to be sprayed with a terrible kind of starchy substance so that it would keep a shine.

Over and over they were told that it didn't *matter* what it tasted like, the audience was not going to eat it, only to see what Tom and Cathy could prepare for the winner. They had to unpack things from refrigerated boxes so that the viewers could imagine them turning up in simple kitchens anywhere in Ireland and producing this gourmet meal. Douglas, the director looked not at all hassled in the studio. Tom and Cathy watched him admiringly; oddly, he seemed equally admiring of them.

'You're naturals,' he said. 'I wouldn't be at all surprised if you are invited back. I bet your guests get well fed in your home,' he said.

They hadn't the energy to disabuse him.

'She's a lovely girl, your friend Marcella, isn't she?' Douglas said.

'Lovely,' Tom said. 'Very special.'

'She's been a friend of ours always,' said Cathy.

And then they were back into countdowns, and settle down studio, and good luck everyone, before they went out live.

The phone hardly stopped ringing the next day. In the front room Lucy sat taking details and sending out brochures. It had brought them right out there into the public eye.

'You'll never be able to thank Marcella enough,' June said.

169

'I'm going to send her a bunch of flowers from all of us,' said Cathy. 'Here's the card, let's all sign it now.'

They let Tom be the last to sign. He wrote: *Marcella, you have been a very generous and good friend, love from Tom.*

Cathy noticed that Lucy was stretching her muscles. 'Here, I'll take over the phone for a while,' she told her.

It was peaceful there in the front room, her punchbowl back on the table, a little Christmas tree in the window. It gave her a chance to think between calls. Last night when she'd arrived home, Neil had been working as usual. He had smiled, glad to see her. And then suddenly a look of guilt came over his face.

'Oh, my God, it was tonight, the television thing.'

'You didn't see it?'

'I'm so sorry . . .'

'Or record it . . .?'

'I can't tell you . . .'

She had gone straight to bed. And she had left this morning before he had got up. Things had never been so bad.

'Mother, did you record Cathy last night on television?'

'No dear, why should I?'

'I just thought you might. Did you see it?'

'Yes, they were surprisingly good, don't you think?'

'Yes, yes, very,' Neil said.

'I'm delighted she finally did something about her hair, I hardly recognised her. I'm glad she finally used that token I gave her, makes a lot of difference, don't you think?'

'Great difference, goodbye, Mother,' Neil said.

'There's nothing I can say except I am so ashamed.'

'It's all right, Neil,' she said wearily, and she actually meant it. It *was* all right. Compared to the much bigger picture, the fact that the programme had slipped his mind was no big deal.

'Look, I know lunch wouldn't make it all right—'

'I don't have time for lunch today, Neil. I'm not being cold, it's just a fact. The phone is jumping off the hook.'

'Congratulations, I'm very proud of you. I'll try to see it today.'

'No, don't, honestly, you're too busy. We'll get a copy of the video from Mam and Dad later on. When will you be home?'

'About seven,' she said. 'But you're going out.'

'I won't tonight,' he promised. 'I'll cancel my meeting.'

Shona Burke was having lunch with James in his flat. They talked about how the television programme could be the turning point for Scarlet Feather.

'If only the insurance would pay up,' James said. 'I don't want to be the spectre at the feast, but it's serious, you know.'

'There's five of them working flat out there today. I called in to congratulate them on my way here . . .'

'What do they think of us going to Morocco for Christmas?'

'I didn't tell them.'

'Why ever not?'

'Well, you're such a private person, I didn't think you'd want them to know . . . about us.'

'I used not to be a private person, Shona, I used to tell everyone everything. I brought your essays to the office to show my colleagues, that's how outgoing I used to be, once.'

'Me too. I just learned to be private. But I suppose we could unlearn it. Will I tell them, or will you?'

'We could even tell them together,' he suggested.

Cathy came in at exactly seven o'clock.

'I have turned the answering machine down, we won't even *hear* anyone if they call.' His infectious smile didn't get a response. 'I got oysters,' he said. 'To try to make amends . . . I don't know how to open them, actually, but I thought you might like . . .'

'To come home from eleven hours in a catering kitchen and open oysters?' she asked.

'No, perhaps not. Not a great idea.'

'It's beyond gestures now, isn't it, Neil?'

'What do you mean . . .?'

'We're much too far apart, there's nothing left.'

'It's a bad patch, certainly. We are missing each other a lot in a way that we never did before, but I *did* say that I was perfectly willing to try for another child.'

'Neil, you can't say you'll "put up" with a baby just to shut me up.'

'I never used those words, nor felt them.'

'You and I used to be able to talk about everything. It was the greatest thing in the world. It's not that we have no time, it's just that we make no time.'

'We can get it back, can't we?' He sounded unsure of himself.

'I don't think so.'

'You're not serious?' he said.

'I am. What you want is a different kind of wife entirely. Someone who idolises you, someone who will stay at home with you and have nice dinner parties for your colleagues. I'm not saying it's wrong to want that, but you don't need someone with a career, you need someone who will give up everything and follow you. I'm not that person, but there are many of them out there. Sara, for example.'

'Sara? What are you talking about? You're not suggesting?'

'I'm just saying she hero-worships you. But that's not the point, that's not what we're talking about.'

'What *are* we talking about?'

'I suppose about what we do now.' She felt exhausted. Somehow, once she had said the words they seemed less frightening. It was out in the open.

'You still care about what I do, the work, don't you?'

'Yes, I do, I really do. But much as I admire you, it seems to me that you bleed for everyone in the world but you can't see the hurts and hopes on your own doorstep.'

'Now that's not really fair, you *said* you supported the same things as I did, then you suddenly went off trying to be the world's biggest caterer. You *said* that you didn't want children, just like me, and then you got pregnant and I was the worst monster in the world because I wasn't suddenly delighted. I said OK, let's have another baby, and apparently that was the worst thing I ever said. So don't throw all the accusations at me. I just won't accept it.'

'What will you accept then?' she asked. 'Are you going to accept that things are very, very bad between us?'

'I can't believe this is happening,' he said, shaking his head. 'This is all brought about by us both working too hard. Cathy, don't let's lose it. Listen, we can start again, leave here, leave all the pressures, start all over. I'll take the job, we can put everything behind us, we'll have space and peace to work everything out, have our baby when we want to. Come to Africa with me, come on, we can make it work.'

'No, Neil.' Suddenly she snapped.

'You're just being stubborn. I'm offering us the chance to save our marriage. We love each other. We're not going to throw it all away just after one bad year are we?'

She said nothing.

'I'll go without you if you won't come. I mean it. I've only been stalling them for you. I don't want to go without you. But this is what I've always wanted. I'm going to go now, before Christmas if I can, and leave it open for you to join me.'

'That's a nonstarter. You can't railroad people into things.'

'Cathy—'
'If you don't mind I won't stay for us both to get more upset.'
'Please don't go,' he begged.
'It's for the best,' said Cathy Scarlet as she packed a bag and left.

Before she lay down on the chintz-covered sofa, she left a message on Tom's phone back at his flat.

'Hope the company doesn't mind. I'm spending a couple of nights on its sofa.'

Then she went to sleep. When she woke to get a drink of water in the night she saw that a fax had arrived. It said simply, 'The company wishes you sweet dreams.'

She had every sign of her overnight stay removed before anyone arrived. And as she had known there wouldn't be, there was no comment from Tom Feather.

'Shona said that she wanted to come and have coffee this morning,' she said. 'James will drop by too, and it won't take long.'

'God, what a morning to choose. We have a team of highly skilled polishers with us today.'

'Oh, yes. Simon and Maud.' She had forgotten.

The twins arrived early. They were wearing their oldest clothes, they said, and could do heavy work. Cathy told them their duties, and stressed the need to keep out of people's way.

'Do we have the relaxing hot drink and a scone like we had before when we came?' Simon wondered.

'Why not?' Cathy said. 'Come on, Tom, let's take five minutes to relax with Maud and Simon.'

The four of them sat in the front room while the twins told them they had shown a video of Cathy and Tom at school. Everyone had loved it, and were very impressed that Cathy was their aunt.

'Do you still have the same code to get in? Nineteen and then six?' Maud asked.

'How on earth did you know that was our code?' Cathy asked, quietly.

'You told us. Remember, one day when you were doing a party, and you told us about the ceremony of the keys.'

Cathy could hardly breathe.

'And did you tell anyone else about it, do you think?'

'I don't think so,' Simon said. 'No point in telling your code to everyone we meet, some of them might be robbers and come in.'

'We did tell Walter that night,' Maud said.

173

'You did?' Tom said, in a deceptively light tone.

'It doesn't matter, does it?' Simon felt uneasy.

'No, it doesn't matter,' Cathy said. 'In fact, it's very good to know that, because a lot of things fall into place.'

'Do you think Walter was your burglar?' Simon asked suddenly.

'I do, yes, Simon.'

'Why?' he asked.

'I don't know, maybe he was short of money.'

'He was always very nice to us, except when we were stupid,' Maud said. 'And he did come to find us that time.'

'I know, of course he did.' They must be allowed to believe that, at least. 'Are you very cross with him?' Maud asked.

'No, not now, but there is something which would help us a lot without getting Walter into any more trouble.'

And in the middle of one of the busiest mornings that Scarlet Feather had ever known, hours were spent while Maud and Simon Mitchell told James Byrne, then the guards and then an insurance official about the night they had wanted to prove to their brother that they knew all about the business. And everyone softened at the obviously true story and the mixed feelings about their big brother.

'It's going to help a great deal, believe me,' James said.

'What were you going to tell us, Shona?' Cathy asked. 'Hold on a minute. Simon, Maud, could you go down to the newsagent, it's at the end of the street, and buy me an *Irish Times*?'

When they were gone, Shona spoke immediately. 'When I was young I was fostered with James and his wife Una in Galway, but I was taken away and brought back to my own home when I was fourteen. We've only just got to know each other again.'

James spoke in a different voice than usual. 'We were told it was for the best that we didn't make contact. I didn't question it; that's what I blame myself for, letting the child we loved go away without begging to have her back.'

'So now we're making up for lost time, meal after gourmet meal . . .' She laughed with the teachers who had taught her lost father to cook.

'And we're going to go away together for a three-week holiday,' James said proudly.

Tom blew his nose loudly. 'If I hadn't another ten hours' work ahead of me today. I'd say that we all went out and got drunk on this.'

'In the New Year,' promised James. 'You come round to my flat, I'll cook a Moroccan speciality for you.'

'Mam, can I have my Christmas dinner here?' Cathy asked.

'Well, of course you can, but I thought the pair of you were going to Oaklands.'

'Neil is, Mam, I'm not.'

'Ah, now, don't tell me you've fought with Mrs Mitchell again.'

'Mam, sit down, I have to tell you something,' Cathy said.

It wasn't really all that much easier to talk in the daylight, but they managed a very creditable performance between them. They spent a few hours sitting peacefully in Waterview and made a list of who would take what.

'Stay here, if you won't come with me. It's your home.'

'It never felt like home. It's too minimalist.' She smiled ruefully when she said it, and so did he.

They decided to put the house on the market in January. Neil said that there would be no problem in putting his share of the furniture in a warehouse. Cathy said she would have found somewhere to stay by then. For the next three weeks she was minding Shona Burke's Glenstar apartment. 'The one thing we should really do together is go to see your parents. We owe it to them,' Cathy said. 'I'd really like to go tomorrow evening, about six.'

'That's fine for me. I will be there, I promise,' he said.

But of course he wasn't. At five, she got a call to say that his meeting was going on.

'We can't have them sitting there wondering what it is,' she said.

'You don't have to go today, you can wait until I'm able to come with you.'

She hung up. She saw Tom looking at her.

'Thanks,' she said. 'For not asking.'

'Ah, Cathy, a drink?'

'Yes, please, Jock, a small brandy would be nice.'

'And is Neil not with you?'

'No, you know the way he always gets tied up at things. Well, today, there's a meeting and he sent his apologies.'

Hannah rushed to defend him. 'He has so many responsibilities, he couldn't drop them for a social call.'

'It's more than a social call, Hannah. We had something to tell you, but now I'll tell you myself.'

Jock looked alarmed. 'Nothing wrong, is there?' he asked.

Hannah's hand went to her throat. 'I know, you've come to tell me that you and Neil are going to have a baby!'

On Christmas Eve they opened a bottle of champagne at the Scarlet Feather premises. And then another. It was a celebration.

The insurance had paid up and they had been booked to do another television show. Between them they had worked all day and all evening for twenty-four days. So they deserved a party.

They were all off now until New Year's Day, when there was a big lunch and the team would gather again, but the main thing they were celebrating was that they had refused eleven bookings on New Year's Eve. They wanted to consider it an anniversary . . . one whole year since they had found the premises. Everyone went home. Tom and Cathy insisted that they do the clearing up.

'It's only putting things in a machine. Don't our arms do that automatically?' Tom said.

Muttie and Lizzie had come with the twins.

'Have you got a present for Hooves?' Maud asked Cathy.

'Would I forget Hooves?' asked Cathy, who had.

'I didn't see it under the tree,' Simon said.

'That's because he might have smelt it,' Tom intervened.

'She's got him a *bone*!' Simon said, excited.

'Or something in that area,' Cathy said.

They went off down the lane from the premises arm in arm with Lizzie. Tom and Cathy waved them goodbye.

'Get me something out of the freezer for Hooves, for God's sake. You're an utter genius, did you know that?' Cathy said.

'I could thaw a fillet steak if you like,' he suggested. 'We froze them in threes, remember.'

'What will we do with the other two?'

'Well, I might eat one myself, I'm not going anywhere,' Tom Feather said.

'Neither am I,' said Cathy Scarlet.

The day passed as Christmas Day passes for so many people, in a sea of paper and presents and fuss about cooking.

Neil had an awkward lunch at Oaklands, where nobody was able to talk about the situation. It seemed very artificial.

Muttie was delighted with his new red overcoat and said he would wear it everywhere. Including tomorrow, when they watched the races on television. He had the accumulator of a lifetime on: everything he won on the first race through the card. It could be millions.

Simon and Maud planned spending the millions. They would get their mother a dressing gown like another lady had in the nursing home. Mother hadn't known it was Christmas Day. It had been a bit sad, but

Lizzie had said that the poor lady was quite happy. Father had sent them five pounds to buy gifts, and Walter had sent them marvellous watches.

Cathy was smiling a lot, even when there was nothing particular to smile at. They had been warned by everyone to be particularly nice to her but she hadn't been cranky at all. It was a mystery.

The next day, Muttie's first horse won and so did his second. They were all standing behind his chair watching the television, willing the horses to win for him. When the third horse won they all began to get chest pains. Geraldine's face was contorted by the time the chosen horse started to pull away from the rest in the fourth race.

'I didn't know the meaning of the word stress until this moment.'

Lizzie said over and over that he should have done the races individually, then they'd have been fine. *Why* had he to do it this way and give them all heart failure? Muttie said he had been studying form seriously. This time he really knew what he was doing. The phone rang just as the fourth horse won. Tom answered it. It was Marian from Chicago. He spoke in clipped tones.

'Marian, no one in this house is able to speak now, we'll call you back.'

During the fifth race he had his arm so tightly round Cathy's neck she thought she was going to choke. When it won, they all leaped up and hugged each other; only one race to go.

Lizzie said, 'I can't believe this is happening.' Tom got Muttie a glass of water, he got Geraldine a whiskey. Muttie's face was ashen, it was within his grasp. Tom and Cathy clutched each other's hands like people on a life raft. The horse was in the last three. One of the others fell.

'I can't *bear* it,' screamed Geraldine.

'Come on, Muttie, come on, Muttie,' shouted the twins. Lizzie had her eyes closed, so she didn't see Muttie's horse come in at thirteen to one.

'That's a hundred and thirty thousand pounds, not bad for a day's work,' said Muttie with a beatific smile on his face.

Tom said he'd drive Cathy back to Shona's apartment in Glenstar.

Just before the turn to Glenstar, Tom said, 'You know we never had any Christmas cake tonight.'

'After all the trouble we took icing it,' Cathy said.

'We could drop by the premises and have tea and a slice of cake there?'

She thought it was a great idea. Neither of them wanted to go home to empty flats, but it hadn't been their custom to invite the other in at night. The premises had always been neutral ground.

They settled into the front room, drank their tea, and talked about Muttie's win.

'We can't take any of his money though,' Tom said.

'We can let him invest,' Cathy said. 'At least that way it's here, rather than in Sandy's hot little hand.'

'I do wonder which is the sounder investment,' Tom said.

'Stop that at once, Tom Feather. We won. We've had a hard year, but in terms of the business, anyway, we won, didn't we?'

'Sure we did. We did win in the end.'

The phone rang.

'Leave it,' Cathy said.

They listened as the twins spoke. They were thanking them for the best Christmas ever. It had been pure magic, they said. And Lizzie had said they could stay up until they were so tired that they fell down.

Tom and Cathy sat side by side on the sofa and listened while the twins talked on. They moved very slightly closer to each other and realised that they were holding hands. It seemed very natural so neither of them moved away.

'Good night, Tom. Good night, Cathy,' the twins said eventually.

'They knew we were here,' Cathy said in surprise.

'Imagine,' said Tom Feather as he stroked her hair.

MAEVE BINCHY

Maeve Binchy was born in Dalkey, a small village outside Dublin, and was educated at the Holy Child Convent in Killiney and at University College Dublin. After a spell as a teacher in various girls' schools, she joined the *Irish Times*, for which she still writes occasional columns. She wrote her first novel, *Light a Penny Candle*, in 1982 and since then she has written more than a dozen novels and short story collections, each one of them a best seller. Several have been adapted for cinema and television, most notably *Circle of Friends* in 1995, which starred Minnie Driver and Chris O'Donnell.

When asked in an interview whether fame and popularity has changed her life, Maeve Binchy answered with characteristic modesty: 'I was forty-three years old when I became a best-selling author. I was already happy then, married to a man I love, the writer Gordon Snell. We had a very good life with not quite enough money to pay the bills. But we didn't buy a new house, we just did up the old one and made it more comfortable, and it's wonderful not to have to worry about providing for our old age any more.'

Sadly for her fans, Maeve Binchy has decided to retire, having reached the age of sixty, and *Scarlet Feather* will be her last novel. 'I'm not going to be like Frank Sinatra with lots of farewell concerts. This will be the one and only farewell,' she says. 'I thought I should stop it while I still had a pulse and was able to get on with things. I've seen too many writers caught up in the treadmill of writing books for the mass market who grow old and crotchety having to deliver so many words every two years and then tramp around the world promoting them.'

Although Maeve Binchy has given up writing her blockbuster novels, she has not ruled out an occasional return to writing on a smaller scale. 'The experts all advise against ever shutting any door too firmly if you can manage it,' she said. 'So the occasional article or short story from time to time would be lovely. I do not believe those who say I will regret it. I do not believe that people get sluggish and brain dead and go round in their dressing gowns when they retire. I think they get better.'

Much of Maeve Binchy's success as a writer has hinged on her extraordinary ability to capture the hopes and fears of ordinary people. Now, in her retirement, she plans to turn her back on the hurly-burly of a best-selling author's life in the limelight and sample, once again, the simple delights of an ordinary existence, such as those of the people that she has depicted in her novels for so many years. We wish her the best of luck.

Jane Eastgate

Susan Lewis

CRUEL VENUS

Tessa Dukes adores her job as PA
to television chat-show hostess Allyson
Jaymes. In fact, her burning desire
is to be just like Allyson—famous and
successful and loved by everyone.
But as her ambition grows, she finds
herself drawn into a fatal minefield of
sexual obsession and psychotic jealousy
that threatens to destroy the lives
of the only people to have shown
her any real kindness.

Chapter One

'IS IT TRUE? Are you sleeping with her?'

The sound of him crunching into his toast followed her question. Then he turned a page of the newspaper to pick up the last part of a story in the sports section.

She didn't look up either, simply continued to gaze at the paper as though absorbed. The question hung in the air with the smell of coffee and the warmth of the heating. She wondered how many women knew what it was like to pick up a paper and read, along with the rest of the world, that your husband was having an affair. She imagined every woman knew exactly what she'd do; she'd always known too, until now.

It was Sunday morning, and the autumn sunlight pinged off the china on the kitchen table. In front of her was one of the more scurrilous tabloids bearing the front-page headline 'Bob's Secret Love'. Not a particularly imaginative headline, but it was a great picture. No surprise there, he was a good-looking man. Had quite a fan club now, especially here, in the village, where they spent most weekends.

Allyson wasn't a lover of sports; couldn't stand football, hated cricket, detested rugby. It had never come between them though; he had his job as a freelance commentator on TV sports, she had hers, hosting *Soirée*, a nightly magazine show. Allyson and Bob Jaymes. They'd been together since their early twenties, had fervently supported each other's careers, and now they were a pretty famous couple. They went to all the right parties, were invited to all the first nights, all the benefits, balls and winter ski trips. They entertained regularly, both here at their farmhouse, and at their London flat. Their lives could easily be described as blessed, though of course they weren't without their problems, but

183

whoever heard of anyone sailing through eighteen years of marriage without problems? Not having children helped, but testing though they were, children were by no means the only cause of marital unrest.

To remain childless was a decision they'd made early on in their relationship, though lately they'd been talking about reversing it and taking the plunge into parenthood. In fact, now she was used to the idea Allyson had to confess she wanted it much more than she'd realised.

Her dark blue eyes scanned the story again. That Bob was being accused of having an affair with Tessa Dukes wasn't something she could allow herself to take in when it was so patently absurd. No, the Sunday papers generally yielded up material worth pursuing for the show, which was why she read them, and it had to be said that this story definitely didn't make the grade. The problem was, was there, and false though it had to be, *please God!* it couldn't be ignored.

Putting the paper down she refilled her cup with lukewarm coffee. She loved this farmhouse kitchen with its handcrafted cabinets, rows of copper pots and arrangements of dried herbs. The view, down over the valley to the village, was spectacular today. The seasonal shift in colours spread over the hillside like a busy artist's palette, and the sky was so clear, just one small mass of fluffy white cloud.

'I think you heard my question,' she said, feeling an odd reluctance in her legs as she got up to make more coffee.

He glanced at the paper and laughed. 'You're taking that seriously?' he said, his amazement sounding comfortingly genuine.

'Are you telling me I don't need to?' she responded.

'Oh, come on, Ally,' he said, 'you know what the tabloids are like. No one ever believes the *News of the World*, so why don't we just let this go?'

'So you don't care what they're printing about you? Or about Tessa Dukes, my *nineteen*-year-old assistant?'

'Why the hell would I care what they're printing about her? I barely even know the girl.'

'So how come they've got a shot of you coming out of her flat?'

Bob turned the paper round and frowned as he looked at the front page. 'You know where that is,' he said, finally. 'It's the building Danny Jacobs just moved into. In Peckham. He's one of the producers at the Beeb, in case you'd forgotten. His flat's on the second floor. You can check easily enough.'

'I know who he is,' Allyson snapped, though relief was starting to release the tension inside her. After all, the tabloids were well known to fabricate scandal in order to increase sales, and she and Bob were nothing if not prime targets. Indeed, all that was really surprising about this was that they had never been targeted before.

He really was handsome, she was thinking, with his large grey eyes, round, rugged face and quirky mouth. He might not be in quite as good shape now as when they'd first met, but who was, twenty years down the line? Allyson couldn't imagine any amount of passing years diminishing the incredible warmth of his character, or the magical intensity of his laughter-lined eyes. Funny, when you'd been married a long time, how you forgot to notice those things. They were just there, like the monthly bills and pile-up of laundry. More diverting of course, but just as constant—except for the times when crises hit. But those times weren't often and when compared to the disasters some couples suffered, Bob's occasional problem with drink and erratic struggles with self-esteem were really very minor. Sometimes he seemed to resent the fact that she came from an established and wealthy family, and had had many of the advantages that weren't available to someone like him. Which was nonsense, of course, because his working-class origins had, if anything, broadened his social skills to a degree many people from her kind of background never got to achieve, and had propelled him into a prominent and highly paid career.

However, it wasn't often that cracks appeared in the famous Bob Jaymes charm, and when they did, she was never backward in reminding him that his inferiority was a product of his own addled mind, and of how incredibly fortunate, and talented, he was. For she knew him to be a deeply caring and sensitive man, with the kind of allure that was extremely appealing to the opposite sex, especially those who were impressed by fame—and plenty were. However, she had long since overcome her insecurity where other women were concerned, for though Bob could be an outrageous flirt, their marriage had never suffered anything even approaching a crisis on that front.

No, they were too much a part of each other now to be torn apart. All right, she was just a teensy bit bored, sleeping with the same partner all these years. Not that he didn't do it for her any more. He just didn't do it so often, or quite so explosively, as he had during the early years. But she truly didn't harbour any desire to engage in sex with anyone else.

As though sensing some of the turmoil going on in her head, he looked up. For a long moment his eyes locked with hers, then leaning forward he cupped her chin in his hand and kissed her softly on the lips. 'It's not true,' he said gently.

She forced a smile, and as she waited for a renewed buoyancy in her spirits, he lifted her feet onto his lap and began to massage them. After a while he turned back to the paper, though he continued to toy with her toes. She watched his hands and wondered if they were hands that had recently caressed the teenage Tessa. The young beauty who Allyson, herself, was grooming for bigger and better things. The question lodged with immense weight in her heart, seeming to depress the beat.

She reached for the *Observer,* and as she started to read about the upcoming American presidential elections she heard the crunch of Sid Carter's milk float on the gravel outside. She padded down the hall to the front door. 'Hello, Sid,' she called, her breath visible in the crisp morning air.

'Hello,' he said gloomily. Sid was always gloomy. 'How many pints?'

'Two, same as usual,' she said. 'And three sliced loaves. We've got the kids from Hobert Hall coming over this afternoon for the cricket match.'

'Your husband there, is he?' Sid asked, in his gruff West Country burr.

'Of course he is,' Allyson replied. 'Where did you expect him to be?'

It wasn't in Sid to look uncomfortable. 'Well, after what we read in the paper this morning,' he said, 'Elsie reckoned you'd kick the bugger out.'

'Come on, Sid,' she chided, 'you know better than to believe what you read in the papers, especially that kind of paper.'

'No smoke without fire, is what I say,' he muttered, and trundled back to the milk float. As she waited she waved to Mrs Briggs, who was walking past the end of the drive with her dog.

'Everything all right, dear?' Mrs Briggs called out. 'Anything I can do?'

'Everything's fine, thanks,' Allyson called back. 'Are you still coming this afternoon to help with the kids?'

'Of course. Still going ahead with it then?'

Allyson hid a momentary irritation. 'I wouldn't want to let them down. Nor would Bob.'

Mrs Briggs only nodded, but Allyson could see she too was surprised to hear that Bob was around.

'Here,' Sid said, thrusting two hand-labelled jars at her. 'Lemon curd. For the kids. Elsie's coming up later with a couple of jam tarts.'

'Thanks, Sid,' she said. 'See you later, if you're coming.'

She waited for him to turn his float round, milk bottles jangling, then turned back inside and closed the door.

She could hear Bob moving about upstairs; the howl and thud of the pipes as he turned on the shower, the hiss and whine of the radio as he searched out a sports station. It was so normal it almost made her shudder, for it made her think of some dreadful sci-fi movie she'd once seen, where the world was going about its day in blissful ignorance of the asteroid that was about to smash it into oblivion. But likening Tessa Dukes to an asteroid was a touch melodramatic; after all, all that had happened was that Bob had been photographed coming out of Danny Jacobs's building, which could be the same building Tessa lived in. Tessa, of whom she was so exceptionally fond. Tessa, the intriguing young girl who'd made Allyson's life so much easier since she'd joined the team. Intriguing, because the girl almost never talked about herself except in the most general terms, was clearly nervous of strangers and had a way of looking at a person as though he or she might prove the hidden key to a mystery. From her much-vaunted work with abused and abandoned children Allyson knew the signs when she saw them, though Tessa didn't strike her in any way as a severely damaged victim, more an extremely bright young girl who might have had to fight an overbearing father for the freedom to shine. Allyson had interviewed more than two dozen candidates for the position of her PA, but she'd known immediately Tessa had walked in the door that here was the assistant she wanted. The dark-eyed Tessa with her shaggy black hair and rosy red cheeks not only exuded intelligence and ambition, she also radiated a clear need to feel she belonged somewhere, which, for someone like Allyson, was an irresistible quality. And not once in the four months Tessa had been with her had Allyson experienced a single moment of doubt over her decision.

Going back to the kitchen she began putting away her groceries and wondering why the phone hadn't rung. True, her parents would never read the *News of the World*, nor would most of her friends, but someone had to know about the 'exclusive' by now. So why hadn't anyone called?

Allyson cleared the table, loaded the dishwasher, then went upstairs.

'Don't you think it's odd there's no press outside?' she remarked to Bob as he stepped out of the shower. She squeezed a line of toothpaste onto her brush and began to clean her teeth.

'Thank God there isn't. Anyway they probably know by now that the *News of the World* got it wrong,' he said, reaching for a can of talc from the antique brass-framed cabinet above the bath.

Loving him for being so unruffled by it all, Allyson went and put her arms round him. He smiled, giving life to the roguish grin she adored. 'You really did take it seriously, didn't you?' he teased.

'No,' she denied. Then, 'OK, perhaps I did, a bit. She's a pretty girl, and the men in the office are all crazy about her.'

Bob grimaced. 'What's the matter with them, looking at her when you're around?'

'She's twenty years younger, and available,' she said, putting her lips very close to his.

He kissed her, then looked into her face, and she wondered if he

SUSAN LEWIS

meant it when he told her she was even more beautiful now than when he'd first met her. She couldn't really be considered a beauty, but she certainly felt more attractive now.

'If it were anyone but Vic Stafford you were going to see,' she said after he kissed her again, 'I'd insist you be late. But Vic won't stand for it.'

'We can always catch up with this later,' he said, smiling into her eyes. 'After the cricket match.'

'If we've still got the energy.'

She moved away and slipped out of her pyjamas.

'OK, I'm off,' Bob said, putting his head round the door, some ten minutes later. 'I'll get the bus from Vic, then go over to the station to pick up whoever's coming. What time does the London train get in?'

'Half past twelve. Take them all straight to the pub. I'll meet you there. I'm going to make a start on the sandwiches, then I'll pop over to the Hall to check how many kids are coming.'

It was only when he'd gone that Allyson remembered Tessa was due to arrive on the train. Her heart reacted with a disturbing lurch as she wondered what it would be like for them, having to face each other after that morning's story. She pictured them meeting, awkwardly, trying to laugh off the absurdity of their rumoured affair. *But maybe it wasn't a rumour! Maybe they were desperately in love.*

No! No, they weren't.

Shelley would be on the train too. Shelley Bronson was *Soirée's* editor and senior producer. She was also Allyson's closest friend. She wondered why Shelley hadn't called. Everyone else on the train would have read the paper—the premier-league footballers, the soap stars and the children's TV presenters Bob had roped into the kids'–celebrity cricket match in the field next to their house. The children at the Hall, who all had Down's syndrome, were already so excited that Mrs Gore was having trouble keeping them calm. Time to concentrate on them now, and abandon this ludicrous mind-trip to the brink of disaster.

She was on her way out of the house when the telephone finally rang.

'Darling, I've just been informed of that nonsense in the *News of the World*. I imagine Bob's going to sue.'

'Hello, Mother. He hasn't mentioned suing, but it could be an option. How's Daddy?'

'He's right here. I called Uncle Cecil and he gave me the number of a good lawyer. Apparently the man has a good record of winning libel cases. You could donate your compensation to one of your charities.'

'Good idea.' Allyson smiled. 'I'm glad you're so convinced it isn't true.'

'Preposterous, darling. Bob would never dream of being unfaithful, any more than you would. Sorry we can't make the match, but we'll be sending a donation. Bye, darling. I'll hand you over to Daddy.'

Her father's voice came on the line. 'Hello? Who's that?'

'Hello, Daddy. It's me. Allyson.'

'Who?'

'How are you feeling today?'

'This is Howard Butler-Blythe speaking. Identify yourself, please.'

'Bye, Daddy. Love you.'

She rang off, feeling a sharper edge to the sadness of her father's fading mind than she usually did. She missed him so terribly, and how hard this had to be for her mother.

Having put on the answering machine, she managed to escape the house before being intercepted by any more calls.

Bob was sitting in the driver's seat of the bus he'd collected half an hour ago. Now, with time to spare before he was due at the station, he'd pulled into this hidden little picnic glade and parked.

It was starting to warm up outside. There was no wind, and the occasional leaf that fell from the densely clustered trees merely wafted to the ground in its own lightness of being. His eyes were transfixed by Tessa as she came towards the bus, her short, shaggy black hair and deeply flushed cheeks making her seem even younger than she actually was. She wasn't tall; her body was plump and soft, like an overripe melon; her normally timid eyes were glittering now with a light that cut right through him. The smile on her full, sulky lips quivered with a lethal mix of modesty and mischief.

By the time she reached the bus his pulses were thick and throbbing. He watched her come up the steps, knowing that beneath her long dark winter coat she wore nothing more than a pair of black vinyl thigh-high boots. Her eyes were on his as she stopped in front of him and allowed him to open the coat. As he pulled it apart desire cut through him in a long, painful groove. Her breasts were fleshy and round, their nipples blood red and hard from the cold.

Getting up from his seat he lifted her mouth to his. She tasted of peppermint and coffee. Her skin, beneath his fingers, was as soft as a baby's. He pulled it, pushed it and squeezed it, while feeling himself swimming in the vortex of emotions she aroused in him, the agonising desire to love her, the fear of its intensity, the horror of its consequence. 'Did you see the paper?' he said gruffly.

'Yes,' she answered.

Her black eyes were fringed with long, dense lashes, her pale skin was blotched with patches of red. He looked at her and felt a thousand knots twist around his heart. He knew he should say more, but he had no idea what to say. All he knew was the glowing allure of her face, the tender trust in her eyes and the enslaving beauty of her body. His need for her was like a silently raging tide, way beyond reason.

Turning her round, he steered her to the back of the bus then stopped and removed her coat. His hands moved to her breasts as he pulled her back against his chest. Then he whispered in her ear what he wanted her to do. Without hesitation she pushed him down on the seat and sat astride him, moving with electrifying vigour, her breasts quivering and bouncing, her black eyes watching him closely. He looked back, feeling the slap of her buttocks on his thighs, and making her pant and groan until their bodies were thrown into the tumultuous sensations of climax.

In all his life he had never known a woman like this. A woman who was no more than a girl, and who was now as consumed by him as he was by her.

'Don't tell me, you've got to go!' She pouted as he gently withdrew.

He looked at his watch. 'I'm due at the station in ten minutes.'

She climbed off his lap and sat beside him, entwining her hand in his. 'How did Allyson react to the paper?' she asked.

He looked at her and wondered what she was really thinking, for everyone knew how devoted she was to Allyson, who had plucked her from some Allyson-imagined hell and was now turning her into a rising star. It hadn't stopped her falling for Allyson's husband though, had it? Nor had it stopped Allyson's husband falling for her. 'I'm not sure,' he said. 'She was prepared to believe it.'

'But you told her it wasn't true.' Her big eyes looked up at his, her kiss-reddened lips were apart and inviting.

Unable to stop himself he kissed them, for a deliciously long time. 'I sidestepped it,' he said finally.

'But you're going to tell her?'

A stab of guilt penetrated his chest, stopping his breath. He looked away. Yes, he'd tell Allyson, if it was the only way to keep this girl.

Tessa's eyes went down. 'I don't think you should,' she whispered.

He was surprised, and relieved. 'I thought it was what you wanted?'

'What I want is *you*,' she cried earnestly. 'Not to hurt Ally. I really like her. A part of me actually loves her, you know, like a sister or something.' She covered her face with her hands. 'God, I hate doing this to her. I hate you for making me.'

'Hey, no one's making you,' he said gently. 'Remember it was your idea to drive down last night and stay in a hotel. Your idea for us to meet here, before I go to the station.'

'You don't get what I'm saying,' she protested. 'I mean, you make me because I can't resist you. Because there's something in me that has to do whatever you want me to do.' She was suddenly very young and confused. 'It's weird. I've never felt anything like it before.'

Two tears trickled down her cheeks. He caught them with his fingers, tilted her mouth up to his and kissed her. 'Come on, I'll walk you back to your car,' he said.

Her Beetle was parked further down the track. They walked hand in hand, through the misty bands of sparkling autumnal sunlight, her coat wrapped warmly around her naked body. 'What's going to happen?' she said, stopping to look up at him as they reached her car.

'I don't know.' He leaned forward and kissed her lingeringly.

'I'll drive straight to the house,' she said, 'as though I've come from London. See you there?'

'We're meeting at the pub,' he told her. Then looking anxiously into her eyes he said, 'This afternoon's going to be tough, for us both. Do you think you can handle it?'

'It'll be tough for Ally too, after the papers.'

He glanced away for a moment, looking back along the hazy, glistening track as though he were looking back at his life. Allyson, his wife, the only woman he had truly loved—until now. How could he do this to her? What the hell was he thinking?

He turned back to Tessa, then putting a hand behind her head he pulled her mouth hard against his, defiance and anger pushing aside the savage onslaught of guilt.

Chapter Two

THE BELL OVER THE PUB DOOR clanged as Allyson walked in, a mobile phone pressed to one ear. She was wearing tight black jeans, snug little ankle boots and a thick cable-knit sweater that seemed to engulf her petite frame. Her sleek blonde hair was swept casually to one side, her neat, attractive features were lightly made up and currently drawn in a frown. 'Can't you just tell her to go to hell?' she grumbled.

At the other end of the line Shelley sighed. 'Wouldn't I love to,' she replied. 'But I'll have to go and find out what the old witch wants.'

Allyson knew that their illustrious programme controller, Stella Cornbright, was unlikely to be summoning Shelley to her home on a Sunday afternoon for tea. Whatever it was, it had to be serious. 'Do you think it's got something to do with what was in the paper this morning?' she asked, keeping her voice low as she dumped her heavy bag on a tapestry-covered stool and sat down on a comfy bench seat.

'No,' Shelley answered, her tone indicating that she'd been expecting the question. 'If it were, it would be you she wanted to see, not me.'

Allyson waited. Shelley said no more.

'Is that it?' Allyson said tightly. 'You obviously know what I'm talking about, so don't you have something to say?'

'Not right now,' Shelley answered. 'What did Bob say?'

'Not much. Except that Dan Jacobs probably lives in the same building as Tessa. If not, the same street.'

'How very convenient.'

Allyson's face darkened as her heart thudded an extra beat. 'I'm not sure I like the sound of that. Don't you believe him?'

'Do you?'

'Why shouldn't I?' she replied. 'Oh God, Tessa's car just pulled into the car park. She must have driven down instead of getting the train.'

'Bet you're looking forward to seeing her,' Shelley remarked drily.

Allyson couldn't help smiling, for she could easily imagine the droll expression on Shelley's beautiful face. 'Even more than you're looking forward to seeing Stella,' she responded.

'Are you going to fire her?'

Allyson laughed. 'Who, Tessa? Not today,' she answered. 'I need to keep a perspective on this, because there's a huge chance the *News of the World* have got it wrong. You know what they're like. Oh shit, I wish you were going to be here. This thing has really thrown me. And here comes *Soirée*'s answer to Christina Ricci, looking like she's just been screwed all the way to senselessness and back.'

'Goodness me, that can't be darling, brilliant, got-to-be-rescued little Tessa you're talking about, can it?' Shelley teased. 'God, she makes me feel old. I could forgive her for a lot, but definitely not that.'

Tessa was hovering uncertainly and, because Allyson was still laughing at what Shelley had just said, it was easy to smile as she waved the girl over. 'Give me a call later and let me know what Stella wants,' she said to Shelley, and put away her phone. She forced another smile as she looked at Tessa. God, this was difficult. What was she supposed to say to a girl who was rumoured to be having an affair with her husband? 'So how does it feel to be famous?' she said, making an attempt at levity.

Tessa took off her coat and sat down. 'Given the choice, I wouldn't have gone for it this way,' she replied, trying to match Allyson's wryness.

Allyson laughed. 'No, I suppose not. But as long as it's not true we'll just have to wait for the fuss to die down, then put it all behind us.'

Tessa's eyes were disconcerting in their frank, searching efforts to gauge what Allyson was really thinking. 'Oh, it's not true,' Tessa assured her.

Allyson smiled warmly, and could have hugged her for sounding so convincing. 'What'll you have to drink?' she said.

'Whatever you're having.'

'Ron,' Allyson said, as the thickly bearded landlord emerged from the kitchen. 'Come and meet my assistant, Tessa Dukes.'

Ron's small, watery eyes rounded with amazement, leaving Allyson in no doubt which Sunday tabloid the paper boy tossed over his garden gate. 'Your . . .?' He looked at Tessa and his normally florid complexion deepened to scarlet. 'Tessa,' he said. 'Nice to meet you.' He glanced at Allyson, as though seeking assurance that it was all right to say that.

Allyson's expression was friendly.

Ron looked at Tessa again. Tessa was smiling, shyly, the way she always did with strangers, especially men, and Allyson watched the cordiality of Ron's smile start yielding to a bemusing haze of unexpected attraction. The girl's appeal was very definitely of the Lolita variety, for there she sat, looking no more than sixteen, skirt barely covering her buttocks, boots tugged up over her knees, and the exposed flesh of her thighs looking as succulent as cake. And as for the big bra-less breasts that were amply evident beneath her tight-fitting light blue sweater, it was enough to make Allyson want to stuff the girl in a sack and smuggle her out of sight for her own protection.

'We'll have two lagers and lime,' Allyson said to Ron. 'I'm reckoning on us being around fourteen for lunch.'

'Roast beef today,' Ron told her, dragging his eyes from Tessa.

'Roast potatoes?'

'Of course. Wouldn't be a Sunday dinner without roasters, would it? And Wanda's doing her home-baked apple crumble and ice cream for pudding. Says Bob called her up and asked special.'

Allyson laughed. 'She spoils him.'

'Well, it's a bit of a favourite with everyone round here,' he said. 'Hope you're going to have some, young lady,' he said to Tessa. 'Can't be doing with all you London types who won't eat a square meal.'

'Oh, I can't pass up on Wanda's legendary crumble,' Tessa responded, peering at him bravely from under her lashes.

Allyson's smile lost some warmth. How did she know the crumble was legendary? Who, except Bob, could have told her? No! No! She'd just said it to be polite.

The pub door opened and a few more locals came in. Then Bob arrived from the station with a busload of celebrities and the small, oak-beamed bar was soon full to overflowing. Allyson watched him as he ordered pints and vodka martinis for their party, then swung behind the counter to mix the martinis himself, while Ron and his two barmen manned the pumps. Allyson's second martini got her joining in with the loud and lively chat that was erupting all around her. Wanda and her waitresses bustled in and out of the tables, taking orders and delivering mouth-watering lunches.

Later, after downing her third martini, Allyson got involved in a rowdy game of darts with two of the footballers. Bob, she noticed, was engaged in some hot dispute with the farmer, Jack Turner. Tessa was listening to the hilariously tall tales being bandied about by a noisy group of locals, where the men involved appeared as keen to make her laugh as they were to ogle the jostling breasts under her tight blue sweater.

It had never been clear if anyone in the village ate Sunday lunch at home, certainly they were all in the pub by one, and no one ever left much before three. Reverend Beesely and his wife Mary were usually the last to go. Today, though, it seemed that the celebrities would be the last out, and, laughing as Bob slipped an arm round her shoulders, Allyson wondered what kind of event the cricket match was going to turn into.

'I'm just off to pick up the kids,' Bob shouted in her ear. 'We should be back at the house by three thirty.'

'How much have you had to drink?' she shouted back.

'Half of bitter,' he answered, giving her a wink, then catching her as she wobbled. 'How much have you had?'

'I stopped counting after three. By the way, can you remember where it was that you and Tessa met?'

Bob looked across the bar to where Tessa was now talking to a couple of the soap stars. 'You know, I'm not even sure that we have,' he said. 'Which one is she? The one over there with Mandy and Frank?'

Allyson knew the devilish spirit of drink was goading her, but she was too far gone to smother it. 'Come on, I'll introduce you,' she said, grabbing his hand. 'She's a great assistant, did I ever tell you that?'

'Yeah, you told me,' he answered, following on behind.

Looking back over her shoulder she gave him a saucy wink and said, 'What's she like in bed? Is she great there too?'

Bob's insides churned, for the tease had barbs and he knew it. Deciding to keep it all on the surface, he said, 'Oh, she's the best. Just the best.'

Though Allyson's heart did a sickening dive, she continued to smile, telling herself that a hot denial might well have been far greater cause for worry. 'Tessa!' she cried. 'I want you to meet Bob.'

Tessa turned round, flushed and sparkling, but her smile was already fading as unease clouded her eyes.

'This is Bob!' Allyson declared. 'Apparently, you're having an affair with him!'

Bob took Allyson's arm and tried to pull her aside. 'The joke's gone far enough,' he said. 'You're embarrassing the girl.'

'No, I'm not. Am I embarrassing you?' she demanded of Tessa.

Those nearby had stopped to listen. 'So you live in the same building as Bob's producer,' Allyson affirmed, slurring slightly. 'Did you hear that, everyone? Just because Tessa here lives in the same building as Bob's producer she's supposed to be having an affair with him. What a joke!'

There was some uneasy laughter as again Bob tried to pull her away.

'No, don't,' she said, shrugging him off. 'I'm just telling everyone that you and Tessa have never really met before today, but you're still supposed to be having an affair. Crazy, isn't it?' she said to Mary Beesely, the vicar's wife. She turned to Tessa and put an arm round her. 'This is my Tessa. She's the best assistant I've ever had. And she's not, I repeat not, having an affair with my husband. Are you?'

Tessa's voice was small as she said, 'No.'

'You see,' Allyson shouted. 'She's not. And just for the record, Bob and I are more in love than we've ever been, and if things work out, we're going to be starting a family. Aren't we, Bob?'

Laughing, Bob pulled her into his arms. 'That's enough now,' he whispered. 'You've made your point. I'm going to get the kids.'

'But you didn't even say hello to Tessa!' Allyson objected. 'Tell you what,' she cried. 'Why don't you take Tessa to get the kids? Then you can actually get to know one another.'

Tessa was looking more miserable by the minute. 'Ally, let's leave it now,' Bob said shortly. 'I'll see you in half an hour, back at the house.'

As he walked away he took Wanda to one side. 'Give her some coffee,' he said. 'She's never been able to handle martinis.'

'Leave her to me,' Wanda said. 'I'll have her sober in no time. What about the lass? She looks a bit lost, standing there like that.'

Bob turned round. Allyson had now moved into the centre of another crowd, leaving Tessa standing alone. Her head was bowed and Bob ached to take her in his arms and soothe away the pain. 'You know what, I think I'll take her with me,' he said.

Wanda watched in confusion as he brushed past her to get to Tessa.

The young girl's eyes looked big and grateful as he spoke to her, and it was only after they'd gone out of the door that Wanda thought it strange that neither of them had looked at Allyson.

From across the room, Allyson stopped listening to those around her and watched Bob lead Tessa to the bus. Her heart was pounding. *It was true! He was sleeping with the girl. Oh my God! Oh my God! It was true.*

She was staring hard at the bus, watching it pull away. Dread was billowing up inside her like a great suffocating balloon. She had to be wrong, it had to be drink that was frightening her like this, because Bob and Tessa both loved her far too much to do this to her.

The spacious sitting room of Shelley Bronson's Kensington flat was littered with the Sunday papers. The remains of a late breakfast were still in evidence, and a stack of hand-labelled video cassettes had broken down into an untidy pile in front of the TV. Otherwise the room was pure elegance and style, with its sensuously lit Icart nudes, stylish thirties furniture and rugs, and splendid original Art Deco fireplace. But not even the tasteful elegance of her surroundings could compare with Shelley herself, whose hauntingly dark beauty, languorous movements and thoughtful, almond-shaped eyes created a woman who was so exotic and sensuous that she aroused interest and caused intrigue merely by existing. But she was a very private woman, and she wanted it to stay that way. And whatever doubts and insecurities she might have were nobody's business but her own.

For Shelley, her outward appearance and the image she created were all that mattered. She was forty-two, almost six foot tall and had the most perfectly formed body it was possible for a woman to have. She was also incisively intelligent, with great poise and confidence, and had very little time for fools, of whom there seemed to be lamentably plenty among the males of her acquaintance. She had yet to meet a man who could match her, in the bedroom or the boardroom, though she wasn't the kind of woman who went for long without sex, she simply indulged herself with the husbands of others, who would naturally want no scandal or commitment. There was only one exception to the non-commitment deal, though not one that she ever discussed, even with Allyson, her closest friend.

Shelley was thinking about Allyson now, as she spoke on the phone to one of *Soirée's* other two producers, Alan Rich, who'd surely seen that morning's exclusive in the *News of the World*.

'So how do we handle the "Secret Love" at the meeting tomorrow?' Alan asked, when he finally got round to the subject of Allyson. 'Is it true, by the way?'

'What do you think?' Shelley responded, enjoying the sensation of her fingers as they moved through her glorious chestnut hair.

There was a moment's silence at the other end before Alan said, 'Have you spoken to Allyson today? How did she take it?'

'Probably the way you're imagining,' Shelley replied.

'Isn't Tessa going down there today?' he asked.

'Mmm.'

'My, she's got guts,' he remarked.

'Why? If she's innocent?' Shelley said.

That stopped the conversation. Obviously Alan had presumed the story was true.

'OK, we'll talk tomorrow and I'll fill you all in on what Stella Cornbright has to say then,' Shelley said.

She rang off and after showering, she dressed slowly, savouring the pleasure of satin, then cashmere, then leather as it covered her lovingly scented body. She wasn't unduly worried about what Stella Cornbright had to say. The show's ratings were down, it was true, and Allyson's popularity had been waning these past few months. However, this scandal would turn that around. The nation would take her right to its heart now, the way it always did when a wife was cheated on by her husband, especially publicly.

Shelley sighed, for she knew that this kind of pain was new to Allyson, and she wondered how she would handle it. Of course, it might all blow over. However, Shelley doubted that, for she knew very well that this obsession had hit the man like a raging tornado, and there was just no knowing how much havoc it was going to wreak.

The cricket match was a triumph for the kids. Despite their handicaps they threw themselves wildly into the game, and came out so far ahead that the losers deserved nothing less than the bombardment of cream cakes and soggy fruit they got.

Allyson rarely loved Bob more than at times like this, for he got so involved with the children, and had such a great time himself. He was their hero. He was the one who visited them each month with Allyson, and he was always interested in what they were doing and what they had to say. He was so good and kind and full of crazy fun that their reward was to make him the prime target when it came time to let fly with the ammunition of cakes and fruit.

She hadn't yet passed comment on how he'd taken Tessa to pick up the kids. She didn't know what to say and the thought of them together on that bus was making her feel sick inside, but she had to keep reminding herself that those torturously erotic images were a product of her rabid imagination, not of reality. Now Bob was making his way towards her with cream all over his face, and looking so wicked and humorous that she had to laugh. As he reached her she began mopping him up with a paper towel, then she shrieked as he suddenly scooped her up and spun her round. The spectators were delighted, and after taking their bows Allyson turned to Bob with a huge, friendly smile and said, 'So, did you screw Tessa on the way over to the Hall?'

His face was hidden as he had resumed wiping the cream from his eyes. When it emerged he was grinning. 'Of course,' he said. 'I wasn't going to waste the opportunity, was I?'

Allyson hoped her look of scepticism disguised her misgivings. 'Out of interest,' she said, 'is she going with you when you take them back? Could be another opportunity, though hopefully not in front of the kids.'

She was already turning away in anger, but he grabbed her arm and spun her back. 'Stop this,' he whispered. 'You're tormenting yourself.'

Guessing they were being watched she put on a showy act of intimacy as she looked up into his eyes. But the caustic response she was planning got suddenly swept away by a wave of unease. 'Can you stay here tonight?' she asked. 'My meeting's not until twelve tomorrow.'

He was still looking at her, and she could see his anger retreating too. 'I'll fix it so I can,' he said, and after giving her a lingering kiss on the mouth he went to start packing the kids into the bus.

'How much do you think we raised?' Tessa said, joining Allyson.

Allyson turned round, concealing the jolt in her heart with a vaguely distracted smile. How close had the girl been standing? she wondered. Close enough to hear what she and Bob were saying? Oh God, this was an impossible situation. 'Five hundred?' Allyson guessed.

Tessa's face broke into a delighted smile. 'Better,' she cried. 'Nine hundred and twenty!'

Allyson was impressed. 'Fantastic,' she said, although it was hard to care about anything else when your life could be falling apart. But it wasn't. *It wasn't!* 'You'll have to get on to Wendy Peacemaker in the morning,' she said, 'find out how much we've totalled so far. We should be up around fourteen thousand by now, almost enough for a bus. My parents are donating, by the way. You'd better call my mother tomorrow and remind her. Oh, and find out what time the guy from Human Rights Watch is flying in from the Balkans on Tuesday. If he's up to it, Bob and I will take him to dinner.'

'Which restaurant?' Tessa asked, as she noted down her instructions.

'Let me see. What about the Pharmacy? No, let's take him to . . . Hey,

Kathy, what was that restaurant you were telling me about?' she shouted to one of the soap stars. 'The one on Fulham Road.'

'It's on Brompton Road,' the actress answered, wandering over, a couple of autograph-hunters in tow. 'I'll call you tomorrow with the number.' She finished signing, then turned back to Allyson. 'This has been a terrific day, Ally,' she said. 'Those kids are something else.'

'Aren't they?' Allyson agreed, smiling. 'Are you going to come into the house for a drink before you leave?'

'Sure. Lead me to it.'

'What about you, Tessa?'

'Um, I'd like to,' Tessa answered, blushing, 'but I don't like driving in the dark, so I should probably start making tracks.'

'OK,' Allyson said. 'Drive safely now, won't you?' she said. 'And thanks for all your help today.'

Tessa smiled a shy goodbye to Kathy, whose eyebrows went up in response, and stayed that way as she watched the girl walk away. 'Tell me it's not true,' she said when Tessa was safely out of earshot.

'It's not,' Allyson responded.

'But you want to kill her all the same.'

Allyson laughed. 'No, of course not,' she said, and went off to find out if anyone else wanted to come back for a drink.

Bob was a long time taking the kids back and returning the bus. Eventually Allyson had to call taxis to take everyone to the station. She'd tried his mobile a dozen times, but he had it switched off, and she'd reached such a pitch of anxiety by now that there was just no way she could stop herself fearing the worst.

She stared down at the bath she'd filled in an attempt to make her guests think she was so unruffled by Bob's disappearance that she was planning, as soon as they left, to take a long, soothing soak before he came home. Then, when everyone had gone, she continued the delusion by returning to the bathroom and taking off her clothes.

This was a horrible, frightening feeling. Her body was rigid, as though tensing for a terrible blow. She looked at the time on the radio clock. Actually, he wasn't that late. He'd only been gone an hour and a half, and he might have stopped in at the pub on his way back. She gave his mobile another try. It rang and rang, then to her amazement he answered. 'Bob?' she cried. 'Where the hell are you? I've been trying—'

'Listen, if you think I'm shagging your damned assistant in some ditch somewhere, then get off the line,' he growled. 'I'm waiting for the AA to call back. Bloody bus has conked out on me.'

'Then why didn't you call and say so? I've been worried sick. What about the kids? Are they still with you?'

'No. They're back at the Hall. I'm about three miles from Vic's, and guess what, his bloody answerphone's on, so a fat lot of use he is.'

His disgruntlement was suddenly making her laugh. 'Do you want me to come and get you?' she offered.

At his end Bob looked down at Tessa. Her ruffled head was resting on his shoulder, her smooth plump legs were curled up on the front seat of his car. 'You could,' he said into the phone, 'but I can't just abandon things here. I'll wait for the AA and they can take me and the bus to Vic's where I'll pick up my car.'

'Did you call your office to let them know you'll be late tomorrow?'

'No. I'll just get up at the crack of dawn,' he said, starting to feel irritated that he'd switched the phone back on, but he'd known she'd be worried and it wasn't fair to put her through that.

'You could be pretty tired,' she said softly.

'I'll survive,' he responded brusquely. 'Listen, I'd better ring off in case the AA's trying to get through.'

'I don't think you got what I was saying,' she said teasingly.

He had, but with Tessa right there beside him . . . Somehow he managed to mumble that he had to go, that the AA had arrived, and he rang off.

'Why did you lie to her?' Tessa said, as he tucked the phone back in its wallet. 'Why did you say the AA was here . . .'

He was incredulous. 'You surely weren't expecting me to tell her *you* were here,' he cried.

'No, of course not,' she answered.

He already regretted his outburst, for the way he'd referred to her had been disparaging and unnecessarily hurtful. In an effort to make amends he reached out and touched his fingers lightly to her cheek. He turned her to face him and kissed her in small, tender touches. She looked into his eyes, and said, 'Do you really love me?'

He answered, 'Yes.'

But she seemed troubled, so he tilted her chin so that she could look nowhere but at him and whispered, 'What is it?'

Bunching her hands around his, she said, 'Allyson said you were starting a family. In the pub earlier . . . Is that true?'

He turned to look at her, letting his eyes roam over the pale softness of her skin. 'It would be irresponsible for me to consider having a baby with Allyson when I feel the way I do about you,' he said tersely.

She was looking at him so intently, immersing herself in his every word. 'But you do want to have a baby?' she said.

'Allyson does,' he answered. 'And yes, I suppose I do too; after all, I'm not getting any younger, and what you see in an old codger like me . . .'

Laughing, she squeezed his hand to her cheek. 'I keep asking myself the same question,' she teased.

'And what answer do you come up with?'

Her eyes slanted out to the night as she thought, then her humour started to fade. 'There are no answers. Not for us.' She sighed. 'Maybe if we could all live together . . . Allyson and I could share you . . .'

His eyes were like saucers. 'Oh, I can see that going down a treat with Allyson,' he scoffed. But of course she didn't mean it.

She laughed, and they sat quietly then, side by side in the darkness, watching the jagged journey of raindrops as they ran down the window. He thought back to the beginning and how this had started, three short months ago, when she'd touched his hand in the privacy of Allyson's office, and smiled as she'd told him how Allyson had confessed to loving his hands, and she, Tessa, could see why. Looking back, there was a chance he'd known then that this girl was going to change his life, though if that were true, he had to ask himself why hadn't he stopped it then? He had no answer for that. All he knew was that of all the women he had slept with throughout his marriage, none had ever been the threat to it that Tessa was now. No one had even come close.

 Chapter Three

The *Soirée* studios were in a converted warehouse in Fulham. Though the programme was owned by one of the large network companies, independent premises had been found to accommodate the many staff and freelancers it took to service a show with four transmissions a week.

Allyson and Shelley had their own offices next door to each other at the top end of the production level, on the first floor of the building, but as the show's main presenter, Allyson also had a dressing room next to the studio on the ground floor.

It was after eleven thirty when Allyson sailed into the open-plan production office, causing an immediate hush which she pretended not to notice. She stopped en route to her office to talk to Jerry Milne, that night's director. As they took a brief look through the opening links, she knew everyone was dying to see how she dealt with Tessa. Of course, there was a chance they'd known for ages about the rumoured affair, which would mean she was now either an object of pity, or a laughing stock because it had taken her so long to find out.

'You know, I think these last couple of sentences don't quite flow,' she said, pointing them out on the script.

'I'll take it back to the subs,' Jerry told her.

Allyson moved on through the random arrangement of desks. 'Hi, Alan. Are you doing Wednesday's show? Great. I'd like to talk about it when you've got a minute.'

Hearing Allyson's voice, Shelley came out of her office and embraced her friend, who, she thought, was looking rather good this morning, considering. 'Are we making a regular thing out of the humanitarian angle on Wednesdays?' Shelley wanted to know.

Allyson's blue eyes were eager. 'It wasn't an intention I set out with,' she responded, 'but I think it could be good.'

'We'll discuss it in more depth later.' Shelley was already heading off towards the stairs. 'We're recording at four this afternoon.'

'Jerry told me. Hi, Tessa,' she said, knowing that every eye in the room was on her now that she'd reached her own office. 'Did you call my mother about the donation?'

Tessa was her usual efficient self. 'I spoke to her an hour ago,' she answered. 'She's sending it over.'

'Good.' Allyson was smiling. Leaning in a little, she put a twinkle in her eye and said softly, 'Everyone's watching us now, so we can either make ourselves look foolish, or them. I say we make it them.'

Tessa's eyes reflected the twinkle. 'How do we do that?'

'Just laugh, and make it look as though we're the great chums we've always been. Which we are, I hope.'

Tessa laughed as though she'd just been told a hilarious joke. A bit overdone, Allyson thought, but it would do.

Allyson was still close. 'If I was horrible to you at all yesterday, then I'm sorry,' she said.

'You weren't,' Tessa assured her. 'Though you had every right to be, if you believed the paper.'

Allyson's smile froze. Picking up her briefcase, she walked into her office and closed the door behind her.

If you believed the paper! Just what was that supposed to mean? Why would she believe the paper? Just who did the girl think she was, coming out with statements like that? It was offensive, the way she'd said it, and arrogant. At least it had sounded that way. 'Looks like a fun day ahead,' she trilled lightly to herself, and taking a steadying breath she crossed to her desk and put down her briefcase. Her chair was occupied by a sack of mail.

'Tessa,' she said into the intercom. 'Could you come in, please?'

The door opened and Tessa was there in all her girlish, tousle-haired splendour and black leather boots.

'Could you get rid of that mailbag,' Allyson said, going to hang up her coat. 'We'll go through it later.'

Tessa did as she was told. At the door she said, 'I've just made some fresh coffee. I'll bring in a cup as soon as it's ready.'

'Great.' Allyson was watching her computer screen as it blinked and whirred into life. 'OK, you can go now.'

Allyson knew she was handling this all wrong and if she'd just calm down she'd remember that she believed Bob when he said he wasn't having an affair. And the way he'd made love to her last night . . . OK, he was tired after the hectic day, so was she, which would account for why neither of them came, but the way he held her and kissed her and then how quickly he fell asleep—a guilty conscience would never have permitted such an easy release. This would all blow over in a day or two and no one would even remember.

A few minutes later she was still at her computer, going through the email, when Tessa buzzed through. 'Ally, Bob's on the line,' she said.

'OK, thanks,' she said. 'Put him through.' She picked up the receiver.

'Darling?' his voice came down the line.

'Hi. Did you get to the office on time?'

'Yep. Sorry if I woke you when I left.'

'It doesn't matter. We're going into the meeting in a minute.'

'Then I won't keep you. I just wanted to tell you that I've been invited to host this year's Sportsman of the Year awards. Isn't that great?'

'Oh, darling. It's wonderful. I'm glad you called. I was just thinking about you and feeling insecure over that newspaper thing again.'

'Then I'm glad I called too. Do we have any commitments tonight?'

'I don't think so.'

'So let's rent a video and have dinner at home, just the two of us?'

'Sounds perfect.'

'OK, got to go. Just wanted to give you my news.'

'Love you,' but he was gone.

'Coffee,' Tessa said, coming in the door.

Allyson looked up and smiled. 'Thanks.'

Tessa put the coffee down and was just about to leave when she said, 'Isn't that great news about the Sportsman of the Year awards?'

Allyson's smile was gone. 'He told you?' she said.

Tessa flushed deeply and suddenly appeared so flustered she could hardly speak. 'No, uh . . . No, I . . .'

Allyson watched her, then a horrible suspicion dawned. 'You were listening in to our conversation!' she said.

'Allyson? You ready for the meeting?' Shelley called out.

Allyson was still looking at Tessa. 'Coming,' she called back. And to Tessa, 'We'll continue this later.'

Allyson's powers of concentration were giving her a rough time as the meeting got going. There were about twenty of them in the room, all with their own agendas, each in need of a green light, a no go, or further discussion. The stories they ran with were usually decided on by Shelley and her, but today Shelley was taking most of the decisions.

For a while, though, Allyson managed to wrench herself out of her inner confusion to take part in the discussion on that night's show. Each episode was set up with Cocktails for the first part, a commercial break, then a filmed insert from one of the reporters, ending with a Nightcap. The most important section was Cocktails. The guests that night were a leading politician and his wife. The filmed report was from Colin Quinlan, who'd been following the rehearsals of a new West End show.

'Terry Black's taken over the lead,' Colin informed them. 'He's agreed to come in for the Nightcap slot. By the way, we're invited to the opening night. By we, I mean me, Allyson and Shelley. For Allyson, read Allyson and Bob.'

'When is it?' Allyson asked.

Colin's handsome face showed his surprise. 'Tonight,' he answered.

Shelley arched a humorous eyebrow. Clearly Allyson wasn't paying attention. As Shelley continued the briefing Allyson found her mind straining back towards Tessa and what it might mean if Bob had told her himself about the Sportsman of the Year awards.

'Ally? Are you OK?'

Allyson blinked, then found herself looking at Shelley. 'Sorry,' she said. 'I was miles away. What were we saying?'

'That the meeting's over,' Shelley replied.

By the time Allyson got back to her office Tessa and the rest of the team had gone for lunch. Allyson made a couple of calls then went down to her dressing room, where Shelley joined her a few minutes later. 'I'm worried about you,' Shelley said bluntly. 'You lost it in there today and that's just not like you.'

'You don't have to tell me,' Allyson responded. She looked anxiously into Shelley's face. 'I hate to admit it, but this is really getting to me.'

'I can see that.'

Shelley walked over to the bar and poured them both a soft drink. No alcohol before a recording, and no alcohol on the show either. All glasses contained coloured water.

She handed the drink to Allyson, who was curled up in a corner of one of the canary-yellow sofas, and went to sit in an armchair. Allyson watched as she crossed her silk-stockinged legs and let one of her black suede Ferragamo shoes dangle. It was probably impossible, she thought, for Shelley to look anything other than supremely elegant. 'Tell me honestly, Shell,' Allyson said, unconsciously attempting to tidy up her hair, 'do you think it's true? Do you think he's sleeping with her?'

Shelley drank.

Allyson watched her and felt the cold burn of dread enclosing her heart. 'Oh my God, you do, don't you?' she said.

'I don't know what to tell you,' Shelley said. 'Have you checked whether it's true about Danny living in the same building?'

Allyson shook her head.

'Is there any other evidence?'

'Not really. Bob treats it all as a joke.'

Shelley's lips tightened at that. 'It doesn't seem much of a joke to me.'

'I was thinking,' Allyson said, after a pause. 'The guy who wrote the story, do you know him?'

Shelley shook her head. 'His name's new to me.'

'But you do know the editor,' Allyson pointed out. 'Could you to talk to him, find out if this guy has any more?'

'I could, but we're talking the *News of the World* here, so you can rest assured that if he did have more he'd have printed it.'

'Oh God,' Allyson groaned. 'Please God, don't let it be true.'

Shelley watched her lean back and close her eyes. She was going to have to confront the truth sooner or later, but to tell her before a recording wasn't a good idea. She could go to pieces, and Allyson wouldn't thank her for that. She leaned forward and took one of Allyson's hands between her own. 'Ally, this is just a minor hiccup,' she said. 'You'll be past it in a couple of days. A couple of weeks at the most.'

'I hope you're right,' Allyson said, suppressing a shudder, 'because the truth is, it's frightening the hell out of me. Oh, Bob and I have had our ups and downs, but there are people out there who'd trade their kids for problems like mine. The Golden Child, is what Bob sometimes calls me. Wealthy parents. No bad experiences with boyfriends. No drugs, no illnesses, no real traumas to speak of. Maybe it's my turn now.'

'I never realised you were queuing up,' Shelley teased.

Despite herself Allyson laughed. Then after finishing off her juice, she said, 'Let's drop it before I drive myself nuts.'

'It's a deal,' Shelley said. 'So let me tell you what Stella wanted to see me about yesterday.'

'Oh my God! I totally forgot!' Allyson cried. 'So?'

'It's a biggie,' Shelley warned. 'The old trout's retiring.'

'No!' Allyson responded. 'Retiring? But she can't be more than fifty. I know she looks ninety, but I always thought she'd go on till the Grim Reaper came to get her.'

Shelley's eyebrows rose. 'Apparently he's on his way.'

Allyson looked stunned. 'You mean she's . . .'

Shelley nodded. 'The big C. She's been told she's got six months or less, and she wants to spend it travelling with her husband.'

'Oh God, that's horrible news,' Allyson groaned. 'And I don't know what's come as the biggest shock, that she's dying, or that I care.'

Shelley laughed. 'I know how you feel,' she said. 'She's leaving at Christmas, but it's all hush-hush for now. She knows I'm telling you, though. She asked me to so you could practise the dance you're going to do on her grave.'

'No! She didn't say that?'

Shelley grinned.

'She did. It's just like her. Oh hell, I actually think I'm going to miss her.'

'There's more,' Shelley said. 'The company's been sold. We've known for ages that it's been in the offing, but now, apparently, it's happened. It's been bought by Leisure and Media Inc.'

'The American cable company?'

'Anglo-American,' Shelley corrected. 'It's based in the States, but it's owned by Nick and Mark Reiner, who are British.'

Allyson screwed up her nose. 'I've interviewed Mark Reiner. Isn't he the one who bought Rowcliffe House in Devon and spent something like five million quid restoring it? The one with the alcoholic wife?'

'The very same.'

'I'm trying to work out whether this is good news or bad.'

'Personally I think it's good,' Shelley responded.

'I'm trying to remember what he looks like,' Allyson said.

'Not typically handsome, but certainly passable. Incredibly powerful of course and . . .' She let the sentence hang.

Allyson felt a canny smile growing on her face. 'Filthy rich,' she grinned. 'Wow, this could be good news, provided he's managed to dump the dipso wife.' She immediately turned to the window and looked out at the sky. 'Oh God, please forgive what I said about dumping the wife. I didn't mean to tempt fate. Honestly.'

Shelley was laughing as she got to her feet. 'If he is available,' she said, 'he's going to be a mighty big fish to land.'

'That's what they say about you,' Allyson reminded her.

'Ah, but what they don't know about me,' Shelley responded, 'is that I keep getting thrown back.'

The door closed behind her, leaving Allyson with a fading smile and a growing wish that she could do something to change Shelley's luck with men. In Allyson's opinion, the problem belonged to the men Shelley got involved with. They were all too often intimidated by her, wanting to reduce her to a level they considered inferior to their own, and Shelley just wasn't the kind of woman ever to stand for that. But it had to be a lonely existence, having so few relationships and none that had ever worked. At least she had the programme, which was like her baby, her lover, her life and ambition all wrapped up into one.

It meant the same to Allyson too, for they'd started it together, had developed it into what it was now, and it was as much a part of their identities as it was of their lives. And when life got really tough or out of control it became their own personal refuge, too.

Allyson was already in the make-up room by the time Tessa returned from lunch. She came bounding into the room, flushed and breathless, and endearingly puppy-like, which was how she generally looked when she wanted to share some good news with Allyson. 'I'm sorry I'm late,' she gasped. 'They said upstairs you were looking for me.'

Allyson eyed her, then realising the make-up girl was watching, she said, 'I was worried. Are you OK?'

Tessa nodded. 'Yes, I'm fine. But I'd like to talk to you when you've got a minute. I've got something to tell you.'

Allyson's mouth dried. Whatever this news was, Allyson didn't want to hear it. 'Go and check on things upstairs, then meet me in my dressing room,' she said. 'Have any of the guests arrived yet?' she asked Julian, the floor assistant, as he came in.

'Lionel Godfrey's in the green room. His wife's on her way. Still waiting for Terry Black. Here's your mic pack,' he added, handing it over. 'Hey, Tessa, are you coming to see the band tonight?'

'I'd love to,' she said. 'Where are you playing?'

'The Man in the Moon at World's End. Eight o'clock.'

'I'll be there,' she promised, and skipped off.

Boy, she was in a good mood. Allyson watched the way Julian looked after her. He was a good-looking kid, shoulder-length blond hair, pale lashes fringing his eyes, and a slim, wiry physique. He was obviously besotted. Was there a man on the planet who wasn't? Still, with any luck, this one would whisk Tessa off into a wild and passionate romance that required far more energy than a man Bob's age could muster.

Ten minutes later Tessa knocked on the dressing-room door and put her head round, her eyes shining. 'I'm just dying to tell you my news.'

Though Allyson was irritated by the way the girl was brushing that morning's eavesdrop aside, she wasn't about to get into a scene when she was due in studio in fifteen minutes. 'So, what is it?' she said.

'I was late back to the office,' Tessa said, her pink cheeks filling up with pleasure, 'because I went to have lunch with my boyfriend and *we got engaged*!' She thrust her left hand forward to show off the jazzy little diamond on her third finger.

Allyson was reeling. Surely she wasn't talking about Bob!

'Isn't it pretty?' Tessa insisted. 'He chose it himself.'

'It's lovely,' Allyson agreed weakly. Then, laughing to cover her awkwardness, she said, 'I'm sorry, it's just, well, I didn't even know you had a boyfriend. You've never mentioned him before.'

'I know, but you're so busy I didn't want to bore you with my love life. Anyway, his name's Phil and he's an interior designer. He's hoping to get enough money together to start his own business. Meantime, he's working for a company over in Battersea.'

Allyson started to laugh. 'Well, I can't wait to meet him,' she said. 'Have you set a date?'

'No, but when we do it would mean the world to me if you were there.'

There was a tap on the door and Shelley came in. 'Shell,' Allyson cried. 'You'll never guess. Tessa's just got engaged.'

Shelley turned a chill gaze on Tessa. 'So I heard,' she said.

'Isn't it great?' Allyson said, taking a script from the PA who raced in.

'Ready to go in ten minutes,' the PA called over her shoulder, as she raced out again.

'I want a quick word with you about the Nightcap,' Shelley said, holding the door open for Tessa to leave.

Taking the hint, Tessa left.

'You didn't congratulate her,' Allyson protested, lifting up her skirt to slot the microphone's battery pack in the back of her tights.

'Here, let me,' Shelley said, turning Allyson round. 'We've just heard that Terry Black's wife's been awarded the Nobel Prize for Literature. She's the writer Anna Godling, in case you'd forgotten. Ross is doing a quick background on her; he'll be down in a minute to fill you in.'

The phone rang and Allyson picked up the handset. 'Ally? I got a message you were trying to reach me?'

'Oh, hi, darling. We'll have to postpone our cosy night in, I'm afraid. We've been invited to Terry Black's opening night. That doesn't feel secure,' she said to Shelley, who was still trying to fix the mic pack.

'OK. Where and what time?' Bob answered.

'I think it's the National, but I'll check and call you back. Got to go now, I'm due in studio.' She put the phone down. 'I've got it,' she said to Shelley, who was pushing the wire round Allyson's waist and up between her breasts. Allyson clipped the tiny radio mic onto her dress.

Quickly picking up the phone, she buzzed through to Tessa. 'Get the details for the play tonight and call Bob with them,' she said.

Shelley walked with her to the studio, then after stopping off at the green room to greet the show's guests, she went upstairs to the gallery to watch the recording. On the way she popped into her office and was on the point of leaving again when she noticed Tessa standing over one of the subs, obviously taking in everything he said, then asking the relevant questions to increase her knowledge of reporting and production. Allyson herself had championed this unofficial training and Tessa's remarkable progress had been the source of much pride on Allyson's part, and encouragement on the part of everyone else. How generous Tessa must think Allyson, providing her not only with the background for a new career, but apparently with a fiancé too. Unless, of course, the mysterious Phil actually did exist. And if Shelley believed that she'd be in even bigger denial than Allyson, though without the excuse.

 *Chapter Four*

LATER THAT EVENING Shelley was with a group of friends in a far corner of the crowded theatre bar when she saw Bob pressing a path towards her. 'Hi, where's Allyson?' he said, raising his voice over the noise.

'Backstage talking to Terry Black's wife,' Shelley answered. She turned to the people she was with. 'I expect you've all met Bob Jaymes.'

Most of them had, either through Allyson, or through their own professional fields, for they were all connected to the Business. 'Can I get anyone a drink?' Bob offered.

'It's champagne, wine, water or juice,' Shelley informed him. 'I'll come and give you a hand.'

As they made their way through the crowd Bob kept very close behind her. 'You're looking sensational, as always,' he murmured in her ear.

Shelley said nothing, just kept working her way through to the bar.

'Have I done something to upset you?' Bob said, as they eventually reached the bar.

Shelley passed him a tray and treated him to a look that penetrated even his thick skin. 'Boy, seems like I'm really in trouble,' he joked.

'Did you buy that girl the ring she's wearing?' Shelley demanded.

His disarming grey eyes dilated. 'What ring? What girl?' he said.

Shelley turned away and reached over for two glasses of champagne. There had been times when she'd understood perfectly why Allyson was so devoted to Bob, for the man had the charm of the devil. But now was not one of them. 'The jailbait you've been screwing for the past three months,' Shelley replied, smiling sweetly, putting the drinks on the tray.

Bob laughed. 'I'm beginning to think you might be jealous,' he said.

Shelley looked at him pityingly, then turned back for more champagne. 'Just exactly what are you trying to do?' she asked. 'How did that story leak out?'

'I rather thought you'd have the answer to that,' he countered.

Shelley rolled her eyes. 'It's an old and trusty tactic to go on the attack when you've got no defence,' she said, disdainfully. 'It just doesn't work with me.' She moved in a little closer and spoke very softly. 'If I were you, Bob, I'd give that girl up,' and sweeping past him she headed back into the crowd.

Tessa was sitting at a small round table in the middle of the packed pub, her hands stuffed into the pockets of her leather jacket, her chubby white knees poking through the frayed holes of her jeans. As Julian carried two halves of lager through the crowd he was frequently stopped and congratulated—the gig had definitely gone down well.

'Everyone's saying you were brilliant,' Tessa told him, as he sat down.

'Yeah, it seems to have got them all going. Cheers.'

'Cheers,' she echoed. 'I'm really glad I came,' she said.

He gave a nonchalant shrug, and as his eyes moved from the radiant loveliness of her face to the ring on her left hand, he said, 'How come your boyfriend didn't show up?'

'He's working. I might see him later though.'

Julian wasn't good at hiding his disappointment. He drank some more lager, then sat staring at the glass as he put it back on the table. 'That thing in the paper yesterday,' he said, 'about you and Bob Jaymes . . .'

'Oh, that was terrible,' she gasped. 'It got me really upset when I saw it. And then I had to go down to Bath to Allyson's place to help with this charity thing. I wanted to die when I saw how hurt she was.'

Though Julian managed to retain his look of understanding and sympathy, he was having a hard time keeping the delight off his boyish face. For some reason the sophisticated Bob Jaymes seemed to be a bigger threat than the mysterious fiancé. 'I'll bet anything the bloke fancies you though,' he said. 'Everyone does. I mean, all the blokes.'

She laughed. 'No they do not,' she said, slapping his wrist.

'Oh yes they do.'

She turned to him and looked frankly into his face. 'What about you?' she challenged. 'Have you got a girlfriend?'

Now he was embarrassed, because the truth was he'd never really had much luck with girls, and it was only because Tessa was always so friendly in the office that he'd found the courage to ask her to come tonight. 'Well, there's this chick I've been seeing,' he said, trying to sound cool, 'but we're not, you know, serious.'

'And what about your career? Are you going to carry on in telly, or really make a go of it with the band?'

'TV pays the bills, but if we could get a good break, you know, sign some kind of deal, I'd be out of that door faster than you could say *Soirée*. What about you, will you stay with the programme?'

'I hope so,' she answered. 'Shall I tell you my secret ambition? Well, I've got this amazing dream that one day I'll be just like Allyson. You know, famous and successful and'—she laughed self-consciously— 'right up there in the spotlight. I've done a few pieces to camera lately, you know. Allyson says Shelley really rates them, but I don't know how much good it'll do me, not while all this is going on.'

Julian suppressed the offer of help that sprang to his lips. After all, there was zippo someone like him could do. Finally, after racking his brains, he said, 'So, are you from London? You sound like you are.'

'Mmm,' she answered, drinking. 'I was born in Wimbledon. I live in Peckham now though.'

'And your parents?'

'They're both dead.'

'Oh. Sorry.'

She was staring down at her glass, so it was hard for him to tell if he'd just sent her off on a downer. 'What about brothers and sisters?' he asked cautiously.

'No, just me.' She turned to him and smiled. 'What about you?'

'Me? Two brothers.'

'Lucky you. I always wanted to have a brother.'

'You could always adopt me,' he said, then groaned. 'God, how corny can you get?'

'You're so funny,' she laughed. 'It would be great having you as a brother. For one thing, I'd get to go to all your gigs.'

'Then don't forget to bring your friends, seeing as you're not available any more.'

Her eyes narrowed with playful laughter. 'It's a deal,' she said. Then, glancing at her watch, 'I think I'd better get going. I told Phil I'd be home by eleven.'

He walked her to the battered old Beetle. After an awkward moment of not knowing whether to kiss her or not and deciding he couldn't because of Phil, he stood watching the car as she drove away. He felt really sorry that he hadn't managed to get in before this Phil bloke, because she was just the kind of girl he could be inspired to write songs for.

'Hi, it's me.'

'Hello, you. Where are you?'

'I just slipped out. The party's still going on. Where have you been all evening? I was trying to call you.'

'I went to watch a band.'

Bob turned sharply as the fire-escape door he was next to crashed open and a drunken couple lurched out into the alley. He turned away, hiding his face in the shadows. 'I miss you,' he said.

'I miss you too. Can you come over?'

'I don't think so. We're going straight home after this.'

Changing the subject she said, 'The Phil thing seems to have worked.'

'You know, I just don't get you,' he responded. 'I thought you wanted me to leave, so we could be together.' Not that he was actually offering, it was just what he'd thought. Or maybe he was offering, for the idea of feasting himself on her completely, knowing how full and different their lives could be if they didn't have to worry about anyone else, if the lies could end and the betrayal could be over . . . He'd even started to feel jealous of this Phil character, fictitious though he was.

'I do want us to be together,' she was saying, 'more than anything, but I can't lose my job. Allyson—'

'I know,' he answered, cutting her off. He had no desire to talk about Allyson. He couldn't stand to be reminded of anything that stood in their way, especially something that could fire up his conscience the way

Allyson did. And as for the job . . . That problem was surmountable. 'They can't fire you,' he said. 'You haven't done anything wrong, not from the company's point of view, and even if they tried you could sue for wrongful dismissal.' Boy, was he glad no one else could hear him right now, not only because of the despicable disloyalty, but because of the way it proved how deeply he'd thought about this.

'I wish you could come over now,' she said.

His head went back against the wall as he closed his eyes. 'God, I wish I could,' he groaned.

'Because . . . Oh, Bob, I don't know how to tell you this . . . Can you still hear me, Bob?'

Fear suddenly plunged into his chest. She was about to tell him it was over . . . She didn't want to wreck his marriage. He felt as though he were suffocating. Panic was close behind . . . Then suddenly everything in him came to a crashing halt as he heard her say, 'I keep trying to find the right time to tell you . . . Oh, Bob, please don't be angry, but . . . I'm . . . I'm going to have a baby.'

His eyes closed and he felt himself being swallowed up by emotions he couldn't even begin to name.

'Oh, Bob, I'm sorry. I shouldn't have told you like that. It just came blurting out and . . .' Her voice was suddenly choked with tears.

'It's OK. You had to tell me some time.'

'I wish you were here. No, I don't mean that. I don't want to put pressure on you. I know you love me and I love you too, but I promise I'll never tell anyone it's yours. If you want, I'll get rid of it.'

'No! That's not what I want,' he said. 'You know what I want. For us to be together.'

'You mean that hasn't changed?' she said. 'You still do?'

'Yes. I still do.'

He stared out into the shadows, knowing only the agonising effort to summon the words that would set in motion the greatest pain and devastation Allyson had ever known. It was hard. So hard. He was going to be turning his back on so much, not just Allyson, though God knew that was going to be the most difficult, but on the lives they had created together, the friends they had, the dreams . . . Oh God . . . How could he tell her that he'd made Tessa pregnant? What was it going to do to her?

As though sensing his dilemma Tessa said, 'It's enough to know you still love me. You don't have to do anything.'

'Yes, I do,' he said, brushing aside her offer of reprieve. Hard it might be, but he didn't want to put it off, he just wanted it done. Then suddenly he was saying, 'I'll talk to her tonight. Then, if you still want me . . .' It was a tease that had found its way stiffly, awkwardly, through the numbing gravity of the crisis they were facing.

'You know I do, silly,' she said. 'I'm just worried about Allyson . . .'

'Let me worry about Allyson,' he said. 'You just worry about you and don't wait up, I'll use my key to get in.'

Allyson was in the bathroom that adjoined their bedroom, dabbing on the expensive perfume Bob had given her last birthday. Their flat, which took up the entire second floor of one of the beautiful listed buildings on Cheyne Walk, had been a wedding gift from her parents. Everything in it she and Bob had bought or designed together; even the exotic French and African antiques had been found during long hot summer holidays together.

She could hear him moving around in the bedroom, picturing him starting to undress. She'd set the heating to come on while they were out so the place was warm, and she'd turned the bedside lights down low, to make it seem even more cosy. She slipped into one of the negligees she knew he particularly liked, and kept the cabinet door firmly closed on her diaphragm.

When finally she went into the bedroom she was surprised not to find him undressed. The unease she'd been trying to keep suppressed all night was starting to stir. His hands were stuffed in his trouser pockets and his head was bowed. 'Mummy called earlier,' she said, attempting to inject some normalcy into what was starting to feel like a horribly surreal situation. 'She's trying to work out the roster for the villa next summer. She wants to know if we want it, and if we do, when?' She was pulling back the sheets, climbing into bed.

He walked into the bathroom, and was fiddling about with his shaving gear, but the door was open, so he could hear her—and he still wasn't undressing.

'Bob? Did you hear what I said?' she asked him.

At last he came into the bedroom, but his whole demeanour was making her wish he hadn't. 'You choose,' he said.

Good. That sounded better. 'OK. Well, I was thinking—'

'And take Shelley,' he interrupted. 'The two of you'll enjoy spending some time together, out of the office.'

Allyson forced a laugh past the clogging in her heart. 'What do you mean? Why would I go with Shelley and not with you?'

He sat down on the edge of the bed, on her side, but he wasn't looking at her. Her heart seemed to be getting more clogged than ever.

'I won't be coming,' he said softly.

She stared at him, knowing exactly what he was saying, yet refusing to hear it. 'What do you mean?' she said, feeling her smile start to hurt.

He turned to look at her and her heart felt as though it were tearing in two. So the story in the paper was true. *But that didn't explain Phil!*

'You're Phil, aren't you?' she whispered.

He nodded.

'Oh my God.' Her hands moved to her mouth. A bolt of desperate denial cleaved through her heart. 'Oh my God!' She tried to get up from the bed, but his weight on the sheets was trapping her legs.

'I'm sorry,' he said. 'I'd give anything for this not to have happened.'

Her chest was heaving. She couldn't make herself think. *This wasn't happening!* 'Why didn't you admit it yesterday, when it was in the paper, when I asked you *if it was true*!' she cried.

He grabbed her fists as she started to hit him, held them to his chest.

But there was only craziness in her head. Fast irrational thoughts erupting from a disabling panic and anger. She wanted to scream and scream. She wanted to tear out the horrible, lacerating realisation that he'd got himself engaged to a *child* when he was married to her! How could he have done that . . . But no! No! She had to put the brakes on this because she knew what it was. Midlife crises didn't respond well to hysterics. So, making a superhuman effort to even out her breathing, she said, in a voice that shook with unsteady courage, 'How long? How long have you been seeing her?'

'Three months,' he answered.

Her heart recoiled from his words, but she made herself nod, as though she were talking to a friend. 'So everyone knew, but me?' she said.

'I don't think so. We've been as discreet . . .'

He stopped as she turned her head away. It was the 'we' that had done it, the 'we' that had joined him to Tessa, and severed him from her. *Oh God, no! No! No! No!* She was biting her lip in an attempt to stop herself crying, but tears were already streaking down her face.

'I don't understand how you could have done this,' she said, her voice breaking with emotion. 'I just don't understand.'

'I'm not sure I do either,' he responded. 'It just . . . it just happened, and it feels, well, right, I suppose.'

She looked at him wildly. 'How can it be right?' she cried. 'You're forty-five years old! You're old enough to be her father.'

'I know. But what we have . . .'

Rage flung out her next words. 'What do you mean, what you have? You have nothing except some deluded middle-aged fantasy that you're the answer to some little tart's dream!'

'Don't talk about her like that.'

'I'll talk about her how I like,' she screamed. 'She's a fucking whore who's putting it out for every man she meets, and you, you fucking moron, are so damned conceited that you think you're different. Well, you're not, because she's screwing half the men in—' The breath suddenly left her body, and not even the sting to her face was as great as the shock that he'd actually hit her. She looked at him, stunned, unable to believe he'd done it.

He stared back, shaken too by what he'd done. Then, dropping his head, he said, 'I wish to God I could take that back.'

Allyson looked away. The slap had deadened her. She was numb, and the deafening sound behind the silence was the slow, devastating explosion of her world. She wanted to reach out her arms, pull it back, hold it safe. But there was nothing there to touch except her husband, who no longer wanted her. Oh God, she wanted this to end.

A few seconds ticked by, then, getting up, he walked into the bathroom and took his robe from the back of the door.

'What are you doing?' she said, following him.

He looked down at her and she was suddenly shouting, 'No, Bob! Please! Just stop this. Our marriage is good and strong, you can't go smashing it up for a passion that's bound to pass, can't you see that? No!' she screamed, as he started to walk past her. 'No, Bob. Please.' She was clutching his arm so tightly her nails were breaking his skin, but she didn't care. She wanted to hurt him, the way he was hurting her.

'Allyson, don't make me say things that are only going to hurt you more,' he said.

Dread of what they might be whipped through her heart. 'You don't have to,' she sobbed. 'All you have to do is tell me you're not going.'

'I have to go,' he said softly. 'I'm sorry, but I have to.'

She was in chaos. She didn't know what to do. She didn't even know she was crying as she said, 'Don't you care what this is doing to me? Don't I matter to you at all any more?'

His grey eyes looked sadly into hers. 'Of course you do.'

The terrible pain of his admission trampled what was left of her hope. 'But she matters more?' she said.

Still he looked at her. Then finally he whispered, 'Yes.'

Her legs suddenly felt so weak she thought they would crumple, but somehow she managed to turn and walk down the corridor to the sitting room, not really knowing what she was doing or where she was going. She stared out of the tall casement windows to the river. She could hear him moving about, putting things into a suitcase. Panic was rising like a storm inside her. She didn't know what to do, how to make any of this stop.

He came into the room. She turned to face him and saw that he was dressed, ready to leave. She couldn't let him go. She'd rather die than let him walk out of that door. 'Don't go,' she whispered. 'Please. Don't go. I'll do anything to make you stay. We need to talk. We should discuss this and try to find a way to work through it.'

'There isn't a way.'

'No! Don't say that! I'm your wife. I love you. I can forgive you for this. Please!' She looked at him with dark, frightened eyes and willed him with all her might to stay.

'I'm sorry,' he said, and picking up his case he let himself quietly out of the door.

'Shelley.'

'Allyson?' Shelley sounded sleepy. 'What time is it?'

'I don't know. Shel . . .' She tried again. 'Shel, he's . . .'

'It's OK, I'm on my way. Just pour yourself a stiff drink and stay in the kitchen until I get there.'

Allyson had gone through half a bottle of wine by the time Shelley arrived. 'I feel so embarrassed now,' she said, 'calling you up in a state like that. I'm fine really. But now you're here, would you like a drink?'

'Just coffee,' Shelley said, 'and the same for you. Hangovers are the worst for dealing with something like this. I'll put the kettle on.'

'I feel really terrible about this,' Allyson said, sitting down at the table. 'I mean, I know it's going to be all right. He'll come back, but it's just a bit tough, you know, tonight . . . In fact, right now I want to *kill him*. But it'll be OK, and before you know it, we'll be looking back on this and laughing. Well, maybe not laughing, but you know what I mean.'

'Allyson, shut up,' Shelley said gently. 'You're still in shock and nothing you say tonight is going to make any sense to you in the morning. What you are going to need to prepare yourself for, though, is the press. They're going to get hold of this so fast that it wouldn't even surprise me if they already know. So, I think you should take some time off . . .'

'No! I'd rather die than let either of them think this was getting to me,' Allyson protested. 'Oh no. I'm going to be on that screen tomorrow night, and I'm going to be my usual dazzling self. I've still got you, and I've still got my job, and I don't intend to let either of you down. So I'll be there tomorrow, and if she's there too, I'll . . . I'll . . . smash her fucking face in, is what I'll do.'

Shelley burst out laughing. 'That's the spirit,' she said. 'But in my opinion, if anyone's face needs smashing in, it's his.'

Allyson was up for being rash. 'Then I'll smash his in too,' she declared. 'I don't need him. In fact, I might not even take him back when he wants to come. Do you think I should tell him that? I've got Tessa's number, I could call . . .'

'No,' Shelley said. 'I don't think you should. I think you should just drink this coffee and then get some sleep.'

At that tears started welling in Allyson's eyes. 'I can't go to bed without him,' she said. 'I know it sounds pathetic, but I just can't.'

'It's OK. I brought some things with me,' Shelley said. 'I'll sleep in one of the guest rooms, so if it gets unbearable in the night I won't have so far to come to rescue you.'

Allyson gave a shaky smile. It was good that Shelley was staying. And it would be good if she went to work in the morning too, because there was just no way her pride could handle it if Tessa managed to turn up and she didn't. But how the hell was she ever going to get to sleep knowing that Bob wouldn't be there in the morning—that he would be in someone else's bed?

 *Chapter Five*

THE PAPERS WERE FULL OF IT. And every time Allyson turned on the TV or radio it seemed that they too had little else to discuss but the break-up of the Jaymeses' marriage. It was as though the entire nation had become obsessed with it. Even journalists and photographers she considered to be friends were constantly phoning, crowding her in the street, demanding to know how she was, if she had anything to say, or if she would take Bob back.

She was under siege, not only in her private life, but in her professional life too, as the programme ratings had shot through the roof. Everyone was watching, looking, she supposed, for signs of how she was handling this. Inwardly she wasn't. But outwardly she was doing everything she could to make it look as though she were on top of the situation and perfectly able to cope. And in its way it was probably being in the spotlight that was saving her; knowing that the whole world was waiting for her to go to pieces was what held her together.

Two weeks passed and still Tessa didn't come into the office. Nor did she call. They were difficult weeks for the whole team, as no one knew quite how to behave towards Allyson. Whenever they were around her they spoke in hushed tones as though she were ill, and if anyone caught her eye she was treated to looks of such sympathy she wanted to scream. She didn't want to be this object of pity. She wanted them to laugh and tease her the way they always did, even though she didn't have it in her to respond.

'If firing the girl wasn't going to land us in even deeper hot water, I'd go right to Stella,' Shelley said.

Allyson shook her head. 'You know we can't do that legally,' she said. 'Besides, it'll just turn me into the villain and I couldn't handle that.'

Shelley went to refill their coffee cups. They were in Allyson's dressing room, where they'd spent a lot of time lately. 'We still don't know for certain that she will be coming back,' Shelley said.

'Oh, she will,' Allyson responded. 'Don't ask me how I know that, I just do.' She took the coffee Shelley was handing her and turned to look at the TV monitors. 'I should start getting ready for the studio,' she said.

'I wish you'd take some time off. You're asking too much of yourself, trying to carry on like this.'

Whether she was right or not Allyson had no idea. All she knew was that if she didn't come to the office, and was forced to spend every day in the home that was still so full of Bob, then she'd probably end up doing something crazy. 'God, every time I think of them together . . .' She had told Shelley more than once, 'Oh, Shelley, sometimes I mean it, you know, I really do want to kill her.'

Shelley smiled. 'Of course you do,' she said. 'You wouldn't be human if you didn't. But I swear to you that relationship of theirs is destined for disaster. We both know Bob, and I'm telling you, once the novelty starts wearing off he'll soon find out that he can't survive without you.'

Allyson sighed. 'Right now, it feels the other way round,' she said dismally. 'But I have to believe what you're telling me, because if I don't . . . Well, there wouldn't seem much point in going on, would there?'

'Don't underestimate your strength,' Shelley said. 'Because you've got plenty more than you might imagine. However, I don't think you can keep Tessa as your assistant. That would be pushing yourself too far.'

Allyson looked away and stared blindly down at the floor. Shelley was right, of course, and Tessa's future with *Soirée* was something Allyson had given a lot of thought to recently and she'd reached a decision that she needed to discuss with Shelley.

Shelley listened quietly, thoughtfully, showing some surprise, even doubt. But by the time Allyson had finished Shelley was ready to accept her suggestion, not necessarily because she considered it the best solution, but it was one that would work. And if Allyson was sure she could handle it, then Shelley would talk to Stella and get it put in motion.

Bob was lying on top of the bed in the cramped bedroom of Tessa's South London flat, feeling clumsily oversized and masculine in among Tessa's fluffy toys and silly girlish fripperies. But, small though it was, they'd spent a lot of time in this room these past couple of weeks as they'd indulged themselves in an orgy of sex that made even his wildest dreams look tame. For days they'd not gone out at all, sending out for food that was delivered, invariably by undercover journos, who'd seized the opportunity along with the pizza to climb the two flights of stairs in the hope of snatching a few shots of the couple.

At first it had been funny, romantic even, fighting the siege together, confined to the badly wallpapered rooms of their 'love nest'. But two weeks on and it was fast deteriorating into a nightmare of frustration and guilt. Frustration because the press just wouldn't let them move, and guilt, obviously because of Allyson, and the cowardice that was stopping him picking up the phone to make sure she was all right.

Of course Tessa was always on hand with comfort and strength, defiantly refusing to accept that either of them had done anything wrong, since they had had no choice in the matter of falling in love. It had just happened and feeling guilty wasn't going to change it. Brave words, considering he knew how terrible she really felt, for he was the one who wiped away her tears every time she cried for all the pain they were causing to someone they cared about so deeply. Yet it couldn't be much longer before those bloodhounds outside found some other juicy bones to unearth and maybe then he and Tessa could start going out again, maybe even return to work. After all they couldn't exist on sex and pizza for ever.

'Guess what?' Tessa said, coming into the bedroom with the mail. 'I've got a letter from Stella Cornbright. She's asking me to go and see her next week.' She looked at Bob apprehensively. 'Do you think they're going to sack me?'

He shook his head. 'If they were they'd tell you in the letter,' he said.

She sat down next to him and smiled as he started untying her robe.

'There don't seem to be any reporters out there this morning,' she told him, as his fingers rotated around her nipples.

'Thank God for that,' he responded.

She grinned. 'Something tells me you're in a better mood than you were last night,' she teased.

'I am,' he said.

She stood up and shrugged off her robe. 'So I thought I might go back to work today,' she said. 'If it's all right with you.'

He laughed. 'You're the one who has to face it,' he said, though he thought it a bit odd that she wanted to go back. However if Allyson was prepared to accept her back then it was hardly his place to argue. 'I don't think we should go public about the baby yet though,' he said.

'Oh God, no,' she gasped. 'You'll have to tell Allyson about that before we even think about telling anyone else.'

He shifted restlessly as though to escape the unease that swept through him. That particular nightmare could wait, though just the thought of it had had a deflating effect on his ardour.

'Oh dear,' Tessa said playfully, looking at it. 'I imagine you'd like me to do something about that before I go.'

Smiling, he reached out and pulled her down on top of him. 'You're something else, do you know that?' he said.

She wriggled a bit, wrapping her feet round the back of his legs until he was inside her.

'Mmm,' he murmured. If only he could feel like this all the time, so right about being here, and so definite that she was everything he wanted. But it was clear that his conscience wasn't going to make this an easy trip, though when it really acted up the whisky helped. Thank God Tessa didn't nag him about that; she never nagged him about anything. She didn't even complain when he started thrashing about in a temper, the way he had last night, when he'd felt so trapped and cooped up, and furious with Allyson because she seemed to be coping so well.

But this morning, hangover aside, he was feeling just dandy as he lay here with Tessa, his gorgeous, insatiable little nymphet, who was carrying his baby. She deserved everything he could give her for the way she made him feel so much better about himself, his decisions, and the whole wonderful life they had ahead of them.

'Oh my God!' Allyson murmured, coming to a halt. 'Tell me that's not Tessa Dukes standing in my office.'

Shelley was beside her. They were at the far end of the production office, just returning from lunch. The rest of the team was busy on the phones or with computers, though everyone had to be acutely aware that this would be the first time Allyson and Tessa had seen each other since the night Bob had left.

'I've got to hand it to her, she's got some nerve,' Shelley remarked.

Allyson was shaking all over. She'd never felt so at the whim of conflicting emotions. But she knew she had to go through with this. She just wished she didn't have to do it in front of an audience.

Before she could give herself any chance of backing down, she started across the room towards her office. Tessa was already watching her, that meek, frightened look she knew so well darkening her eyes.

'Hello, Allyson,' she said softly, as Allyson stalked into the room. 'I think we should talk . . .'

Allyson's eyes closed, then suddenly she seethed, '*Get out of my office.*'

Everyone outside stopped what they were doing. Then Shelley was there, grabbing Tessa by the arm and pushing her towards the door. 'Clear out your desk,' she said. 'We'll find you another.'

Closing the door she turned to Allyson, who was chalk white and shaking so badly she had to sit down.

'I'm sorry,' she said. 'I swore to myself that when this happened I wouldn't make a scene, but . . . I don't know if I can handle this . . .'

'You are handling it,' Shelley told her. 'You're handling it better than anyone I know.'

Allyson shook her head. 'It's all show, and you know it.' Suddenly her face crumpled and only with supreme effort did she manage to stop herself crying. 'Oh God, it's all so horrible,' she choked. 'I hate him, I despise him, but I still can't stop going over and over in my head all the things I wish I'd done, or hadn't done. What I should have said . . .'

'It's still early days,' Shelley reminded her. 'These things take time.'

Allyson blew her nose. 'I wish to God I could stop imagining them together. It's enough to know, without reproducing it in my own private Technicolor.'

Shelley smiled and said, 'It's not a programme day so you can just go home if you find the sight of her starts really getting to you.'

When Shelley had left she sat staring at the phone, her heart thudding away like a drum as she tried to pluck up the courage to call him. Tessa was here, so he could be at the flat alone . . .

Only after she finished dialling the number did she realise how badly she was shaking, and when his voice suddenly came down the line her heart gave such a horrible lurch she thought she was going to pass out.

'Bob?' she said, fighting to stop herself imagining his face. 'It's me.'

Silence.

He was shocked. He needed a moment. OK, she'd give it to him.

'What do you want?' he said finally.

Suddenly she was reeling, knocked so off course by his abruptness that she didn't even stop to consider that it might have been caused by nerves or caution or guilt, she only knew anger. But remembering that everyone outside would hear, all she said was, 'I want the rest of your belongings out of my home by the end of the day! I'll send it all round in a taxi.' And she slammed down the phone.

A few minutes later she was down in her dressing room, stretched out on the sofa, utterly drained. But it was OK. At least the hurdle of seeing Tessa for the first time was behind her. It could be she was going to regret the decision she'd reached about the girl's future on the programme, but for the time being she didn't have the energy even to think about changing it, so she'd just have to let events take their course.

Stella Cornbright's secretary Melissa put down her phone and nodded to Tessa. 'You can go in now,' she said.

Melissa watched the door close behind Tessa and fervently wished that she could be a fly on the wall. She'd only met Tessa a couple of times, as she rarely had reason to visit the *Soirée* studio, but there'd been so much about her in the papers these past few weeks that Melissa, like many others, almost felt she knew her. She couldn't help wondering if Tessa was about to find herself out of a job.

Stella Cornbright was staring frankly into Tessa's face, framed in its unruly thatch of shiny black hair, and pondering on what she'd done to Allyson and Bob Jaymes's marriage. Stella could only lament the idiocy in a man that made him behave like a prize buffoon. In her opinion Allyson was probably better shot of him. Still, that was Allyson's business, and this, for the moment, was hers.

Tricky. At least it would have been had Shelley Bronson not come up with a solution, one she had formulated with Allyson herself. Stella wasn't sure she approved, but she was prepared to give it a go if Allyson and Shelley were.

Launching straight into why Tessa was there, she said, 'So, what are we going to do about this unholy mess you've created?'

As it seemed like a rhetorical question Tessa didn't answer.

'I'll be frank with you, if Allyson had personally requested it, I'd be firing you right now. What do you have to say to that?'

Tessa was momentarily thrown, then, clearing her throat, she said, 'I feel terrible about what's happened, but . . .'

'If you had any real sensitivity you'd be leaving of your own accord,' Stella barked. 'But I can't force you, nor will I try. What I'm going to do is act on the reports I've had on your work performance, all of which are good. That means, young lady, that instead of being thrown out on your ear, you're being promoted.'

Tessa's eyes flew open. 'Promoted?' she echoed.

'To the position of researcher and occasional reporter. Your potential,

I'm told, is considerable.' Her bulging eyes were fixed on Tessa, demanding a response.

'Thank you,' was all Tessa managed.

Stella closed the personnel file. 'OK, you can go,' she said shortly, and after her beady eyes had escorted Tessa to the door she picked up the phone to call Shelley.

'Promoted?' Bob echoed.

Tessa nodded. 'I've been dying to tell you. Where were you?'

'On air,' Bob reminded her. 'I don't understand. Why the hell would they promote you with all that's going on?'

'You were probably right, they were afraid I'd sue if they fired me.'

He grunted and went to pour himself a drink. He'd had a godawful day with one of the sports editors at LWT. Sure he'd let them down these past few weeks, but what the hell was he supposed to do with the press camped out on his doorstep.

They made him sick, the whole damned lot of them. Subs messing about with his scripts, producers giving his matches to other, less experienced reporters, his agent calling up to tell him that the new deal they had in the offing with Sky had hit a few problems. Well, let his bloody agent sort it out, it was what he paid him for, wasn't it?

'She's up to something!' he snapped, suddenly remembering Allyson as he emptied what was left of a bottle of gin into a cheap glass. 'Haven't we got any more?' he growled, looking at the empty bottle.

Tessa smiled benignly. 'It's in the cupboard,' she said. Then, lifting her face, 'Don't I get a kiss, Mr Grouch?'

Reaching out, he dragged her towards him and pressed his mouth hard against hers. She snaked her arms round his neck and pushed her groin against his. Since all she was wearing was one of his shirts, he had only to lift her onto the counter, unzip his trousers and enter her.

It was over quickly, and what followed, the tenderness and the giggling, the teasing and the cajoling, went a long way towards working him out of his bad mood. Though she hadn't long gone off to take a shower before he started feeling sour again, so he opened a fresh bottle of gin and drank a bitter, bolshy toast to Allyson, who had refused to talk to him when he'd phoned about picking up more clothes. The taxi she'd threatened to send over had never materialised. Maybe the answer was just to get himself a whole load of new gear and let the past stay where it was.

After pouring himself another drink Bob slumped down in front of the television. His head was spinning and he felt nauseous, which was something Tessa never seemed to feel, given her condition. He hated even to think it, but lately he'd found himself wondering if she'd made it up about the baby. Not that it would change anything.

He took a large mouthful of gin. Why the hell did she have to go off and see this bloke Julian when she had him? He'd given up his wife, was getting regularly dumped on by the press, and she gets promoted and goes off to celebrate with *Julian*. It didn't seem fair.

His glass hit the floor and broke. He left it where it was, too drunk and worked up to care.

'Here, drink this,' Shelley said.

Allyson took the brandy. She was huddled into a blanket on Shelley's sofa facing the sluggishly flickering fire. Shadows from the fire danced around the softly lit room.

Allyson drank and sat quietly watching the fire. 'I keep asking myself, what it is about her?' she said after a while. 'I know she's young and pretty, but so are thousands of girls. So what is it about Tessa Dukes?'

'You could ask what is it about any of us,' Shelley said. 'No one knows what attracts us to the people we're attracted to.'

'He's never done anything like this before,' Allyson protested. 'We've always been so close. And it wasn't as if he wasn't getting sex at home. So why did he need to go elsewhere? And why to *her*?

Shelley, too, had often wondered what Bob saw in Tessa, for she knew how many affairs the man had had during his marriage, but not even Shelley had been able to bring him close to leaving Allyson, and she was certainly much more Bob's type . . .

This led her on to Allyson's belief in his fidelity, which was an aberration that should be addressed, for it was only a matter of time before the press would be trumpeting his serial adultery all over the front pages.

Give him his due, Bob was pretty discreet, but this *was* the British press they were talking about.

So, bracing herself with the reassurance that in the long run it was the kindest thing she could do, Shelley said softly, 'Ally, Tessa isn't the first.'

Allyson was about to drink, but her hand stopped in mid-air.

Shelley looked at her. 'I'm sorry,' she whispered. 'I wish to God I wasn't the one to tell you.'

Allyson leaned forward and put down her glass. Her whole life was crumbling again, but she had to let it happen; there was no way she could stop it. 'How do you know?'

Shelley steeled herself again. 'I was one of the women he tried . . . Well, let's just say, he tried with.'

Allyson took a sharp, quick breath. Her eyes remained focused on the exquisite Night and Day clock by Lalique. After a while it felt strangely soothing, the way the two female figures, engraved so gracefully in the glass, were entwined. Shelley had so many beautiful things, but of all of them this was the one Allyson loved the most.

'I always turned him down,' Shelley said.

Allyson's eyes left the clock. 'I suppose it was why he always had such a hard time with you,' she said. 'His ego probably couldn't handle the rejection.' She turned her head and Shelley saw the tears starting to fall from her eyes. 'Men like Bob never can handle women like you. You intimidate them because you're so strong. Oh God, Shelley, how is it possible to love someone who treats you like this?'

'You'd be amazed how many women do. I've been there myself, but never again.'

'No, never again,' Allyson said, a fierce determination in her now.

 *Chapter Six*

'HELLO, TESSA. How are you?'

'I'm OK. Got stuck in traffic, that's why I'm late.' The rosiness of her cheeks told how cold it was outside, but her smile, when it came, was like sunshine.

'Sit down.' Laura Risby's wiry brown hair was tucked behind her ears, exposing the calm warmth of a face that was in the twilight of a serene and understated beauty.

Tessa sat in a leather wing-backed chair, her face gently illumined by the muted light of the desk lamp.

'I'm glad you came,' Laura said. 'I've been reading about you in the papers.'

Tessa grimaced. 'I guessed you might,' she said sheepishly, 'but I didn't really feel like talking about it.'

'Do you now?' Laura asked.

'I'm not sure. It's all been pretty, well, you know.'

No, Laura didn't know, but she could guess, and though, as a psychotherapist, it wasn't her place to approve or disapprove of this affair with Bob Jaymes, she was fond enough of the girl to be more than a little concerned at the way events appeared to be unfolding.

'You're still at the same job?' she asked.

'Yes and no,' Tessa answered. 'I'm with the same programme, but I'm a researcher/reporter now.'

'What about Allyson? Do you come into much contact with her?'

'A bit. But mainly I'm out, you know, on location, getting together material for the filmed insert that comes after the commercial break. It's really cool. I did one of the inserts myself the other day, just for practice, and they're letting me have the tape to give to my new agent.'

Laura's surprise showed. 'You have an agent?' she echoed.

'Yes. Julian, he's this kind of friend, he introduced me.'

'I see.' Laura drank some coffee. 'You were always very fond of Allyson,' she said. 'Has that changed?'

'Oh no!' Tessa seemed genuinely distressed by the idea that Laura would even think it. 'She's the kindest, most wonderful person I've ever met, and I can't tell you how terrible I feel about everything that's happened. And sometimes she looks so cut up about it all that I just want to put my arms around her and cry with her.'

Laura waited to see if she wanted to expand on that, but she seemed not to so Laura said, 'What about Bob? How do you feel about him?'

'Oh, he's wonderful. I really love him. And no one's ever made me feel that special before.'

Given her case history, Laura didn't doubt that. 'Does he love you?'

Tessa blushed. 'He says he does.' She paused, then nodded happily. 'Yes, I think so,' she said. 'I mean, sometimes he gets in a bad mood, not with me, but because he feels terrible about Allyson, and he gets angry with himself for not being able to handle it better.'

'How do you think he should handle it?' Laura asked.

Tessa's head went to one side as she thought. 'Well, I think it's better that he's not lying any more,' she began, swerving away from the question. 'I know Allyson probably didn't want to hear the truth but when things like this happen, it has to come out some time, doesn't it?'

Laura's professional antennae were suddenly alert. 'Like it did before?' she said carefully.

To her dismay Tessa looked sharply away, rejecting the bait. Laura tried again. 'Do you feel at all responsible for what's happened?'

Tessa reached into her bag, pulled out a bunch of grapes and began to eat. Laura was familiar with this method of defence, an attempt to appear nonchalant and detached, when in truth she was anything but.

'Yes, of course I do,' Tessa said, chewing. 'It wouldn't have happened if it weren't for me, it might still not have happened if I hadn't told him I was pregnant.'

Laura nodded slowly. 'And are you?' she asked.

Tessa inhaled deeply. 'I wasn't when he left,' she admitted. 'Well, I might have been, but I didn't know it then.'

'But you are now?'

Tessa nodded.

Laura sat quietly for a moment. This manipulation of older people was typical of someone with Tessa's background, so Laura wasn't particularly surprised this was happening, though she could wish that it wasn't proving so costly, tragic even, for those who were involved.

Laura changed the subject. 'You mentioned a friend just now. Julian,' she said.

'Oh, yeah, Jules. He's great. He's my brother. Not officially, obviously. I've adopted him.'

This new piece of information immediately set off all kinds of alarm bells for Laura. 'How old is he?' she asked.

'Same age as me. I think he wants us to be, you know, closer than brother and sister.'

Laura wasn't liking the sound of this at all. 'Is that what you want?'

Tessa wrinkled her nose as she thought. Laura watched her, knowing that behind her frank expression and simplistic manner there was a maelstrom of complexities that had no moral compass to guide them. It wasn't that she didn't know right from wrong, it was simply that she had difficulty in attaching much importance to either. Although Laura was well aware of the reasons behind this disconnection from her conscience, she'd made small progress in its repair. It didn't help that Tessa had been such an irregular visitor over the past two years, but these things couldn't be forced, unless of course Tessa became a danger to herself or society, and as yet she wasn't that.

Finally Tessa answered the question. 'No, it's not what I want,' she said. 'I've got Bob. Although Jules is pretty cool. We've kissed a couple of times.' She giggled. 'Bob would go ballistic if he found out.'

Laura regarded her with unease. 'Tell me,' she said, 'does Bob remind you of anyone, someone you know, maybe from your past?'

Tessa screwed up her nose again, then shook her head. 'No.'

'What about Allyson?' Laura asked.

Again Tessa shook her head.

'Have you ever told Allyson about your mother?'

'Oh no. I never tell anyone. That's all in the past.'

Laura said, 'Did it come as a complete surprise to Allyson when she learned of your affair with her husband?'

'I don't think so,' Tessa answered after a moment's reflection. 'I think that she knew, but she was turning a blind eye.'

Laura almost groaned. This was worse than she'd expected. 'So you told Bob you were pregnant, which then forced him to make Allyson face the truth?' she said, spelling it out.

Tessa frowned. 'I suppose so,' she answered.

'Are you recognising any similarities here?' Laura challenged.

Tessa stiffened and suddenly the grapes were out again.

Laura allowed several minutes to tick by, and was on the verge of asking the question again when Tessa said, 'You know, I've been in a bit of a state since everything blew up.'

'In what way?'

'Well, because of Allyson mainly. I wish it hadn't happened to her. Everyone but Allyson knows Bob's been sleeping with other women for years. It was kind of an accepted thing, you know, that no one would tell her. I expect she knew though, and pretended not to.'

Laura inwardly groaned, for there were those fatal words again.

'So what now?' Laura said.

'Now,' Tessa responded, 'I think I'll have to get an abortion. I mean, I can't have a baby when I've got a whole new career starting up, can I?'

'What about Bob? Does he want the baby?'

She nodded, and looked away. 'I'll have to tell him I had a miscarriage,' she mumbled, digging back into her bag of grapes.

'Tessa,' Laura said firmly, 'I want you to tell me who you think Bob and Allyson are representing in your life.'

'You think Bob's the father figure and Allyson's the mother.'

'Don't you think that?'

'I can see why you do.'

Laura said gently, 'Can you see that you're punishing them for something they had nothing to do with?'

Tessa's lips trembled as she tried to laugh. 'I don't think Bob's being punished, not with all the sex I give him.'

Laura looked at her until Tessa's eyes dropped.

'It's been almost two years since your breakdown,' Laura reminded her. 'You've come to understand a lot about yourself and what happened in that time. So why are you denying it now?'

'I'm not,' Tessa responded.

Laura fired the next question. 'Then why did you have to make Julian your brother? Why not just a friend?'

'I don't know. What difference does it make? I suppose because I always wanted a brother who was a friend.'

'Unlike the one you had.'

'Totally.' Tessa looked at her watch. 'I'm going to have to cut this short,' she said. 'I promised to be home early. Bob's been told he's not hosting the Sportsman of the Year awards now, and he's really upset.'

In dismay Laura watched her go for her coat. 'Would you like to make another appointment?' she said.

'I'll have to give you a call,' Tessa replied. 'I'm so busy these days I might not have the time,' and with a hurried but extremely polite good-bye, she was gone.

Laura sat staring at the door, and shaking her head in frustration. She needed to see this girl more often, especially now she'd got herself embroiled in this horrible mess that had such sinister similarities to what had happened in her past. In fact, Laura believed that Tessa, with the extraordinary power that a bruised and damaged mind often had, had manipulated the entire affair, setting it up to be a sad and poten-tially disastrous restaging of earlier events. Not that Laura thought for a moment that Tessa's love for Bob and Allyson wasn't genuine, because it almost unquestionably was; it just wasn't always easy for her to apply her emotions in a normal way.

Where's the gin?' Bob shouted from the kitchen.

Tessa lay in bed, idly stroking the pink, fluffy squirrel that was squashed between the pillows. 'I threw it out. You drink too much, and then you get angry,' she replied.

He appeared in the doorway, clearly straining to hold onto his temper. 'Have you got any idea what kind of a day I've had!' he demanded. 'First of all I'm told I'm no longer needed for the awards. Then I find out that Duncan Grueber, a snot-nosed kid half my age, is covering the big match for Sky tonight. Then you throw away the gin. God, I need a drink.'

'More than you need this,' she teased, stroking him.

He'd liked to have said no, but it would have been a lie. He needed a drink, and he needed one badly, because on top of everything else that had happened today, he'd been notified by the bank that all the funds in his and Allyson's joint accounts were frozen until their marital difficul-ties were resolved, one way or the other. Which meant that Allyson must have contacted them to make the break-up official.

Inside he was panicking. It was as though everything were slipping away from him. Christ, he needed to get to his money. He was practi-cally broke already and the hundred and fifty quid that was in his own account was going to get him about as far as the middle of next week, if he was lucky. It was all right for Allyson, with her inherited wealth to bail her out, but it sure as hell wasn't all right for him.

He went to find his coat. He had to have a drink, and maybe, if he drank enough, he'd manage to link up with the feeling of liberation he'd had when he'd actually believed that Tessa's pregnancy was a God-given sign to the path of his destiny, providing him not only with the permission to walk out on his marriage, but with an absolution from guilt. Well, it certainly didn't feel like that now, in fact it was so far from anything that even resembled liberation he might just as well consign himself straight to hell and be done with it.

A few miles away, in the centre of London, Allyson and Shelley and a few of their friends were applauding loudly as the final curtain came down on a spirited and imaginative production of *La Bohème*.

As they made their way outside, Allyson was only too aware of the way people were whispering to each other, making her feel so horribly pitied that she could feel cracks appearing in the veneer of airy laughter and interest she was affecting as she and her friends discussed the performance. This wasn't her first excursion back into the social scene, but tonight was proving particularly hard, because she was feeling so awful about what she'd done today. At the time she had felt so driven and vengeful that she'd derived a deliciously vindictive enjoyment from instructing the bank and her lawyers. It had taken all of ten minutes for that to wear off, and now she hated what she'd done.

Everyone had said it was too soon, that she didn't need to do anything yet, but they were wrong. She had needed to do something, and if that was what it took to get Bob to face the reality of what he had done, then so be it. But when she replayed her messages when she got home, she discovered that it hadn't paid off in the way she had hoped.

As she listened, she could be in no doubt that he was drunk. But through the slurred words his fury reached her loud and clear; so did the fact that he had somehow twisted events round in his mind to enable himself to blame her for the break-up. He should have left her years ago, he ranted. She'd always considered herself to be better than him, just because her family had money and his father was only a labourer on a building site. Well, she could stick her money. He was well out of it, and happier now than he had ever been.

Though the harshness of his words cut right through her, the very fact that he was so drunk told her that his own hurt and suffering was perhaps greater than she'd imagined. But the sudden recollection of where he was and who he was with ripped any impulse to feel sorry for him out by the roots, providing even more space for the fiercely bitter urge to cause Bob and Tessa every bit as much pain as they were causing her.

 *Chapter Seven*

THE NEWS OF STELLA CORNBRIGHT'S retirement and impending death had brought the *Soirée* offices to a standstill. Shelley had told them all just after the previous day's recording, and now, after a night to think about it, everyone had something to say. With Allyson and Shelley yet to put in an appearance that morning, they were free to air their views and recycle the gossip they'd already managed to glean about Stella, and about Mark and Nicholas Reiner, whose takeover of the company was going to be announced the following week.

'Someone told me the Reiners are actually British, not American,' Debbie, one of the researchers, said.

'They are,' Jerry Milne confirmed. 'I directed the show that Mark Reiner appeared on back whenever it was. He sounds American, but that's because he grew up over there.'

'I remember him,' Hayley Brocket, one of the programme's producers, said. 'He's quite young, isn't he?'

'If you call thirty-six young,' Frankie, the production manager, who rated anyone over thirty as past it, said bitchily.

'More to the point, what's he going to do with the company?' Edmund, another programme researcher, demanded.

'I can answer that,' Marvin said, coming through the doorway.

They were all ears. Marvin was Shelley's assistant.

'Apparently,' Marvin said, enjoying the attention, 'he's moving the transmission to eleven thirty and bringing in another presenter.'

Tessa's eyes rounded.

'Don't listen to him,' Alan Rich chided. 'He doesn't know any more than we do.'

'Straight up,' Marvin insisted. 'My sister's friends with Melissa, Stella's secretary. I got it from her.'

They all looked at each other, not sure whether to believe him. Even so, they were impressed with his source.

'I also heard he wants the programme to go live,' Marvin added.

'At eleven thirty!' Jerry exploded. 'Does the man think we don't have lives?'

'Say it a bit louder and you'll save *Variety* the print space,' Shelley commented as she and Allyson walked in. 'The official announcement's not until next week,' she continued, 'so if anyone calls from the press, trying to get some inside information, play dumb. As for any of the rumours you may have heard, I'll be better placed to put you in the picture after my meeting with Mark Reiner today.'

Allyson was staring across the room at Tessa, whose shaggy dark head was bowed over a newspaper. Allyson was certain the engrossment was feigned, and felt a dizzying rush of hatred, for it was thanks to that little bitch that she and Bob wouldn't be spending today, their *nineteenth wedding anniversary*, together. And the story the bitch was reading—was it the one about Bob's drunken rampage last night, when he'd got himself thrown out of a pub and threatened to beat up a policeman? How was she feeling about that? Allyson wanted to know, sitting there looking like butter wouldn't melt. Did she feel any kind of responsibility for the state Bob was in? Did she know what the word meant, even? Maybe Allyson should go and drum it into her head with a blunt object. Then Tessa looked up, and Allyson turned away, saying, 'Marv, I've got a mountain of mail to get through, can I hijack you for the morning?'

'If it's OK with Shelley,' he answered.

Shelley waved an assenting hand. 'OK, everyone, we've got a show to get on the air. And today's guests are?' She looked at the board. 'Mmm,' she grunted when she saw the names that were chalked up for Cocktails. Then her face brightened. 'Josh Burrows is coming in for the Nightcap. New film?'

Edmund nodded. 'I gave Ally the video . . .'

'Which she sat up and watched last night,' Ally finished. 'Totally absorbing, absolutely forgettable.'

'And the film insert?' Shelley enquired.

'We're shooting it this morning,' Edmund answered. 'It's Tessa's story.'

Shelley's eyes lost their warmth as they moved to Tessa.

'Uh, it's this writer in North London,' Tessa said, stammering slightly. 'She's got one of the world's biggest collections of dolls. It's seriously spooky. The neighbours swear they hear them screaming in the night.'

'OK. Shoot the story today, then let's schedule a couple of interviews around it and use it another night. I'll take a look at the inserts on the shelf and see if there's something we can use for tonight.'

'Debbie, did you manage to get a selection of reviews for Josh Burrows's film?' Allyson asked.

'You'll have them by lunchtime,' Debbie replied.

Allyson stayed in her office all morning. She knew Shelley was on edge about her lunch with Mark Reiner, but they were both too busy to discuss it. However, no amount of work was going to allow Allyson to forget the significance of the day, nor would it stop her remembering that cold sunny afternoon, nineteen years ago, when her father had walked her down the aisle and she had looked into Bob's eyes and known, beyond any doubt, how deeply she was loved. And that was the same man who was probably too hung over today to read the date on the newspaper, never mind remember the details of the obscene spectacle he'd made of himself the night before.

Obviously he was in a much worse state than she'd imagined, to be going around getting himself into fights and threatening to assault a policeman, and the anniversary present she'd sent him, a taxi full of his bills and belongings stuffed into bin liners, wasn't going to do much to cheer him up either. Especially coming on top of the blow she herself had dealt him yesterday with the bank . . .

She looked out of her office, across to where Tessa was talking on the phone. Her heart twisted. Was she talking to Bob? Was she trying to soothe the humiliating effects of the article? The very thought of such an intimacy sent all sympathy for Bob fleeing for cover as another storm of hatred broke.

'Allyson Jaymes,' she snapped into the phone.

'Hi. It's me.'

Her heart stopped dead, as the sound of his voice slammed a lid on all the raging frustration and anger. God knew how she had hoped for a call this morning, though in truth she'd never expected it to come. In her best neutral voice, she said, 'Hello. How are you?'

His laugh was dry-throated and achingly familiar. 'Lousy, actually,' he admitted. 'Did you see the *Express*?'

'Yes.'

There was a long, tense silence as she waited for him to apologise for the offensive diatribe he'd left on her machine last night. But instead he said, 'Can I see you? I want to talk.'

Allyson's chest was suddenly so tight, it was hard to breathe. Eight long and bitterly hard weeks she'd waited to hear those words, and now he'd spoken them she didn't know what to say. It wasn't that she didn't want to see him, she was just afraid of what he might want to talk about. Please God, not divorce. 'Can we talk?' he repeated into the silence. 'I'll come over to the flat this evening, if you're free.'

It was on the tip of her tongue to remind him, gently, what day it was, but her self-protective hostility barged its way through instead. 'If you think you can control yourself,' she said.

'What the hell kind of an answer's that?' he snapped.

'The last time I saw you, you hit me,' she reminded him. 'And you haven't exactly been behaving in a way that suggests I'd be safe around you since,' she added.

'Are you going to be there, or aren't you?' he growled.

'Come about seven,' she said.

After putting the phone down she went straight into Shelley's office and closed the door.

'So, what do you think he wants to talk about?' she said breathlessly, when she'd finished recounting the details.

'Could be anything,' Shelley answered. 'What if he wants to come back?'

'Oh God, I don't know.' Allyson groaned as her stomach churned. 'Obviously I want him back, but . . .' She dashed a hand through her hair and started to pace. 'What if he turns up drunk and we have a horrible fight and he beats me up.' Her face turned pale. 'Oh my God,' she gasped. 'Are you doing anything this evening?'

Shelley almost laughed. 'Are you serious? It'll send him right off his head if he sees me there,' she said.

'You could hide,' Allyson suggested. 'He won't even have to know you're there. Think how you're going to feel if he does beat me up and you weren't there to stop it.'

Shelley laughed. 'OK. I'll be there,' she said. 'But I'm not hiding.'

Allyson grinned, and was on the point of leaving when she turned back. 'Good luck with your lunch.'

Shelley's smile vanished. 'Don't!' she groaned. 'I haven't been this nervous in years. I'll let you know how it goes.'

Though Shelley was five minutes late, there was no sign of Mark Reiner at the Pharmacy, the clinically styled restaurant in Notting Hill, West London, that Mark had chosen for their lunchtime meeting.

Shelley looked businesslike and beautiful. She wore her luxuriant hair in a chignon, allowing full view of her exquisite, finely honed features. The silk shirt beneath her soft black suede suit was vaguely transparent, with no lace bra to spoil the smooth plane of the fabric, nor was there any unbecoming trace of a panty line beneath her skirt. It made her feel more powerful and feminine knowing how she was, or wasn't, dressed beneath her outer garments.

As she glanced casually at the menu she was mulling over the rumours that were circulating about the changes Mark Reiner was planning. Though they were probably less than 10 per cent accurate, she was fairly certain he'd want to make some changes, so she was ready to put forward her own proposals. The documents in her briefcase contained ideas and budgets that were audacious, though conscience and loyalty made her hold back slightly.

A few subtle enquiries had told her that the current Mrs Reiner had recently returned to the States and a divorce was in the offing, so Shelley had taken home a videotape of the *Soirée* programme he'd featured in, and watched it several times in order to acquaint herself better with the man who was about to become her new boss. It was why she was experiencing such anticipation and even apprehension about this meeting, for there had been a lot in the programme, which had been recorded during one of her rare absences, to convince her of how appealing he was. And the first glimpse of the tall, extremely striking and well-dressed man, as he walked into the restaurant and was greeted warmly by the hostess, did nothing to alter Shelley's view.

He had to be at least six foot three, which was extremely pleasing, as it was rare for Shelley to meet a man she didn't have to look down on. And the fluid movements of what was clearly a well-toned and muscular physique, clothed in a black Armani suit, were so entirely male that the sexuality he seemed to exude was, though subtle, totally compelling.

Shelley stood up as he approached the table and smiled as she shook his hand.

'Shelley,' he said, his deep-set brown eyes looking directly into hers. 'I'm sorry if I kept you.'

The American accent she had expected, even though she knew he was British by birth, but the warmth of his tone and the intensity of his gaze unsettled her slightly. Though it wasn't possible to tell what he was thinking, her instincts were responding with the kind of shivers that suggested he too was making an assessment not entirely professional.

'I'm glad to meet you,' she said, humour flashing in her eyes.

His hand was still holding hers, but he let go as he waved her back to her chair. 'Did you order a drink?' he asked, sitting down too.

'Evian for me,' she said to the waiter.

'For me too,' he said. He looked at her again and raised a single eyebrow in a mock-conspiratorial kind of way, which made her smile.

His face was slender, his eyes narrow and quietly assessing. Though in his way he was strikingly handsome, his nose was slightly hooked and his mouth was too wide. Yet these imperfections were obscured by the magnetic potency of his smile. And as their eyes continued a friendly, yet explicit appraisal, Shelley could feel small waves of pleasure eddying through her. 'May I offer my congratulations on your acquisition of the company?' she said, her dark eyes showing irony.

'I'll accept them if you're offering,' he replied, matching her expression.

Barely two minutes had passed and already the chemistry was loading the air.

'Shall we decide what we're going to eat first?' he suggested, as he was handed a menu.

His manner had taken a few paces back from the intensity, which allowed an easier, less demanding tenor to the proceedings, so that by the time their meals arrived they were talking about music and Shelley was forced to dab away tears of laughter as he told her some outrageous Country and Western song titles someone had recently sent him.

'You're making this up,' she accused, breathlessly.

'I swear,' he protested. 'Apparently they're all genuine. What about this one? "Mama Get the Hammer there's a Fly on Papa's Head".'

Shelley had just taken a mouthful of water, and almost choked. 'Stop,' she gasped when finally she could. 'Stop, I can't laugh any more. Anyway, I thought we were here to discuss the future of *Soirée*.'

'Indeed we are,' he agreed and took a mouthful of food.

'Do you want to give me your comments first, or shall I start with my proposals?'

He seemed amused. 'You're that confident that I intend to keep the programme going?' he said.

Shelley didn't miss a beat. 'Do you?' she said.

He arched an eyebrow. 'Let's hear your proposals. Just give me bottom lines. We can go into detail later.'

She cut a slice of veal and ate it first, giving herself a moment to regroup her thoughts, for that hint about axing the programme had momentarily thrown her.

'To begin with I'd like to propose a fifty per cent increase in budget,' she said, expecting an immediate protest. However, she received none, so she continued. 'The extra funds would enable us to travel around the country and transmit from other cities, maybe even other countries, lending a more international appeal.'

He nodded for her to go on.

'That's it,' she said. 'We're a successful programme, so I don't see any reason to make changes just for the sake of it.'

He picked up his glass, finished eating, then drank.

He had now become impossible to read, which perversely, considering the threat he might be posing to the programme, was making him more attractive than ever.

For his part, though he was looking into her face, at that moment he wasn't really seeing her. He was thinking, considering what she'd said, and evaluating the body language that wasn't at all hard to read. He'd heard what a powerfully sexy and intelligent woman she was, and he admired women like her, who made their sexuality work for them. It was going to be interesting to see how far she would go with it.

'I've been watching the programme these past few weeks,' he said, and his eyes drifted upwards to hers again. 'I've also looked at the ratings and read the audience straw polls,' he continued evenly. 'Unless you can convince me otherwise, I think the programme should be reduced to three nights a week, and a new presenter should be brought in. Cocktails is too stuffy. It should be reinvented as Happy Hour with younger guests and a much younger host.'

Though she didn't show it, Shelley was reeling. 'What brought you to these conclusions?' she asked.

Impressed by the deliberate mildness of her tone, he said, 'The general trend of the ratings is down. Some shows do well, but the figures indicate that the programme, if it's to continue, is in need of a shake-up. I'm not criticising you as a producer. Everything I've heard about you assures me you are excellent at your job, and I think, hope, you will find the challenge of a new shape to your programme stimulating as well as rewarding. To focus on three nights a week will make your team sharper in their choice of material, and to bring in new, and certainly younger, blood is vital for the image of the programme.'

Shelley might have laughed had it not seemed so inappropriate, for what he'd just outlined were all the changes she longed to make herself, but loyalty to the team, and particularly to Allyson, had always prevailed. 'Are you suggesting we get rid of Allyson Jaymes?' she said.

His eyebrows rose. 'Not at all,' he answered. 'What I'm saying is we need someone younger to front the show.'

'So where does Allyson fit in?'

'She could continue with the Nightcap slot.'

Shelley lowered her eyes. His determination, tinged with ruthlessness, was pushing her loyalty to Allyson into a distant second place. Then her head came up as he said, 'I'm afraid we'll have to postpone the details of my proposals to another time.' He was taking out a credit card and signalling to the waiter. Then, looking across the table, he let his intense gaze rest on hers once again.

'I've a feeling we're going to get along well,' he said. 'I'm certainly looking forward to finding out.'

The evening was chill and dark as Allyson tramped through the drizzling rain from her car to the flat. Rumours of Mark Reiner's takeover had already made the papers; the *Standard* was full of it tonight, along with all the speculation she'd got wind of in the office earlier. So now she was convinced that everyone thought that, on top of everything else she'd been through lately, she was about to be removed from her job. And if she didn't have such great faith in Shelley she might have been more worried about that too. If that wasn't bad enough, one of Tessa's film inserts, with Tessa appearing, was being aired tonight. It would be Tessa's first time on screen and Allyson was deriving a certain comfort from the fact that Bob was going to be with her this evening, instead of out celebrating with *Soirée's* very own Tellytubby.

Opening the front door, she heard the telephone start to ring. She dumped her shopping on the floor and picked up the phone.

'Hi, it's me,' Shelley said.

Relief expelled Allyson's pent-up breath. 'Hi. Just got in. How was lunch?' she asked.

'I've got a lot to tell you,' Shelley answered.

At that Allyson's imagination erupted and within milliseconds she was being dumped from her job, divorced from her husband, rejected by the public and utterly destroyed by a killer nervous breakdown.

'What time's Bob supposed to be getting there?'

'In about an hour. You know, I was thinking, you don't have to come. I'm sure I can handle it.'

'I'll come,' Shelley said. 'If it's a reunion he's after and you find you're interested I'll leave. But if he turns up drunk—'

'OK,' Allyson said, cutting her off. She didn't want to think about Bob being drunk.

'Listen, we're about to go into the underpass, so I'll lose you. I should be there in half an hour. Maybe less.'

Allyson rang off and went to put on the kettle. Then, smothering her face with her hands, she fought back the sudden urge to weep. In the past her father had always been the one to make things better. Now he barely remembered who she was, and her mother was so upset by Bob's desertion that Allyson was usually the one to comfort her.

Forgetting about the kettle she went to put on the heating, then still wrapped in her coat she lay down on the bed. The phone rang several times, but she let the machine pick it up, as she sank deeper and deeper into despair. She had no energy, no fight. Things weren't going to work out with Bob tonight, she just knew it, and she wished to God now that she hadn't agreed to see him.

However, by the time Shelley arrived she'd managed to force herself into the shower, which had somehow manoeuvred her out of the bleakness and back towards a few daring rays of hope. It was possible that

Bob might be wanting a reconciliation, and Shelley wouldn't really allow her to be thrown off the programme. She was even able to laugh at Mark Reiner's Country and Western song titles when Shelley repeated them as she poured her a generous glass of Merlot. Shelley had let herself in while Allyson was still in the shower, so was already halfway through her own glass by the time Allyson put in an appearance. They always had keys to each other's flats, in case of emergencies.

'Sounds like you two hit it off,' she said, sitting opposite Shelley.

'We did,' Shelley confirmed, and the glimmering light in her eyes for some reason made Allyson's heart contract.

'Tell me more about lunch,' she said.

Shelley's eyes moved to her reflection in the night-blackened window. Allyson was bound to have read the paper by now, so there wasn't much doubt about what she was really asking—and Shelley couldn't have felt worse, for she knew that Allyson would be trusting her to keep the programme format exactly as it was. Prevaricating, she said, 'There's not much to tell. We mostly talked generally. About TV in the States compared to here, that sort of thing.'

'Nothing about the future of *Soirée*?'

Shelley continued to avoid her eyes. 'Only in the abstract.'

Allyson was quiet, and Shelley felt a crippling guilt when she looked up. 'He wants to replace me, doesn't he?' Allyson said.

Shelley reached for Allyson's hand, but Allyson moved it away. 'It's not that bad,' Shelley said. 'He wants you to continue with the Nightcap.'

Allyson felt sick. 'And Cocktails?' she said.

Shelley was searching desperately for a way to postpone this, but it seemed her hesitation had already answered.

'He wants someone younger, doesn't he?'

Shelley nodded.

Allyson stared at her, ready to crumple beneath the weight of rejection. Then anger and bitterness swept into her heart. She wasn't just going to sit here, getting bashed to a pulp by a fate that deserved, at the very least, to be battled. 'It's different for you, isn't it?' she cried. 'You're not getting pushed aside to make room for some airhead with stardust in her eyes. Did you fight for me, Shelley? Did you tell him it's *my* show?'

Thrown by the outburst, Shelley said, as calmly as she could, 'We didn't get down to specifics. He just gave me his thoughts.'

Allyson started to speak, but seizing the ground Shelley stopped her. 'Listen, I believe he's a reasonable man. If we can come up with something, if we can think of a way to make your age work for you, instead of against you . . . he'll give us a hearing. I'm sure of it.'

'*Soirée* is my programme!' Allyson cried. 'Why the hell should I be trying to come up with something?'

Not wanting to get into an argument about whose programme it actually was, Shelley said, 'We've been using this format for eight years. Maybe it is a bit tired. Maybe what we need is a new concept.'

The doorbell sounded, announcing Bob's arrival.

'Oh God!' Allyson cried, as a whole other fear sprang up inside her. 'Just what I need.'

'Shall I tell him to go?' Shelley offered. 'You don't have to see him.'

'No. I do.'

'Why?'

'I don't know!' Allyson snapped angrily. 'Maybe to get it all over with at once,' and getting up she went to the entryphone and buzzed him in.

As she opened the front door she could hear his footsteps coming up the stairs. Suddenly she wished Shelley wasn't there. Bob had never liked Shelley, and right now she didn't either.

'Hello,' he said. Though he was still in shadow, she could see he looked terrible, but then she probably did too.

She attempted a smile. She wanted so badly to walk into those arms that she knew so well, but it might not be what he wanted. So she stayed where she was, listening to the unsteady thump of her heart. 'It's still raining out,' he said awkwardly.

She nodded.

'Is it OK if I take off my coat?'

That made her want to cry, because he was her husband and this was their home, but all she did was nod.

'Are you going to say anything?' he demanded.

She jumped at his tone, but realising his belligerence was caused by nerves she said, 'How are you?'

He came forward. The light moved across his face and her heart twisted. His belovedly familiar features were ravaged with exhaustion. She wanted to sit him down, soothe him and tell him it would be all right, yet somehow she knew already it wasn't going to be.

'It's money, isn't it?' she said. 'That's why you're here.'

His eyes went down and she wondered how much pride he had left.

'I think the BBC are going to drop me,' he said. 'Permanently.'

It was probably the wine that almost made Allyson laugh, for she wouldn't normally find their imminent state of unemployment funny. But she didn't want to tell him about her, so all she said was, 'I'm sorry.'

He waved a dismissive hand, then followed her into the kitchen. He was almost at the table before he saw Shelley, and the aggression and anger that leapt into the air the instant he did told Allyson that she had made a disastrous mistake in asking Shelley to be there.

'Hello, Bob,' Shelley said mildly.

He turned to Allyson. His face was twisted with rage. 'You can't make a move without her, can you?' He pushed his face up to hers. 'I thought we were going to talk?' he hissed.

Allyson wiped the saliva from her face. None of it felt real. 'What do you want to talk about?' she asked.

He turned to Shelley. 'Not with her here. Either she goes, or I go.'

Shelley stood up. 'I'm going to wait in the sitting room,' she said to Bob, 'because I can see that as long as I'm here you're going to carry on behaving like the asshole you are.'

Allyson saw his fist tighten and grabbed it with her hands. As soon as Shelley was gone she let go and said, 'What do you want to talk about?'

He slumped down in the chair Shelley had vacated. 'Why did you ask her to be here?' he said. 'It would have been all right if it had just been me and you.'

'Would it?' she said. 'Did you read the *Standard* tonight?'

He seemed thrown for a moment, then said, 'No. Why? What are those bastards saying about me now?'

'Actually, it wasn't about you, it was about me. And the programme.'

'So what's new? The darling of the press gets herself a few more pages of free publicity?'

Allyson looked at him and through the muddle of hostility and confusion she tried to find the man she loved. 'Bob, what have I done to make you hate me like this?'

His eyes were refusing to meet hers, but she could see they were burning up with frustration. 'What you did with the bank,' he mumbled. 'You've really fucked me up.'

'Bob, you left me for a girl barely out of a gym slip,' she reminded him sharply, 'a girl who I trusted every bit as much as I trusted you. So do you think I give a damn what you might be suffering now? And look at you! What the hell's happened to you? You're a mess!'

'I don't have any fucking money, that's what's happened to me!'

'Not all your work's dried up, you must be earning something . . . Or no, don't tell me, what you are managing to get you're spending on booze. Well, let's see how good Tessa is at bailing you out, shall we?'

'OK, go right ahead and gloat, because you're right, we're squashed up in a shithole of a bedsit somewhere at the back end of nowhere, while you're here in *my* home, sitting on *my* money . . .'

Fury blazed from her eyes. 'This is *my* home,' she seethed.

'Wrong!'

'It was a wedding present from *my* parents!'

'But it's in both our names. And I've checked with a lawyer. This flat is as much mine as it is yours, and I want to sell. I've got an estate agent coming round'—he glanced at his watch—'in about twenty minutes.'

Allyson was white. Dimly she wondered how much more she could take. First her husband, then her job, now her home. Suddenly she was on her feet. 'Get out!' she spat. 'Just get the hell out of here and don't contact me again unless it's through a lawyer.'

'I told you, I've got someone coming . . .'

'I don't give a damn. You've got no right to do this.'

'You're the one who wants a divorce,' he reminded her.

'Because you left!' she screamed. 'Because you're the one who's sleeping with a kid half your age. And what about all the other women, Bob? What about all the years you deceived me, made a fool out of me? So don't come snivelling to me now that you haven't got any money. Because I couldn't give a fuck. And where's your precious little baby whore tonight? Why aren't you with her, celebrating? Surely she told you she's on the telly tonight. Hah, you didn't know, did you? Seems like things are working out really well for you, Bob.'

'Bitch!' he snarled. He lunged across the table, but he didn't reach her. 'She told me,' he spat.

'Oh yeah, right,' she said.

'*She told me!*' he thundered. This time the table skidded across the floor, and before she could move his hands were round her throat. 'You bitch!' he sobbed. 'What are you doing to my life?'

'Let go!' she gasped. 'Bob, let me go.'

'Let her go!' Shelley yelled, coming in the door.

His grip loosened and, struggling for breath, Allyson wrenched herself away and went to stand over the sink.

Bob and Shelley were motionless in the silence, both staring at Allyson, until Shelley turned to Bob and said, 'Just go.'

Visibly shaken, and still breathing hard, he brushed past her and went to get his coat. 'Tell her,' he said, suddenly turning back at the door, 'she's got to sell. Tessa's having a baby, we need a decent home.'

Shelley spun round to look at Allyson, then suddenly she was behind Bob, physically shoving him out of the door.

For a long time after he'd gone neither Allyson nor Shelley spoke. Shelley put an arm round Allyson's shoulders, but though Allyson didn't push her away, she didn't welcome the comfort either. Her eyes were dry, the shock, the utter devastation, was almost palpable on her face. In those few short words Bob had not only annihilated any hope she had that he might come back, he had destroyed everything they had ever meant to each other.

Chapter Eight

THE UK HEAD OFFICE of Leisure and Media Inc was on the south side of Russell Square in the centre of London. It was from here that Mark Reiner ran the successful media and catering empire he and his older brother, Nick, had built up. Though Nick was headquartered in New York, they met up at least once a month, more often than not in New York. This month, however, Nick had flown to London. His wife Claudia had come with him. She had wanted to shop and catch up with old friends. Mark's wife, Heather, had checked into the Betty Ford Clinic six weeks ago and didn't expect to be out in time to celebrate their divorce. Not that she'd have celebrated with Mark; more likely she'd fly straight to the Hollywood mansion she and her budding movie star lover had recently acquired—at Mark's expense.

Though his marriage had been a resounding failure, the business triumphs of the past twelve years had been spectacular. He and Nick had come a long way from the lowly West Country roots that had been transplanted to Idaho, USA, when Nick was twelve and Mark was eleven. After college they'd headed straight for New York. Within a year they'd owned one small restaurant on the Upper West Side, not as fashionable then as it was now. Nick had persuaded a local radio station to promote them heavily, and, to cut a long story short, they'd ended up buying into the radio station, opening up more restaurants around the city, gradually going into hotels and then into television. Claudia, Mark's sister-in-law, now ran the cable TV company the two brothers owned in the States, while Nick concentrated on their catering interests. For his part, Mark had been working for some time on the acquisition of the British TV station. Now the takeover was assured he would remain headquartered here, making the restructuring of the station his priority.

And boy, was he making himself unpopular. Already he'd announced plans to axe two current affairs shows, a struggling drama serial and two spectacularly bad situation comedies.

Oddly, the programme that was giving him the greatest pause for thought was *Soirée*. His first inclination had been to cancel it altogether, but after watching for several nights he'd decided it had a certain style and the ratings were still respectable. The lunch he'd had with Shelley Bronson a couple of days ago had also gone some way to persuading him that it was worth keeping the show going. If she'd given any sign of resisting his changes he might be taking a different view right now, but his guess was that he'd suggested changes Shelley had long wanted, although until now she'd allowed her friendship with Allyson to take precedence over her judgment. So he was going to be the bad guy, which was fine by him; he was in this to make money, not friends.

'Get Shelley Bronson on the line,' he said through the intercom to Corinne, his assistant.

While he waited he turned to his computer to pull up the company's investment portfolio. As he perused it he rocked gently back and forth in his giant leather chair. Mark's office was on the first floor of an old Regency building that still retained all the charm and character of its original high ceilings and creaking wooden floors, though the floors were now covered with luxurious carpet and the furniture was of the highest quality and outstanding workmanship.

He was still scrolling through the latest figures when his assistant buzzed through to announce that Shelley was on the line. Picking up the phone he connected himself to the call. 'Good morning,' he said.

'Hello,' came a sultry voice.

He smiled and sat back in his chair, picturing the fullness of her lips as she spoke. 'I enjoyed our lunch,' he told her. 'Sorry I had to rush off.'

She said nothing.

Amused by the silence, he said, 'I watched the show the night before last.'

'And you want to talk about Tessa.'

Of course, she would know that; it was almost certainly why she had slipped the girl into the programme, to show him that she already had young talent on tap. 'How much experience does she have?' he asked.

'Virtually none. But that needn't be a problem.'

'I'll trust you on that. Would the start of the New Year be too soon to turn things around?'

'No,' she answered.

'Send me a breakdown on what you'd do with a fifty per cent increase in budget,' he said.

'You'll have it by the end of the day.'

'Then we'll discuss it over dinner,' he said. 'Bibendum. Eight thirty,' and without waiting for an answer he rang off.

Allyson had spent the past two days, and nights, trying to come up with something sensational with which to impress Mark Reiner. It was either that, or five bottles of paracetamol and the lower oven of the smart Bosch unit. Indeed, there had been plenty of times over the past forty-eight hours when the second option had seemed the better of the two, and in truth she was so exhausted now, as she sat blurry-eyed at her computer, that the desperation and tiredness were threatening to make her emotional. But she didn't want to cry, not here in the office, where people would see her. Tears were for the privacy of her bedroom.

She was about to print out the proposals she'd drawn up to show Mark Reiner, when she found herself looking across the office to where Tessa was sitting. A wild and raging hatred surged into her heart. Then came the panicked terror of the months ahead, when she'd have to watch that girl growing big with Bob's child. Somehow she had to find the energy to fight back and make something work for herself.

She turned back to her computer, and after printing out her proposals she concentrated on that night's show. Somehow she managed to get through the programme. It wasn't clear how she did it, she was in such a daze. She simply responded to the countdown, spoke to the camera and interviewed her guests.

'Do you know what?' Allyson said when she found Shelley waiting in her dressing room afterwards. 'I think I'll have a drink. What about you?'

'Vodka and tonic. Light on the vodka,' Shelley said.

Wearing a fabulous floor-length Ungaro creation, with a slit up the front to mid-thigh and a drop back that descended to her waist, Allyson crossed to the drinks tray. She'd spent some time after the show talking to the guests, and seemed slightly calmer than she'd been an hour ago. As she poured, Shelley was chattering on about how well the recording had gone, so maybe there was nothing to worry about yet.

How was it possible to be so wrong?

As Shelley told her the news, that Mark Reiner wanted to try Tessa out for Cocktails, Allyson could feel the blood draining from her face. Her drink remained in its glass. But her hands wouldn't move, her voice was gone. Her entire world was moving to a place far beyond her reach. First her husband, then her home, now her programme. Was there anything left for Tessa Dukes to take?

Her eyes were dry as she turned them to Shelley. 'And did you agree with him?' she said. 'Do you think Tessa should take the first half of the show, leaving me the Nightcap?'

'It's my belief that if I don't agree, he'll axe the show altogether,' Shelley confessed.

Leaving her drink Allyson walked over to the clothes rail and started to change. Shelley was shocked to see just how thin she had become.

When she was dressed, Allyson picked up her bag and started to leave. 'Don't you want to discuss it?' Shelley said.

'What's there to discuss? It seems you've already made up your mind.'

Shelley was shaking her head. 'Look, I know you think I've betrayed you,' she said, 'and if you want me to put up a fight for you to keep Cocktails, I will. But trust my instincts on this, Ally. If I do, Mark Reiner will just pull the plug.'

Allyson's eyes went down. 'Why Tessa?' she said, her voice shaking with emotion. 'There have to be a thousand other girls out there who could bring youth and talent to the show. And what about the baby?' she demanded. 'What are you going to do when it starts to show?'

Shelley's eyes remained on hers. She'd already thought of that. 'I'll need to discuss it with Mark. It could be a problem.'

Allyson stared at her hard. Was Shelley saying what she thought she was saying? Without another word she turned and walked out of the door. She didn't know where she was going, but she had to get away from Shelley, from this building, and from the girl whose youth and good fortune were taking over her life.

'So how did she take it?'

'Badly, I think,' Shelley said. 'She left the building and I haven't been able to find her since.'

Mark Reiner waited as the waiter poured a little Bordeaux into a glass for him to taste. After approving it, Mark said, 'Are you worried?'

'A bit. She's been having a rough time of it lately. Tessa Dukes is living with her husband.'

'Allyson's husband?' he said, showing surprise.

Shelley nodded. Clearly he didn't read the tabloids.

'Is she going to accept the Nightcap slot?' he asked.

'I don't know. She probably needs time to think.'

'Of course. Have you spoken to Tessa yet?'

'No. Not until I've found out what Allyson intends to do.'

He seemed thoughtful for a moment, then raising his glass he touched it gently to hers, and Shelley could sense the subject of Allyson's position on the programme sliding down his list of priorities as he allowed his eyes to roam the smooth, candlelit planes of her face. She knew she intrigued him, as he intrigued her, and she wondered how ruthless he could be. How professional? How controlled? All the time she'd been dressing for the evening she'd felt the sharp bite of lust. Her knee-length dress was halter-necked. Knowing the selection she had made to go underneath would drive him wild, were he to see it, was enough. But she had no intention of seducing him yet, for toying with him this way, and with herself, both satisfied and intensified the desire. It also added an edge to their discussion that meant no matter how professional the subject, the personal was always there, flowing like a slow, sultry river through the *double entendres* of their softly spoken words.

'I've looked at how you would spend the budget increase were you to get it,' he said.

'And?'

'I'm impressed,' he responded.

Her dark, sensuous gaze remained on his as the compliment folded its promise warmly around her. 'So do I get the increase?' she said.

'Not as much as you've asked for, but I imagine you figured that into your request.'

Shelley's eyebrows flickered upwards. Though there was an unquestionable irony in his eyes, the harsh masculinity of his body was inviting her imagination to experience the force, maybe even the violence of his passion. A small sigh of anticipation shuddered through her.

'How did you become a producer?' he asked.

'The usual way. Through researching.'

'You didn't want to present?'

'If I'd chosen presenting, what's happening to Allyson would be happening to me now,' she said.

'But you're not married.'

'I was referring to the programme.'

'Were you ever? Married?'

'No.' Then she added, 'The last significant relationship I had ended eight years ago.'

He was clearly surprised. 'I find it hard to believe that a woman like you has lived all that time without a man.'

Her eyes were burning. 'I haven't,' she said.

He cocked a single eyebrow, telling her he had received the message, then their food arrived and as he watched her eat, the fork gliding smoothly from her lips, the wine moistening them, her fingers circling the stem of the wineglass, she knew the power of her sensuality was affecting him. They continued to talk, about the programme, about life, until their plates were taken and they were offered a menu for dessert.

He declined for them both. She looked at him in surprise, then felt her skin start to burn as he said, 'I think it's time I fucked you.'

Her lips parted as her breath became heavy. 'Yes, I think it is,' she said.

He drove them to her apartment. Neither of them spoke, except for her to give him directions.

She led him up the single flight of stairs and unlocked the front door. Her heart was pounding. She was on fire for him, and the moment they were inside he grabbed her and crushed her mouth with his. Drawing the hem of her dress up to her waist, his hands moved over the gossamer-fine rubber straps that were binding her body, and as she sensed the sudden charge to his lust, she began tearing at his shirt, pushing it with his jacket from his shoulders.

He rammed her up against the wall, and as he pulled the dress over her head he saw more fine rubber straps. They circled her waist, her breasts, and disappeared between her legs. They covered nothing. She was revealed to him in a cage of black rubber. It was blowing his mind.

In her high heels she matched his height. She took him by the hand and led him to the sitting room. Everything there was as elegant and benign as she was bewitching and brazen. She reached the sofa and glanced over her shoulder. Her dark eyes were smouldering with immeasurable lust.

Parting her legs she bent over the sofa. She was speaking to him now, telling him what she wanted in a language that was inflaming him beyond any point of control. He came up behind her, stooped and bit into her flesh. She moaned and writhed and bent more steeply. Suddenly he thrust his cock to the core of her and her legs lost power. She was dizzied by lust, breathless with pleasure as he pounded into her with unmerciful force. His orgasm was explosive. She was bucking beneath him, shuddering with the might of her climax. He pulled out of her quickly, spun her round and pushed her to the floor. He lay over her, entered her and began a new journey to the end. Her legs and arms entwined him, her mouth and tongue assailed him. She stayed hot for him all night, matching the harsh demands of his body with her own.

The next morning she woke him with fresh coffee and croissants. As he ate she did things to him, and to herself, that stole his appetite for food and concentrated it solely on her.

When the time came it was all he could do to drag himself away. She was sensational. She oozed more femininity than an overcrowded harem. She walked him to the door, kissed him, and before he knew it he was inside her again. She was incredible. Indescribable. Insatiable.

It was the middle of the afternoon. Allyson hadn't made an appointment. She simply turned up at Mark Reiner's office and demanded to see him. She'd worked out what she was going to say, was determined to deliver it as calmly and succinctly as possible and then listen quietly, unhysterically, to his response.

Last night had been one of the worst of her life. If it were possible, literally, to cry oceans, she felt she'd shed every one of them, and her entire body felt bruised now from the power of the storm. Around midnight she'd driven to Tessa's flat half-demented with grief, so desperate to see Bob she hadn't cared what kind of scene she might cause. When she'd got there she'd sat outside, feeling herself filling up with so much hate and despair that all she'd wanted was to go in and kill them both. But even if she could come up with a perfect plan, she knew she didn't have what it took to go through with it. So she drove home again, acknowledging that these thoughts were nothing more than the wild ramblings of a rejected, middle-aged woman.

She'd spent this morning at home, working frantically on the plan to save her career. Today was Friday and there was no programme, which was why she was able to be here in Mark Reiner's office now.

The last time they'd met was when she'd interviewed him, but that was some time ago and she remembered almost nothing about it now.

After she'd been waiting about half an hour, his door suddenly opened and the jolt of her heart made her queasy. She turned to look at him and immediately felt worse, for his towering height, dark good looks and inscrutable manner were all reminding her of his power, and she felt appallingly wrong-footed and diminished by it.

'Allyson,' he said, smiling. 'I'm sorry to have kept you. I was on a conference call to New York. Did you get some coffee?'

Allyson shook her head. Oh God, she remembered now, he was younger than her, only by two or three years, but those years suddenly seemed to be a tangible threat to her existence. She said, in her best affable voice, 'How are you? It's good to see you again. How's the house? It was in Devon, wasn't it?' Too much. Too many questions.

'It still is. It's my wife's now. Soon to be ex. Come in.'

She followed him through and smiled politely as he waved her to a chair. She was OK now, past those initial ravings, and slipping calmly back into the steadying grip of poise and control. For some reason his eyes had made her feel better. They were knowing, unreadable, so why they'd soothed her she wasn't entirely sure. She thought he seemed a good match for Shelley and she wondered how they'd got on last night. But she didn't really care. All she cared about was saving her job and with that her sanity.

As he watched her sit down he could see how much this was costing her. There was so much pain etched in her eyes, and fear, that he was reminded of what Shelley had told him, that her husband had just left her, for a younger woman, for Tessa Dukes.

Trying not to flinch under his scrutiny, Allyson began her pitch. 'Shelley's told me about your plans for the programme,' she said, her voice sounding oddly harsh and discordant.

He nodded, and waited, politely, for her to continue. She'd said nothing that he could respond to—when she did he would reply with the truth, which he knew was going to be brutal for her.

'I think,' she said, 'that you've probably got a point. The show does need a younger image.'

His surprise showed. 'I hope that means you're willing to stay with the Nightcap,' he said.

'Maybe.' She took a breath. 'I would like you to consider using someone else to host Cocktails,' she said. 'Happy Hour,' she corrected.

'You mean instead of Tessa Dukes?'

She nodded.

He didn't answer straight away, so she continued.

'I'd also like to become one of the new-style programme's producers.'

His eyebrows went up, then, looking at the pen he was holding in both hands, he said, 'Have you discussed any of this with Shelley?'

She shook her head. 'No.'

He nodded. On the face of it he didn't consider this to be a bad idea. 'What would you bring to your producership?' he asked.

'A long-time knowledge of the programme, and the business,' she answered, wishing her heart would stop thudding so loudly. 'Many contacts from just about every walk of life . . .'

'In terms of programme content.'

'In terms of programme content,' she echoed, 'I'd like to produce a weekly round-up of how young people are getting involved in helping others. Whether it's the sick, the elderly, or the homeless.'

He thought about this for a few seconds. 'It's not the direction we're going in. In my opinion, people don't want to hear about those who are worse off than themselves. 'Soirée is a light-entertainment programme . . .'

'It's always had style and sophistication,' she protested. 'What you're aiming to do is bring it downmarket . . .'

'My aim is to up the ratings and attract a broader cross-section of the viewing public. Right now it appeals primarily to your age group and older.'

'OK, I accept that. But a broad section of the viewing public does care about those worse off than themselves. I believe that a light-entertainment show, if it handles the subject correctly—'

'I don't want to argue about this,' he interrupted.

Suddenly she was on her feet. 'Then what do you want to do?' she shouted. 'Throw me out like I don't matter? And you're wrong about what people want, do you know that? You're all about money, but the people out there, they're about care and compassion. They want to help, they want to make life better for themselves and for those worse off than they are. They need to know where they can go to get help, or give help. We can show them how to do that, in an informative, entertaining way. But you don't want to, because you think young people only want gossip and music, light, inconsequential rubbish to escape into. And you're right. They do want all that, but they need more. However, you don't believe it'll bring in the advertisers, which is all TV is about to you people from America. Well, I'm a shareholder of this company and I'm telling you this is what I want to do, regardless of how much money it makes. And it *will* make money. I'm telling you now, it *will*.'

Her cheeks were flushed with anger, her body was vibrating with passion. He was surprised how much her attempt to make herself heard was affecting him, though it would do nothing to change his decision. 'Being a shareholder isn't going to help you,' he said gently.

'Why don't you at least give it a try!' she implored. 'Test it out until the end of the season. If it doesn't work we can drop it next year.'

He was shaking his head and suddenly she couldn't stand any more. 'Then fuck you!' she yelled. 'Fuck you to hell.'

'Allyson, I didn't come to my decisions with the intention of hurting you.'

'Then give me a chance! Don't throw me on the scrap heap.'

'You've still got the Nightcap slot,' he reminded her.

'Don't you think I've got my pride? Imagine how I'm going to feel, sitting at Tessa Dukes's feet four nights a week down in the Nightcap slot, while she stands tall with the rest of what's always been *my* programme?'

'Three,' he corrected. 'I'm reducing the transmissions to three a week, so there won't be enough airtime to pursue your proposal.'

Allyson looked at him. Her taut, tired face was ashen, defeat was crawling through her limbs like lead. She looked so small and vulnerable, so weighted by loss, that it could only be pride that was holding her erect. He spoke her name without really knowing why, or what to say. 'Allyson.'

She turned back. She looked so fragile she might break.

In the end, she was the one to speak. 'The next time you look in the mirror,' she said, 'I want you to ask yourself, are you really always right, or are you just in a position that makes it that way, regardless of truth?'

# Chapter Nine

TESSA HAD NEVER BEEN comfortable around Shelley. Shelley was one of the few people who'd seemed to dislike her from the start. In fact, it was amazing to Tessa that Shelley hadn't found a way to sack her when Bob had left Allyson. Instead, weirdly, now she was making all Tessa's wildest dreams come true with this giant leap to hosting the first half of the show starting in January.

'Under the new format one report a week will come from somewhere else in the country,' Shelley was saying, 'and once a month we'll transmit from a location in Europe. How up are you on the rest of the world?'

'I read the papers every day,' Tessa answered.

'Do you have views?'

'Usually.'

Shelley wasn't interested in what they might be. The girl was intelligent, a quick thinker and an unusual personality. She also had the right measure of naiveté to strike a note in her interviewing that made a refreshing contrast to those who'd been at it for years. Nevertheless she would need some intense training between now and January. I'm hiring a number of experts in all fields to get you ready,' she said. 'You'll also get an image enhancer and a personal publicist.'

Tessa was grinning widely. 'Wow,' she said. 'What about my own dressing room?'

'Let's concentrate on the important issues first, shall we?' Shelley responded coldly.

Tessa flushed. 'Sorry,' she mumbled, retreating into the persona of a shy, anxious-to-please beginner.

Shelley fixed her with a harsh, relentless stare that, after a while, made Tessa squirm. 'Is it true you're pregnant?' Shelley suddenly demanded.

Tessa's face drained. 'Yes, it's true,' she said. 'But if it's going to get in the way of this job, I'll have an abortion.'

Just like that. Not a second thought. Shelley wasn't surprised, but she was disgusted. 'It'll get in the way,' she said.

The meeting was suddenly over and Tessa was back at her desk. She looked around for Allyson, but there was no sign of her. Did Allyson know about this? Was that why she wasn't here? She had to be livid. But it was hardly Tessa's fault that she was getting all these breaks, was it?

Before she called Bob to tell him her news she booked herself into a clinic. She'd always thought it was a shame her mother hadn't done that when she was pregnant with her, but the way her life was going now she was glad she hadn't. It was all turning out OK at last.

It was nine o'clock and Bob was still waiting for Tessa to come home. She'd left a message on the machine to say she had some great news but wanted to wait till she saw him to tell him. But she wasn't back yet and when he called they said she'd left the office around six.

He hated being alone, for unless he was drunk he became easy prey to his conscience, and found it almost impossible to blot Allyson from his mind. He nearly went off his head thinking about her, wanting her to understand why he'd done what he had. But she wouldn't speak to him any more, so there was no point getting himself into a state about it.

In the end, he went out to look for Tessa. But she wasn't in the pub and he didn't know where else to try. As far as he knew she didn't have any friends, except Julian, and Julian was in the pub.

'I haven't seen her today,' Julian said. 'There's no programme on Fridays so I don't go in.'

Bob nodded. Now he was here he might as well have a drink. He ordered himself a large gin and a Guinness for Julian.

By the time Tessa found them at half past ten they were both roaring drunk, and discussing Chelsea's latest performance as though it were the most important issue on the planet. She watched them from the door, slamming their fists on the table, shaking their fingers. They appeared to be doing some serious male bonding over there. A bit like father and son. That might have been funny had she not just come from a session with Laura Risby, but she didn't want to think about that now, it had raised too many issues that really ought to be forgotten.

'There you are,' Bob said, when he saw her. 'I was worried.' He pulled her mouth down to his and kissed her. 'Are you OK?' he asked.

She nodded, and sat down next to him. 'Hi, Jules,' she said.

'Hi.'

She was tired, and strangely, considering what a great day she'd had, a bit depressed. 'You seem in a good mood,' she said to Bob.

He shrugged, as if to ask why he shouldn't be. She could think of plenty of reasons, but she wasn't going to remind him.

'So, do you want to hear my good news?' she said, her face brightening. 'As of January I'm going to be presenting the Cocktails section of the programme, which they're going to call Happy Hour.'

Julian's eyes grew wide.

'Shelley told me today. And my agent's going to ask her for a great big fat fee, which means, Bob, that we might be able to buy Allyson out of the flat and live there after all. Wouldn't that be great?'

Bob's brain wasn't working as fast as it should. Tessa moved over to sit on his lap. 'Aren't you proud?' she said.

He was looking at his empty glass. 'Her parents gave us that flat when we got married,' he said weakly.

Tessa smiled. 'Which makes it half yours, silly,' she reminded him. 'So we'll buy the other half and make it all yours. After all, I deserve a nice place to live in, don't I? And you were all for it a few weeks ago.'

'Yes, but . . . There are thousands of nice places. I don't see why it has to be that one.'

'I thought it was what you wanted. And if you're worried about Allyson . . . Well, just remember that it's because of her that you can't get to your money, and if you're right about her putting a word in with the producers not to give you any work . . .'

A dark flush spread over Bob's face. Had he said that? He couldn't remember, but it seemed likely. 'Get me another drink,' he slurred. 'And you don't have the money yet, so before you start thinking you can afford even a quarter of a flat on Cheyne Walk . . .' He lost his train of thought.

Tessa laid her head on his shoulder. 'Please don't be angry. If you don't want us to buy the flat, we won't.'

His head was spinning now, and she was feeling heavy on his lap. 'OK, then we won't,' he mumbled.

Her eyes drifted across to Julian and she winked.

'Hi,' Shelley said. 'How are you?'

'Pretty good,' Mark responded, sliding into the other side of the banquette. 'Did I keep you waiting?'

'I was early,' she told him. Though her smile was warm, waves of unease were threatening to trespass on her cherished serenity. They'd spoken a couple of times on the phone since Thursday night, calls she had made, neither of which had elicited a desire on his part to see her again. So she'd invited him to her flat for Sunday lunch, which he'd accepted, but suggested they ate out.

So now, here they were, being so formal with each other, when all she wanted to discuss was their night together, and how ready she was for it to happen again. 'I'm getting a team together for Tessa's training,' she said. 'They start work on Tuesday.'

255

His eyebrows went up. 'Does that mean Allyson's made a decision about the Nightcap?'

'She's letting me know tomorrow.'

They took the menus from a waitress and ordered drinks. Shelley chose wine. She felt she needed something stronger than water.

Mark ordered a vodka. He too felt the need for something stronger than water. He'd given a lot of thought to what had happened between him and Shelley on Thursday night, and he was furious with himself now for having allowed himself to get involved in personal matters, when he'd only just taken over the damned company. There was no doubt in his mind that this thing with Shelley had to stop.

'Did Allyson tell you she came to see me?' he said.

Shelley's surprise showed. 'No. When?'

'Friday. She tried to talk me out of using Tessa for Happy Hour.'

Shelley digested this. 'And you've had a change of heart?'

'No. The show needs a younger image, and Tessa's the answer if we want to turn it around fast.'

'So?'

'So nothing. I was merely wondering what Allyson had decided.'

Shelley got the feeling there was more, but for some reason she didn't want to ask. Instead, she fixed her eyes on his. 'It's Sunday,' she said, 'why don't we forget about work and talk about . . . other things.'

Their drinks arrived, then the food, and despite all her attempts, he stubbornly refused to move from the general to the personal.

In the end, embarrassed and angry, she said, 'Am I supposed to be pretending that Thursday never happened?'

She saw his discomfort. 'Shelley, listen,' he said. 'What happened on Thursday, well, it was something else. The best. I don't know anything, anyone who can compare.'

'But?' Her heart was pounding.

'I don't think it should happen again.'

She felt her face drain. At last she'd found a man she could call her equal, a man she already knew she wanted to share her life with, and he was telling her he didn't want her. It didn't make any sense.

'Is there someone else?' she said.

He glanced up as their coffee was delivered. 'Shelley, you're a beautiful and desirable woman,' he said. 'But if we're going to have a relationship that works, it should remain professional. I'm sorry,' he said.

'Sorry that it happened, or sorry that you're a bastard who led me to believe you felt the same way I did?'

'I don't recall us discussing feelings,' he countered.

'Oh'—she laughed angrily—'so you think I put out like that for every man I meet?'

'Frankly, I don't know,' he responded. 'All I know is that you blew my mind, and I'm not sorry it happened. You're a unique and beautiful woman, but as for anything else, well I'm afraid that's as far as it goes.'

She was so stunned she was unable to make herself think. She had to find a way to talk him round, and being hostile wasn't going to do it. So she managed to smile, winsomely, seductively, as she said, 'Why don't we go back to my place and talk this over?'

He smiled back. 'If we went back to your place the last thing we'd do is talk.'

She laughed. So he did still want her. 'We could be really good together, can't you see that?' she said.

'We already were,' he responded. 'But it's not all about sex.'

'I wasn't just talking about sex.'

He glanced at his watch. 'I've got to go,' he said, signalling for the bill.

It was like a slap. A slap that reverberated right the way through her. And later, back at her flat, she didn't want to think about how she'd pleaded with him, tried to cajole and seduce him. The humiliation of the way she'd behaved was so great it burned her all over.

As Allyson walked down the stairs of the farmhouse, she was remembering the hot summer's day when she and Bob had first found it, and how thrilled they had been to discover their dream home in such idyllic surroundings, despite its dilapidated state. Then had come the long and arduous task of restoring it, and there wasn't a single cushion or rug, painting or book they hadn't chosen together.

She'd filled two suitcases with her personal belongings. Bob's were still there. She'd considered packing his too, but in the end had been unable to do it. Maybe he wanted them to stay here. Maybe he was planning to move Tessa in and make this a home for their baby.

Over her dead body.

Her mother was waiting outside by the car. Her father was in the front passenger seat, staring blankly down over the hillside. A few meagre Christmas lights twinkled over the church spire, but it was a grey and cheerless day. She put her cases in the boot, then got into the driver's seat. She didn't look back as she drove away. She simply kept her eyes on the road and tried not to feel what was going on in her heart.

The drive back to London took less than two hours. She went to her parents' house first to drop them off. 'Thanks for coming with me,' she said, kissing her mother goodbye at the front door.

'I wish you'd stay,' Peggy said. The trip to Wiltshire had been almost as difficult for her as it had been for Allyson.

Allyson hugged her again and was about to walk away when Peggy started crying. 'I'm sorry,' she sobbed. 'I just can't bear seeing you hurt like this. I wish Daddy understood.'

Allyson smiled. Driving down to Wiltshire had been hard for him too, in his own way. He hadn't known who they were, or where they were taking him. 'Poor Mummy,' she said.

'Call me when you get to the flat?'

'Of course.'

Shelley was the only one who knew why Tessa wasn't in the studio today. The team of hand-picked gurus who were coaching Tessa in interviewing subtleties had been given the day off, they thought, because Tessa needed a break. It was a plausible enough excuse, for they'd been hard at it this past week.

At the moment Shelley was in a screening room viewing videotapes of the results of Tessa's training so far. They were even more impressive than she'd expected, for the girl looked so fresh she might burst, and seemed so strikingly unfazed by the celebrity guests Shelley had talked into rehearsing with her that she could have been at this for years.

Someone knocked on the door and Shelley looked up as a shaft of light from the corridor outside cut across the darkened viewing room.

'Have you got a minute?' Allyson said.

Shelley hit the VCR's pause button. 'Sure,' she said.

Allyson glanced at the screen.

Realising the frozen image was of Tessa, Shelley turned the monitor off. 'Come in,' she said.

Allyson let the door swing closed, but stayed where she was. 'I just wanted you to know I've decided to continue with the Nightcap,' she said.

Shelley's expression only partially relaxed. 'I'm so pleased,' she said.

Though Allyson's smile was weak Shelley couldn't help noticing that there was more colour in her cheeks than of late, and her hair looked newly cut and styled.

'When it came down to it,' Allyson said, 'it was that or nothing. I don't think I could handle nothing, even if it means having to remain in the same vicinity as Tessa Dukes.'

Shelley removed the files on the chair next to her. 'Come and sit down,' she said.

'I can't. I've got to go up to town to have lunch with Mark Reiner. Do you know anything about it?'

Shelley's smile drained. 'No.' Her voice was harsh.

Allyson attempted a shrug. 'He called yesterday and asked me to lunch. I thought you might know what it was about.'

'No idea,' Shelley said, attempting to sound casual.

'Then let's hope it's not to rescind the offer of the Nightcap,' Allyson ventured.

'No, let's hope not,' Shelley responded, unable to give the reassurance Allyson was searching for.

Allyson was almost out of the door before she turned back and said, 'How are things working out for you two?'

Frustration and anger dug into Shelley's heart as she playfully rolled her eyes. 'Oh, it's still early days,' she said.

Allyson smiled and nodded, then closed the door behind her.

Shelley started up the video again and Tessa's face filled the screen. But her mind was still angrily exploring the many paths of doubt and suspicion that were opening up all over the place. This was the second time Allyson had been to see Mark in a week. Had something happened that neither of them was telling her about? Except that was crazy, for Allyson appeared genuinely anxious about today's invitation.

Realising she was getting carried away, stirring up fears and insecurities that had nothing to do with reality, and everything to do with the carefully suppressed rivalry she felt with Allyson, Shelley attempted to ground herself in reason. After all, it wasn't often that she felt this rivalry. Yet even though Shelley would never have allowed Bob to leave Allyson during their long, bittersweet affair, the fact that he had never even shown any signs of wanting to had confused and angered her, for she simply couldn't imagine why any man would rather be with Allyson than with her. But that was as nothing to how she would feel if Mark were to suffer a similar aberration.

But no, she wasn't going to allow herself to continue with this. It was crazy to be thinking this way, when people in their positions had lunch all the time, with nothing more personal on the agenda than a shared liking for fish.

Laura Risby, Tessa's psychotherapist, led Tessa to where the car was waiting on an expired meter, a few doors down from the clinic. The wind was blowing a bitter gale through the parallel terraces of Harley Street, scattering clouds of dust up into the elegant façades.

'OK?' she said, settling Tessa into the front passenger seat.

Tessa nodded. She was pale, but that was only to be expected. She was going to tell Bob she'd suffered a miscarriage, though Laura wondered if he'd guess the truth, with the baby's loss coinciding so neatly with Tessa's new status on the programme. Either way, Laura was curious to see if he stayed with Tessa once it sank in that there was no longer a child. Laura had to hope he didn't, for this wasn't good for Tessa, sleeping with a father figure. And the substitute brother could prove disastrous too. But it was the punishment Tessa was unconsciously inflicting on Allyson that was the most disturbing. Fate had rather played into Tessa's hands by promoting her into Allyson's position on the programme, but the rest of it, like Allyson's husband, Allyson's flat and even the complex need for Allyson's approval and affection, was forcing Laura to wonder if it would be wise for her to talk to Allyson. However, considering this new turn of events, she felt it was probably better to wait and see if the relationship broke up of its own accord, for then there would be no need to step outside the bounds of professional confidentiality and interfere.

Mark was watching Allyson as she chose which of the three vegetables the waiter should put on her side plate. The man was clearly delighted to be serving someone famous and had made such a performance out of filleting her sole, he might well have been auditioning.

She handled the situation well, Mark noted with amusement, and brought it to such a well-practised and smooth conclusion that not for a minute would the waiter consider he'd been dismissed.

'So,' she said, picking up her cutlery, 'we've talked about America, we've discussed the earth-shattering prophecies for the new millennium, we've established that neither of us cares much for Christmas, what comes next?'

He laughed. 'To be frank,' he said, 'I'd like to be able to tell you that I'm going to give you the airtime for your social issues. But I'm not.' She might still look like an injured bird, he thought, with her tired, watchful eyes and unsteady smile, but she was staging a remarkable show of togetherness considering how tough life must be for her right now. 'I just don't think they've got a natural setting in *Soirée*,' he continued. 'But as a presenter, you do. Which is why I want you to continue with the Nightcap—and why I think you should become a producer, as you yourself suggested.'

Allyson's eyes widened with surprise. Elation was a beat behind.

'As you know, we're going to have a slightly new-look programme, and I think your experience and high profile would serve us best for the monthly international transmissions.'

Allyson blinked. This was too much. She wasn't sure what she'd been expecting, but with the way her luck had been going lately, it wasn't this. She put down her knife and fork and lifted her napkin. Then, realising she hadn't eaten anything yet, she picked up her fork again. Only when she looked at him did she realise he was laughing, and she laughed too. 'Have you discussed this with Shelley?' she said.

'I'm discussing it with you,' he responded. 'Does it interest you?'

'That's like asking me if I'm interested in living,' she told him. 'Yes, I'm interested. Though a few days ago I might not have been, but we won't get into that.'

He'd seen the newspapers, so he knew she'd moved some belongings out of her country home at the weekend, but he had no intention of trespassing on that hallowed ground. 'Would it be possible for you to produce the monthly slot, as well as presenting the Nightcaps?' he asked.

She was nodding. 'I think so. But we'll have to discuss this with Shelley. After all, she's the boss.'

He waited, with ironic eyes, for her to remember to whom she was talking. When she did, she seemed absurdly confused for a moment, until she realised he was teasing her. 'OK, you're the boss,' she laughed. 'But I think Shelley would like to be consulted before she gets me foisted upon her as her new producer of international programmes.'

Sidestepping the Shelley issue again he said, 'Maybe you could think about the kind of shape you'd like your programmes to take. Whether you want to keep the same style as the domestic transmissions, or—'

'I think it should stay the same,' she interrupted. 'At least for the first few months. Coming from a different European city each time is going to make it individual enough.'

'And of course you realise that Happy Hour is something that occurs all over the Continent,' he said, looking right into her eyes.

Allyson flushed slightly, and looked down at her plate, for she realised that this was a gentle reminder that, if this did all come off, she'd be travelling with Tessa and would have to find a way of working with her. A second later her head was up again and she was smiling. 'Of course,' she said, 'which is why we should stay safe and in style for the moment. Shelley will probably be happier with that too.'

He nodded.

She wondered why she kept bringing Shelley's name up. Perhaps she was unconsciously trying to get him to say something about Shelley that might give some clue as to what his feelings might be, which was not only unprofessional of her, it was also disloyal. Yet right at that moment Shelley was preparing the source of all Allyson's misery to take over the main part of Allyson's programme. So where was the loyalty in that?

Mark's eyes were watching her closely as she looked at him again. They were steeped in humour and had that knowing sort of look that seemed to suggest he was reading her mind. Allyson smiled, a little self-consciously, but she had to admit she was rather enjoying the interest he seemed to be taking in her, and picking up her fork she took a delicious mouthful of fish.

He asked her then if she had had any early thoughts on publicity. Ideas soon began spilling out of her, almost faster than she could think them, and bouncing them around with him was turning out to be an extremely exhilarating and often hilarious process. The glass of champagne he ordered to mark the launch of her new, jet-setty career slipped down rather easily too, as did the next glass, which was to celebrate Christmas and the fabulous start of their very special friendship.

Realising that she'd got a bit gushy and over the top with that particular toast, she blushed and winced and said, 'If I'm embarrassing you, I promise it's nothing to what I'm doing to myself.'

Laughing, he clinked his glass against hers again, and replied, 'It's better than when you yell at me. Now, instead of ogling my dessert like that, why don't you just have it?'

'Oh no!' she cried as he started to pass over his banoffi pie. Then, grinning, 'Well, maybe just a taste.'

Not until they were leaving did she realise that she'd eaten an entire meal for the first time since Bob had left. She'd also drunk three glasses of champagne and was feeling considerably warmer towards Mark Reiner than she had a week ago. In fact, as he handed her into the back of a taxi she was starting to see why Shelley was so attracted to him. She might be too, were it not for the way her heart plummeted at the very idea of anyone other than Bob occupying that place in her life.

The week leading up to Christmas was pandemonium on all fronts. The *Soirée* set was transformed into a wonderful Alpine cabin, with snow on the windows, a fire in the hearth and a ready supply of hot toddies at the bar and twice the number of guests as usual flooded in for the extra recordings to cover the holiday period. Being so rushed off her feet Allyson had yet to tell Shelley about the new producership she had discussed with Mark, so she was relieved when out of the blue Mark called to say he was going to talk to Shelley himself. 'I think it should be put to her in a way that the idea seems to come from her,' he said.

Allyson was intrigued. She hadn't been looking forward to talking to Shelley about it. 'How will you do that?' she said.

'Leave it to me. Just act surprised when she offers you the job.'

Allyson laughed, but there was so much noise going on in the office outside that she missed what he said next. 'Hang on,' she said, closing the door. 'What did you say?'

'I was wondering how Tessa's doing with her training?'

The warmth instantly drained from Allyson's smile. 'You'll have to ask Shelley,' she said coldly. 'I'm not involved in the training.'

'I see.'

She imagined he did. 'Is there anything else?' she asked.

'No. Well, I guess, Merry Christmas if I don't see you before Friday.'

'Thank you. To you too.'

After she rang off she regretted sounding so sharp. Still, she didn't imagine he'd lose any sleep over her tart little responses, so she wouldn't either, and picking up her script for the next recording, she switched her phones through to Marvin, Shelley's assistant, and made her way to her dressing room.

Shelley was in a great mood. She had just attended a producers' lunch that Mark had hosted at the Mirabelle, and now, at his invitation, she was leading the way up the stairs to his Russell Square office for a pre-Christmas drink. Thanks to the lengthy conversation they'd just had in the restaurant she was no longer having to feel quite so bad about Allyson, because after tossing around several different ideas, they'd decided to give Allyson a shot at producing the new continental trans-missions as well as presenting the Nightcaps. Whether or not she was interested in producing, or even up to it, remained to be seen. But at least Shelley had some good news to be going back to her with, some-thing that would hopefully help to ease the tension between them.

'So what are your plans for Christmas?' Mark was asking as they walked into the reception area of his office.

As he'd already told her he was spending the time with his brother and sister-in-law who'd just flown in from New York, Shelley didn't mind admitting to spending the time with her family too. 'My mother and stepfather have a place in the New Forest,' she said. 'I'll probably drive down there. My stepsister and her husband usually come too.'

He stopped to speak to Corinne, his assistant, and Shelley used the opportunity to go and powder her nose. When she returned she could see him already in his office pouring them both a drink. The intention now was to watch the two pilot programmes that had been recorded the day before, with Tessa as the Happy Hour host, and Allyson at the foot of the show taking care of the Nightcaps. Personalities and all other issues aside, the new-style programmes were even better than Shelley had hoped for. Tessa's magical quality on screen was richly enhanced by the girl's wonderful gift of getting people to say or do things as though the camera wasn't there. And Allyson was perfect in her new role. Shelley had no doubt that Mark was going to be impressed.

Closing the door behind her, she put down her bag and took off her coat. She was wearing a close-fitting black cashmere dress and a gold silk scarf. He smiled as he handed her a drink, then touched his glass to hers. 'Merry Christmas and Tessa's success,' he said.

As she drank she kept her eyes on his, and was pleased to see that he didn't look away.

'Did you bring the tapes?' he asked, opening the TV cabinet.

She watched as he ejected a cassette from the machine, then putting her drink down she pulled her dress over her head and laid it beside her coat. Wearing only the gold silk scarf, black hold-up stockings and high-heeled shoes, she handed him the videos.

'Merry Christmas,' she murmured.

He started to speak but her hand was already twisting round his tie, using it to pull his mouth to hers. He thought to push her away, but as he touched her and felt the intense hardening of his cock he found himself kissing her back. 'Someone might come in,' he said gruffly.

'I locked the door.'

Her tongue moved back into his mouth as she unfastened his trousers, then holding his cock with both hands she sank to her knees and began to moisten him.

He could stop this, and knew he should, but he also knew he wouldn't, for she had the power to arouse him like no other woman, and if this was what she wanted then he sure as hell was going to give it to her. 'Merry Christmas,' he murmured.

 ## Chapter Ten

IT WAS CHRISTMAS MORNING. The floor of Tessa's flat was strewn with torn wrapping paper and breakfast dishes, and the tree Bob had brought home a few nights ago was standing in the corner, its blinking lights reflecting in the shiny surfaces of the red and gold frosted balls.

Bob had given Tessa a bottle of Estée Lauder perfume. The slim gold necklace that had accompanied it was back in its velvet pouch on the coffee table, waiting for a special occasion that Tessa would probably also have to pay for, but that was OK, she didn't mind. She'd given him a pair of Ralph Lauren cuff links and a book on how to stop smoking. It should have been drinking, but she'd obviously picked up the wrong book, which had made them laugh when he'd opened it, quite an achievement for Bob, considering his hangover.

Now the presents were open, Tessa was in the kitchen, flicking through a cookbook to find out what to do with a turkey. Bob was lying on the sofa, still struggling with his hangover. Tessa, a regular little nurse, had brought him coffee and Alka Seltzer, but despite her show of concern he knew she was worried that he'd spoil the day.

'I've always hated Christmas,' she'd told him last night. 'But this year I'm going to love it.'

And he wanted her to, especially after the miscarriage. He'd come home a few nights ago to find her tucked up in bed, eyes red from crying, and fearful that he was going to be angry. It had upset him immensely to think she was afraid, though it had been a timely warning of just how violent his drunken tempers must be getting. Wanting only to comfort and reassure her, he'd slipped into bed with her and held her until they were crying together. Not until later, when she had fallen asleep in his arms, had he given any thought to the fact that he was now free to leave her. But at the time he had brushed it aside, because he couldn't just up and go while she was still so upset about the baby.

Fortunately she had this new job to keep her mind busy now, and though she still seemed a bit shaky at times, she was throwing herself into all the training and rehearsals to such a degree that he really hadn't seen much of her since the baby had gone. It was a busy time for sport too, but he had yet to hear back from any of the contacts he'd phoned.

'Why don't you come and help,' Tessa grumbled. 'I've never cooked a turkey before.'

'Just leave it,' he said. 'Who wants turkey anyway?' It wasn't what he'd meant to say, but the last thing he wanted right now was to start playing happy Christmas cooks.

Coming to kneel on the floor in front of him, she looked up at him, and said, 'It's our first Christmas together. We should be doing all the things everyone else does at Christmas.'

But in the end it was too much effort, so they went to the pub and Bob had a few stiff gins, while Tessa sipped a Coke, and they poked fun at all the men who turned up wearing their new Christmas sweaters.

'I should have bought you one,' Tessa declared. 'Did Allyson ever buy you one?'

He knocked back another gin. Yes, Allyson had bought him sweaters. He could hardly remember buying anything without Allyson being there, except surprises for her, of course. He hadn't got her anything this year, though. How could he when he'd have to ask Tessa for the money?

'Let's have another drink,' he growled, angry now that Tessa had made him think about Allyson, whose fault it was that he hadn't got her a present, since she'd got the bank to freeze his money. 'What will you have?'

'Another Coke.'

'It's Christmas Day,' he reminded her testily. 'Why don't you have a sherry, or something?'

'I've told you before, alcohol makes me unhappy.'

He was feeling belligerent enough to press it, but then she grinned and kissed him on the mouth, and by the time he went off to get a refill he'd forgotten all about her abstinence and was thinking more about when she might be ready to have sex again. But that was soon forgotten too, and Julian's arrival on the scene a couple of hours later was well timed to help Tessa get Bob home and into bed.

With Bob safely tucked up, Tessa smiled brightly at Julian. 'Let's go out somewhere and leave him to sleep it off in peace.'

'OK. Where do you want to go?'

She shrugged. 'For a walk. That's what people do on Christmas Day, isn't it? Come on, let's wrap up warm and go for a walk by the river.'

Half an hour later Julian was edging his ancient BMW into a parking space on a Chelsea side street, and after locking up he and Tessa, who was colourfully dressed in a bright red Santa's hat, Bob's huge black padded jacket and an outrageous pair of Christmas-tree leggings, strolled out along the Embankment beside Cheyne Walk.

'Do you think she's up there?' Tessa said, gazing at Allyson's windows.

'No lights,' he answered, resting his elbows on the river wall.

'I might ask for her dressing room,' Tessa said. 'Now I'm doing most of the show, I think I should have the big one. What do you reckon?'

'Where would she go?'

'She could have the one I've been using. It's nice. It's got its own shower.' Tessa tucked her arm through his as she walked him on towards Battersea Bridge. Despite the bitter cold the sun was shining, and there were plenty of people about, walking off their Christmas indulgences, or watching out for children on new bicycles or skates.

'Shall I tell you something?' she said as they stopped to look over the side of the bridge. The water that flowed beneath was shiny and black. 'Sometimes Allyson reminds me of my mother.'

When Julian said nothing she turned to look at him, her luminous eyes combing his pale, handsome face. 'My mother killed herself, did I ever tell you that? She got this gun and she just blew out her brains.'

Through his shock she could see him struggling to find the right words. 'Why?' he finally managed.

'I think it was because she couldn't forgive herself,' she answered, then turned to look back at Allyson's flat.

'Had she done something . . .?' he said.

Tessa smiled. No one ever really knew what to say. 'It was more what she didn't do,' she answered. She linked arms again. 'Come on, we ought to be getting back. If Bob wakes up he'll wonder where we are.'

With the day's festivities at an end Allyson was tidying up in the kitchen with her mother. Her aunt and uncle were still there, snoozing on the sofa, while a repeat of *Only Fools and Horses* played on the TV. Her father had retired to his study to write a letter to *The Times*.

Allyson had spent every Christmas she could remember in her parents' Chelsea home. Though she hadn't wanted to be anywhere else this year, it had been almost unbearable without Bob. And she knew that Christmas hadn't been the same for her family either, without his teasing and taunting and outrageous games to liven up the day.

'Daddy's had another bombing,' her mother said, as Allyson started to pack away the cake. It was Peggy's way of saying her husband's incontinence pad needed changing.

Allyson stopped and looked at her mother. Then quite suddenly she started to laugh. After a moment her mother started to laugh too. It had been an awful day, so awful Allyson had almost wanted to put a gun to her head as she tormented herself with images of how cosy and romantic Bob and Tessa probably were, over the river in their love nest. And now here she was at the end of it all, standing in the kitchen with her mother crying with laughter at how wretched their lives were, thanks to the men they loved.

Five days later Allyson was back at the office. Normally she and Bob drove down to the country on Boxing Day and stayed until New Year, but even if she hadn't closed up the house she wouldn't have wanted to go alone, it would have been just too depressing.

She had no more programmes to record before January, they were all in the can, so she'd come to the office to start getting things ready for her first meeting with her new research team. Thanks to Mark's skilful handling of Shelley, Allyson had been able to have a long and productive talk with her on the phone over Christmas, when Shelley had been very enthusiastic about the few sketchy ideas Allyson had thrown in for discussion. And to Allyson's relief they'd also agreed that she should keep her office, her salary and dressing room, all of which was going to save her an enormous amount of face when her new role on the programme was made public some time in the next few days.

Shelley arrived in the office just before lunchtime, so they ran through the rain to the wine bar where they ordered shepherd's pie and chips and a bottle of red wine.

'So, how was your mother?' Allyson asked as they waited for the food.

'As witchy as ever. Probably where I get it from. What about yours? Still cut up over Bob?'

Allyson felt the bottom drop out of her carefully constructed resolve. Quickly she recovered it and rolled her eyes. 'And some,' she said. 'But it's only been a couple of months. You can't expect her to be over it yet.'

Shelley smiled wryly. 'No, of course not.' She was looking curiously at the package Allyson was taking out of her bag. 'So, have you spoken to your research team yet? Any decisions on where you're going to record your first programme?'

'Nothing's settled yet,' Allyson answered, 'but it should be by the end of next week.' She set a beautifully wrapped package on the table in front of her, then looked into Shelley's face. 'Listen, I know things have been a bit strained between us lately,' she said, 'and it's probably mostly my fault. No, please, hear me out,' she said when Shelley started to protest. 'We've come through difficult times before and no doubt we will again,' she said, 'but right now, I just want you to know how much this new job means to me. It's exactly what I need, something fresh and challenging to focus on, and I'm flattered you think I could do it.'

Shelley smiled. 'Just don't prove me wrong,' she warned. 'I really stuck my neck out with Mark Reiner to get you this position.'

Allyson looked down at the package. The lie irritated her intensely, but she let it go unchallenged. She handed the package over. 'This is not just a Christmas present, it's a thank-you present too.'

Shelley looked delighted, but that was nothing to how she responded when she opened the package and saw what was inside.

'Oh my God, Ally,' she breathed.

'It's a Marcel Bouraine fan dancer,' Allyson said. '*Circa 1920.*'

'This must have cost you a fortune,' Shelley protested. She was lifting the heavy, bronze figurine from the box. 'It's exquisite.'

'I'm glad you like it,' Allyson said, smiling.

'Like it! I love it.' The slender female body and open bronze fan were almost animated by the glinting winter sunlight coming through the windows. They were still admiring it when their food arrived.

'OK, so tell me about Mark,' Allyson said as Shelley packed the figurine away. 'Did you see him over Christmas?'

Shelley's eyes started to shine. 'Just before,' she said. 'We had the most amazing session in his office.'

'No!' Allyson cried, covering her true reaction well. Not that she wanted to have a session in his office, it was just that . . . somehow Shelley's involvement with him felt like a threat to her own friendship with him. Laughing she said, 'What if someone had come in?'

'The door was locked. But to be honest I don't think either of us would have noticed even if someone had. I'm telling you that man is something else.' She sighed ecstatically and picked up her wine. 'You know, I was really beginning to think there was no one out there for me. Well, I can tell you Mark Reiner is definitely worth the wait.' She took a sip of wine, then abruptly changed the subject. 'New Year's Eve,' she said. 'Will it be the Roof Garden, or Jemima and Phillip Gunter's? They always have a good bash. Which do you fancy?'

'I hadn't given it much thought,' Allyson answered, trying to steer her mind away from the image of Bob embracing Tessa at midnight.

'Well, you decide. I'll ask Mark if he wants to come too.' Shelley looked quickly at Allyson. 'You don't mind, do you, if he comes?'

'Why should I? No, that's fine.' She was lying, because it wasn't fine, but she didn't know why.

After lunch they returned to the office. With so few people there to distract her she'd managed to achieve a great deal by the time she packed up. She was on the point of walking out of the door when her phone rang.

'Allyson Jaymes,' she said.

'Allyson Jaymes. It's Mark Reiner.'

Her heart skipped a beat. 'Mark!' she cried, unable to keep the pleasure from her voice.

'How are you?' he asked. 'Did you have a good Christmas?'

'Yes, thank you,' she lied happily. 'How was yours?'

'My brother's here with his wife. It's good to see them.'

'Oh,' was all she could think of to say to that.

'I was wondering,' he said, 'if you're doing anything New Year's Eve. Nick, that's my brother, has got a table at the Grosvenor House ball, and, well, I'm in need of a partner.'

Allyson's mind went straight to Shelley.

'It's for charity,' he said, as though that would persuade her.

'That's good,' she responded.

He laughed. 'I can come by and pick you up.'

Allyson's thoughts were in such a commotion that she truly didn't know what to say. She wanted to go, of course, but if she did what the hell was she going to tell Shelley?

'Mark, I . . .' she began.

'. . . would love to come?' he finished.

She laughed. 'Yes, but . . .'

'You've got other plans?'

'No. It's just . . .'

'Then I'll be by around nine,' he said. 'I'll be the one in the tux,' and the line went dead.

She had to call him back. Right now. She had to explain that she simply couldn't do this to Shelley, even if he could. And, anyway, though she found him attractive, there was simply no way in the world she was ready to go out with other men.

Her dilemma seemed only to increase as she wandered down to her dressing room to get her coat. Bob was going to be with Tessa on New Year's Eve, so why the hell shouldn't she go out with someone too?

Her heart turned over as she suddenly realised she was sifting through the gorgeous creations on her clothes rail, picking out something that was suitable for a ball. Did that mean she'd already made a decision? No, it simply meant she'd have a dress to hand if she did decide to go.

At nine o'clock on New Year's Eve, dressed in a black Gianni Versace tuxedo, a long black cashmere overcoat and white silk scarf, Mark rang the doorbell to Allyson's flat. A few seconds later the buzzer sounded to release the door, and he climbed up to the second floor.

He stopped when he saw her waiting on the landing. 'You look beautiful,' he said. And she did, with her fine blonde hair scooped up in a diamond-studded net, her face exquisitely made up, and her slender shoulders bare to the tight black bodice of her dress and tops of her over-the-elbow gloves. From the waist to the ground the dress was a magnificent array of black taffeta petticoats.

'Thank you,' she smiled. 'Would you like to come in?'

He followed her inside, to where her black fur coat was lying on a chair in the sitting room. 'It's only a fake,' she said, meaning the coat.

He smiled. 'But this isn't,' he said, taking a small boxed orchid from his inside pocket. Allyson's eyes widened with surprise and pleasure. It was such a touchingly old-fashioned thing to do, bring a girl an orchid to pin on her dress.

'Perfect,' he said, when she'd finished arranging it.

She looked up into his eyes, then felt herself blushing. 'Thank you,' she said again, and hoped he didn't realise how awkward she felt, and how wrong it seemed for him to be in her flat without Bob being there too. In an attempt to cover it she said, 'You look very dashing.'

'Come on,' he laughed, 'the car's right downstairs.'

It was a black Aston Martin with a cream leather interior and every conceivable electronic gadget right at his fingertips. As he drove they talked about recent films they had seen, what had been in the news that day, everything but why he'd invited her tonight, instead of Shelley. She really wanted to ask, but she was afraid it might sound as though she were seeking comparisons or compliments, and maybe she was.

When they reached the hotel, they left the car with a valet, checked their coats, then followed the crowd into the huge, baroque-style ball-room. The orchestra was playing a Christmas tune, while waiters in smart white jackets and tartan bow ties wove between tables with trays of drinks. Nick and Claudia were already there, and to Allyson's surprise she recognised Claudia from school.

'You were in Miss Egger's class,' Allyson laughed. 'The year above me.'

'And I remember you. You were Rachel Wainwright's best friend,' Claudia declared.

'That's right,' Allyson confirmed. She didn't want to spoil the moment by telling them that Rachel had died over ten years ago. Instead she accepted the glass of champagne Nick was offering her, and sat down.

The two brothers were very similar to look at, she noted, both being dark-haired and dark-eyed, with chiselled features that, while not conventionally handsome, were, in her opinion, strikingly attractive. But there the similarity ended, for Nick was much shorter than Mark and carried considerably more weight. There was no doubt they were close, and as they baited and rallied each other, and went out of their way to make her feel welcome, she started to relax and feel glad she had come.

They ate smoked salmon and three different types of caviare, followed by roast duck and the most delicious mustard and honey sauce. A tenor from the English National Opera joined the orchestra, then another band took over and soon people started to dance. Allyson stopped thinking about Bob somewhere between the baked alaska and her fourth glass of champagne, and was feeling so alive she could probably dance until dawn. But, before she knew it, the countdown to midnight had begun and suddenly she was thinking about Bob. She wanted so desperately to be with him that, despite her efforts to hide it by cheering in the New Year along with everyone else, she could feel herself reeling off into the black depths of despair.

Sensing her distress, Mark pressed his lips to her forehead and hugged her gently. 'Happy New Year,' he whispered.

'You too,' she said, embarrassed for him to see the tears in her eyes.

He smiled. 'I'll get your coat.'

As Bob pushed his way through a loud, smoky pub in South London he had no clear idea of where he was going, he just knew that he didn't want to be there any more. Tessa was on the stage with Julian and his band, helping them bring in an extremely rowdy New Year, and though Bob had had far too much to drink, it wasn't enough to stop him feeling ridiculous. Everyone there was at least half his age.

He couldn't help wondering which party Allyson had gone to and he felt sick inside at the way all his old friends were probably laughing now, as they pictured the pathetic farce of his life, and assured Allyson she was better off without him.

As he stumbled out of the door the freezing night air hit him, sobering him enough that he could hail a taxi and get in the back.

It seemed like a long time later that the driver finally came to a stop. For a moment Bob was confused. Though his surroundings were unquestionably familiar, this wasn't Tessa's street, this was the Embankment, between Albert and Battersea Bridges.

He blinked at the driver, who was watching him in the rearview mirror. 'You OK, mate?' the driver asked.

Bob turned to look up at the windows of Allyson's flat. In his drunken state he must have given Allyson's address instead of Tessa's.

'That'll be seventeen fifty,' the driver told him.

Bob got out of the cab and started digging in his pocket for the twenty-pound note Tessa had given him today.

'Come on, mate, I haven't got all night,' the driver grumbled.

Bob found the note and was just handing it over when he saw a flash black Aston Martin turn into Cheyne Walk. The taxi driver offered him some change, but Bob wasn't looking. So the driver pulled away into the night, leaving Bob swaying on the edge of the pavement as he watched Allyson and another man getting out of the Aston Martin.

'Would you like to come up?' Allyson was saying, as Mark opened the car door for her to get out.

'No,' he said, knowing it was the answer she'd hoped for.

She looked up at him. 'I had a lovely time. Thank you.'

Though he didn't smile, his eyes were on hers. 'The photographers upset you as we were leaving,' he said.

She nodded. 'We'll probably be in all the papers tomorrow.'

'Probably.'

'So what do I tell Shelley? She's going to wonder why you invited me instead of her.'

'That's an answer I should give Shelley,' he said.

'But it'll be me she asks.'

'Then tell her why you accepted.'

Allyson's eyes were confused. 'I'm not sure I know,' she said softly.

Still he didn't smile. 'I'm sure you can work it out,' he said.

He walked her to the front door, hugged her good night, then turned back to the car. She stood watching him drive away, then taking out her key she let herself into the building. Right now it was hard to know why she'd gone. Certainly she'd had a good time, but had it been worth it for all the problems this was going to create with Shelley?

But when she got inside and saw the pale lilac and white orchid pinned to her dress in the mirror, she smiled, and felt her heart fill up with gratitude for the man who had gone out of his way to make her feel special for those few short, but deeply significant hours as one year blended into the next.

Across the street Bob was trying to focus on the light at the window, angry that he was standing out here in the cold while she was inside.

He wiped a hand across his face, staggered, then looked up at the window again. She had their flat to live in, and a private income that didn't touch their joint accounts. And now she had some rich bloke taking her out on New Year's Eve, while he stood in the street outside, like some tramp without even the money to get back to Tessa's.

After a while he slumped back against the wall and pulled his coat more tightly around him. Then he remembered he had the keys to his and Allyson's flat in his pocket.

Thrusting himself away from the wall he started across the pavement, heading towards the blinding lights of the traffic. He rolled back a few paces, then pushed forward again. Someone honked their horn and he shouted some unintelligible abuse.

The last thing he remembered was hearing himself grunt as he hit the ground. When he awoke the next morning he was fully dressed, stinking and dry-mouthed on the hard wooden bench of a police cell.

Though New Year's Day was a bank holiday there was a transmission that night, which was to include Tessa's debut as the Happy Hour presenter. This meant there was a meeting that morning to fill everyone in on who the guests were, which film insert was being included, and all the endless other minutiae that went into making up the studio day. Also on the agenda today was a preliminary discussion on the European-based programmes. Probably because it was a novelty it engendered some lively debate and excellent input, which Allyson and her two researchers, Justine and Zac, were thrilled about. Tessa hardly contributed, and Allyson was pleased to see her showing signs of nervousness. Until now it had all been playtime, but today's studio recording would be the real thing. Had it been anyone else she might have offered some encouragement; as it was Tessa she simply willed her to die.

However, an even greater concern right now was Shelley, who was at a meeting in town and not due in the office until eleven. It was a moment Allyson was dreading, for, as expected, one of the papers had announced Allyson's 'new love' that morning, with the headline 'Happy New Year, Ally!' above a lead-in telling her that she deserved to be loved after the terrible time she had been through. Just thank God Shelley hadn't been there first thing, when the others had been ribbing Allyson about her 'dashingly romantic millionaire prince'.

Shelley arrived as the meeting broke up and cut Allyson dead as she called that day's production team into her office for a briefing. She then went out of her way to avoid Allyson until just before the recording, when she walked into her office and slammed the door shut behind her.

'So,' she said, tight-lipped, 'I call your flat at midnight to wish you happy New Year and you're not there. I, of course, think you're in bed, hiding from the world, but no! Cinderella's flaunting herself at some fancy ball, having a fabulous time in the arms of her new love, who, as far as I knew, was just getting started on a relationship with me. So do you want to give me some explanation of what's going on?'

'Don't condescend to me like that,' Allyson snapped. 'I'm not a child you're reprimanding. I'm a grown woman and as far as I knew Mark Reiner *was*, and *is*, getting started on a relationship with you.'

'So how come *you're* at a ball with him on New Year's Eve?'

Allyson had thought about this, and was pretty sure she knew the answer. 'He invited me,' she said, 'in an effort to divert some of today's press attention from the way I'm being pushed down the agenda on my own show, and having to suffer the humiliation of my husband's mistress taking over the spotlight. I don't know why I didn't tell you. I suppose because I knew you'd be upset.'

'You're damn right I am. You know how I feel about him, yet you go out with him on one of the most romantic nights of the year. So let's have the real truth, shall we? If you're having an affair . . .'

'We're not having an affair.'

'So why didn't you tell me about going to his office? What are you trying to hide?'

'You're making this sound like a conspiracy! I've done nothing to hurt you, nor would I. OK, I should have told you about last night, but, to be frank, you pissed me off when you said you'd stuck your neck out to get me the producer's job. The job was my idea, which is what I went to see Mark about on the day you think I started on some clandestine affair.'

Shelley's face was white.

'Look, I'm sorry,' Allyson said. 'Can we try to forget this has happened? For God's sake, we can't fall out over a man. A man who means nothing to me. Who was just being kind.'

'But why? Why would he care about the way *you* feel?'

Allyson's eyes flashed. 'Well, thanks for that,' she snapped. 'It's just what I need, right now, to feel as though I'm not worth the effort.'

'Oh, let's make this all about you, shall we?' Shelley cried. 'You and your heartbreak. Why deal with your disloyalty and lies, they don't paint such a great picture, do they?'

'Shelley, do you really think after what's just happened to me I'd walk off with the man you're crazy about? Besides, I'm so far from being ready for anything new . . .'

'But that's you, not him.'

'Shelley, I've yet to meet the man who can resist you. And believe you me, he's no exception.'

Shelley despised the weakness in her that so desperately wanted to believe that. And in her heart she just couldn't stop herself believing that Mark Reiner was the one who was going to make some sense of all the waiting and rejection, all the confusion and trying, that until now had never brought her anything but pain.

In the end all she said was, 'I hope you're right.'

'I am,' Allyson assured her. Getting to her feet, she walked round her desk and put her hands on Shelley's shoulders. 'If it makes you feel any better, think of this: I've now got the overwhelming joy of watching Tessa Dukes make her glittering debut on what was always my programme, before she no doubt goes off to celebrate with my husband.'

Shelley groaned. 'How could that make me feel better?'

'OK, not better,' Allyson responded, 'just aware that Bob Jaymes still very much dominates my life, which is the main reason I went last night, in the hope of making him jealous.'

Shelley smiled. She wasn't sure it made it any better, but that was at least something she understood.

The cameras were moving into position. In the gallery the production team was getting ready to record. Tessa's face was on every monitor. She looked cute and sexy in a skin-tight catsuit. She'd already met the guests, a flighty actress who was playing the bitch in a new teenage soap, and a car-wrecking stunt man who'd just cut his first single.

'OK, recording in one minute,' the floor manager announced.

Tessa peered through the lights and found Shelley walking towards her, smiling her encouragement.

'Are you OK?' she asked.

Tessa nodded, but she looked as scared as Shelley had expected. 'The pilots were fantastic,' Shelley told her. 'You're a natural when it comes to letting your guests talk. It took Allyson a long time to learn that.'

Tessa knew then that she was going to be brilliant.

Satisfied that the compliment at Allyson's expense had worked, Shelley squeezed the girl's hand and disappeared into the darkness surrounding the set.

'OK, studio, stand by.' The director was speaking into the talkback.

'Good luck, everyone,' Shelley said. 'Be brilliant.'

Tessa smiled, and the production assistant began the countdown.

'OK, on you, camera two,' the director said as the countdown ended. 'And cue Tessa.'

Tessa's first real recording was a triumph. She was entertaining, energetic and impressively professional. She caused an audible gasp in the gallery when she asked the actress, point-blank, how much her new breasts had cost, and made them all laugh when she got up to jig about to the stunt man's new hit. As a performer she was outlandish, unconventional, surpassing even Shelley's expectations.

The reviews next morning were brilliant, though, ironically, Tessa's limelight was somewhat stolen by Bob Jaymes's appearance in court for being drunk and disorderly. But as his arrest had happened on New Year's Eve people were more inclined to laugh than condemn.

Allyson was one of the few who didn't find it funny, and might have called him, had she not been flying off to recce the Sporting Club in Monaco as a possible venue for her first foreign programme. That must take priority. Bob's increasing problem with drink was no longer her concern. Let Tessa deal with his mess, she was the one who'd created it.

Getting Bob out of bed after a heavy night was no easy task, but Tessa had gone to a lot of trouble organising things, so she had no intention of letting him spoil it, even if it did mean giving him a breakfast of thick black coffee followed by a fortifying gin.

By ten o'clock he was showered, shaved and dressed ready to go. His face was a bit pale, but he looked pretty cool in his Hugo Boss jeans and a white Armani shirt, though definitely his mood could have been better. Tessa had intended to drive, but he insisted he would, so, as soon as she'd finished putting their belongings in the car, she slipped into the passenger seat and soon they were heading towards Chelsea. Tessa started chattering on about Allyson and how she'd gone to France on a supposed recce, but, according to office gossip, she was meeting up with Mark Reiner.

'Just shut up about her, will you?' Bob snapped. 'I'm doing what you want, aren't I? So you don't have to wind me up any more.'

'Sorry.' Tessa looked out of the window and said no more.

The photographers and a reporter from *Hello!* were already waiting when they drove into Cheyne Walk. Though Bob had qualms about what they were doing, he was still angry enough with Allyson to go along with it, and since this was his home too, he reminded himself that he had every right to be there.

Once inside, the photographer started setting up in the kitchen, while the make-up artist took Tessa into the bathroom. This was the first time Tessa had ever been inside the flat, so it was all she could do not to give herself away by drooling over the amazing draperies around the bed, or the size of the rooms, or the incredible marble bathroom.

Very soon she was helping herself to Allyson's cosmetics, then rummaging through her underwear drawer looking for clean tights. It was like a game as the photographer clicked away, taking shots of her and Bob hugging each other in the amazing designer kitchen, and of Tessa curled up on one of the creamy yellow sofas in the sitting room. No one mentioned the silver-framed photographs of Allyson and Bob on their wedding day, or the photographs of Allyson's friends and family.

All the time the photographer worked the reporter was asking questions about how it felt to be famous, and other trivial stuff that Tessa could handle easily. There was an awkward moment, though, when the photographer asked her and Bob to pose on the bed and Bob flatly refused. Knowing that there would be no point in arguing, Tessa took the reporter and photographer to one side and said, 'He's very private about our life together. In fact, I had a hell of a job getting him to agree to this at all, so, if you don't mind, we'd better call it a day.'

The photographer and make-up artist started packing away their gear while the reporter asked Tessa a few final questions. When they were ready to leave Tessa walked to the front door with them.

'Wonderful place you've got here,' the reporter said, as Bob walked into the hall. 'Isn't it where you and Allyson lived?'

'Yes, but we live here now,' Tessa answered, pulling open the door. 'Thanks for coming. Let me know which issue it's in, won't you?'

Their footsteps could still be heard on the stairs as Tessa closed the door, then turned to Bob. Her eyes were glittering brightly. 'See, I told you,' she laughed. 'We've only been here a couple of hours and already everything feels better.'

She looked into his face and saw how troubled he was. 'Oh, Bob,' she groaned. 'You're home. I thought it was where you wanted to be.'

How could he say, 'Yes, but not with you?' How could he say anything now the photographer had gone with evidence of their unforgivable intrusion into Allyson's life? But if Allyson was down there in the South of France with another man, a man who might already have spent the night in his bed . . .

'Do we have to go?' Tessa whispered, her disappointment showing.

'No,' he said. 'I'm just trying to decide whether we should bring our bags in first, or . . .' he was turning into the bedroom.

'Or?' she said, starting to laugh.

'Or whether I should make love to you right now.'

'I'd say there's no contest,' she said as he carried her into the bedroom and dropped her on the bed.

Allyson was sitting at a table near the empty stage of the Monte Carlo Sporting Club. With her were Justine and Zac, her researchers, and Monsieur Thibault, a representative of the Société des Bains de Mer, the organisation that controlled everything in Monaco, including the permissions needed to film.

The Sporting Club was an ambitious target for Allyson's first transmission, and although her first efforts to book it had met with a disdainful no, after two days' negotiation they appeared to be making some headway. Allyson hardly dared to imagine what a coup it would be if she could pull this off, for the large, circular room, with its spectacular views of the Mediterranean, was a location like no other.

'You say you will need the club for three days,' M. Thibault purred. 'One to set up, one to rehearse and shoot, and one to de-rig.'

'That's right,' Allyson confirmed. 'There'll be about twenty crew in all, and fifty invited guests to make up an audience. Obviously, there'll be the programme guests too, which should number around six, I believe?' She was looking at Zac and Justine, seeking confirmation.

Zac, the lanky Irish lad who was the senior of the two researchers, pushed a sheet of paper across the table. 'Here's a list of those we've approached,' he said. 'They all live here, in Monte Carlo. I'm still waiting to hear back from a couple, so I'll confirm nearer the time who we're actually going to use.'

'And the audience invitation obviously extends to you and a guest,' Justine added with a fetching smile.

Whether it was Justine's invitation or her smile that Thibault appreciated was hard to tell, but after giving Zac's list a look-over, Thibault turned back to Allyson. 'You understand that we make you a special rate because it is winter,' he said.

'We're very grateful to you,' Allyson said, knowing she'd have to cut into the budgets of future programmes to cover this 'special rate'.

Thibault nodded graciously, then returned to his perusal of the documentation in front of him. 'You are returning to London tomorrow?' he said, after a while.

Allyson replied, 'We leave Nice at midday.'

'Then I shall have an answer for you before you leave.'

Half an hour later Allyson was at the wheel of their hire car driving back to the auberge in which they were staying. All three of them were having trouble containing their excitement. 'I don't know what I'm going to do with you two if this doesn't work out,' Allyson laughed, as she pulled up outside the inn. 'Will you be able to handle the disappointment?'

'We won't have to,' Zac assured her. 'Thibault's going to come through, I just know it.'

And M. Thibault did not turn them down. At ten the next morning he called Allyson on her mobile to announce that he was delighted to offer the facilities of the Monte Carlo Sporting Club to her programme under the terms and conditions they had agreed. The second she rang off Allyson gave a scream of joy, then flung her arms round Zac and Justine. Losing her status as a presenter was hard, but if this first real experience as a producer was anything to go by, then Allyson suspected that working behind the scenes was going to prove more rewarding than anything she'd done before. And that in itself felt like a triumph over Tessa Dukes, not to mention a poke in the eye for Bob, who might have been deluding himself that she couldn't survive without him.

By the time the plane touched down at Heathrow, Allyson was so exhausted by all the elation and intense hard work of the past couple of days that instead of going straight to the office she went home first to shower and change.

After the taxi dropped her off she hurried up the stairs, only to find that for some reason her key wouldn't turn in the lock. Baffled, and not a little irritated, she was about to call a locksmith when, to her amazement, Julian came bounding up the stairs behind her. He stopped dead when he saw her.

'Julian?' she said. 'What are you doing here?'

He looked ready to bolt. 'I just, well, uh, Tessa left something here. I've come to pick it up.'

Allyson stared at him, not sure she'd heard right. 'Tessa's been here?' she said, her heart starting to thump. 'How were you going to get in?'

He looked at her wretchedly.

'You've got a key, haven't you?' she said. 'They've changed the locks.' Her knees had turned weak with the shock, but her voice was icily determined as she said, 'Give me the key.'

He didn't put up much of a fight.

Allyson took the key and turned to open the door. 'Come with me,' she said. She was so angry she felt violent.

The place was a mess, newspapers and unwashed dishes all over the floor. She stalked straight into the laundry room, grabbed a roll of black plastic sacks and began filling them.

'Help me,' she snapped at Julian.

Obediently he took a bag and began filling it.

When Allyson was satisfied that everything of Tessa's was gone, she made Julian help her carry the sacks to the bins.

'You can go now,' she said when they'd finished.

Returning to the flat she called an emergency locksmith who came within the hour. When he'd finished she drove into the office.

Tessa was just coming out of the studio. Whether Julian had had time to get to her before she'd gone in to record wasn't possible to tell. Allyson didn't care. She grabbed hold of Tessa's arm and flung her up against the wall. 'If you ever set one foot inside my flat again I'll have you arrested,' she hissed. 'Do you hear me?'

'Let go of me,' Tessa cried. 'Just who do you think you are, pushing me around!'

At that Allyson dealt her such a resounding blow to the face that Tessa staggered sideways.

Allyson turned and walked away.

'Bitch!' Tessa screamed after her.

Allyson kept going, past those who had stopped to stare, and upstairs to Shelley's office.

Shelley looked up. 'What's happened?' she said.

'Nothing. I just wanted to let you know that I'm going to tape our first foreign programme in Monte Carlo. Oh, and if—'

The door crashed open and Tessa flew at her.

'What the hell?' Shelley cried, leaping to her feet.

Tessa was on Allyson's back, clawing her hair and trying to bang her head against the wall. 'Bitch!' she was screaming. '*Bitch!*'

'Get her off,' Shelley demanded as Alan and Jerry ran into the office.

Quickly they prised Tessa away. Allyson stumbled against the desk and brushed the hair from her face. 'I'm warning you,' she shouted at Tessa, 'stay away from me and what's mine or I'll kill you.'

The others watched in silence as she walked out of the room.

Shelley caught up with her in the car park.

'She tried to move into my flat,' Allyson gasped. 'I got back to find the locks had been changed and her and Bob's things were all over the place. I wanted to kill her, Shell. I swear, if I had it in me . . .' She took a breath. 'And as for him, I was considering giving him some money, but he can rot in hell now. They both can. They've turned my life upside-down, they've mocked me, humiliated me and now they're trying to destroy me.' Fury was making her breath short, tears streamed down her face. 'How does a man you've loved for more than twenty years suddenly turn into this monster?' she raged.

'Because he's weak,' Shelley answered. 'He saw something he wanted and took it, without thinking about you or anyone else. And this is what it's got him. No job, no money and a stupid little cow of a girlfriend who he probably can't stand any more.'

'Then why doesn't he leave her? He's got me.'

Shelley looked at her. 'Are you sure about that?'

Allyson looked back, her eyes dark with confusion. In the end she closed them. 'God, I hate her,' she said. 'I hate her so much it scares me.'

Chapter Eleven

'MARK? IT'S SHELLEY.'

'How are you?'

'OK. I was wondering if you watched the recording last night.'

'From Monte Carlo? It worked very well. Congratulations.'

'Thank you. But it was Allyson's programme.'

'Your idea to go international,' he reminded her.

Shelley appreciated his remembering, but could think of no suitable response. It had taken her three weeks to pluck up the courage to make this call, rehearsing what she would say. It all worked very well in the planning; right now though she couldn't think how to proceed.

'Is the crew back yet?' he asked.

'Tonight. Uh, I was wondering, would you be free for dinner?'

'Tonight? I'm afraid not.'

The pounding in her heart increased. She wanted to pretend this call had never happened. 'I was hoping,' she said, 'that we could talk.'

'About?'

'Us.'

Another silence. Panic rushed to fill it, sweeping aside her dignity and forcing words from her lips that she knew already she was going to regret. 'I thought it meant something to you, when we made love,' she said. 'You seemed to enjoy it.' Oh God, where was her pride?

'It was sensational,' he said.

'So why don't we do it again? You've got to admit we have fun together.' Was this begging? Could this go down as begging?

Another pause before he said, 'I'm sorry, but I'll have to cut this call short. I have someone with me.'

'Is Allyson with you? Is that why you won't talk to me?' What wretchedness was making her behave like this?

'No. I believe you know where she is.'

Of course she did. Allyson was on her way back from France, aglow with the success of her first programme as a producer. Shelley had invited her out tonight to celebrate, but Allyson had said she was having dinner with her mother . . .

'I have to go,' he said.

Shelley put the phone down. Her hand wasn't steady, shame was burning her all over. Oh God, why couldn't she just accept that he didn't want her? Maybe she could if it didn't seem to be Allyson he wanted instead. Of course she had no actual proof of it, but she'd always trusted her instincts in the past, and this time they were signalling her loud and clear. It was too hard to take, too cruel of fate to give the man she wanted to Allyson Jaymes.

After ending his call with Shelley, Mark replaced the receiver and looked across at the frankly questioning eyes that were watching him. She'd just returned on an early flight from France and still appeared flushed with the success of her visit.

Tessa smiled. She had no idea who he'd been talking to as he had carefully avoided mentioning any names. Maybe it had been Allyson.

Certainly he'd spoken to Allyson while they were in Monaco, because to Allyson's obvious displeasure, she, Tessa, had answered Allyson's mobile when Allyson had been over the other side of the Club and no one else had seemed inclined to pick up the phone.

After the call Allyson had announced that he'd rung to wish them all good luck. But there had to have been more to the call, simply because of how long it had gone on. And the way Allyson had laughed, then taken herself off into a corner so she couldn't be overheard, went a long way towards confirming the rumours that there really was something going on between them.

Now, as Tessa looked into his watchful dark eyes, she smiled and revealed more of her legs because men usually enjoyed being teased. He didn't smile back, nor did he look at her legs.

'Well,' she said, getting to her feet, 'I suppose I'd better be going. I only came to give you my new address and make sure you were happy with the way I'm presenting the programme.'

'Very,' he said, though there was no warmth to his assurance.

She looked a little lost. 'You seem as though you're cross with me,' she said. 'If I've done something wrong, I'm sorry.'

He seemed to thaw a bit at that. 'No, Tessa, you haven't done anything wrong. But I have to be somewhere . . .'

'Oh, yes, I'm sorry. Thank you for taking the time to see me. I really appreciate it.' She watched him as he came round his desk to see her out. Then as he passed she reached for his hand and looked up into his startled eyes. 'If there's anything I can do to say thank you, you know, for the chance you've given me . . .'

'There's no need,' he informed her. The door was open, he was standing aside for her to go. 'Just continue to do a good job.'

'Of course,' she smiled, walking past him. Then at the last moment she turned to look over her shoulder. 'Until the next time,' she said playfully, and after a quick glance at his assistant she left.

Bob was holding the note in his hand, staring at it, and hardly believing it. Yet the words were right there, in Tessa's girlishly round writing. He sat down on the sofa and read.

Dear Bob,

I'm really sorry to leave without talking things over, but we both know how unhappy you've been lately, and nothing I do seems to help. I wish it did, but I think we both have to accept that there's no point pretending any more. I may or may not have mentioned to you how I thought my

*new boss, Mark Reiner, was interested in me, and I've decided I'd like to
give that relationship a chance. I think the only reason he's been holding
back is because I'm living with you. So, I've found myself a new place in
Knightsbridge, where you'll be welcome to come and visit any time you
like. I really love you and care about you.*

    Tessa.

*PS: I've left twenty-nine pounds on the table, which is yours from my
bank account. Big kiss and good luck. T.*

He went into the kitchen and saw that she'd left him a glass, a cup, a
plate, two knives, two forks and a spoon. She'd also left him some bread
and cheese, and a bottle of gin.

He was halfway through the gin when suddenly he couldn't stand any
more. He had to get out of this prison. He had no clear idea where he
would go, except he knew it couldn't be to Allyson. Since he and Tessa
had tried to move into the flat his shame was so great he didn't have the
nerve to face her. There was only one other place he could go, and fortunately he had just enough money to cover the cab fare.

'Oh my God,' Allyson murmured, as she and Zac and Justine wheeled
their luggage into the noisy arrivals hall at Heathrow Airport. 'I don't
believe it.' She was smiling all over her face, and the closer she got to
where he was waiting, the deeper she was blushing.

'Hi,' Mark said, handing her the flowers that he was holding.
'Congratulations.'

Allyson started to laugh, and glanced self-consciously at her colleagues who were clearly enjoying the moment. 'Thank you,' she said. 'I
wasn't expecting . . . I mean, I didn't know you'd be here.'

'I had a meeting at a hotel nearby,' he said, his eyes holding onto hers,
'so I checked what time your flight was coming in and . . . Here I am.
Can I give you a ride into town?'

Allyson looked at Justine and Zac again, then threw out her hands.
'Why not?' she said. 'Yes, that would be lovely.'

'It certainly would,' Zac agreed, starting to head out.

Justine kicked him. 'We'll get a cab,' she said, smiling through her
teeth.

'But . . .' Zac complained.

'Take no notice of him,' Allyson told Mark, 'he's always like that. He's
Zac O'Reilly by the way, and this is Justine Webb. My researchers.'

Mark shook their hands. 'I'll be happy to drive you into town too,' he
said. 'We'll all fit in.'

'Oh no!' Justine cried. 'We wouldn't hear of it.'

'Why wouldn't we?' Zac demanded.

'Listen, please come with us,' Allyson said. 'This is too painful to go through any more.'

Zac and Justine were still arguing by the time they reached Mark's car. 'Just shut up, will you?' Allyson said, as they got into the back seat.

Mark was laughing, and after holding the door open for Allyson to get in too, he slipped into the driver's seat and started up the engine.

'It was a great programme you shot in Monaco,' Mark said, clearing the ticket barrier. 'The congratulations are extended to all of you.'

'Does that mean we get a share in the flowers?' Zac wanted to know.

'Give me a moment and I'll work out a quiet way to kill him,' Justine said. Then both Mark and Allyson burst out laughing as they heard her whisper, 'You're going too far now. I mean it, Zac, button up or I'll do something drastic.'

'Oh, what a temptress she is,' Zac intoned, but after that he managed to keep quiet, and Mark began asking the researchers what they were working on for their next foreign transmission.

Allyson contributed little, for she was happy just to sit and listen, and allow the pleasure she'd felt at him being at the airport wash over her. Though how the hell was she going to explain it to Shelley?

Shelley was staring at the exquisite bronze fan dancer Allyson had given her at Christmas. It was one of her most prized possessions, a generous gesture of friendship, but now Shelley was wondering if it wasn't really a means of trying to buy off her guilt.

Shelley wondered where Allyson was now, if she really was spending the evening with Mark, as she'd suspected. Her eyes moved to the elegant Lalique clock that Allyson loved so much. It was the only thing Shelley had that Allyson wanted, whereas Allyson had virtually everything Shelley wanted. Or that was how it felt tonight.

Around nine o'clock someone rang the doorbell downstairs. When she heard Bob's voice on the entryphone she almost laughed. All that surprised her about him being there was that he hadn't come sooner. She'd have liked to tell him to get lost, but suddenly she felt in enough need of company to make even his acceptable.

A few minutes later he walked into the sitting room, bringing a cloud of chill night air with him.

'So what do you want?' she asked, from where she was sitting.

He seemed to flinch at the bluntness of her words, then obviously decided to match them with a bluntness of his own. 'Money and somewhere to sleep,' he answered.

She laughed incredulously. 'And you came here for it? You must be desperate. What happened to Tessa?'

'She left. Got a new place in Knightsbridge. Seems I'm too small-time for her now. She's set her sights even higher.'

'Not difficult to get higher than you, Bob,' she remarked.

His mouth twisted, and the old fire she was used to made a fleeting return. 'It was good enough for you once.'

'A lot more than once, as I recall,' she said. 'Do you want a drink?'

He looked tempted, so tempted that she was amazed when he slumped down in a chair and said, 'No. I'm trying to get off it. I'm in a bad way, Shelley.'

There was only disdain on her face as she looked down at him. 'Spare me the self-pity,' she said. 'You were the one who started screwing around with a kid, and you've got some nerve coming round here now that it's all fallen apart. What did you expect, a sympathy fuck?'

Raising his head, he looked at her with cold, hostile eyes. 'It wasn't so long ago you were begging me for it,' he reminded her. 'Did you ever tell Allyson that? No, I bet you didn't. You got the papers to tell her about Tessa though, didn't you? It was you, wasn't it, who tipped them off?'

'Yes. It was me. She deserved rescuing from you.'

'Oh, is that what you're telling yourself? If you ask me it pissed you off big-time that I wouldn't leave Allyson for you, so you reckoned you'd pay me back by making my affair with Tessa public. Must have come as a real blow to you when I actually left Allyson for Tessa.'

'You're pathetic,' she said. 'To think of everything you've lost for the sake of a fat little teenager. And now she's famous you're left with her footprints all over your face.'

His head came up and she saw something of his pain as he looked her straight in the eye. 'Can I stay here tonight?' he said.

'No.'

From his expression it was the answer he'd expected, but he seemed crushed nevertheless. 'What about some money?'

'No.'

'Shelley, I'm destitute. I can't even afford the rent on the little shithole she left me in.'

'Talk to your wife. Oh sorry, her lawyer. Pity I can't do the same, and make you talk to me through a lawyer.'

'You're such a bitch,' he said, getting to his feet. 'I'm wasting my time here. I thought you might take pity on an old friend, but you don't know what pity is, do you?'

Shelley picked up the phone as it rang.

'Shell? It's me. Mummy's cancelled on me. Do you still want dinner?'

Shelley's smile grew as she realised what this meant. 'My treat,' she said to Allyson. 'I'll meet you at San Lorenzo in half an hour.' She hung up and turned back to Bob. 'Are you still here?' she said.

Shoving his hands in his pockets he walked towards the front door. She reached for her bag and took out her purse. 'Here,' she said, handing him a fifty-pound note. 'Don't spend it on booze.'

Taking the note he said, 'Was that Allyson on the phone?'

She nodded, and he looked so dejected that for a moment she really did feel sorry for him. Then, remembering something he'd said earlier, she said, 'By the way, you didn't tell me who Tessa's sights have risen to.'

He slammed the door in her face and, laughing, she went to freshen her make-up.

Allyson watched Shelley coming towards her. Though she was anxious about how the evening would go, she was glad Shelley had come, because the last thing she wanted was for her to find out through office gossip that Mark had been at the airport earlier. He'd dropped Allyson at her flat an hour ago, with no mention of going on for dinner, which she'd half expected, though he had asked her to come to his office at five tomorrow. She had no idea what that was about, and hadn't asked because Zac and Justine were still in the car. Heaven only knew where he dropped them, though she couldn't imagine he'd played taxi service right to their doors.

'Hi,' she said, getting up to embrace Shelley as she reached the table. 'I'm on such a high that I just couldn't have stayed in this evening.'

'I'm not surprised,' Shelley smiled. 'It's a pretty impressive debut. I hope you've ordered champagne.'

She nodded. 'I see the ratings were up again last week, which must mean that even if I can't stand her, the world loves Tessa.' Though she was still smiling even she heard the edge to her voice. 'She was good in France,' she said. 'I'm just wondering what we're going to do when the baby starts showing.'

Shelley smiled, but she could see that Allyson was fast coming down from her high. Tiredness would do that of course, and the reminder of something she'd obviously rather forget. 'About the baby,' she said.

Allyson's eyes flickered off to one side. 'Let's not talk about it,' she said. 'Not tonight.'

'I think we should,' Shelley replied. 'Mainly because there is no baby. Not any more.'

As the words reached her Allyson felt herself go very still. No baby?

Did that mean . . .? Her eyes came up to Shelley's.

'I think she told Bob it was a miscarriage,' Shelley said. 'Did you know she's left him?'

This was all too much for Allyson to take in. The shock was so great that she didn't seem able to grasp what any of it might mean. 'When?' she finally managed.

'I'm not sure. I only heard myself today. Apparently she's living in Knightsbridge.'

The champagne arrived, and as Allyson watched the waiter open it she had to remind herself what they were celebrating, because suddenly everything felt very different.

'Here's to you,' Shelley said when their glasses were full. 'And to many more programmes like your first one.'

Allyson smiled as they touched glasses. But the Happy Hour at the Monte Carlo Sporting Club felt like an entire world away now, another lifetime even.

Bob and Tessa were no longer together!

'Did you see the spread in *Hello!*?' she said.

Shelley nodded.

'I still can't believe her nerve,' Allyson said. 'She's just not normal.'

'She's found someone else, apparently.'

Allyson's surprise showed. 'Oh? Who?'

'No idea.'

Allyson drank some more champagne. 'Let's stop talking about her,' she said. 'I only want to deal with her as some kind of prop on the show. Tell me about you. Did you hear from Mark again? Have you seen him?'

Shelley was shaking her head, then looking Allyson frankly in the eye, she said, 'To tell the truth I thought you were seeing him.'

'Me?' Allyson responded. 'What made you think that? Just because he gave us a lift in from the airport?'

Shelley's mouth had turned dry. 'You mean he came to meet you?'

'No. Not really. He was out at the airport anyway, and knowing we were about to fly in, he came to offer us a lift into London. Zac and Justine were there too.'

Shelley looked away. She felt as if her feelings had been ripped away from their centre, were hanging jagged in a vacuum of confusion.

'He's asked me to go and see him tomorrow,' Allyson said, desperately wishing he hadn't, for she could see how much this was upsetting Shelley.

'What about?'

'He didn't say.'

Several seconds ticked by before Shelley looked up and said, 'So, do you think you'll go back with Bob?'

Allyson knew what answer Shelley was hoping for, but it wasn't an answer she could give, not yet. So all she said was, 'If I do, it's not going to happen immediately.'

 ## Chapter Twelve

IT HAD BEEN A HECTIC DAY recording six Nightcaps, catching up with correspondence and starting plans for the next transmission, which was coming from the ski slopes of Austria.

Allyson gathered up her briefcase and coat and ran out to her car.

On the way up to town, still buzzing from her day, she called in at the women's refuge, where she was welcomed with freshly brewed tea and the latest news on funding. She'd had so little time lately that she'd been unable to visit as regularly as usual, but she'd been in contact by phone, getting updates on how they all were and trying to offer some comfort and sympathy. She understood that her being a celebrity made them feel special, which was probably one of the best parts of being famous. Of course, one of the worst parts was being hounded by the press, as she had been today, now it was known that Tessa had left Bob.

They were in Tessa's hair too, of course, but Shelley had been quick to bring in a publicist to handle the calls, as Tessa had nothing like Allyson's experience in dealing with the press

Leaving her car at the refuge she hailed a cab and gave the driver the address of Mark's office. She could do with these few minutes of peace to collect her thoughts. However, they had barely pulled away from the kerb when her cellphone rang. It was Shelley, pointing out the duplication of a celebrity guest who was being talked about for the ski programme, but was already pencilled in to appear on one of the regular shows the previous week.

It was a problem soon settled, for Allyson was willing to find someone else, and Shelley put forward a few suggestions that could easily work. The call then ended on a friendly note, but there was no mistaking the chill of politeness that had crept into the usual warmth between them.

After paying the driver Allyson walked the few paces to Mark's office, still wondering why Mark had invited her here.

'He's with the finance director,' Corinne, his assistant, told her when she walked into the reception area. 'I'll let him know you're here.'

As Corinne picked up the phone, Allyson could feel the flutterings in her heartbeat. Although she felt nervous, she really was looking forward to this meeting, for reasons that weren't entirely professional.

Allyson wandered over to the window. Rush hour was already under way, though she was hardly registering it. In fact she had no idea how much time had passed before she became conscious of Corinne's voice again, and realised she was talking to Mark.

Allyson turned round and was aware of the way he seemed to dominate the room and reach everything inside her with his dark eyes.

'I've put the tickets on your desk,' Corinne was telling him as he looked at Allyson. 'Your flight's at eleven in the morning, arriving in Paris around noon.'

'Great,' he said. Then to Allyson, 'Hi. Come in.'

He held open the door, and as she passed she caught the warm, male scent of him. His tie was loose and his white shirt was crumpled. 'Can I offer you a drink?' he asked.

'Thanks. I'll take a vodka martini.'

Noticing the way the corners of his eyes creased as he smiled made her smile too. 'I'll join you,' he said, walking over to fix the drinks.

Allyson was about to sit on one of his guest chairs when he said, 'If we're having martinis we don't need to be formal.'

So she went to sit on one of the comfy black leather sofas. There was something quite exhilarating about being here, and allowing herself to sink into the attraction, even though she was far too unsure of herself to permit the kind of thoughts she was having to become a reality.

'Thanks for coming,' he said, as he sat down. 'I know how busy you are. Anyway, here's to you and your continued success.'

'Thank you,' Allyson responded.

As they drank she dropped her eyes from his, not wanting him to see how aware she was becoming of his body, but it was hard not to be when his proximity was dragging her shy and battered libido out into the light and giving it all kinds of ideas on how to get going again.

'Did I tell you, my family enjoyed meeting you on New Year's Eve?' he said, with intimacy in his voice.

'I enjoyed meeting them,' she answered. 'And I'm sorry if I wasn't, well'—she gave a playful raise of her eyebrows—'quite myself.'

'You're going through a tough time. I heard about the spread in *Hello!*.

Allyson coloured, and felt ashamed for him to know that Bob had treated her so badly.

'I need to ask you a favour,' he said, changing the subject. 'Nick and I have a hotel in Ravello, Italy. The renovation is complete and it is due to open some time in March. The favour I'm asking is if you'd consider making the hotel's launch the subject of one of your programmes. From my point of view the publicity would be excellent, and from yours the party would be worth going to. The guest list will be suitably celebrity-heavy, and the setting on the Amalfi Coast is extremely picturesque.'

Allyson was laughing. 'You're the boss,' she said. 'If you want us to go to Ravello then to Ravello we shall go.'

'It's not an order. It's a request. As the producer you tell me if you're happy about making it one of your programmes.'

'I'd be very happy,' she said. 'Obviously I'd want to be involved in drawing up the guest list, but on the face of it it sounds perfect.'

Though he was still smiling, he appeared to look at her in a way that seemed to be moving past the veneer of professionalism and politeness. 'There's something else I'm going to ask,' he told her.

She waited, feeling a shortening of her breath and a wonderful antici-pation tightening her insides.

'Nick normally takes care of the hotels and restaurants,' he said, 'but he can't get over in the foreseeable future, so he's asked me to take care of the pre-opening business. And as you'll need to recce the place I thought we could go out to Italy together.'

Allyson's breath had stopped. This was clearly a romantic proposal and she wanted more than anything to say yes. But how could she when she knew how much it would hurt Shelley? 'If . . . If you're meaning what I think you might be meaning,' she said, looking at him again, 'then I'm afraid I can't.'

He seemed neither surprised nor put out by her response. 'Because of Shelley?' he said. 'Or because of Bob?'

'Because of Shelley,' she said frankly.

It was nine in the morning when Tessa rang Mark Reiner at his flat.

'What can I do for you?' he said.

'I've been invited to this charity dinner at the Inn on the Park next Thursday and I was hoping you'd come with me.'

'I'm afraid that's not possible. You should ask one of the directors to go with you, or a reporter.'

'I'd prefer it to be you.'

He looked at his watch. 'Tessa, I have to go. I've got a plane to catch.'

He put down the phone and walked along the hall to where he'd left his luggage, just inside the front door. He'd like to think he was wrong about this, but if his suspicions were correct, and Tessa had transferred her affections to him, then he was a very long way from being flattered. In fact, he was far closer to being angry and concerned, for it certainly hadn't escaped his attention that her interest in him had neatly coincided with his in Allyson. Exactly what that meant he wasn't yet sure, but he'd no doubt find out soon enough—just as Tessa Dukes would find out that he didn't respond to the whims of a teenage girl as though they were some kind of irresistible magic charm.

A week had gone by since Shelley had learned about the proposed programme in Italy. She knew she should tell Allyson to go on the recce, that it was the only honourable course to take, but she just couldn't make herself do it. Instead, she kept her distance and made a great show of having far more pressing matters to deal with, like supervising Tessa's progress as a presenter, which was why she was with her in her dressing room, late one afternoon, when Tessa took a call from Mark Reiner.

'Oh, hi, Mark,' Tessa cried cheerfully. 'Did you see the programme?'

Shelley couldn't hear the response, but she saw the glow on Tessa's face. 'So when am I going to see you? . . . Tomorrow? . . . Great. What time?'

Shelley continued to look at the script, stunned by what she was hearing. Surely Tessa Dukes wasn't setting her sights on Mark Reiner? She suddenly turned cold as she remembered that was the phrase Bob had used when he'd told her Tessa had found someone else. But Mark Reiner? She had to be into self-delusion in a big way if she thought she was going to get anywhere with him.

'OK, well don't forget to come and say hi to me,' Tessa said. 'I'll pass you over to Shelley.' She held out the phone. 'Mark Reiner, for you.'

Shelley's heart skipped a beat. This would be the first time they'd spoken since the day she'd all but begged him to see her, and she'd have preferred it not to be in front of Tessa. 'Hello,' she said coolly.

'Shelley. I'd like to see you,' he said. 'I thought I'd come over after the recording tomorrow. Will I catch you?'

'Of course. Shall we roll out the red carpet?'

'Keep it low-key. It's a personal matter.'

After he'd rung off Shelley could feel an unsteady sensation swirling through her insides, then, noticing that Tessa was watching her, she picked up the script and said, 'I think we're finished here, don't you?'

After the recording the next day Shelley took advantage of Allyson's absence in Austria by using her dressing room to change into something less formal than the suit she'd been in all day. As she was pulling on a pair of cream leather trousers and a black silk shirt Marvin rang to tell her Mark had arrived.

'Could you show him down here?' Shelley said. In the time since Mark had called to fix this meeting she had driven herself half crazy trying to guess what personal matter he wanted to discuss.

Minutes later there was a knock on the door, and, with a calmness she was far from feeling, she called for him to come in.

'Hi,' she said, looking up from the pile of paperwork she'd provided herself with. 'It's usually noisy in the office, so I thought we'd talk here. Did Marvin offer you some coffee?'

'I'm OK,' he said.

She waved him to a seat, wishing she didn't feel quite so uptight. 'So, are you impressed with the way things are going?' she said. 'Tessa seems to be proving a good choice.'

'Her novelty value appears to be paying off in terms of increased ratings. The real test will come once that runs out.'

'I think she'll keep it going. She gets better all the time.'

He didn't argue with that, he simply took the conversation to where he wanted it to be. 'Can I presume that Allyson's spoken to you about the hotel in Ravello?' he said.

As she nodded she could feel her insides tensing. 'It's a good idea,' she said mildly. 'It should make an excellent programme.'

'I'm glad you think so.' He paused. 'I need to visit the hotel prior to its opening,' he told her, 'and I want to take Allyson with me. I think she'd come were she not afraid of upsetting you.'

Shelley could feel her smile fade and the skin under her clothes cringe with the shame of rejection.

As though sensing how badly she'd taken it, his voice seemed much softer as he said, 'I want you to know that I'm truly sorry if I led you to think there might be something between us. It wasn't my intention, but I understand that you might have read it that way.'

'Has it crossed your mind that maybe she doesn't want to go to Italy with you and she's using me as an excuse?' she snapped waspishly.

His eyes showed his regret that he was hurting her. 'If she needed an excuse she'd have used her husband,' he said.

'From whom she is still very much on the rebound.'

'I know.' He got to his feet. 'I hope when I next speak to Allyson she'll tell me she's coming to Ravello,' he said.

Shelley remained where she was long after he'd gone, hot tears scalding her eyes. Of course she had no choice now but to tell Allyson she didn't mind about Ravello. And if she didn't there was every chance she'd end up losing her job. Where would she be then, with no man, no best friend, and no *Soirée*? Oh God, she hated the world. Hated it! And it was only by some miracle of self-control that she stopped herself smashing the dressing-room mirror in a fit of uncontrollable rage.

The sun was warm on her face, the breeze gentle in her hair as she stood on the balcony overlooking the village below. They were surrounded by ripening orange and lemon groves, that stepped down to the glittering sweep of an impossibly blue sea. Immediately behind her was the arched doorway that led back into her room, which was cool and airy, with white marble floors and elegant Italian antique furniture.

Her feet had barely had time to touch the ground from Austria before she'd taken off again to fly here. They'd arrived last night, in the dark, and the general manager, Giovanni, and his wife had been waiting at the door of the magnificent palazzo to greet them. The smell of freshly applied paint assailed them as they walked in, along with the glossy, airy vision of an exquisite white marble floor, stark white walls, two polished mahogany reception desks and a new delivery of beautiful silk-upholstered sofas that were yet to be arranged in the piano bar.

The recently appointed chef had prepared a light supper of baked sea bass and grilled vegetables, while Giovanni had briefed Mark on the current state of affairs, which was fraught with typical Italian chaos, and some gloriously theatrical accounts of the tantrums being thrown by everyone from the landscaper to the interior designer. After a while Allyson left them to it, and followed Chiara, Giovanni's wife, upstairs to her room. Everywhere there were gorgeous gilt-framed mirrors, green palms and ferns still in their wrappings, and expertly restored antiques that ranged from elegant silk-upholstered *chaises-longues* to Renaissance-style cabinets containing alabaster sculptures.

Her room was one of the few that was ready, and though small, everything in it, from the pale lemon silk bedspread to the dark walnut nightstands, bespoke an exquisite elegance of taste. She was both pleased and disappointed to find she wasn't sharing with Mark, for despite the yearnings of her body she doubted she'd have appreciated it if he had just assumed she would sleep with him.

Now, hearing a knock on the door, she went to open it and found a maid with a large tray of breakfast. In her broken English the maid said, 'Mr Reiner say he will be joining you.'

Allyson slipped one of the thick white towelling robes over her pyjamas and, as she watched the maid lay the table on the balcony, a sudden guilt smothered her tremors of anticipation. Shelley had insisted she come here, that she'd blown him up in her mind to be something he wasn't, and that she was quite happy to let go. Allyson didn't believe it, but she'd come anyway, and now she was wondering what kind of friend that made her.

The phone rang on the wall beside her.

'Did the maid bring breakfast yet?' he asked.

As her heart tightened her face broke into a smile. 'Yes,' she said.

'Then I'll be right there.'

She hung up and took a breath to steady her nerves. Then she looked at herself again. She was probably imagining that the haunted look that had deadened her for months was now lit up with a radiance that made her want to laugh out loud. It was so wonderful to feel this alive again.

When he came he was dressed in chinos and a black polo shirt, and raised a droll eyebrow to find her still in pyjamas.

'Good morning,' she said, opening the door wide.

'Good morning. Did you sleep well?'

'Very.' It felt so gloriously wicked and tempting being in the same room as him and a bed. 'Are you ready for coffee?' she asked. 'It's outside.'

They went onto the balcony and he joined her at the table. 'I've asked the company publicists to fax over the provisional guest list,' he said. 'We can go through it while we're here.'

'Great.' She passed him a coffee. 'I've been having some thoughts on it, and I've left Justine and Zac making tentative enquiries to find out who's free.' Her eyes were drawn back to the spectacular view of mountains and sea. 'I've got such a good feeling about this place,' she said.

He was watching her with dark, humorous eyes, which made her laugh when she looked back at him.

'Let's just hope the paparazzi don't find out we're here,' she said, 'because the last thing we need is them chasing us about the place.'

'I've arranged for a car and driver to take you around,' he said, breaking open a crusty roll. 'Someone who knows the area and can give you all the information you need.'

'You mean you won't be coming with me?' she protested.

He laughed. 'Not all the time. There are things here I have to attend to, although Giovanni seems to have everything well in hand.'

'So I can count on you for Pompeii and Capri?'

'You can,' he grinned, then groaned as his cellphone rang.

It was Corinne, his assistant, with the messages that had come in overnight. He hadn't finished the call before the phone rang inside the room. It was Chiara letting Allyson know that a fax was coming through for Señor Reiner, which she'd send up to Allyson's room.

An hour later, after a quick jacuzzi shower that did nothing to pummel any sobriety into her simmering state of excitement, she was walking along the narrow cobbled lane with Mark to where the car was parked, in a small piazza in front of the church.

'What time shall we meet?' she said, getting into the back of the Mercedes.

'One. Then after lunch we'll go to Pompeii together. Did you remember your camera?'

'It's in my bag. By the way, do you speak Italian?'

'*Un peu*,' he answered, making her laugh. 'How about you?'

She pulled a face.

'Domingo'll take care of you.'

He closed the door, then after a few words with the cheerful Domingo, he stood aside for them to begin their tour of the surrounding countryside. Allyson was researching the vantage points that would offer the best exterior shots of the hotel and the ancient hilltop village. She clicked away happily with her camera, hoping that the weather was going to be this gracious when they came to shoot, for though there was no great heat to the sun, its quality was so mistily beautiful as it bathed the ancient walls in a glistening treacle of light that she could almost feel the cameraman's excitement.

They returned to the small church piazza around eleven, and she walked past the hotel, down through the narrow, steeply sloping streets that led to the main square, where tables and chairs were set up outside the cafés, and tourist shops spilled their wares out onto the street.

The magnificent *duomo* with its wide sweeping steps and decorated façade dominated the piazza, and the ancient stone arch and clock tower set at an angle beside it looked so inviting that she drifted through the arch and into what turned out to be the magnificent Rufolo gardens. After taking her time to look around, she parked herself on a bench overlooking the sea and began working out a schedule for the programme. Happy Hour she'd already decided would be in the hotel's piano bar. The filmed insert would be either Pompeii or Capri—she'd know once she'd done the recces. And the Nightcap could be done in the gorgeous little alcove she'd discovered here in the gardens, which had a small fountain at the centre, lush green plants all around it and ancient circular stone walls protecting it.

'Did you know,' she said to Mark later, as a waiter set two chilled glasses of local wine on the pink tablecloth between them, 'that Wagner got his inspiration to write the music for *Parsifal* here, in Ravello? We should use some extracts from it in the programme,' she decided, sipping her wine. 'So what have you been doing this morning?'

He grimaced. 'Definitely not having as much fun as you,' he responded. 'For instance, I've just fired the chef.'

Her eyes rounded. 'The chef?' she said.

'What we had last night wasn't up to standard,' he explained.

'But it was only a snack.'

He merely looked at her, allowing his silence to state the standards of excellence.

'OK,' she laughed, and they opened their menus. A few minutes later, she asked, 'What are you going to eat?'

'Spinach ravioli,' he answered. 'You?'

'Parma ham and mozzarella.'

After they'd ordered they carried on discussing the hotel, then moved on to the programme, concentrating mainly on the logistics, as well as the cost, of getting so many names over to Italy.

'The best answer,' he said, as their food arrived, 'is to charter a plane. I guess the crew will fly out a day early to get everything set up?'

She nodded, and ordered two more glasses of wine before the waiter went away. As they ate, their conversation meandered away from the programme, moving easily from one subject to another as they made each other laugh with all manner of stories, and, for Allyson, this journey of discovery into his character was so fascinating she could have continued it all day. There was so much she wanted to know about Mark Reiner that, in the end, he laughingly held up his hands, saying, 'I refuse to believe I'm as interesting as you're making me feel, so stop before it goes to my head.'

Smiling, she finished her salad and reached for her empty glass.

'More wine?' he offered.

'Oh God, I'd love more wine, but if I do I'll never make it through the rest of the day.'

A teasing light came into his eyes. 'This is Italy, siestas are permissible,' he reminded her.

'Permissible?' she said, tilting her head to one side. 'I thought they were obligatory.'

The way he looked at her then caused all kinds of sensations to ignite in her body. 'Nothing's obligatory,' he said.

She smiled and was trying desperately to think of a suitable *double entendre* when his cellphone rang and rescued her from the brink of potential disaster.

She watched as he listened to the voice at the other end. 'That's great,' he said, starting to laugh. 'Do it.' He was looking out across the square, giving Allyson the impression he was avoiding her eyes. 'OK, I'll see you when I get back,' he said, then signalled the waiter for the bill.

By the time they got to Pompeii, Allyson could have wished he'd dropped off his cellphone too, but she wasn't going to let the constant interruptions spoil the experience, for she'd long wanted to visit this historical site.

A gentle breeze carried the rank, earthy smell to her senses as they strolled along the cobbled roads and walkways, tramping the journey that nineteen centuries ago had been so routinely taken by a people that were to meet such a terrible end. They walked through the ruined basilica, the central baths, the gymnasium, and stopped at what had once been the Temple of Apollo. A bronze statue of the god himself, now green with age, stood in front of an amazingly preserved portico and faced a bust of Diana across the dusty forum.

After a while they walked on, down what had once been a busy market street that still bore evidence of the graffiti and advertising that were splashed in Perspex-covered colour on the decaying walls.

'You know, I had a past-life regression once,' Allyson said, as she stopped to get a shot of Vesuvius. 'I did it for the programme.'

'Oh?' Mark said, settling comfortably on a bench and stretching out his long legs. 'Did it work?'

'Oh yes,' she answered, sitting next to him. 'It was amazing. It was like I was here, living that life all over again.'

'You were here? In Pompeii?' he said, surprised.

She nodded. 'At the end, I was,' she said. 'It's where I died, or, as they say, left that particular life.'

He glanced at her, waiting for her to go on.

'I was a dancing girl,' she said. 'In Rome. I danced for the Emperor Titus. I was also his mistress.'

He looked at her again, not sure whether to believe this or not.

'My family lived in Pompeii,' she went on. 'I was trying to persuade them to leave the town when the mountain exploded. Everyone knew it would explode, it had been spewing out lava and rocks for days, but my family were among those who wouldn't leave. And then it was too late. We tried to run, but . . .' She paused for a moment, then said, 'After I died, when I left my body, I could see the Emperor Titus in his palace in Rome, and do you know the most remarkable thing?' Her eyes were trained straight ahead, but appeared to be seeing nothing of what was in front of her. 'He looked exactly like you.'

Mark blinked, looked at her incredulously, then, instinctively knowing he was being had, he said, 'So that's what happened to you! I always wondered. You were a great mistress, but boy were you a lousy dancer.'

Allyson burst out laughing at the way he'd managed to get the last word, then picking up her camera and guidebook she walked on towards the Amphitheatre.

By the time they started back to the hotel it was already getting dark, and the effects of the Campari they stopped for en route were making her yawn as she said, 'I'm thinking about dressing up Tessa and a couple of actors and re-creating a street scene for the film insert.'

'What about Titus and his dancing girl?'

She grinned. 'What about them?'

'Well, if you can improve on your act, I don't mind stepping in to become the man I once was.'

A teasing light shot to her eyes. 'Sounds more like a scene for siesta,' she commented.

His eyebrows made a sardonic arch. 'Now you're talking,' he responded.

Laughing, she rested her head against the back of the car seat and turned to look at her reflection in the window while allowing herself the heady delight of imagining where the evening might end.

Shelley regarded the outside of the garish pub and wondered what artless soul had named it the Romeo and Juliet. Not the kind of place she would normally be seen in, but when needs must . . .

Leaving the relative safety of her car, she ran across the deserted South London street, towards the door. Warmth, and the smell of beer, assailed her as she looked around the dimly lit room. The bar was an island of tawdriness, with mock Shakespearean props and posters of Gwyneth Paltrow and Joseph Fiennes plastered to the pumps.

Spotting the person she was looking for, alone in a dark corner, she headed straight towards him.

'How did you find me?' Bob said when she reached the table.

Shelley sat down and unfastened her coat. 'It wasn't hard,' she said. 'I had Tessa's old address, and there aren't too many pubs in the area. I got you on my third attempt.'

'What do you want?' he growled.

'Apart from a vodka tonic, I want to talk to you. Don't worry, I'll get it.

'So,' she said, when she sat down again, 'you've been on my mind quite a bit since you came to see me.' She picked up her drink. 'Would I be right in thinking you'd go back to Allyson if you could?' she said, coming straight to the point.

'I'd go back to a lot of things if I could,' he snarled. 'Why do you ask?'

'Because I don't think I played fair with you when you came to see me. Not that I care about you, you understand, but I do care about Allyson. And if I led you to think she wouldn't take you back, then I'm sorry, because the truth is, I think she would. Because I believe in her heart she still loves you.'

He was shaking his head. 'I think there's a much bigger chance she hates my guts,' he said.

'No. She doesn't hate you. She's just angry with you. If she hates anyone, it's Tessa.'

'She's not the only one,' he snarled. 'What I wouldn't like to do to that bitch for the way she's screwed up my life.'

Shelley said nothing. It was typical of the Bobs of this world to absolve themselves of all responsibility for their own spineless behaviour. 'I think you should try talking to Allyson,' she said after a pause. 'Tell her you still love her and ask her to forgive you. You might have to do it through the lawyer, but you know Allyson as well as I do. She's got a very forgiving nature and, despite outward appearances, I'm telling you she's falling apart without you.'

'What about Mark Reiner, then?'

'It's all a front. She's seeing him to make you jealous.'

He reached for his glass but didn't pick it up.

'Bob, look at yourself,' she said with feeling. 'You're a mess and you know it. You've got no money, no job, no real home. So don't you think your pride's a bit out of place? And that's all that's stopping you, isn't it? You couldn't stand it if she rejected you. But she won't. You belong together, you two, and you know it.'

His upper lip curled in a snarl. 'What's in this for you?' he demanded. 'You never do anything without there being something in it for you.'

Her lovely eyes narrowed as she regarded him, seeming to weigh up how much she should tell him. In the end she said, 'All right, to be blunt, I've got three programmes a week to get out, with an increased workload since the international theme started, and I can't go on carrying Allyson. That's one reason. The other is, she genuinely does love you, though you sure as hell don't deserve it. And I think these past few months have shown you just how much you love her too.'

He looked despondently down at his Coke.

'You just lost sight of it for a while,' she said comfortingly. 'So think about it. Work out what you're going to say and then contact her lawyer. I'm convinced you can win Allyson back.'

In fact Shelley was certain he would, because there was no doubt in her mind that nineteen years of marriage was going to mean a whole lot

CRUEL VENUS

more to Allyson than a few heady days in Italy, however romantic they might be. And Shelley couldn't even be persuaded they'd be that romantic, for, when it came down to it, Allyson just didn't have what it took to satisfy a man like Mark Reiner.

'Stand over there. No, not there. There,' Mark said, trying to get Allyson in the right spot to be photographed outside Capri's beautiful baroque cathedral.

'Are you trying to get it so that campanile is sticking out of my head?' she accused.

He laughed. 'Just take a step to your left. OK, that's it! Smile!'

He took the picture, then, turning the camera towards the vast, glittering expanse of the Mediterranean, he took another.

'Mmm,' she murmured, inhaling deeply of the wonderful spring blossom that was wafting from the trees. When she opened her eyes it was to find him watching her with that lazy, gently mocking humour she was coming to know so well. In its way it seemed to suggest he wanted to kiss her, yet he never did.

'I don't think this island is going to work for the programme,' she said, stirring her cappuccino. 'It'll take too long to get here and the budget won't stretch.'

Nodding, he said, 'I guessed you might decide that, but it was worth coming, just to make sure.'

'Of course,' she replied, smiling. 'I'm having a wonderful time. I feel as though we're on holiday, don't you?'

His eyes were dancing, but he only looked past her as their driver approached to ask what they would like to do next.

Mark looked at Allyson, and to her horror she felt her cheeks burn. Yes, that was what she wanted, but surely she hadn't said it aloud.

'Maybe we go take a look at where Tiberius fling his wife over the cliff,' the driver suggested with a grin.

'No,' Mark said, still looking at Allyson, 'I think you can take us back to the ferry now.'

It was already dark by the time the ferry sailed into Amalfi. They were leaning against the deck rail, huddled warmly in the sweaters they'd thought to take with them and gazing out at the glittering lights that shimmered like fireflies at the foot of the hillside. She was so aware of him standing there beside her, and so tensed by desire, that she almost gasped when he slipped an arm round her and pulled her in closer.

For a moment she was rigid. Then she turned to look up at him, her hair blowing in the wind. He lowered his eyes to hers and gazed deeply into them. With all her might she willed him to kiss her. But he only brushed the hair from her face and hugged her.

They drove back to the hotel in silence. Tonight was their last before they returned to London in the morning, and she just couldn't bear the idea of leaving without knowing what it was to make love with him. As they walked upstairs she resolved to tell him what she wanted. And if she ended up making a fool of herself, then so be it.

When they reached her door he unlocked it for her, and she took a moment to summon her courage before lifting her head to look into his eyes. 'Mark,' she said.

He raised a hand to her face, brushing his thumb over her lips. 'Are you sure?' he whispered.

'I'll go mad if you don't,' she answered.

As he continued to look at her, she drew his thumb into her mouth. The symbolic meaning of what she was doing inflamed them both, and suddenly his lips were on hers and he was pulling her to him with all the force she had longed for.

He took her into the room, closed the door and pulled her to him again. His mouth was tender and probing, commanding and harsh. He kissed her neck, and she unbuttoned her dress, letting it fall to the floor, then unhooked her bra. He slipped it down over her arms, then smoothed her surprisingly full breasts with his hands, teasing their tight, rosy nipples and watching the desire cloud her eyes. Then he undressed her completely and ran his hands all over her nudity in a way that almost sent her out of her mind with longing.

The bed was just behind her and pushing her back he stood over her, looking at her, as he undressed himself. He lay down with her, pulling her to him and feeling her fingers grip the solid stem of his erection. The tenderness he felt curled through his heart and was belied by the urgency of his need. He sensed the powerful need in her too and knew that whatever the truth of her feelings, in this moment she was his.

She lay over him and pushed her tongue between his lips. Her small body was light on his chest, her legs were open. He pushed himself into her and watched as she rode him, his eyes moving between her face and where their bodies were joined. Feeling the mounting pressure inside her, he rolled her onto her back. She gripped his shoulders and stared up at his face. Then, as he looked at her too, she seemed to lose all sense of where and who she was as he began moving his hips in a way that bathed her in sensations that were almost too powerful to bear.

'Oh my God, my God,' she murmured.

Time and time again he took her to the point where she felt her entire body might explode with the ecstasy. She wanted to scream, to rage, to draw him in tighter, but she was so lost to anything beyond what he was doing, she could only cling to him and beg him for more, and yet more.

Then at last he let her fly, and as the climactic rush soared through him too, he pressed his mouth needfully to hers, wanting her cries inside him as he was inside her.

They held each other long after their heartbeats were calm. Though he said nothing he knew it was love that he felt for this woman, who was still so injured inside that she might be his for only one night.

Chapter Thirteen

THE ONLY GOOD THING about leaving Ravello was knowing that now she'd rejigged the schedule and put the Italian programme ahead of the Austrian, they'd be back again in less than two weeks. The closeness Allyson was starting to feel with Mark was something she wasn't ready to put into words; it was enough just to feel it and know that he felt it too. Self-effacement definitely wasn't her thing, but even without the horrible battering her confidence had taken recently, she'd never imagined a man wanting her rather than Shelley. And though she knew that there had been no actual relationship between Shelley and Mark, she still felt bad about what had happened because she knew she was trampling her friend's dream.

However, despite feeling that she had her emotions under control, Allyson had to confess that their parting, when they returned to London, was a much greater wrench than she'd expected. And the flat, when she walked in, seemed empty and cold, so that for a moment she felt herself sliding towards depression, as the confusion of what had happened with Mark, and what it might mean for her and Bob, started to engulf her. But then the phone rang, bringing a call from her mother, which was quickly followed by a call from Justine wanting to know how it had gone in Italy. Half an hour later she was on the point of heaving her suitcase onto the bed to empty it when the phone shrilled into life again. This time it was Mark.

'I promised myself I wouldn't do this,' he said, 'but as I'm at a loose end for dinner, I was wondering if you were free.'

'I promised myself I'd say no if you asked,' she replied, 'but if you bring the wine I'll cook.'

He arrived an hour later and they made love straight away. She sensed a new urgency to their passion that must have been incited by the parting, for the lazy tenderness of Italy was replaced by an aggressive need to be as close as their bodies would allow.

Only afterwards, as they lay in each other's arms, did Allyson think of Bob, and how no other man but him had slept in this bed. But that was going to change now if she could persuade Mark to stay.

It was never discussed, he just did.

The next morning as she drove to the office she relived every smile and caress, every word and sensation of the night before. Though she knew there were still many complications to overcome, she allowed herself these few precious moments of believing that the worst was behind her and that everything would work out perfectly in the end.

Zac and Justine were already at their desks when she walked in, but there was no sign of Shelley. This was no surprise, for she'd left a message on Allyson's machine to say her mother had had a mild stroke so she was going to be in the New Forest for the next couple of days. Not for a minute did Allyson think Shelley would lie about something like that, but she couldn't help wondering if Shelley hadn't welcomed an excuse to avoid hearing about Ravello.

After checking her email, she went back out to the main office to sit with Zac and Justine. They would need to be in each other's pockets during the build-up to the Italy show, since there was an endless number of details and suggestions that needed to be discussed, and before long half the office had managed to join in the planning. It quickly deteriorated into a ludicrous free-for-all, providing a convenient platform for the wits among them. The party in Ravello was going to be an impossible act to follow, was almost everybody's opinion, until Zac came up with a brilliant idea that made everyone roar with laughter. It was at that point that Tessa walked into the office to find Allyson in the midst of a hilarious group.

Turning, Allyson saw Tessa and said, 'Ah, just the person. We're talking about doing a programme from Transylvania at the end of April. There's a convention of vampires.'

Tessa's face froze. Were they calling her a vampire?

'What happened to the piece you did on those dolls?' Allyson said. 'The ones who belonged to that writer? It could be perfect for this programme. Did you ever edit it?'

'No,' Tessa said.

'Well, there's plenty of time. Just make it good and scary.'

Allyson turned back to the others, and Tessa walked over to her desk. She still felt shaken, even though she knew she'd misunderstood. It was reminding her of all the times she'd thought she was being laughed at at school, even when she wasn't. But all that was in the past now, so there was no reason to get angry, especially not when it sounded like the trip to Italy was going to be a lot of fun, and when she, as the presenter, would naturally be at the centre of it all.

Three manically busy days had passed since their return from Ravello, and Allyson had barely had a minute to herself. Every time she snatched a few moments to call Mark, who had flown to New York on business, he was either in a meeting or on another line. She'd got him once, on his mobile, but the reception had been so bad they'd had to ring off. He'd said he would call her later, at home, but she hadn't got in until late and there was no message waiting.

The company publicists who were handling the hotel's opening extravaganza were beginning to put together a guest list boasting some pretty impressive American names.

As far as the UK went, since promos for the programme had started to air she'd been inundated with requests for invitations to the party. She was going to have to stop answering her phone, for it seemed everyone she'd ever known wanted to speak to her now, or take her to dinner, or invite her to a party of their own.

'No! No! No!' she cried, clasping her hands over her ears as Zac and Justine teased her with yet another chorus of offers.

She ran into her own office to grab the phone that was ringing there. 'Allyson Jaymes,' she said into the receiver, then spun round to hold up a hand to whoever was calling her name. 'Sorry, who is it?' she said, blocking her other ear.

'It's Bob, your husband,' he answered.

Allyson's eyes closed as the world outside seemed suddenly to recede and the guilt flowed in. 'Bob,' she said. 'You're supposed to . . .'

'. . . speak through your lawyer. I know, and I'm trying, but you're not being very responsive.'

'Because I'm really busy at the moment. I can't discuss anything until after this next programme's out of the way.'

'Allyson! For Christ's sake! What can be more important? Surely you can spare a few minutes . . .'

'No! It wouldn't do any good.' Then, realising how much this must be hurting him, she said, 'It's our marriage we're going to be talking about;

it deserves more than just a few minutes, surely.'

He said nothing, and a few seconds later she heard the line go dead.

'Allyson!' Justine yelled. 'Giovanni from the hotel's on the line, he has to talk to you. Now!'

Allyson went to take the call and almost collided with Shelley, who was about to come into her office.

'Hi!' Allyson cried. 'I thought you weren't back until tomorrow.'

Shelley's smile was ironic. 'I told you that yesterday,' she said. 'Go and take the call and I'll catch you later.'

Allyson spent the next few minutes jotting down Giovanni's latest list of complaints, then zoomed off to find the production manager who was organising the crew.

The rest of the day continued at the same frenetic pace until, at seven thirty, Shelley walked into Allyson's with a bottle of wine and two glasses.

'So, tell me all about Ravello,' Shelley said, pouring the wine and handing Allyson a glass.

Allyson took a sip of her drink. 'Ravello was great,' she said. 'We had a really good time.'

'How lovely,' Shelley remarked. 'So are you in love?'

Allyson bit back the response the sarcasm deserved, and reminded herself how hard this must be for Shelley. So all she said was, 'I wouldn't go that far.'

'So how far did you go?' Shelley enquired, picking up her wineglass.

'We slept together, yes,' Allyson responded. Then, attempting to soften the blow she added, 'But he went off to New York the day after we got back and I haven't heard from him since.'

Shelley frowned. 'So he's dumped you too?'

'I'm not sure, he might have.' It wasn't what Allyson thought at all, at least she hadn't until now.

After a moment Allyson asked, 'Are you coming to Italy for the party?'

'I'm not sure,' Shelley responded. 'I might not have the time.'

'I wish you would,' Allyson said, her eyes taking on a mischievous glow. 'Just think about all those gorgeous American movie stars and obscure European royalty. Not to mention the smouldering Italian waiters.'

Shelley's eyebrows flickered, a disdainful attempt to join in the spirit of it, so Allyson steered the conversation out of the danger zone by saying, 'Bob's trying to get in touch. I think he wants to come back.'

Shelley's eyes widened. 'Well, there's a turn-up,' she commented. 'Though I can't say I'm really surprised now that Tessa's no longer on the scene.' She topped up their glasses. 'How do you feel about him now?'

Allyson sighed. 'I don't know. I mean I care about him still, obviously, and God only knows if I'll ever be able to stop thinking of him as my husband . . . I suppose I did in Italy, though, but in the end what happened there might just turn out to be a much-needed boost for an ego-crushed woman on the rebound.' She looked at Shelley. 'Do you think I should give him another chance? Bob, I mean.'

'I don't suppose there's any harm in talking to him,' Shelley said.

'Anyway, I've told him I'm not going to decide anything until after Italy—as though Italy's going to come up with all the answers!'

'You never know,' Shelley responded, 'it might.'

Later, when Shelley got home, she undressed and wrapped herself in a white silk robe. Then she sat in front of the mirror, staring at the face of a woman who was suppressing so much rage it was a miracle it didn't show. But she couldn't let it show, could she? Not to anyone. Particularly not to Allyson, because if there was a breakdown in their friendship, or even the slightest fracture, there was every chance that the results would be so disastrous for Shelley that they hardly bore thinking about. She pondered the unconscionable spite of fate, or was it God, that had brought Mark Reiner into her life, showing her everything she'd ever wanted, only then to snatch him away and thrust him into the arms of her best friend. A friend whose injuries seemed to matter so much to God that he was salving them not only with a new love—*a love that should have been Shelley's*—but with the return of the old love too. So now Allyson could choose, and while she was making up her mind it seemed that God was going to fly her higher and higher in her new career as well. Well, Shelley could handle it. She'd had years of practice, after all, since the sparkle of love and shining light of happiness had died with her father, when Shelley was twelve and God had first decided to show her the darkness. That, emotionally, was where he had left her, for there had never been anyone who could replace her father. But who the hell cared? What impact did her misery have on a God who wasn't even listening? And why should he listen when Venus had bestowed all her bounteous gifts on Allyson Jaymes?

Allyson was laughing and shrieking as the ice-cold champagne trickled down over her body into the madly whirling jets of the jacuzzi bath she was standing in. Mark was beside the bath, a half-empty bottle in one hand, a full glass in the other, as he lowered his mouth to her breasts and licked off the champagne. Then, seeing how aroused she was becoming, he stepped into the jacuzzi and settled himself onto one of the bench seats and drew her down onto his erection. He increased the speed of the jets until she was moaning with ecstasy. The sensations were so intense, cutting through her with such harsh, insistent power that an orgasm was devouring her almost before he could move.

'Oh God, yes, yes,' she cried, as his mouth sought hers. Then he was carrying her into the bedroom and lying her down on the bed. As he came into her again she could feel the immense hardness of him filling her, then pulling back gently before sharply filling her again. The pace of his thrusting began building until he was crying out her name as the explosion of his climax erupted into the renewed torrents of hers.

Minutes later, as they were still breathless and clinging together, he kissed her on the mouth, then rolled onto his side so he was no longer crushing her. Morning sunlight streamed through the open curtains, early-morning traffic honked and roared its way along Eaton Terrace.

'I could get used to this kind of homecoming,' he told her.

Laughing, she kissed him again, then went into the bathroom to fetch what was left of the champagne. 'Are you going to fall asleep on me?' she asked, when she came back and saw that his eyes were closed.

'It's four in the morning, New York time,' he reminded her.

'And nine o'clock here, so I have to leave for work soon.'

He watched her as she sat naked and cross-legged on the bed and refilled the glass with champagne. 'Did you see your husband while I was away?' he asked.

She shook her head. 'No. I've decided not to see him until after Italy.'

'We leave tomorrow,' he said.

'You think I don't know that?' she laughed.

'Did you consider that he might have erased all the messages I left you with his remote?' he said.

Her eyes came up to his face. 'Yes,' she answered, though she had only begun to suspect Bob of tampering with her machine in the last day or so. Naturally, she was glad to have a reason for why she hadn't heard from Mark while he was away, but she couldn't help feeling sorry for Bob that he had felt compelled to do something like that.

'Have you reached any decisions?' Mark asked.

She looked away, staring at the luggage he had brought in from the airport. He'd called her as soon as he'd landed, demanding to know how they'd managed to miss each other's calls for almost two weeks. She'd been so thrilled to hear him that it had been her suggestion to meet this morning, and now here she was, not wanting to be anywhere else in the world, yet still managing to feel worried about Bob.

'Only that I'm not ready to make any yet,' she answered.

'Then don't,' he said gently.

Much later, after they'd showered and dressed for the office, he went to check on the messages that had come in since he'd arrived back. The earlier calls he'd picked up on his way in from the airport, but the phone had rung a couple of times in the past two hours and he needed to satisfy himself there were no emergencies. There weren't, but Allyson was standing right beside him as the machine replayed Tessa's jubilant voice welcoming him back from the States and telling him how much she was looking forward to seeing him in Italy.

Chapter Fourteen

THE MAJORITY OF THE SIXTY specially selected guests began arriving in Ravello at midday. Most came on the chartered plane that flew into Naples from London, while others motored down under their own steam. The American guests, who included a Pulitzer Prize-winning author, four internationally renowned movie stars, and a teenage rock legend, would be flying in later that day.

The weather couldn't have been better, as the sun blazed down on the steep, winding roads that led up to the village, and the wild spring flowers that were shooting up all over were as uplifting as the heady promise offered by the terraces of blossoming vines. Allyson couldn't help being thrilled by all the delight and enchantment as she and Shelley stood in the small church piazza and welcomed their guests.

Tessa was in the hotel lobby with Zac and Justine, feeling totally blown away by so much style and grandeur—and all the incredibly famous faces that were flowing in through the giant carved-oak doors.

'My feet are killing me and my jaw's starting to ache,' Alan, the pro-gramme's director, complained to Shelley as she and Allyson finally wandered in to join them.

Laughing, Allyson said, 'You can stand down for a while. The next lot aren't due to arrive until six. Are you OK?' she said to Tessa, who was starting to yawn.

'Sorry, yes,' Tessa answered.

'What time did you leave the bar last night?' Shelley asked.

'It was about two thirty,' Tessa confessed. 'But I wasn't the last to go up. Some of the crew were still there . . .'

'But they don't have to appear on camera today,' Allyson reminded her. Turning to Alan she said, 'When are you setting off for Pompeii?'

'About four,' he answered. 'We should be back around nine.'

'Then make sure Tessa goes straight to bed when you get back, she's got a busy day ahead of her tomorrow.'

Tessa was grinning. 'You sound like my mum,' she said.

Allyson's answering look was so withering that Shelley actually laughed. 'Nothing ever seems to faze her, does it?' Allyson grumbled, as they strolled down the white marble steps into the piano bar.

'Which is something you should feel glad about when you've got her hosting a programme featuring this many VIPs,' Shelley commented. 'That reminds me, I've brought in Terri Jankler, one of the more informed diarists, to coach Tessa on how to address the royals . . . Oh, smile, we're on Candy's camera.'

'Great!' Candy Egan, a freelance showbiz photographer, declared, still clicking away. 'Now, get back to work, I want some shots of the heads together, like you were in the planning stages of this shindig.'

'Did you get all the guests as they arrived?' Allyson asked.

'Every one of 'em. It's going to be quite some show. Where's the man, by the way?'

'If you mean Mark Reiner,' Allyson answered, 'he's arriving tomorrow.'

'So is it true you two were here together a couple of weeks ago?' an *Express* reporter asked, as he came to join them.

'I was here on a recce,' Allyson said, smiling sweetly, 'and Mark Reiner happened to be here too, sorting out last-minute details.'

'So the answer's yes,' the reporter declared, 'and straight from the horse's mouth.'

'Charming,' Allyson muttered. 'Now push off and interview some of the guests who're outside on the terrace, we've got work to do here.'

After further conferences with the publicists, and with Giovanni and his staff, Allyson went to see Tessa and the crew off to Pompeii, then before anyone else could waylay her she darted up to her room to get out of the formal suit and tight shoes she'd been in all day, and work on the seating plan for dinner.

As it turned out, her careful structuring of the evening soon dissolved into a wonderfully convivial flow that saw the *crème de la crème* of international society moving with effortless charm from one table to another, exchanging anecdotes and memories, and drinking the champagne cocktails that were travelling freely about the room on shiny silver salvers. Though no one had bothered with formal attire, it was easy for Allyson to get an early view of just how spectacular the party would be in this magnificent airy hall with all its white arches, cherubic fountains, marble floors and exotic greenery.

And once all the glitter and dash of fame, noble birth and sheer magnetism were added, along with the exquisite designer gowns, beautifully tailored tuxedos and expensive jewels, it couldn't fail to be anything but the party to end all parties.

Allyson smiled as she experienced a pleasing glow of satisfaction, for though she had no idea what the future held for her and Mark, it was good to be playing a part in the birth of the splendid Palazzo. The thought took her mind instantly to Shelley, who was perched on the edge of a fountain, talking to a distinguished Italian tenor and his wife. She looked lovely, in a pale blue silk dress that buttoned down the front, and silver Chanel pumps that were as elegant and graceful as Shelley herself.

Allyson watched her for a moment more. They'd known each other for so long, had come through such a lot together, that even if this was starting to prove the toughest test yet to their friendship, Allyson felt sure they both wanted it to survive.

However, focusing her attention on their relationship was doing nothing to help the programme, so putting down her champagne she slipped out to reception to see if the crew was back from Pompeii yet. It was perfect timing, for Alan, the director, was just coming in the door.

'How did it go?' she asked.

'Great,' he answered, handing her a cassette. 'Tessa did a great commentary, by the way. Did you write it?'

'Yes. Where is she?'

'She was behind me a moment ago . . . Ah, here she is.'

Allyson followed his eyes to the door, then went suddenly still with shock. Mark was walking in behind Tessa. She felt slightly disorientated for a moment, but the feeling started to ebb as his eyes found her and the space between them seemed to close even before he moved.

What seemed like seconds later, before anyone else could register his arrival, they were in one of the offices behind reception and she was laughing as he kissed her, and loving the tumultuous urges that made these early stages of their relationship feel so risky and exciting.

'I thought I'd surprise you,' he was saying.

'Well, you definitely succeeded,' she scolded. 'I thought for a minute, when I saw you, that I was losing my mind . . .' His lips silenced the rest of her words, and the pressure of his body began igniting responses that needed much more immediate attention than her state of mind.

When they emerged, a few minutes later, there was no one near the reception desk, and they were soon melding once more into the dinner crowd. But now and again they caught one another's eye and couldn't stop themselves exchanging glances that would have given them away to anybody who was watching, and, with so many reporters present, plenty were.

Though Allyson and Mark slept in separate rooms, he delivered her breakfast personally the next morning, at the ungodly hour of six, when everyone else was still sleeping. This gave them a precious hour together before Allyson had to meet the crew at the Rufolo gardens to start recording the Nightcap. Though they made love passionately, it was the memory of what they'd talked about afterwards that lingered with her as she sat waiting for the crew to set up in the leafy glade.

'I had a call from your husband before I left,' he'd told her, as she poured the coffee. 'He wanted to know how I feel about you.'

Allyson's heart tripped. 'What did you tell him?'

'That considering his reasons for wanting to know, it would probably be more helpful to find out how *you* feel about *me*.'

Allyson looked away. 'I'm sorry he did that,' she said.

Reaching for her hand he pulled her down on the bed beside him. 'I could tell you right now how *I* feel about *you*,' he said softly, 'but it's not going to help. If anything it'll only complicate things further.'

She hadn't asked him to elaborate on that, there had been no need to, for the tenderness of his kiss had told her all she needed to know. And now, sitting here, in this beautiful Italian garden, with the sunlight streaming down through the trees, she could feel herself coming to the decision she knew she had to make. She smiled, for a part of her wanted to go to Mark right now and tell him, but she wouldn't because she owed it to Bob to tell him first. It was awful to think of how much it was going to hurt him, but she had to follow her heart.

'OK?' Zac said, coming to sit beside her. 'You've got a bit of a daft look on your face, so I thought I'd ask.'

Allyson laughed. 'Has Lenny Blomfeld come down from the hotel yet?' She was referring to the Scottish composer who was to be their guest.

'He's on his way.'

Allyson looked up and saw Alan heading towards them. 'Ready?'

'Five minutes,' he answered. 'Our guest arrived yet?'

'I'm here,' Blomfeld's voice boomed out behind them. 'And I've brought someone to join us.'

It was America's latest teen pop phenomenon, who was no mere product of the electronic age, but a gifted musician who had won Blomfeld's heart the night before when she'd sung, unaccompanied, an aria from

Aida. An interview with the two of them would provide the perfect finale, particularly if Allyson could persuade them to perform together.

While the interview took place, Zac and Justine were outside in the piazza burning the phones to agents and managers in an attempt to get the go-ahead for a closing performance, but it simply wasn't possible to obtain permissions in such a short time. So it wasn't long before Allyson and her two guests, having completed an extremely entertaining exchange, strolled back out to the square to find Shelley and Mark drinking coffee together outside one of the cafés.

Allyson stopped mid-sentence, for the picture they painted, of a couple who seemed so relaxed with each other, caused such a jolt in her heart that it was a moment before she could make her thoughts move beyond it. But then she reminded herself of how much easier it would be, for all of them, if Mark and Shelley could be friends.

'Darling,' Mark said when he saw her, and getting to his feet he took her hand in his and looked into her eyes.

Allyson's hostility instantly melted, not only because it was the first time he had called her that, but because he had said it in front of Shelley. 'Hi,' she whispered, still looking at him.

Shelley picked up her cup. 'I get the feeling I could be extra to requirements,' she said, finishing her coffee.

'No, don't go,' Allyson protested. 'I'd really like you to take a look at the guest running order,' she said.

Zac and Justine joined them at the table. 'We're making some progress for the closing number,' he told Allyson. 'With any luck we'll be able to record something first thing tomorrow before we leave.'

'Great,' she said. 'Are you leaving us?' she said to Mark, who was on his feet, with a cellphone at his ear.

'I'll catch you later,' he said to Allyson. 'OK, Giovanni, I'm on my way. Sure, it shouldn't be a problem.' Allyson watched him as he headed off up the cobbled steps that led up to the hotel, then Shelley was starting to remark on the running order and before Allyson knew it they too had returned to the hotel, with the running order still in hot debate.

Through all the mayhem of caterers, decorators, cleaners, musicians and electricians, Allyson spotted Tessa being coached by Terri Jankler, the freelance society writer. Great, that was under way; now she needed to find each of the featured guests and run through their questions.

'Ally, here's the list of what everyone's wearing,' said one of the wardrobe assistants, handing her the names of the designers who needed to be credited. 'The princess is wearing Gucci after all.'

'Great. Give it to Justine,' Allyson said.

By five that evening, by some miracle of organisation, all the guests were assembled ready for a rehearsal. This was merely for position and timing, so they were through by six, at which point everyone vanished to their rooms to start dressing for the great occasion.

At eight o'clock the guests started filling the bar, many of them looking every bit the royalty or movie stars they were. The women wore gowns of silk, taffeta, satin and lace, and jewels that sparkled off the exquisite crystal and gold chandeliers above. The pop of champagne corks mingled with muted voices and occasional laughter. The band started to play and the director's assistants began guiding everyone into place.

Allyson stood in the lobby looking down at the scene. Her fine blonde hair was swept up into a cluster of diamonds, with loose, curling tendrils tumbling around her neck. Her eyes glowed in their dark rims of kohl and her lips were moistened by a delicate frosted pink gloss.

She started to move down the stairs and felt as sensuous as she looked, in her figure-hugging black dress that fishtailed around the ankles and revealed her delicately tanned skin through the shimmering transparent panels that snaked around her body. She was looking for Mark, and when her eyes finally found him it was as though he sensed she was there, for he looked up from the people he was with and her heart swelled with emotion. .

He met her at the foot of the stairs and drew her into his arms to kiss her. 'I wish everyone would vanish so that I could just carry on looking at you,' he murmured.

'Doesn't she look stunning?' Shelley said, joining them.

Allyson turned to her, smiling. 'So do you,' she said, glancing at Shelley's white silk trouser suit whose jacket was slashed open almost to the waist. Very elegant, very sexy.

'And you look so dashing,' Shelley said to Mark, 'that I absolutely have to insist on the first dance once the party gets under way.'

'Consider it yours,' he told her. Excusing himself, he went off in answer to a signal from Giovanni.

'Where's Tessa?' Allyson asked, peering into the darkness of what was now the set.

'Through there,' Shelley said, pointing. 'At the bar.'

Allyson found her, and her eyebrows rose in approval of the way Tessa looked. Her strapless red-sequined dress showed off her fleshy shoulders to perfection, and curved over her round, girlish hips in a way only she could carry off.

'I'll have a quick word with her before we start,' Allyson said, and squeezed her way through the guests to where Tessa was being miked up ready to record. 'Are you OK?' Allyson asked her.

Tessa nodded. 'I've got the order glued in my head now, so please don't tell me you're about to change it.'

Allyson smiled. 'No,' she said. 'Now remember, just be yourself, and if you screw up someone's title, or even their name, don't worry, they've come to expect it.'

Tessa giggled, then said, 'You look fab, by the way. I'll bet Mark Reiner thinks so too.'

Allyson didn't reply.

'He said he liked my dress,' Tessa said. 'I expect he was just being polite though, because I don't look anywhere near as glam as you.'

'Just concentrate on the show,' Allyson advised.

'OK, everyone, stand by!' Alan's assistant shouted.

Allyson made her way back to the lobby, where she was able to look down on the scene and see everything that was happening, from the moment Tessa delivered her opening link to camera, to her first over-played shock at finding a couple of film stars relaxing on the sofas she'd reserved for herself, to the introduction of the garish Happy Hour cocktails. It was all going so smoothly that Allyson could sense already what a triumph the programme was going to be. Of course, she had no way of knowing then that it was a show no one would ever get to see.

Not even when the cameras were taken away and the dancing began were there any signs that anything was wrong. Allyson watched Shelley in Mark's arms, then turned away, refusing to be jealous. The next time she saw Mark he was smooching with Tessa, who seemed drunk and vaguely out of control, but was making him laugh, so Allyson didn't bother to step in. Later, she danced with him herself, but was soon whisked away by an insistent politician. Then towards midnight she couldn't find him, but the sight of Shelley, sitting with a German count and his gay lover, quelled the sudden burn of dread in her chest. Shelley waved, but Allyson didn't go over.

'If you're looking for who I think you're looking for,' Zac said in her ear, 'he carried our pretty little presenter up to bed. Too much champagne!' he expanded, his eyes twinkling with humour. 'Ah, here he is.'

Allyson turned round to see Mark coming towards them. 'How is she?' she asked when he reached them.

'She'll survive. Are you OK? You look pretty tired.'

She smiled. 'You offering to carry me up too?' she teased.

Mark looked at Zac, who for once took the hint and discreetly backed away. 'You don't have to stay to the end,' he said to Allyson.

'Do you think it would be terrible if I didn't?' she said, stifling a yawn.

'No. You've had a long day and the adrenalin's run out . . .'

'You're right,' she said. 'Will you come and say good night before you go to bed?'

'Of course. But I won't wake you if you're sleeping.'

'Just bring me breakfast at the crack of dawn!'

Still smiling after they gave each other a friendly kiss on the cheek, he watched her as she made her way to the top of the stairs and turned back to blow him a kiss. Then he rejoined the party.

As the clock ticked towards two in the morning the last of the revellers began finding their way back to their rooms. Shelley strolled among the remaining few, still sipping champagne, still smiling, talking, laughing, while all the time she was crying inside.

She thought back to the times she and Mark had danced throughout the evening. It had felt so right being with him, touching him, that she just couldn't accept that they weren't destined for each other.

'You look lovely,' he'd told her as he held her in his arms.

She'd wondered if he was just being polite. But no, she did look lovely, and the expression in his eyes had suggested that he was remembering just how lovely.

'Thank you,' she'd said, and when the music slowed he'd pulled her closer and she'd been so intensely aware of his body that she'd lifted his hand and placed it inside her jacket, over her breast. His eyes were burning into hers as he said, 'I've never denied how sexy you are.' Then it was over and he was moving away to dance with someone else.

Shelley looked around for him now, but apart from the staff she seemed to be the only one left. A tall, lonely figure amongst the debris of the night.

She walked slowly up the stairs, past the door to her room. Allyson was in the room next to hers. Shelley had seen her go to bed earlier, so she was probably asleep by now. She wondered if Mark was too.

She moved, hardly knowing it, along the dimly lit hallway, towards his room. Maybe he was expecting her, certain she would come, the way she was meant to, for that was how it felt, that this was meant to be.

Then she was suddenly disorientated by the sound of his voice. She looked to one side, and saw that the door she was passing was open. There were voices, speaking so softly she couldn't make out what they were saying. But one of them was Mark's, she knew that. And the other sounded curiously like a child. This was Tessa's room. For some reason, Mark was in Tessa's room.

Shelley's heart was banging against her ribs. She should leave, turn away, but something was compelling her to stay. She stepped closer to the doorway. Her eyes suddenly dilated. Reflected in the mirror she could see Tessa, on her knees, gazing up at Mark. He was looking down at her, but it was too dark to see his expression. Then Tessa spoke again, in a meek and tearful voice.

'Please,' she was saying tearfully. 'Please don't be angry with me.'

Mark stooped to draw her to her feet.

Shelley remained rooted to the spot, too appalled even to breathe. She heard his next words but hardly registered them as Tessa moved into his arms. Still Shelley listened and watched, then, finally, she turned and walked silently back to her room.

The next morning Shelley and Allyson had breakfast together on the terrace. Allyson's face was white, her eyes were blinded by shock.

'I'm sorry,' Shelley said. 'If I hadn't been coming back from Janie's room then I wouldn't have seen it. But I did and . . .'

Allyson picked up her coffee. She didn't drink, she simply stared down at the cup. She didn't want to believe it, was resisting it hard, but images and memories kept flashing through her mind: Tessa's voice on his machine; Tessa arriving at the hotel with him; Tessa dancing with him; Tessa being carried up to bed by him . . . And now this . . .

'You say she called him Daddy?' she said, feeling confused and sick and horribly distanced from reality.

'That's what it sounded like,' Shelley said. She too was pale, having hardly slept all night.

'You don't think . . .?' Allyson couldn't finish the question.

'That it was a sex game?' Shelley said. 'I don't know.'

Allyson's eyes closed, but she couldn't stop herself picturing the scene, nor could she stop the revulsion. 'Why's she doing this?' she said. 'First Bob, then the programme, then my flat, now Mark. What is it with the girl? And how the hell do I handle it?'

'Maybe you should talk to him,' Shelley suggested. 'Ask him what it was about?'

'He left early this morning, for Rome. He's on a midday flight to New York.' He'd come to kiss her goodbye, but she was still so tired she'd barely known he was there. She wondered now why he hadn't told her before that he'd be leaving so early. Or maybe he had and she'd been so busy she hadn't heard him.

'Oh God,' she groaned. 'Why did I ever let that girl into my life? Or more to the point, how the hell do I get her out?'

Chapter Fifteen

TWO DAYS HAD GONE by since they'd returned to London, and still Allyson didn't seem able to shake herself out of this trance-like state. But life was easier to deal with that way, just going through the motions.

Mark was still in New York. He'd rung several times, but if she was in the office she cut him short by saying she'd call back, and if she was at home she listened to his voice on the machine without picking up. She didn't want to talk to him, because she didn't even want to think about asking him if anything Shelley had said was true. Besides, even when she was ready to talk, she wouldn't do it on the phone. She'd make herself face him, which shouldn't be as hard or as devastating as when Bob had betrayed her because she hadn't known him so long. But the hatred she'd known for Tessa since Bob had left was magnified to a degree that consumed her. She couldn't look at the girl without thinking monstrous thoughts, couldn't hear her voice without wishing her dead. Yet she still had to work with her, still had to see her every day.

Yet Tessa too seemed different, strangely cowed. But Allyson wasn't interested to know anything about her, except to understand whatever insanity it was that was making her want everything that was Allyson's. For one wildly insane moment she'd even considered asking her. But what good would it do? She couldn't be relied on to tell the truth, and even if she could Allyson didn't want to hear it from her.

Nor did she want to hear from Bob. She just wanted him out of her life, expunged from existence, along with his pathetic pleas to come home. But she couldn't put off seeing him any longer, and reluctantly she agreed to meet him.

It was evident right away that he'd made an effort, for he was wearing the cologne she liked best, and a shirt she had bought him. He looked haggard though, and was so apprehensive that ordinarily she'd have wanted to hug him. Tonight, she simply stood aside and tried not to wish that he would go away. 'Would you like a drink?' she offered as he walked into the sitting room ahead of her.

'Maybe some wine,' he said.

She went to get it and came back to find him sitting on the edge of a chair, his hands clamped together. 'Did your lawyer tell you . . .?' His voice was hoarse. She could see how hard this was for him. He started again. 'You know why I'm here?'

She nodded, then seeing his eyes fill with tears she put down the wine and went to him.

He clung to her as he wept, bitterly, full of shame. 'I'll do anything,' he sobbed. 'I'll get counselling, anything. Just please say it isn't too late.'

She looked at his tormented face. She knew this man so well. Yet at this moment she felt so remote from him. 'I'm sorry,' she said, her voice seeming to come from a long way inside her. 'You made this happen, Bob, and nothing I do can change it.'

'But we can put it behind us. I'm starting to get some work again now, so we can move forward and be together the way we should.'

'Until when? The next Tessa?'

'No! I don't want any other woman. Leaving you has made me understand that in a way I never did before . . .'

'But what about all the other women? Shelley's my best friend.'

He looked shocked and hurt. 'Are you saying you'd rather give me up than her?'

'She didn't betray me.'

Disbelief widened his eyes, and as she looked back at him she could feel something horrible rising up inside her, something that had always been there but she'd never wanted to face. 'She slept with me all those years, but the betrayal was only mine?' he said incredulously. And there it was. Shelley, her best friend, had been sleeping with her husband all along. Shelley had betrayed her too.

Her head was spinning. 'What are you talking about? She said you tried . . .' But she couldn't go any further.

Realising what had happened, he dropped his head in his hands. 'Oh God,' he groaned.

Allyson got to her feet. 'You should go now,' she said.

'No. Allyson, please.'

She pushed his hands away and walked to the door. 'There's no one I can trust,' she said unsteadily. 'No one.'

He wasn't listening. 'Tell me you'll think it over,' he begged.

'Just leave me alone,' she said. 'All of you. Just leave me alone.'

Bob was standing in Shelley's sitting room. He felt foolish, unmanned, yet so desperate that even now he was still clinging to the hope that Shelley would know how to repair the damage he'd done.

But when he'd finished Shelley looked so angry he thought she might strike him. 'You fool,' she spat. 'You bloody fool!'

'But she made it sound like you'd told her.'

Contempt twisted her face. 'Are you out of your mind? She's my best friend. God, you're pathetic!' she seethed.

'I should never have left her in the first place. And I wouldn't have if Tessa hadn't been pregnant. It's all her damned fault. Everything was all right before she came into our lives . . .'

'You self-pitying piece of scum!' Shelley spat. 'You always were a cheating bastard. You'd screw anyone who'd lie down for you . . .'

'Including you, you stuck-up, self-righteous bitch! You lay down often enough, didn't you? That's how good a friend you are. And I'll tell you this, if it was you who'd been pregnant, I still wouldn't have left, because Allyson's worth ten thousand of you, Shelley . . .'

'No, you gave Allyson up for a silly little tart who didn't give that for you, or your kid . . . You *do* know she had an abortion, don't you . . . What are you doing? Get away from me!' She was backing across the room, but he kept on coming.

'I said get away!' she shouted.

His fist knocked her flying back across the sofa, then picking up a photograph of her and Allyson he flung it violently into the fireplace before snatching up her purse, helping himself to the money and storming out of the door.

Shelley lay breathlessly where she was, her hand covering the throbbing in her face as his footsteps thundered down the stairs. Nothing was happening the way she had expected and she didn't know how to turn it around. But maybe she didn't need to. For though it didn't seem likely that Allyson would take Bob back now, there was nothing to say she'd take Mark back either. So maybe she should wait, let events unfold a little further, until she had a clearer idea of what she should do.

The following morning Shelley was already at her desk when Allyson arrived at the office. The strain in Allyson's face was plain to see, and it was clear to everyone that something had happened.

Shelley considered going to talk to her, but this was not the place to have the kind of showdown to which they were heading. How must she be feeling, with Tessa sitting out there, Shelley in here . . . So maybe Shelley *should* go and talk to her, if only to help her connect to something as superficial, yet stabilising, as the day's needs.

But as Shelley reached her door Allyson was calling across the room to Tessa. 'Have you edited the piece about the dolls yet?' she was asking.

'No, not yet,' Tessa replied. 'But if you're in a hurry I can do it tonight,' she said, a kind of frightened eagerness in her eyes.

Shelley knew Allyson wasn't due to shoot that show for another three weeks, so it surprised her when she snapped, 'Yes, do it tonight.'

As she turned back into her office her eyes met Shelley's, and Shelley could see how deeply her pain was cutting. Then she disappeared, and Shelley returned to her desk to pick up her keys.

'I've got to take my car in for a service,' she told Marvin, 'then I'll be popping home for a few minutes. I'll be back before lunch.'

It was early in the afternoon when Allyson answered the phone in her dressing room to find Mark at the other end. 'I don't know why you're refusing to speak to me,' he said, 'but I'm outside, and if you're not here in the next five minutes I'll come in and get you.'

Allyson replaced the receiver, stared at it for a moment, then walked upstairs, where she found Shelley alone in the screening room.

Allyson walked straight in and said, 'Did you really see Mark and Tessa together in Italy? Or were you lying about that too?'

'I wasn't lying,' Shelley cried. 'I swear I saw them.'

'Do you have any idea what all this feels like?' Allyson said. 'Knowing there's no one you can trust?'

'Yes. I know what that feels like,' Shelley answered. 'But listen, we have to talk. Not now. Later. Will you let me at least try to explain?'

Allyson didn't answer, and suddenly Shelley was afraid. Everything seemed to be slipping away, moving beyond her reach, and she wanted desperately to bring it back.

'Think of loneliness, rejection, never feeling as though you matter,' Shelley cried. 'You know now how some of that feels. That's how it's been for me. All my life I've never known what it was like to be truly loved by a man. You had that and I wanted it. I resented you for it and at the same time . . . I loved you.' She was choking with emotion. 'I'll book a table in Dolphin Square for eight thirty. Please say you'll come.'

'I'm looking after Daddy until then.'

'Then I'll book it for nine. If you're not there, I'll wait.'

Allyson sat in the passenger seat of Mark's car, numb with exhaustion. So many betrayals, so many lies, could there ever be any trust again?

She'd already asked him about Tessa and he'd explained, but the words didn't seem to have reached her.

He said them again. 'She was very drunk and when she passed out I carried her up to bed. She was out cold when I left her. Then later, when I was in my room, I heard her crying. She sounded hysterical, so I went in. It was like she was hallucinating. She seemed to think I was her father and that I was going to hurt her. She offered to have sex with me if I promised not to beat her. I couldn't get her to understand who I was. Then she started talking in a childish voice and calling me Daddy.' He was shaking his head. 'I don't know what was going through her head. What I do know is it wasn't coherent and it wasn't particularly sane. Then she threw up all over us both, so I called someone from downstairs to come and take care of her, and went back to my room.'

Allyson was staring straight ahead. She was hearing the words now, but hardly knew what they meant.

'Allyson, you've got to know how much you mean to me,' he said. 'I don't want to push you, I know you've been through a lot, but for God's sake, I love you . . .'

She turned to look at him. So Shelley hadn't lied. He had been in Tessa's room. Tessa. Tessa. It always came back to Tessa.

'I have to go now,' she said, and before he could stop her she opened the door and got out of the car.

The day's recording was over, and there was nobody in the building now except Tessa and Will, the editor, who were editing the film about dolls together, and Shelley, who was almost ready to leave.

It had been the strangest day. It was as though something bizarre and pivotal were happening, something that was going to move with a silent and mighty force to change their lives completely.

Shelley knew Allyson had seen Mark earlier, but had no idea yet of the outcome. She kept wondering what she would do if Allyson told her later that everything was all right, that she and Mark were staying together and that they didn't want her in their lives any more.

She felt suddenly breathless, and there was such unease in her heart that each thud felt like a blunted blow.

She should leave now, go home and change. She'd just check on Will and Tessa first, find out what time they'd be finished.

The edit room door was closed, but Shelley could hear the squealing whir of the videotape rewinding. She opened the door and walked in.

'Oh, Shelley!' Will said in surprise. 'I didn't know you were there.'

'Just checking on how you're getting on,' she said, looking past him to where Tessa was sitting at the control desk.

'It's great,' Tessa told her. 'Really scary.'

Shelley smiled. 'I'll leave you to it, then,' she said.

Allyson was standing next to her mother's car in the garage, waiting for Peggy to start the engine.

'Are you sure you're all right?' Peggy asked, peering up at her anxiously. 'You seem . . . distracted?'

Allyson forced a smile. 'I've got a lot on my mind. But I'm OK. You have a good time with Aunt Mary. It'll do you good to get out.'

'We'll just get a quick bite. I should be back by eight thirty.'

Allyson looked at her mother's ageing, kindly face and felt a lump rise in her throat. The one person in the world she would never doubt, would always be able to trust.

Going back into the house, she went to check on her father and found him sleeping peacefully on a sofa in his den. She wondered what happened to the lucidity when the confusion took over. Was it still there somewhere, operating on another level? Or was it tangled so deep in the subconscious that it could never be found?

Kissing him on the forehead, she closed the door quietly behind her, then returned to the kitchen. The clock said six thirty. That should give her plenty of time to do everything she had to do—she'd just sit down for a few minutes first though and try not to think any more.

The lights in the edit suite were off. All eight monitors glowed in the darkness, each projecting an identical image. Tessa was alone for the moment. Will had received a call from the car-parking attendant, reminding him that the barrier went down at eight so he should move his car out to the street.

Tessa was seated at the console, watching, enthralled by the house that was filling up the screens in front of her. It was tall, gothic, with stained-glass windows and a forbidding air. The effect on the sound track whistled the same eerie cry as the wind that was sweeping through the streets outside. Naked tree limbs swayed across the face of the moon, fallen leaves gusted over the brittle, frosted lawn. Footsteps crunched on the dark, gravelled path. The front door was opening, the dubbed effect of a creak stretched with the ominously slow swing.

This sequence was a cheat. It wasn't the author's North London home, it was footage imported from Hammer. But the next mix, as the camera inched along the hallway and a hand pushed open a door, revealed a huge, brightly lit room full of every imaginable type of doll. This was the writer's home.

The dolls lived on every shelf, every chair, every surface of the high-ceilinged room. A thousand staring eyes, unseeing, unspeaking, yet all-knowing. Dressed in delicate, hand-sewn clothes; small, malignant spirits locked in wax, china and porcelain forms. The discordant music dipped and swayed as the camera panned sharply, then settled in benign observation of inscrutable Orientals. A sudden screech emanated from the frame of a spiteful Turk. Tessa's concentration was total as the thrill of fear stole through her senses. Behind her the door opened quietly.

'This is brilliant, Will,' she murmured, eyes still riveted to the screen.

Faces flashed across the screen. Ugly, old, tormented, sad. She felt Will standing behind her. Her heart was thudding.

The first blow knocked her unconscious.

The grating, staccato squeals from *Psycho* knifed through the room. A shadow bulged on the wall, a nefarious enactment of the final four blows that took her life.

Allyson was running. When she reached her car she took out her phone and dialled as she got in. 'Shelley?'

'Ally? Where are you? You sound upset.'

'No. I fell asleep and Mummy was late back. I didn't want you to think I wasn't coming.'

'It's OK.' Shelley's voice sounded strained too. 'I'm stuck in traffic. I should be there just after nine.'

Allyson rang off and pulled away from the kerb.

By the time Shelley arrived at the restaurant Allyson was already sitting at the table. Both women looked pale and strained.

'There's a bomb scare somewhere in Chelsea,' Shelley said. 'They've closed off half the roads.'

'I heard it on the news,' Allyson said. She felt strangely groggy, as though she'd been asleep for days.

Shelley ordered a drink while Allyson toyed with her own.

'About Bob,' Shelley said.

Allyson closed her eyes. She didn't want to hear it.

'I'm not stupid enough to think you can forgive me,' Shelley said, emotion acting like a burr on her voice. 'I just want you to know that your friendship has been more precious to me than anything else in my life. I wish I'd known how to value it. I wish I wasn't realising how much I value it now that it's all too late.'

Allyson's eyes were shining with tears, but none fell.

'Jealousy is a powerful monster,' Shelley said, 'and I've always been jealous of you. But I've loved you too.' As she spoke she was reaching inside the large carrier bag on the floor beside her. She took out a box and said, 'This is for you. A token of our friendship.'

As she pushed it across the table Allyson suddenly laughed.

Shelley looked at her curiously.

'I'm sorry,' she said. 'It's just been . . . Oh God, I don't know how much more of today I can take. Thank you. What is it?' But as she started to unwrap it Shelley covered her hands.

'Maybe you'd better wait until you get home,' she said. 'It might make us both cry.'

Allyson looked into her lovely face and felt her heart filling up with emotion. Everything that had been so familiar and cherished, so central to them and who they were, was about to change, and there was nothing they could do to stop it. 'I don't want to lose you,' she whispered.

Shelley swallowed the lump in her throat, then looked up as her drink arrived. She was about to make a toast when her phone started to ring. 'Shelley Bronson,' she said.

Allyson watched her face as its expression turned from surprise, to confusion, to horror and shock. 'What is it?' Allyson said, feeling her blood run cold. 'What's happened?'

Shelley was ending the call. 'Of course,' she was saying. 'I'll come right away.' She clicked off the phone and stared at Allyson, her face bloodless and stricken. 'It was the police,' she said. 'Tessa's been murdered.'

Allyson's head started to spin. She thought she might faint.

'They want me to go back to the office,' Shelley said. Her eyes drew focus on Allyson. 'Maybe you should come too.' She stood up. 'I had to park miles away. Where are you?'

'Just down the road,' Allyson managed to say.

'Then let's take your car. Don't forget your parcel,' she added, then turned to lead the way out.

By the time they got to the office the place had been cordoned off and the press was starting to gather. A couple of policemen spotted them and ushered them through.

Inside there seemed to be policemen everywhere. They saw Will sitting at a desk with a detective. He looked as though he'd been crying. A short man with cropped red hair and a stern face approached them. 'Mrs Jaymes,' he said, recognising Allyson. 'Detective Inspector Hollander.'

Allyson shook his hand. 'This is Shelley Bronson,' she said.

Hollander shook hands with Shelley.

'Where did it happen?' Shelley asked.

'Through there,' he answered, and as he pointed towards the editing room another man and a woman joined them, whom Hollander introduced as Detective Constable Geoff Maine and Detective Constable Sheila Lister.

'We're going to need you to answer some questions,' Hollander told them. 'Mrs Jaymes, perhaps you can take Detective Lister somewhere quiet. Miss Bronson, Detective Maine will take a statement from you.'

Allyson took Detective Lister to her office, where she answered the detective's questions as succinctly and helpfully as she could. After hours of questions and black coffee and watching her colleagues come in and out, they told her to go home. She drove in a trance back to the flat. All she could see in her mind's eye was the image of them carrying Tessa's body away in a bag. It was an image she would never forget.

When she got home the message light was blinking wildly on her machine. Ignoring it she poured herself a drink and sat in a chair, her coat still on. Everyone thought she had done it. They all believed she had finally flipped and smashed Tessa's brains in. She started to cry, so afraid she didn't know what to do.

After a while she went into the hall and stood over the bags she'd carried in from the car. Two of them were from Waitrose. The other contained Shelley's gift. She stared at it for a long time, bizarre and frightening thoughts whirling round in her head. Finally she knelt down on the floor and took the gift out.

Minutes later the wrapping on Shelley's gift was open, the lid of the box was cast aside. Allyson looked at the ugly brown marks on the wad of rolled-up fabric it was wrapped in. She looked at the heavy object in her hands expressionlessly, breathlessly. It was the elegant Marcel Bouraine figurine Allyson had given Shelley at Christmas . . . The fandancer . . . Her chest was heaving, her hands were shaking . . .

Then suddenly the monstrous reality of what had happened erupted like a bomb in her head and as the figurine fell to the floor, she slumped back against the wall, gasping uncontrollably.

 *Chapter Sixteen*

THE FIRST SIGNS of spring had been swallowed into a dark and chilling late afternoon. Detective Constables Lister and Maine had been up all night, so had many of their colleagues. This was a high-profile case and the boss wanted an arrest by the end of the day. It was looking increasingly likely that would happen.

Inspector Hollander was scanning the early statements they'd taken, and listening closely as the two detectives briefed him.

'The time of death has been established as being between seven fifty and eight o'clock,' Maine said. 'Cause of death was pretty obvious, list of suspects tentatively increased to three after Shelley Bronson called late last night to report a bronze figure missing from her flat. She says she first noticed it had disappeared after a visit from Bob Jaymes, Allyson Jaymes's husband.'

'And this figure was a gift from Allyson Jaymes?' Hollander said, looking at the note that had been added to Shelley's statement.

'Yes. It's also now been confirmed as the murder weapon since Allyson Jaymes brought it in this morning.'

It was DC Lister's turn. 'She says she gave the figurine to Shelley Bronson at Christmas, but Shelley gave it back to her last night, wrapped up in a bloodstained make-up gown.'

DI Hollander's face showed his dislike of the way things were going. 'Has someone talked to Bronson since we got the figurine?' he said.

'I did,' Maine answered. 'I went over to her flat earlier. When I told her we had the figurine and what Allyson had said about it, she got pretty upset. She says the gift she gave Allyson last night was a Lalique clock, an item from her own collection that Allyson had always admired.'

'So where's the clock now?'

'No one seems to know,' Maine answered.

Hollander tugged at his lower lip. 'Things aren't looking very good for Mrs Jaymes, are they?' he commented. 'We all know her husband left her for the girl and now, according to Shelley Bronson, she believed her new boyfriend, Mark Reiner, was also having an affair with the girl. Has anyone talked to Reiner?'

'I did,' Lister replied. 'He says he wasn't having an affair with Tessa Dukes, but that Shelley Bronson had intimated to Allyson that he was.'

'Oh, the tangled webs,' Hollander remarked, sighing. 'And Bob Jaymes? Do we have a statement from him yet?'

'Yes, it's there, sir,' Maine answered. 'He says he was at the Arsenal match last night and reckons the first he heard of anything was when he got home and turned on the news. We're still checking his alibi.'

'And the cars?' Hollander asked.

'So far we've checked out Allyson's, Shelley's and Bob Jaymes's,' Lister answered. 'Oh, and the Butler-Blythes', Allyson's parents. All have come back with clean bills of health.'

Hollander looked up. 'So what we're really saying here is that our chief suspect is Allyson Jaymes, whose only alibi for between six and nine last night is a father who doesn't know what day of the week it is.'

'That's right,' Lister confirmed. 'She says she was looking after him while her mother went for a bite to eat with her sister-in-law.'

'Mmm,' Hollander grunted, looking at Allyson's statement.

'Meanwhile, Shelley's stuck in traffic caused by the bomb scare in Chelsea last night,' Maine added.

'She was on her way from the office?'

'Yes. She says she left around eight with the intention of going home to change. But when she saw the traffic she decided to go straight to the restaurant. She arrived just after Allyson.'

'Did she see Tessa before she left?'

'Yes. She went to check on her in the editing room and that was the last time she saw her.'

'And there was no one else working late?'

'Apparently not. Except the editor, of course.'

Hollander was reading again. Then, sighing, he looked at Lister. 'What a bloody circus this is going to be,' he grumbled.

Maine rubbed a hand over his face. 'I say everything points to Allyson Jaymes. Let's wrap this up and get some sleep.'

'Hey!' Lister protested. 'Let's not make any hasty decisions. After all, Shelley Bronson we *know* was at the scene of the crime.'

'And three hours is plenty of time for Allyson Jaymes to get in her car, go to Shelley's flat and get the figurine, take it to Fulham, bash the victim's head in, get back in her car and drive back to Chelsea. And the old boy wouldn't even know she was gone.'

'But we've checked her car. And her parents' car too,' Lister reminded him. 'They're clean. Forensics have been over her flat, but we knew the murder weapon was there.'

'What about Shelley Bronson's flat? Are they checking that?'

'Nothing,' Maine informed him.

'Yet,' Lister added.

'But where's her motive?' Hollander asked.

'Allyson claims Shelley was having an affair with her husband, prior to his affair with Tessa. She also claims that Shelley was jealous of her relationship with Mark Reiner.'

'Leading us to?'

'A frame-up, according to Allyson. In other words, if Allyson's sent down on a murder charge then Mark Reiner might rediscover his interest in Shelley. Apparently they had some kind of fling prior to Reiner getting involved with Allyson. Both he and Allyson say that he dumped Shelley in favour of Allyson.'

'Ah, the "hell hath no fury" motive,' Hollander declared.

'But what we all seem to be forgetting here,' Maine pointed out, 'is that there's not a shred of evidence pointing to her. Unlike Allyson Jaymes, who not only has motive and opportunity, but actually turns up with the murder weapon. What more are we looking for?'

Hollander turned to Lister.

'The restaurant owner's confirmed that he saw Shelley handing Allyson a box that was large enough to have contained the figurine,' Lister said, looking up as a policeman put his head round the door.

'There's a woman downstairs claiming to be some kind of therapist to the deceased,' he told them.

All eyebrows rose with interest. 'I'll talk to her,' Lister said. 'Don't get carried away with any arrests until I'm back.'

The longer DC Lister listened to Laura Risby the more she was being forced to admit that things were looking grim for Allyson Jaymes. It seemed that Tessa Dukes had had some kind of fixation on Allyson, which in itself didn't amount to much, but when weighted with everything else could easily add another motive for the killing.

'It was all rather tragic,' Laura Risby was saying about Tessa. 'She grew up in a household where both her father and older brother regularly abused her, sexually, and her mother either turned a blind eye, or simply didn't know. Then they had a terrible fight, during which Tessa tried to strangle her mother. The father broke it up and the next day the mother shot and killed both her husband and her son and then herself. Tessa was sixteen when it happened. When she was eighteen, just after she started university, she had a breakdown, which was when she first came to see me. Tessa truly loved her mother, even though she blames her for what happened. I think what she's been doing since is trying to re-create her family. Bob the father, Julian the brother and . . .'

'Julian?'

'A young man who works for the programme too. But he was with me last night, talking and trying to understand why Tessa's the way she is.'

Lister wrote Julian's name down, then nodded for Laura to continue.

'He told me he'd been worried about her lately. She'd seemed depressed and withdrawn, and more preoccupied with Allyson than ever. You see, she'd cast Allyson in the role of her mother, someone she loved deeply, but wanted to punish too. She blamed herself for her mother's suicide, and with Allyson she was trying to see if she could do it again. I don't believe she wanted to succeed, quite the reverse in fact. She wanted Allyson to be stronger than her mother; that way her own faults might not be so much to blame for the suicide.'

Lister inhaled. 'Sounds like she had a lot of problems.'

Laura nodded. 'In recent weeks Tessa and Bob broke up,' she went on. 'It appears that when Allyson's interest in him had faded, so Tessa's did too. Going after Bob had been an attempt to become a part of the love Allyson shared with him, to feel as though she belonged to them both, as she had to her parents. Then, when it became known that Allyson was involved with Mark Reiner, Tessa tried to get involved with him too. As far as I'm aware Mr Reiner never allowed their relationship to go beyond the professional, but maybe something did happen between them, and maybe that's why Allyson . . .' She stopped, suddenly uneasy, but Lister knew what she'd been about to say. *Maybe that's why Allyson finally lost control and killed her.*

'So there you have it,' Lister said, finishing Laura Risby's story for Hollander and Maine. 'One severely damaged teenager with a mother fixation on Allyson Jaymes, whose life she was systematically taking apart.'

They were silenced for a moment by the tragedy of it all.

'So do we arrest her?' Maine said.

Hollander nodded. Then rubbing his eyes he said, 'It's not every day we get a suspect who brings in the murder weapon themselves then sits in our canteen all day with her mother, waiting to be cuffed.'

'Which is what bothers me, sir,' Lister said.

'I know. It bothers me too. But you've heard the evidence. Give me one good reason why we shouldn't arrest her.'

Lister's eyes remained on his, until finally, feeling heavy with fatigue and defeat, she stood up and walked to the door.

Allyson and her mother were in the station canteen. They'd been there ever since they'd brought the figurine, together with the make-up gown it had been wrapped in, to the station. Neither of them had slept after Allyson had driven over to her mother's last night to tell her what had happened. It had taken a while to calm Peggy down, but then they had both tried to make her father remember that she had been there the entire time between six and nine last night. But of course he didn't. He didn't remember her at all.

'You should go home and see to Daddy,' Allyson said now.

'I'm not leaving you,' Peggy said. 'Aunt Faye is looking after Daddy.'

DC Lister came into the canteen. 'Hello,' she said.

Allyson's heart was in her mouth. Something had happened, she could tell. 'I'd like you to come with me,' she said, looking at Allyson.

Allyson glanced at her mother and stood up. 'You're going to arrest me, aren't you?'

Lister nodded.

'No!' Allyson cried. 'I didn't do it. I swear I didn't do it.'

Lister looked into her terrified face and wished there was something she could say, but all she managed was, 'I'm sorry. I'm truly sorry.'

After Allyson's personal effects were taken she was led to a cell and locked in. Her mother sat on a bench outside and refused to leave.

DC Lister made the call to the Butler-Blythes' family lawyer on Peggy's behalf. He was going to sort out the best man for the job, then come with him to the station. After that, the detective returned to her desk and went over the statements again, trying to find something that would satisfy that niggling doubt in her mind that some crucial factor was being overlooked. But there was nothing to support any doubt.

Maybe it was simply that she didn't want it to be true. She didn't want the shining image of a woman, known for her compassion and kindness, to turn out to be the glittering front for a monster.

Lister turned her thoughts to Shelley Bronson, the wronged and rejected woman. The only one who really stood to gain with both Tessa and Allyson out of the way. The gain being the eligible Mark Reiner.

She read Shelley Bronson's statement again, then on a hunch she picked up the phone and called the uniformed officer who had driven Shelley home after her initial interrogation at the *Soirée* offices. By the time their call was over Lister's adrenalin was starting to pump. The young officer had merely confirmed everything in his report: how he'd driven Shelley back to the restaurant she'd been at earlier with Allyson, watched her get into her car and drive off, then he'd returned to the scene of the crime. The only thing he'd omitted from his report was the make of Shelley's car. Armed with this new information Lister made a few more calls, then consulted a map of London pinned on the wall.

It was just before two in the morning that Lister got a call back from the owner of a car-hire company confirming that one of his staff had rented a black Audi to Shelley Bronson on the morning of the murder. She'd returned it early the next day, already washed and vacuumed, and had paid in cash. The car the young uniformed officer had returned Shelley to, which had been parked a few streets from the restaurant, was a black Audi. Shelley's own car, the one that forensics had gone over, was a silver Lexus.

Lister got on the phone to her colleague, Geoff Maine. 'Shelley Bronson hired a car on the day of the murder,' she said. 'She returned it the next day, already cleaned, and paid for it in cash. The roads between the office and her flat weren't affected by the bomb scare, so she had time to get home, change and drive to the restaurant by nine fifteen.'

'Jesus Christ, Sheila,' he grumbled. 'What time is it?'

'The reason we couldn't find anything in her car was because she was driving a rental!' Lister almost shouted.

Maine was still coming to. 'So we talk to her in the morning, right?'

'No. Trust me on this, Geoff. We need to go now.'

Even with no make-up and her hair tousled from sleep, Shelley Bronson still managed to look gorgeous. As Lister had expected, this dead-of- night visit had unnerved Shelley, though of course that in itself proved nothing. And despite her unease, Shelley was perfectly polite as she invited them to sit down and asked if she could get them a drink.

They sat, but refused the drink. Shelley sat too, drawing her fine satin robe more tightly around herself.

'So, what can I do for you at this hour?' Shelley asked.

Lister smiled. 'We just need you to clear something up for us. You said in your statement that you left the office around seven fifty, possibly a little after, and were stuck in traffic until you got to the restaurant.'

Shelley nodded. 'I was going to go home, but when I saw how bad it was I decided I wouldn't . . . have enough time.'

'Can you remember where you were when Allyson called you on your mobile to say she was going to be late?'

'I think I was by the cinema in Beaufort Street.'

'And that was about what time?'

'Just before nine, I think.'

'You knew Allyson was babysitting her father that evening?'

'Yes. She told me earlier in the day.'

Lister smiled. 'Good, that all checks out.' She glanced over at Maine, noting the relief in Shelley's eyes.

Shelley was about to get up when Lister said, 'Why didn't you mention you were driving a hire car on the day of the murder?'

Panic stripped away the relief. Shelley's face went deathly pale. 'My car was in the garage. I always hire another when mine's in the garage.'

'And do you always clean it before you take it back?'

Shelley's eyes darted to Maine. 'Sometimes,' she said.

Lister could almost smell her fear. 'We'd like to take a look at the clothes you were wearing that day,' she said.

Shelley's eyes were almost wild. 'They're at the cleaners.'

Of course.

'I think I should call a lawyer,' Shelley said.

'Yes, Miss Bronson,' Lister responded. 'I think you should.'

Chapter Seventeen

MARK REINER got out of his car and looked across the cemetery to where a small, huddled group stood in the rain. Further away, at a distance that was almost respectable, was a much larger group, most of them clutching cameras and notebooks. It was a horrible, bleak day in every way, for no one could help feeling the terrible sadness that came with the senseless and untimely death of a young girl who had suffered so much in her short life. The papers had been full of her story since the details had come out, the nightly news never failed to mention it.

'Are you OK?'

Mark looked at his sister-in-law, Claudia. She'd insisted on coming to the funeral with him, and now they were here he was glad that she had. Holding an umbrella over them both, he steered her towards the mourners who were starting to file into the chapel. They consisted almost entirely of the *Soirée* team, with the exception of the two detectives who were involved in the case, and Allyson's husband and mother. Shelley was still in custody, but of Allyson herself there was no sign, though he guessed she was already inside.

The chapel was cold and dark, but the candles cast a warm glow over the altar. Mark and Claudia slipped into a pew near the back, and knelt to pray. With his eyes closed Mark thought of Tessa and felt the profoundest regret that he had done nothing to help her, for that night in Italy had surely been enough to show him how disturbed and desperate she was. Now it was too late. Accepting that was almost as hard as accepting everything else, but how much worse it must be for Allyson considering the complex role she had played in Tessa's life—and ultimately in her death.

Seeing her at the front, dressed in black and seated between her mother and husband, he tried to imagine the aching futility of what they had been through, unwitting pawns in a game they hadn't even been aware of until it was over. The trauma of her arrest must have been hard for Allyson, but the worst of this now, apart from the tragedy of Tessa's death, must be knowing what Shelley had tried to do to her. Friends for so long and now this. He couldn't help wondering if Allyson blamed him in some way too, holding him accountable for the pain he had caused Shelley, which in the end had driven her to do what she had. It was impossible to know, for they hadn't spoken since the murder.

The organ droned on, merging finally into the opening strains of a well-known hymn as the minister entered, the coffin and pallbearers behind him. As everyone rose, Mark watched the small procession pass by. He tried to sing, though he barely heard the words leaving his lips.

Everyone sat, and in their still fragile stupor listened to the minister as he read from the Bible. A while later he asked everyone to pray, then Julian, a young boy from the programme, read a piece he'd written himself. Like everyone else, Mark was profoundly moved, not only by the words, but by the relief of knowing that someone had cared, and apparently very much.

Then the worst moment was upon them, as the coffin moved slowly away from them, taking with it the young girl no one had ever really known. She hadn't deserved such a life, and it was inevitable that each in their own way would feel they had failed her.

No one hung around for long after the service. Eager to be out of the rain and away from the grim rituals of farewell they were soon finding their way back to their cars.

'I feel I should go and say something to Allyson,' Claudia said, as Mark opened the door for her. 'Do you mind?'

'Of course not,' he answered.

She looked up at him. 'You won't come with me?'

'No.'

He watched as Claudia ran over to where Allyson and her mother were talking to a few of the *Soirée* team. Bob was talking to the detectives. No doubt the press would be drawing their own conclusions from what they were seeing today, and it was partly because of them that Mark didn't want to go over there now, for he didn't want the event of Tessa's funeral to be upstaged by speculation on where Allyson's relationships with her husband and Mark Reiner might now be going. And as his eyes met Allyson's for a long and torturous few moments he knew that no matter how hard this was for him, for her it was nothing short of hell.

It was hard to believe that three weeks had gone by since the funeral, though in some ways it felt like three years. Or maybe it was another lifetime, for there was something strangely disconcerting about standing here with Bob, in the front porch of their country home, facing a battery of press who had come to witness the Jaymeses' reconciliation being made official.

Bob's arm was wrapped protectively around her as she blinked at the flashbulbs and he dealt with the barrage of questions, confirming that they were now back together and intended to stay that way.

'Bob! Is it true you're about to sign a deal with Sky?' someone shouted.

Bob laughed. 'It's being talked about,' he answered.

'Allyson! Now that *Soirée's* been cancelled, can you tell us what you're going to do?'

Bob's arm tightened around her. 'She won't be doing anything until after the trial,' he told them. 'She needs to rest now, and be looked after.'

Irritated that he'd answered for her, Allyson continued to smile, demonstrating a lightness of spirit she was so far from feeling. A young girl was dead and her best friend was in prison. There was nothing to celebrate in that, and it felt horrible, callous even, to be standing here pretending everything was all right, when it was so very far from being all right that there were times she felt she might be going out of her mind.

Her biggest enemy was fear, for she was so afraid now of what the future might hold, for her and for Shelley, that she could think about nothing else. She tormented herself night and day with the horror of being arrested again, of being locked in the prison where Shelley was now, of not being able to prove her innocence.

She was startled back into the moment by someone calling out, 'Allyson! Are you in touch with Shelley at all?'

She started to answer, but Bob said, 'Come on, you guys, you know we can't discuss anything to do with the case. How about you ask us where we're planning to go for our second honeymoon?'

Allyson stopped listening again. She was thinking now about the letter she'd received from Shelley, two weeks ago, the first communication they'd had since the murder. All it had said was: *Dear Allyson, I am enclosing a visiting order. Please come. Shelley*.

Allyson had meant to go. She'd even got as far as the prison itself, but at the last she'd turned away. She just hadn't been up to dealing with it then. She'd been too afraid, too disorientated still to grasp the steadying hands of reason. She'd tried to remind herself that she had no need to fear Shelley. And even if Shelley persisted with her claims of innocence, there was still nothing to say Allyson had done it, nothing even to put her at the scene of the crime. But at the time the thought of seeing Shelley, of looking into her eyes and knowing . . .

Suddenly aware of what Bob was saying, Allyson felt herself cringing. This ludicrous charade, she knew, had been staged as much for Mark's benefit as for anyone else's, to let him know that Bob and Allyson were still very much in love, despite everything. She prayed to God that Mark wasn't watching, and if he was she willed him to know it was a lie. She was only here because she couldn't bear what the press would make of it if she was with him so soon after Tessa's death.

Would he understand that? Would he know how desperately she wanted to be with him? Those moments at Tessa's funeral, when their eyes had met, were all she had to persuade her that he still cared. But now, after three weeks of anxiety and self-doubt, she no longer knew what to believe, especially when he'd made no attempt to call her.

At last the questions began to peter out, and Bob announced they were going inside. Allyson looked out at the ragged group with their cameras and notebooks. How loyally they had all rallied behind her, hardly even questioning her innocence, and seeming so eager to believe that she, the model of compassion and stability, was wholly intact. Even those who had attempted to put her in the frame of guilt had been unable to prove she was anywhere but at her parents' house during those crucial three hours.

'Well, I think that went well, don't you?' Bob said, following her into the kitchen. 'So what do you think of the second honeymoon?' he said, starting to kiss her neck. 'Bali OK for you?'

She wondered how he was going to pay for it when his work was still so thin on the ground. But of course they wouldn't be going, so all she said was, 'We can't go anywhere until the trial's over.'

'I know,' he murmured, still kissing her. 'God, I've missed you.'

She knew exactly what that meant, for though he'd been with her virtually every day since the murder, they'd been staying with her parents and until now she'd insisted on sleeping alone.

'Bob, don't,' she said, shrugging him off, and to give herself something to do she plugged in the kettle.

She allowed several seconds to pass, staring down at nothing, and feeling his eyes caging her in. Then she made herself turn round, and to her surprise her heart contracted when she saw how hurt he looked.

'I'm prepared to wait,' he said. 'It doesn't matter how long.'

She reached for his hand. 'Bob, I know this isn't what you want to hear, but I've already told you I don't know if this can work. I'm not sure I love you any more. And sooner or later I *will* want to go back to work.'

'There's no programme any more,' he reminded her, 'so what do you think you're going back to?'

'I don't know. But I'm still under contract and maybe . . .'

'Maybe what?' he said sharply. 'You'll see Mark Reiner?'

Yes, of course it was because she might see Mark; was he such a fool that he had to ask? But she smothered the anger and said, 'I keep trying to tell you how afraid I am of this trial, how terrified I am that there

won't be a life for me after, but you don't listen, do you? You don't
understand why I need to project my hopes beyond the next few weeks.
You can't imagine what a huge thing it is for me to dare to be hopeful,
because all you can think about is your jealousy of Mark.'

'Oh God, Ally,' he groaned, 'I'm sorry. You're right, I am being selfish
about this, but only because I'm so afraid of losing you.'

'But you only think about me leaving you for Mark!' she cried. 'Me
being locked away in prison for something I didn't do is more acceptable than me leaving you for another man . . .'

'No! No, you've got it wrong. I do understand what you're going
through. But Shelley's going to be found guilty, you know that, so . . .'

'No! I don't know that and nor do you. But let's drop this now, shall
we, because I just can't keep going through it.'

Much later that day, as they were lying side by side in the darkness of
their bedroom, he said, 'I love you.'

She braced herself and prayed that this wouldn't turn out to be the
lead-up to sex she feared it was, because right now she couldn't even
bear the thought of him touching her. But it seemed God wasn't listening to her prayers that night, because it did turn out that way, and not,
she thought, because Bob was particularly in the mood, but because it
enabled him to pretend that they really were pulling through all this.

But they weren't, not at all. She could see now that their life together
had rescued him from the destructive side of his nature, because she
had given him a belief in himself. But it was time to put herself first and
she was going to begin tomorrow.

'Hello. Mark Reiner's office.'

Allyson's heart was thudding so hard that she almost put the phone
down. 'Hello, Corinne,' she heard herself say. 'It's Allyson Jaymes. Is
Mark there?'

'I'm afraid not,' Corinne answered. 'He's in Los Angeles until the end
of next week.'

Disappointment seared through her.

'Can Clive Dansing help?' Corinne suggested. 'I can put you through.
I'll tell him you're on the line.'

Of course she should speak to Clive, who had recently taken over from
Stella. But it was Mark she so desperately wanted to speak to. The trial
was only two weeks away now, and . . .

Clive Dansing's voice came brusquely down the line. 'Allyson. How
are you? I've been waiting for your call.'

Startled, Allyson said, 'Clive, uh . . . I'm fine. How are you?' She'd met him before, a couple of years ago, at the MIP TV Festival in Cannes. He'd been the head of a rival TV station then. 'My leave of absence expires in a couple of weeks,' she said.

'Which is why I've been waiting for your call,' he said. 'Let's meet to discuss what you're going to do. How's your diary looking for next week? I can make Wednesday at four or Thursday at ten thirty.'

She opted for Thursday, because it was the last thing he said and Bob was walking in the door so she wanted to get off the line.

'Who was that?' he said, coming into the kitchen.

'No one. Wrong number.'

He looked at her with reproachful eyes. 'You were talking to him, weren't you?' he said.

God, this was so hard, living in the same house as someone who already belonged to the past. 'No,' she answered.

He seemed to take no comfort from that, probably because he knew that it was only a matter of time before she would contact Mark.

For a long time they only stared into each other's eyes. Finally he was the first to speak. 'Tell me the truth, Allyson,' he said, 'do you know where that clock is?'

The question was so unexpected that for a moment she was sure she hadn't heard right. Then suddenly she began to shake with fury.

'I'm sorry,' he said. 'I had to ask. And if you do, then I want you to know that I'll stand by you—'

'Stop!' she seethed. 'Before another word comes out of your mouth.'

'Allyson, I'm just trying to say—'

'I know what you're saying,' she yelled. 'You're saying that you think I might have done it. *Oh Christ!* Tell me this isn't happening!'

'I'm sorry,' he cried. 'I didn't mean it to come out that way. I was just trying to show you how much I love you, and I chose a really stupid way of doing it . . . Allyson, you've got to forgive me, please—'

The telephone cut him off, and snatching up her keys she wrenched open the front door and slammed it behind her. The clock! The bloody clock! She wished she'd never set eyes on it.

Shelley was looking at her lawyers, listening to every word they uttered, memorising every twist and turn that was ultimately going to provide her path to freedom. There was less than a week to go now, and the madness of her not-guilty gamble was eating away at her, crushing her belief in herself. At the beginning her lawyers had tried to persuade her to enter a plea of diminished responsibility, in the hope of reducing the murder charge to manslaughter. But perversely they seemed more confident now than they had at the outset, were willing to believe they did have a case they could win. After all, no trace of Tessa's DNA had been found in Shelley's apartment, unlike in Allyson's, and the clothes Shelley had worn to the office that day had been retrieved from the cleaners and whisked off to the lab, but they'd failed to produce any damning evidence. Allyson's clothes hadn't yielded up any incriminating results either, so everything still hinged on what had been in the package Shelley had given Allyson that night at the restaurant.

'Such a shame you didn't let her open it right then,' Ed, her solicitor, remarked. 'Someone would have been sure to spot it. Still, you didn't,' he said, noticing the barrister's reproachful look. 'It would just be very helpful if that clock could materialise before the trial began.'

'I think we can feel confident it won't,' the barrister responded. 'So let's go over the witness statements again and make sure all inconsistencies are noted.'

It was a long and painful process as she read what people had said about her. Worst of all was going over Mark Reiner's version of their brief affair, and discovering how little she had meant to him. Of course he didn't phrase it that way, in fact he blamed himself for handling the situation so badly. But his chivalry made her feel even more humiliated and foolish. How very alone she felt now with no one to support her, no one to care whether she was found guilty or not. Even her mother had disowned her.

So maybe, she thought, it would be better for her to stay here, condemned to a world where there were no men; at least then she wouldn't have to suffer any more of this pain. But just a single thought of Allyson brought her indomitable spirit back to its fighting best, for nothing in the world was going to induce her to let Allyson walk away from this without, at the very least, being made to face the hell of the trial.

'Ah! Allyson!' Melissa cried, jumping up. 'Have you been there long?'

'Just walked in.' Allyson smiled at the girl who used to be Stella Cornbright's assistant and was now Clive Dansing's. 'How are you?'

'Frenzied. Clive is . . .'

'Right here.'

Allyson turned round. Clive Dansing was walking towards her. 'Hello, Allyson,' he said, holding out his hand. 'It's good to see you again.'

His smile was friendly enough, his handshake was firm, almost warm.

'Would you like to go in?' he said, indicating his office. 'I've just got a couple of things to sort out here.'

Allyson went in and sat down on one of the guest chairs. She'd just come from an interview with Detectives Lister and Maine, so it wasn't really surprising that she was feeling drained. But it was OK, everything seemed to be in order, they'd said.

The trial was set to start next Monday at ten, but right now the thing that was causing her the most concern was how her sudden split from Bob was going to be perceived, virtually on the eve of the trial.

Obviously all manner of suspicions and assumptions were going to be drawn from it once it became public, but she'd finally realised that she could not pretend that she and Bob were a loving couple any longer.

But she had to put all that out of her mind now and run through a final rehearsal of everything she was going to say to Clive.

'I'm sorry,' Clive said, coming in but not closing the door. 'Mark should have been here by now. Must have got caught up in traffic.'

Allyson couldn't move. Her heart was thumping wildly. Oh God, she wasn't ready for this. She'd had no idea . . .

'Perhaps we should start,' Clive was saying. 'I know there are certain things Mark wants . . . Ah! Here he is.'

Allyson turned round, knowing that all her apprehension was there to be seen.

'Hello,' he said. His eyes were on hers.

'Hello.' Her voice was throaty and faint.

'I wanted to be here when you came back,' he said.

'You could have warned me,' she said, attempting a smile.

His eyes darkened with the irony she loved, then he turned to Clive. 'I think the programming can wait,' he said.

'Of course,' Clive responded. Then to Allyson, 'If you'll excuse me.'

The door closed behind him. Mark said, 'So how are you?'

'OK. I think.' She laughed. 'You've really thrown me.'

'Am I allowed to ask how things are working out with Bob?'

Shaking her head she said, 'They're not.' She longed to tell him why, but wasn't sure she dared.

He nodded.

She looked into his face. His eyes were still on hers, and she could feel their intensity reaching into her. She wanted to touch him so badly.

As though reading her mind he took a step towards her, and then she was there, in his arms, holding him tightly as he kissed her with such tenderness and passion that she could feel the love searing through her.

'We'll just get this trial out of the way,' he said, when finally they were able to speak steadily again, 'then we'll go back to Italy and take some time for ourselves.'

'Yes, Italy,' she said. 'Let's go back to Italy.'

Chapter Eighteen

THE PRESS WAS WAITING at the entrance to the court; she could hear them from the back of the prison van. And she was swamped by shame that she, Shelley Bronson, wasn't permitted to walk free and enter the court with everyone else.

Just before ten thirty the guards took her upstairs to the court. Her lawyers were already there. As she was led in, a terrible silence fell over the room. She kept her eyes straight ahead and walked steadily, rigidly to the dock. It was horrible. She wanted to scream, or run.

She inhaled deeply.

The room was crowded with people, so many it was as though she were suffocating in their macabre fascination. But she didn't look back. She was alone in a room full of strangers. And those twelve empty places over there were going to be filled by more strangers, who would decide whether she should regain her freedom or return to living hell.

'All rise.'

The judge entered and the indictment was read.

'Shelley Bronson, you are charged upon an indictment containing one count, that of murder. In that, you, on the 14th day of March, did murder Tessa Jane Dukes. How say you? Guilty or not guilty?'

'Not guilty.' Her voice was an echo in her ears. She was shaking hard, her legs were barely able to support her.

The jury was sworn in. The prosecution counsel outlined the case, then the first witnesses were called. They were police officers, whose testimony took up most of the day. Shelley had always known that DC Lister had no doubts as to who had done it, but hearing the story told Lister's way was scaring her to death. Until now she had dared to believe that this nightmare would end, that she would be given a chance to pick up her life. By the end of the day she hardly believed it at all.

Before they took her back to the prison she was allowed to speak to her lawyers. To her amazement they seemed in good spirits. 'All that testimony,' one of them explained, 'and they've still failed to come up with any kind of evidence that connects you to the crime.'

Shelley looked at her solicitor, Ed. He nodded and smiled.

'But all that about me leaving the office and going home to shower and get rid of the bloodstained clothes, when all the time I was stuck in traffic,' she said.

'Hypothetical. They've got no proof. Everyone knows there was a monumental jam that night, thanks to a bomb scare, and it's not up to you to prove you were in it, it's up to them to prove you weren't. So far they haven't managed to do that.'

'And the car? God, that all sounded so much worse than I'd expected. I wish to God I'd told them straight away.'

'Don't lose any sleep over that,' the leading counsel told her. 'The owner of the car-hire company is going to testify that you generally rent from him when your car is in for service. And that you generally give the rental back already cleaned.'

Shelley covered her face with her hands. What she wouldn't give to be able to go home to her own bed. 'Was Allyson there today?' she asked.

Ed nodded.

'You're going to ask her what she did with the clock, aren't you?' she said, turning to counsel.

'What do you think she did with the clock?' he asked.

Shelley's eyes were burning.

Allyson wasn't called until the afternoon of the third day. By then both Bob and Mark had been in the witness box, and the tabloid press was going crazy. That she and Mark were arriving and leaving together had been noticed, so the second breakdown of her marriage was being crudely splashed over the inside pages, while the trial retained its hold on the headlines. Pictures of Shelley graced every newsstand; mounting belief in her guilt loaded every story.

Despite everything, Allyson's heart went out to her. She could imagine what it must be like to be in Shelley's shoes, though she hoped she would never find out.

When her name was eventually called it was as though everything inside her drained away. Her mouth turned dry. Her legs became weak. Mark was beside her, his hand on hers, filling her with his strength. Thanks to his own testimony the world now saw him as the great seducer of his employees. He claimed not to care, that all that mattered was that she got through this so they could get on with their lives.

Bob was nearby. As she stood up and walked towards the courtroom she could feel him watching her, could feel his pain and bewilderment.

An usher was holding the door open for her. It took only seconds for her eyes to find Shelley's and when they did Allyson felt the room start to spin. It was as though Shelley's hatred was streaming into her like a paralysing venom, and her instinct for survival took a stultifying blow as she realised how determined Shelley was to see her pay for this crime. But she wasn't going to let Shelley win, because they both knew the truth of that night, and they both knew who had killed Tessa Dukes.

Allyson took the oath and answered the questions quietly, firmly and always succinctly. Yes, she had been looking after her father that night. No, she hadn't left the house. No, her father was in no mental state to understand whether she was there or not. No, she hadn't gone to the accused's apartment. No, she hadn't taken a bronze figurine from the apartment. No, she did not return to the office after she'd left at around five thirty. Yes, she did know that the deceased would be working late, because she had instructed her to.

They wanted to know if it was easy to get a taxi around where her parents lived. Generally it was. She knew what they were driving at: neither her car, nor her parents' car had yielded up any evidence, so perhaps she had taken a taxi back to the office that night. If she had, they had been unable to find a driver to confirm it. The question of how she might have returned, covered in blood, wasn't addressed.

They moved on.

Yes, she had met the accused for dinner at around nine fifteen, when the accused had given her a gift. She hadn't opened it until later, because the accused had asked her not to. No, the gift was not a Lalique clock. Yes, it was the murder weapon, wrapped up in one of her own make-up gowns. No, she had no idea where that clock was now.

And was it her belief that the accused had tried to frame her for the murder of Tessa Dukes?

Objection!

So many objections. Some accepted, plenty denied. They journeyed through her husband's betrayal with her assistant, Tessa Dukes, and with her best friend, Shelley Bronson. They made much of the loss of her senior position on the programme, the downsizing of her public profile. Yes, she had felt humiliated. Yes, she had hated Tessa. Yes, she had threatened to kill her.

Yes to everything.

She had known about Mark Reiner's affair with Shelley. She'd also known that Mr Reiner had been in Tessa Dukes's hotel room while they were all in Italy. No, she didn't believe they'd had sex. Was she afraid of losing Mr Reiner to Tessa, the way she had lost her husband? Had she hatched a plan to kill Tessa Dukes and make it look as though Shelley had done it? With Tessa dead and Shelley in prison, history would be prevented from repeating itself.

Allyson was breathless. The faces in the courtroom were swirling around her. Her skin was on fire.

In the end it all amounted to motive, means and opportunity. She had them all.

She had to be guilty.

It was time for Shelley to enter the witness box. She'd hardly slept last night. Not even the convincing ring of Allyson's guilt, nor the murmurs of doubt that were finally being voiced in the press, had been enough to stop the trample of panic inside her head. She wouldn't get a second chance at this. She had to do everything she could to persuade the jury that though she might have had the means and opportunity, she simply had no reason to kill Tessa Dukes.

There seemed to be even more people in court today. Shelley was wearing a beautiful navy silk suit with a rose-pink shirt. Her demeanour was composed, her dignity was quiet and modest. She knew that many were still disturbed by the shock that they might have judged her wrongly, that their beloved Allyson was really a monster who had killed an innocent girl.

There was no other sound in the room as she took the oath. Inside her was an emptiness that kept flooding with fear and foreboding.

'What time did you leave the office on the night in question?'

'A few minutes before eight.'

'Was anyone else there?'

'As far as I knew only Tessa and Will, the editor.'

So many detailed questions. About what she was wearing. The car she was driving. At what point she hit the traffic jam. Where she was when Allyson called to say she'd be late. Did she have a gift for Allyson? Yes. Why? Because relations had been strained between them lately, and she wanted to do something to repair them.

'Why were relations strained?'

'Because of my affair with Allyson's husband. And then hers with Mark Reiner.'

'So you were jealous of her affair with Mr Reiner?'

'Yes.'

'What was the gift you were hoping would restore the friendship between you and Mrs Jaymes?'

'A Lalique clock. Allyson had always loved it.'

The lawyer turned away for a moment to speak to junior counsel. Shelley's eyes moved across the courtroom until she was looking at Allyson. Her face was pale, but her eyes didn't falter from Shelley's.

Suddenly Shelley felt a hot, uncontrollable rage well up inside her and before she could stop herself she was shouting, 'Ask her where the clock is now. Ask her! She knows where it is!'

The judge was calling for order. His reprimand was short and harsh. Her lawyer's eyes showed his dismay.

The questions kept on coming.

Had she really been in that traffic jam? Wasn't the truth that after she had brutally killed Tessa Dukes, while wearing Allyson Jaymes's make-up gown, she had driven back to her home in Kensington? The record showed that the roads between Fulham and Kensington were unaffected by the traffic jam, so she would have had plenty of time to drive home, clean herself up, and the car, make a parcel out of the murder weapon, and drive over to the restaurant to meet Mrs Jaymes.

'Why did you suggest that Mrs Jaymes should wait until later to open the gift?'

'It had been an emotional day and she seemed agitated about some-thing, so I thought it might be better to wait.'

'When the call came to tell you Tessa had been murdered, why did you suggest you return to the office in Mrs Jaymes's car?'

'Because she was parked the closest.'

'Not because you didn't want her to see that you had a hire car?'

'I thought we should get there as quickly as possible, and I'd had to park several streets away.'

'Going back to the gift. A Lalique clock, you say. How much would such a clock be worth? Roughly.'

'Somewhere around twenty thousand pounds.'

There was an audible gasp, followed by murmurs that were silenced by the judge.

'A very generous gift. And where, Ms Bronson, is the clock now?'

Shelley's eyes returned to Allyson. The tension between them cut through the room like blades of light. 'I don't know,' Shelley answered.

It wasn't over yet. Her innocence, like Allyson's, was far from estab-lished. The means and opportunity were still as easily hers as Allyson's. But what about the motive? Didn't that start with her self-confessed affair with Bob Jaymes? Wasn't it the truth that she had been trying to break up his marriage for years?

'How did you feel when you discovered that Mr Jaymes was sleeping with his wife's assistant?'

'Upset for Allyson.'

'Who contacted the press to expose the affair?'

'I did.'

'Why?'

'Because I thought Allyson should find out what kind of man she was married to.'

'You could simply have told her that. Was it not because you wanted to punish Mr Jaymes?'

'Possibly.'

'And you wanted to punish him because he'd broken off his affair with you?'

'No.'

The lawyer allowed his scepticism to hang in the air, before moving on to her relationship with Mark Reiner. She'd already heard Mark testify to the power and immediacy of their attraction, and she said nothing to contradict it. Nor did she deny that she was jealous when she found out that Mark had transferred his affections to Allyson. It was all true, but none of it made her a killer.

'How did you feel when you realised that Mr Reiner was in Tessa Dukes's hotel room?'

'Upset, for Allyson.'

'Like you were when you found out about her husband's affair with Tessa? When you alerted the press?'

Her face turned hot. 'I suppose so.'

'So what did you do this time?'

'I told Allyson myself.'

'And how did she react?'

'She was extremely upset. She said that she wished to God the girl had never come into her life.'

The lunch recess was over. Shelley was back on the stand. She was feeling light-headed, as though she had been there for days, maybe weeks.

'Did you harbour a hope that Mr Reiner might, at some point, rediscover his attraction to you?'

'No. I knew he wouldn't. It was obvious that he was in love with Allyson.'

'But if Allyson were no longer in the picture?'

'Objection!'

'So this was the second time you'd been passed over for Mrs Jaymes? First was when Mr Jaymes refused to leave her for you. Then, when Mr Reiner dropped you for her?'

Shelley didn't answer.

'Let's go to the clothes you were wearing on the day of the murder. Are they the same clothes as those collected from the cleaners two days later, by the police?'

'Yes.'

'How many black trouser suits do you own, Ms Bronson?'

The air was suddenly trapped in her lungs. 'Three,' she said.

'So you could have substituted the suit that became stained . . .'

'Objection!'

The point had been made. Counsel paused for a moment, spoke to his colleague then turned back to Shelley. 'Was it your impression that Mr Reiner was engaged in a sexual encounter with Tessa Dukes on the night you happened upon them in Italy?'

'Yes, it was.'

'And why, exactly, were you there at the door?'

It was pointless to lie, for the friend she'd told Allyson she had visited had testified that it wasn't true. She said, 'I hoped to talk to Mr Reiner.'

'About what?'

'The programme.' It didn't even sound true!

'At two in the morning?'

'Yes.'

'I suggest to you, Ms Bronson, that you were there in the hope of rekindling your affair with Mr Reiner. And that when you found Mr Reiner in Tessa Dukes's room, giving comfort to a girl who was in an inebriated and distressed state, you decided to twist what you'd seen and use it to try to break up Mr Reiner and Mrs Jaymes. But even if you'd succeeded in that there was still Tessa to contend with, wasn't there? Because if that was a sexual encounter you had happened upon, it could be that Mr Reiner would abandon Mrs Jaymes in favour of Tessa instead of you. And you couldn't let that happen, could you? Not again.'

It was as though the ground were shifting beneath her. Questions. Distortions. Allusions. A stampede of fear. A pit of despair. She was no longer reaching the jury. Now they saw her only as a rejected, bitter woman. The woman who'd twice tried to steal her best friend's man. Who twice had failed because of a teenage girl. Didn't she have a history of failures with men? What about her jealousy of Allyson? How many years had that resentment been building? And what about Tessa? Was it Tessa's youth and freshness that had poisoned Shelley against her? How hard was it for her, a forty-two-year-old woman, to watch Bob Jaymes, whom she'd pursued for years, becoming besotted with a nineteen-year-old girl? Had she felt used up? Discarded? She'd certainly felt bitter. Why else would she have gone to the press? What had she cared about on the night of the murder? Certainly not Tessa Dukes. Nor Allyson

Jaymes. All she'd cared about then was talking Allyson out of opening a gift in the restaurant, and then making sure they used Allyson's car to return to the office once it was known Tessa had been murdered. And what was the last thing Shelley said to Allyson as they'd left the restaurant that night? 'Don't forget your gift.' Certainly she'd be concerned if it contained such a valuable clock. But wouldn't she have been equally concerned if it contained the evidence that was going to remove Allyson from Mr Reiner's life as effectively as she, herself, had already removed Tessa? There was only Shelley's word that there was a clock in that box. And no one seemed to know where that clock was now.

'Or maybe, Ms Bronson, you do know where it is.'

'No, I . . .' She stopped as panic welled in her chest.

'Yes, Ms Bronson?'

Her eyes fell away and she shook her head. 'I don't know where it is,' she said, but her voice didn't have the conviction it needed to persuade anyone she was telling the truth.

Nor, when all her lies were summarised, was there a single benign face remaining among the twelve who were watching her so closely.

In the rooms beneath the court Shelley broke down and cried. Hope had gone now, all that was left was despair, swallowing her up and suffocating her with fear. She would grow old and ugly in that dark cold place that smelt of raw vegetables and unwashed skin.

Ed tried to comfort her by reminding her that the picture of Allyson's guilt was every bit as strong, if not stronger. But his words didn't help her to sleep that night, nor did her knowledge of the truth.

Total silence accompanied the jurors' return to the court. After two days of deliberation a verdict had now been reached. Shelley was unable to look at them. She kept her eyes lowered and her prayers intense.

A clerk of the court was speaking, asking the jury if they had reached a verdict.

The foreman of the jury stood. A small woman in her fifties. 'We have.'

Shelley stopped breathing.

'Members of the jury, on the count of murder, do you find the defendant guilty or not guilty?'

'Guilty.'

Shelley's eyes opened. She was starting to shake. Convulsions were rushing through her. She could hear herself screaming, feel them struggling to hold her down. Panic and denial drove through her. *No! No! No!*

The judge was calling for order.

Mitigation began. But what difference did it make now? They'd found her guilty. Shelley Bronson, the producer, was now Shelley Bronson, a convicted killer. *Oh God, don't let this be true!*

Someone was holding her. The judge was ready to pass sentence.

Now he was speaking, but she seemed not to be hearing. Some words broke through. '. . . I sentence you to life imprisonment . . . Recommendation to serve a minimum of fifteen years . . .'

Life! Oh my God! Oh my God!

There was a commotion near the back. Allyson had collapsed. Everyone watched as she was carried from the court. Shelley watched too. The reporters were rushing to get out, desperate to be first with the news. No one bothered to watch as she was taken from the court.

And only she remembered the clock.

Chapter Nineteen

ALLYSON TILTED BACK HER HEAD and felt the sun burn hotly on her face. The air, the sea, the sky were so dazzlingly bright it was as though it were all brand-new. She could see for miles. Orange and lemon groves cascaded down the hillsides, silent waves broke over the shore below. She inhaled deeply, as though she could take the beauty inside her and hold it there. It might act as a balm on all the ugliness and fear that had blighted the past few months.

She looked down at the courtyard below where a fountain of lions' heads spurted water into the glistening trough, and smart cane furniture was spread out between towering ferns and palms. The hotel was still in its first season, but already word had spread. It was *the* place to stay.

Allyson and Mark had arrived two days ago. Stepping off the plane into the welcoming warmth of the Italian sunshine had felt like stepping into another world. It was what she had needed, because although the nightmare of the trial was over, the wounds, the fear, had left scars that were going to take a long time to heal.

But mercifully there were moments when she was able to forget.

Now was one of those moments, for she was smiling as she watched the car winding its way up the hill. Mark had been to Naples for a meeting, he'd said, though she hadn't believed him, because today was her fortieth birthday and she had gone along with the charade because she knew he was planning a surprise.

The car disappeared as it headed round to the church piazza. Eager to see him, she ran down to the reception. She arrived just as he was coming in through the door. There were others around, talking quietly, browsing through guidebooks out in the courtyard, but Allyson didn't care who saw her embrace him and it seemed he didn't care either.

'Hi,' he murmured, holding her close and smiling down into her eyes. 'I get the feeling you missed me.'

She laughed. 'How did it go?'

'OK. The deal's all but done. But now, there's somewhere I want to take you. Are you free?'

It turned out not to be far, just along the dusty lane and back into church piazza.

The church door was open. Inside was cool and shady, with a damp, earthy smell. Rays of sunlight streaked through the windows and across the magnificent Byzantine pulpit. Holding her hand he led her up the centre aisle, towards the lifesized crucifix suspended above the altar. When they stopped she looked up at the face of Christ.

'Don't you think it's beautiful here?' he said.

She was still looking at Christ. 'Yes,' she said, smiling.

'I'd like to marry you here,' he said.

Her heart suddenly swelled, and her eyes were disbelieving as she turned them to him.

'When you're ready. When it's possible,' he added.

'I love you,' she whispered. 'And if there's a question in there, the answer's yes.'

His eyes were full of irony, as, pulling a small box from his pocket, he took out a large, oval-shaped diamond ring and lifted her left hand.

She watched as he slid the ring onto her third finger, and felt an unbearable happiness filling her heart. Then she raised her eyes back to his as he said, 'Happy birthday.'

A while later they walked slowly back down the aisle, arm in arm. At the door she turned back for a moment to look again at the striking image of Christ. 'Thank you,' she said softly.

When they got back to the hotel the concierge called them over. 'Señor Reiner,' he said. 'I forget this parcel arrive for you. It come a long time ago. It say to wait for your arrival.'

Mark picked it up curiously and looked it over. Then, grinning, he turned to Allyson. 'What is it?' he said.

She frowned.

'It says here that you sent it.'

She looked at the sender's name. *Her name!*

He put the parcel on the desk and began tearing off the wrapping paper. But though she couldn't yet see it she already knew what it was. The walls were closing in, her heart had stopped beating.

Her name on the parcel. She was the sender.

He turned to face her, deathly pale and uncomprehending. In his hands was the exquisite Night and Day clock by Lalique.

Allyson's eyes were huge as she looked at him. The drumming in her ears was starting to fade, the nausea in her stomach was receding. She could sense his resistance to what this must mean, and wanted desperately to go to him. 'I didn't send it,' she said. She needed air. She needed desperately to be able to think. 'Look at the date. When was it sent?'

He looked at the date. 'March the 16th.'

Two days after Tessa was killed. Shelley was in custody then.

His eyes were on her again. Not yet accusing, only questioning.

'If she posted the clock late on the 15th,' Allyson said, 'it would have been postmarked the 16th.'

He was still staring at her.

'Darling, listen,' she said, struggling to remain calm. 'Just ask yourself, why would I send it to you? Why would I even keep it, if what you're thinking was true?'

She could see he wanted to believe her.

'Darling, don't you understand what she's doing? She sent the clock to you knowing you would react this way. Oh God, Mark! Don't let her do this. Please, don't let her do it.'

After an interminable, unbearable time he put the clock back on the desk. Then turning to her he pulled her into his arms and held her. 'It's all right,' he said. 'It's all right.'

She clung to him and felt the air returning to her lungs. He believed her. *Oh thank God, thank God.*

'What shall we do with it?' she said, looking at the clock.

'I guess we have to tell the police it's turned up.'

She looked up at him again, uncertainty still darkening her eyes. 'You really scared me,' she told him. 'I thought . . . I thought maybe she was going to win.'

He smiled. 'It scared me too,' he confessed. Then, turning her to the door, he said, 'Come on, let's get a drink. I think we both need one.'

'Do you think it's all over now?' she said, after he'd asked the concierge to lock the clock in the safe.

'I certainly hope so,' he answered.

A smartly dressed woman, who'd arrived the day before, was coming up the steps towards them, and broke into a smile as she saw Allyson. 'Oh, my dear,' she gushed, 'I just wanted to tell you how much I used to love your programme, and how sorry I am for all that you've been through. I never believed, even for a minute, that you could have done such a terrible thing, but it must have been a very difficult time for you.' She glanced approvingly at Mark. 'I'm so glad it's working out for you now.'

Allyson smiled. 'Thank you,' she said.

The woman moved on, flushed with the pleasure of having spoken to Allyson Jaymes.

Mark's eyes were teasing as he left her to go to the bar.

Laughing, Allyson wandered out to the terrace to watch the sunset. It was incredible, she was thinking, the power of fame. Would she ever have had such support without it? Everyone felt as though they knew her, like a sister, a daughter, a mother, who had known pain and betrayal, who needed to be shown the same compassion she'd always shown to others. It wasn't possible for her to be a killer, not only because there had been no evidence to say she was, but because they just couldn't believe it of someone they knew to have such a kind heart.

Yes, it really was incredible, because despite the investigation, despite the trial, the fact still remained: she could have done it . . .

SUSAN LEWIS

Strangely enough, it was a youthful ambition to become a TV producer that launched Susan Lewis on her successful career as a writer. After leaving school, she worked in television until somebody told her that, if she really wanted to become a producer, she should hone her writing skills.

'So off I went and wrote myself straight out of TV!' she comments wrily, although she admits that she had always had a strange feeling at the back of her mind that writing might one day take over her life. Looking back on her decision to concentrate on writing, she believes that events in her personal life also played a large part in it. Around that time she was working through a broken love affair and needed to fill her days with something that would take her completely out of herself. 'Probably there is some autobiographical material in my first book, *A Class Apart*, though it certainly wasn't intentional. In fact, I believe it's impossible for a writer not to exist somewhere in her characters. But of course people I meet often inspire me greatly, either with personality or look. For instance, the divinely beautiful Shelley in *Cruel Venus* was inspired by the look, rather than the personality of someone I know.'

These days, after fifteen years of writing and an amazing twelve novels, Susan's life is every bit as glamorous as those of the people she writes about. 'Yes, my life can occasionally be like one of my heroines—though thankfully not the screwy ones who go through such pain and tragedy,' she jokes. Most of her year is spent in Los Angeles where she lives with her two dogs Casanova and Floozie, but she also has a home in London. She remains single and says that there haven't been many occasions when she has been tempted to give that up. However, there is a man in her life who, she says, is pretty wonderful and fun and likes being single too.

When she is in the middle of writing a book, Susan is incredibly dedicated and hard-working, rarely socialising or even breaking for weekends, but generally she only works between October and May, taking the summers off to recharge and get back in touch with life.

'Before moving to Los Angeles, I lived for four years on the French Riviera, so I often spend time there during the summer, relaxing with good friends, great gossip and too much wine!' Susan says. She likes to travel, too, mainly as research for her books. 'I have had many wonderful adventures, sailed some beautiful seas and met some fascinating people, many of whom remain friends.' Among the places she's visited most recently are Bogotá, Rio de Janeiro and Zanzibar, so it seems likely that we can look forward to some colourful reading from Susan Lewis in the near future.

Christine Craig

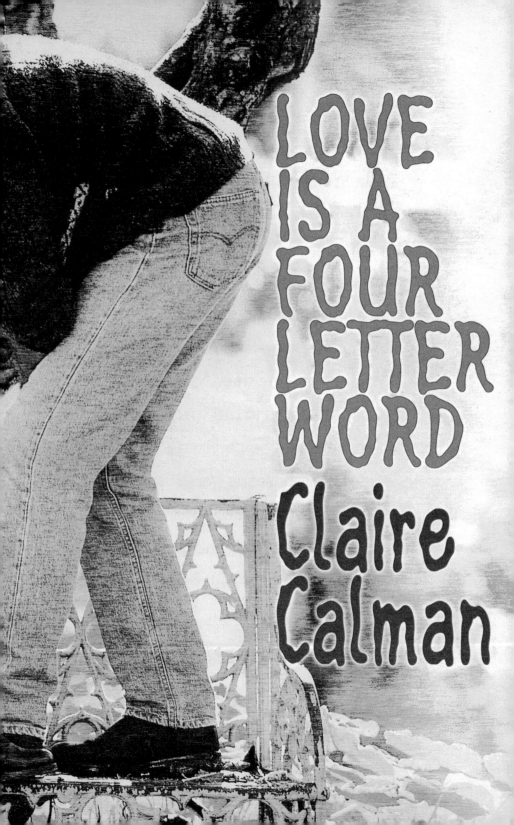

LOVE IS A FOUR LETTER WORD

Claire Calman

Bella Kreuzer has compartmentalised
her life into two sections—Before and
After Patrick. For Bella the second section
has been far harder to live with, but she
has finally moved out of the city and
bought a new house in the country.
But her new home needs so much work
that Bella decides to tackle the garden
first and calls in the services of a local
expert. As landscape gardener Will
Henderson prunes, weeds and plants he
tries to restore not only the garden to its
former splendour, but Bella too.

Prologue

SHE SEES HERSELF fall in slow motion, the toe of her shoe catching on the edge of the paving-stone, her arm reaching out in front of her, her hand a pale shape like a leaf against a dark sky. The pavement swims towards her, its cracks the streets of a city seen from a skyscraper, the texture of the concrete slabs suddenly sharply in focus.

It is not a bad fall: a swelling on her left knee destined to become an outsize bramble-stain bruise, a stinging graze on the heel of her hand, a buggered pair of decent tights. Back at home, Bella balances half a bag of frozen broad beans on the knee and sips at a glass of Shiraz. She tells herself it is not a bad fall, but when she wakes the next morning it is as if a switch has been thrown, draining off all her energy in the night. She leans against the kitchen worktop to drink her coffee, not daring to sit down because she knows she will never get up again.

Overnight, London seems to have become a grotesque parody of a metropolis, no longer bustling and stimulating but loud and abrasive. Litter flies up from the gutters. Grit pricks her eyes. She feels fragile, a rabbit caught in the target-beam of headlights. Buses loom out of nowhere, bearing down on her. Cyclists swerve to avoid her, bellowing abuse. She tenses each muscle in her body when she crosses the road, imagines she can hear the thud-thudding of her heart. When someone bumps into her in the street, she thinks she will splinter into tiny fragments.

Her doctor is unsympathetic, sighing through his nostrils as she

357

answers his questions. Months of overworking, he says. Prolonged stress. What else did she expect? Did she want to have a serious collapse? If so, she was certainly going the right way about it. No tablets, he says, no prescription. Time off. Rest. Rethink your life. That's it? she asks. That's it.

Her boss is unsurprised.

'You're no use to me half-dead,' he says. 'Sod off to the Caribbean for a month and drink Mai-Tais till dawn.'

The Caribbean? She is so exhausted she'd be lucky to make it down the road to the travel agent. Perhaps they could administer her Mai-Tais via a drip.

Visiting her good friends Viv and Nick in the Kentish city where they now live, she wanders at convalescent pace through the web of narrow streets, past lopsided houses and ancient flint walls. She focuses on one task at a time, as if she were a stroke victim learning afresh each skill she had previously taken for granted. Then, meandering down a quiet side street near the river, she sees the For Sale board.

Compared with the London flat she had rented with Patrick, this is a delight. Sunny. Spacious. With a proper garden rather than a sad, overshadowed strip of concrete. Yes, says Viv, a fresh start is just what Bella needs. Plenty of companies would jump at the chance to have someone with her experience.

She seems to enter a trance then, dealing with the solicitor, the building society. Writing job applications. Forms become a welcome distraction, tangible things to focus on—things she can solve. You take a pen, fill in the spaces in neat block capitals. The questions are straightforward: Name. Address. Bank Details. Current Salary. You do it all properly and you get the result you were aiming for. It feels like magic.

She moves smoothly through the weeks on automatic pilot, gliding through her notice period at work, her smile efficiently in place, her projects on schedule. Now that she knows she is leaving, she cuts down on her hours, and fills her evening with paperwork and planning, relishing each hitch and setback—the vendor's pedantry about the garden shed, the surveyor's discovery of damp—as something she can get her teeth into.

She transfers her accounts, her doctor, her dentist, sends out exquisitely designed change-of-address cards. This is easy: making phone calls, folding A4 letters into three and sliding them into envelopes, measuring for curtains. And it fills her head.

NOW THAT SHE WAS HERE, this didn't seem like quite such a brilliant idea. Around her, on all sides stretched a cubist landscape of cardboard boxes. The removal men had thoughtfully set them down in such a way as to make traversing the room an epic expedition, necessitating the use of ropes, crampons and teams of huskies. And the heating had decided not to work. Of course. No doubt the vendor had extracted some vital organ from the boiler the moment they had exchanged contracts. He had taken the art of pettiness to new heights, arguing over every fitting and fixture, frequently phoning Bella, his manner swinging between smarmy and covertly aggressive. He was sure she would like to buy his wrought-iron wall lights; they were practically new. No, she said, she wouldn't. The built-in shelves? She had assumed they were, well, built-in. What about the stair carpet? It still had plenty of wear in it, he insisted. 'Mmm,' she agreed noncommittally, deciding its durability was a disadvantage unless you wanted to design your decor around a theme of khaki ripple. He was obviously attached to it, she pointed out, clearly he must take it with him.

Now, sitting on the stairs, trying not to catch her jeans on the exposed gripper strip, she stretched out one foot to flip open the lid of the nearest box. Loo brush, bubble-wrapped mirror, squeaky rubber crocodile. Oh-oh. She checked the label on the side: BTH. Marvellous. That was supposed to be upstairs. Something else to add to The List: lugging downstairs boxes upstairs and upstairs boxes downstairs.

Her gaze fell on the puckered and peeling paintwork above the skirting board. The only house in the street with psoriasis. The damp. That ought to be top of the list—certainly above getting the sash cords fixed or Polyfillaing the crack in the studio or painting a mural on the end wall of the garden or . . . In her mind, The List stretched out before her.

There was a banging on the front door.

'Why didn't you use the bell, you old bag?'

'I did. It obviously doesn't work, slag-face.' Viv gave Bella a hug and pushed a gold cardboard box into her hands.

'Just what I need. A cardboard box. I was running dangerously low on them. How on earth did you guess?'

'It's cakes. Emergency rations. My God—are all the rooms as full as this?' Viv waggled her head in disbelief, sending her precariously pinned carroty hair lurching from side to side.

'I seem to have more stuff than I thought.' Bella shrugged.

'What's in them all?'

'I don't know. Books. Paints. Kitchen things. Families of refugees. You know, stuff. Make yourself useful, can't you? Help me look for the kettle. It's in a box marked KTCH, which stands for kitchen not kitsch before you make any smart-arse comments—it's probably in the BTH.'

That first night in her new home, Bella left a light on as she always did. She lay awake, looking at the slit of light under the bedroom door. I ought to be feeling excited, she told herself. New house. New job. New city. I mustn't be so negative. So what if I've only got one week to sort out the house before I start at Scotton Design? So the house needs a few things seeing to? That's why it was so reasonable. A counter voice cut in: As if you didn't have enough on your plate without turning your life upside-down. Now you'll be living in mouldy chaos for ever and you don't even know anyone here except for Viv and Nick and you can't expect to see them all the time. They've got each other. They don't need you.

As her eyelids drooped, she thought of Patrick. If he'd been here with her now, what would he be doing? Snoring, probably, she reminded herself sharply. He'd have liked the house, she decided, yawning and snuggling down under the duvet. That was the bugger about not having a chap around the place. He would have got the damp sorted. And the boxes. No, she thought, he wouldn't: Patrick would have stepped over the boxes, saying, 'We really must sort these out.' But at least he would have rubbed her cold feet to warm them up.

Right. Pens, briefcase. Shoes polished. Lipstick. Hair. Oh, bollocks. It wasn't supposed to do that. It made her look like a sheepdog that had been lolloping through the undergrowth. Perhaps her hair would be better pinned up? She scooped it up off her neck and made what she hoped was an elegant face in the mirror. Tremendous—now she resembled a coiffured poodle. She stood at the kitchen sink and drank a glass of water to settle her stomach. Good grief, this was worse than preparing for her first day at school. You're thirty-three for God's sake, she told herself. They're not going to pick on you or try to nick your pencil case.

It took her longer to find Scotton Design than she had expected. She stood still for a moment, trying to ignore the flutter of panic rising in her stomach. A passer-by sighed loudly as he detoured around her, impatient at yet another gawping tourist blocking the pavement. The tower of the cathedral loomed large to her left—ah-hah, cathedral on left, so—yes, past greasy chip shop and Waterstone's.

Renewing old London habits, she veered automatically into a café as she neared the office, to pick up a cappuccino and a Danish. Excess froth splurged out of the steam hole in the lid, sidling lava-like towards her fingers.

She was still licking her fingers as she entered the reception area to be greeted by her new boss.

'Bella! You're here! Great!' Seline checked her watch. 'New client meeting at two! But I'm out most of the morning so I'll have to brief you in two mins! OK!'

'Fine!' Bella lifted her voice, attempting to interject exclamation marks to match Seline's tone. Had she really been like this at her two interviews? 'Of course!' She looked around for somewhere to set down her cascading coffee.

'Gail! Do the honours, will you!'

'Here—let me take those.' Gail disentangled Bella from her cup, her coat, her briefcase. 'Pay no attention to Seline. She's just trying to impress 'cause you're t' swanky art director from t' big city. There's the loo, by the way—kitchen—coffee-maker—tea bags in there. Now come and meet the other inmates . . .'

'Sorry, sorry, sorry.' Viv swept into the tapas bar twenty minutes late. 'There was a complete *crisis* at work. The entire network crashed because some total arsehole plugged in a hair dryer and overloaded the electrics.' Viv loved a good crisis. They ordered a couple of beers, and debated over whether the *pinchos morunos* or the *pollo al ajillo* was a better bet.

'What do you think?' Viv indicated the waiter with her eyebrows. 'Bit tasty?'

Bella wrinkled her nose.

'You're *so* fussy. I thought you liked Latin men?'

'He's probably from Bromley,' Bella said. 'I know, I know. I'll never get anyone at this rate. You sound just like my mother.'

'Did I say that? Of course you'll find someone else. No need to panic—not for ages and ages. How are the parents anyway?' Viv said. 'Have they been to view the new Kreuzer estate yet?'

'Fending them off as long as possible. *Alessandra* asked after you, as always, last time we spoke.' Bella coloured her voice with theatrical timbre as she said her mother's name. 'I can just see her peering at the damp—"Oh is that a *deliberate* paint effect, Bella-darling?"'

'What you need,' said Viv, 'is an action plan. To meet men.'

Bella took a swig of her beer straight from the bottle. 'I'm not bothered. I like being on my own.'

'Liar.'

'I do. Why shouldn't I? Just because you've found Mr Perfect, you think anyone single must be some pathetic half-person. I hate all that couply stuff anyway.'

'Which stuff?'

'You know. All that having joint opinions about everything: "*We* think this and *we* do that . . ." Their personalities go all amoebaed into one like a matching pen and pencil set.'

'That's such crap. We're not like that.'

'See? *We're* not . . . ? Whatever happened to *I*?'

'Anyway.' Viv sighed and signalled to the waiter for another two beers. 'There's lots of good bits: love, companionship, sex for a start.'

'Sex? Ah, yes, I had some of that once . . .'

'So, have you not—' Viv nodded euphemistically, 'since—?'

'No. No one since Patrick.'

No one since Patrick. She could remember the last time. It was Christmas. Boxing Day. They'd just got back to the flat after a slow and drizzly drive home from visiting his parents in Norfolk.

The flat is cold and unwelcoming.

'I think I'll slope off to bed,' she says, half suppressing a yawn.

'Good idea. I'll come too.'

She undresses slowly, pulling off her things distractedly. Reaches for her big black T-shirt under her pillow, her fluffy bedsocks. Pads through to the bathroom to brush her teeth.

'You reading tonight?' asks Patrick.

Her Christmas books are still in a carrier bag in the hall. She shakes her head. A click as he switches off the light.

She feels his hand snake over her side, under her T-shirt, cupping her tummy from behind.

'You're nice and warm.'

She turns over to kiss him good night.

She feels his tongue push tentatively between her lips; starts to murmur that she's really too sleepy, it's been a long day. He strokes her hair, tells her he loves her, how soft her skin feels, how sexy she is.

Her body starts to respond automatically to his touch, his hand moving between her thighs; she feels herself growing wet, hears his low sigh as his fingers find her.

Boxing Day, the year before the one just gone. That's when it was.

They walked as far as the cathedral together before their routes took them separate ways. How stunning it was lit up at night—and not a tourist in sight to appreciate it. Bella walked across the bridge. The river glinted darkly below. A few boats bobbed gently, clunking woodenly against each other.

A young couple wove towards her, stopping every few feet to kiss, veering erratically in their path like drunken crabs; an older pair, in their fifties she guessed, passed by holding hands. When she was first with Patrick, she had usually felt glad at the sight of other couples laughing and kissing and canoodling. There seemed to be a secret bond between them all.

Now, it just made Bella depressed. God, how smug couples were. If she were ever stupid enough to be in a couple again—that sounded dreadful: *in a couple*, like *in* prison, *in* detention, *in* a mess—she would shun smugness. How can you be so ungenerous about other people's happiness? she reproached herself. She lengthened her stride and resolved to be more positive. Things were fine. Time for herself so she could concentrate on her house. She could slump about all weekend in slobby clothes. Go out with lots of different men. No need to keep tidying the towels because he couldn't grasp the concept of folding. No need to buy that ridiculous, expensive, three-fruit marmalade just because he liked it.

But I grew to like that marmalade too, she reminded herself. And I don't seem to be going out with lots of men, do I? That was true, she admitted. But she could if she wanted to; it was the principle that mattered.

Beneath the two words 'YOGHURT—IDEAS??' on her notepad, a sketch of Bella's new boss was taking shape nicely. The gap between her neck and her shirt collar, the glasses propped on top of her head apparently watching the ceiling. As if it were a thing apart, Bella watched the line of her pencil re-create the angle where Seline's chin jutted forward in eagerness, a chicken heading for corn.

'Bella?' Seline raised her eyebrows at her.

Bella clunked her coffee mug down on top of the sketch and tried to look thoughtful, as if weighing up all the various options before giving her opinion. Could they possibly still be talking about the yoghurt campaign or had they moved on to the corporate design deal for the country-house hotel?

'Erm . . .' she volunteered, trying to peer sideways at Anthony's pad to read the note he was scribbling for her.

'Lifestyle Yoghurt?' Seline prompted. 'Any more thoughts on the redesign? The focus groups research suggests it looks too healthy. The client wants a new look.'

'Yes.' Bella nodded wisely, every inch the creative director. 'I certainly think we could strengthen the idea that these yoghurts are fun and sensual, too. The customer—consumer—wants to feel that she can be healthy yet self-indulgent and just a bit sinful at the same time. I'll do some roughs tomorrow, with a sexier typeface.'

'Great!' Seline clicked her pen against her teeth, pleased.

Bella told herself she shouldn't knock it. On a good day, she prided herself on her ability to know exactly which typeface looked more carefree than any other. Besides, it kept her off the streets, and someone had to pay for all that damp treatment—and the extractor fan, and replacing those two sash cords, and the doorbell, and she could do with a freezer, too . . . On cue, The List of Things to be Done appeared in her head, winding itself around her, binding her like an Egyptian mummy. She closed her eyes at the thought and comforted herself with the knowledge that she could go and see Viv soon if she could escape without Seline heading her off at the pass.

'Bella! What a surprise.' Nick came into the kitchen and started filling the kettle. 'It seems like only yesterday that we saw you. Ah. It *was* yesterday. So, how've you been in the last twenty-four hours?'

'I'm going, I'm going. It's her fault. She made me come.' Bella pointed at Viv.

'I did. It was me.' Viv held Nick round his waist. 'But she's doing it for you. She's showing me how to make her posh fish pie so I can do it for your parents at the weekend.'

'Correction. I am in fact making the fish pie for the freezer while Viv stands there and nods and says "Oh, I think I see. Show me how to peel just one more potato and then I'll have a go".'

'Cup of tea, anyone? No? You found the wine then?' Nick topped up their glasses, then went and stretched out on the sofa.

'I'm out of earshot now if you two want to talk about men and sex and girlie stuff.'

'Shoes, Nick!' called Viv from the kitchen.

There was a discreet rustling, as of the sound of a newspaper being tucked under feet.

'Nick, imagine you're a proper man for a minute.'

'Cheers, Bella.'

'Oh, shush. You know what I mean. Viv says I should get your advice on how to attract a bloke.'

'No. People always say they want your advice and then they get pissed off with you.'

'I promise not to, Nick. Scout's honour.' Bella held up her hand in a three-fingered salute.

'When were you ever a scout?' hissed Viv. Bella waved her away.

Nick sighed. 'At your own risk then. Of course, it's only my opinion and I realise I'm not a *proper* man or anything, but if you really want a man, then get your legs out, woman. Wear a short skirt and laugh at our jokes. Aside from that—' Nick started counting off on his fingers '—one, you wear too many dark things. It's depressing. Two, do something about your hair—it's great but half the time no one can see your face, which seems a bit of a waste. Three, you could try smiling from time to time. Men like that. It makes us feel wanted.'

'Like this?' Bella adopted an enormous toothy grin.

'So, I suppose it wouldn't be a waste to cover *my* face with hair then?' said Viv.

'I knew this would happen. I hate both of you.' Nick heaved himself up from the sofa. 'If anyone wants me, I'll be pretending to be a proper man, reading my car magazine in the bog.'

There were two messages on her answerphone when she got home: one from the damp man, saying he couldn't do the damp until the weather was better; and one from her father, Gerald: 'Just calling to see how it's all going. Do you fancy coming for a visit at the weekend? Be lovely to see you. Mum says you're welcome to bring anyone, you know. If you want to. Well. Or just your good self of course. More than enough. Oh, and we've still got your house-warming present. Give us a ring. Lots of love, Dads.' He always finished like that on the answerphone, as if he were writing a letter.

Bella rolled her eyes at an invisible audience. Still, she hadn't visited the House of Fun for quite a while. She couldn't fend it off for ever.

2

'EV'RY TIME WE SAY GOODBYE, I die a little . . .' Bella sang along with Ella Fitzgerald while sucking on a sherbert lemon, then cursed at a driver surging onto the roundabout in front of her. '. . . why a little, why the gods above me . . .' She should have left at lunchtime to miss the Friday exodus but she'd got caught up all afternoon with Seline. Since Bella had moved, it was barely more than a fifty-mile journey to her parents' place, a wisteria-covered house in a pretty-pretty village in Sussex, but it was turning out to be a slow drive, much of it cross-country on minor roads.

It was always strange returning to the parental home, immersing herself in that peculiar mixture of pleasure and frustration. There was delight in the house itself: the gleam of well-polished furniture, its quiet colour schemes, its tidiness and orderliness—so different from the flat she had shared with Patrick, and from her new house with its brilliant cushions and exotic rugs, the pictures, still packed in boxes, that would line the walls; there was enjoyment of her mother's cooking, one thing they shared, and of her father's easy good humour, his guilelessness, his pleasure in seeing her.

Irritation was never in short supply either, however. The way Dad was so infuriatingly fair all the time, seeing everyone's point of view; and, most of all, her mother's unruffled efficiency, her air of stoic disappointment.

Going back home, Bella felt the inevitable yet unspoken questions hanging in the air:

Have you got another boyfriend yet? shone out at her from the ivory silk lampshade in the hall. *Are you making enough of an effort?* peeked at her from behind the velvet curtains. *You're running out of time*, glinted at her from the silver saltcellar. *How much longer must we wait?* whispered the soft carpets under her feet.

Alessandra, Bella's mother, was more subtle, of course, with a diploma in Reproach by Implication so that even the most innocuous topic of conversation could become a minefield, hidden dangers lurking beneath every cautious tread.

'Do you remember Sarah Forbes, from the year below you?' she had asked on Bella's previous visit. 'Who used to live in that house off Church Street with the fake bay window? Just married a lovely young man. She had such a pretty headdress for the wedding—and it drew attention away from her nose.'

The subtext was elaborate, but crystal clear: *She's a year younger and she didn't have your advantages, but even she's managed to get married. And she's not even nice-looking. You should do better than her.*

Bella had sidestepped the shots neatly and returned fire.

'How lovely. I'll send her a card. Will she keep on her job at the shop, do you think?'

She may as well get married. She's not exactly firing on all cylinders on the career front. Can't you at least be proud of my talents and achievements?

'Oh, I shouldn't think she'd need to do that, Bella-darling. Her husband's a lawyer; a junior partner in a very reputable firm apparently.' Alessandra smiled serenely. 'He's doing very well. Still, men can afford to concentrate on their careers, can't they? They don't have the same pressures as we women.'

Impressive: an attack on two fronts. 1. She's hooked someone not just with money, but a professional with good prospects. 2. Men don't have a time bomb nestling in their reproductive organs, so it's fine for them to be ambitious and successful. Can't you hear that clock ticking?

Feebly, Bella had lobbed back a boulder, a heavy, clumsy last shot.

'A lawyer, eh? Oh, never mind. Couldn't she find someone with a respectable profession? You know that old joke: What do you call a hundred lawyers chained together at the bottom of the ocean?—A good start.' *Pathetic. A damp squib.*

It didn't even merit a countermeasure. Alessandra had sighed softly, unimpressed, and patted the back of her hair, smoothing her already perfect chignon.

'Perhaps you wouldn't mind making some coffee, Bella-dear? There are homemade *fiorentine* in the blue tin.'

The *coup de grâce.*

If you can't manage to find a man and give us grandchildren, you can at least be useful by making some coffee. Perhaps if you could be bothered to make your own biscuits, like I do, you would have a man.

And the way she pronounced foreign words so overperfectly, as if she were a newsreader. Especially Italian, although Alessandra had actually been born in Manchester, her parents having come to England several years before. The way she said 'Bella'—with that preposterous lingering on the double 'l', the way an Italian waiter would as he poked his outsize pepper-phallus under your nose: 'Black pepper, *bella* signorina?'

It was late when she arrived and her mother had already gone to bed. Bella peeked into the utility room to say hello to Hund, the dog, but he was asleep in his basket, curled into an old childhood blanket. Her father had waited up, however, and was sitting in the kitchen reading a glossy women's magazine. He hugged her fondly and put on the kettle.

'Met anyone, um, interesting recently?—he asked in his interfering-old-parent way.'

'It's OK, Dads. I don't mind when you do it. Fraid not. You can keep your morning coat in mothballs for the foreseeable future. Might as well flog it, in fact—I can't see it happening.'

'Well, you know we love you whatever you do. We just want you to be happy.'

'Yeah, yeah. Dutiful parental speech duly acknowledged. But you want grandchildren. You all do. My friends say the same. It's just a phase—you'll get over it,' she said affectionately.

Bella slept in her old room. It was very different now, rather more restful, she mentally conceded. Alessandra had had it redecorated the week after Bella left to go to art school in London, covering with tasteful tones of subdued peach the ambitious mural of a Rousseau-style jungle painted over one wall. *Of course, you're welcome to do another if you like, Bella-darling, perhaps something a little more simpatico, hmm? A spray of lilies could be very pretty on the wardrobe door*. It had been getting very tatty anyway and she wouldn't have been bothered to retouch the whole wall. The room had been altered at least twice since then, although it wasn't even used very often. The bed was in the same position, though, next to the window, snug between the wall and the side of the wardrobe. Lying in it now, Bella felt she wanted to be tucked in tight and read to. She pulled up the quilt over her chin and turned off the light.

'No rush to get up,' Gerald said, as he poked his head round the door with a cup of tea. 'Your mother's had to go into town to have her hair done, so you're a free woman.'

'Nice of her to put out flags and form a welcoming committee.'

'Fancy some breakfast?'

On her customary stroll round the village, Bella bought a couple of postcards of endearingly awful watercolour views of the high street and the church, and wandered along to The Whistling Kettle to write her cards and have a coffee.

'Mum's back,' said Gerald, on her return.

Bella tugged at a pucker in her shirt and knocked on her parents' bedroom door.

'Mmm?'

She opened the door a little way and craned her head round it.

'It's only me. Just come to say hello.'

'Oh, *hello*, Bella-darling.' Alessandra glanced up at her from the dressing table. 'Why are you hovering there? Come in, come in. Lovely to see you.' Bella dipped to kiss her mother's proffered cheek.

'The hair's great. Very elegant. Colour's nice, too.'

Alessandra scanned Bella's face as if to check her expression, then turned her head this way and that in the mirror.

'I think I'd have made a better job of it myself. Anyway, how *are* you, darling?'

'Fine. Yup. I'm fine.'

Alessandra's threefold reflection peered up at her expectantly from the triple mirror.

'We haven't seen you for ages,' said the full face from the central frame. 'You really must come more often.'

'I'd love to, but—' Bella shrugged. 'There was the move. There's still loads to do, and you know how busy it gets with work and all.'

'Well, of course, we can't compete with the excitement of the rat race,' said the right profile, briskly dusting its cheek with translucent powder.

'The house is looking lovely. As always. Is that a new vase in the hall?' The reflection nodded and glanced at her sidelong.

'Your father misses you terribly,' said the left profile. 'You should really try and think of him sometimes.'

'I *do*.' Bella hooked her thumbs in the belt loops of her jeans and focused on the toe of her left boot. How nice the worn leather looked against the soft green pile of the carpet, like a piece of fallen bark on a floor of springy moss.

Alessandra's mouth formed a rictus-smile as she applied her lipstick.

'What do you think, hmm? It's new. Amber Spice.'

'Lovely.' Bella nodded at the reflection. 'Brings out the colour of your eyes, too.' Alessandra's glittering eyes, flecked like tortoiseshell, brightened in the mirror.

'Do you really think so?' She smiled, her feathers smoothed. 'Let's go down and have some coffee.' The reflection blotted its lips. 'I've made some new *biscotti*. You must try and guess what's in them.'

Alessandra walked towards the kitchen. 'Amuse yourselves, and keep out from under my feet, both of you. I'm just going to prepare a few bits for dinner. Nothing special as it's just us.'

'Nothing special' turned out to be individual asparagus and Gruyère tartlets followed by a layered terrine of smoked chicken and spinach with salad.

'Any news?' asked Alessandra to the air in general once they were safely on the home stretch of dinner, warm pears poached in port served with crème fraîche.

Are you seeing anyone? Bella sensed the silent question crawl across the starched linen tablecloth, edging its way round a china bowl of tight apricot rosebuds. *Are you even trying?* crept in its wake.

'Nothing major,' said Bella, concentrating on scooping up a wayward piece of pear, while redirecting the conversation with the practised ease of a politician. 'The house needs some work to eradicate the damp.'

'Sounds expensive,' Gerald said. 'Do you need any help?'

'Have you—' Alessandra began.

'Thanks, but I'm fine money-wise . . . and Seline seems to be very happy with me so far, probably because I've brought some juicy clients with me ready to be squeezed. She said if all goes well, we might discuss setting up as a partnership next year.'

'But that's wonderful. Shall we drink a toast?'

'Of course it's good that they appreciate your talents, but isn't that rather risky?' asked Alessandra. 'Wouldn't you be liable if the company went bankrupt?'

Bella took a drink of her wine.

'Well, of course, it's always good to look on the bright side,' she said, starting to get up from the table. 'Shall I make some coffee?'

'Perhaps I'd better make it, Bella-dear. The percolator's being rather temperamental.'

'It has my sympathy,' Bella said under her breath.

In the garden on Sunday morning, Gerald took Bella for the traditional guided tour. They stood together by his vegetable patch, pointing, assessing, as if judging it for a medal at a horticultural show.

'I'm planning to grow some squash this year. Your mother says they make good soup.'

'Oh? Don't they make an *eccellente* soup?'

'Behave yourself, daughter dear.'

'I'm wondering whether I should have my garden redesigned—make it easier to manage somehow?' she said. 'It's getting out of hand already.'

'Very sensible. I'll have a look if you like, or get someone who actually knows what they're doing.'

'**Of** course, I've no idea what's fashionable any more,' Alessandra said, plucking a blouse from her walk-in wardrobe to offer Bella. 'But this has always been useful.'

And it has to be better than that awful shirt.

'It's gorgeous,' Bella said, stroking the slippery satin sleeve against her cheek. 'Are you sure you don't want it?'

'We don't go out as much as we used to. I've far more evening clothes than I can use.'

Bella held up a silk chiffon top and looked at herself in the mirror. It was delicious, red and rich as cherries.

'The colour's wonderful with your hair. Take it.' Alessandra pulled out a matching skirt from the rail. 'Here—I can't get into it any more. All part of the joys of ageing.' She patted her still-slender hips.

You won't be young for ever.

'And you could do with some decent things. With your looks, it's such a waste not to make the most of yourself.'

Why don't you try harder? You won't catch a man if you don't.

With the blouse and skirt on, Bella felt different—unfamiliarly elegant, graceful, grown-up. The skirt swirled softly about her legs as she walked up and down the bedroom.

'That's really very glamorous on you,' said Alessandra, assessing. 'Lovely for a special occasion. It needs high heels, of course,' looking down at Bella's weekend boots.

'I do have some smart shoes, you know—just because I don't—'

'No. Well, of course, we can't expect you to waste your best things on us.' She turned and left the room.

Alone in her parents' bedroom, Bella faced herself in the mirror. Her reflection looked back, coolly appraising. The cherry top and skirt seemed suddenly ridiculous, absurdly glamorous, too obviously not her own. She tugged at the zip, jamming it in the fabric before pulling it free, and reached for her jeans.

'**Don't** forget your house-warming present,' Gerald said.

She didn't need to unwrap it to see what it was. There were two bits: one large and heavy piece that was evidently some kind of lamp base, and one awkward-looking shade. Even without seeing it, Bella could tell it wouldn't look right in her house. It was too large and, knowing her mother, too grand. It was bound to have been expensive. She could have had some decent new towels for the money. Or a couple of seriously good saucepans.

'Gosh,' she said. 'How exciting to have a proper present.'

'Aren't you going to open it?' Alessandra stood poised behind it proprietorially. It was evidently of her choosing.

'But it looks so well protected as it is. I'd better transport it wrapped, I think. Then I can have it to look forward to when I get home.'

'Of course.' Alessandra smoothed back a wisp of hair and folded her arms. 'Well, safe journey then.' She hovered forward, printed a birdlike kiss on Bella's cheek.

Gerald handed her an envelope once she was in the car.

'Not a big fat cheque, I'm afraid. Something for the garden.'

'Looks a bit flat for a cherry tree.'

'Be off with you.' He bent down to kiss her goodbye. 'The receipt for the other present's in there too, in case you want to exchange it for whatever we should have got you in the first place. Feel free to invite us to your housewarming. If you're not too embarrassed by your crumbly old parents. We'll come early and lend a hand.'

'Don't be daft, Dads.'

No chance, she thought. Come early and lend a hand? Thanks, but no thanks.

Bella gave a peremptory toot as she drove out of the gate. In the rearview mirror she saw her father's arm raised high, as if signalling from a desert island to a distant ship, her mother's hand tentatively lifted, stretching out for something she couldn't hope to reach.

'Why not do an evening class—that way, you'll meet people and learn something at the same time!' The advice in women's magazines was always the same: whenever someone wrote in saying they wanted to meet people, the answer was predictably of the get-out-and-join-clubs variety. But did you ever meet likely men at an evening class? Bella sounded out Viv and Nick later while at their place for supper. Nick decreed it was a rational approach and asked what subject she planned to take: carpentry or car maintenance? Bella had rather fancied stained glass or patchwork; she whimpered at Viv, who would have none of it.

'Look, do you bloody want to meet men or don't you? Go to patchwork classes if you want, but don't come running to me afterwards whinging that the best bet in the class is a forty-seven-year-old midwife because at least she's got hair on her chin.'

'That'd do. I want to meet more *people*, otherwise I feel like I'm just a visitor here.'

Leafing through the booklet of adult education courses from the library while she was supposed to be working, Bella thought she could do with lessons just to make sense of the brochure. Was there some logical reason for the range of subjects, prices and locations to be encrypted in quite such a complex way? She was tempted to leave it till September. Maybe she'd have more energy for deciphering it after the summer and she could start afresh with the new academic year. But, knowing her, she would have forgotten all about it by then. She should definitely do it NOW.

Car Maintenance/Complete Beginners was due to start on Tuesday evening at half six. Bella dashed home after work to pick up her car. It wouldn't start. Ha-ha, ha-ha. Very droll, she thought, slapping the dashboard. How cheering to witness that God obviously did have a sense of irony after all. And, of course, she panicked, and kept revving it, and the engine flooded.

She turned off the engine and sat there for a few minutes. Marvellous. Another element in her life that didn't work. The evening-class thing was a stupid idea anyway, she'd obviously never meet anyone like this; she probably had mildew between her legs by now. Why couldn't she simply accept the fact that she was a sad, pathetic spinster who would never have a man or children.

One last try. It started. Of course. Glanced at her watch—it might still be worth it; she could still enrol at least. By the time she got there, and found a parking space, the lesson was half-gone. She found the room and, wisely as it turned out, peered through a pane in the door before plunging in.

A group of about a dozen people were clustered round what she assumed must be a car engine. They suddenly parted to let a fiftyish man in blue overalls get to the centre. As they moved aside, they turned in Bella's direction. All except two of them were women. The two that weren't huddled close together and looked very awkward; neither could have been a minute over seventeen. She pressed herself back against the wall like a B-movie spy. A narrow escape. Hell, who wanted to learn about engines anyway? That was what mechanics were for.

It seemed a bit of a waste, however, now that she was there. The noticeboard's list of classes for that evening included Life Drawing/All Levels (starting in thirty seconds). Probably not many men, but she would enjoy herself anyway, and she needn't tell anyone; she hadn't sat in an actual class since she'd been at art school but she had loved that complete absorption in the task. She hurtled along the corridors, trying to find the right room.

She finally tracked it down in an annexe and leapt into the room in the middle of the tutor's introduction. He said they must all call him JT and ask as many questions as they liked. Despite the fact that the tutor insisted on calling himself by initials, he seemed to be OK. He suggested they all start with a quick fifteen-minute study before moving on to a longer pose.

The model disrobed and moved into a standing position, leaning forward with his leg on a chair. There, she was getting to be with a naked man after all, and without any of that awful awkwardness or having to introduce him to her mother. Marvellous.

When it was time for the model's break, Bella noticed the room around her, the other people in the class, as if she had awoken from a trance, forms coming into focus. Blinked as if the lights had been switched on suddenly. Found it hard to speak for a moment or two, her head still filled with pictures, shapes. Drawing was rather like being in love, she decided, the completeness of it, no need for anything else.

She was aware of a presence at her left shoulder. JT, checking her progress. He nodded, approving.

'I take it you're not exactly a beginner,' he said.

3

SUNDAY. THE DAY designed for the sole purpose of reminding all single people on the planet just how sad and lonely they really were. It wasn't as if she had a shortage of things to do. There was the small matter of the boxes, for a start. It was weeks now since she'd moved in and she was still surrounded by her cardboard cityscape. But what was the point of unpacking everything when it would all have to be repacked when she got round to having the damp done? She couldn't descend on Viv and Nick again. Viv kept saying it was fine, but the other evening Nick had remarked that they needn't bother having any children now because they had Bella: no need to worry about getting her into a decent school—no need to fund her through college—no arguments about her staying out late or hogging the phone for hours. Fantastic, he'd said, why hadn't anyone else thought of it? Why put yourself through all those years of anxiety and heartache when you could just adopt a thirty-three-year-old who could cook and everything? Hilarious. My, how she'd laughed.

She got out her list. 'Sort out house', it said. 'Sort out garden'. They both seemed a bit epic for a Sunday morning. 'Damp'. She underlined it firmly to give herself the feeling that she was somehow hastening its progress. Added 'Chase Mr Bowman again' as a subentry beneath it. 'Crack in wall/studio'. That was obviously more than a DIY project, more of a get-someone-else-in-to-sort-it-out sort of thing. 'Shower curtain', the list continued. 'Blind for bathroom'. Ah, that was more like it. She could manage a little light selecting of shower curtains. Habitat wasn't open till noon. Plenty of time to whiz round and have a quick tidy-up. After a spot of breakfast.

A breakfast tray was assembled with cornflakes and cold milk, tea, a toasted muffin; she whopped a tape of *The Philadelphia Story* into the video and settled back into the sofa.

Bella clicked off the television. Good grief, it was nearly noon. She must, must, must do something constructive. She remembered about the quest for a shower curtain. She would go to Habitat now, right this very minute, then come back and take a good hard look at the garden.

Patrick had hated Habitat, loathed it as he loathed any kind of shopping that didn't involve the acquisition of food, claiming colour blindness, taste blindness, any impairment he could think of to be excused—'You go, Bel. You're good at that sort of thing. It all looks the same to me.' She had been genuinely baffled, as if he'd claimed not to be able to tell the difference between fruit-cake and prawn cocktail. How could someone not mind what their surroundings looked like? 'A quilt's a quilt,' said Patrick. 'If I'm underneath it and asleep, why should I care what it looks like?' Bella bit her lip; why did she always miss him most when she was remembering something annoying about him?

If Bella had thought about it properly, she'd have realised that Habitat was no sensible place for a single person to go at the weekend. Now she knew the dark and horrible truth: Habitat was the core, the pit of woe at the centre of Sunday Hell. She had never seen so many couples; they must be growing them in pods in the basement, extruding perfect, ready-made families onto the shop floor so that you, the Sad Single, will be inspired by these visions of familial bliss. You start to feel warm, broody, generous; if only you buy a set of rustic peasant coffee mugs, a Mediterranean juice jug and a checked tablecloth with matching napkins, surely you too will acquire a coordinating Perfect

Husband and Children set and resulting Perfect Life.

Bella resolved to restrict future visits to late-night-closing day, which was when professional, single women who wore smart, co-ordinating items with proper lapels and waistbands rather than big, shapeless sacky things over leggings went to look at lamp bases in the evening because they had no one to eat dinner with.

Annoyingly, the prospect of sorting out her studio looked just as daunting that afternoon as it had every other day. What about the garden? That was marginally more appealing. She went to see the current state of play from behind the safety of the French windows. No doubt about it, it was getting worse. She must exert some sort of control.

Where on earth should she start? She'd need a machete, a compass and a Boys' Own Survival Guide out there. Have to tie a length of string to the door handle so she could find her way back to the house. The lawn looked as sad as uncombed hair scraped across a bald patch. It desperately needed mowing—all she needed was a mower. And that enormous monster bush needed hacking back—if only she had a pair of secateurs. She retrieved her list from the kitchen drawer. 'Garden centre', she added, '—get tools.'

The garden centre was busy; there were people buying sheds and hefting sacks of compost into car boots and tying trellis panels to their roof racks, a hive of industry. Even watching them made Bella feel tired. Retired couples bent lovingly over shrubs and rosebushes, as curious and nurturing about a prospective purchase as over a new grandchild.

Perhaps she should simplify the whole garden—just have lawn and a small tree and a couple of tubs. She would definitely have to sort out the garden properly before it was worth spending much on plants, she realised, because there was nowhere to plant them in its current state. In the meantime, she chose a few small pots of herbs to cheer herself up. While paying, she noticed a sign by the till advertising the services of a garden designer: 'Time to turn over a new leaf? If your garden's more of a jinx than a joy, don't stay indoors and cry. Whether your taste tends towards the traditional or the avant-garde, simple or stupendous, I'll help you create your ideal garden and turn your dreams into reality—at a reasonable cost.' It offered a free initial consultation, without obligation. She noted down the name and phone number.

Planting out her herbs to avoid the greater evil of doing her laundry, Bella resolved to phone the garden man immediately. It was Sunday, so he probably wouldn't be there, was probably yet another person out having a wonderful day in the bosom of his family, but at least she could leave a message, and it meant she could cross off something from The List. His answerphone said to leave a message for 'Will Henderson or Henderson Garden Design'.

'I need a man with a machete and a vat of weedkiller,' she said, 'oh, yes, and a new garden.'

She went and extracted her list from the drawer again. Damn. Added 'Call garden designer' to the bottom, then crossed it off firmly and went upstairs, feeling positive enough to face her studio.

The crack in her studio wall was longer than she had remembered. It was the kind of crack to be tutted at, the kind to make you say, 'Something should be done about that' as if you were an authority on such matters. Bella did both of these things, then stood back to squint at it through half-closed eyelids. It seemed a shame to fill it in with boring old Polyfilla; plus there was the minor fact that she didn't have any. She nodded to herself, as if she had come to a decision, then began to delve into the boxes, foraging for her paints.

'No, no, no, no, and no.'

'I'll take that as a no, then?' Bella said.

Something gave her the feeling that Viv wasn't mad keen on the idea of going to a poetry reading.

'But it's not *poetry* poetry, Viv, not wandered-lonely-as-a-cloud wafty stuff. She's really funny. Some of it's rude. You'd love it.'

'Can't be done, babe. Friday's our takeaway and video night.'

'But this is Culture,' Bella said. 'You remember Culture. You had some once, about four years ago.'

Viv remained immovable. All couples have a regular evening together when they sit glued to a movie, chomping their way through chicken chow mein and beef in black bean sauce or Special Set Meal No. 2; it was a Universal Law, like gravity, not to be questioned.

'You're very sad. Anyone would think you were joined at the hip. No, no, don't try to protest.'

'You should go anyway,' Viv said. 'There might be some nice men there.'

'Right. What kind of man goes to a poetry reading?'

Most of the seats were already taken by the time Bella arrived at the poetry reading, having extricated herself with difficulty from a conversation with Seline about the prospect of going into partnership as things were going so well. Bella hoped to defer the moment of actually Making a Decision for as long as possible. Or longer. She didn't know what she wanted, other than not to have to decide. She helped herself to a glass of wine and covertly peered over the rim in quest of any lone, attractive men. It would be considerate if they could carry a small sign or wear a lapel badge: 'Available' or 'Married but looking for a leg-over' or 'In relationship but keeping my options open'.

There was quite a crowd. She settled by a table piled with Nell Calder's books, and looked around for somewhere to rest her glass. There was an empty corner on a table nearby—she reached for it at exactly the same moment as someone else. Their glasses clashed.

'Oh, sorry,' they said in unison.

'Er, cheers then.' The man smiled, looking directly into her eyes. Nice face, she thought, and looked away quickly. She didn't want to give him the wrong idea. His hair could do with a bit of a brush. It was strangely springy, sticking up at odd angles here and there. She peered at him sideways. He caught her at it and smiled.

There was an amplified whoompf and whine as the microphone was wrestled from its stand at the front.

'Oh, hello, signs of action, I think,' said the springy-haired man at her side, stretching to see over a woman wearing a peculiar patchwork hat with a ludicrously high crown.

'Do you think she's got planning permission for that hat?' he whispered to Bella, indicating the woman with a nod. 'This is a conservation area.' Mid-swallow, Bella laughed, spraying her wine with a snort. Oh, terrific. Well, it was one way to attract attention.

Embarrassed, she looked away. Nell Calder was being introduced. Applause.

'This one was inspired by my ex-husband,' said the poet. 'It's called "Can I have custody of the egg timer?"'

Conscious of Springy Hair's presence by her side, Bella made a sweeping I'm-just-looking-for-my-friend cast of the room, trying to see round the woman in front. Suddenly, across the room, half-hidden by a woman holding her glass in front of her, Bella caught a glimpse of a man. Dark, floppy hair. The edge of a face with horn-rimmed glasses. Patrick? A jolt. Dry mouth. Thudding heart. Even now. Craning her head to see, the memory caught her unawares, flooding over her in a wash, leaving her pale and breathless.

She catches herself looking round the room for him. Perhaps he is in the kitchen, rootling about in the fridge, or in the loo absorbed in a copy of the *National Geographic*. Of course he isn't here. She *does* know that. And yet. These people—his sister, Sophie, who suddenly looks so slight and frail as if the lightest breeze would carry her off, her right hand clasping her left arm behind her back, holding herself; James, one of Patrick's oldest friends, uncomfortable and aware of his paunch in a too-tight borrowed suit; Rose, Patrick's mother, immaculately turned out as for a wedding, solicitously anticipating the needs of every guest— 'A drop more dry sherry? Another smoked salmon canapé? Everyone's been marvellous, really. I've hardly had to do a thing. Do let me get you something. Just a little bite?'; his father, Joseph, held together by his crisply tailored suit, dark as wrought iron, staring down into his heavy glass at the ice boulders floating and colliding in their enclosed lake of Scotch—he looks as if he would gladly join them, slide into that welcoming liquid and feel it flow round him, through him, in him, pushing out the warm blood that obstinately completes another tireless circuit of his body, swooshing through him, steeling his arteries with its icy anaesthetic, until he is numb and feels no more.

But, of course, *he* isn't here. Bella knows it, and yet still it seems as if these people who were closest to him—people who had helped him take his first stumbling steps, compared scabby knees with him in the playground, coughed over a first stolen cigarette with him, worked with him, argued with him, laughed with him, kissed him, loved him—they seem between them to make a shape, a Patrick-shaped space, so that really she feels he must be here. Surely they would only all be here because of him?

Ting, ting. A strange sound, metal on glass. A knife tapped against a wineglass, edge on; a sound effect to punctuate every wedding, every anniversary, to herald every speech, a sound of celebration. Someone is saying something. Yes, faces are all turning in one direction.

Alan, Patrick's brother, is speaking:

'. . . all for coming, many from a great distance. I have—we have all— been immensely pleased. Touched. To see so many of you here. So many friends. Family. I—well.'

He clears his throat, presses his lips firmly together, sealing in the words.

'Anyway,' he smiles tightly, 'I know Patrick wouldn't have wanted us all to be mooning about with faces as long as a wet weekend, and he would have hated to see good liquor go to waste, so please, raise your glasses. To Patrick.'

'To Patrick,' they echo.

Alan raises his glass again, the ice tinkling softly like a half-heard bell blown by a distant breeze.

'May his memory live on,' he says.

Someone is hugging her. She squeezes the navy-suited body back softly, politely, unaware of who it is yet grateful for its solid warmth. A hand pats her consolingly on the shoulder, a master rewarding his faithful dog for carrying out a trick well. And it was a trick. Sip your sherry, nibble a canapé, proffer your cheek to be kissed, shed a silent tear or two. No screaming; no wailing; no ugly, wrenching sobs dragging her whole rib cage; no face bizarrely painted with black mascara trails, streaked by tears that seemed as if they would never run dry; no sitting curled up on the floor, head tucked tight to her knees, clutching herself, holding herself together in case she falls apart in sharp, brittle fragments, or subsides slowly, sliding across the floor in a pool of tears and pain. No. She could accomplish this trick very well indeed. She smiles and kisses the cheek, wondering how soon she can leave.

'Isabel, isn't it?' A hand was waving in her face, claiming her attention. Recoiling slightly, Bella craned again to see the man. His face turned: a longer nose, thinner mouth. Quite different. Not Patrick at all. No. Of course not. She shook the thought away and turned to concentrate on the person standing rather too close in front of her. It was the woman in unlawful possession of an offensive patchwork hat.

'No,' said Bella, automatically. 'It's Bella.' Who was this woman? Under the brim, her face did look familiar, but Bella couldn't quite place it.

'Well, that's short for Isabella anyway, isn't it?' The woman glared at her almost accusingly.

'Not in my case. It's just Bella.' She smiled. 'I'm so sorry—I'm terrible with names—'

'Ginger Badell. We met at Scotton Design just the other week. I create concepts for Benson Foods.' The woman clutched at a tall, thin man hovering in a nervous orbit around her and steered him by his elbow towards Bella. 'And this is Roger, my *amore*.' She looked to either side of Bella, and pulled the stringy *amore* closer as if worried that Bella might suddenly grab him in a passionate embrace.

They chatted politely for a few minutes, while Bella tried to glance round unobtrusively for Springy Hair. Had he gone?

'So nice to see you again,' said Bella, backing away. 'I must just grab this chance to buy a signed copy—do excuse me.'

There were three other people in front of her waiting to have their books signed. Bella looked round the room while she waited. Springy Hair had obviously left. She would have thought he might say goodbye. Not that she'd been interested. Probably hadn't fancied her anyway, he was just being friendly out of pity. Must be on his way home now back to his wife. And his four children. And their dog. Bloody hell. Even that bonkers Ginger woman with the world's worst taste in millinery had a man. She probably looked down on Bella, pitied her because she was obviously alone.

When Bella got back home that evening, there was no message from the damp man. How dare he? She had come to expect the little flashing light on her answerphone that indicated another exciting episode in the life and work of Mr Bowman. Her favourite so far was that the lodger had left without giving notice. Quite why this should prevent Mr Bowman from hacking off her plaster, she was unsure, but he was adamant on the matter.

There was, however, another one from that Henderson person, the garden designer; they had been playing answerphone tag for days. Will Henderson's message said his man with a machete was still chomping at the bit, but that they didn't seem to be having much luck getting each other, her life was obviously one nonstop glamorous social whirl. Perhaps he would pop round on Saturday morning, around ten-ish, but if not OK, could she phone and leave another message. Actually, could she phone anyway because she hadn't given him her address.

She phoned in the morning, from work.
'Hello again. Bella Kreuzer here again. Just calling—'
'Hello?' The phone was picked up.
'Mr Henderson? In the flesh? You do exist, then. You've completely thrown me now. I was getting on so well with your answerphone. Best relationship I've ever had.'
'Shall I hang up and leave you two alone together?'
She gave him her address, agreed that Saturday would be fine.
'And please can I beg you not to cut anything back before then,' he said. 'It's so easy to lose something wonderful because it doesn't look like much and you might not recognise it.'
'I promise. Scout's honour.'

Saturday morning. The doorbell rang. Was it really that late or was this Henderson character early? She ran down the stairs, buttoning up her jeans. Shoes? Never mind.

'Springy Hair!' She tried to turn it into a cough. The funny man from the poetry reading.

'It's you,' said Springy Hair. 'What did you say?'

'Nothing. Just a tickle in my throat.' She cleared it loudly. Very alluring. Why not just hawk phlegm all over him. 'What are you doing here?'

'I've come to blowtorch your garden. Will Henderson.' He smiled. 'Hello. I'm glad I've bumped into you again.' He apologised for having dashed off after the reading without saying goodbye. He'd been embarrassed when he saw her talking to the woman with the hat after he'd been so rude about it.

'So, have you just moved in, then?' He waved at the multistorey box park in her sitting room.

She explained that there was no point unpacking everything because there was still the DAMP to be done. 'I see it in capital letters in my head now because I've been meaning to have it done for so long. Mr Bowman's more elusive than the Scarlet Pimpernel.'

'Bowman, eh. Hmm-mm. You're not in a hurry are you?'

She explained that she'd already been waiting for over two months, then launched into a tirade about Mr Bowman and his imaginative range of excuses. Was he a local legend, Bella asked, was that why Will had heard of him?

'No. He's my brother-in-law.'

'Yeah, right. Very droll.'

'No. He really is. Sort of. Well he's my brother-in-law, in-law. My sister's husband's brother. What does that make him?'

'A very annoying person who hasn't done my damp, I'm afraid.'

They went out to the garden. He nodded in places, humming, clucking his tongue in others, making a running commentary to himself. She saw him make scribbly sketches, numerous notes, tiny diagrams. He would come back and measure properly if she wanted to go ahead, he said.

'OK if I ask you a few questions?' Will put down his mug and took out a notebook from one of the bulging pockets of his jacket.

'Sounds ominous.'

He looked up from his notebook. 'Trouble is, the reason people end up with a garden that doesn't suit them is they plunge straight in without thinking about what they really want.'

Bella shifted in her seat. 'I feel as if I'm in an exam.'

'You are.' Will rolled up his sleeves. 'If you get too many wrong, my fee goes up. Ready? Right, question one. What do you want to do in this garden? Judging from the state of it, can I assume you're not a veteran plant collector? So do you want somewhere for eating out? A bolt hole from the rat race? Place to sunbathe in privacy? All of the above?'

'I don't know. But privacy's a must. I want a secluded corner somewhere with lots of traily things hanging down. I hate feeling people are looking at me. Does that sound terribly paranoid?'

'It must make life pretty awkward.' Will jotted something down in his notebook.

'What? Being paranoid?'

He shrugged as if it were obvious.

'No—just—well, I imagine you get looked at quite a lot.' He raised his eyes from what he was writing.

Bella looked down into her mug of coffee. He was obviously only saying it to wind her up. No one could find her attractive the way she looked this morning in these grotty old jeans and baggy jumper.

'Any kids?'

'Nope. What's that got to do with it anyway?'

'Play space. You might want a sandpit. Swing. Any on the horizon?'

'The Vatican will declare me a modern miracle if there are.'

'You're not keen on kids then?'

'It's not that I don't like them. I just . . .' she shrugged. 'I . . . anyway, I'm— More coffee?'

'Don't bother. Really.' Will got up to go. 'I've been here way too long already. So, think about exactly what you want in the garden, any must-haves and so on. Make a list.'

'Right. List-making, I'm good at that. Will you really design it to suit my every need?'

'Not at all. I'll nod and say, "I see. No problem," a lot, then ignore you and do whatever I thought of in the first place.'

Will held out his business card.

'Call me. Here—let me give you a few in case you want to pass one on.'

Bella smiled. 'You had too many printed, didn't you?'

'Well, it's ever so cheap if you have a thousand done.'

'A thousand? Give me a stack. I can do shopping lists on the back.'

'They're good for sticking under wobbly table legs in restaurants too.'

There were no spare drawing pins on her kitchen pinboard, so Bella tucked one of his cards behind the corner of a photograph. The one of her and Patrick. Her finger rested for a moment on the pin, feeling its cold hardness solid beneath the fleshy pad of her fingertip.

She had been cooking when she heard the news.

Bella is stirring her sauce, giggling at Viv's description of some pompous pillock she has had to endure at her all-day conference.

The telephone rings.

'Get that, will you? I have to keep whisking—this is looking a bit blobby. It's probably Patrick.'

'Good evening, Kreuzer and Hughes residence.' Viv's overcorrected receptionist voice is spot-on.

'Yes, yes, she is. She's just here.'

Viv hands her the phone, saying it is Patrick's father, and takes the whisk.

'Hello, Joe? How are you? Patrick's not back yet. He—'

She is silent.

There is only the ticking of the kitchen clock.

Viv stops whisking and looks up. Bella's face is a mask, pale and blank.

'Mm-mm. Still here. I'm OK. Where are you? Hang on.' She casts about for a pen. 'OK. Where do I come to?'

Her writing scrawls unevenly across the bottom of a shopping list on the back of an envelope. Looking at the loops and lines of ink as they appear on the paper, she knows she will remember this moment for ever: standing in this kitchen, seeing the name of the hospital as she writes next to words that suddenly seem pointless—butter, potatoes, coffee. The look on Viv's face, the way the whisk falls from her hand into the sauce. How loud the kitchen clock is. Why is it so loud?

She is shaking. This is probably normal, she tells herself. She feels as if she is outside her own body, watching her hand clutching the phone like a life belt, looking at her bare feet on the floor. She cannot feel the floor properly beneath her; presses her soles hard into the cork tiles, making contact with the ground. She is nodding, saying yes, yes, she is on her way, she will be there as soon as she can.

'It's Patrick, isn't it?' Viv says.

'There's been an accident. On a site.' It sounds like a line from a poor movie. She wishes she could rewind the tape and say something more meaningful, more poignant, *better*.

'Is he . . . ?'

Patrick is alive but unconscious, suffering from severe head injuries and internal haemorrhaging.

'Shoes?' Bella is saying. 'I need some shoes.'

Her legs start shaking compulsively as she sits and tries to lace up her boots, her knees pumping up and down like pistons. Viv kneels by her feet and ties the laces, holds Bella steady by her shoulders.

'You can't drive like this,' Viv says. 'I'll take you.'

'Sorry if I'm boring you. It's just that now's a good time to get your garden under way, so call me soon. Yes? Am I being too pushy?'

'No. Yes. You're right.'

'I am pushy?'

'No. About coming back. Next weekend? Or perhaps that's not—'

'Fine. It's fine. See you then, then. Never sounds right, that, does it?'

'Which?'

'Then then.'

'Have you thought of having treatment? They're working wonders with laser surgery these days. Burn whole lobes of your brain right off.'

'Thank you. I'll bear it in mind. I'm going now, but don't forget.'

'I won't.' She nodded decisively. *Forget what?* she wondered.

'CROISSANTS,' SAID WILL, waving a paper bag under her nose as she opened the door. 'As I've made you get up early.'

'Nonsense. Been up for hours. Done my ten-mile morning run. Hundred press-ups. Hoovered the house. Licked the windows clean. Retiled the roof.'

They took their croissants and mugs of tea out to the garden, stood talking as they leaned with their backs against the French windows, pleasantly warm from the spring sun. What kind of plants did she like, he wanted to know.

She closed her eyes to picture it, to see it fresh and alive in her head: grasses, she said—feathery heads waving in the wind, catching the light—different textures, felty foliage and shiny stems and those plants with the downy, pleated leaves that held the raindrops like glass beads—drifts of colour—scented things, roses and lavender and jasmine—herbs for cooking—dramatic, spiky jobs, maybe a yucca, something that could be lit up at night, throwing its shadow on the wall.

They talked of shapes, proportions, styles, materials. He sketched ideas, paced up and down, swirling his arms like a manic conductor, showing her, squatting to model the position of an urn, standing tall like a tree for her to assess the effect from the house. Discussed the budget. He asked her even more questions, how much time would she spend looking after the garden? 'Be honest,' he said. Was she lazy? What else did she do with her time?

'Is this OK? My mother calls me the Spanish Inquisition.'

Would he like a bite to eat, only odds and ends from the fridge, she said, embarrassed that she had taken up so much of his time again, but perhaps he would have a proper lunch waiting for him at home?

'No chance.'

'Help yourself.' She set out dishes on the kitchen worktop. 'This is sort of a grazing lunch. Just pick at whatever you fancy.'

'What a treat. Like a midnight feast—I love picking.'

'Me too.'

'Me three.'

Bella looked at him. 'I used to say that when I was little.'

Will insisted it was a banquet: cold chicken with basil dressing, homemade coleslaw, hot ciabatta bread, runny Brie. She shrugged.

'Just leftovers. Don't you eat properly?'

'I *do*. Why do women always imagine that men don't cook? I can do a good roast chicken. A stew sort of a thing.' He seemed to be thinking. 'Chops!' he said triumphantly. '*And* I do a mean stir-fry.'

'All men say they can do stir-fries. Didn't you see that documentary? Apparently, the Y-chromosome is linked with the ability only to cook over a high heat—that's why men like barbecues.'

Back outside, Will drew her to the far end of the garden. He stood behind her, pointing back at the house over her shoulder. She could feel the warmth of his breath in her hair. Imagined for a moment she could hear him swallow, hear the double beat of his heart.

'There. See? What I suggested before about the patio? With wide steps.' She moved away, scraped her fingers through her hair.

'Fine. Now, what about this awful lawn?'

Will stamped on it.

'Get rid of it. It's in a chronic state. We can returf, of course, if you want, but I wouldn't bother. It's not a good use of space here. Just think—' He gestured in a broad arc, a wizard weaving a spell. 'No mowing. No edging. More space for interesting plants . . .'

'Won't it look too hard? Like a car park?'

'Not unless you specifically want Tarmac. I was thinking of a sweep of shingle, so we can plant directly into the soil below—ornamental grasses, herbs, whatever. Or big, clunky grey cobbles, with water . . .'

'Like a beach? I'd love that. My dad used to take me when I was little. I still go to the seaside when I feel crappy.'

'Same here. Oh—look at that—' He strode off and plunged into the border between two overgrown bushes.

Bella stared at the ground, remaking it as her own private beach in her head, a stretched-out curve, water lapping at the stones, the wetness bringing their colours to life, the surf frothing at her feet.

She leaves the post-funeral 'do' as soon as she decently can and drives to the coast. Patrick had taken her there a few times, when they'd gone to stay with his parents. Now she needs the sea air in her lungs, the sting of salt in her nostrils, the wind to blow away the surface of her skin, leaving her purged, raw but renewed.

Turning into the road that leads to the beach, she is surprised as always by the sudden emptiness at the end of the road where it curves sharply round. The car slows and she concentrates on turning left into the cul-de-sac to park. Pulls her old, crushed mac from its permanent home in the boot of the car. She scrunches down onto the shingle, her black suede court shoes sinking into the pebbles. Slips them off and walks a few steps further. Struth, these stones are hard; she wishes she'd brought some other shoes. Still, it's not normally what you think of when you go to a funeral: 'Have I got everything? Tissues? Black hat? Beach shoes?'

The wind flicks her hair across her face, into her mouth, and she huddles closer to the breakwater for shelter. How weathered it is; the wood is smooth to the touch, sanded by the waves and—well, sand, she supposes. She leans her head against it and wiggles her toes down into the shingle, incongruous against her sheer black tights.

'Fuck, fuck, fuck,' she says, under her breath. 'Bugger, bugger, bugger.' How could he do this to me? That's just so typical of Patrick, it really is. Only he would go and get himself killed in such a ridiculous fashion and with such bad timing. There is a kind of pleasure, a comfort in this facetiousness. Better to be pissed off with him, better to rail against his annoying habits than to allow her mind a stretch of silence, where the darkness lies in wait, curled up patiently, ready for the moment when she would let it in.

'Bloody Patrick.' She shoves the shingle down sharply with her foot.

'OK with that then?' Will stood close, looking down at her. He seemed to be expecting something.

'Mmm?'

'Welcome back. Are you happy for me to take out those shrubs? They're eating up space.'

'Won't it feel very exposed?'

'Trust me. There'll be plenty of seclusion. We can put a pergola across that corner, with a purple vine and some spring clematis. Oh, I know—' He ran to the end of the garden and Bella found herself following. 'Say just here—a secret hideaway seat with a living willow roof. Just wide enough for you and whoever to sit—'

'Yes.' She turned away from his gaze. 'I'd love that. And I was wondering about having a mural on this end wall.'

Will said, sure, she could have what she liked, but it could be expensive. His artistic skills didn't extend that far so he'd have to subcontract it. Bella explained she was planning to do it herself.

'Your *face*.' She laughed. 'It's such an open book. I can see you thinking, "Oh no, a client who thinks she can paint. She's going to mess up the whole garden with some terrible scene of Tuscan olive groves."'

'Not far off. I thought you'd favour a Gothic folly actually, covered in creepers. Some wild romantic fantasy.'

'*Touché*. You're pretty close.' She described what she planned: a *trompe-l'oeil* crumbling archway, framed by a real climbing rose perhaps, revealing a tantalising glimpse of a sunlit secret garden beyond, with a path curving off into shadows. He didn't mean to be rude, he said, but it sounded like quite a tricky feat to bring off.

'I can always paint it out if it looks hideous.'

'Or train the rose right over it.'

'Are you this rude to all your clients?'

'Only the ones on a tight budget. Add another couple of grand and I can be a real smoothie: "A mural! What an inspired idea! And you'll paint it yourself? How delightful! That will give it your own *unique* stamp."'

'Doesn't suit you. I'd rather have the rudeness, thanks.'

'Erm, your downstairs loo seems to have been invaded by boxes. Where are they all coming from?' Will asked.

'I had to clear some space. Surely you can manage the stairs?'

He explained that many clients didn't like the gardener to use the upstairs one. Some of them wouldn't even let him in the house. He always took a flask because he could never count on even being offered a cup of tea.

Bella was outraged. Didn't it make him angry?

He shrugged. 'Some people are like that. It's no good getting yourself worked up about every little thing that annoys you.'

'But I love ranting about things that annoy me. It's practically my favourite pastime.'

'Hmm? What's your favourite then?'

His words were accompanied by that look again. That peculiar, assessing look as if he were trying to see inside her head.

'Arguing. The bathroom's round to the right.' Bella pointed up the stairs. 'Oh, hang on.' She followed him. 'I think I used up the soap.'

He watched her foraging in boxes.

'Why don't you just blitz all the boxes in one go and unpack everything so you know where it is?'

'Because of the DAMP!'

'Ah, now I know why you're letting me use your posh loo. You want me to have a quiet word with my brother-in-law-in-law, don't you?'

Bella opened the door to her studio to look for another box. There was definitely some soap somewhere.

'But this is fantastic!' Will was standing in the doorway, looking at the almost-completed mural on the wall with the crack. 'You realise I feel like a total prat now? Why didn't you say you were a professional?'

'But I'm not really. I only paint for me. You can't earn a living at it.'

The crack had been incorporated into a painting of an old, peeling wall including a half-open window. On the windowsill there stood a small stoneware pot. Part of the wall was brightly lit, as if illumined by the fake window, the part beneath the sill in deep shadow.

'I bet you could earn a crust doing murals.' He pointed at the window. 'I thought the pot was real. And this bit of tree that you can see through the window. It's a winter-flowering cherry, isn't it?'

'I haven't a clue. It's whatever that is out there, in the neighbours' garden. It was in bloom when I first moved in.'

'This is bloody good, you know. I bet you I could get you a couple of commissions if you're up for it.'

'You mean I'd be a proper artist?' Bella clasped her hands together. 'Oh, I've dreamed of this for so long! Slaving away in my humble garret over a hot paintbrush. Going without cream doughnuts in order to buy paint. At last my genius has been recognised!'

'Do you do this about everything?' Will shook his head. 'I'll tell you one thing though . . . if you always joke about something that's really important to you, you're selling yourself short.'

'What makes you think painting's important to me?'

He said nothing. He leaned against the door frame and just looked at her. She felt herself flush as if he had accidentally caught sight of her naked.

'So what if it is?' She crossed her arms and bit her lip. 'Still got to eat, haven't I?'

'Of course. But if you don't take your work seriously, you can bet your bollocks no one else will either.'

Bella laughed. 'Bet your bollocks? Good grief. Where on earth did you get that from? Haven't got any bollocks. I'm a person of the female persuasion, in case you hadn't noticed.'

Will went into the bathroom and closed the door.

'Your metaphorical bollocks,' he called from the other side. 'Which you certainly have got.' Bella started to go downstairs. 'And, yes, I had noticed,' she heard his voice from above.

Over a number of phone calls, a few faxes, and many cups of tea in the following fortnight, the garden plan was finalised and a modest budget agreed. Some of the construction work—the patio, the pergola—was to be carried out by Will's subcontractor, Douglas. Will explained that he could keep the costs down if Bella helped with the clearing and planting, and it would speed it up. 'My other projects are all civic stuff at the moment, so we could do most of it at the weekends if you'd prefer it,' he said. 'Then you can help and oversee it. You sure you're happy? You can do any amount of fiddling with the details later but we've got to get the foundations right at the beginning or it'll never work.'

'So,' said Bella, 'the acid test: do you share your brother-in-law-in-law's belief that work is more of an interesting concept to be discussed rather than something to be actually done, or can you make a start soon?'

He could. He would. He was raring to go, he said.

'So what's he like then?' Viv leaned back in her chair at the tapas bar.

'Oh, hello, this is a bit of all right.' Bella turned round the wine bottle to examine the label. 'Who?'

'Your garden man. Is he a rugged man of the soil? Tough, but secretly sensitive underneath?'

'Not as such. I think Will and sensitive are not words that would naturally fall in the same sentence.'

'Still, you seem to be spending a lot of time in his company. I miss you. And Nick's hankering for your prawn thing again.'

'Glad you both appreciate me for my lovable qualities and not just my magical way with a piece of ginger root.'

'So, when are you next seeing him?'

'I am not "seeing him" at all. He is coming to start *work* on Saturday morning.'

'Bet you get up early to put on your make-up. Tastiness quotient?'

'You're obsessed. You're supposed to be past all this.'

'I have to have some vicarious pleasure, don't I? Anyway, you must have thought about it.'

'Why must I? I'm not the one who's obsessed. I told you, I haven't got the energy to have a relationship. Don't look at me like that.'

Viv sighed. 'So, is he tasty or what?'

'He's not really the kind you have mad passionate fantasies about. Not handsome, but quite attractive. Cuddly. His eyes are nice. He's sort of solid-looking, like a tree, as if you could lean on him. And he has this little scar—here.' She raised her hand to her eyebrow.

'Not that you've spent any time looking at him at all.'

Bella wrinkled her nose. 'His hair's a bit peculiar, springy, bits of it stick up oddly.'

'Golly. Wild hair. How awful.' Viv's eyes widened, taking in Bella's sprawling curls.

'Very droll.' Bella knocked back the remainder of her wine. 'Anyway, he's certainly no dashing Mr Rochester. He's just an ordinary bloke.'

'Do I get any wine at all? Don't write him off though, babe. Remember, Mr Rochester did have a bonkers wife locked in the attic. There's a lot to be said for an ordinary bloke.'

The week at work stretched out, a predictable cycle of meetings, designing, staring glassy-eyed at her computer, and chatter, nipping out for cappuccinos—*I think you mean cappuccini, Bella-darling.* She found herself drawing more often. Her layout pad filled with sketches of her colleagues in a gallery of postures, her pen moving at speed over the paper, capturing the way they stood, sat, leaned, stretched and worked.

On Thursday, Viv phoned.

'Are you all right? You sound terrible.'

'This just feels like a very, very long week. Finding it a struggle to feign enthusiasm about Buck's-fizz-flavoured yoghurt.'

'You're kidding?'

'No, I'm just not in the mood for it, you know.' Bella was already wishing she'd asked Anthony to get her two Crunchies on the chocolate run.

Viv invited Bella to a party on Saturday.

'Nick's cousin Julian has just breezed in from Rio and we're trying to show him that we have an exciting life, too—'

'But you don't.'

'You know that, we know that. He doesn't. Nick says he can't bear Julian being all smug because we're so settled and couply and boring.

Say you'll come. You're not doing anything else, are you?'

'Charming. I could be. Masked ball. Movie premiere. Romantic week-end in Hull.'

'So you're free then?'

'Unbelievably, yes.'

Bella offered to turn up early, to lend a hand.

Saturday. At last.

'No croissants?' Bella peered at Will from behind her front door.

'I knew I'd spoiled you too early on.'

'Oh, well, you're here now. Come in anyway.'

She passed him a plate. And a croissant. Tried to stop herself from grinning like a fool, biting her lip. Annoyed with herself for being pleased to see him. Surprised. Bustled into the kitchen, speaking to him over her shoulder, avoiding his gaze. *Don't be too keen.*

'Went out early and got them. Hardly slept anyway, so thought I might as well get up.'

'Oh? Why's that?'

'Oh, you know . . .' She turned the tap on full, filled the kettle, con-centrated on scrubbing the sink.

Plastic sheeting topped with dustsheets was spread all the way from the front door to the French windows; everything—bricks, rubble, shingle, plants—would have to go through the house because it was mid-terrace.

They set to work, clearing the brambles, moving plants to protect them from the debris.

'Don't overdo it,' he said. 'You'll do your back in if you're not used to this kind of work.'

'I suppose you think I'm just a fragile female?'

'Why are you so defensive? It's nothing to do with what sex you are. It's what you're used to that matters. You can't spend all week sitting at a desk and then leap straight into heavy physical work.' He leaned his garden fork against the wall. 'Time for a break anyway.'

Douglas arrived at lunchtime, to lift the turf from the lawn and pre-pare the sub-base for the patio. He was a quiet man and merely nodded hello to Bella.

'Very shy,' Will whispered. 'Frightened of attractive women.' Will marked out on the ground where the pergola would go.

'And this is where your little bower will be. See? You'll be invisible even from a few feet away once the plants are in.'

'Perfect,' she said.

Bella seemed to have been staring into the black hole of her wardrobe for a very long time. She could really do with some new clothes. It was basically down to three options: black silky trousers with brown wrapover top or cream silk shirt, short red skirt with sexy black top which helped divert attention away from the fact that her stomach stuck out, or purple dress that was too clingy.

Her gaze fell on the cherry-red two-piece that Alessandra had given her. The fabric was glorious. She took it out and held it up against herself. It was beautiful; too good for her really. She didn't feel smart enough to do it justice. Besides, it was probably way too dressy for the party. The purple. At least it was a change from black. What the hell, she'd hold her stomach in. It was a good dress to flirt in. It made her feel more forward, more daring.

'I'll be off then,' Will called up the stairs.

'OK. Hang on a sec. I'll be right down . . .' She thundered down the stairs.

'Ah, do I hear the patter of a tiny buffalo stampede? Are you—' He stopped.

'What? What's the matter?'

'Nothing. Sorry. Haven't seen you in all your finery before. Didn't recognise you without mud on your face.'

'Er—do I—look all right? It's not too—?'

'Too what?'

'Well, too clingy. See—' she turned side on, 'my stomach sticks out.'

'My God! You're right. People will be whispering in corners about it. Perhaps you could hire a small marquee to wear instead.'

'We are not amused. Just answer—does it make me look fat or not?'

'Unbelievable.' Will shook his head. 'Why does every female on the planet think she's fat?'

'So is that a yes, then?'

'Mind-boggling. Have fun, Moby Dick.' He turned to go. 'I'm off to fight my way round Tesco's.'

Odd. She was sure she had a couple of bottles of wine left. The mice must have drunk them. Now she'd have to go via the supermarket on the way to the party.

It was surprisingly crowded. Who on earth would choose to shop on a Saturday evening? she wondered. Maybe they were all swinging singles out looking for action. She was always reading that supermarkets were a great place to meet people. Was that so you could see in advance whether you had compatible tastes? Never mind whether you had any interests in common or similar politics, values, ideologies. Did he buy gravy granules, chicken nuggets or Quorn burgers—that was what you really needed to know. She started peering into people's trolleys; what she wanted was someone with fresh pasta, decent wine and plenty of chocolate, who kissed sexily and could make her laugh.

Suddenly, there, at the far end of her aisle, Bella thought she saw Will, apparently absorbed in his shopping list. She could sneak up behind him and pinch his bum. No. She could pretend to be a normal person and say hello in a friendly manner. Yes. She would do that.

As she moved towards him, Will abandoned his trolley for a moment and disappeared round the corner. She wondered what kind of things he bought, bet it was frozen lasagne, beer and probably something unexpected—Battenberg cake, maybe. A look into his trolley. Apples. Bananas. Frozen lasagne—hah! Tins of things. Nothing exciting. Two large plastic packets: Newborn Ultra-Dry, they said. Unisex. Soft and Snug. A large blue plastic bottle: Johnson's Baby Bath.

She recoiled as if she had been bitten. Backed away into a gangly youth in a bow tie who was rearranging the shelves.

'Sorry,' she said. 'Sorry.' Turning, clutching her basket, swinging it into a woman. 'Sorry, sorry.' Heading for the wine, the till, the exit.

5

'AH-HA!' SAID VIV when she opened the door. 'The sexy purple. Are you out to entrap someone in particular or is it just a lure for any unsuspecting male who happens to be passing?'

'It's either part of a cunning plot to overthrow the government and change civilisation as we know it or a sad and desperate attempt to inveigle some feeble-minded myopic man with excess testosterone into chatting me up. You choose. So you don't think it shows off my stomach too much?'

'I see there's been no unexpected rise in self-esteem on the stock market then.' Viv waved her in.

Bella raised one eyebrow. 'Call yourself a hostess?' she said. 'I've been here forty-five seconds and not been offered so much as a Twiglet.'

Viv slavered garlic and herb butter onto slit baguettes while Bella tipped pistachios and olives into dishes.

'Getting enough to eat there, are you?' said Viv as Bella cracked open yet another pistachio nut. 'Are you all right? You look a bit peaky.'

'I'm fine. Give me a top-up, will you?'

'Steady on. You've got a whole evening to get through. What's up?'

'Nothing. Everything. It sounds stupid.'

'What's stupid?' Nick breezed into the kitchen.

'I just saw Will in the supermarket with a trolley full of nappies.'

'What a bastard!' Nick shook his head. 'What? I thought that's what I'm supposed to say. Thought I'd get it in before you did. Who's Will anyway?'

'Bella's garden man. I said you bloody liked him. Well, he's obviously not worthy of you, then.'

'I feel such a fool. Ever since I met him, there seemed to be this thing between us—'

Nick raised his eyebrows suggestively.

'Go away,' said Bella and Viv at the same time.

'This unspoken assumption that we like each other. I bet he flirts with all his clients just to butter them up. He's probably turning to his wife and cooing over their baby—and laughing about me and my stupid boxes and my stupid mural—and I hate him now only not as much as I hate me and I wish I'd never met him. It's really all my fault because I allowed myself to like him which was stupid, stupid, stupid. And I can't even send him away because he's started and there's soil everywhere and if he doesn't finish the garden, it'll look like a total tip and the house already looks like a warehouse. More wine, please.'

'Oh, babe. I'm sorry. We'll find you someone nice, won't we, Nick?'

'Me? What are you looking at me for? You're always saying my friends are clueless.'

Bella dug into the pistachios again. 'Forget it. It's a lost cause. I don't care any more. I'm going to be celibate for ever and devote myself to art.'

The doorbell rang. Nick was making the French dressing, and Viv was 'elbow-deep in bloody lollo rosso', so Bella went to the door.

It was Sara and Adam, a couple whom Bella had already met, and Nick's cousin Julian, who had been sent out for more paper napkins and arrived back at the same time. Bella offered them drinks and tried not to look at Julian too much.

More people started arriving and Bella got hooked up in an argument two couples were having about nursery schools. When she ventured an opinion, all four of them turned as one and gave her that look; one woman voiced the predictable statement on their behalf: 'Of course, when you have children of your own, you'll feel differently.' How could she argue with that? She was tempted to embarrass the couples, to tell them that, tragically, she could never have children because . . . because she had some horrible disease, she had donated her womb to science, her Fallopian tubes had been mangled by a mad surgeon, her ovaries refused to release any eggs without written authorisation.

From the other side of the room, Julian caught her eye, raised his glass, and beckoned her with his head. God he was tasty. Bella hastily excused herself and tried not to appear to be rushing over towards him.

She should definitely have stopped drinking at that stage because she'd already had more than she was used to. At some point in the evening, she noticed a burst of too-loud laughter and was inwardly curling her lip in smug disapproval when she realised that it was her own; but she didn't seem to care any more. For once, she wanted to forget about being sensible and act the bimbo, flirt outrageously and simply enjoy the obvious effect it had on men. So she found herself laying her hand on Julian's arm and gazing at him with rapt attention while she asked him to tell her all about his travels. He returned her eye contact with frank interest and happily talked about himself.

It was well after one in the morning when the last guest had finally been folded into a taxi, and Viv had ushered her into their spare bedroom. 'Don't argue. You're in no condition to go anywhere,' she scolded affectionately. 'Julian's volunteered to have the sofa bed, so you're in here, though I think he'd have been more than happy to squeeze in here with you judging from the way he's been eyeing you all evening.'

Viv started to make up the bed. Bella pulled pathetically at one side of the sheet but subsided into giggles and keeled slowly over onto the bed while it was still only half made. 'Do you think he fancies me then?'

'Shift off. If he'd stood any closer he'd have been in that dress with you. But I wouldn't bother if I were you—he's off to Washington in a few days. Anyway, he may be quite hunky, but he's not all that interesting really and he's got an ego the size of the EU butter mountain.'

'Nice shoulders.' Bella smacked her lips in appreciation. Viv sighed and pulled the quilt over her. 'Night-night,' she said.

'You said you'd show me around town.' Julian's voice on the phone was confident, expecting assent. 'I'm only here for a few days and I've got to shoot up to Coventry tomorrow. How about Friday, after work? I'd love to discover all those secret places the tourists never see.'

I bet you would, Bella thought, hearing herself accept with a flirtatious laugh. Why bother with innuendo when you could be blatantly suggestive? God, she had been so drunk at the party.

Friday morning was bright and sunny, definite skirt weather. Shaving her legs in the shower, Bella told herself it was just because of the skirt. She certainly had no intention of letting Julian run his warm male hands all over her silky-smooth calves, no siree. Similarly unconcerned about which underwear to put on, Bella foraged through her top drawer then scooped up the contents and chucked them onto the bed. Her decent cream-lace set and her sexy dark red bra and pants were in the linen basket. She should have done a load of washing yesterday; too late now. She picked through the garments, holding them aloft between finger and thumb. Three pairs of ageing, greyish, allegedly white cotton briefs; a Valentine's Day pair emblazoned with a red heart on the front and the legend 'I'm Yours'—*I don't think so*. She dropped them back into the drawer. A pale pink pair with too-loose elastic. Black lacy knickers that were so skimpy that knickers seemed too big a word for them; they had been a present from Patrick. She stuffed them back into the drawer. She could nip to the shops at lunchtime and pick up a plain pair of cotton pants to change into at the office. This was ridiculous, she reproved herself, no one would be looking at her knickers; this was a stroll around the city and perhaps a spot of supper—theoretically, no underwear assessment would be involved. Still, she really could do with some new tights and things anyway, and it wouldn't take long.

As she was dashing out the door to go to work, the phone rang. It was Will.

'Oh, hello you. I'm glad you're there. Are you in tonight?'

'No, I'm not for once. Do you need to get in?' *How's your wife?* she wanted to say. *Baby doing nicely?*

He only wanted to check those shrubs they'd transplanted, he said, and had she remembered that he couldn't work tomorrow but that he might pop in, and that Douglas should be coming at eleven? Was she off somewhere nice?

'Mmm. Just, you know. Out.' Bet he thought she had some pathetic crush on him. 'On a date actually,' she added.

'Oh.' He coughed. 'Have fun then.'

Julian wasn't there when she arrived by the east door of the cathedral, a little breathless as she was slightly late, so she leaned against a bollard and simply enjoyed the sun on her face while she watched people walking by. A mumbling man marched by in a battered straw panama and a blazer that had long since shrugged its shoulders and given up any thought of passing for smart; he seemed to be towed by his unlikely-looking companion, a small, snuffling terrier that resembled a shaggy bathmat gone grey in the wash. She should have brought her sketchbook. This was a perfect spot to catch people. She closed her eyes, trying to imprint the pictures in her mind.

A shadow stepped into her sun.

'Do you know you look even more delectable today than you did in that sexy dress?' said Julian. 'So, do I get a kiss?'

It went on and on. Julian seemed to be taking immense pride in the fact that he could carry on for a long time, as if a marathon were in some way inherently better than a sprint, no matter how dull it was. Boring sex was bad enough, but if the person had staying power as well . . . Bella felt she was starting to go numb.

Her gaze roved around the room. That lampshade wasn't ideal in here. The shape was a bit odd and you could see the bulb, especially from this angle. Perhaps she could make one from that parchmenty stuff and draw on it? She'd better get some shopping in tomorrow, too—she was definitely running out of loo paper. And bleach. More olive oil. She mentally sifted through the kitchen cupboards. Pasta—rigatoni or tagliatelle? Shells? Better check detergent, too.

He was still going. What did he want—a medal? She closed her eyes, letting her mind drift, her thoughts float free, watching herself from the outside. She willed Patrick to be here, warm and alive, reassuring and known, loving her, absolving her.

His face before her, now, smiling his familiar smile. He kisses her once, hard, then reaches up under her skirt. As he lifts it, she feels the thrill of their long-disappeared brocade bedspread, textured like a low-relief map, rough beneath her naked thighs. Surprised by his sudden urgency, she starts to pull away, to look at him, read his eyes. But, even as he touches her, his brown eyes swim to sea-grey, his jaw broadens, his hair gets lighter, shorter, growing springy as cushion-moss beneath her hand—and it is Will's face she sees. His tender face. She feels her eyes well with tears and she moves towards him then, her lips on his, their mouths hungry, greedy, grateful.

'Well, well,' said Julian, 'you certainly warmed up all of a sudden. Bit of a slowcoach, eh?' He slapped her bottom playfully.

'Guess so.' She lay back, flushed with lust and pleasure and guilt. She rolled over then on the rumpled sheet, suddenly appalled at its unfamiliar softness, her body still alive to the touch of the rough brocade.

Waiting for the kettle to boil, Bella stared down at her feet, pale and soft against the cold quarry tiles. Her toenails could do with a trim, and her nail varnish was chipped.

What on earth did she think she was doing? She had just leapt into bed with a virtual stranger and had to fantasise about another man—two men—she was getting seriously weird—and yet here she was thinking about her toenails. Still, it was better than thinking about how extraordinarily, incredibly, mind-bogglingly stupid she'd been. And it hadn't even worked anyway. She still felt horrible about Will, worse if anything because thinking about him had made her so turned-on, only now she felt bad about Julian and guilty about Patrick as well. Three for the price of two. Marvellous.

But what if she could never enjoy sex again without pretending it was with Patrick or someone else? Her sense of shame stung her afresh.

The doorbell rang. She rolled over, dopey from lack of sleep. The shock of another face on the pillow next to hers.

'Expecting visitors?' asked Julian. 'Not the vicar, I hope.'

Bella laughed and shook her head. Why was she humouring him? Glanced at her watch. Nearly ten thirty. Could be Douglas a bit early. A horrible thought: it might be Will. Perhaps she should ignore it.

The bell rang again. No time to get dressed. Well, what did it have to do with him anyway? It was certainly none of his business whom she chose to sleep with. Have sex with. Absolutely none. She pulled her robe close around her, crossed her arms over her chest and stomped downstairs to open the door. Framed her face in a look of defiance.

'Morning,' Will said. 'Sorry if I got you out of bed, but you should be up anyway. Glorious day. Come out to the garden.' He steamed through to the kitchen.

'Any chance of a cup of tea?'

'Why? Have you lost the use of your hands?'

'I didn't want to just barge in and make myself at home.'

'Why not? You do normally.'

Will turned to look at her.

'You're as prickly as a hedgehog holly this morning. What's up?'

'Nothing's *up*.' Why couldn't he go away? She crossed her arms again and looked down at her feet. 'I'm just in the middle of something.'

'In your dressing gown?' Will laughed, then flushed. 'Oh. Right. Sorry.' He clunked the kettle back down on the worktop. 'Why didn't you say? I'm only the gardener after all. You don't have to pussyfoot around my feelings.'

'No, I—it's not. I—'

'There's no need to look embarrassed.' He was looking at her directly now. 'I'm sure you don't need to justify yourself to the hired help.'

Bugger him. How dare he try and make her feel ashamed?

'No. I certainly don't. You've got a fucking cheek, trying to make me feel guilty when you've been flirting with me all this time and you've got a wife and babies and everything.'

'What?' Will looked behind him. 'Are you talking to me?'

'Yes, don't pretend. It doesn't suit you. You didn't exactly advertise it, did you? How very peculiar that this minor detail of your life seemed to have slipped your mind during all the talks we've had. But I *saw* you. In Tesco's with *millions of nappies*.'

He sighed loudly and shook his head.

'Have me put down now and put me out of my misery. Did it not occur to you to speak—try communicating some time, why don't you? Try saying: Will, why have you bought a load of nappies? Then I say: Bella, I'm glad you asked. It's because I'm a proud and devoted uncle. I was helping my sister out because what with her five-year-old girl, her baby boy and her workaholic husband, she's bloody knackered. OK?'

Bella was silent, bunching and unbunching her fists by her sides. Her breastbone felt tight, as if it were clamped against her lungs, squeezing, pressing the breath out of her.

'I just sort of assumed . . .' Her voice a croak.

'Why didn't you ask if it was bugging you?' Will took a step towards her.

'Why on earth should it bug me?' She rallied, defiant once more, moving away. 'It's nothing to do with me how many babies you have. You could have a whole crèche-load for all I care.'

'Thanks. Anyway, for the record—not that anyone's remotely interested in me or my life or my marital status—I am: a) childless, b) single, and c) open to offers. Thank you. I am now going into the garden to check those shrubs, then I'll be out of your hair.'

'There's no need. Take as long as you like.' She bit the inside of her lip. She wouldn't cry. Would not. Dug her fingernails hard into her palm. *I don't care*, she told herself, *I don't care, I don't care, I don't care.*

'Just make sure you drag yourself out of bed to give them another watering tomorrow if there's no rain. I'll be back on Monday anyway before you go to work—eight sharp. Please make sure you're up.'

'A SMALL TOKEN of apology.' Will pushed a small plastic bag into her hands. 'Still a bit early for roses.'

The bag was filled with stems of rosemary from his garden. Rubbing it between her fingers, she dipped her head to breathe it in: heavenly—rich and pungent, but a clean smell, almost antiseptic.

She should apologise, she knew. It had been entirely her fault. Making assumptions. And then she'd practically thrown herself at Julian to make herself feel less crappy. What was the point of a brief bout of meaningless sex if it made you feel so bloody miserable afterwards?

Once Will had stomped off on Saturday morning, she couldn't get Julian out of the house fast enough, babbling about vital work—she had to go into the office, she'd said—ushering him down the stairs—giving him coffee in a small cup so he'd drink it quickly—kissing him in the hallway, her hand already on the doorknob—saying yes, yes, it had been wonderful—would love to see him next time he was over. Bye-bye.

'I know you're a bit of a foodie. Sorry about the inelegant wrapping.'

'Thank you. I love it. Why are *you* apologising anyway?'

He gave a small cough. 'I'm just sorry if I was a bit snotty on Saturday.'

No sweat, she said, it didn't matter.

Definitely, she should apologise. She scrunched her toes in her shoes at the thought of it, the shame, admitting she'd been wrong. As a child, her head dipped like a wilting flower, she'd seemed to be having to say sorry almost every day. Sorry, Mummy, I didn't mean to—sorry, I forgot—sorry, I didn't know—didn't realise—thought it would be all right—sorry for being a nuisance—sorry for being naughty—sorry for being me. Her mother's mouth, twitching in silent triumph, suddenly gracious in victory: *That's all right, Bella-dear. You'll know better next time, won't you?*

'Yes,' Will nodded, 'it does. I—was—well. I apologise.'

'Me too. Really.'

'Me three.' He smiled. 'Really.'

'You can make the tea—if it'll help you feel better.'

Will said he couldn't stay now, had only come to check a couple of things and drop off the rosemary, but was she still all right for Saturday?

'Or are weekends likely to be a problem in future?'

'Is that Will-speak for is there likely to be a recurrence of last Saturday? I'd say it's about as probable as my being commissioned to fresco the dome of the Albert Hall.'

He shrugged. 'So quite possible then?'

'And you say *I'm* a dreamer?' She shoved him playfully.

'You *are*. Now, have you started the mural on the far wall yet?'

'It's still in the planning stage.'

'That'd be a no then, as you would say.' He turned to leave. 'Better get on with it, hadn't you? I need you to be useful at the weekend.'

'But I'm not designed to be useful.'

'You'll love it. It'll be a new experience. Trust me.'

Starting the mural on the garden wall, Bella felt once more that old rush of excitement, giddy and disturbing. Years before, when she'd been accepted for art school, she'd considered herself a lucky fraud: being allowed—encouraged!—to draw and paint all day! A licence to play. Remembered Alessandra's baffled smile, explaining Bella's peculiar peccadillo to the neighbours. 'Of course, dear Bella could have gone to university, but she's set her heart on being an artist!' It sounded no less ludicrous to her own ears, like wanting to be a ballet dancer or an astronaut, a silly childish fantasy. She'd kept herself in check. Opted for graphic design. Practical. Commercial. Focused on building her career.

On Saturday morning, Will stood back to admire the beginnings of the *trompe-l'oeil* arch on the garden wall. 'You probably want to carry on, or shall I show you how to plant and stuff?'

'The Henderson patented Instant Green Fingers Course? Will that really make me a proper gardener?'

'Oh no, my lovey, takes years 'n' years to become the real thing. See? Look at those hands.' He held his palms outstretched towards her. 'That's ingrained that is, never come out.'

Bella started to stretch out her finger, to trace the lines in his hands. She wondered what his skin would feel like beneath her fingertip, how he had got that scar at the base of his thumb. Their eyes met.

'Nonsense,' she said, withdrawing her hand and diverting its direction to push back a strand of hair from her eyes. 'You just need a good scrubbing, that's all. Show me the secrets of the soil then. I can't paint with someone else watching me anyway.'

'Really? Why's that?'

She stopped, not having really thought about it before.

'I think it's a bit like having someone in the same room when you're in the bath or on the loo. Kind of—'

'Intimate?'

'Mmm-mm.' She nodded. 'Does that sound wanky?'

Will laughed through his nose.

'Tremendously, you old pseud. No, not at all. Makes sense. But what about once you've finished a painting? People are going to look at it then, aren't they? It's still revealing.'

'Ye-e-e-es. But it's separate from you then. Like an ex-husband or something. You had a relationship once, but he no longer has quite the same power to embarrass you in public.'

He showed her how to plant, carefully firming the soil around a lemon verbena, giving it his undivided attention. He passed her another pot.

'Here. Your go. About there, so it has room to grow.'

'You really love this, don't you?' she asked, looking across at him. The tips of his ears went slightly pink, then he nodded.

'Always have. Ever since I was a kid. Used to sow sunflower seeds, radishes, anything I could get my hands on. My mum gave me my own little patch of garden when I was eight. And Hugh, my stepdad—ex-stepdad now, I suppose, as he died a few years back. Whatever. He helped me lay a course of bricks all round the edge to make it my own little kingdom.'

'They sound nice. You must miss him. My dad's a keen gardener.' Bella got up from where she'd been kneeling on the ground and stretched herself. 'You'd like him.' She said it without thinking, seeing Will and Dads in her mind, the two of them together, bending over plants, pointing, talking, at ease. Swung her arms, pushing the thought away.

'Are you stiff? Sorry if I've been too much of a slave-driver,' he said. 'And your mum? Does she garden too?'

'Ha!' The thought was amusing, absurd. She looked down at him. 'She might snip a few flowers, but the rest of it—too messy. Might spoil her hands.' Bella held up her own hands and stroked one delicately against the other, as if admiring their charms in the sunlight. 'Oh no! National crisis! Call the Emergency Services! Bella-darling, I've chipped a nail!'

Will laughed.

'I'm sure she can't be all bad as she produced you.'

'I'm a changeling. Didn't I tell you?'

They fell into a routine over the following month, working each weekend, stopping too often to talk or to survey their progress, adjusting the plan slightly here and there as they went. As she dug her trowel into the soil, she could hear the confident clipping of his secateurs, methodical and comforting, his quiet humming as he tied in a climber or cut back a wayward stem.

The mural was completed, the painted arch offering a glimpse of another garden beyond, with a moss-cushioned woodland floor opening to a sunlit clearing, at once tantalising and out of reach.

Silently, he leaned past her, stretching into the cupboard for two mugs. They moved around each other in the narrow kitchen, a silent dance, sidestepping, anticipating, not touching. The gaps between them fizzed; she felt the air charged and trembling, making her skin prickle, her body light and buoyant. She wondered what he would do if she were to touch his back as he stood by the sink washing his hands, imagined his warmth beneath her palm, her fingers. She swallowed. A hollow ache in her gut. A slight feeling of nausea. Low blood sugar, she told herself, that's all it is. Wished he would go away, leave and not come back—ever. Wanted him to stay—always. Wanted him to hold her, stroke her hair, make her safe.

The work, inevitably, took longer than he had originally estimated. 'It's your fault, of course,' he said. 'Too easy to talk to'—but, finally, it was done.

'Well then.' Will lingered on the doorstep. 'I'd better be off.'

She thanked him again for all his hard work. It was stunning, she said, she would try to look after it properly.

'You better had or I'll come round and deface your mural. Oh and—nearly forgot.' He turned back towards her.

Her heartbeat quickened.

'Would it be OK for me to come back soon to take some photographs? For my folio?'

Bella stood at the door for a moment, then went into the kitchen to fill the kettle. Wiped the surfaces, opened first one cupboard then another, as if looking for something. Padded through to the sitting room to plump the cushions. It was a good thing, she told herself, pounding the cushions, tweaking at the corners to make them pointy, that he hadn't kissed her goodbye or anything silly like that because then he would still have left and she'd be feeling a whole lot worse.

Yes, all things considered, she was very lucky that he hadn't kissed her. She picked up the phone and called Viv, to see if she wanted to come and admire the garden before Bella had a chance to mess it up.

'Wow. It looks stunning now it's all finished. Lemme out there.' Viv rattled at the French windows. 'Is this all the work of the wunderkind Will?'
Bella unlocked the doors. 'Yup. And me.'
'So, tell me more. Since you found out he was single—has he—'
'Declared his intentions? No. I think I've lost the knack, Viv. Anyway, it's too late to impress him. He knows me too well.'
'But?' Viv raised her eyebrows into an exaggerated arch.
'But what? I told you before, he's not drop-dead gorgeous or anything . . .'
'Orange toupee? Nicotine teeth?'
'I admit I do think he has a nice face—the kind that makes you think you must always have known him. And he's got this little scar here—'
'I know, I know—you told me, it makes him look vulnerable. You're bloody smitten woman. Admit it.'
'Nonsense.'
'Yes you are. You're all glowy and smiley. You're in l-u-u-r-r-v-e.'
'Am not. You know I'm immune to that sort of thing. And please don't use the "l" word before the nine o'clock watershed or I'll report you.'

'Hello.' It was Will. 'It's me,' he said.
'You're right,' she said. 'How could you tell?'
'Don't be annoying. You're probably wondering what reason I could possibly have to call you when I only left your house a few hours ago and the garden's all done?'
'You're calling to tell me to check the peonies every half-hour and to tie in any traily bits on the clematis. You told me.'
'Did I? Good.' There was a pause.
'And I've got a possible commission for a Kreuzer mural.' He told her about an urgent civic project he had, two alternative designs for part of the area behind the mayoral offices. It was a plum job, high-profile, could bring in lots of new clients. Would she be interested in coming up with a couple of ideas for a mural at the back? Only on spec, but could be worth it.
'Thing is, we'd have to meet up to go through the brief. I could pop round or we could go out. How would tomorrow suit you? Evening?'
It was a first-rate opportunity, so why did she suddenly feel disappointed? A large-scale commission—what could possibly be better? You're just scared, she told herself, scared to try anything new.

Could it really be true? *Another* spot? Smack dead centre on her chin. It couldn't have been more perfectly centred if she had used a measuring tape and painted it there herself. The spot gleamed back at her from the mirror. Will wouldn't be able to take his eyes off it.

If she wore the black top that was quite low-cut, he might not notice the spot. Sort of like creating a diversion. Good grief, it was a meeting, not a seduction. Will you be sensible, she told herself. Her fingers wandered over her smart charcoal suit: too formal. Back to the black top, teamed with a sober skirt to show that she was capable of being a serious, professional person. She looked at herself in her old barley-twist mirror: first, the top half—the black top clung as closely as a drunken friend. Better cover herself up with a jacket. She tilted the mirror to inspect her lower half. Perhaps she should go wild and buy a full-length mirror one day. Then again, perhaps not; she felt she was best seen only a small portion at a time.

The doorbell rang.

'Wow—have you dressed up just for me?' he smiled.

'This is my official impressing-a-prospective-client outfit, not that you bothered when it was the other way round. And it's to distract people from the repulsive spot on my chin. Don't worry—it's not contagious.'

Shut up, shut up, she told herself. Just try to be normal.

Drinks drifted into dinner. Dinner stretched into coffee. More coffee. It was getting late. He said he would walk her home. They meandered through the streets, talking, walking slowly. Zigzagged along the high street, pointing out their favourite hideous objects in shop windows and searching for the ultimate Gift You'd Least Like to Have to Display in Your Own Home.

'So then.' Bella paused, eventually, at her door. 'Can you stand yet another coffee? Or will it keep you awake?' What the hell was that supposed to mean? Now he'd think she was trying to seduce him when she was only being friendly.

'It's late.' He smiled. 'I'd better get back.'

She turned to put her key in the door.

'Still. If you insist. Just for a minute.'

When Bella came down from the loo, Will was looking at the kitchen pinboard while drinking his coffee.

'Sweet-looking kid.' He nodded at the picture of Patrick's nephew, which was still attached to the board, having survived the move from

London. 'I always meant to ask you who he was.'

'Yes, isn't he? That's Lawrence in his school nativity play. My old boyfriend's nephew,' she continued. 'Patrick.' She gestured at a photo of a drenched Patrick standing by a Scottish loch, his straight hair plastered to his skull by rain. 'There. That's Patrick. Not looking his best there though. One of those Scottish holidays where it rains nonstop. We got soaked. Rain, rain. Endless.' She must stop talking about Patrick. She was starting to babble. *Will you shut up, woman?*

'Oh? Right.'

She saw his eyes drop to the picture at the bottom of the board, the one of her and Patrick together, sporting red Christmas antlers in bed.

'That looks horribly aren't-we-wacky.' She made a face. 'I must take it down some time.'

'I've got a bit of a confession to make,' Will said.

'I knew it. You used to be a woman. You're an international drug-smuggler. Out on parole. Worse—you're really a journalist?'

'The roughs for that project. I may have exaggerated its urgency.'

'When are they needed by?'

'Not for six weeks. I got home and then realised I didn't have an excuse to see you again. And I felt lousy.'

Her stomach felt tight, knotted. She couldn't do this—she couldn't have this kind of conversation—she must stop him—she'd thought she was ready for this, but she wasn't. She turned to the sink, poured herself some water, holding on to the cold metal of the tap.

'Do you think you could turn round, Bella? I'm trying to talk to you.'

'OK, OK. I was just thirsty. You're supposed to have eight glasses of water a day. I read it somewhere. Good for the skin.'

'Thanks for letting me know that. Nice timing. Now I've started and I don't know how to—I've never, you know, really *liked* a client before, but there's always been—something—between us, hasn't there? I'm not very good at this, am I?'

Bella crossed her arms and shrugged. 'Good at what?' Behind Will's left arm, she could see part of Patrick's photograph.

'Oh, shit. Good start, Will.' He clunked down his mug on the worktop. 'I feel like such a prat. So you don't think there is?'

'Why should there be?'

'All the hours we've spent talking meant bugger all to you then?'

She shrugged.

'And every time we've looked at each other, that meant nothing either?'

He moved towards her.

She would not look at him. Could not. Opened her mouth to speak. He was standing close, so close. She could feel the warmth of him, smell his skin, his Will-smell that she had sniffed a hundred times in the garden, when he'd leaned close to her, showing her how to prune correctly, when he'd squeezed past her in the kitchen to get to the sink. She pressed herself back against the draining board, clutching the curved edge of the worktop. Noticed her knees were shaking. Surely she would pass out. If only he wouldn't stand so close.

'Oh, Bella . . .' His voice quiet. Then, he held her suddenly by her arms, anchoring her to the ground. His skin touching hers.

'Look me in the eye and say, "Will, you're imagining the whole thing. I'm not interested. I never have been." Come on. Say it. I'll believe you.'

At last, she raised her face to look into his eyes. She couldn't speak. Her lips parted, but there were no words. Her throat felt tight and full as if she were about to cry. Once more her mouth opened, forming a single silent word: *Will*.

And then she was in his arms. He was holding her, drawing her tight to him, his face buried in her hair, her neck, saying her name again and again. She tilted her face up towards him and his face was so close. He was kissing her now, his mouth warm and real, and she was drunk with it and the two of them were gasping and laughing and kissing. She pressed herself against him, feeling that he was indeed like some great tree, standing firm, safe and strong and true.

There was no way he would phone the next day. *You phone him if you want to. You're thirty-three for God's sake.* Well, she might just do that. But not yet. If he didn't phone her at work, then she would give him until, say, nine this evening, OK, eight thirty. After that, she could legitimately call him to ask vital questions about the mayoral mural because they hadn't really gone through the details properly and she wasn't sure if she'd noted down the dimensions correctly and she ought to be making a start on it; yes, she decided, she probably should give Will a ring.

She had awarded herself bonus points for not going to bed with him straight away, propelling him out of the front door, telling him she wanted to take things slowly. Her mother would have approved, she thought.

Even from the other side of the office, she saw that she had a message, signalled by the semaphore flag of a yellow stickie. She tried not to run to her desk. It was probably only a client. Clients always loved to phone first thing in the morning to catch people out when they were late in, while a colleague covered—'She's not at her desk right now. I believe she's in a meeting.' Or Viv, wanting to know whether Bella had at last broken the longest snog-free spell in recorded history. Bella had managed to suppress the urge to recount the full hideousness of the Julian saga, but Viv had given her that pursed mouth, something's-going-on-and-you're-not-telling-me look.

WILL PHONED. PLEASE CALL ASAP.

'Hi,' she said, phoning him while she was still standing, her bag hunched on her shoulder. 'It's me. Anything wrong?'

'Hello, you. No. Just being a sad sod who can't get enough of you. When am I seeing you? I need to kiss you again.'

'One moment, Mr Henderson. I'll have to put you on hold while I check Ms Kreuzer's diary . . .' She clucked her tongue officiously. 'Looking very busy, Mr H, especially with dull clients having just come into season. Oh, but, there may be a small *window* this evening.'

'I'm not sure I could fit into a small window. I'm not the svelte little snip I once was, you know.'

He was working outside the city in the afternoon, he said, overseeing the landscaping of the area round a swimming pool at a swanky health club, but he could be back a bit after seven. They arranged to meet in the little garden behind the cathedral.

There was still over an hour to spare after Bella had left work, so she went to the cathedral and leaned against one of the massive pillars to draw the tourists. She quickly sketched a couple pointing up at the carved masonry, a toddler journeying across the central square of grass. As she looked up from her pad, a woman settled to lean on one of the stone ledges, crossing her arms over her body like an Egyptian mummy, holding her shoulders. She stood watching the child for a little while. *Please don't move*, Bella willed her, *please don't move*. Speed gave her strokes greater boldness, confidence, mapping the angle of the woman's arms, the shape they formed round her neck, capturing the tilt of the chin, almost defiant. Her pencil set down the symmetry of the arch, framing the woman, echoing the line of her arms.

If only she had her paints with her; the evening sun falling at an angle seemed to pick out every element: the single strand of hair in front of the woman's eyes, the shadow her arm cast, the drape of the fabric round her shoulders, the shape of her elbow leaning on the flat stone. As if Bella had willed it, the woman suddenly looked up and straight towards her, without moving her head. There was something wistful about the angle of her head, as if she were trying to catch the faint strain of far-off music. Bella's pencil moved over the paper once more; she must paint this later, must, must, *must*. She closed her eyes, drinking in the image, the light, the shadows, feeling the picture sinking into her skin in thousands of points of colour like a tattoo.

'You've missed a bit.' Will's chin appeared over her shoulder. 'I may be a complete oik where art is concerned, but that's bloody good. Why aren't you in the little garden where you should be?'

A glance at her watch. 'I'm only five minutes late. Sorry. I got immersed.'

'Just as well I spotted you on my way there.'

'What do people *do* on dates? We should probably go see a movie or something.' Will rubbed his chin.

'You're hardly a toy boy. What do you normally do? Even you must have found the occasional female to take pity on you.' She felt his hand gently laid on the small of her back.

'So you're just doing this out of pity? Excellent. If I'm truly pathetic, will you seduce me?'

'Nope. It's just part of a local initiative to help keep our city clear of roving bands of garden designers rampaging along the high street, dead-heading the petunias. Shall we get a paper? See what's on?'

'We don't really want to go to the cinema, do we?' Will lightly nuzzled her cheek. 'You're probably desperate to invite me back to your place, but worried I'll lose all respect for you, so I just want to assure you . . . that I've never respected you anyway.'

'Thanks for reassuring me on that point. Come on, you. We're going to your place, I want to see *your* garden.'

'Oh, Will . . .' Bella laughed with the pleasure of it.

'I thought you might like it.' She had never seen him look so pleased.

It was like stepping into the most beautiful countryside. There was a pool, fringed with rushes, irises and a clump of giant gunnera, like an alien forest, each leaf an inverted umbrella; this melded seamlessly into a bog garden, filled with lush foliage plants and candelabra primulas, as neat and straight-backed as convent girls.

A small dining table and two simple benches were set beneath a pergola swamped in blue and white clematis and the acid-green leaves of a twining golden hop.

'Now it's warm I'll bring out my lanterns so we can sit here after dusk.'

After supper, Will pulled her onto his lap.

'Is it too soon to whisk you into bed?' he asked, kissing her.

'Oh, stop beating about the bush, Will. I have a teeny hunch you're trying to make a pass at me.'

'Well, is it? Not that I've been thinking about it nonstop for two months or anything.'

'Why? We're not in a rush, are we? Have you a plane to catch?'

They kissed and Bella stroked his back, as if she could absorb him through her fingertips. His hands stayed at the sides of her rib cage for a moment, not quite touching the soft rise where her breasts swelled away from her body. She drew his bottom lip gently between her teeth, sucked its fullness briefly, opened her mouth to his. His thumb eased across her left breast, circling the nipple. Their hands roamed over each other, exploring, stroking, teasingly avoiding erogenous zones, creating new ones. 'So much for not rushing,' she thought.

He gathered her to him in a tight squeeze, then pulled away.

'You'd better go while I'll still let you. I'm getting too turned-on.' He adjusted his jeans.

'I dare say you can handle the problem.'

He laughed, pulling her close for another kiss.

'Don't get me started again.' He removed his lips with a loud smack, as if they had been stuck together. 'And call me, Gorgeous.'

'You're gorgeous.'

'That's comma, Gorgeous—Gorgeous.'

'I know, Gorgeous.'

'Thank you and good night.'

She stood on the doorstep.

'Hang on,' he said. 'I'll just get my jacket. I'm walking you home. That way we can spin out this good-night kiss for at least another hour.'

7

'I COULD LIE LIKE this stroking you for hours. Days.' Will's finger paused in the dip above her collarbone. 'On the other hand . . .'

'Mmm-mm?' She spoke as in a dream.

'. . . I also want to shag you senseless, so get your knickers off.'

'I could tell you were a hopeless old romantic.'

Bella reached for the top button of his shirt. Her top came open and he peeled it off, traced the curve of her breasts through her silky camisole and lace bra. He raised her arms above her head and the camisole poured off her like cream.

'Slow down a sec, will you?'

'Sorry. Am I rushing?'

'No, but—new underwear—appreciate it, damn you.'

'You went and got new underwear? Just for me?'

She tried to backtrack—not really, she needed some anyway, she hadn't got round to doing her laundry.

'Uh-huh. I believe you, really I do. So, in fact, you were planning to get me into bed all along? Jury, please note.'

He bent to kiss her breasts above their frame of lace, reaching round her back to unhook her. His voice was low, deep in his throat. His chest felt warm and hard, solid against the soft swell of her breasts.

'God, you make me so nervous,' he said. 'Look at my hands.'

'Me too.'

'Me three.'

His fingers moved over her leg, stroking upwards, then exploring, teasing her through the lace. He traced the boundary along her thigh. Pushed aside the fabric, questing for her. She inhaled sharply and pushed against him.

A line of light squeezed through the gap in the curtains, slanting across the bed. Bella lay on her front, half-asleep. Will leaned towards her and blew the ghost of a breeze on her lashes. Her eyebrows dipped and furrowed in the centre, puzzled, then she peered at him through half-open lids. She smiled, a cat gorged on cream.

'Hello.' Her voice soft with sex and sleep.

'Hello, you.' Will brushed her lips in a morning kiss. 'Do you have a permit to look so sexy in the morning? Shall I make some coffee or do you want to take advantage of me again first?' He flopped back on the pillow. 'I'm completely defenceless.'

Her lips curved again.

'Mmm. Coffee.'

'I can see I'm not going to get much intellectual discourse out of you at this hour. Or unbridled passion. Coffee it is.'

He got up and tucked the duvet carefully round her shoulders.

She nipped to the loo and brushed her teeth. Glanced in the mirror. Oh terrific: mascara smudges under her eyes. She hopped back into bed as Will reappeared with a tray: coffee, toast, apricot jam. He was wearing her crimson kimono, which reached only to his shins.

'Make yourself at home, why don't you?' Bella nodded at the kimono.

'These sleeves are impossible. I'm afraid I may have dipped them in the coffee. How on earth do you manage with them?'

'I have slaves who come in to do my every bidding.'

'Ah-ha. So that's the secret. Need any more?'

'Yes, but you will be expected to perform certain *personal* favours.'

'Well, if I must, I must,' he said, reaching for her.

'Such as pouring me some coffee. Thank you.'

Will went through to the bathroom to shave and shower. Bella lay back against the pillows and closed her eyes. She let herself relive last night, savouring the best moments again and again. A world away from that fiasco with Julian. What the hell was all that about? she wondered. Why couldn't she have been more patient? Waited for . . . for. The long-banished phrase *The One* stubbornly resisted eviction from her head. *Don't be so stupid*, she told herself. *Don't be such a pathetic, fairy-tale-fantasising girlie. There's no such thing*. Still, at least this time there had been no group orgy with Patrick roped into the proceedings.

She regretted the thought as soon as it had popped into her head, knowing at once that she couldn't banish it now that it was there. And now he was there, conjured up like a genie in a bottle, waiting for her.

In her mind, she calls him, her voice echoing in shadowy recesses.

'Patrick!' she calls softly, then louder, 'Patrick?'

When she enters she sees he is reading, lounging with his legs over the side of the armchair. He doesn't look up when she opens the door, but she knows he must have heard her.

The fire is lit in the grate, but the flames yield no comforting heat.

'Busy?' he says.

'Mmm.' She stands facing the fire with her back to him. 'But I do think of you. Often.'

'Yeah.' And now she senses him look up. 'Right.'

'I'm sorry.' She turns to face him.

He shrugs and returns to his book.

'Doesn't matter. You can't be bothering about me all the time.'

'Don't be like that. I'm with you now. I'll stay for a little while.'

'If you like,' he says, not looking up from the page. 'It's up to you.'

Will came into the bedroom with a towel over his head, drying his hair.

'Hey—you OK? You look a bit pale.'

'Fine. Don't fuss.'

Will made a face and asked her what her plans were for the rest of the weekend. Painting, she told him, working up one of the drawings from her life class or the one she'd done in the cathedral cloisters.

'Good. Why don't we meet up later then? This evening?' He buttoned up his shirt.

'Mm. Quite a lot to do. Maybe another day.'

She sensed his eyes scanning her face, trying to read her.

'Shall I call your secretary? Sorry. Am I being too intense? I sort of assumed . . .'

Bella laughed and patted him lightly on the head.

'Relax, will you? What's the rush? At this rate, we'll be married by next week and divorced the week after.'

The phone rang. It was Viv.

'I was going to call you anyway,' said Bella. 'It's official. I've finally lost my virginity. Again.' She refused to count Julian, mentally sweeping the incident under the mat, best forgotten. The management cannot be held responsible for the occurrence of embarrassing one-night flings.

'Oi, Nick!' Viv shouted away from the phone. 'Guess what? Bella's got herself a shag at last!'

'Oh, feel free. Tell everyone, why don't you?'

'Nick's not everyone. He's really an honorary girlie. Garden man, right?'

'Garden man it is.'

'You really like him. I can tell.'

'No, I don't. Well. I do a bit. But don't tell anyone.'

'OK, OK. But, Bel—don't forget to let *him* know you like him, will you?'

'I'm sure he does.'

'No, really. Men can be amazingly stupid about things like that. You sound a bit miserable. You're supposed to be full of post-shag afterglow.'

'I am, I am. I just feel a bit, you know . . . Weird. Like I've been un— I can't explain it. Got to go.'

Three o'clock in the morning. The yellow light from the bedside lamp shone on a tangle of limbs, heavy with sleep. Bella shifted and took in an eyelid-slit view: the light, the pillow by her cheek, Will's face from below. The stubble on his chin, dark pinpricks. Even his nostrils were lovable, she thought. She moved slightly to nuzzle his neck.

'Hello, you,' he said, opening his eyes a peep to match hers.

'Hello, you.'

'You know—' He yawned, catlike. 'You know when I first realised I

414

was in love with you? You had this incredibly sexy dress on and you came running down the stairs and—you looked—so—beautiful I couldn't speak.'

'Makes a change.'

'Shut up. Then you started wibbling on about your tummy and you suddenly seemed so young and vulnerable, as if you were going out with the grown-ups for the first time.' He closed his eyes again and his mouth smudged a kiss across her left eyebrow before he settled back to sleep.

She nuzzled closer to his chest, as if she might absorb him through every pore in her body. Her eyelids shut tight, clenching onto the moment, feeling tears start to well. *Let me have this*, she prayed silently, like a child not daring to jinx her wish by speaking aloud. *If I'm good for ever, can I? Please let me have this. Please.*

Bella woke first and slid out of bed, carefully lifting the covers so as not to wake him. She made a pot of tea and brought it up to the bedroom. He was lying on his back in a straight line instead of his usual diagonal sprawl, taking up most of the bed. His body was absolutely still, his face expressionless. She put down the tray and drew closer, leaned over him.

'Will?'

No response. Her brows bunched into a frown. Dry mouth. Her hands clammy and cold, heartbeat loud in her ears.

Patrick's father gets slowly to his feet as Bella is shown into a side room. He holds her by her upper arms.

'I'm too late, aren't I?'

Joseph nods.

'He never woke up. They said he didn't suffer.'

She hears the words. *He didn't suffer.* Does that mean you're supposed to feel OK about it? Joseph crushes her in a tight hug so she can barely breathe. Rose, Patrick's mother, looks blank and numb. Bella dips to hold her and they clasp each other for a minute, survivors in a storm.

'Do you want to see him?'

A silent, screaming 'NO' echoes inside her head, ricocheting round her brain. She is afraid and then ashamed. 'What would Patrick want?' she asks herself. 'What would Patrick do if it were me?'

She nods once and a nurse leads her to just outside the room, saying she can take her time, have as long as she likes.

She peers through a small glass panel in one of the double doors. Patrick is lying on a narrow, trolley-type bed in a small room. She breathes a slow breath, squashing down a wave of nausea and palpable dread, and pushes open the door. A side table covered with a crisp white cloth holds a cut-glass vase of fresh flowers.

She looks down at Patrick. He looks slightly paler than usual, as you might expect under the circumstances. And there is a padded bandage covering half his head, though Bella suspects that, as this looks pristine, it is to protect the bereaved from the sight of their loved one with a squished skull. Aside from the bandage and two scratches on his forehead, Patrick looks surprisingly normal, as if he's dropped off, as he tends to do, for a quick doze. Perhaps if she prods him, he'll sit up with a jolt and say 'I wasn't snoring. I was just breathing deeply' the way he does. Did, she corrects herself.

One arm lies outside the crisply turned hospital sheet. She wants to touch his hand, reach over and give it a reassuring squeeze, though whether for Patrick or herself she can't be sure. She wants so much to feel his warmth, to feel him return the pressure of her hand. Perhaps she should touch it? Shock herself with its coldness, its waxy softness, so she would understand that it was true, know that he was really dead.

But she can't. She pats the other arm, the one safely under the sheet.

Her voice, when finally she speaks, is a hoarse whisper, sounding to her ears as if it comes from someone else.

'I'm sorry,' she says.

'Will?' Silence. She tweaked his nose. 'Will.'

He opened one eye.

'Boo,' he said.

'You pig.' She pinched him. 'You bloody scared me.'

'Hey, sorry. Ow. That hurt.'

'Good. Don't do it again. I'm confiscating your tea now.'

'Tea in bed?' He lifted his head from the pillow. 'Oh tea, tea, oh please.'

She poured it out, then took her own cup to the bathroom.

Will picked up her post from the doormat. As he handed it to Bella, his gaze dropped to a postcard on the top. His eyes met hers, then he glanced down again. She looked at the card: *Hi, Sexy!* it said in large capitals. Bella felt herself flush slightly and Will quickly turned away. The card was postmarked Washington. Julian. *Sorry we couldn't get it together again before I had to leave—the price of being a jet-setter! Great to spend time with you. See you on my next visit!?! Luv, J XXX.*

She put the card on the mantelpiece, next to one she'd recently received from Patrick's parents—'Very glad to hear you've escaped from the big smoke. We did worry about you in London on your own . . . Do keep in touch . . . visit any time . . .' As well as the occasional card or letter, there were still periodic phone calls.

She felt she should ask them for permission to be happy. Knew, of course, what they would say: 'You've got your own life to lead now, Bella. Don't waste it. He wouldn't have wanted that, not Patrick.' And no, she realised, he wouldn't, not exactly. How would she feel if it had been the other way round? 'You wouldn't feel anything, stupid, you'd be dead,' she told herself. But still—what if she had died and Patrick had been left alone? Or—her scalp prickled—what if it were Will? Would she want him to grieve for ever? In a horrible way, she would—at least in some small corner of himself. What a vile, mean-spirited person she was. How could she ever want Will to be unhappy? No. She'd want him to remember, that was all, only so she wouldn't be lost without trace. She wouldn't want to have him hunched over his grief, treasuring it and hoarding it like a miser, allowing no one near—a second death.

'Can I ask you something?' Will said after breakfast. Then, without pausing, 'Are you seeing anyone else?'

'No. Whatever gave you that idea? I can barely cope with you.'

'Nothing. Just a feeling.'

That postcard from Julian, she thought. He must have read it.

'Um, do you still see your ex at all? Patrick. You look like one of those civilised types that manages to stay on good terms with their exes.'

Bella rootled in the fridge for some mineral water.

'Hmm?' Her voice floated from inside the fridge. 'No, I don't. Do you want some water?'

'No, thanks. Sorry. I didn't mean to be nosy.'

Bella shrugged. 'Doesn't matter. Anyway—do you still fancy seeing a film tonight? I could give Viv a call, see if she and Nick want to come too. We don't have to be stuck just with dreary old us all the time.'

'Is that how you see us? Dreary old us?'

'No, course not.' She banged the fridge door closed. 'Still, we don't want to get too couply, do we?'

'Why ever not? I like being couply.'

'Oh, Will. I'm just teasing. Where's your sense of humour?'

'Had to give it back. Only got it on loan.'

Viv rang the next day to recap on their cinema outing.

'Lousy film,' said Viv. 'But, Will—he's so lovely! And he's got you sussed, hasn't he?'

'Meaning?'

'Meaning he knows how to handle you.'

'You make me sound like a deranged leopard.'

'Well, you're no giggling pushover, matey, are you? You need someone like that to stand up to you. But the way he *looks* at you. A child of
three could've seen that you were mad about each other.'

'Get me a child of three then. You read too much into everything.'

'Bel? You do know about being happy, don't you?'

'Is this a trick question?'

'No. It's just—well, it is *allowed*, you know.'

'WHICH IS MY BEST SIDE, do you think?' Will turned his head this way and
that.

'It's a well-kept secret apparently.' Bella balanced her sketch pad on
her knee.

He got up and went to the window, gazing down at his garden. 'That
honeysuckle needs a good prune.' He half turned to look back at her.

'Stop! There, like that. No, no, don't move.'

Standing by the window, his face half in light, half in shadow, his
body twisted towards her, he looked alert, expectant, as if he had heard
an unfamiliar sound, or suddenly noticed the extraordinariness of
something ordinary.

'Can I see some of your paintings yet? I know you've been secretly
beavering away.'

'Not secretly. And no you can't.'

'Yes secretly. And why not? You must have enough for an exhibition
by now.'

'Don't be absurd. Anyway, will you ssshh! Concentrating.' Looking
down at the drawing, she sensed his making stupid faces at her. Patrick
used to do that, too, when she sketched him. Her gaze flicked up to
Will's hairline, the clear shape of his brow where the hair jumped up
from his scalp, looking eager to grow, to get on with it; she smiled to
herself, trying to let its enthusiasm run into the line of her pencil.

Patrick's hair was soft and fine, flopping down over the left-hand side of his forehead. She remembered the way he reached his hand up, pushing it back off his face, the way he fidgeted annoyingly while she drew, even in his sleep, never entirely at rest, never, until . . . She swallowed.

'Sssh!' she said again.

'What?' Will frowned. 'I never made a sound.'

When they stopped for a break, Will told her how weird it was to be looking at her looking at him as she drew.

'You seem to look at me so intensely, but right through me at the same time. I see your eyes flicking over me, scanning me, but you don't seem to be registering me as *me*.'

'Don't take it personally. Drawing's like that. You just become *a* body, *a* face, not Will, the man I know and—so forth.'

'Excuse me? The man I know and so forth? You can't say it, can you? Not even casually.'

'What? The "l" word? Of course I can. Don't be silly.'

'The "l" word. That's exactly what I mean. Love really is a four letter word to you, isn't it?'

'I'll do the jokes, thank you.' She rummaged in her pencil case for her putty rubber. 'The man I know and love. See? OK?'

He staggered backwards.

'Overwhelmed with the force of your passion. Look, ease up on the slushy stuff, will you? I'm not sure I can handle it.'

Bella sharpened her pencil into the bin.

'Yes, dear. Pose, please. Left arm round a bit. Yup. And could you twist a little more this way. Whoa, not too much. Yup. That's it.'

Will asked her if she would be free at the weekend.

'Yes. No. Yes. I should be doing some painting—I want to work up that drawing of you. *What is it?*'

'I thought you might like to meet my mother.'

'Do I have a choice?'

'Oh, charming. She's lovely. She's just like me.'

'Smug with stupid hair?'

'No. Easy-going. Loves plants.'

'It's really a bit tricky this weekend. Got loads to do.'

'Such as?'

'*Will*. I'm not on trial. I don't have to account for my movements every second of the day. You know—*things*. Washing and stuff.'

'Oh, *washing*. Well, obviously that comes first. Heaven forbid you should actually put yourself out to meet my family.'

'Deep breaths. I'm sure she's not exactly sitting there, crocheting in her rocking chair, wondering how much longer she can carry on without meeting me. Of course I'd like to meet her some time. I can't imagine the paragon of patience and fortitude who could have put up with you for so long. Now, will you please get back to your pose.'

Over supper that night, Will got out his diary and raised the subject again. 'If it really is that you're just busy this weekend, let's make it another time.'

'We don't have to do all that meeting-the-parents stuff, do we? I'm in no rush for you to meet mine.'

'Have I ever asked to meet yours? We'll come to that when you're ready, but Mum's dying to take a look at you.'

'Why? What have you told her about me?'

'Nothing. Well, I may have gone on about you a bit, well, a lot. I couldn't help it. It'll be painless, I promise.'

'All right, all right. Don't go on about it. Next weekend, OK? Let's get it over with so you'll stop nagging me.'

She hadn't seen Patrick's parents for quite a while; looking back, she was worried to realise she couldn't remember exactly when her last visit had been. In the beginning, she had gone almost every weekend.

At his parents' house, the family photo albums have taken up permanent residence on the coffee table.

'Look,' they say. 'Here he is ready for his first day at school. That grey cap kept sinking over his eyes. Remember when he went off to college and he was tall and lanky but he suddenly looked like a little boy again.' *Do you remember?* they say. *Do you remember?*

Fran's cottage was set back a little way from a narrow track with three other houses. It looked old to Bella, perhaps seventeenth-century, with a low doorway and steep 'catslide' roof that swept right down to her eye level. Succulent houseleeks clung to the roof-tiles in compact clusters. An uneven brick path led to the front door, flanked by beds packed with scented clove pinks, outsize Oriental poppies with petals like salmon-pink tissue, a haze of pale blue love-in-a-mist. Will dipped to smell the pinks as he passed.

'Here, have a sniff,' he said over his shoulder to her.

There was no answer when they knocked, so they went to the back.

'Hello-o-o-o-o,' Will called down the long garden.

A figure sprang up from a fuzz of fennel halfway down.

'Hello-o-o, yourself.'

Will led the way along a narrow path that wove between lavender bushes, feathery artemisia, waving blue delphiniums.

'Hello, Ma.' He gave Fran a big bear hug.

'Willum,' she said fondly, squeezing him back. She was wearing a voluminous blue boiler suit, and what looked suspiciously like a pair of men's leather slippers. Her grey hair was piled on top of her head in a rough heap. There seemed to be a pen stuck into it, though Bella couldn't tell whether it was to anchor the hair vaguely in position or if it had just been poked in there as a temporary resting place. Will reached forward and removed a bit of twig from her hair.

'So you're Will's light-o'-love then?'

Will rolled his eyes.

'Ma, do make some effort not to embarrass me completely.'

Fran took both Bella's hands in her own and looked at her.

'Will said you were a beaut but I presumed he was biased. What wonderful eyes. Tell me—do you like rosemary?' She waved her secateurs around alarmingly.

Bella was grateful for the sudden change of tack.

'Here, have some cuttings. This one has the bluest flowers ever. Do you know which it is, Willum? I never remember the names.' She leaned towards Bella. 'I'm sure he must despair of me.'

'Nonsense. I do not. The plants don't know their names either, do they? I only need to know to impress my clients. It might be *Rosmarinus officinalis* "Primley Blue"—that's very blue.'

'Certainly worked with me, at any rate,' Bella said. 'He bewitched me with his talk of *Meconopsis* and *Salix* and *Lavandula* whatever it is.'

'*Angustifolia*, mostly.' He looked suddenly very serious and very young. 'This one,' he patted a nearby bush with wing-tipped purple flowers as if it were a small child, 'is French lavender, *Lavandula stoechas*. Like we put in your garden. And I thought you'd fallen for my brains, wit, charisma and dashing good looks.'

'And simple humility, obviously.'

'Obviously.'

Fran laughed and linked her arm through Bella's.

'How nice to see he's met his match. Lunch isn't quite ready, but come in and have some tea. You must both be gasping.' She stuck her secateurs into her pocket. 'There's a casserole on the go, but the meat's a bit tough, so we'd best leave it as long as we can stand it, I think.' Fran lit the gas under an outsized enamel kettle. 'There're some scones some-where if you want to keep yourselves going. Have a rummage in the bread crock there—they're fresh today. Or yesterday.'

'They're not homemade, are they, Ma?'

'No, you needn't worry, rude boy. I knew I should have paid more attention to your manners when you were growing up.' Fran's voice echoed from the depths of the larder. 'My scones are legendary, Bella— flat as steppingstones and twice as hard. Hughie cracked a tooth on one once. The dogs used to love them, though. But these are proper shop-bought ones as you're a real guest.'

'Consider yourself honoured,' Will said. 'Any jam, Mother dear?'

'Strawberry and elderflower. And that is homemade.' Fran caught Will's look. 'Recent vintage, so don't look like that, but it might be a bit gloopy; it didn't seem to want to set. It's fine. Just eat it with a spoon and alternate it with bites of scone.'

That night, Bella lay cuddled up close to Will in the narrow double bed in the 'rose room'. Fran had said they could have the proper guest bed-room, but they'd have to shove the beds together, or they could squeeze in here.

'It's very cosy, but—be warned—the walls are a bit thin and I'm right next door.'

'God, Ma, you are so embarrassing.'

Fran breezed on, unabashed.

'I only do it to annoy. I know, how hideous—a parent alluding to sex.'

Will pulled Bella by the elbow into the room.

'Fine, fine. We'll have this one. Thank you. Come on, otherwise she'll be off on her I've-had-quite-a-few-interesting-escapades-in-my-time speech.'

'I'm paying no attention.' Fran skipped downstairs. 'Kettle's on.'

Bella told him he was being rude.

'No, I'm not. We love each other to death and we both know it. So we can be as rude as we like.' Surely her family weren't *polite* to each other all the time?

'Dad and I tease each other. We always have.'

He asked about her mother.

'Do you know, you almost never mention her.'

'I'd never talk to her the way you just did. You can't tease her, it would be bound to upset the planet's orbit or something. We try to be quite civil most of the time. Like in an armed truce.'

He raised his eyebrows.

'Mmm. If we let down our guard, boy the knives'd be out.'

'Aah, how sweet. The joys of the mother-daughter bond. I see it now: Madonna and child with beatific smiles, a small dagger glinting discreetly beneath flowing robes.'

'Hilarious.' Bella left the room. 'Coming down for some tea?'

9

AFTER ONLY MINOR arm-twisting, Will had volunteered to speak to his brother-in-law-in-law about the DAMP. The phone call was made, unknown leverage put into action. Mr Bowman had moved her from his black book to his red book, the actual one where real jobs were written in with dates and everything. It would take four to five days; once the treatment had been done, the walls would need replastering then drying out before they could be repainted.

Life became even more impossible. Boxes were squished into the bedroom, pictures stacked like dominoes on the landing, pot plants gathered in a leafy convention in the bathroom.

'You oughtn't really to stay in the house while all that's going on; the dust can't be good for you,' Will said.

'I know. Viv said they'd put me up.'

'Right. Or—you could, ah, stay with me.'

Although they usually ended up at Bella's house, she had stayed the night at Will's place several times before. He had bought her an extra toothbrush to keep at his place because he thought it ridiculous that she kept taking hers backwards and forwards. He had cleared a drawer for her, in which she kept one large T-shirt and one pair of pants. But staying the night casually was different, supper followed by sex followed by falling asleep. This was planned, official. Living together for five days solid—well, it was . . . domestic, wasn't it? It would involve couply conversations, cohabiting-type rituals: who would pick up something for supper; you-cook-I'll-wash-up routines; she'd become involved in the minutiae of his household: where he kept the spare loo rolls, which day the rubbish was to be put out.

'That's very kind of you. You don't have to do that. You've earned your scout badge, talking to Mr B.'

'I'm not being kind. I know I don't "have to do that"—I want to do that. What I mean is—I'd love you to come and stay. With me.'

Warning bells. What if she got to like it? Got used to seeing his face and his adorable, funny eyebrows on the pillow by hers when she closed her eyes each night? Each morning, there his face would be, her first glimpse of the world, already familiar. She'd know if he was in by the feel of the house when she entered the door, the smell of him in the air. How quickly might she adjust to his tread on the stair, his voice calling hello, the change in his eyes as they met hers? And then? Then the DAMP would be done, the walls painted and there would be no reason for her not to go home. That first evening she would go back to her own house. It would be like the first time she had gone back to the flat after Patrick. *After* Patrick. That was how she saw her life sometimes: Before Patrick/With Patrick/After Patrick; divided into neat sections like a pie chart, with no space left over for anything else.

She turns her key in the lock, half expecting him to call out 'Hiya. Good day?' The silence is like water, filling the rooms right into the corners. She moves through it with slow limbs, feeling it part and reseal itself behind her. In the kitchen, there is an unfamiliar stillness, a cold tidiness; nothing has moved. There is no marmalade jar sitting on the worktop with its lid off. No half-read paperback spread-eagled on the table. Automatically, she looks down. Patrick has an infuriating habit of leaving his heavy brown lace-ups in the middle of the floor where she frequently trips over them. *Had* an infuriating habit, she corrects herself. She is tempted to go and fetch his shoes and place them on the floor, then dismisses the thought as silly, mad even.

The bathroom is worse. Four disposable razors, all apparently on the go at once. Her fingers run over the head of Patrick's green toothbrush, splaying the bristles to and fro. She lifts her purple brush from the tooth mug and holds one in each hand, face to face, bouncing them up and down the way Patrick used to, giving them voices. 'Are you talking to me yet?' he'd say as green toothbrush, putting on an extra-deep voice, pogo-ing it along the edge of the basin. He'd twist the purple one from side to side, shaking its head, until Bella laughed.

She head-butts green toothbrush with purple toothbrush.

'Why'd you have to go and die on me then? That was pretty dumb.'

'Yeah.' She switches to goofy, green toothbrush voice. 'Guess I just didn't see it coming, a-her-her.' She leaves them intermeshed—'Kiss and make up?' Patrick used to say, pushing their bristles together. Wipes her stupid tears away with her hand. She can feel ugly sobs stirring, churning around in her, threatening to lurch out of her uncontrollably, tearing the fragile silence. She rubs her rib cage; it is so tight, it is painful, aching for release. Her teeth clamp tight shut and she bites the inside of her lip hard, desperate for some tangible, lesser pain to cling to.

In the bedroom, the curtains are half drawn and the dim light is welcome. She undresses slowly, by rote. As she pulls back the quilt to get into bed, she stops, then crosses to the linen basket and digs down, dropping socks, towels on the floor. Patrick's blue shirt—crumpled, soft with wear. She sinks her face into it, and breathes in.

She slides beneath the quilt and folds the shirt into a bundle by her face. Fingers one of its pearlised buttons, tracing round and round the rim, until she slips into sleep. It is twelve hours before she wakes again.

Will took her in his arms, scooped her close.

'What's up, sweet pea? Have you disappeared again, dreamy?'

She rallied a smile and kissed him. Shook her head. *I must try. I must.* 'I don't want to put you out.'

'You're right. It would be a huge hassle, having to lie next to a gorgeous naked woman every night, having to wake up each morning to see the face of the woman I love on the other pillow. What a drag.'

'Oh, is someone else coming too?'

'Shut up. You're staying with me. Don't argue.' He held her by her upper arms, making her face him straight on. 'You just don't get it, do you? I'm afraid you're stuck with me.'

'Why, Mr Henderson, this is so sudden.' She fanned her face with her hand.

He let go of her and held her hands.

'No, it isn't actually. I thought that before I'd even kissed you.'

He caught her expression.

'You look like you're about to see the dentist. I'm not rushing you, just telling you. I want to spend the rest of my life with you.'

The rest of my life. But how long would that be? Could be forty, fifty years, sure. Or ten years, five. Or one. Three weeks. If only there could be some sort of guarantee.

'Once you've had me stay for five days, that'll cure you.'

'Oh, you can come again.' Will relieved her of the bottle of wine she had brought, the beribboned box of truffles. The big kitchen table had been freshly covered with a bright madras check cloth. On it stood a stoneware jug of scented white roses and sprays of foliage from Will's

425

garden. Bella bent to sniff one of the blooms and sighed with appreciation. Will opened a kitchen cupboard and gestured. Blackcurrant tea, her favourite.

'And, and . . .' He towed her round the house: recycling crates finally shifted from the hallway where they always snagged her stockings to miraculously tidied cupboard under the stairs; more flowers by the bed in a blue glass tumbler; hangers vacated; folded towel laid out, topped with a boxed hotel guest soap; a foil-wrapped chocolate on the pillow.

'Wouldn't spoil me too much. Might get used to it.'

'That was the general idea.'

'This is weird,' Bella said as they were stretched out on the sofa after supper.

'What is?'

'This. Being with you and it feeling so normal. Almost as if we're a real couple. Can't we have a row?'

'Whatever for?'

'So I can relax. I feel so *nice* when I'm with you, just as if I were a normal person. Really quite lovable. It's most disconcerting.'

'You *are* lovable, you noodle.' He blew a raspberry into the side of her neck. 'Anyway, we are a real couple. You've been in a couple before. You remember how it's done, don't you?'

She nodded. *But*, she thought, *but*. This is *different*.

'So, why aren't you married then, Mr Perfect?'

'Nearly was. You're lucky to get me.'

'Yeah? How nearly is nearly? Were you jilted at the altar?'

'No. It was Carolyn—we were together for years: Will and Carolyn, Carolyn and Will, like fish and chips or—'

'Burke and Hare.'

'Hush up, you. But you know when things are the same year in, year out so you never question it?' Will told her that they were getting on OK, not arguing or anything, but not really talking either, their conversations were just the exchange of information about work or gossip about their social circle. They went out frequently, together and separately, rarely staying in on their own, surrounding themselves with people, with events, with busyness. Still, they were trundling towards marriage. Arrangements were being discussed. Then Carolyn was offered a three-month contract in New York.

'Did she take it?'

'Yes, she did. And I encouraged her. I was the ultimate unselfish fiancé—"You must take it, Caro. It's such an opportunity. It's only three months." I didn't realise for ages that I was kidding myself. I think I was relieved when she decided to go.'

Bella nestled against him. 'So then what happened?'

'So, she went to New York and she met someone else within a month.'

'You're kidding? How awful.'

'No, not really. I just think neither of us could see a sensible way out. We needed—' he laughed—'outside help.'

He tucked Bella's head closer and stroked her hair.

'After she'd been gone about a fortnight, I was pottering about at home in a lethargic kind of way one weekend. I remember thinking, it's still so clear in my mind: "I'm feeling sluggish because I must be missing Caro." And then it hit me. I thought, "No. You're *acting* the part of a man missing his girlfriend because you don't want to face the truth."'

Bella rubbed at her arms, suddenly chilled.

'Which was?'

'Which was that I *wasn't* missing her, which was much, much harder to deal with. Because then—then I started looking back at our relationship and I couldn't remember the last time either of us had shown any real interest in each other. Or how long it was since I'd stopped loving her.' His fingers rested still on her hair. 'I felt horrible. Scared. Ashamed. And when her letter came saying she'd met this other bloke, God, the relief! I had been let off the hook and I hadn't even had to *do* anything. I felt like a fraud.'

Bella nodded slowly. Her mouth felt dry. She kneaded at her stiff neck, then twisted to look up at him.

'Wasn't your fault though.' Bella cleared her throat. 'It's just life.'

'Confucius, he say "It's just life." Thank you for your words of wisdom.' She punched him softly.

'Oof.' He held her hand. 'And, *now*, I cannot believe that I could ever have thought of marrying her for even a minute. I can't explain—this is *so* different. It's like all your life you've been given strawberry-flavoured, I don't know, bubblegum or something and told "This is strawberry". Then, one day, when you weren't expecting it, a beautiful, brilliant red fruit is popped right into your mouth and it's like nothing you ever saw or smelt or tasted. Or—or *knew*. And then you suddenly get it: "Oh my God, *this* is a strawberry."'

Bella bounced the flat of her hand lightly on Will's head.

'I love this. First thing I noticed about you. I even thought of you as Springy Hair in my mind after that poetry reading.'

He tilted to look at her.

'You never said you'd thought about me after that first time. Tell me something nice. What else did you think?'

'Well, I thought you were funny and what bright eyes you had. And, what? Your eyebrows. Definitely your eyebrows. Very sexy. And you had this sort of amused look, as if you found the world a fascinating place.'

'I do.'

'I know. That's what I love about you.'

'You just used the "l" word.'

'It slipped out. I'm not responsible.'

'How long were you with Patrick?' Will asked the next evening as they were finishing supper.

'Five years, three months and eleven days, since you ask.' Bella started clearing the table.

'Not that you were counting or anything. Can I ask why you split up? Do you mind? Did you just get bored of him or what?'

'Why do you assume that? It could have been the other way round.'

Will pulled her away from the sink and back to the table.

'Uh-uh. Not possible.' He picked up her hand and lightly nibbled it. 'Infuriated, yes. Mystified, certainly. Bored, never.'

'Thank you. I think.'

'You never mention him.'

'I thought it wasn't considered polite to talk about one's exes.' She withdrew her hand and started whacking the place mats together like cymbals. Dislodged crumbs fell from their spiral grooves. 'Where do you keep these?'

'Wherever. And the answer to my question is . . . ?'

'You were wrong. He did get sick of me.' Bella tucked the mats into a drawer, and stood at the sink, looking out at the garden. 'He did the ultimate escape trick. He died. Men, eh? So unpredictable. Just when you think you know where you are with one, he goes and gets himself killed. Still, it's cut down on the ironing.' Will came and stood behind her. His arms encircled her, held her tight. She remained rigid.

'God, I'm sorry. I'm so sorry. I wouldn't have teased you. I'm an idiot.' He whispered into her hair. 'Why on earth didn't you tell me before? Do you mind talking about it? Of course. What a stupid question.'

She told him the bare facts. One paragraph. News in brief. In her head, she saw it typeset on a newspaper page:

DEATH FUELS CONCERNS OVER SITE SAFETY

The death of a surveyor has reawakened concerns over safety

standards in the construction industry. Patrick Hughes, thirty-four, died late on Tuesday evening after sustaining severe head injuries and internal haemorrhaging when part of a brick chimney stack collapsed on him on a building site in Vauxhall, south London. He was rushed by ambulance to St Thomas's Hospital, but doctors were unable to revive him and he died without regaining consciousness. Mr Hughes was assessing the stability of an adjacent wall when the accident occurred. The Health and Safety Executive has launched an inquiry.

Was that Patrick, those neat, flat little words in black on flimsy newsprint? When it had appeared in the newspaper, she had wanted to buy up every copy. Tomorrow, people would be using it to protect their floors, stuff into wet shoes, line cat-litter trays; tomorrow, it would be thrown away, old news, forgotten.

'Bella?' Will started to turn her towards him.

'I'm OK. Honest.' An automatic smile.

'Are you?' His voice was low and gentle.

She could feel his warmth, solid and reliable at her side as he moved to see her face. She wanted to lean against him. How good it would be just to let go, give herself up to him, let herself be held and comforted.

Her head moved a fraction, barely discernible, and Will clasped her more tightly to him. For a moment, for one moment, he felt her give and he held her as tenderly as if she were a frightened child; his hand stroked her hair. Then she stiffened and drew herself straight, shook her head with small jerks. Patted his arm with distant affection.

Will sighed. 'Can I just ask—I mean, you must miss him, right?'

'It's not—you don't—you couldn't understand. I'm sorry.'

'I might. I lost my stepdad, remember? I'm not a bereavement virgin. Won't you even let me try? How do you know if you won't tell me?'

'Will. Please don't.' She closed her eyes.

'I'm sorry, Bella. I'm sorry. The last thing I want is to hurt you. I'm being selfish, I know—but I just want you to love me—as much as you obviously loved him.'

There was a barely discernible shake of her head, then her eyelids flickered and she was silent. She felt his soft kiss on her brow, the breath of his silent sigh.

'I wish I could really know you.'

She was aware of the brief pressure of his hand on her arm, then he turned to the sink and covered the silence with the reassuring clatter of washing-up.

Could she use the phone, she asked Will.

He shook his head, amused. 'I keep saying, treat the place as home.'

'Hi, Dads. It's me. I can't be long.'

Will made a 'T' sign. 'Take as long as you like. No rush.'

She nodded and pouted him a kiss.

'No, it's just I'm on someone else's phone.'

She heard Will's voice, deliberately audible from the kitchen: 'Yes, folks, that's me. Someone else. Not "my boyfriend", not "my partner", not "Will" even, just "someone else". She loves me, nah, nah, nah . . .'

Fine, she said, she was fine—house fine—damp actually being treated and soon it would be done and she could unpack and live like a real grown-up—yes, work fine, bit dull but paying the mortgage and keeping her in croissants—painting, surprisingly fine, she was less rusty than she'd thought—no, silly, not nearly good enough for that—yes, of course he could see them some time.

'How come I'm not allowed to see them, then?' Will called through.

'Don't be so nosy,' she called back. 'Get on with the tea, boy.'

'Oh. That's Will,' into the phone. 'Well, he's—y'know . . . hmm . . . yes, I guess he is really.' She might as well admit it. She couldn't sidestep the issue for ever.

'Quite a while. He originally came to do the garden, which, incidentally,' she said as he came back into the room with two mugs of tea, 'is in dire need of attention. He's falling way behind in his duties.'

Will came up behind her, put his arms round her and whispered in her ear, 'That's because I keep getting distracted.'

She shook him off and waggled her fingers at him to wave him away.

'Yes, yes, he is.'

Will was standing very close.

'Is what?' he said. 'Gorgeous? Most Rampant Man on the Planet?'

'Is right *here*,' she hissed at him. Will wrinkled his nose.

'No, no, don't be leaping ahead, Dads. That's not on the agenda.'

'What isn't? What isn't?' said Will, nibbling at her neck. Bella covered the mouthpiece.

'Go away, Annoying Person. I'm trying to have a sensible conversation with my esteemed father here.'

Will smiled and shrugged.

She dropped her voice and turned her back to him.

'Funny, playful—yes, hmm-mm, very bright, thoughtful, direct. Sensitive, too. OK, if you like that sort of thing, I guess.'

There was a pause. A long pause. Bella was frowning.

'It's a bit tricky. He's very busy.'

430

'No I'm not,' said Will.

The volume dipped again. Will tried to get closer to hear. Bella kept him at elbow's length.

'She *is*. You know what she's like. Mmm. You always say that. Possibly. I'll consider it. No promises. Yeah. Bye, Dads, bye.'

Will was standing with his arms folded.

'They want to meet me, don't they? You can't hide me from them for ever.'

'It's the other way round, silly. I'm protecting you from them. Her. We'll go if you insist, but don't blame me when it all goes horribly wrong.' She stomped upstairs. 'Can I run a bath?' calling back over her shoulder.

'You don't need to ask, for the forty-fifth time.'

AFTER A MERE EIGHT DAYS rather than the promised five, the DAMP was done, the walls replastered and painted, and there was no excuse for her not to return home. Bella repacked her clothes into her holdall.

Will watched her as she retrieved her bits and pieces from the bath-room, as she zipped up her toilet bag with a final flourish.

'Come on, sweet pea. I feel like we're getting divorced or something. You don't have to take every little last thing with you.'

She laid a hand on his arm.

'Thanks, Will. But I need to have my things around me at home.'

'I—well—I thought, maybe . . .'

She stretched up to reach him, silencing him with a kiss.

'Come and stay with me this weekend. I can spoil you for a change. I want to paint you anyway. And you can help me unpack the dreaded boxes.'

He gathered her into a hug.

'If you really want to spoil me, will you do that duck thing again? With the sauce?'

'You're squishing me. Yes, you can have the duck thing, but you'll have to do extra box duty.'

'It's a deal. And don't forget your promise.'

'I won't. Which promise?'

'About the galleries. You said you'd take in your pictures.'

'I will. At some point. There's no rush. Don't go on.'

'There is a rush. Life's short, you know.' He saw her eyes flicker. 'Sorry. But you must . . . otherwise I'll be forced to suck your toes until you beg for mercy.'

'So?' asked Will, manically raising and lowering his eyebrows at her when he met her from work on Friday evening.

'What?'

'Did you go and see any galleries?'

She kept it brief. Yes, she had, so could he please now stop nagging her about it. At the first gallery, the manageress had said they were certainly 'well painted, very well executed, but slightly disturbing'; they preferred still lifes, landscapes, more conventional interior scenes. At the second, the decision-making person had turned out to be away for a week and she couldn't see why they hadn't just told her that on the phone because she had dragged out of her way to go there.

'Did you go to that Mackie one, what's it called? The top one?'

'MacIntyre Arts. No, I didn't. What would be the point?'

Will shrugged. 'Can't see what you've got to lose. Don't be so negative. They've got to hang somebody's stuff on their walls—why not yours? We could go there now, just for a look.' He stopped in the street, blocking the narrow pavement.

'No, we couldn't. Why have you stopped? Can't you walk and talk at the same time? Does it run down your batteries?'

'Yes, it does. I stopped because I like to see your face when you talk. Can I see any of your paintings yet, by the way?'

'OK, but no smart-arse comments.'

'But these are stunning.' He held a small canvas up to the light to see it more clearly.

'What's the "but" for? No need to sound quite so surprised.'

'Don't be annoying. I'm not surprised that they're so good, Paranoid Person. But I can't *believe* that anyone could produce anything so beautiful and—and powerful and want to keep them under wraps. I love the colours. I'm glad I nagged you to try the galleries now. You're bonkers.'

'Thank you for your support.'

'You have to try that top gallery. You know that, don't you? If you don't, and you exhibit in some ordinary, run-of-the-mill place, you'll always know you *settled*, that you didn't go for what you really wanted, never even tried to see if you could have it.'

'It doesn't bother me that much. Anywhere would be wonderful.'

432

Monday lunchtime. She stood looking in the window for a long time. Good stuff, very good: a first-rate portrait of a slightly cross-looking woman in oils, rather quirkily done; two small pastel nudes; a set of four woodcut landscapes—beautifully stylised, accomplished. She tried to look beyond the window, to see inside.

'Going in?' A tweedy, middle-aged man about to enter the gallery was holding open the door for her.

'No. I just—' Why not? She was here now. Nothing to stop her from having a quick look.

She went from picture to picture, her mood swinging from elation—'this is wonderful'—to depression—'I haven't got a hope in hell'. Even the pictures that weren't to her taste were at least well done. They would never take her work here. She couldn't possibly ask.

The tweedy man was standing by the desk, talking to the assistant.

'So.' He swung round towards her while looking through his post. 'Have you come to see me?' He nodded at her portfolio, her brown paper parcel.

'Let's have a look then.' He held out his hands.

Mr MacIntyre nodded as he looked through, without speaking. Oh God, she thought, he couldn't even think of anything polite to say. This was awful. She focused all her attention on her toes, clenching and unclenching them inside her shoes. He hovered a long time, looking at the five cathedral paintings she had brought. Were there any others? he wanted to know. Yes, several, more than a dozen she thought, and some other watercolours. Was she planning to do more? She couldn't stop at the moment, she said.

He flicked through his calendar.

'We're booked solid for the next ten months or so, pretty much.'

He was letting her down gently.

'But, but, but,' he said as she retaped the brown paper round the paintings. He ran his finger along the dates. 'It's decidedly tight time-wise, but we do have a mixed show in three months. Three artists. It was supposed to be four anyway, but one dropped out to have a nervous breakdown. You'd fit in.' He laughed. 'The show's called Visions, which covers anything we fancy really. But these—' he patted the parcel. 'These *are* visions.

'Have a think anyway. I'd understand if you wanted to hold out for a solo show—if that's the case, we'd be looking at next year, say early autumn and, obviously, we'd need quite a lot more. I'd like to come and see the others. Give us a ring tomorrow if you can, Thursday at the latest, and we can talk about framing and so on.'

Did that mean he liked them? Had he said? Had he just offered her a joint exhibition or had she imagined it? Could she possibly ask?

He smiled, his sober face suddenly bright and youthful.

'They're superb, by the way. Really.' He nodded. 'Let's talk tomorrow.'

Bella was 'in conference' with Seline. She had put off making a decision for as long as she reasonably could, but Seline had finally pressed her: was she interested in the possibility of a partnership next year or not?

'I really appreciate your asking me . . .'

'But you've decided against it? I'm sorry but I suppose it's not a huge surprise. Can I ask why?'

Bella explained about the exhibition and wanting to spend more time painting. Perhaps Seline would like to come? She'd love to.

'I don't think I'd really be able to put in more time here. In fact,' she heard herself say, 'I was wondering if you'd let me work part-time. Say, three days a week? So I'd have time to paint. Anthony could take over when I'm not here. He's got the experience. Or I could leave altogether if you think that would be better?'

'Don't you dare!' Seline clicked her pen against her teeth. 'We'll take whatever time you can offer. I guess we can get it to work as long as we don't have to lose you completely.'

Now that the words had been said aloud, Bella realised that the idea had been lodged in her head for months. Now it had been spoken, it was Out There, no longer safe in silence. She agreed to carry on full-time for the next couple of months while she trained Anthony in the small but vital matter of diplomacy when dealing with awkward clients.

Bella closed the door behind her. *Did I really say that?* Her knees seemed to be trembling slightly but her body felt lighter, clear and fizzy, as if her veins were flowing with lemonade—was it oh-shit-what-have-I-done nerves or something not unlike excitement?

Will's sister Helen was coming over with her two children the following Sunday. Would Bella join them?

'Could be a bit tricky. Got stuff to do.'

'Oh, stuff. Right. Sounds important.' Will puffed out his cheeks. 'Do we have to go through this every time I want you to meet my family?'

'I'm working on a painting, Will. It's your fault. It was your idea to send me to the gallery in the first place.'

'*Send* you to the gallery? So it's my fault that you're in danger of being fulfilled and successful? What a bastard. I don't know how you put up with me.' He reached for her. 'Of course you must put your painting first, sweet pea. I only meant if you weren't doing anything special.'

'Perhaps I could pop in and say hello briefly at teatime?'

'Mmm. Do that. Offer me crumbs—old Will'll lick 'em up.'

'I don't have to come at all.' She started to turn away.

'Yes, you do have to come at all. Didn't you read the job description? Will's partner—Official Duties. Number 1: Love me hugely. Number 2: Have lots of sex with me. Number 3: Meet my family. It's not as if we're down to Number 54: Meet my boring cousins from Uxbridge, is it? This is actually important to me, for two of the people I love most in the world to get to know each other. Can you not understand that?'

'OK, OK. Remain calm. I said I'd come.'

Helen shifted her baby to balance him on her hip so she could shake Bella's hand.

''Scuse the sprog. I can't remember the last time I had both hands free. I always seem to be holding one or restraining one or hoiking one back from near-death.'

Bella looked at the baby. He looked back.

'Leo, is it?' she asked.

'That's right. The munchkin trying to scale Mount William over there is Abigail. Come and say hello, Abby.'

Abigail looked round, saw a New Person, and buried her face in Will's leg.

'Don't take it personally. She's going through a shy phase.'

'That's OK. I'm still waiting to grow out of mine.'

Abigail stretched out on the floor, surrounded by paper and crayons. Bella took Leo's foot in her hand and gently squeezed it.

'Hello, Leo.' She puffed out her cheeks and blew her breath out in a raspberry. His little cheeks bulged into a smile.

'Here, cop hold of him a minute, will you? God, he's so heavy now. I'll just get some cups.'

He was heavier than he looked for such a small person. How was it possible for hands to be so tiny, yet still be hands? He grabbed her outstretched finger with surprising strength.

'He's got quite a grip,' said Will. He held up his hand with one finger bent down. 'See, lost one last week.'

Helen swept back into the room with the cups.

'Oh, he likes you. Normally, he'd be bawling his fat little head off by now, wouldn't you, chubs?' She touched her baby softly on the nose.

Helen started pouring the tea.

'So, you planning to do all this nonsense? Do you look forward to the delights of Motherhood or are you sensibly relishing your peaceful existence while it lasts?'

'I think I'd be a lousy mother.'

'No you wouldn't!' said Will. 'You'd be brilliant. Why d'you say that?'

'I'd be bound to mess them up and they'd grow up resenting me—they'd need decades of therapy and then send me the bill. Or I'd be too anxious and overprotective. I'd lie awake all night to check they were still breathing.'

'Believe me, after a few nights of no sleep, you'd find yourself dropping off in the middle of the supermarket. Anyway, babies are tougher than they look, but, yes, it's a worry. Mum says she still worries about us and look how old he is.' Helen nodded at Will. 'What about your lot—do they nose into your life all the time?'

'Dad can be a bit of a fusser. My mother likes to interfere but not to the point where I might think she actually cared one way or the other. As for worrying about me, the only reason she'd mind if I was squished by a truck tomorrow is because then she'd have to put up with pitying looks from the neighbours.'

'That's a horrible thing to say.' Will's voice was quiet.

Helen was silent.

Bella shrugged. She had intended it as an amusing hyperbole, but said out loud it had suddenly seemed not very amusing at all.

'You sound very angry,' said Will.

'I didn't come here to be analysed. Don't patronise me, Will.'

Helen topped up their cups.

'Well, it's none of my business,' she said, 'but I'd be angry if I thought *my* mother didn't care. So would you, Will. Course you would. Anyway, you can share our mum, Bella. She obviously thinks you're the best thing since sliced bread. Went on about you for hours after Will took you to see her. I felt quite jealous, I can tell you.' She paused. 'Have you ever tried to talk to your mum about how she is?'

'What would be the point? She's not going to change magically just because I ask her to.'

'No, she probably won't. That's not what I meant. But *you* might. If you talked to her, you might start to understand why she's like that. What have you got to lose?'

Abby gave Bella a drawing as they were leaving—one she had done of Bella, with huge eyes and a red smile.

'See, she's got your hair spot-on,' said Will, pointing at Bella's head in the drawing, covered with a tangle of lines like unravelled knitting.

'Shut up, you.' She squeezed his arm. 'I'm glad I came. Thank you.'

'I knew you would be. Have you got to dash off to do "stuff" or do I get the good of you on my own for a while?'

She checked her watch.

'Hmm. I ought to be getting back.'

'Can't it wait?' He drew her towards the stairs. 'I've got something to show you . . . upstairs.'

'I bet you have. OK. On condition I can watch *Jane Eyre* here—starts in forty minutes.'

'Forty minutes, hmm? Look, she gets him in the end—there, you don't need to watch it now.'

They were lying in his bed in a tangle of pillows and duvet.

Will turned towards her. 'I—' he kissed her nose, 'love—' another kiss, 'you—' kiss, 'bigly.' Kiss.

'Bigly?' She snuggled closer to him, rubbing her face against his chest.

'Yes. Very bigly. I know this has all been—well—it has, really, hasn't it?—quite quick and intense, not just the sex—which is certainly intense but not too quick I hope—and anyway, the thing is—'

'You're wibbling, Will.'

'That's true. I am wibbling. I want to say something, but I don't want you to panic. I don't want to scare you off. You know how I feel about you.'

He took her hand, looked down at her fingers as he squeezed them in his own, ran his thumb over her knuckles, her fingernails as if he had never seen them before, then looked up and straight into her eyes.

'I want to marry you.'

For a tiny fraction of time, she felt herself flooded with warmth. Her face must be glowing. For one moment, light shone from her eyes. Tears pooled softly below the rims.

Yes, yes. Love me, marry me. Yes.

Then a wisp of cold blew down her neck. She shivered. Her skin was clammy, pale, her mouth dry. For a moment, her eyes closed. And there was Patrick, his back turned towards her. But she dared not reach out to him. What would she see in his eyes? She clenched and unclenched her fists, digging her fingernails into her palms.

'Er, does your silence mean you'd like some time to think about it? I sort of thought you might feel the same way. Shit, I knew I shouldn't have rushed. I'm such a dickhead. Forget I said it.'

'How could I? It's fine. Really. I'm flattered. I'm just not sure yet. Sorry.'

Why could she not say what she wanted to? *Yes, yes. Love me, marry me. Yes.*

He managed a smile.

'Will you think about it at least? At some point, as you would say.'

'At some point.' She smiled and kissed his cheek. 'Thank you.'

She met up with Viv on Monday lunchtime. They sat on a park bench eating sandwiches.

'Oh-oh, you've got that strange mask look.' Viv's eyes narrowed. 'What's occurring? You've not had a fight with Will, have you?'

'Uh-uh.' Bella shook her head. 'Quite the contrary. He proposed.'

'Proposed? What, like marriage you mean?'

'No. He proposed we start drilling for oil in my back garden. Yes, of course marriage. Is that so ridiculous?'

'Of course not. But that's brilliant!' Viv clasped Bella in a big hug. 'I'm *so* pleased, you know I am. Oh, a wedding! I may have to cry.' She took a bite of her sandwich, then chewed slowly. 'Hang on—shouldn't you be looking a bit more ecstatic or something? You did say yes, babe?'

'Not as such.'

Viv stopped mid-chew.

'I'm not hearing this.'

'Well, it is quite quick. I thought you'd be all in sensible mode—now don't rush into anything—take your time—it's a big decision.'

'So why *did* you turn him down?'

'Don't know, miss.' Bella picked at a bit of lettuce from her sandwich and kicked one of her shoes with the other.

'Bel? Is it . . . ? Is it, well, because of Patrick? Oh, *babe*. I'm sorry.' Bella was shaking her head, her eyes scrunched tight.

'I don't know, I don't know. I just can't. I can't—'

'Bella, can I ask you a favour?' Will called up from her kitchen.

'Sure. Why so serious?' She ran down the stairs. 'You don't want to borrow my life savings, do you?'

'No. Now don't go ballistic on me, but is there any chance—would you mind moving those photos of Patrick from the pinboard, up to your studio say?'

'Really, Will. You can hardly be jealous of a dead person?'

'No. I'm not jealous. But every time I come into the kitchen I'm confronted by this picture of you in bed with someone else.'

'Will, we're wearing toy antlers. It's not exactly a writhing bodies shot, is it?'

'Now you're deliberately missing the point. I don't think I ask for much. But, seeing as we're practically living together, I thought—'

'We're not living together.'

'Oh, aren't we? Forgive me. There must be some mistake. And what would you call spending every night together and every weekend and me having shirts in your wardrobe? That is my jacket out in your hallway, isn't it? My shredded wheat in the larder? My razor in the bathroom? Or is it Patrick's?'

'No need to shout. Now you're just being offensive.'

'I'm sorry. I didn't mean that.'

She shrugged. 'No big deal. I meant to take them down anyway.'

'No. Leave them. It's OK.'

She shook her head. Carefully prised out the drawing pins and took the photographs upstairs. Standing in her studio, she hovered between her desk drawer and the mantelpiece above the fireplace. She looked down at the photographs, the one of the two of them together and the one of Patrick on that Scottish holiday soaked to the skin. How peculiar it was to have a photograph of someone who no longer existed. It was as if he were an actor in a film only now it was over and the lights had gone up in the cinema. She propped them up on the mantelpiece.

'I JUST KNOW I'm going to regret this.' Bella put down the phone and scrunched her forehead into exaggerated furrows. Will kissed it and cupped the back of her neck in his palm.

'Stop worrying so much. Everyone's embarrassed by their parents. That's what parents are for. You met my mother and survived, didn't you—and she's pretty odd.'

'On your own head be it. Just remember that it was your idea.'

The drive was punctuated by Bella's explanations of the various idiosyncrasies of the house and her parents.

'Oh, oh, I forgot—most important of all, don't forget to be nice about my mother's cooking. That should be easy because she's an exquisite cook—'

'Do you know, I think that's the first time I've heard you say anything complimentary about her?'

Bella shrugged. 'You have to be specific. About the cooking. Don't just say, "That was lovely" or she'll think you've been coached. And ask her questions—give her a chance to show off.'

'I should have come in black tie. Then I could have written notes on my stiff cuffs.'

They turned into the drive through an open white, five-barred gate; the tyres crunched on the gravel, signalling their arrival. Hund lolloped round the corner of the house to greet them. Bella bent down to hug him.

'Hello, Hund.' She fondled his ears. 'You lovable old thing.'

Will hunched down to check his hair in the wing mirror and pressed it with the flat of his hand to smooth it down. It bounced back.

'C'mon, Springy Hair. Into the lion's den.'

Alessandra smiled and extended her hand. 'You must be William. Do come in. We've heard so *little* about you.'

Will joined in as she laughed at her jest. Bella dipped forward to exchange dual cheek kisses with Alessandra.

'It's Will,' Bella said. 'Not William.'

'Whatever.' Will waved his hand.

'Perhaps you'd like a sherry?' Alessandra ushered him by the elbow towards the drawing room. 'Of course, we rarely drink this early ourselves, but we're rather green when it comes to sophisticated city habits. Perhaps you'd prefer coffee?'

'Yes, whatever you're making. Coffee, of course.'

Gerald came in from the garden and shook Will's hand and patted him on the arm.

'So you're Will. Good, good. We're very pleased to see you here.'

There was a promising clinking as Gerald delved into a cupboard. 'Say you'll join me in a Scotch. Or would you prefer gin and tonic? Bourbon?'

'Just a small Scotch, then. Thank you.'

'This is a beautiful room, Mrs Kreuzer.' Will crossed to the corner cabinet. 'Is this eighteenth-century?'

'It is. I do hope Bella hasn't schooled you to be so formal, William—'

'*Will*,' said Bella.

'—Gerald and I are very easy come, easy go, aren't we, darling?'

'Hmm?' said Gerald.

'Please do call me . . .' she took a breath as if about to launch into an aria, '. . . Ales*sandra*.'

To Bella's surprise, they were shown to the guest bedroom.

'I dare say you'll want to *share*, will you?' Alessandra said, giving a little, indulgent laugh, making it sound like a perversion.

'It is pretty normal for people in their thirties.'

'I dare say it is, Bella-dear.' Alessandra closed the curtains and moved a vase of spiny sea holly slightly. 'I'm sure I'm hopelessly out of touch.' She straightened the guest towels by the washbasin. 'Towels. Soap. Yes. Wait until you have children and they start telling you off every time you open your mouth.'

Bella started to unpack her holdall.

'I'm *not* telling you off,' she said at her washbag. 'I'm just *saying*—it'd be abnormal if we slept in separate rooms at our age.'

'Well there's no problem then, is there?' Alessandra paused by the door. 'You're not in separate rooms.' She smiled at Will. 'Do just say if you need more towels.' The door closed behind her.

'For God's sake! *I dare say it is, Bella-dear.* And *more* towels!' Bella thumped a plump pile of them laid on a chair. 'Whatever for? What *does* she think we'd be doing in here? Having babies? Covering ourselves in maple syrup? What?'

'Oh, keep calm.' Will looped his arms round her. 'Now, about this maple syrup . . .'

'I can see where Bella gets her culinary finesse from,' Will said at supper, grinning as if he'd had a whole bowlful of manna. 'This is superb.'

Bella mouthed 'Crawler' at him.

Back in their room, Will sat on the bed and asked Bella what was the matter.

'I can see where Bella gets her *culinary finesse* from,' she parroted. 'Culinary finesse? Whatever happened to good old cooking skills, Mr Lover-of-Plain-English?'

'Why are you having a go at me? I'm not your mother.'

'Very funny. I'm not, anyway.'

'Yes you are. I thought you wanted me to praise her cooking. That's what it said in the manual: Bella's Parents—A Visitor's Guide.'

She could see the corners of his mouth curving, expecting her to laugh with him.

'It didn't say be a slimy, goody-goody, suck-up sycophant, did it?'

'Oh, charming. I love you too.'

'I just think it would be appropriate if you were to show me some support while you're here.'

'Appropriate? What? I'm not *not* showing you support by being nice to your mum. It's a common custom when you're a guest. It's called Getting On with People. You should try it some time.'

'Ssh! Will you keep your voice down. And I don't Get On with People, I suppose?'

'Well, you could try the revolutionary new tactic of being pleasant to your mother. It wouldn't kill you, would it?'

Bella fiddled with the stiff latch and opened the window.

'I knew you wouldn't see what she's really like.'

He crossed to her and put his hand on her shoulder but she shrugged it off.

'I can see that she's awkward with you. Not relaxed. I've no idea why. But you're making it worse, can't you see that? She looks nervous around you, almost as if she thinks you might hit her.'

'*Her* nervous around *me*. Hah!'

Will nodded, serious.

'Yes, that's how it looks.'

'I do try actually.' Bella folded her arms, holding herself. 'You've got no idea. You don't know anything about it.'

'Yes, well, I wouldn't, would I?' His voice became brisk. 'I'm just an outsider. I guess it's none of my bloody business.'

'Guess not,' she said, staring straight ahead.

She heard him let out a breath as if his whole body were sighing, then the quiet click as he closed the door behind him. She stayed completely still, seeing herself as if she were in one of her own paintings, leaning on the window ledge, looking out to the garden in a dream.

By Sunday lunchtime, Alessandra was patting Will's arm and laughing at everything he said. Gerald took him on a tour of the garden and pronounced him 'a breath of fresh air and robust enough to stand up to Bella'. He laughed when he said it, so Bella was sure he must have been joking. Will found Bella in the sitting room after lunch, curled up in an armchair reading a book. Was she coming to join them, he asked; there was fresh coffee.

'No, thanks.'

'Would Madam like a cup brought through before the staff go off duty?' He smiled and leaned down to see her face.

'I'm fine, thanks.'

'What's up?'

'Nothing. I'm reading.'

'Rightio. You're reading. Of course. We trail miles across country so that you can introduce me to your parents then you spend the entire time skulking in corners like some snotty adolescent. Do you always visit people then ignore them when you get there?'

Bella continued to stare at her book.

'I think it's very rude. To me as well as your parents. I'm here only because of you but you've practically abandoned me.'

'You seem to be managing very well without me.'

'I'm trying to be sociable enough for two people to compensate for you.'

'Please don't bother on my account.'

'Come on. Will you please at least look at me?'

Bella raised her eyes from the page. They were like glass.

'I hate it when you do that.' He shoved his hands down deep into his pockets. 'I hate it when you shut me out like that. Go all icy. I don't know how to get through it.'

'Better not waste your energy then.'

'What is all this? What's the matter?' Will moved towards her and laid a hand on her hair.

'Don't do that. Flattens it.' She flicked her head.

His hand dropped back to his side. 'Come through when you're planning to rejoin the human race, why don't you?'

Bella deposited a single kiss on Alessandra's right cheek and promptly stepped backwards, stranding her mid-ritual. Alessandra hovered, then tugged at her silk cardigan draped over her shoulders and crossed her arms. A hug and kiss for Gerald, then Bella squatted to clasp Hund in a warm embrace. She heard Will kissing Alessandra and her light laugh, heard Gerald clapping Will affectionately on the back. She kissed the top of Hund's head again and showered him with extra pats.

'You must come and see us again, dear Will. Don't wait for Bella to bring you—we'll be quite old and grey by then!' Alessandra laughed.

Will got into the front passenger seat and balanced a tin of homemade biscuits on his lap. A jar of cherries macerated in brandy was wedged between his feet.

'Enough going-home presents there, have you, *dear* Will?' Bella turned the car and gave a cursory wave out of the window.

'I thought it was very kind of her. She was only trying to make me feel welcome.'

'Welcome? She practically offered to adopt you. I'm surprised she didn't just swap me for you, old for new: "Don't throw that old, unlovable child away. Trade it in for an easier, more adorable one."'

'You *are* angry, aren't you?'

'As you well know, nothing is more guaranteed to make a perfectly calm person angry than telling them they're angry. You're so—so *fucking* smug sometimes.'

'I'm afraid you've lost me. I really don't understand why you're so upset.'

'Don't you? Don't you really? You've just spent all weekend forming a cosy little mutual fan club with my parents, especially my mother, and you've no idea why that would upset me?'

'Not really, no. Well, I could hazard a guess.'

'And what would that be, Mr Smug?'

'Cut it out. Don't push it, Bella.'

'Bella. Oh, you do know my name then? But only when you're telling me off? The rest of the time it's "sweet pea" or "pumpkin" or some other type of vegetable matter.'

Will was silent for a minute.

'That's just me being affectionate, you know it is. Why didn't you say if it annoyed you? I thought you liked it.'

I do like it. She felt as if she were at the bottom of a pit and could see no way to scale the walls; what could she do but dig deeper?

She exhaled shortly through her nose. Will ignored it.

'I think you're pissed off because I got on OK with your mum and that's blown your guiding theory of life out of the water—that she's the Wicked Witch of the West and you're sweet little Dorothy.'

Bella raised one eyebrow.

'Oh, the famous Kreuzer look. I *am* scared. I think you'd actually rather be right than happy, wouldn't you?'

'That does sound likely, doesn't it?'

'OK. Why are you so upset then?'

'I'm not "upset"—I might be justifiably pissed off that you smarmed up to *Alessandra*,' her voice quivered dramatically. 'So that I was made to look like the bad one, a naughty misfit schoolkid.'

'You were acting like a stroppy brat, so what do you expect?'

'I really fail to see the point of this conversation.'

Will rested his hand on her leg.

'C'mon, you.' He moved her leg to and fro playfully. 'Let's not fight.'

Bella reached to change gear and nudged his hand away.

''Scuse me. Could you . . .? Thanks.'

He withdrew it and clucked a quiet rhythm to himself for a minute, then he turned to look out of the window.

The rest of the journey passed in near-silence.

Bella stopped the car outside Will's house and kept the engine running while he unloaded his bag from the boot.

'Well then,' she said.

'Bella? Could you park the car and come in for a minute?'

'I'm really tired.'

'Aren't we all? Just for a minute. I want to talk to you.'

'Why? Not if you're going to tell me off. You're doing your schoolmaster voice.'

'Give it a rest.' Will let out a breath. 'Right.' He got back into the car and slammed the door.

Bella sat facing straight ahead, feeling his eyes on her.

'Hello?' Will ducked his head from side to side to try to make eye contact. 'Hello? Am I going to get any response or what? It's like you're not even *here*. You've gone off to Kreuzer Dreamworld again, haven't you?'

Anger rose inside her, bubbling up through her body like boiling milk, threatening to spill over in a hiss of scalding steam and acrid smells. How could he? How dare he? She wanted to let it out, scream at him, rage at him. She dug her fingernails into her hands, felt her fury wind tight as a spring, coiling around her in wiry bands; she clung onto it, buckling it around her so it would hold her together.

'Just don't.' She raised her hand in front of her face as if he were about to strike her.

'Have you any idea how cold you seem when you do that? How on earth is anyone ever supposed to get close to you if you keep shutting them out?'

'I don't imagine anyone is *supposed* to get close to anyone else. You either are or you aren't.'

'Fine. And I never have been?'

Bella shrugged and folded her arms.

'Right. No need to put up a placard. I think even thicko Will has finally got the message.' He fumbled for the door handle. 'I love you to pieces. You know I do. But I can't—'

She could see him trying to swallow.

'Whatever.' He clenched and unclenched his hands. 'Why didn't you just say you didn't love me? Is it so hard? Will, I don't love you, please go away. There. I feel like—I don't know. Jesus. I—' He ran his fingers through his hair and was silent for a moment. 'It's Patrick, isn't it? You're still in love with him. And how the *fuck* is anyone supposed to compete with a *dead* guy on a fucking ginormous pedestal?'

Bella held herself still as he opened the car door. A wall of cold air hit her, surrounding her. She felt it was coating her, pouring over her like chilled liquid glass, sealing her in.

'I do love you,' she spoke quietly.

The door clunked firmly behind him. And then there was nothing, only the sound of his footsteps walking away.

Of course, it was impossible NOT to think about a particular person or a particular thing just by deciding to. The very act of NOT thinking about—brought his face bright and alive before her. She would not name him to herself as if even the letters, the sound of them in her head, held the power of a spell. His scent seemed to hover in the air, catching her unawares when she entered the bedroom. She felt she could see the imprint of his footsteps on the floors, the whorls of his fingerprints on furniture, objects, as if she had infrared vision. She must fill her head with something else, anything else, to oust him.

Thank God she had her painting to focus on. The date of the exhibition private view gleamed in red pen in her diary; she forced herself to keep it in her sights, a brilliant buoy in a dark ocean. When she got home from work, she dumped her bag on the floor, clunking her keys on the table, sloughing off her jacket like a snake eager to slither from its old skin. She ate standing at the cluttered kitchen worktop, shoving aside coffee cups and old newspapers, hunched over a dish of pasta—bored with cooking, bored with eating, bored with herself. Then she climbed the stairs to her studio and sank into her paintings, losing herself in colour and shadow, letting the smell of paint and turpentine fill her head, her brush jabbing into the paint, swirling onto canvas, blotting him out.

Bella started getting into work crisply at nine instead of breezing in towards ten with the rest of them, paring down the hours to be endured alone at home. Work was dull but safe and she was grateful for the routine and the office banter. She shunned socialising, pleading the need to prepare for her exhibition, even avoiding Viv.

Seline had agreed that it would be worth attempting to train Anthony as Bella's deputy, if she could get him to act a little more responsibly and not refer to his pierced nipple in front of clients. Bella concentrated on 'grooming him for stardom' as he put it.

'Other boys wanted to be astronauts, footballers,' he said, 'but I dreamed of becoming a megalomaniac.'

'All in good time,' she said. 'Don't let them see the power-crazed glint in your eye until it's too late.'

She closed the door from Seline's office with a too-loud clunk, after yet another meeting that had once again been sidetracked from the insignificant issue of future projects to the far more important one of the redecoration of Seline's house.

Two yellow stickies on her phone: 'Your dad called. Have you remembered your mum's birthday? Please call back.' Another Duty Visit, that would be fun; she flicked through her desk diary—it was a Friday, she'd have to book a day off. And a message from Viv, saying hello and goodbye before she went off to work at head office in Birmingham for three weeks. It was too late to ring her back anyway. Viv had been strangely unsympathetic when Bella told her about Will—'You're a bloody idiot if you've shoved him away, Bel. That man is a gem.'

A series of sketches were spread out on her studio floor and she was about to start painting when the phone rang. It was Fran's voice on the answerphone; Bella stood at the top of the stairs, wanting to run down and pick up the phone. Fran went on at length—she was ringing to see how Bella was, to tell her she was still very welcome, she didn't have to come with Will. Bella crept downstairs as if Fran could detect her presence, and rested her hand on the phone.

'I know I can be a bit of a nosy old bag, but I promise not to interfere. I'd just love to see you. Besides, I have an ulterior motive. I'd love some more of that flan you made. The upside-downy one . . .'

The tarte Tatin?

Bella thought about standing in Fran's kitchen, rolling out pastry while Will peeled the apples, dipping a piece into the bag of sugar before slipping it into her mouth; his look of childlike wonder when she had turned the tin upside-down and there was the tart, warm and brown and smelling of caramel; his face as he smiled at her across the kitchen table.

'I dare say you must be up to your eyes preparing for your exhibition. Will told me—he sounded so proud of you . . .'

Should she pick up?

'Anyway, sorry to blether on, hope I haven't used up your tape. Do ring me any time you want to come. Don't wait to be asked.'

And then she was gone.

Donald MacIntyre phoned from the gallery. How were things progressing, he wanted to know, and could she supply a brief biography of herself. She sat slumped on the stairs, lulled by the rich maleness of his voice.

'. . . you'll need to have them here by then at the latest so they can go to the framers . . . or would you like us to pick them up?'

'I think—there—might—I think there could be a bit of a problem.'

'Oh?' His tone was cool.

'Um, yes. I'm not sure if they're—well, I might not be ready for the exhibition. I think perhaps you should just count me out.'

'No.' He spoke with authority. 'Sounds like classic pre-exhibition jitters to me. Let me come and see what you've done.'

'I'd rather you didn't.'

'I'm afraid I think I'll have to. Say this evening? Around eight?'

Donald MacIntyre was taller than she had remembered, filling the sitting room with his presence. His smart suit made her suddenly self-conscious about her appearance—her hair hauled back roughly into a clip, her faded leggings and slipped-down socks.

'They're upstairs.' Bella led the way.

She was sure he would hate them, anticipated his embarrassed look of disappointment, the shrug of his shoulders as he searched for the most tactful phrases. Best get it over with.

'There are just a few watercolours.' She gestured. 'Some line drawings as well. The rest are oils, as before.'

He squatted, incongruous in his beautiful tailoring among the oily rags and half-squished tubes of paint. He paused by a large painting, the one based on her very first sketch of Will.

'This.' He nodded. 'For the window.'

'No!' She coughed apologetically. 'It's not for sale.'

He laughed drily to himself and shook his head.

'We can fight about that later. Anyway, what was all that nonsense about your not being ready?'

Bella shrugged.

'With the others you brought, there's more than we have space for anyway. However . . .'

Here it comes, she thought, he hates them.

'These are better than a couple of the other ones, so we might have a

448

bit of a swap round before they go to the framers, OK?' He straightened up, then looked at her. 'Is there a problem?'

'No. Yes. Are they—all right then?'

And then he laughed. A great big, generous, booming laugh. Bella giggled nervously, unsure why he was laughing, surprised that such a sound could emanate from this quiet, elegant man.

'I do apologise,' he said. 'Forgive me. Do you think for one second that I would exhibit them if I didn't think they were "all right"? Why would I? I'm not running a charity for unemployed artists. All right? No, they're not all right. They're bloody good. Really. Consider yourself told.' He shook his head, laughing again. 'I love this business,' he said. 'If only I didn't have to deal with artists.'

12

'YOU'LL BRING WILL, of course, won't you?' Gerald said on the phone when Bella finally returned his call about Alessandra's birthday.

'Hmm. Possibly not.'

'Oh? How's it going with him?'

'Going, going, gone, since you ask.'

And, no, she didn't want to talk about it and please would he not tell Alessandra, because she wasn't feeling up to that stoic, 'my-daughter-is-the-cross-I-bear' look.

She had already bought Alessandra's present—an antique serving platter, its edge patterned with clusters of deep pink rosebuds and touches of gold, but she spent almost as long hunting for the perfect wrapping paper to go with it. Although she usually gave her own hand-made cards to friends, she had long since switched to shop-bought ones for her mother. It was easier, none of that 'how charming, so lovely to have a homemade one' insincere bollocks, and she was very busy anyway what with trying to fit in some painting most evenings. Friday, the birthday itself, was booked off, so she loaded the car late on Thursday evening—her clothes, the present plus a graceful weeping-fig plant as an extra, a new thriller (unbirthday present for Dad), a bottle of decent claret—and set off.

Still wearing the baggy T-shirt she had worn in bed, Bella quickly pulled on her jeans and thick socks to come downstairs. She let out Hund from his preferred sleeping place in the utility room. Aside from the clicking patter of Hund's paws on the floor, the house was hushed and still, with the particular quietness of the hour before anyone else is up.

The kitchen, as always, was pristine, with the slight chill of a very tidy room. She was glad of the socks—even through them she could feel the cold hardness of the quarry-tiled floor. She pulled out the prettiest cups and saucers from the glass-fronted cupboard, filled a milk jug, foraged in the cutlery drawer for the best tea strainer. Now, tray? And a cloth. She found a fresh linen napkin and laid that on the tray and set out the cups on it, pilfered a single bloom and a frond of foliage from the arrangement in the hall to add to a tiny vase.

She heard soft footsteps on the stairs, then Gerald came in.

'Morning, Dads. Back to bed with you. Go on. I'm bringing you both up some tea.'

He spotted the tray.

'What a treat, to have it made. Did you find everything you needed?' He paused at the door. 'Oh, did you know, your mother will only drink Earl Grey in the morning now? I prefer the ordinary, but don't worry.'

'No, no. That's fine. I'll just find a second pot.'

Balancing the tray on her raised knee and steadying it with one hand, she knocked on their bedroom door.

'Birthday tea in bed, madam?' Bella bent down to kiss her mother's cheek. 'Happy birthday. Your present's in the car; I'll go and fetch it in a minute. Your hair's looking nice.' Even first thing in the morning, it was already pinned up neatly.

'Thank you, Bella-darling. How lovely. Pretty anemone—I have some just like it in the hall. Is this Earl Grey?' Alessandra peered at the tray.

'Yes, Dad warned me. Shall I pour?'

'Best leave it for a minute. Oh, could you not find the tray-cloths? They're in the drawer.'

'No.' Bella turned her back to busy herself with pouring the tea, placing the strainer on each cup with infinite care, remembering to put the milk in last as was correct, carrying the cups over to the bed like a child, her brow furrowed in her eagerness to please.

'Marvellous,' said Alessandra. 'Perhaps I could have just a drop more milk?' Bella followed instructions with the milk jug then turned to go.

'No Will this time?'

'No.'

450

'Oh. Everything all right?'

'Fine, thanks. Why shouldn't it be?'

'Sorry. I didn't mean . . . Give him our best, won't you?'

Bella had insisted on cooking the birthday banquet. They started with hard-boiled quails' eggs, sitting on a salad of mixed leaves, fresh rocket, shreds of purple-red radicchio, blanched sugar snap peas, strips of grilled red and yellow peppers, with a warm sesame oil dressing.

'Is this from that cookery book I gave you at Christmas?' asked Alessandra at supper, cocking her head to one side, assessing.

'No, actually, I just made it up. What do you think?'

'Delicious!' said Bella's father. 'The peppers are lovely cooked like this.'

'It's very good. But the *rucola* must have been expensive,' said Alessandra.

The main course was poached salmon, served warm with a watercress sauce, pommes Anna, layered with translucent slivers of onion and moistened with milk, and fine French beans with glazed carrots. Nothing innovative, nothing risky, nothing with too much how-interesting-I-never-cook-it-*that*-way potential.

'You still haven't opened your present from me yet. It's in the hall. I'll go and get it.' Bella rose from her chair.

'Please don't bother, Bella-darling. I'll open it later.'

'Please open it now.'

Bella cleared the plates and placed the present in front of Alessandra.

'Well, isn't this wonderfully wrapped? What pretty paper.'

'I hope you like it.' Bella straightened the salt and pepper in front of her, brushed crumbs from the cloth into her palm.

Alessandra delicately picked off the sticky tape. 'Well now.' The platter lay exposed in its nest of pale pink tissue and rose-covered wrapping paper. 'That's really very charming, Bella. Thank you.'

'We must give it pride of place,' said Gerald. 'Why don't we move that boring green one and put it in the middle of the big dresser?'

'But Gerald-darling, that was Mamma's. Perhaps we could fit this one on the dresser in the hall.'

Bella went into the kitchen to get the dessert.

'I hope you'll use it sometimes,' she called through as she looked for the silver cake slice.

'Well, of course we don't entertain as much as we used to, Bella, not like I did when I was your age. It's a bit big just for the two of us.'

Bella appeared bearing her chilled lemon mousse cake, circled by a red moat of raspberry coulis. The perfect, smooth surface was piped with a large A in curlicued chocolate script.

'Dah-dah,' said Bella, flatly, a token fanfare.

'That looks simply delicious, but you know I don't think I could manage another mouthful just now. You and Dad have some.'

'It's very light,' said Bella. 'It's mostly air.'

Alessandra smiled, gestured gracefully with her hand in refusal, and wiped her lips conclusively with her napkin.

'Now, I'll make the coffee,' she said, getting up from the table.

Bella looked down at the mousse cake. There seemed to be a large drop of water on one twirl of the A. Another. Her tears fell as she stood, poised with the cake slice.

'Oh, Bella, sweetheart, don't,' said her father. 'She can't help it.'

She was gulping now, her breaths coming in great waves, pulling at her rib cage.

'She—never—' Bella slapped at the top of the cake with the flat of the cake slice, hitting it as she gulped in air. 'Says—anything—nice.'

'Hush, now.' He put his arm round her stiff shoulders. 'That was a delicious meal you made. Of course she liked it.'

'She—hates—me.'

Alessandra swept in with the tray of coffee.

'Oh, have I interrupted something? What happened to that lovely-looking cake? I was just about to have a piece.'

Gerald silenced her with a look.

'Well, I'm sure I don't know why she's crying. It ought to be me. I'm the one who's a year older.'

'Ali! That's enough now.'

She sighed and shrugged. 'All this fuss . . .'

Bella turned on her, shouting, choking out words:

'Yes, all this *fucking* fuss. Nothing's ever good enough for you, is it? No matter what I do, it's just wrong because it's me.'

Bella looked down at the cake slice clutched tight in her hand; it felt hard, solid—comforting. The cold glint of metal. She couldn't seem to let it go.

'What do you *want* from me? What can I do that would be *right*? You don't even like me, never mind love me. Why did you bother to have me? *Why?* You've never wanted me, have you? *Have* you?' Bella screamed into her mother's face.

Alessandra's eyes looked huge, flecked with shock and fear; she recoiled in tiny flinches as the words struck her.

Bella raised the silver cake slice high and slammed it down hard into the middle of the cake, splattering great gobbets of mousse across the table. Raspberry coulis spurted blood-like over the crisp white cloth.

Gerald folded his hand round hers, firmly guiding it down to the table, releasing her fingers.

'No,' said Bella, wiping her nose with the back of her hand, and laughed. It seemed so obvious. 'You never have. It's as simple as that.' She looked down at the smashed cake, the silver slice, the white cloth with its splatters of violent red.

She was too weary to drive back now. She'd go in the morning, as soon as it was light. Now, all she wanted was a long, hot bath and some sleep. Her ribs seemed to hurt from crying, but there were no tears now. She was calm. The unsayable had been said, and it was a release.

Gerald came up to her room as she was getting ready for her bath.

'Your mother wants to talk to you. She wants to explain. Just talk to her. Please.'

'I'm sorry, Dad. I've had enough. I'm not in the mood to hear her justifying the way she is.'

'I know it's hard. She does try. She can't help it really.'

'Dad. Let's just leave it, OK?'

'All right.' His shoulders sagged and he looked tired. 'Maybe in the morning though, hmm?'

'Maybe.' She smiled, and gave him a hug. 'I'm sorry about the mess.'

He shooed away her apology with a wave of his hand.

'Forget it. Still—mostly air, indeed!' He patted her cheek.

In the morning, when her father knocked on her door with a cup of tea, she was gone.

The light on her answerphone flashed manically, the tape full of unreturned calls. Her father phoned most of all, leaving weary messages. She didn't want to phone in case her mother answered and she couldn't see the point of talking to Dad either. He'd only try to coax her into coming for a visit, assuring her it would be different this time, apologising for Alessandra at the same time as justifying her, defending her.

The post plopped onto the mat. A postcard on the top caught her eye. She picked it up, with a few envelopes beneath it.

The postcard was from Viv, still in Birmingham spending some time at head office—'Hello, snotface. Hope you're OK and not brooding too much about Will. Sorry if I was bit of an insensitive so-and-so—it was only because I thought you two were so right for each other. Now I suppose I've only gone and made it worse. Sorry, sorry again. Do go and see Nick if you need cheering up (he'll need it if you don't and he loves your spicy prawn thing). Back next week.' Estimate for replacing broken sash cords on three windows. Credit-card bill—open that later.

Oh, hello, she hadn't seen that elegant script for quite a long time: Letter from Her Mother. What beautiful handwriting she had, but no doubt the letter within was packed with poison, a razor-sharp dagger in a jewelled scabbard.

She hotted up her coffee with water from the kettle and then opened the letter.

Dear Bella
I'm surprised she didn't put the Dear in quote marks.
I am unaccustomed to writing, or indeed talking, about my emotions so you may appreciate how difficult it must be for me.
Indeed? How difficult it all is—poor Alessandra, got at by nasty Bella.
I think we are so alike in so many ways.
Alike! Ha! Bollocks we are. We're completely different.
I know we both tend to shut ourselves off from those we love most when we feel hurt or vulnerable.
I do not. I'm very open. Will's face came into her mind, his voice: 'I wish I could really know you.' She saw flashes of herself: her own averted face, her pinched-shut lips, her swift exits through doorways, leaving awkward conversations behind.
I apologise . . .
Couldn't she actually say 'I'm sorry'? Did she have to be so formal all the time?
. . . if you feel let down by me or that I have not shown you as much love or warmth as you would have liked.
This could have been worded by a lawyer. Wouldn't she take some responsibility for being so cold? Some—some blame?
I do not believe that I have been such a bad mother.
Ha! You wouldn't, would you?
I wish I could have been a better one. Perhaps all mothers do. We both did our best to feed and clothe you, provide a safe and stable home for you. We always welcomed your friends, encouraged you to develop your talents, allowed you a great degree of independence.

Hmm. Only because you didn't give a toss.

All I can say is that I did the best I could—being the person I am. I would never deliberately upset you. I dare say I could have been a 'better' mother . . .

Ah-ha. Interesting you put that in quotes—definitely an alien concept.

. . . and I will try my hardest. I do not want to justify myself or feel that I ought to . . .

But you will anyway.

. . . my own upbringing was very different. We had very little money, as is often the case with immigrants, so perhaps I gave too much importance to providing for you rather than giving you the attention you feel you needed. Later, there were other problems too that affected me very badly. Perhaps, one day, I will tell you about them.

Oh, a cliffhanger? Very slick. Problems, such as? Lost a lipstick when you were twenty? Curdled the hollandaise once fifteen years ago? Won't specify because you know it would sound feeble?

You are wrong in thinking I don't love you. Very wrong. I'm sorry if I do not show it as much as you would like—or as much as I would like.

Why couldn't you put you do love me? I love you. Is that really so hard to say, to write? (She thought of Will: 'You can't say it, can you?' and her response, 'What? The "l" word?') But surely only her mother could manage to phrase it so that it actually appeared on the page in the negative.

A quiet voice in her head asked, 'And have you ever told her you loved her?'

I hope we can both try to be better friends to one another. With much love, Mum.

Bella refolded the letter to put it back in the envelope. There was something else in there; she shook out the envelope. Two photographs fell onto the table. She had never seen them before, nor any like them. Most of the family photos were slightly formal, awkward poses or ones of Alessandra looking glamorous or a few of Bella on her own or playing with a friend. Her father had taken most of them, so was hardly in any himself. But these were different. One of them was slightly out of focus: in it, Alessandra stood, looking pretty and relaxed in a summer dress with her hair loose; she was carrying Bella on one hip, apparently tickling her under her chin; little Bella was laughing. When had it been taken? Bella turned it over. No date. She looked about two, maybe three.

The other photograph was sharper, clearer. It was a beach. Alessandra was kneeling on the sand, holding her hair out of her face and watching Bella, who was just sticking in a flag on top of a large sandcastle that reached up to her shoulders. It had turrets studded with shells, and a moat. Again, there was no date, but Bella thought she couldn't have been more than three. Looking at it more closely, she recognised the little swimsuit she was wearing in the picture. It had been navy, she remembered now, with a little white skirt and a stripy, V-shaped bit at the top. She'd forgotten all about it until now, although she'd been absolutely thrilled when her mother had bought it for her. It had been so grown-up, her first proper swimsuit.

Perhaps she would ring Dad and ask him if he knew the date and where it had been taken. Bella stared deep into the first photograph. What was so odd about it? It was like a thousand family photographs. It was delightful, but ordinary. She looked more closely at her mother's face. There, that was it. Although it was slightly blurred, she could see that Alessandra was looking at the young Bella with rapt attention. The photograph was a whole little world, with only Alessandra and Bella in it, mother and child completely absorbed in each other. She shut her eyes as if she might recapture it.

Warm arms around her. The smell of jasmine and face powder and sea. Rubbing noses.

She looked down at the photos in her hand, then propped them up on the mantelpiece.

Bella went round the supermarket in a daze. What did she need? Why was she here? She picked up a pot of yoghurt and stood staring at the label, biting her lip as if considering her selection.

Again and again, Will filled her thoughts, her vision. She saw him asleep, his irrepressible hair curling against the pillow; out walking, stopping frequently when he got excited by their conversation. In the shower, letting the water stream over his face, running down his chest, washing the lather down his legs; in bed, his face relaxed, his eyes shining as he looked at her, wound his finger into a lock of her hair—'See? We're entangled. You'll never get shot of me now.'

She tried to push the thoughts away, as solid as if they were boulders. Then the photos flashed into her mind, the ones of her and her mother. Impatient with herself, she concentrated on the chill cabinet in front of her. What else did she need? She stared at a carton of orange juice as if the answer might be written on its side.

456

She manoeuvred around the one-way system of the car park, driving at a snail's pace, forcing herself to notice people backing out, shoppers with uncontrollable trolleys, below-eye-level children. She saw his face clear in her head, his half-smile as he listened, his eyebrows straightening as he thought. She blinked hard and swallowed. She didn't have to think of him. Wouldn't. Anything else. Anything.

Then, as if through mist, she thought she saw Patrick ahead of her, walking away. He half turns as if he senses her behind him, but still she cannot see if it is him. As she breathes in, her nostrils flinch at the smell of damp, a sly odour of mould. The hairs rise on the back of her neck, goose bumps freckle her arms. Perhaps he will turn round, beckon her so she can follow him. Chill and dank, fear crawls over her, creeping across her shoulders, scuttling down her spine, sliding towards her knees. Patrick! she wants to shout after him. Patrick!

A sudden bang. The crunch of metal. The sickening screech of rubber on road. She was jerked forward and left, then jolted back as her seat belt held her fast.

'You fucking *stupid* cow! What do you think you're doing?'

A man was bellowing at her through her window. There was a bang as he slammed his hand down at the side of her bonnet. If she could just hold on to the steering wheel everything would be all right. Her hands felt numb. Beneath the wheel, her legs shook uncontrollably.

A policeman was talking to the bellowing man, laying a hand on his arm, drawing him to one side. A tapping on her window. Another policeman was making a circling motion with one finger and pointing.

Open your window. She could almost hear the cogs in her mind slowly whirring. She watched her arm move through the air as if wading through water; it stretched out for the handle, grasped the knob.

'Switch off the ignition and get out of the vehicle, please.'

Bella looked back at him. His expression shifted and he reached across her to turn the key. The door was opened.

'Are you injured, miss? Hang on. Don't move. Stay there.'

Someone else was squatting down beside her, asking her questions. Had she any pain anywhere? How did her neck feel? Could she move her legs? Her feet? What was her name? Did she know what day it was?

'Okey-dokey. Let's get you out of there. You're going to be fine.'

A soft spongy collar was carefully placed round her neck. A click as her seat belt was unfastened.

'. . . badly in shock,' a voice said.

The policeman spoke to her slowly.

'Is there someone you need us to call?'

Will. I want Will. Someone pressed a wad of tissues into her hand.

She couldn't call Will. Mummy and Daddy ought to come and fetch her. They would make everything all right again. No. No, they wouldn't. Wouldn't want to see her now. She shook her head. A policeman gave her a small tube to blow into; a little green light glowed and he said she was 'all clear'.

'We'll have to ask you some questions,' said the policeman, 'but you need to be checked over first. OK?'

Yes, she nodded. She understood. There were questions to be asked. She needed to be checked.

First she was to climb into the ambulance. Had someone been hurt? As she was helped up the steps, she looked back at her car and saw that a small white van was embedded in the front right wing. *That is her car. She was in that car.* Her whole body started to tremble, as if a tremor were shaking the earth beneath her feet.

At the hospital, she was given the all clear.

'You really ought to have someone fetch you,' the nursing sister said. 'Is there someone you can call?'

'It's fine. Really. Thank you. I'll just phone a taxi.'

The sister points to the payphone.

'There's a number on the wall there. Will anyone be in when you get home? You shouldn't really be on your own when you're in shock.'

'No. Yes. My—there'll be someone there when I get in.' Nodding now, backing away. 'I'm fine. Honestly. I'm fine.'

13

THERE WAS A STRANGE ringing sound. Bella flapped vaguely at the side of her head to make it go away. No. There it was again. A ringing. Definitely a ringing. And now banging. Bloody neighbours. Noisy people. It was very noisy around here. Someone should complain. Yes.

She would write to them. To the people. The people you complain to. That's what she would do. More ringing. She stretched out for her alarm clock and hit it. The button was already down. Still ringing.

Bella swivelled her body around and slowly lowered her legs to the floor. Shoes. She should find some shoes. Looked down at her feet. In shoes. That was handy. Banging again now. Right. She would go and sort them out. She pushed herself to her feet. Wandered out to the landing. Noisy people.

'Sssh!'

She stood at the top of the stairs. Below her, the stairway stretched, elongating itself so that it seemed as deep as the Grand Canyon.

'Hell-o-o-o,' she called.

'Bella? Hello! It's me!'

It seemed an awfully long way to the bottom. She sat down abruptly and started to make her way down on her bum, step by step.

Near the bottom, she was confronted by a pair of eyes looking at her through the letter slot.

Bella waved.

'Bella! Thank God.' Viv's eyes widened. 'What *are* you doing?'

'Why are you in my letter box?'

'I'm not in your letter box, you idiot. I'm trying to look through to see if you're there.'

Bella looked around. 'But I am here.'

'Yes, I can see that now. Babe—it's bloody cold out here. Could you let me in, d'you think? I'm getting cramp.'

'You should take salt for that. And not be getting into people's letter boxes.'

As Bella opened the door, Viv practically fell inside onto the mat.

'Gone numb,' she said. 'I've been kneeling on your doorstep. What the hell's the matter with you? Why haven't you been answering your phone? Your answerphone tape's full. Bel? You haven't—' Viv suddenly grabbed her by the shoulders '—had anything, have you?'

'Yes, thank you. Do you want some?'

'What? Tell me—exactly—what you have eaten or drunk.'

Bella thought for a minute.

'Bikkits. Jaffa Cakes.' She held up three fingers.

'Three Jaffa Cakes?'

Bella shook her head.

'Three packets.'

'They've never had this effect on me. What else?'

'Wine . . . and some Bailey's . . . and a fuck of a lot of vodka.'

Bella sat on the stairs, watching Viv dash from room to room, listening to her babble on: why hadn't Bella phoned someone? Nick would have come round—could have given her the number in Birmingham—was this all about Will—what on earth was going on—unbelievable—all this mess—pile of mail—her office said—phoned in sick—she'd been frantic—she'd no idea—how long had Bella been—water—drink loads of water—how could Bella have been so stupid.

Viv squeezed past her to run upstairs, opening drawers and cupboards. Reappeared stuffing clothes into a bag.

'You're coming to stay with us for a few days. No arguments. You had me shit-scared, you know. I just got back to discover you'd disappeared off the face of the earth.' Viv hugged her. 'You've got no idea, have you?'

The police were very polite. She had been on the main road, the other driver turning out of a side street. He thought she had stopped, he said, she was obviously letting him go, any idiot could see that; then she'd suddenly moved forward so he'd gone straight into her. Anyone would have done, he said, she must be a loony. Eyewitness reports conflicted. One thought she had almost come to a halt. Another said the van had swung out way too fast, she couldn't have avoided it. And it had been indisputably her right of way.

Viv asks if Bella has told Will.

'Why would I? Why would he care?'

'God, you can be irritating. Because he's probably still mad about you, that's why. I've never seen anyone so in love.'

'Oh, do you think so?' Bella's voice is flat, expressionless.

'You know he was. And so were you. You were sickening to watch, the two of you, like cute puppies falling over each other. Bleugh.'

Bella opens her mouth to speak.

'And don't even think about denying it.' Viv cuts her off. 'I've never seen you so happy. Sorry to say this, but not even with Patrick—nothing like. You had this incredible sort of—radiance. Your skin glowed.'

'Too much blusher.'

'Shut up. You always do that. Joke about stuff that really matters to you. Just stop it for once. Don't you remember Nick teasing you because you wouldn't stop talking about Will? How can you forget?'

'I know. I haven't forgotten.'

'Can't you, well, ring him up or something?'

Bella shakes her head.

'It's too late.'

He won't want me now. And I don't know how. I haven't the words.

'How you doing there, babe?'

'Marvellous. Loving every second.' Bella closes her eyes and starts to cry. 'Peculiar. Crap. Shaky. Glad to be in one piece. Can I have a hug?' she says.

Viv holds her tight.

'Don't you dare scare me like that again—or I'll have to shoot you.'

They laugh together, tears streaming down their cheeks.

'Of course you can. I told you—any time.' Fran sounds genuinely pleased.

Bella explains about her knock in the car.

'I still feel a bit shaky, but I know I have to drive soon or I won't be able to do it.'

The insurance company are processing the claim; they will decide on the value of her car and, eventually, send a cheque. She intends to start looking at second-hand cars in a week or so, when she feels a bit more robust. In the meantime, she is planning to hire one for the weekend.

Fran is out in the garden, apparently undeterred by the damp—'Perfect for planting.'

She hugs Bella.

'You must take some redcurrants when you go. I've a freezer full. I know you'll think of something interesting to do with them. There's only so much redcurrant jelly one person can get through.'

Bella works alongside Fran in the garden, now adept at spotting which are weeds and which are not, what to cut back and what to leave. The sound of secateurs reminds her of Will, the way Fran dips in and out of the borders, casually pulling up a weed as she passes, snipping off a faded bloom. Fran avoids talking about him, Bella notices, and speaks instead of her late husband, Hugh.

'I still miss him, y'know? It's over five years ago now. I used to wonder when I'd "get over it"—as if it were some kind of obstacle course. I remember seeing it in my head like a great, craggy rock I'd have to climb. I thought I'd get to the other side, then maybe life would go back to normal. No bloody idea.' She laughs at herself. 'Come in out of this drizzle and let's get some tea.

'I went through all these different feelings. At first, I just could not believe it. Hughie was so alive, do y'see? I kept thinking I saw him. I followed some man in a similar sort of corduroy jacket halfway round Sainsbury's. Daft I know.'

Bella shakes her head. 'It's not daft.'

'And I was so angry with him. Why hadn't he looked after his health better?—he'd already had a minor stroke before—how dare he leave me alone? Then I felt it was all my fault. I should have done something, anything. When it really sank in, I kept crying in all the most unlikely places. In the garden, I'd be digging up potatoes for supper and I'd suddenly look down and see that I'd dug enough for two and I'd be off again.'

Bella tops up their mugs.

'But—it did get better.' Fran waves a hand at Bella's eyebrow, twitching into a doubting arch. 'No. I know what you're thinking. It used to make me so angry when people patronised me with all that time's-the-best-healer stuff. But my feelings did shift. I haven't forgotten him, God knows. Things can never go back to being as they were before. Life's different. I'm different. But the pain's not sharp now. I can *enjoy* my memories of him without feeling wretched all the time. And, somewhere along the line, I let myself off the hook.'

There is a silence. Fran gets up and refills the kettle.

'You've lost someone, too, haven't you?'

The clink of the kettle lid. The striking of a match. The soft hiss of the gas.

'I'm sorry. Perhaps you prefer not to talk about it?'

'I—it's not—I find it hard. I don't. It's so—' She presses her lips tight shut, to hold it in, then, suddenly, her mouth trembles and opens, gaping wide. And Bella is babbling. She is so scared—she couldn't let go of Patrick—she didn't dare—it would be like a betrayal—he needed her to cling on or he'd be really, really gone.

Around her, the kitchen swims into a blur.

And then she'd met Will and she'd felt bad, guilty for loving him so much—then terrified she'd lose him as well. She wouldn't be able to bear it—not Will—she couldn't—she'd be eaten away by the pain of it—cease to exist. And she'd messed things up and driven him away and it was awful. He didn't even know that she loved him because she couldn't say it, she was so afraid. She just knew if she owned it, admitted it, he'd be taken away—she'd be punished—she wouldn't be allowed to be so happy, not for long—just enough to lull her into a false sense of security. She'd get used to him, and life would be rosy, then—BAM—and he'd be hit by a truck or get cancer or flit off to Auckland—and she wouldn't be able to stand it. Only now she'd lost him anyway, but it wasn't so very bad because at least she'd expected it, engineered it—at least she knew where she was this way. Really, it wasn't so very bad. Not so very bad.

And Fran's arms are round her; she is stroking her hair and holding her. She is making comforting, ssshusshing sounds into her hair.

Bella's breaths lurch from her lungs. Her shoulders shake in spasms. Unleashed sobs wrench at her chest. She tries to gulp them down. Tears scrawl mascara in a spidery calligraphy over her cheeks; she wipes her nose with the back of her hand.

'But it's much worse than that—m-much worse.'

Fran is still holding her, and Bella looks up at her.

'I've never told anyone. You'll hate me when you know.'

'Hush, hush. I could never hate you.'

Bella is quiet now, even calm. She blows her nose and lets out a long sigh as she remembers. At last, it is time to tell.

The knowledge has been swirling through her for weeks now, maybe even months if she dare admit it. When had she framed that first thought? Allowed herself to think it? Now it is like a prickling itch beneath her skin, refusing to be ignored. She can only create the luxury of forgetting when she hurls herself into something else, so she spends long hours at work, gets up early to go swimming, relishing for once the smell of chlorine, climbing up her nostrils, stinging her eyes, scouring her shameful, selfish thoughts.

Patrick comments with a laugh, 'Anyone would think you had a lover, Bel. All this staying late at the office.'

'Er . . . nonsense, darling. Important client, that's all.' She had pretended to be flustered to tease him, as if he had found her out, unearthed her great secret, and he had laughed.

But he hasn't discovered it. Doesn't seem to have a clue. Bella almost wishes she did have a lover, a proper reason, something tangible, someone else she could point to and say, 'See? That's why.' How simple that would be.

As each day passes, she can feel the gap widening between her intentions and her actions. She watches herself moving around the flat, one step behind her false ghost image, sneering at its bright manner, its smiles. Why can't Patrick see it? Surely he will suddenly catch a glimpse of her there, shivering behind that horrible smiling façade?

She starts to timetable 'Telling Patrick' in her head, then in her diary. Not this weekend because we're going up to his parents. Not in the week because he'll be coming back late from that job in Walthamstow every night. Next weekend? Maybe. Then next weekend comes and they have friends for supper or Patrick seems under the weather or she has a period pain. Maybe she'll do it Tuesday, quickly before it's in the run-up to his birthday or, oh my God, then it'll be Christmas. Maybe it'd be better to wait till after then.

And so, now it is January 18 and she is standing in a small white room, looking down at Patrick's body spread out before her.

'I'm an impostor,' she tells herself, 'a cheat who didn't deserve him.' But still, through the shock, she knows she is glad she didn't tell him, didn't spoil his last few months; she is glad she never said the words:

'Patrick. I can't do this any more. I don't—I don't love you.'

Fran comes to say good night, tucking her in tightly as if she is a child. Bella pokes her chin over the turned edge of the sheet, comforting as a folded sandwich, and looks around at the rose-patterned wallpaper, with its oddly cheering misaligned joins and irregular edges. The bed-side lamp shines on a few bright buttercups, sprawling in a tiny blue jug with sprigs of feathery fennel and daisylike feverfew. Funny, she thinks, I've never noticed how pretty buttercups are before—how perfect each petal is, how smooth. She drifts into a doze, their yellow heads like tiny suns warming her as she closes her eyes.

She rummages through her sketchbooks. Somewhere here, yes. Here. There are several sketches—and her memory.

She begins to paint. It is as she remembers him best, his long form awkwardly folded into an armchair, one leg draped over the side. If only she could capture the way he rotated his foot as he read, first one way, then the other; she could draw it at an angle to suggest it, perhaps. She knows she must paint it all in one sitting, now while he is so clear in her head. She lets his voice wind its way into her ears once more, recalls now his touch with simple fondness, lets the essence of him quicken the sinews of her hands, spilling out onto the paper.

It is good, she realises, better than she could have hoped. Sometimes, painting was work, work and more work, a battle with the limitations of the paint, the paper or canvas, frustration with the gulf between the image in her head and the insipid translation of it that she set down with her brush. But, occasionally, rare and precious, one came as a gift, flowing from her eyes, her mind, down through her hand, capturing her vision in front of her like a butterfly come to rest.

She phones first, to make sure it will be all right for her to come, saying she won't stay long, she doesn't want to impose, feeling her way through the pauses, wondering if she is welcome. The picture is carefully wrapped, laid on the back seat of the car.

As she raises her hand to the knocker, the door sweeps open.

'Bella!' Joseph, Patrick's father, gathers her close.

'Is that Bella here already?' calls Rose, running through and undoing her apron.

Their delight in seeing her stings her with shame. There is no word of reproach, no veiled hints that she might have visited sooner. Their apparent gratitude that she's bothered to drive all that way to see them is more mortifying than any criticism could have been. How could she have been so selfish?

'Come in, come in—and look who's here.'

Sophie, Patrick's young sister, jumps up and throws her arms round Bella.

'Soph! I didn't know you'd be here.'

'We haven't seen you for months. I thought you'd forgotten us.'

'Sophie!' Rose frowns at her. 'Don't be so rude.'

'Oh, Mum. Bel doesn't mind.'

Bella catches a look between Joseph and Rose.

'Oh, Bel! Don't cry. Shit. What have I said now?'

'Language!' says Rose. 'Please excuse her, Bella.'

'No. It's not that. It's not you, Soph, really. It's just me. And you're all being so *nice*.' She takes Joseph's proffered handkerchief.

'I brought you something, but I don't know if it's the right thing.'

'No need to bring anything,' says Rose.

'Just a pleasure to see you,' says Joseph.

'Is it your sticky lemon cake?' says Sophie.

Bella goes out to the car to fetch it. What if they hate it? What if they burst into tears? This could be a horrible mistake.

She holds it close to her body.

'I hope it doesn't make it worse. But I did it for you and I want you to have it.'

Bella hands the picture to Joseph. His eyes start to pool above the rims. He nods without speaking. Rose, close beside him on the sofa, clutches his arm. Tears spill down her powdery cheeks, run along the creases round her eyes.

'I didn't mean to upset you. I'm sorry. I thought—I don't know what I thought.'

Rose and Joseph are both shaking their heads.

No—they say—that's not it—they love it—hadn't expected it—there is nothing they could have loved more—nothing better she could possibly have given them—it's just, you see—Joseph looks round for his hankie—it's just so *Patrick*.

Sophie agrees, it is *very* Patrick, look at his foot there, you just know he's winding it round and round like a bloody clockwork toy the way he always did. Won't Alan love it when he sees it?

Alan is not expected until teatime, so Bella stays for tea. When he arrives, he kisses her cheek and holds her arms awkwardly for a few moments. He looks at her half-sideways, the way Patrick used to.

'The folks have missed you, you know.'

She nods, abashed.

'The picture. They're really chuffed, you can tell. It was a good thing to do. The right thing. Thank you.'

Rose won't hear of her driving back all that way at night. Bella must be exhausted. The bed's all made up anyway. They couldn't possibly let her go back so late. Absolutely not.

'But I haven't got my things . . .'

A clean nightie is presented, a new toothbrush found. She lets herself be fussed over for once.

After breakfast, Joseph walks round the garden with her, impressed by her new-found knowledge as she admires his plants by name. She holds their leaves between her fingers, comforted by the familiar feel of them, letting the names, the scents, roll round her head: thyme, she thinks, lemon balm, rosemary. *Rosmarinus officinalis*. Ah, rosemary.

'I'm glad you came. I don't imagine it's been easy for you either.'

'I'm much better than I was.'

Joseph clears his throat and leans over a plant to pull off a dead leaf.

'You wouldn't ever have married him, would you?'

Bella is silent, then lifts her gaze to meet his.

'It's all right.' He digs his hands down deep into his pockets. 'I think I knew quite a while ago. Rose doesn't. She thinks you were just being young folk, doing the modern thing.'

'I'm sorry.'

'You don't need to be. It's no good cheating on how you feel, is it?'

'S'pose not.'

He folds her in his arms, patting her back.

'Is that why you've kept away?'

She nods into his shoulder.

'I couldn't. I felt such a fraud. I thought you'd hate me.'

He tuts quietly into her hair, shaking his head.

14

'THAT IS COMPLETELY GORGEOUS, much too nice for you, you old slapper. I want it.' Viv lets the sleeve of the cherry two-piece slither between her fingers. Bella had worried that she would look ridiculously overdressed for her private view, especially when she had arrived and met one of the other artists who is wearing denims and what Bella mentally catalogues as a mixed-media waistcoat, a garment that might be interesting if it was framed but looks ridiculous on an actual person. Fortunately, Donald MacIntyre is wearing an immaculately pressed suit and a snazzy red-and-black silk tie and Fiona, the gallery assistant, is in a smart little black dress. Both approve heartily of Bella's outfit, Fiona with a sidelong flare of her nostrils at Mr Wacky Waistcoat.

'You look stunning,' says Viv. 'Give us a twirl then.'

Bella obliges and the skirt softly swings out round her legs.

'You must have splashed out. That never came from Oxfam.'

'It was Alessandra's. Mum's.'

Viv raises her eyebrows without comment.

'Too glam for me really.' Bella looks down at herself.

'Nonsense. It's very you.'

Nick gives an appreciative whistle and kisses her on the cheek.

'Show us some o' yer art then.' He feigns a nose-wipe-with-sleeve.

She points out her section of the exhibition and the two paintings in the window.

'I thought that looked like Will,' says Viv. 'Not his face exactly but something about the posture, the way he's standing. Shit, you *are* good. Why've you been footling about all these years when you're a bloody genius, woman? Well, at least you're winding down at Scotton Design.'

'Ssh.' Bella nods towards Seline.

'Where're the proud parents then?' asks Jane, a friend from London.

'Not here.'

'Oops, sorry, have I put my foot in it?'

'You *did* ask them, Bel, didn't you?' Viv joins in, narrowing her eyes at Bella.

'I did send them an invite.' Bella reaches for another canapé. 'But I forgot to post it till this morning.'

'Forgot, yeah. You meanie. They'd have loved to come. Don't scrunch your nose like that—it makes you look like a pig. Well, more fool you—they might have bought one.'

It should be one of the best evenings of her life. It almost is. She has good friends around her. Her work is on show in the best private gallery in the city and people are praising it. A pleasant, fizzy feeling hovers just beneath her skin. People are showering her with compliments, but she finds it hard to let them sink in. She feels herself discounting them, repelling them like water bouncing off an oilskin. *They're just being polite. They have to say something nice. They've drunk too much wine.* She smiles and nods and says her thankyous, makes self-deprecating jokes, on guard against feeling too pleased.

But all she can think of is Will. She is glad *his* picture is in the window, facing the street, so she doesn't have to keep catching sight of it as she looks around the room. She keeps thinking how much he would have enjoyed this evening, what he would have said: he'd have been amused by that man over there, inspecting her brushwork at such close range that he is practically wiping his nose on it. She thinks of the way Will's hand would rest on the small of her back for a moment as he passed her, how he would stroke her hair away from her face casually, almost without noticing. He'd have liked Donald MacIntyre with his dry wit and keen intelligence. And they even had canapés and dippy things. Will loved food on sticks.

'Sign mine on the back for me some time, will you, Bella?' Seline says. 'You've only initialled it on the front.'

Seline has bought a picture. Spent money—and quite a lot of money—on a painting by Bella, a person she actually knew. How could you take someone's work seriously when you'd argued together, fought over chocolate biscuits, borrowed Tampax from each other?

'But they're so expensive—you mustn't—the gallery sets the prices—and their commission is high—I must do you another one.'

Seline tells her to shut up and stop babbling.

'I love it and I have the perfect spot for it, so let me enjoy it.' She smiles. 'And I also suspect that I have made rather a wise investment.'

She spots Nick writing out a cheque and runs over to try to stop him. Fiona threatens to lock her in the kitchen—'People are supposed to buy them. That's the point of having an exhibition.' Bella corners Viv.

'You're just doing it because you feel sorry for me, aren't you? Confess.'

'You're right. That's the only reason. We're even going to put it over the fireplace—that's how sorry we are for you. Don't be daft, babe. Nick's never polite, you know that.'

'True.' Nick gargles briefly with his wine. 'I can't be arsed. We're just cynical collectors, snapping you up while you're still cheap. Well—not that cheap . . .'

'Shut up and have one of these mushroom thingies.'

Work the next day flies by for once, with Anthony returning from lunch with a beret which he plonks on her head—'You are now officially a bona fide *artiste*, and must wear this at all times.' Back home, she sinks onto the sofa to relive yesterday evening. The doorbell rings.

She opens the door.

'And what exactly is this, Ms Kreuzer?' Gerald is waving the exhibition invite under her nose.

'Oh, hi, Dads. That's an invite.' Her shoulders drop in disappointment. 'They have them for exhibitions. Just passing by, were you?'

'Most amusing. When did all this happen? And any idea why ours should have got to us so late?'

'Can't imagine. Post, eh? Terrible.' She tuts and shakes her head.

Over her father's shoulder, she sees her mother. Alessandra hovers outside in the street, wondering whether it is safe to venture into the bear's den.

'Hi!' Bella's voice sounds artificially high and bright in her own ears. She clears her throat. 'Er, hi. Hello. Mum. Come in, come in.'

'Thank you, dear.' Alessandra steps cautiously into the hall. 'But the invite was postmarked yesterday. Surely the gallery should send them out much earlier?'

'Mmm.' Bella helps her off with her coat. 'Just an oversight, I suppose.'

'We went to see it,' says Alessandra. 'It was marvellous. We loved it.'

Yeah. Right. Course you did.

Gerald is off now: it's fantastic—why hadn't she told them?—she must be over the moon—he is over the moon—they should both have been at the private view—would have been, of course—and the pictures— they were extraordinary—unforgettable—why did they bother having those other people's stuff in there, cluttering up the place—only to be interrupted by Alessandra saying she had thought them beautiful—the colours so rich—the textures so real she wanted to touch them—and they had argued over which one to buy because of course they must have at least one, would have bought one even if she hadn't been their daughter—and the young girl there had been ever so sweet and offered them coffee when they'd said who they were and made a fuss of them— and Alessandra had bought one for Gerald's birthday in advance and would Bella be sure to bring it next time she visited—if she thought she might be visiting—if she had time at some point.

Then there is silence. Gerald coughs.

'We don't want to interrupt you if you're busy.' He looks around the room. 'But we were curious to see the house. Didn't think we should wait for a formal invitation—what with the *post* and all.'

'No sweat.' Abashed, Bella crosses her arms in front of herself, then lets them drop to her sides. 'Tea or coffee?'

'Tea, please,' Gerald says just as Alessandra speaks.

'Coffee would be marvellous.'

Alessandra's gaze meets Bella's.

'Tea's fine.'

'Or coffee,' says Gerald.

Alessandra opens the kitchen drawers and cupboards, like any keen cook. It is small, she agrees, but seems well laid out, very easy to work in, was Bella doing much cooking or was she too busy painting? Looking through the French windows, they exclaim over the garden with its architectural plants dramatically lit up, casting shadows onto the walls. Then they rather obviously try to play down their praise, switching their attention to the drama of the sweeping curtains framing the view outside, how light the house was, what fine details, the fire-place, the cornices, much more spacious than they had imagined.

'Can I poke about in the garden?' Her father stands at the French win-dows, unable to contain himself any longer. Bella unlocks the doors to let him out.

'Can you see all right? Feel free to weed while you're out there.'

They are alone.

'Do have a look too if you'd like.'

'Maybe in a minute.' Alessandra follows her through to the kitchen.

'I'm sorry about last time.' Bella forces herself to look at her mother. 'I didn't mean—I went a bit overboard. Well, a lot overboard. I was, well, things with Will had—but I don't want to make excuses.'

'I didn't know at the time. I am sorry. I'd have tried to be a bit more . . .' Alessandra shrugs, Italian-style. She seems to be especially fidgety, repinning strands of her hair that are already neatly in place.

'Your father says there's something I ought to tell you. I ought to have told you a long time ago.'

'I'm adopted? I'm the last remaining granddaughter of the lost Czar? I was born a boy? Dads isn't my real father; it was the milkman and that explains why I've got curly hair and can whistle so well.'

Alessandra is silent, waiting for her to finish.

'Sorry,' says Bella.

'It doesn't sound so very big now. Seems silly to have hidden it for so long.'

Alessandra asks if she remembers how, when she was a little girl, she was always asking why she didn't have any brothers or sisters.

'In fact, well I . . . I did get pregnant again. When you were nearly three. But it didn't feel the same.' She shifts in her seat. 'It was six, nearly seven months, but I couldn't feel the baby moving. And with you—well, you were always kicking me.' Her eyes flick over Bella's face. 'You were very mobile.'

They had examined her again.

'And I was right. She—the baby—was dead.'

Alessandra starts to fumble in her handbag.

'Here.' Bella tears her off a sheet of kitchen roll.

'So silly after all this time.' Alessandra shakes her head, impatient with herself. 'And. Well. I'm sure they wouldn't do this now. They couldn't. I hope they don't. But then—they induced me. I had to—you see—go through labour knowing she was already dead.' She seems to subside in her chair, deflated.

'That's horrible.' Bella swallows. 'You shouldn't have had to go through that.'

'Did you try to have another one?'

Alessandra shakes her head slowly.

'They said there was no reason why not. Your father was so keen. I could see it in his face, even when he forced himself not to say any-thing.' She blows her nose on the kitchen roll surprisingly loudly and laughs. 'Not very elegant. No. No, I couldn't. I couldn't face it. In case, you know. Not again.'

She clicks open her powder compact and pats at her cheeks.

'And were *you* all right?' Bella says quietly.

Alessandra seems to drift off for a moment, ahead, as if hardly aware of Bella's presence.

'Mmm. Physically. I suppose so. I came home afterwards. From the hospital. We went to pick you up from Mrs Mellors next door and—and you stretched your arms up to me. You were so adorable but so, so—*little*, do you see? You looked so small and I . . . I couldn't bear it. Gerald always told me I wasn't—wasn't the same after that. With you.'

'So, shall we join Dad in the garden?' Alessandra rises to her feet. At the French windows, she pauses and lays a hand lightly on Bella's arm.

'I'm glad I've told you.'

'So am I.'

'But still—I'd prefer it if you didn't keep bringing it up. I really can't—you know.' Her head on one side, eyes wide like a child's. 'You do see?'

'Sure.' Bella places her hand on top of Alessandra's and smiles.

Alessandra steps out into the garden.

'Well now. Isn't this quite splendid? The lighting! *Magnifico!* Gerald-darling, you must be green with envy.'

Bella notices Alessandra peering round the room. She seems to be looking for something. Oh-oh, the lamp. Their house-warming present.

'These are very elegant, aren't they?' Alessandra gestures to the uplighters on the wall.

'If you're wondering where your lamp is, just say so. The fact is it looked like it belonged in a stately home. It didn't fit in, OK?'

She scans their faces, expecting outrage or that wounded look.

'It's fine.' Gerald is smiling, brows raised in amusement. 'I did give you the receipt in case you wanted to change it.'

She uncrosses her arms and lets her hands fall to her sides.

'It just wasn't quite me. I'm sorry.'

'So what did you get instead?' Alessandra casts around as if she might guess.

Bella's face lights up. 'Here. Come and see.' She tows them upstairs.

They stand in her bedroom, the three of them in a semicircle as if assessing a prize thoroughbred.

'I've never had one before.' Bella suddenly feels embarrassed, like a child showing off her favourite doll while wondering if she were too old for such things.

'I should have thought of it,' says Alessandra. 'Why didn't I think of it? Everyone should have one.'

Gerald steps forward and poses in front of the full-length cheval mirror, holding his lapels.

'I feel quite the gent seeing myself in this.'

Bella and Alessandra stand behind, flanking him. In the mirror, their eyes meet. A cautious half-smile from Alessandra, like a boy asking a girl out for the first time; the smile returned, then both are eclipsed by Gerald, adopting a certain swagger and beaming fit to bust.

Downstairs again, Alessandra spots the old photographs of herself and Bella on the mantelpiece.

'Oh! That reminds me.' She opens her handbag and starts to search for something with her long, elegant fingers. 'They are lovely, aren't they? You look so sweet in them. I'm so glad you have them up. Gerald-dear, we should have them framed. You'll never guess what I found at the back of my dressing-table drawer. I was having a tidy-up. Wait a minute. Here—here it is.'

She hands Bella a small ring box covered in soft blue velvet. Alessandra nods for her to open it.

'The family jewels?' says Bella.

Inside, lying on a bed of pale pink cotton wool, as if it were a precious stone or a valuable ring, is a shell.

She takes it out and gently probes the inside, at the edge before it starts to curl in on itself; it is touched with pink, and very smooth. She turns the shell over and over in her fingers.

'Beautiful,' she says. 'Where's it from?'

'Don't you remember?' Alessandra is half smiling, half frowning. 'I thought you might. You gave it to me when you were only small. From the beach. It was on that day.' She picks up the photograph again. 'Yes, I'm sure it was. I'd just been told I was pregnant—before—yes.' Alessandra nods.

And you've kept it all this time?

Her dreams of those early days. *Warm arms around her. The smell of jasmine and face powder and sea. Rubbing noses.* They were memories.

The sky is the pure, fierce blue of a child's best summer. It is so blue, it almost hurts to look at it. Still, she tips her head back, trying to swallow the whole sky inside her so that she can have this colour always. She closes her eyes tight shut now to check, her legs carrying her erratically crab-fashion along the beach. Inside her eyelids, the blue stays clear and strong.

'Shall I show you how to build a castle?'

Mummy kneels beside her on the hard sand. She scoops sand into the brand-new yellow bucket until there is too much, then shows Bella how to slap it down flat with the red metal spade.

'Now.' She turns the bucket upside-down with one deft movement like a conjuror, and sounds a fanfare. 'Dah-*dah*.'

Daddy comes back, holding three ice creams as carefully as if they were Mummy's best crystal glasses. Strawberry sauce trickles down onto one of his hands, chocolate down the other. He hands them over and licks his fingers. Mummy breaks off the bottom of her cone and shows Bella how to make a mini-cornet with it, topping it with a tiny portion of ice cream and dab of sauce. Then she sucks the broken end of her big cone. Bella watches, fascinated, and copies her, dribbling ice cream down her chin and getting it all round her mouth.

'You look like a clown.' Daddy laughs and Mummy licks a hankie from her bag and wipes Bella's face.

'That's beautiful, Bella.' Mummy cups the perfect shell in her palm like a little mouse. It is a curly-wurly shell no bigger than Mummy's thumb. It is almost white, weathered by the salt and the sun. At the opening, it is smooth against her finger, and slightly pink as if reflecting her peachy skin.

'Will you use it to decorate your castle?' Mummy offers it back.

'No.' She shakes her head. She looks at Mummy and not at the shell so she won't be tempted to change her mind. She has decided. ''s for you.' Warm arms round her. The smell of jasmine and face powder and sea. Being squeezed, squee-ee-ee-eezed. Rubbing noses, now. The bright gurgle of sudden giggles.

The click of the camera.

FIVE PICTURES HAD been sold at the private view ('An auspicious start' and much nodding from Donald MacIntyre), and her parents had bought one the next day, but there is absolutely no reason whatsoever to imagine that she could have sold any more. However, the gallery is hardly out of her way at all. Besides, it is near the better fishmonger, so it makes sense. She rephrases it in her head to prevent probable disappointment: she ought to pick up some fish from the good fishmonger and, while she is passing, she might as well poke her head into the gallery.

There are two of her paintings in the window: one small one, the first she had painted, of the woman holding herself, and a larger one, based on her first drawing of Will, which she had finally worked into a painting. It shocks her afresh to see them there, her own work. It is like entering a clothes shop and suddenly coming across a rail with the contents of your own wardrobe. It is slightly embarrassing in a way; she half expects people to come up to her and say, 'We *know* you now. We've seen inside your head. It's no use trying to hide.' She looks at the Will painting, as if she is seeing it for the first time. The set of his head on his shoulders there, that is really very Will-ish, better than she'd thought. His face, half in shadow; the light falling behind.

'Hey there,' says Fiona, 'come to check the sales tally?'

'No, no. Just passing by.'

'Uh-huh? Don't be embarrassed. If it were my stuff, I'd be phoning in every half-hour to see if I'd sold anything.'

Bella does a tour of the exhibition, checking the red spots. There are eight on her pictures. It doesn't seem like a lot, but she knows that it is good, better than she has a right to expect so early on. Still she tells herself that she can't count the ones bought by Viv, Seline and her parents, so it's really more like five.

Fiona is flicking through the sales book.

'Nine. That's pretty good. Very good in fact. You should do well next time when you have your own show.'

Next time.

'Nine? I only made it eight.'

'Did you count the one in the window?'

Had the little one sold? That would be good, the very first one she had painted.

'No, the bigger one. It's my favourite, I think. I love the way you can sort of almost see what the man's thinking, but not quite. It makes me go quite shivery.'

The bigger one? Not the one of Will?

'There must be a mistake. That one's not for sale. I told Donald before it went up but he said he wanted it in the window anyway because it would draw people in.'

'Oh-oh. He didn't tell me.'

Fiona cannot apologise enough. Is there any chance Bella would reconsider?

It's only a painting, she tells herself. What's the point of clinging on to it? It'll only make me miserable if I have it hanging about the house. But—*but it's all I have of him.*

'Well, I really . . .' she starts to say.

Fiona interrupts her. She will try calling the customer, explain the situation. Maybe he'd buy another one instead and they wouldn't lose the sale altogether. She'll see if there's a daytime phone number for him if Bella doesn't mind waiting.

'Hello. Oh, good morning. It's Fiona at MacIntyre Arts here. Is that Mr Henderson?'

Mr Henderson. Oh my God. Will.

'. . . if you still definitely want it?'

Will.

'. . . bit of a mix-up . . .'

Will.

'. . . any chance you might reconsider . . .'

Bella waves at Fiona and gestures for a pen, scribbles on the top sheet of the memo pad: LET HIM HAVE IT.

'Er, sorry, Mr Henderson. Apparently it is OK. Yes. Completely my fault. So sorry to have taken up your time.' She laughs. How many times had he made Bella laugh on the phone? 'Yes. Sorry again. Yes. Any time after the 18th. Thank you. Bye.'

'Phew,' says Fiona, shaking mock sweat from her brow. 'Nice bloke, but didn't sound keen to let go of the painting. Thank you so much for changing your mind. Donald would have done his dour John Knox face at me for the whole of next week otherwise.'

Bella is just leaving when Fiona asks if she has had a look at her comments as well. Comments? What comments? Fiona hands her the visitors' book. There is the date of the private view, where the guests had signed in. Some had added a brief note: Viv—'Stunning! Should be in the National Gallery.' Nick—'Buy now while you still can.' Jane—'I may not know much about art but these are fabby.' Seline—'Haunting and atmospheric.' Anthony—'Beats Vermeer into a cocked hat.' Even her parents, her father's minute writing, detailing his proud views, her mother's exquisite script: '*Magnifico!* A new diva of the art world.'

There are a few others, written by people she doesn't know; real actual people had taken one or two minutes out of their own lifetime to write something about her pictures, things she had created. It is an extraordinary feeling, as if she had trailed through all her life like a ghost, her presence registering no more than a wisp of a breeze, then suddenly she is physical, here, incandescent and alive, and everyone has turned to see her. She scans the comments, wanting to note them down so she will remember them but feels too embarrassed; she blinks her eyes closed at each one, as if photographing them, committing them to the vault: 'Unforgettable and exciting', 'Brooding, mysterious', 'Like a dream, a fantasy', two more 'Atmospheric's.

She flicks forward to yesterday's date. Will Henderson. The feel of the page beneath her fingers, the slightest indentations where he had leaned his pen to write. Even his signature makes her want to cry. She moves her finger along the line, tracing his words: *I still love you.*

Sunday morning. Normally, this would be pottering day, but today, this morning, now, I have something to do. The walk is not far and the sky is bright and clear. The nearer I get, the more nervous I feel, as if I am about to sit an exam or enter onto a stage, and will suddenly blunder out there, blinking in the bright lights and opening my mouth in goldfish O's because I don't know my lines.

'There is no answer when I ring the bell, only the sound of my heart thudding in my ears. I should have phoned first, of course, but what could I say? It seems silly to lug the package home again; perhaps I will leave it in the garden under the pergola and call later.

Through the side gate, along the path. I breathe in the swoony scent of a pink viburnum. I don't see him at first, but I hear the clipping of his secateurs and his breath as he tugs at a stubborn weed. He is there, beyond the garden seat, half hidden by plants in the far border as if he had grown there. Through the slatted back, I see stripes of Will, rectangles of black jeans and that needlecord shirt that I never really liked; now I want him to wear it always—this is how I will see him when I picture him in my head. He is working with his back turned towards me and I watch for a minute as he dips and leans into the plants, pruning with his secateurs, his movements fluid and precise.

I am tempted to creep up on him, to reach out and touch him, scare him with a lover's certainty, but I am not sure how he will respond, so I call out.

'You've missed a bit.'

He starts slightly and stands up, then slowly turns round, twisting in the way I once drew him, as he does in the painting I have in my arms.

He looks at me and he does not speak and I do not speak.

I walk towards him, then, and hold out the package. He smiles as he realises what it is and he peels back the paper.

'I wanted to call you so many times,' I say.

'Me too.'

'Me three.'

He reaches out to tuck a strand of my hair back from my face.

'So, are you here just as a courier or have you got time for a proper visit?'

I look at my watch and suck in my breath.

'Hmm, always time for a cup of tea . . . say about fifty years or so?'

'So, is that like a yes then?'

'That is very like a yes then. A YES of skyscraper dimensions.' I reach up and stroke my fingertip across his eyebrow, pausing at his scar. 'Did I mention that I actually "l"-word you quite a huge amount? Will that be a problem at all?'

'I guess I can handle it.' He smiles and takes me in his arms.

I cup his dear, precious face in my hands and stretch up to kiss him. 'Can we start now?

CLAIRE CALMAN

I met Claire Calman at the Oxo Tower in London when she was travelling from her home near Ashford, Kent, via London to Bournemouth. Later that day she was going to participate in a book-signing session for *Girls' Night In*, a short story anthology with contributions from thirty-one of today's most successful women novelists.

'I seem to spend most of my life on the train at the moment,' Claire said with a laugh. 'However, it's all in a good cause. At least one pound from the sale of every copy will go to War Child, a charity that provides assistance for children caught up in the horrors of war. I am very proud to have been a part of it.'

Claire Calman has worked on women's magazines and in book publishing. She is also a poet and broadcaster and has written and recited her comic verse on radio, including Radio 4's *Woman's Hour* and the comedy series *Five Squeezy Pieces*. Eight years ago she decided to quit nine-to-five working and set herself up as a freelance editor, specialising in nonfiction titles, especially gardening, cookery and self-help books. 'All of which has provided excellent background material for *Love is a Four Letter Word*.' She jokingly told me that she decided to take up writing as a career when she discovered that it mainly involved drinking

cups of tea and looking out of the window. It was some time later that a real writer friend pointed out that if she were to select an assortment of words and arrange them in some kind of order, this would speed up the process no end! In fact, Claire has developed a unique way of writing which works successfully for her. She is the only author I have ever met who doesn't write in sequence. 'There are bits of the story I can see very clearly, so I start writing those scenes first and then fill in the gaps. It's very illogical and is not a technique I would recommend to anyone else.'

The germ of the idea for *Love is a Four Letter Word* lay dormant in Claire's head until she decided to sign up for a writing course. 'I had always been very anti doing a course. I always thought you either knew how to write or you didn't. A course was cheating. But then came a chance to spend five days writing in a relaxed setting and I thought "what the hell" and signed up for it immediately. The only drawback was you had to take something you had written and I had only one short story to my name. So I thought I had better write something quickly and it became part of *Love is a Four Letter Word*, although I must admit it was part of the novel I ditched when I put all the pieces together.'

The daughter of the late cartoonist Mel Calman, Claire confesses that she cannot paint or draw. 'The gap between how I can see it in my head and what I can produce on paper is so enormous that I find it depressing. But with writing fiction, I feel I can narrow that gap through many drafts.'

Claire's second novel, *Lessons for a Sunday Father*, is to be published in January. Until then she simply aims to relax and enjoy her new house and garden 'and pray I get another publishing contract!'

Jane Eastgate

601-008-1